I0604113

UPHEAVAL

UPHEAVAL

MANABOUND BOOK 3

TRAVIS ALBRECHT

Podium

For my family. You know why.

All rights reserved. No part of this publication may be reproduced, stored in a retrieval system, or transmitted in any form or by any means electronic, mechanical, photocopying, recording, or otherwise without prior written permission from Podium Publishing.

This is a work of fiction. Names, characters, places, and incidents are either products of the author's imagination or used fictitiously. Any resemblance to actual events, locales, or persons, living, dead, or undead, is entirely coincidental.

Copyright © 2025 by Travis Albrecht

Cover design by Antti Hakosaari

ISBN: 978-1-0394-5433-0

Published in 2025 by Podium Publishing
www.podiumentertainment.com

UPHEAVAL

TREMORS OF WAR

SOME TIME AGO

The Empire of Vlaredia was in many ways a lesson in opposites. The nation and its people were simultaneously warlike and isolationist. When faced with what they perceived as existential threats, they riled up their citizens into a furor that was almost like bloodlust. This was compounded by the fact that the people resisted outsiders almost religiously and thus saw any attempt at foreign control as existential. They lived by a very simple mantra: leave me alone, or I will burn down everything you hold dear.

Some might say that conflict between the Empire and the Sovereign Cities was inevitable. The Sovereign Cities played host to the guilds at a level not seen in other regions of the continent, and the guilds used that ubiquity to push their influence and agenda with little impunity. Such an infringement of imperial culture and sense of self ironically made the Empire seem more sovereign than the very cities they found themselves at odds with.

For the Sovereigns had long been manipulated and led to believe that the guilds were an integral part of the independent mindset of the Cities. The guilds surely ensured that those who had a craft were able to resist being trampled by those above them. Right?

It was this idea that lay at the foundation of why the Sovereigns seemed befuddled when the Empire pushed back on the guilds' attempt to impose their authority within the nation. For it seemed that minor deviations of viewpoints were all that caused such a drastic and visceral reaction. Such a viewpoint was being discussed by the imperial war council. The emperor had summoned his economic and interior ministers, his generals and their advisors, key commanders, and even the priests.

Commander Ressa sat off to the side and quietly observed as they spoke of skirmishes, disposition of forces, economic impact, and potentialities. The empress, in her role as the head of the imperial intelligence ministry, discussed opportunities and the weaknesses her agents had found. The surprising weakness and corruption at the heart of their other longtime rivals could potentially cause those forces to either take advantage of hostilities or simply dismiss the Sovereigns outright—a risk the council was willing to take, but not without approving a mission for the diplomatic ministry to undergo. Just because one was filled with bloodlust didn't mean they couldn't enact a fail-safe and strategy.

Ressa knew they discussed all this for one reason. The economic war the guilds waged in the shadows had gone too far. The Guild of Blades had struck at imperial free merchants and absconded with their goods as a tax.

Those gathered had all worked tirelessly into the night while the council discussed options, using their aids to supply needed context. Ressa herself provided desired information based on her position within the military arm of the Empire.

In the end, only one solution could be made. The guilds had drawn their line in the sand, and the Empire would not acquiesce to the demands of foreigners willingly. To any other nation, such a reaction would have provoked a different response—they would have seen the guilds as the entity they were. They would not have associated the actions of one power-hungry regional head of the guilds with an act of all of the Sovereign Cities. Ressa wondered if perhaps that was a failing of the Empire, or maybe her countrymen had the keen ability to identify a rot that could not be allowed to afflict them again. Whatever the reason, her leaders had made their decision.

As the meeting concluded, small discussions broke out among various members, while others yawned, desiring sleep. The empress called upon the elite soldier.

"Commander Ressa."

The orkun woman stood, saluted, and bowed her head. "Your Majesty."

"Walk with me."

Ressa followed the empress out of the war room. She kept her gaze forward, walking behind the woman, taking note of the imperial guard that trailed them. The man moved past the two of them and opened a door. He bowed his head as the empress and Ressa walked inside.

They entered a small sitting room with a large set of windows that overlooked the private imperial gardens. Ressa quietly sat next to the empress and waited to be addressed.

"These gardens were originally planted by my mother-in-law just before my husband was coronated. She did it out of spite because while she permitted our marriage, she never liked me. She felt that giving me this garden would require me to take my attention away from the duties I have given myself."

Ressa didn't know how to respond, so she remained silent. The empress looked up as if contemplating and continued.

"The woman had very different thoughts on how an empress should act. When I became empress, I had the entire garden burned. Then I had it replanted the way you see now, and people maintain it for me. They know to keep it this way, and I let them do their duties. I have zero intention of micromanaging a garden. My purpose isn't to be some socialite that keeps apprised of the pulse of the nobility. My husband prefers the social aspects of ruling and the day-to-day minutiae, whereas I thrive in sculpting and perfecting the big picture. In this way, we are different. I understand this. As does he. We do not care."

She must have seen the confusion on Ressa's face because she smiled softly. "The reason I tell you this is simple. I do not care about 'the way things have always been.' I will burn the past to the ground and rebuild something greater. I will appoint those who fit any given situation best. The future is uncertain. Our very way of life has been threatened by the changes brought by the Flash and the appearance of these terrans—or *humans*, as some call themselves.

"You belong to one of these situations. I require you to assemble a team. You will ascertain the extent of the changes and research the Sovereigns have put into this new reality we find ourselves in. Your own changes have been followed with great interest, and I expect you to take note of how to counter others such as yourself.

"If the Sovereigns field any such individuals, you will track them down and eliminate them. I predict that we are only just skimming the top of the potential of what is to come. Underestimating those with abilities could spell the downfall of our armies."

Ressa slowly nodded. "I will do as you command, Your Majesty." Her eyes narrowed as her thoughts went to everything she would need to accomplish.

"Good. You will have access to whatever you require, and you report directly to me. If you encounter the need, you have the authority to redirect any assets along the front. Do not abuse this. Ensure you requisition couriers, as I expect monthly reports."

"Understood, Your Majesty."

"The guard will give you your orders on the way out."

Commander Ressa stood and bowed to the empress. She was already thinking of how best to prepare; her team would likely move into enemy territory. This would need to be accounted for.

Ressa smirked as she received the orders from the man outside. She felt her magic ripple within her chest as a feeling of resolve overcame her. She would not fail her empress.

Far from the Imperial Palace of Vlaredia, in the city of Marketbol, members of the Church of the Celestials were hard at work. The high priest for the city's primary temple had been changed by the Flash. Insight from the gods had graced him and a few others. The church had once again been blessed by the ones they worshipped.

However, while the temple was awash with activity, the Paladins of Alos were on a mission. Several villages had been attacked recently, and the shrine priest had called for aid since the Sovereign Cities had not sent any. Leading the response was Shalas, accompanied by a cohort of six from the order, both men and women alike.

They were nearing the mountains south of Marketbol. All of the villages hit were within half a day's ride from the range. Based on descriptions they had received from the villagers, this was the only place where the thing that had attacked could hide. Their first encounter with evidence of the beast's presence occurred during an overnight halt—though, fortunately, they were not attacked.

Under normal circumstances, such a quest would fall outside the Paladins of Alos's purview. Nonetheless, the disunity among the Sovereign Cities compelled Shalas, both as praetor of Marketbol and its environs, to uphold her duty to safeguard the innocent, a duty magnified by the city leaders' indecision. That responsibility of protection was a core tenant of the order. Their purpose was to have the strength and initiative to protect the innocent and bring impartial justice to those who would violate the decrees.

Shalas had been a member of the order for most of her life. Yet, in all of that time, none of it had compared to the challenges brought upon them since the Flash.

Beasts changed by something new. Something within the very air. Praetor Shalas was another such person who had been changed. Her changes, however, did not help her with her current predicament.

As they approached the mountains, the group fanned out, vigilant for any trace of the creature. It wasn't long before they found what they were looking for.

"Praetor."

"What is it, Evocati?" she inquired, joining him.

"I have tracks," Evocati Mori announced, indicating the ground in front of him.

The tracks, to Shalas's astonishment, were enormous, measuring two hands in width. She summoned the rest of the group, and with weapons at the ready, they followed Mori's lead deeper into the mountainous terrain.

It took them much of the day, but they eventually found the cave in which the tracks led. The smell hit them almost immediately when they entered. Spotting a pile of bones, Shalas tightened her grip on her spear. With a silent command, her team advanced in formation. Two of her people held out their bows, arrows already nocked, while the others stood at the ready.

A deep growl echoed from the depths of the cave, leading them to a vast chamber. Across a small pond, atop a hill, loomed a creature of monstrous proportions, likely once a wolf, now standing over two meters tall with fur that glistened with a yellow sheen—another victim of the Flash's corrupting touch. Twisted.

Whatever it was now, it was feasting on the bodies of a family, a scene that prompted Shalas to whisper a prayer to Relena for the repose of their souls. She raised her hand, signaling readiness, preparing to initiate the assault.

As they advanced, the beast's gaze met theirs. With a swift motion, Shalas dropped her fist, and arrows soared through the air in rapid succession.

Her battle cry resonated as she led the charge into combat.

Marketbol was an important city in the central plains, and like other prominent cities, it was host to multiple temples. There was, of course, the primary temple to the Family: the Temple of the Celestials. Although much smaller than Strathmore's great temple, the Golden City of the Plains had a beautiful structure dedicated to the four major gods. Unlike Strathmore—which was the seat of the Church of the Celestials—Marketbol's primary temple did not have dedicated facilities for each major god.

However, like most other places, Marketbol had temples for select members of the remainder of the pantheon. The city had chosen Dylenia, the goddess of commerce, and Erbium, the god of crafting, as its patron gods. These two minor gods had two small, dedicated temples within the city, while the other minor gods were represented within the consolidated Temple of the Stars.

It was rare that members of the Family had their own dedicated temples. This was by design, for it was as they desired when they spoke the First Decree. Alos, Eona, Relena, and Tenera were all to be worshipped together. In fact, there were only five locations in the world that had individual temples for them. In addition to the great temple within Strathmore, there were the Seats.

Relena's Morthenon had been rebuilt by the ancient raithe after the Loreni Diaspora in the northwestern mountains of Ikios a millennia ago. The goddess visited the archpriest of the time in her raithe avatar and pronounced her decree.

Tenera's Templum Tenebris sat in the frozen north of the elven continent, Loren. The oldest of the temples, it rested within the ancient home of the night elves.

The World's Womb, the Seat of Eona, sat deep within the Solana Rainforest in central Loren. The location was said to be the birthplace of all life—or at least of the Loreni.

Alos's Sedes Solaris sat on the island of Torid between the southern coasts of the two great continents—Loren and Ikios. It was the home of the Paladins of Alos.

It was also Shalas's home, and it was on days like today that she missed it. Once again, it was raining, which it did in Marketbol far too often, and today it had begun as soon as she and her paladins returned from their hunt, as if to spite her. While the others left to perform other duties, Shalas went to clean up to meet with the high priest.

She grabbed a towel from one of the attendants of the temple and wiped her face. As she performed her ablutions and fixed her hair, two other attendants dried her armor. She bowed her head and thanked them for their service and headed to where she knew the high priest would be.

Most temples had private chapels where the members of the church could worship. The high priest had one of three such chapels within the temple cleared out of all furniture. Shalas walked into the empty room and noticed a new fix-ture centered within: a pedestal, elegantly crafted and decorated with various likenesses of the Family's Avatars on its shaft. The high priest stood next to it as he awaited her.

She bowed respectfully to the man as she approached, and he smiled.

"Praetor, welcome back. How did your hunt go?"

Shalas reached into the sack she carried and pulled out a large yellow core. "It went well in two ways. We ended the monster that preyed upon the innocent, as Alos wills. And we procured an orb I believe will suit the ceremony."

She handed the orb to the high priest and watched as he channeled his gift into it. The orb swirled with a yellow mist and the man smiled.

"This will work perfectly. Now, we should work out the details of the ceremony."

He placed the orb at the top of the pedestal and moved so that it stood between them. Gesturing to the side closest to her, he said, "Come, Shalas. Let us establish the Ceremony of Paths. You will be the first."

She bowed. "It would be my honor, High Priest."

PRESENT

Shalas walked into the meeting chambers within the temple. The high priest was present, as were two dwarves she did not know. One was obviously a priest, while the other was perhaps a temple guard.

It was rare that she saw dwarven priests. While the dwarves did worship the same pantheon as the rest of the world, they quite often placed more prominence upon Erbium, the god of crafting, and Lysstus, the god of the hearth.

The high priest wore a solemn expression, but she'd worked with the man for many years now and knew there was a hint of sadness in him he was attempting to hide.

"Praetor, thank you for joining us. Please, sit. We have some grave news," the high priest said.

Shalas nodded and took the indicated seat. The dwarf priest glanced at his friend and took a deep breath.

"Praetor. Thank you for coming," he began. "We have come from Dheg Malduhr. It . . ." the priest choked up and his companion placed a hand on his shoulder and leaned in close. She couldn't hear what was said but the priest soon nodded.

"Dheg Malduhr is no more."

Shalas gasped in surprise. Her mouth opened and closed several times, but she could not speak. *A city . . . gone? A natural disaster? The mountain? What . . .*

The priest continued. "A terran created a weapon, one that uses the energy of the gods that was brought by the Flash."

"A weapon?" she managed to ask.

The dwarf nodded. "Yes. There was an accident. I know not what exactly occurred, but the result was that the city was destroyed completely. That we lived was due to visiting the shrine near the pass."

So the other dwarf was a guard.

The guard turned toward her. "There is more. The Vlaredian Empire approached the pass. They are currently helping survivors, but I do not doubt that they will soon use it."

Shalas's eyes widened. *If the Vlaredians get through the pass, they'll attack Goosebourne . . .*

The high priest sucked in a breath. He looked at Shalas. "You know the Decree. We are to remain neutral." Clearly, he knew what she was thinking.

"High Priest—"

"Praetor. We must not interfere within the matters of nations."

She bowed her head. "Of course, High Priest. However, as praetor, I must protect the church. After this meeting, I will send out the paladins to the temples of the region. They will have orders to provide security to our people."

"Of course, I would expect nothing less," the high priest agreed. He turned back toward the dwarven priest. "Now, please, tell us everything you know about these terrans. We had many here in Marketbol, but they recently left. Some are with the army."

She heard the guard gasp lightly. It seemed that the thought of terrans with the army did not sit right with him. After some of the promises she'd heard them make, she didn't blame him.

A knock sounded at the door to her small office. Shalas looked up to see the high priest entering with one of the priestesses-in-training behind him—young Mariel, a raithe girl she'd seen often around the temple and one of the more studious of the lot, if she remembered correctly.

"Shalas, I am glad I caught you."

She tilted her head. "Of course. Where else would I be, High Priest?"

"Were you not going to prepare the rest of the order?" he asked.

She smirked. "It is done, High Priest. They have already departed."

He nodded absently. "My apologies, Praetor. How long was I in seclusion?" He glanced at the young girl.

Shalas looked toward the window, gauging the time. She didn't remember when the last bell had sounded.

"No more than a few bells, High Priest," the girl, Mariel, said.

The older high elf looked weary. He sat in an extra chair off to the side and leaned his head against the wall behind him. "I have drafted a request for the archpriestess on behalf of the Church within the Sovereign Cities."

Shalas gasped. "High Priest, is that not . . . beyond your station?"

He actually shrugged. "Perhaps. However, due to the seriousness of the situation, I feel that I am within my bounds. These terrans pose a greater danger than we know. Her Holiness must enact a Decree to protect the people of our world."

"What are you suggesting, High Priest?" Shalas glanced at the raithe girl, wondering why she was present.

"We must limit how much influence they can hold over our world. Particularly when it comes to weapons. What happened at Dheg Malduhr cannot be allowed to happen again."

Shalas agreed. Some terrans remained within the city. She'd had some of her people subtly reach out to them, and they'd learned much. Terrans came from a variety of different societies and cultures. That was not inherently dangerous, but the ones who came from civilizations that were far more advanced were. The high priest was right. They had a duty to uphold.

"I agree, High Priest. I have two men who can act as couriers. However, if I may, why is the priestess-in-training present?"

A hint of yellow flickered across his eyes. "I have begun performing the Ceremony of Paths upon members of the temple. Mariel shows great . . . promise. I would like you to work with her. However, I believe her gift may require her to seek experts."

Shalas scrutinized the girl. "What is her gift?"

The high priest's eyes closed. "I am not entirely certain. I just know that she has been blessed by more than one of the gods."

The girl fidgeted slightly. "They have not spoken to me, High Priest," she said.

"Ah, my girl. They speak to us in many ways. They have given you their gifts. In time, you may hear their voice."

"Where would she go for an expert?" Shalas asked. "Strathmore? Unfortunately, it will be some time before I can arrange travel. I simply do not have paladins to spare."

Surprisingly, he shook his head. "No, I do not think there is any need for that. There is an . . . order . . . within Calling that I believe would suit our needs."

Shalas squinted, trying to remember anything about a holy order within the city of Calling. The Kingdom of Rosale was small, fairly wealthy, but not necessarily noteworthy for the church. "I am unaware of any order within Calling, High Priest."

"That is expected. It is small. We will simply have to look out for a way to get her there. In the meantime, I would like for her to train with you."

Shalas glanced at the girl and nodded. "I can do that, High Priest. In my spare time, at least."

"Good, good. We will have need of your gift as well, Shalas. We will need to prepare for what is to come. Now, about the Decree . . ."

She took a deep breath. "You are correct that one will be needed. If Dheg

Malduhr is any indication, it is that we must be prepared. However, we cannot let ourselves become blinded. We will ensure the trustworthiness of any terran who enters our city. There are bound to be some we can work with. We do this to ensure the safety of our people."

The high priest nodded. "Good. Let us get to work. We need to prepare the Ceremony for use by the public. The guards will need to be aware and know their role."

"I will see it done, High Priest."

He nodded and stood to leave.

Shalas glanced at Mariel one last time before the young raithe girl followed the high priest out. She looked back down at what she was working on—a list of known terrans and their origins. Along with how dangerous they were to their world.

CHAPTER ONE

UPHEAVAL

Ikios has seen its fair share of wars, but the war that began between the Empire of Vlaredia and the Sovereign Cities set alight a wildfire that would tear nearly the entire western region asunder for many years to come. It was a fire that would spread and consume as it evolved into a truly regional conflict with nearly every nation affected.

What came over the next decade drew in every regional power even as the so-called sides changed constantly. This created a level of distrust that would breed instability for decades and set up the stage for what came next.

The Many Parties War became what is now the most studied war in history due to being the earliest modern example of arcane warfare. As the use of mana increased, the greater cost of warfare in lives quickly became evident. Subsequent research into both offensive and defensive uses of mana created a foundation that lasts to this day.

Mana and War: The Many Parties War, 179 SA

Sometimes all it takes is an outside spark. In others, a healthy dose of flight-or-flight response. Change, inevitable as it is, often arrives unannounced, unwrapping the path to a new normal amid chaos and uncertainty. Reactions vary, molded by circumstances and character, and though the journey may be tumultuous, hindsight often paints a clearer picture, delineating blurred lines that once seemed insurmountable.

Change came in many forms. Some magical and some more . . . monstrous.

Just beyond the fringes of the Westaren kingdom, a modest assembly of wagons had halted for the evening. Their gradual journey from the ruins of Thirdghyll had spanned arduous weeks, paralleled by other survivors venturing toward the hamlet of Vilstaf. The caravan's members, still reeling from the attacks of monsters that bore the mark of pure malevolence, remained vigilant.

A cadre of fatigued knights convened in hushed tones, discussing their path forward as the knight-captain of their order spoke with the woman who led the other half of the caravan. That woman's house had grown, now including five others, and would only increase from there as she sought a way to sustain all that was required to effectuate her mission.

Their encampment lay amid the desolate expanse of arid, rolling plains, a stark contrast to the bustling life once found here. Scattered remains of bygone settlements dotted the landscape, relics of an era when Westaren was merely a fragment of the Sovereign Cities. In the wake of a fierce conflict that carved out their new sovereignty, these borderlands stood as silent witnesses to their tumultuous past.

In a camp alongside the only road that led out of the Kingdom of Westaren, Lady Sloane Reinhart calmly stood and scrutinized the map sprawled out before her.

"We're still a couple of weeks from the town, but Tiberius noticed troops here, here, and here," she said, pointing her dagger at areas where she had seen forces blocking their route to Goosebourne. The bird was able to cover the vast distances quickly, making scouting almost comically simple. *Nothing is gonna be able to sneak up on us easily. Well, unless invisibility magic is real . . . or Tiberius isn't flying.*

Gisele nodded slowly as she examined the rough map that Sloane had sketched. It depicted the area between where they currently rested and the immediate surroundings of Goosebourne. A town they had planned on stopping in for resupply, and so Sloane could pass on a message.

Yeah, I'll let Gisele handle everything.

Before the events that led to the fall of Thirdghyll, Sloane had met with a man who was from the secretive order of spies and assassins the Kingdom of Westaren maintained. That Order of Secrets had condemned an entire city to monsters, solely to ensure they could end the reign of the corrupt count who ruled it. She wondered what had happened to Giallo, who had mentioned that his people would take advantage of the chaos to enact their plan.

I never saw what happened to the count after the monsters attacked his small army.

She knew there were survivors from the city. After learning how to do it, Sloane sent Tiberius back and used her **[Golem Sight]** to watch the East Fort. The soldiers under Captain Jorin had repelled five attacks by the monsters, finally evacuating survivors from the city on the third day. She had Tiberius drop off a note to the captain explaining what they knew of Goosebourne, hoping it would find its way to Giallo.

In reply, Captain Jorin had passed along a message for Nemura containing orders that provided a discharge of honor from the Thirdghyll Guard. They released her of any oaths or commitments to the group to which she had dedicated over half a decade of time. He also provided access to a small amount of funds within the Banking Guild for the former guardswoman.

The tall telv had definitely teared up a little when she had read the message. *I need to discuss the future with her and the others*, thought Sloane.

She shivered and pulled her cloak a little tighter around herself as she waited for Gisele to come to a decision.

Finally, the orkun woman sighed. She looked up from the map. "We do not have a choice, really. If what you described is true"—she lifted a hand to stop Sloane from interjecting—"and I do not doubt that it is, then Goosebourne has already or nearly fallen. We have noncombatants with us, and nine people wouldn't make any true difference, anyway. Plus, neither we nor your house should take a side in this war. I believe we should try and bypass the city by going . . . here," she said, indicating a point on the map.

Sloane leaned forward, seeing that their path would come close to where she saw troops. "Why there?"

"The land farther west is rocky and not suitable for the wagons," Gisele explained. "There is a small road here that we can take to bypass Goosebourne. Then we will need to skirt the edge of the forest down to Marketbol."

"We may run into troops here, though."

"There is nothing we can do about that. We will show that our origins are Blightwych and as such are not part of either side. Explain that we are simply heading through to Rosale."

Sloane squinted. "Rosale? But—"

Gisele shook her head. "We do not want to tell them we are staying in the Sovereign Cities. Rosale is a safer option. They don't need to know where we are actually heading for us to get past them."

"Ah, yes. That makes sense."

Gisele pushed off her knees and stood. "You should discuss with your house members. We'll set up watches. I would appreciate it if you could have Nemura and Stefan take shifts to patrol inside the camp itself."

Sloane nodded. *It seems she is already trying to distance herself,* she thought. She watched as the woman walked away, and was about to stand when Adaega sat down next to her. She gave the woman a once-over as she shuffled around, trying to get comfortable. Sloane's observations since leaving the city had revealed an unsurprising amount of trauma in her companion due to the time Adaega had spent in the count's dungeon being tortured, but the dark-skinned woman was getting better, seemingly, day by day, and it was due, in no small part, to Ernald.

"Lady Sloane? May we talk?"

"Miss Merbaker. Please, call me Sloane. What can I do for you?"

The woman fidgeted slightly, seemingly nervous. "Ernald has told me some, but could you tell me more about yourself? Where do you come from?"

Sloane relaxed and smiled. "Of course."

Their conversation lasted nearly an hour. Sloane told her about her version of

Earth and about Gwyn. They finished with the plans and goals Sloane had. It felt good getting most of it out, especially to another human. Even if that human was from somewhere vastly different. The calendar in the woman's world was another point of divergence, but Sloane was able to guess that the world was at somewhat the same stage of development as hers had been in the fifties.

Adaega shook her head. "It is just so hard to believe. We're here, in this fantasy world, but come from such dissimilar worlds ourselves."

"You don't say." Sloane chuckled. "Your nation is a mouthful! The Unified Kingdom of . . ."

The woman next to her huffed in amusement. "The Unified Kingdom of Yoruba and Dahomey. We simply call it the UK."

The woman's world had some crazy divergences compared to Sloane's. Her nation was African on a continent that vaguely resembled the one Sloane knew. The nation sat within a large area surrounding the Gulf of Guinea—which Adaega called the Yoruba Gulf—that occupied land as far west as Ghana in her world to Niger in the north, and even as far south as Cameroon. The massive divergence from Sloane's Earth was that Europe had a cataclysmic volcanic event occur that caused it to be mostly uninhabitable. Evidently, it was a very active volcano zone still. That led to cooler temperatures over Africa, volcanic ash that settled into the soil, and an ironically better climate overall. It also shifted the landscape fairly substantially such that the Mediterranean and Europe as a whole was barely recognizable.

"What did you do for a living, Adaega?"

That made the woman straighten her back, as if they had finally reached the purpose of her coming to meet Sloane. "I was the director of operations at the Lokoja University."

Sloane perked up. "Oh? That sounds fascinating. What does your university specialize in?"

Adaega launched into an explanation of her institution, speaking about the many different colleges of study that made up the school and how it was one of the preeminent universities in the world. As the woman described it, Sloane realized why it sounded so familiar. It was essentially her world's Oxford.

"What are your goals?" Sloane asked, trying to cut to the heart of the matter.

"I-I want to be safe. I can't follow the knights. They do not know where their path will take them, and it will likely be dangerous. As much as I sympathize with your search for your daughter, I . . . I just cannot do it. Maybe in the future, but I do not want to put myself in danger again. Ernald says that Marketbol is a well-developed city and, most importantly, safe."

Sloane understood completely. It was what she wanted for herself and her daughter. After she found her, that is. Safety was important, and not everyone was cut out for what the knights could do. Sloane didn't think she was either, but she'd be damned if she wasn't going to do it anyway.

"I see. The knights will be with us until Marketbol. It's okay, Adaega. Just ask what you wish to ask."

The woman nodded and took a deep breath to compose herself. "You are correct. I am prevaricating. My apologies. I believe I would be a beneficial addition to your research center as Ernald described it to me. Looking at those you currently have in your employ, I believe that I am uniquely suited to manage it."

Sloane raised a brow. She had expected something after hearing what the woman did for a living, but outright asking to manage her center hadn't been it. There was potential there. *I hope she will be a good fit because it would be nice to already have someone lined up. Elodie can't do everything.*

Adaega must have taken her silence as hesitancy instead of the contemplation that it was, because she glanced back at the knights and then leaned forward.

"I know it's a bit forward of me. Ernald suggested I talk with your . . . retainers, and I did. They all seem genuinely nice. I think I can do some good there. I have experience with running something like this, and with Miss Elodie's financial acumen, we can really expand your business and pursue some great things. Especially into materials research."

Sloane thought back to Giallo and how the man had seemed especially concerned about Adaega. He had asked Sloane to bring her, to get Adaega to safety. Sloane wasn't sure why she was hesitating; she'd quickly agreed to add everyone else. It wasn't as if she was the first person to be uniquely qualified for what Sloane needed.

Sloane took a deep breath. "Let's get there first and see what we can set up. There's no telling what we can start with."

Adaega's shoulders sagged.

"I'm sorry, that came out a bit differently than I had intended. I think we can come to an arrangement, Adaega," Sloane quickly clarified. "I'm not sure what position will fit the center best just yet, is all I mean. There's definitely a spot for you, I just need to decide on the structure." She smiled. "Maybe that's something you can help me with."

"Ah, that makes sense. Thank you, Sloane. I'd like that." She went silent for a moment, looking away. Then she turned back toward Sloane. "I have had a lot of time to contemplate the existence of magic. Especially during my time with the count . . ."

Sloane remained quiet as Adaega collected herself. Based on her facial expressions, Sloane imagined the woman was having a fierce internal debate with herself. She straightened, and Sloane smiled softly as Adaega looked her in the eye. "Ernald has told me a lot about what you have discussed with them. I wanted to pose a question, and you don't have to answer now, but think about it."

"Sure, anything. What's your question?"

"You designed the rings to help people with their magic, right? And help them awaken it."

Sloane wondered where the woman was going with this line of questioning, but went along with it. "I did, yes."

"Then why do only a few of you have access to magic and mana? Is there a connection you haven't seen yet between a person and the domains you spoke of?"

Sloane froze. With all of the stuff that had happened, she had never truly gone back and worked with the knights on their magic.

"I . . ." she started.

Adaega held a hand up. "I had a thought: What if a connection to these domains you discovered is what facilitated someone to perform magic? Like a genetic disposition, for example. Otherwise, mana is just affecting them physically."

"That . . . seems sound. I will need to test that."

Adaega smiled. "Absolutely. I suggest testing on someone who hasn't been practicing as much as the knights have. Then let them know what you find. I believe they're working under the assumption that they can all eventually do it."

Sloane instantly felt guilty but didn't say anything. She definitely owed the knights enough to put in the effort to figure it out.

The woman searched Sloane's face for a moment, then added, "I believe the Reinhart Center can expand into mana research like that in time. Or you could even establish a second center dedicated solely to it."

Sloane's head whirled as she considered everything. She definitely felt better about Adaega, and she could see how she may have been incorrect in her initial theory. *Yeah, definitely need to test that, and I know just the person to use.*

Sloane smiled. "You know, I think you're going to be great for the center. I will test this now. Let me know if you think of anything else."

She stood and held out a hand. Adaega smiled and got up as well. The two women shook and parted. Sloane walked to her wagon, where she could find her guinea pig.

Stefan leaned against the wagon as Elodie spoke with the former Thirdghyll guardswoman. Nemura was asking about finances she could use to hire more guards, and it seemed that they would have enough to maintain a standing guard for the center, but not much beyond that for some time. Stefan and Elodie both knew that the situation would be changing, especially if the Banking Guild approved Lady Reinhart's project. He only hoped the terran noble was prepared for that meeting.

He had discussed their plans with Elodie extensively. The two of them felt that with the baroness's pivot toward the guilds in general, Stefan should stay with Lady Reinhart after she moved on from Marketbol. He would work with the local guild there to provide protection for Elodie, but her safety would be well in hand if what he heard from Nemura was going to happen.

Guildmaster Romaris's niece had a level of excitement that amused him. It seemed that the prospect of running the runecard business for the baroness, along with managing the finances of the Reinhart Center, was enough for the sun elf to all but pledge her firstborn to the terran.

He heard footsteps and glanced over and noticed Lady Reinhart herself approaching. He pushed off of the wagon and stood straighter.

"Hey guys, how is everything going?" Lady Reinhart asked, in her typical informal way.

"It is well, my lady. We were just discussing security requirements for the center," Nemura explained.

"Oh! That's good." She squinted, focusing on Elodie as she paused. "We can afford that. Right?"

Elodie smiled. "We can. The house has funds to support a modest research facility within the Merchant Quarter."

The baroness tilted her head. "Is there an education quarter? Um, something with a place of learning, like an academy?"

"There is the Scholar's Quarter. It hosts the Marketbol School of Economics. It is smaller than Thirdghyll's, but it is still a fairly respectable institute," Stefan assured her.

"Good. We should find a location within that quarter," she said.

Elodie seemed confused. "But why? Isn't the center meant to create opportunities for investment and business?"

Lady Reinhart smiled. "Yes, it is. However, the center can create a relationship with the school. It is primarily a place of research in nature. This will allow us to attract talent from graduating students, who can immediately go to work in the center. You should purchase a small location in the Merchant's Quarter solely for managing the customer relations business. Then expand from there."

Elodie nodded. Stefan glanced up at Nemura and saw that the woman seemed bored. *I cannot blame her there.* He was about to try to excuse himself when Lady Reinhart changed topics.

"I actually came over here for another reason. Miss Merbaker had a thought that I wish to experiment . . . er, test with Nemura and Stefan," she said.

Stefan raised a hand and opened his mouth to object but couldn't think of anything to say. The glint in the baroness's eye was a bit disconcerting as he lowered his hand.

"She theorizes that mana affects physical users differently than mental ones." Lady Reinhart lifted her hand to stop Nemura from interrupting. "Basically, I am going to give you a ring that helped me access my magic. I want to see if it does the same for you. If it doesn't, I want to know exactly what you feel."

"How will this affect us?" Nemura asked.

That is a great question.

"I don't know, other than potentially letting you use magic? If not, then we're going to find out!"

Stefan groaned. "Fine, I'll go first. Nemura, you get my sword if I die."

The tall, muscular telv grunted. "I don't want that toothpick."

He feigned hurt but smirked and turned his back to her. "Here's my back if you want to stab it again."

"No need. You are about to die anyway. Waste of energy."

Lady Reinhart did not look amused. "Really, guys? You're not going to die. If anything, it'll just make you . . . uhhh . . . better?"

"Was that a question or a statement, my lady?" Elodie asked.

Nemura chuckled, and the baroness groaned. "Not you too. Here, Stefan, try this on," she said, holding out a diamond ring.

He pretended to hesitate, then grabbed the ring. "Just put it on?"

"Please."

Nodding, he slipped it onto his index finger, and when nothing happened, he looked at her. "You have big fingers. This fit easily."

Nemura started laughing.

"I Altered it to make sure it fit you!" Lady Reinhart said with exasperation.

"I don't—wait." Stefan felt a slight change. Almost like he had more energy than usual. He bounced on his feet and pursed his lips when he went slightly higher than he thought he would. He would have fallen if Nemura hadn't placed a bracing hand on his shoulder.

He huffed. "Huh. That's different. It's slight, but it feels like it's giving me a bit more energy. Barely noticeable, though, kind of like when one stair is slightly lower than the rest and you misjudge it. And . . ." He hopped again. "Yes, already used to it."

Lady Reinhart was staring at him with her arms crossed. "No magic?"

He shook his head. "None."

"Do you mind if I examine you?"

His eyes shot wide and he glanced at the other two women. "Uh, excuse me, my lady?"

She raised a brow. "Stefan. You know very well that is not what I meant. Focus on yourself. Try to trace the feeling inside of you. Remember the rushes we had? Try to remember how they felt."

He did what she said and tried to feel anything within. Lady Reinhart peered at him, and suddenly her eyes began to glow, and any concentration he had vanished. "W-what are you doing?"

The glow disappeared and she snapped up her head. "What? I was trying to see if any mana was flowing within you."

"Ah. My apologies."

She threw her hands up and stomped away.

He looked at Nemura. "Did I do something wrong?"

She shrugged. "Nobles. I don't try and guess at what is going on in their minds."

Elodie sighed. "Just look."

He and Nemura turned and saw that the baroness was returning, carrying Nemura's shield and a sword. She handed the shield to Nemura. Three symbols that she had engraved in it were glowing white with a hint of blue. "Step back, hold it up, ready to take a hit," Lady Reinhart commanded. "Don't worry, any damage can be fixed."

She turned to Stefan and flipped the sword around, then held it out hilt first. "Take this."

He grabbed the sword and looked down at it. It was hers, and he noticed that the symbols on the blade glowed a bright blue. "Now what?"

"Focus inside again. Feel for the mana; it's there. You want it to make you hit harder, faster, and better. Nemura, be ready."

The telv nodded and settled into a stance that would let her withstand the hit. Lady Reinhart stood back and her eyes began to glow again as she watched. Elodie took a few extra steps back to observe.

Stefan bounced on his toes and took a couple of practice swings. *This is going to be embarrassing. I swear, if Nemura laughs, I am going to sprinkle floren root in her food. She'll be shitting nonstop for weeks.*

"Swing already," Nemura taunted.

He narrowed his eyes. *Remember the rush. Mana is making me better. Faster . . .*

Stefan struck. There was a rush that surged through him. A moment later, his **[Sudden Strike]** caused the entire sword to take on a shadowy appearance as it lashed out faster than he could comprehend. It struck against the shield with such force that his arm jolted, and he heard a grunt from the guardswoman.

Lady Reinhart's eyes were big and round, and Stefan froze in shock. Nemura was the first to react.

"That was a good hit!"

He looked at the sword with incomprehension. Nemura slapped his shoulder, jolting him back to reality.

"We're gonna work well together, Blade." She was smiling fiercely. "Later, we spar."

Stefan groaned. That wasn't the intent. *Maybe the root is still an option.*

Sloane smiled. "That was great! Thank you!" She pulled out her notebook and started flipping through it. She turned and started walking away, before stopping and turning back to them. Stefan smirked and held out her sword with one hand and the ring with the other. The baroness grabbed them and returned to her notebook as she walked away.

"Didn't she want to test both of us?" he asked with a chuckle. Nemura huffed her own amusement. He turned and looked up at her. "You want to take the first shift tonight?"

She set down her shield and rolled the arm that had held it. "I can. I will go ask the knights where they would like us."

"How much do you want to bet she was supposed to tell us?"

Nemura shook her head, smiling. "I wouldn't take that bet. But I do want to get her to let me put on that ring," she said offhandedly, as she too walked away to meet with the knights.

Stefan looked down at his hand and flexed it before glancing up at the departing noble. *Looks like I am in for the long haul.*

CHAPTER TWO

AIN'T AFRAID OF NO GHOST

Amid the rustling hues of autumn, the caravan veered southward, skirting the besieged town of Goosebourne. Tiberius soared through the sky, pinpointing increased signs of activity from above. The bird had already proved itself indispensable, its sharp eyes guiding the caravan past three wary patrols that might otherwise have caused problems.

Unfortunately, it seemed that the luck would not hold. The Empire of Vlaredia had moved a massive force into the area, and the knights were not sure how everyone had managed to miss it. Which is what they discussed as they stopped for the night.

"There is no way they were able to bypass Dheg Malduhr so easily," Cristole mused, his gaze lost in the distance. "The dwarves there would have been able to hold the pass for years without support. Sloane, did the man from the order say anything else?"

Beside Sloane, Nemura expressed her astonishment. "I knew you received intelligence from somewhere, but from them?" she asked, referring to the Westari Order of Secrets.

Sloane nodded, the details of her correspondence with Giallo surfacing in her mind. "Yes, he was the one who gave us the information, which I used to alert Captain Jorin. I do not think the man will hold a grudge, but he specifically told me to inform only Guildmaster Romaris."

Nemura took a deep breath and narrowed her eyes as she realized what Sloane had left out—that the organization could have retaliated against her for going against their wishes.

Sloane looked over at Cristole. "Now, on what you asked, no, nothing. They obviously knew the army was meant to make its way through the pass. He didn't mention anything about them *actually* accomplishing it."

The high elf shook his head. "I have no idea how they could have managed to even make it through the pass with such a large force. The dwarven fortress should have stopped them, or at the very least diminished the numbers substantially. They then somehow also managed to make it all the way to besiege Goosebourne without the Kingdom of Westaren even knowing."

"At least they know now," Gisele said.

During their initial trek over, Sloane had sent messages concerning how everyone was doing along with a letter to Guildmaster Romaris. She'd also sent letters and documents to Reanny with ideas for a business—she'd thought of a lot since she'd last seen her dwarven friend. Lastly, Gisele and Nemura had helped her compose and send notice to Captain Jorin about the Vlaredian troop movements and the fate of Goosebourne.

While her experience in the Kingdom of Westaren had been rough, there were some positive connections that she had made. Giving Jorin information would hopefully allow them to make whatever preparations they needed, since the war had clearly moved into their neighborhood unexpectedly.

"For all of the good it will do them," Cristole added with a scoff.

"You did say that this 'Giallo' mentioned that the Crown had mobilized an army. Perhaps the true reason for such was not just to stop the monsters but also to discourage any actions of the Empire," Nemura said.

Gisele nodded. "That is possible. Your kingdom is—"

"A mess," Stefan said from behind Sloane.

Sloane sighed. "This is all fascinating, but it does not help us right now. What are we going to do tomorrow? We're going to run into at least one squad of troops."

Gisele shrugged. "We stick to the plan and hope for the best. We will handle it if they prove belligerent. Hopefully, they understand that we are not from here."

Deryk huffed, having remained quiet during the meeting thus far. "If we are lucky."

Gisele shrugged again. "I did say *hopefully*."

Stefan moved into the circle and glanced at her. "I believe we should have Ser Ismeld ride with Lady Reinhart tomorrow in her wagon," Sloane's raithe guard said. "No offense to your order, but it's a bit better equipped for two nobles. I will drive it, and Nemura can ride the wagon with Koren. Then the remaining members of House Reinhart can ride inside the knight's wagon as well."

Gisele nodded. "That is a good idea. We'll continue as if we are employed by House Reinhart. We need to ensure everyone keeps cool heads. We act the part and it should be fine. Hopefully with no more than some toll or fee."

"Is it common in these situations to obtain documents from them that will allow us past any other troops we run into?" Sloane asked.

Cristole shook his head. "That is not a common thing unless it's through their actual front lines. With luck, we will only have to make our way past one group. We *are* moving away from the front. That is another thing we can claim: we had no idea we were near any front lines and wish to avoid the war."

"With how covert they managed to keep their movements, that is believable. Or rather, *because* they have been so secretive, they will wish to keep that secret," Stefan said.

"Then we will deal with that situation if it arises. For now, we have a plan. The order will split off into two shifts to maintain an outer watch. Nemura, could you and Stefan please split as well?"

"We will do that, Ser Gisele," Nemura said.

With a nod, Gisele and Cristole stood and began walking back to their wagon. Sloane got up and rushed behind them. "Gisele? Cristole?"

They stopped and turned around.

Sloane tilted her head, her eyes flicking back and forth between them. "Why are you separating yourselves?"

Cristole pointedly stared at Gisele, gesturing as he did. Gisele took a deep breath and looked at Sloane. "Walk with me?"

Sloane nodded and fell into step with the orkun woman as they walked to the edge of the camp. The camp sat on a hill next to the road that dipped down before it continued south. All around them lay nothing except hilly grasslands with sparse trees that lined a small creek that snaked in between the hills. She knew that in the distance there was a forest they had to avoid. Cristole had asked her to send Tiberius to scout it and she had seen evidence of monsters within, along with strange concentrations of mana visible to the naked eye. She wanted to investigate them but knew that such an expedition would be very dangerous.

The two of them stood there and looked out into the twilight upon the plains. The first bit of frost was starting to settle during the night. It seemed winter would soon be upon them. Gisele seemed to hesitate, so Sloane nudged her. "What's wrong? Why are you avoiding me?"

Gisele sighed and rubbed her arms together, her breath visible as she exhaled. "I realized that we were becoming too attached. Ernald is already considering staying in Marketbol with Adaega. The woman has traumas that will likely never heal, and he has been doing what he can to help her. He believes she needs someone she is comfortable with for a while longer."

She sighed again, her eyes searching the darkening horizon as if the answer she needed lay beyond. "He says he isn't sure, but we know. That man was never meant to travel all over the world fighting other people's battles in search of some lost glory and honor. That made us—made me—realize that we'd lost our way. We came here searching for something that was missing, only to find—" She turned her head and looked Sloane in the eyes. "We found you. With you, we found an entirely new world, it seems." Gisele flexed her fist, a shimmering of red energy surrounding it and traveling up her arm, creating a thin shield that reminded Sloane of something out of science fiction. "This is all so new. It's also something we need to take back to our home. They need to know about all of this."

Sloane nodded. "I understand. I am truly grateful for all you have done for me, especially for helping me look for Gwyn. I know it's difficult for all of you to continue on nothing but my blind faith. I have no proof she's here and no proof she's safe. There are monsters showing up everywhere, and what if some of them attacked wherever she is? Then there's this whole war . . . Will she be somewhere that's attacked? Is she safe?" Sloane trailed off, taking a deep breath and collecting herself. Then she continued, consciously avoiding that emotional rabbit hole: "Still, I get it. Even though I constantly bury these worries and force myself to ignore them, I know you guys have probably been thinking about them too."

"Sloane, I . . ." Gisele's eyes fell and her shoulders drooped. "I will admit that there have been doubts. The world is so vast. Humans have appeared all over; some have even been killed. I know you do not like to hear it, but anything could have happened. Still, I—I believe in *you*. We know you have been doing everything you can." She smirked. "Even if your swordplay hasn't improved as much as you'd like during all our training sessions," she said, clearly trying to relieve the tension that was building.

Sloane huffed a laugh, again forcing her thoughts into their tiny box in the corner of her soul. "I feel so *stiff* when I fight like that. I keep naturally going back to my bad habits from fencing. Ugh. I don't think I'll ever be good at using a sword."

"Don't worry. If all else fails, just hide behind a wall."

Sloane raised a brow. "A wall? Is that a joke about that wall I destroyed?"

Gisele laughed. "No! I had forgotten all about that! I meant *Nemura*."

Oh! Sloane gave a half-hearted laugh, mostly directed at herself. "She is definitely a wall, but she's a softie once you get to know her," she said, feeling a need to defend her guardswoman.

The orkun knight nodded, turning serious. "I know. We are leaving you in good hands. Stefan as well. That Blade isn't half bad. He turned out differently than I had originally imagined. I . . . I am not looking forward to saying goodbye, Sloane. I know I have to, but I am going to miss you."

Sloane stepped closer to Gisele and put her arm around the knight's broad shoulders. "You guys are my friends. It's not goodbye. It's just a 'see you later.' We still have months together. Let's make the best of it, yeah? I am sure there is much more we can figure out together. Plus, I still need to figure out a way to give Ismeld magic."

Gisele snorted and nudged her with a shoulder. "You have *no* idea. That woman has been insufferable in training. I expected her to point out you being wrong long before now."

Sloane smiled. "Ah yes, the old 'I told you so.' Of course, it's a universal concept. I guess I deserve that. I tend to get caught up in my projects. Has anyone else been showing magic use?"

"I figured out how to use mana to strengthen myself and my attacks. Deryk and Ismeld have as well," Gisele said.

"That's a *type* of magic. Eh? Eh?" she said, squeezing Gisele's shoulder.

"If she can't make magical shields or shoot purple orbs of exploding death, she won't be swayed. I know Ismeld wants it desperately. She has trained incessantly since departing the city."

Sloane sighed and pulled her arm back. "I'll figure something out. I owe her. Especially after Thirdghyll." She lifted a hand and formed several orbs of arcane energy, letting them orbit each other as she stared into the soft light they emitted.

Gisele placed a hand on her forearm. "You do not. You fought together, as warriors should. That woman trusts you. She'll appreciate anything you do, but she'll simply show it in her own way. She feels inadequate right now. Just do not tell her I told you."

Sloane shook her head. "I won't, but I will come up with something. Then she'll have until I see you all again to become the biggest badass fighter in the world."

Gisele laughed. "That will never happen."

Sloane raised an eyebrow and looked at the orkun woman. "Why not?"

Her friend puffed her chest out. "Because that is clearly me!"

Sloane snorted. "I'm glad we're friends, Gisele. Just don't pull away again. I'll have to kick your ass."

Gisele reached over and squeezed her arm. "I won't. I'm sorry. Come on, let's go make fun of Cristole." The knight turned away, and Sloane smirked.

"You know, making fun of him doesn't hide the fact that you like him. You know everyone knows, right?"

Gisele froze. "Who is gonna kick whose ass, again?" The shielding spread out around the woman's entire form, giving her an almost spectral look with the hazy energy tinted with a light red hue.

Sloane lightly punched Gisele's shielded arm. "I ain't afraid of no ghost! That's all show—I know you can't keep that up. Wait—*Shit. Gisele! Stay away!*" She dodged the hand that swatted at her and ran toward the other knights, laughing the entire way, her emotional compartments holding strong.

Commander Ressa walked into the command tent, her second a step behind her. The general's presence was expected, but not with so few attendants and others. The man looked up from the map he was examining and at her as she entered. His bushy gray eyebrows scrutinized her with the same level of attentiveness that he was giving the effects in front of him.

"Commander, thank you for joining me."

She looked around, taking note of the others in the room, then stopped in front of the man and saluted.

"General, am I early? I was not expecting a private meeting," she said, giving her second a glance, who gave her a slight shake of his head. *Hmm. He thought the same as I did.*

"This should be quick, Commander. I have been looking for opportunities to assist you with your mission for my cousin, and I think I found one," he explained.

The old general was notably a second cousin of the empress and had been appointed to his current position due to his loyalty to her. This did not mean he was any less effective at his role. General Razane was a highly skilled tactician who had been selected for his ability to both command an army and maintain operational security. Those with loyalties to other clans or houses might be tempted to report back to them on their movements. Especially when the empress herself had planned this prong of their assault into the Sovereign lands.

After several secret envoys, the empress had devised a suitable bribe for the dwarves of Dheg Malduhr to utilize their pass. They had all felt the event before arriving, the ground shaking and a flash of light emitting from just over the mountains, and they had entered the pass on guard. When the army arrived and found the ruins of the city, it—while horrific—provided a boon they could not ignore. The army had saved those they could and then sent for specialists to assist the survivors, of which there were few.

Commander Ressa looked down at the map he was examining, trying to see what he meant. Little figures marked the disposition of his troops. Another small figure was placed on a road that bypassed Goosebourne; it was heading straight for two separate groups. The first was a light cavalry detachment that had been sent ahead to create a checkpoint and hopefully catch anyone fleeing from the siege. The second was a more recent addition that had been sent ahead to build a small watchtower at a key intersection in the merchant road.

He pointed at the small figure. "My scouts have been tracking this group here. They have been avoiding Goosebourne and my troops rather effectively. They never came within sight of the city, so I am inclined to let them go, but they will be stopped pending your arrival."

"Who are they?"

"I am not sure. They have been effective—to an almost excessive amount, mind you—at avoiding any patrols. Only two squads have even *seen* them from a distance, but none have gotten close enough to stop them. They will meet the light cavalry I have set up here tomorrow. They have orders to waylay any group that comes upon them."

Ressa nodded, following along. "How does this assist in my mission?"

General Razane pointed at the second group. "That will give you time to get here. Pass orders to the unit there to let the wagons go, then head southwest. Set up a believable way for them to come upon you naturally. Then pay to join their caravan. That should get you into the Sovereign Cities with little scrutiny. You just need to make sure they come upon *you*, not the other way around."

She looked up at him. *That is a surprisingly good plan.* "I think we can make that work. Thank you for your assistance, General. This was outside what was requested of you, and I am sure Her Highness will be pleased," she said.

He chuckled ruefully. "This is my last campaign. There is no need to expound my usefulness to my cousin. Just make sure you get what she needs. I know I do not command you, but if you could send a runner with any information that would affect my men, I would appreciate it."

She nodded slowly. "I understand. I will keep an ear and eye out for anything that may affect your forces here."

"That is all I ask, Commander." He turned and one of the aides moved forward with a scroll case. General Razane took it and handed it to her. "These are the orders for the watchtower. Please pass it to them on your way through."

She turned and handed the case to her second, then gestured toward the door. The man nodded and quickly exited the tent. Commander Ressa scrutinized the little figure once more, then looked up at the general, who stood silently watching her.

"We will prepare and move out tonight." She reached out her hand. "For the glory of the Ror, General."

Razane grasped her wrist. "And the longing of Vlaredia skies, Commander. Be safe, and return with honor."

Ressa gave the man a curt nod. *We have a way in. Now to take advantage of it.*

Sloane sat with Ismeld in her wagon as the caravan traveled toward the place Tiberius had seen a few scouts camped out the previous night. While her elven companion was trying to appear calm, Sloane knew she was ready to go charging out of the door into action. It was obvious in the woman's body language that she was a little on edge. She bounced a knee and tapped against her other leg with a finger while looking toward the small window to her right.

Sloane sighed. "Ismeld. Relax. Everything will be fine. There were only four men. They will let us by after Gisele shows all of our documents."

The knight looked at her. "I know it will be fine. I am just . . . I am at war with my thoughts currently."

Sloane lifted a brow. "At war with your thoughts, Ismeld? Really?"

"Yes. I do not wish to discuss it," she said.

Shrugging, Sloane said, "Alright. Then don't."

"I will not."

"Fine."

The high elf shifted and pointedly looked out of the window for a moment before shifting back. "Gisele told me about your talk."

"Oh?"

"Yes. What else were you wrong about?"

Sloane sighed again. It seemed the woman wanted the ability to use magic more than she had known. "I don't know what I don't know, Ismeld. It's always been nothing but theories and experimenting. I heard you got *something*."

Ismeld's eyes narrowed. "It is not the same."

"Ismeld, you are a brilliant swordswoman. What does it help you do?"

The woman tilted her head. "I feel a surge of energy and can react more quickly and my movements are more fluid. I don't know how, but I know it is **[Arcane Control]**. I felt what was almost a click in my mind and knowledge of what it was, and its function filled me," she explained.

Sloane nodded. "I have always felt something similar when I learn new things. You focus and push your intent on what you want to happen, pulling at mana as you do. Mana then fills you to perform the function you want. It doesn't always work, but I know that every time I *really* push myself, it has. My **[Runic Knowledge]** is a good example of this, I know more about the runes I work with than I have any right to know. It's like mana is giving us these—"

Her eyes shot open. *No. There's no way.*

She channeled mana, feeling it fill her. Sloane looked around. "Menu." She paused. "Screens. Status. System . . . *Framework?*"

Ismeld looked confused. "What are these things? Are you ill, Sloane? Should I get Maud?"

Sloane squinted as she thought. *Why didn't I see it before? How do I test this? Think.*

She blinked as Ismeld snapped her fingers in front of her. "I am getting Maud. Are you having a . . . what was it you called it? A stroke?"

Sloane narrowed her eyes. "I'm fine, Ismeld. I just had a revelation that is both world-shattering and making me question everything."

The high elf crossed her arms. "Dramatic much?"

What if this is just some simulation? Am I hooked up to some computer?

"You wouldn't understand. There is no parallel in this world."

Ismeld gave her a look. "Are you calling me stupid?"

Sloane jerked her head back. "What? No. What?" *Oh.*

Ismeld must have noticed her expression because she huffed a laugh. "Good. I know you did not mean anything by it. Please, explain your thoughts. You were nearly spiraling there."

Sloane considered how to respond, then decided to just keep it simple instead of launching into a long, drawn-out explanation, as was her instinct. "This whole time I've known mana has intent. What if that intent is because there is an underlying system guiding everything? These spells? Your ability? Could it all be a part of this system?"

"System? You mean like one of your computers?"

Sloane groaned. *Of course. They have no true concept of the idea.* "Yes. Essentially."

"You believe mana is controlled by a computer?"

Is it? No. The cores aren't technology. They're organic.

"I don't believe so. I have zero way of testing this." *Wait.*

She looked down at her watch and had an idea. Sloane pushed mana into it, trying to give a general idea of the intent she wanted. Nothing was happening, so she pulled more blue mana, filling her with as much as she could, then pushed it into the watch with one thought. *Show me my attributes!*

The usual swirl of mana appeared, but this time, it moved and formed a shape. It looked like a rough scalene triangle. She glanced up at Ismeld, who was watching her intently. "What did you call your ability?"

"[**Arcane Control**]."

"Control." *Is one of these points control? What are the other two points, then? Why can't it just list the damn things? Hmm . . .*

She pushed more mana, focusing on her intent. *Tell me my—*

A bang at the wall made her jump and she lost all of her focus. The small shutter on the window opened and Stefan's head poked through. "There's a group ahead. They've set up a checkpoint. Be ready, miladies."

Ismeld thanked the raithe and pulled on her glove inserts, then her gauntlets. Sloane looked down at her watch, seeing it swirling with the usual mist as it searched for mana use.

"It is so fascinating to watch you in these moments. Grand revelations usually follow," Ismeld said quietly. Sloane ignored her.

So close … it's something, though. I have attributes, and one has to do with my control. She was lost in her thoughts when Ismeld spoke again.

"Sloane, it's time."

Sighing, Sloane looked up and, too internally focused to respond verbally, nodded. Now to just figure out what it meant.

Just one more thing for the list.

CHAPTER THREE

SHOCK AND AWE

R elax and breathe. You're tense now. You were much calmer when you were distracted by your thoughts."

Sloane glared at Ismeld. "I am not tense. I am nervous. There is a difference."

The knight shrugged. "If we have to go bursting out of the wagon to fight off people, you want to do so as relaxed and confident as possible. Breathe. Can you hear what they're saying?"

Sloane put her head closer to the door, cupping her hand over her ear. After a moment of hearing only muffled voices, she pulled back and shook her head. "Nope. At least, no one is raising their voice. That's a good sign, right?"

Ismeld nodded and went back to cleaning and oiling her sword. The soft glow from the runes that Sloane had engraved into the blade reflected off of the woman's gauntlets.

"Should you be doing that right now?" Sloane asked her.

The high elf shrugged. "We will hear if things get to a point where we are needed," she said.

Sloane sighed deeply, then sat back. She had just managed to relax when a light knock came at the door and Stefan poked his head in. He cleared his throat. "Miladies, if you could spare a moment to speak with the captain of this checkpoint."

Sloane smiled. "Certainly, Guardsman Stranca." She shifted in her breastplate, adjusted her cloak's hood onto her head, and then exited the wagon. Sloane squinted into the sunlight as she moved out of the way to allow Ismeld to descend as well. She nodded at Nemura, who stood next to the entrance. The woman smirked and returned the nod. That smirk alone eased much of her tension. *Nervousness, not tension.*

They followed Stefan to the front, where Gisele was standing with Deryk and Ernald. Sloane looked around, catching Stefan's eye. He nodded behind them. She quickly glanced back and saw Cristole and Maud standing near the third wagon with the orkun alchemist, Rel, and her crossbow.

In front of Gisele stood seven armored men, clearly equipped to be light and quick. Horses were tied to a wooden hitching post that had been set up to the side of the makeshift barricade the men had made. Next to the horses were another four men who were also armed. It seemed that the majority of the soldiers were orkun, but there were some telv as well.

Every fantasy stereotype she had ever seen before arriving in this world hadn't prepared her for how professional and *normal* the orc-like orkun seemed. She had thought Gisele and Deryk were different mainly due to being from a predominantly elf nation. The imperial guards wore a mail hauberk and conical steel cap, and were equipped with a shield and spear. Seeing soldiers from a nation built around the orkun culture wear what could have fit in a European military from a similar era was interesting. The more she saw, the less threatened she felt. *The only thing to worry about at this point is whether any of them could reasonably get away to call reinforcements.*

That was not something the Sloane of Earth would have ever even considered worrying about. *Oh, how things change.*

"Ser Gisele," she said with a nod to the woman.

"Lady Reinhart, thank you for joining us. Captain Mor'rek and I were just discussing our business," she said with a quirked brow.

"Ah, yes." Sloan turned to the man standing in front of Gisele and tilted her head at him. "It is a pleasure to make your acquaintance, Captain. What can I do to alleviate any concerns you may have?"

"We are simply inquiring as to your purpose in this area, milady. We do not wish to hold you longer than necessary," he said, with a hesitant glance at Gisele.

"So you *do* wish to waylay us? For what purpose?"

"What is your business in the Sovereign Cities land, milady?"

"That is none of your concern, Captain. However, in the interest of transparency, we are simply traveling through. I have business in Avira before we return to Blightwych. The events of the past season have been a bit much for my constitution."

"Surely, you do not plan to reach Avira before wintering?" He looked around them at the caravan. "I do not believe you will make it in time."

She narrowed her eyes. "Of course we would not make Avira by land before winter, Captain. Do you believe me a liar? We *will* make it to Rosale, however. Our ship will be there awaiting us."

"So you have no business within the Sovereign Cities?"

"I believe I have answered that question, Captain. The Sovereigns are an acquired taste, one that I do not wish to partake in."

One of his men snorted from behind and mumbled something to the man next to him, who chuckled.

Sloane tilted her head and scrutinized the two men. "Is something I said funny, sers?"

The first man shuffled in place. "Not a ser, milady."

She raised a brow, internally laughing at the situation. "Oh? So you must be a lady. Surely. There is no other reason you would believe it your place to interject into our conversation."

"Uh . . . yes. No! What?" The man next to him jabbed him with his elbow and he shut up.

The captain glared at the two before turning back to Sloane. "My apologies, milady. I have one more question. Could you lower your hood?"

Sloane slowly turned her head from the two chucklers and regarded Captain Mor'rek. "Excuse me?"

"We have also been asked to look for certain individuals. Could you please lower your hood?"

Ismeld stepped forward. "Captain Mor'rek. My cousin here, the baroness Lady Reinhart, has a delicate constitution. The weather has become quite chill and she would like to return to the warmth of the carriage. Now, would you like to check *my* identity? I am Lady Ismeld d'Argin of Blightwych. I am fully aware of why the empire is here. Your grievances are of no concern to me," she told him with an air of superiority.

The man's eyes widened slightly. "My lady—"

Why is that still *such a big deal? And she really dislikes discussing it, let alone using it. I bet she's cringing on the inside.*

Sloane took over to give Ismeld a break from acting in a way she was not comfortable. She herself rather enjoyed acting imperiously.

"What is *my* concern," Sloan said, "is that you are hindering our ability to reach our destination before we are caught in the middle of a conflict we are not party to. I do believe Ser Gisele has shown you all of our documents that speak to who we are. That should be all you require. Anything else is simply criminal. Are you bandits, Captain? Or are you professionals from the Empire?"

Captain Mor'rek stood straighter. "We are professionals. I am simply following orders, milady."

"Many great atrocities were the result of men simply following orders, Captain. As my cousin said, Blightwych is not a belligerent in this conflict. I have nothing against you personally; however, we will not be deterred."

The captain sighed and looked between his men, who stood lazily awaiting his word, and the knights.

Sloane scanned the four with her and saw all were at the ready. Nemura and Stefan stood next to the wagons behind her. *Nemura's looking intimidating, as usual.*

"Fine," Captain Mor'rek finally acquiesced. "You may go."

Sloane nodded. "Thank you, Captain." She spun on her heel and returned to the wagon without a glance behind. She heard the quiet chuckle coming from Nemura as she walked by.

I think I am getting the hang of this noble shit.

* * *

Sloane groaned. After leaving the checkpoint, everything had been going smoothly. That is, until she had sent Tiberius up to scout ahead. The falcon had quickly seen something they hadn't previously. Standing on a hill that overlooked the road was a wooden watchtower about seven to eight meters tall. Below the hill on the opposite side of the road they saw what looked like a traveler's area for rest and camping. The area was surrounded by a small stone wall, which seemed more like something to deter wildlife than anything defensible. The tower had likely been built there deliberately.

Around the tower were a small fence and storage overhang, likely just to keep anything under it relatively dry in the rain. Tents dotted the area and several cooking fires were going. Several men were performing various tasks, while others sat together near the fires talking and eating.

About half a kilometer away from the rest area and the road was the forest Sloan and her company sought to go around. Through her watch's |**Golem Sight**|, Tiberius was able to show her where trees had been cut down. Fresh logs and cut planks still lay about.

The tower is clearly new and a rushed job.

The tower's line of sight allowed it to see fairly far down the road around the forest and then to the east along the northern border of the tree line. Its vantage point would allow the soldiers stationed there ample forewarning of any approaching forces. *Good spot to put a frontier fort.* Sloan had her falcon take note of the number of soldiers and some basic positioning of their patrols and guards while he was overhead. But one thing she saw was surprising.

When Tiberius turned back, she looked up from her watch and noticed Stefan staring at her.

She put her hand up to her cheek. "What? Is there something on my face?"

The man sighed. "No. What did you see?"

"One sec." She lifted slightly on the bench and looked around, seeing Gisele on her horse alongside the second wagon. "Gisele! Come here, please!" she called out.

Gisele had her horse catch up at a trot and slowed as she reached them. "Welcome back. You found something?"

Sloane nodded. "Up ahead at the next traveler's rest area. There's a watchtower and thirty-two soldiers. Six archers at the top of the tower and twelve, in groups of three, patrolling. Last fourteen are working on building up the camp and the area, including what seem to be support functions," she explained.

Gisele tapped a finger as she held the reins of her horse. "We should be able to get by them. We just let them know the previous captain let us pass. Was there anything else of note?"

She smiled. "Yes. There is no one watching the road in the direction we are coming from. There are signs of fighting something from the south."

"So, they aren't expecting to stop people from behind their area, necessarily.

That could be good news. Perhaps they must simply stop anyone from arriving and watch for retaliatory forces. If true, it makes our approach easier," Stefan said—a bit loudly so that Gisele could hear him from next to Sloane.

Gisele nodded sagely. "That is the ideal outcome. We should prepare for the worst, however. Sloane, I believe you should be out here ready this time. If it turns hostile, I want you to—what was the phrase you said?"

Sloane tilted her head. "Uh, shock and awe?"

Gisele snapped her finger. "That is it. I want you to pound them into submission. From what Ismeld tells me, you held off a lot more people than this with just the two of you. Don't hold back."

"Why does everyone tell me to not hold back?"

Stefan chuckled. "You are not a fighter, Sloane. Despite your apparent propensity for overwhelming attacks."

"I . . . resemble that remark."

"We know you do, Sloane. But you also get inside your own head. If it comes down to it, always do what you need to in order to keep your people safe," Gisele said.

Sloane nodded. "Fine. I will."

The caravan came within sight of the watchtower in a couple of hours. Seeing something in person that she had already viewed through the sensory gems installed in Tiberius was always interesting. It was almost like when you got your phone out to film a concert or something, but then looked away from the screen to see it properly, in real life. Things just felt . . . *right*.

As expected, the number of people looking their way was zero. They were about fifty meters to the area when the sound of the wagons and horses caught the attention of one of the archers.

"Troops from behind! Knights!"

"Peace, friends! We are just passing through!" Cristole yelled out from in front.

Chaos and a cacophony of shouting ensued. Soldiers from the area all came rushing back toward the tower, and those above drew bows and aimed down at the group. The soldiers from the camp formed up in their chainmail armor with their spears and shields, all yelling at each other in a completely disorganized way.

Cristole backed up and called out behind him. "Shields! Gisele! Get up here!"

The knights rushed to get in front of the caravan and brought out their shields. Stefan grabbed the large one from the back of the bench and set it up in front of himself while Sloane brought out the buckler from behind her. She wasn't sure what was going on, and she turned to Stefan.

"Why aren't they listening?!"

"They were surprised! I don't know what has them on edge, but we need to stop this now!"

Sloane nodded and stood, holding her buckler in front of her. She held her other hand up to her mouth and yelled. "Stop! We don't want to fight!"

"Form up! They want to fight!"

"That's *not* what I said!"

The men organized, but then an orkun man who looked like an officer rushed out of the tower, yelling at the soldiers. "Hold! Hold! Do not attack!"

Sloane took a deep breath and sat down. She heard a twang and out of the corner of her eye saw an arrow flying toward them. Stefan shoved his shield up and the arrow slammed into it with a thud. Her eyes went wide.

"They shot at us!"

The yelling started on both sides, and Sloane could barely hear what was said on the other side except snippets in between the knights' yelling.

"Shields up!"

"I said hold! Do not fire!" The man frantically tried to get his men to back down, and those on the ground seemed to be listening. Some even started lowering shields, but there was yelling at the top of the tower.

"Maud, get over here!"

A telv stood at the top of the tower. Sloane could just make out the fear on his face. He looked young, and he was pointing at them. He clearly wasn't listening or hadn't heard the officer on the ground.

"Loose!" she heard him order.

"Arrows! Shields!"

"No! Hold! Hold your fire!" The officer looked up and yelled one last time for his men to stop. Those on the ground became more confused as their archers continued firing on Sloane and the knights.

Six arrows went flying, each aimed at a different person, and shouts from the soldiers in front of Sloane told her that they were not backing down. Four of the arrows missed their targets, the last two hit the shields of Ismeld and Deryk. Suddenly she heard another, louder twang that came from behind her, and a bolt went flying and hit one of the archers. The man twisted and then fell over the side of the tower, bouncing off of the wall as he tumbled, before landing on top of a soldier who was standing below.

The chaos went from bad to worse. The soldiers around the officer who was yelling to hold remained where they were, but soldiers returning from patrol came running from the side and charged at the caravan, shouting as they did. Six soldiers came from the side and Sloane knew it was time to stop this mess. She stood and channeled some mana, and then fired off a **[Flashbang]** at the charging men.

The men cried out but were stopped.

"I said, stop!" Sloane yelled as loudly as she could.

"Sloane! Get down!" Stefan yanked her back down to the bench and behind his shield just as more arrows hit it. Her buckler fell away as she lost her grip on it. She moved to get it and saw another man grab a javelin and pull his arm back to throw. He stepped forward and a bolt appeared in his chest.

Gisele yelled for Rel to stop firing, but that was it for the other side.

The orkun officer who had tried to halt his men must have changed his mind after a second soldier was hit by a crossbow bolt. He yelled and the men brought up their shields and started to move forward, cautious of the mounted knights.

Gisele looked at Sloane with a helpless expression on her face.

"Do we fall back?" Sloane called to her.

The orkun knight ducked under an arrow as soldiers on the ground started taking potshots from a distance of just over half a football field. Another arrow caught Ernald's horse between its armor, causing it to rear up and cry out in pain. The sun elf nearly managed to hold on but then the horse came down hard and Ernald fell from his saddle. He managed to roll out of the way of another arrow and then hopped up, seemingly fine.

"Shit! That's it. This ends now!" Sloane yelled.

Stefan looked at her with wide eyes. "What are you doing?!"

Sloane ignored the raithe as she stood up and channeled mana. She had made a new spell specifically for grenades, but her first attempt at using it inside the inn's tavern area had been pitiful. She knew that she had looked at it incorrectly in attempting to change it to fit a medium it was never meant for.

The spell wasn't meant to be contained in a small grenade—it was meant to be fired. It wasn't the type of explosive spell she had needed. That failure had helped her realize there were different types of spells. She focused on the ones more relevant to her now.

With her new theory of a system-like framework to mana, she had started thinking of her spells in similar ways. More and more, it seemed to just *fit*. There were Sustained spells that also gave passive effects. These fell into their own categories like Knowledge or Utility—which for her meant her **[Runic Knowledge]**, **[Golem Sight]**, or like Ismeld's **[Arcane Control]**. These seemed to always give her an innate ability, but then there was an increased effect if she was focusing on them. The effect provided added benefits, but it seemed to mentally drain her as the spell was sustained.

Then there were the active spells. Of these, her **[Mana Bolt]** and **[Arcane Barrage]** were Missile-type spells, while her **[Flashbang]** and **[Starburst]** were Utility ones. While she was sure there were more, another type she had learned was Artillery.

Sloane felt the mana churn in her core as she pulled more and more into her and pushed it into her spell. She raised her hand as if she were going to throw a baseball and pulled her mana into an orb. She then **[Altered]** the Artillery spell the way she wanted and threw it—or rather, she simply performed the motion. A blob-like orb the size of a basketball did not need to be physically manipulated as it launched into an arc high above everyone.

All of the yelling and movement halted as everyone gaped up at the large, pulsing purple blob. With unnatural acceleration, it streaked toward the tower, its deep-purple hue intensifying as it neared its target. The impact was sudden, the spell penetrating the structure with ease before detonating in a brilliant flare of arcane energy.

But the explosion, while potent, wasn't as destructive as they might have expected. The focal point was the tower, which shuddered under the spell's force. The wooden beams groaned, struggling to withstand the magical onslaught. When Sloane cast the spell a second time, the tower could no longer bear the strain. Creaking, it succumbed, collapsing in a cloud of dust and debris.

Sloane drew and shoved more mana into the third cast of her [**Arcane Explosion**]. The resulting detonation was greater than the previous two combined. Everything in her vision flared with purple light.

Gisele, quick to react, conjured a formidable shield that formed a barrier to cover the caravan. It glowed a fierce red as it absorbed the brunt of the shockwave, funneling the turbulent air and particulates around them in a vortex of protection.

As the turmoil subsided and the dust began to settle, the aftermath was starkly revealed. Where once the tower stood, now only scattered remnants remained, strewn across the landscape. The camp, too, had been devastated, its fabric structures obliterated, leaving behind a scene of desolation.

What she didn't see immediately were people. Maud's sharp intake of breath drew Sloane's attention to the first fallen figure, half-buried in the dirt. She froze as she took in the scene. The sight was grim—some bodies were incomplete, and thanks to the spell's ruthless efficiency, there didn't appear to be any survivors. Yet the damage was controlled, confined mostly to the target area, sparing the caravan from the worst.

A feeling of deep exhaustion suddenly overtook her and seemed to bore into her all the way to the bone. Every muscle in her body ached and she started to feel dizzy. Sloane remembered holding her breath, but not when she finally breathed again. She didn't remember when she closed her eyes.

When she finally opened them, it was dark. The caravan was moving along a road with the only light coming from lanterns swinging from the wagon. They slowly passed the forest to their left, and Sloane caught her breath as she realized Gisele was driving the wagon next to her. She felt something on her shoulder and realized then that she was crammed into the center of the bench. A bundle of red hair and soggy fabric on her shoulder was the only way she could tell Maud was there, asleep and drooling on her shoulder.

"Gisele?"

"Shhh. It's late. We need to get as far away from the area as possible."

"What happened?"

"You went into shock. I am sorry. I pushed you too hard," she whispered.

"Would they have stopped before attacking us?"

"No. They were panicked by something. We passed a site of what appeared to be heavy fighting. Not to mention, their archers took their own initiative. Then especially not after Rel also panicked. They may have fired first, but we killed first. There was no turning back from there. We would have ended up dead or as prisoners."

Sloane took a deep breath. "Then I did the right thing."

"You did the *best* you could do under the circumstances. That's all I can ask. Right? Wrong? It's best if we do not focus on it. The world is not black and white, and it is not nearly as civilized as your world sounds."

Sloane tried to nod but couldn't move without bouncing Maud's head around. She felt a pit in her stomach start to form.

"Gisele?"

"Yes, Sloane?"

"If that was the *best* option, why does it feel so bad?"

"You are not used to this life. You'd never killed before coming here. That you are managing so well is a testament to your strength. There will be more situations like this in the future, that is certain. You will not always pick the correct option, but you must choose *something*."

"I don't think that's it. I think—I am struggling to see the Sloane that I was with the Sloane that I've become. My daughter is out there. If I have to kill a thousand people to get to her, I will. I just . . . I never thought it would be this easy to do it, or this difficult to rectify my actions with my sense of self. I look in the mirror and I don't recognize myself, Gisele."

"You're a strong woman, Sloane. You have more tenacity and perseverance than anyone else I know. I wish I could say that it gets easier. It won't. I don't mean to be blunt, but you need to figure that out. You have persistently been able to act in the moment. It's these moments afterward that are going to get you or someone else killed."

Sloane leaned her head back against the wagon. "You're right. I'm sorry, Gisele."

"Don't tell me sorry, Sloane. That's something you need to fix within yourself. This didn't happen in the inn, or as we were escaping the city. Why not? What are you doing, feeling, or thinking differently that is causing this reaction? Don't tell me, but that's what you need to figure out."

Sloane closed her eyes. *What is it? I didn't freeze in the city. I had a reaction after the thugs that attacked me in the alley, and now this. Why?*

She sat and tore through her thoughts and emotions. Struggling to figure out why she felt—*guilt. I feel guilty for killing them so . . . easily.*

She turned her head slightly, looking at the bundle of hair that was shifting to a more comfortable position. Sloane looked at Gisele out of the corner of her eye and saw the knight smirk as she watched Cristole ride ahead of them.

I shouldn't feel guilty about that. My actions are keeping them safe. I am the same woman I was before. Guilt won't help me find Gwyn. I swore to myself that I would turn this world upside down if I had to.

She rolled her shoulders and felt a bit of tension leaving her as she let them relax. *No more. I am coming, Gwyn. It's time I stopped standing in my own way and do what needs to be done.*

Sloane felt determined for a moment. But that feeling passed quickly because then she felt something she didn't want to feel at that juncture of deep introspection.

She squirmed. "Gisele?"

"Yes? Did you figure it out?"

"Yes . . . but . . ." Sloane started. She coughed slightly. "I can't move, and I have to pee."

Gisele let out a deep, exasperated sigh.

CHAPTER FOUR

THE VAL FORESTS

In the earliest days after the Flash, mana caused minimal changes to the various fauna. Like all beings, the wildlife of Eona gained a core and access to mana. However, as was later discovered, mana was not spread over the world equally. It pooled in places, and these "wells" caused numerous mutations within beings local to the areas. Luckily, this predominantly occurred far from civilization, as those effects were even more disastrous.[1]

The prevalence of the mana wells within the Val Forests is subject to many debates, including how much they contributed to the extreme changes in its denizens.

[1] Suya, A. (168 SA). "Examples within Civilization." In *Mana and Its Effects*, 142–68. Text, Royal Academy of Avira.
A History of Monsters, 173 SA

Sloane found Deryk and Ismeld with Cristole at the edge of the forest. She looked around in confusion before walking up to them, stepping over some brush as she exited the tree line. The wagons were in a decidedly different position from when she had left. The remaining knights and her guards were armed and spread out around everything.

"Hey, what's up? Why's everyone on edge?"

Cristole continued looking at what was in his hand, but Ismeld turned toward her. "*Sloane*, there you are. We called for you, are you okay?" The woman's face was full of concern.

Sloane tilted her head. "I didn't hear anyone. I wasn't that far, I just had to go relieve myself."

Cristole stood and turned toward her. In his hand sat something that looked like a scale. "Did you hear anything at all?"

She shook her head. "No . . ." She let out a nervous chuckle. "You guys are worrying me. What is wrong?"

"We heard something that sounded like a large growl coming from the tree line. There was rustling and then it disappeared. I thought I saw something move toward where we saw you last. We yelled, but nothing. We were just about to enter the forest to search for you."

She squinted her eyes. "Uh . . . yeah guys, sorry. I got nothing."

Cristole looked around. "We should move away from the forest. Come on, back to the wagons."

Nemura and the knights met them as they walked up, and everyone started talking over each other.

"You found her. Everything alright?" Gisele asked.

The group entered into a rapid-fire conversation that confused Sloane.

"She just came walking out. Didn't hear anything."

"—Strange—"

"—see a place to stop—"

"—sure we should. There's something out there—"

"Lady . . ."

". . . and it doesn't seem small."

". . . Sloane didn't see anything either?"

"She said she didn't. She also didn't hear us—"

"I even heard it, and we were over here."

"Guys! Everyone stop. I am right here," Sloane said, starting to get exasperated.

Everyone paused and looked at her. She decided to push some organization into the conversation. "Look. There are way too many people trying to inter-ject in this. Gisele, do you think we should stop for the night? No? Okay. Let's get moving. If there is something hostile out there, standing here is helping it. Cristole, do you think it's a big animal or is it a monster? Is it alone?"

He shrugged. "From the size of the scale and the prints I saw, I'd say a mon-ster. I only saw one set of tracks."

"Good. No one stays alone. Buddy system. Let's load up and move out. Now."

Gisele huffed out a laugh and looked around. "Lady Reinhart has spoken. Let's go. I am sure she means that we should all stick with at least one other person." She waited for Sloane to move closer, then leaned over to her as they walked toward Gisele's horse. "Well done. You're becoming comfortable in your new role in life."

"What's that? Lording over people?"

Gisele shook her head ruefully. "Being a *leader.* Seriously, thank you for your help there."

Sloane nodded. "You're usually the commanding one. Figured you were a good person to emulate."

Gisele's smirk transitioned into a focused squint, her attention shifting past Sloane with an intensity that raised the hairs on Sloane's neck.

"Sloane, stay perfectly still," Gisele commanded in a tone that brokered no argument.

Sloane felt something crawling on her. "Oh my god, oh my god. What is it?" Her voice crescendoed into a near-shriek, laden with rising alarm.

With deft precision, Gisele extended her hand and swiftly but gently plucked the creature from Sloane. Sloane spun around, her expression a blend of horror and curiosity as she confronted the source of her fear.

Sloane's eyes went wide. "What is that thing?!" she screeched.

Gisele's expression softened, a mix of amusement and mild reproof playing across her features as she held her palm open for Sloane to see. Nestled within was a tiny, winged reptile, quivering subtly under their gaze. Lacking forelimbs, it possessed instead a pair of diminutive clawed wings, and it peered up at them with an almost imploring look.

"You don't recognize your cloak's clasp? This is a wynver. They're native to this area. Little guy is probably cold."

"A wynver?" *Sounds awfully similar to a . . .* She leaned closer and examined the little thing. *Yup, it looks like a palm-sized wyvern.* She then looked down at the clasp on her cloak. "Huh. That's a funny coincidence . . . He's cute with his little squiggly tail. Do they get bigger?"

"No, this is about as large as they get."

Gisele smiled as she placed the reptile on the wagon. The tiny wynver crawled closer to the lamp that hung from the corner, trying to feel the heat. The knight untied the reins of her horse from the side of the wagon.

Sloane leaned in, her earlier terror giving way to fascination as she observed the tiny, trembling creature, its delicate wings fluttering weakly. "A wynver, you said? It's actually quite adorable, isn't it?" Her initial fright now a distant memory, she watched the thing try to warm up.

Hopping onto the wagon, Gisele pointed down at Sloane. "Let's head out. Keep an eye on that watch. It's saved us more than I care to admit."

A metallic screech sounded from above them.

Sloane and Gisele looked up at Tiberius who was perched on the wagon's roof. "What is it, buddy?"

She tapped the rune on her watch for |**Golem Sight**| and watched as the screen showed the world through the falcon's eyes. In the forest, off in the distance, she noticed movement. Something large and filled with black mana was moving away from them, heading south.

Sloane gasped and let go of the spell. "I saw it. It's out there deep in the woods and is heading south."

Tiberius chirped a few times, bouncing as he did.

Gisele glanced between her and Tiberius, then sighed. "It seems Tiberius is proving to be a valuable team member. Can you point to where you saw it?"

Sloane scrutinized the tree line, trying to estimate where it was based on where Tiberius had been. When she thought she had it, she indicated at a point slightly southeast of them. "That way."

Gisele nodded. "Please have Tiberius fly ahead and above us. Can he notify you somehow if he sees something?"

Sloane nodded. "Yes, we figured out a way." She had managed to connect the watch to Tiberius so that if he noticed something deemed a threat to her, the watch would pulse. She looked at him and gave him the orders Gisele requested. Tiberius chirped as he took off, seemingly understanding the necessity to remain quiet.

"Sloane, get up on the bench. Stay alert. If there is anything big, you're going to be our heavy hitter."

It was several hours later when the caravan finally found a place to stop for the night. There was a campsite on top of a hill with a steep face parallel to the road and the forest beyond. No light from the moons shone through the overcast sky and the site was cast in darkness. They lit a fire and tied the horses close by.

The camp was mostly silent, with everyone drained after the long night on the road. Adaega, the two alchemists, Koren the smith, and Ernald had commandeered the center of the site. The group spoke quietly as they ate their first warm meal in a day. The rest of the knights and the two Reinhart guards had already set up a schedule to sleep and keep watch so those who needed to rest could do so without feeling they might miss something. Sloane was relieved that they had finally stopped; she wanted to be somewhere somewhat defensible during the night in case there was something out there.

Tiberius occasionally caught sight of the monster in the forest but as the night dragged on, Sloane was finding it more and more difficult to stay awake and Gisele had told her to go to sleep. Still, Sloane made sure Tiberius knew to come back as quickly as possible to warn the knights if the monster moved toward the camp.

Sloane climbed into the wagon and her cot and reflected on how poorly the day had gone. *This day really sucked*, she thought. Exhaustion quickly settled in, and her thoughts slowly drifted as she felt herself falling asleep.

Sloane blinked into wakefulness as a small stream of light shone on her face. She let out a yawn, covering her eyes for a moment to adjust to the brightness in the wagon. Sloane turned her head away from the sun laser attempting to burn her eyes out and stretched. After getting up, she looked around and noticed Maud was sleeping close by. Sloane gingerly stepped over the redhead and made her way out of the wagon.

It was early morning, and she was immediately noticed by Nemura, who was standing right outside. "Good morning, milady. Did you sleep well?"

"I did. Why didn't anyone wake me? I should have been up just before sunrise, right?"

The muscular telv woman waved her off. "It was nothing. We didn't see any more signs of whatever was stalking us for the rest of the night."

Sloane nodded. "That makes sense. Thank you. Have you slept?"

Nemura nodded. "We swapped on and off. I am good."

"Good. How long until we leave?"

"A couple of hours. Ser Gisele wanted to let everyone eat first," Nemura said. "*Gisele! Get over here!*"

Sloane jerked her head toward the noise. "Was that Cristole?"

Nemura turned as well. "I think so."

"Let's go see what's wrong."

"Follow behind me, please, my lady. Just in case there is danger."

Sloane nodded, content to let the woman do what she knew best, and fell in behind her. Looking at Nemura's muscled arms, she thought, *Plus, if there really is a system, she's got to be the tank.*

They made their way to the edge of the camp, where Cristole sat on his horse. Gisele and Ismeld stood next to him.

"Everything alright, Cristole?" Sloane asked.

"No. There's something everyone should see," he said.

"*Everyone*, everyone? Or just us?"

"I will remain here. Unless it is dangerous?" Ismeld said.

"We will be fine with just the four of us. In fact, I suspect the danger has passed. Ismeld, you may want to wake the others."

Ismeld looked at Gisele, who gave her a slight nod.

"We will return as quickly as possible," Gisele said.

Cristole got down from his horse and handed the reins to Ismeld. "We won't need to ride, it's just up ahead."

Ismeld led the horse away as the rest of them followed Cristole up the road. Sloane was able to get a good look at her surroundings as they walked. They seemed to be leaving the rolling plains area that had been all they'd known since leaving Thirdghyll. The fields of grass here were drier, yet the forest to her left was vibrant and lush. The road they walked on provided a stark contrast in the environments.

Twenty minutes later, Sloane was wondering why they hadn't just ridden horses. "Cristole? Why did we walk? How much farther?"

The elf looked at Gisele and they shared a look that resulted in Gisele answering for him.

"Sloane, you are terrible at riding horses."

Sloane gasped. "*What?* Et tu? I fell off . . . one time."

Nemura turned and gave her a look. "You do not know how to ride a horse? There . . . there are stirrups . . . How?"

"Look. Riding horses isn't something most people do often on Earth," Sloane explained without admitting how painful that occurrence had been.

Nemura looked confused and opened her mouth to speak, but Cristole cut her off with a raised hand.

"Later, please. We are here."

Sloane looked around and immediately noticed a difference in the area. It was damaged, almost as if a tornado had gone through. Trees were split and leaned on each other. Dirt was upturned everywhere, and as they walked around the crown of a tree that lay along the side of the road, she saw it.

"What. Is. That?" she asked. *No way. What?*

"*That* is a mutated drakyyd lizard," Cristole explained.

Nemura narrowed her eyes. "That looks different from the monsters that were in the city. I thought *those* were drakyyds," she said.

Gisele approached the dead monster. "It is different, but it's clearly mutated from the same animal."

Sloane was staring wide-eyed at the beast. "That looks like something we know of in stories on my world."

That seemed to surprise Cristole slightly. "Really? What do you call them?"

She thought. "It's called a *drake*, or as many people would know it, a wingless dragon," she said, still disbelieving what she was looking at. "The closeness of the names is surprising. Oh hey! Just like the wynver, Gisele!"

Gisele turned her head and gave Sloane a *look* from where she was examining the creature.

Cristole tilted his head questioningly. "Wynvers are small."

Sloane nodded. "Yeah, just imagine if one of those were as big as this!"

Cristole grimaced and shook his head as if considering the potential.

Nemura slowly turned toward Sloane. "You have monsters like this in your stories . . . *that have wings?*"

Sloane nodded. "Yes, they were bigger too. Many stories had them as sapient and incredibly intelligent. Others simply considered them apex predators. They would—"

"There are piercing wounds all over. The core was cut out as well," Gisele said from where she was examining the drake.

"I'll tell you more later," Sloane said in a hushed voice to Nemura. The guardswoman nodded.

Sloane always felt a little squeamish when looking at dead animals, but even she could see that it had indeed been killed by what seemed like man-made weapons. *Elven made.* The wielders of those weapons, however, were nowhere to be seen.

"Cristole, are you thinking what I am thinking?" Gisele asked.

The high elf nodded and pulled out his sword, looking back in the direction they'd come. Gisele and Nemura followed suit.

"What are you two thinking? What is it?" Nemura asked.

Sloane placed her hand where her sword should have been and mentally cursed herself after realizing she had left it behind. Compromising, she chan-neled mana through her and prepared to cast a spell if needed.

Moments later, she heard Tiberius's cries from behind her and the thwap of a bowstring being released. The four of them quickly turned. Almost instantly after it was released, a blur snatched up the arrow and let out a cry. Tiberius flapped his wings and flew higher, avoiding another arrow as he did so. Sloane followed the trajectory of the projectile back and saw five elves. Tiberius snapped the arrow in two and flew down to land on her shoulder.

"Hey, buddy. Good catch. Thank you."

Tiberius turned his head slightly and chirped at her before turning to focus on the elves.

Gisele must have noticed the elves as well because her hand shot up and she cast a shield between them and the other group.

Sloane looked at her. "Who are they?" she asked, louder than she'd meant.

"They're Valeni. The Guardians of the Val Forests. They *hate* outsiders."

Sloane used **[Golem Sight]**, choosing to skip straight to the spell instead of using her watch—and looked through Tiberius's eyes to see the group closer. Immediately, she noticed that the five weren't elves but telv. They wore leather armor and were armed with bows and curved blades on their hips. They were all male, and each had a bow drawn but seemed to be discussing something. *Likely what to do about us and Gisele's shield.*

As if summoned by her thoughts, another one drew back his bow and let an arrow fly, hitting the shield dead center to no effect. Nemura looked at where it hit, then glanced at Gisele. "Your shield alright, Ser Gisele?"

The orkun nodded. "It is fine. We need to make sure they do not try and flank us, though. We should get—"

Sloane turned as she heard a commotion behind her again. Her stomach dropped, thinking that they *had* been flanked, only to see the caravan approaching. Ismeld and Deryk led the way on their horses, with Stefan driving the first wagon. Ernald and Maud rode two other horses on either side of the three wagons.

Gisele seemed conflicted, and Sloane understood. On the one hand, they had more people there to help them, and on the other, it simply gave more targets for the Valeni to hit. *We need to resolve this without attacks.*

"Gisele! Where do you need us?" Deryk called out.

The knight-captain was still maintaining a shield, so Sloane responded for her. "Just come pick us up. Then we are going to move forward *really* slowly."

The wagons slowed as they reached Sloane and Nemura, and the guards-woman helped Sloane up onto the wagon with Stefan. Sloane watched the Valeni, who seemed hesitant to do anything and looked as if they were arguing.

"Gisele, hop up here with us," she said. "Keep focusing on the shield. I'm going to do something. I'll tell you when to drop it."

As she stood, Tiberius took off from her shoulder and flew up to the roof of the wagon. Sloane cast a series of weak **[Mana Bolts]** and Altered the ten of them to hover and follow them. She then aimed away from the Valeni and fired off a weaker [**Arcane Explosion**]. The siege spell arced and exploded away from everyone, but with a large enough blast, that dirt fell near the group of Valeni.

The Valeni's surprise was evident in how their arms simply dropped to their sides and they stared wide-eyed and slack-jawed at where the spell had gone off. Sloane narrowed her eyes.

"Gisele. Drop it."

The woman nodded and lowered her hand, the shield collapsing as she did. Sloane made her [**Mana Bolts**] move in large circular patterns as the wagons started moving forward. The Valeni stepped backward off of the road, and Sloane was finally able to get a good look at them as the caravan passed them. The five men each had short, pointed ears like a telv, except unlike most of the people she had seen, they had beards. Two of the men in the back whispered to each other, one pointing at Sloane. Another raised his hood, almost as if he were trying to hide from her sight.

She almost spoke, but then the man in the front said something in a language she did not understand. The man to his left said something as well, and the first gave her a slow nod. The Valeni's eyes never left her own, and she nearly gasped in surprise. *They have cat eyes!*

There was no conflict as their caravan passed, but the knights on horses made sure to follow from behind and keep an eye on the five, who remained where they were. When Sloane looked back after Ismeld rode by on her horse, there was no sight of them.

The group seemed to breathe a collective sigh of relief after that. Sloane leaned back and looked behind a tense Stefan over at Gisele. "Did you see their eyes?"

Gisele nodded. "Yes. That . . . that was *strange*. I have only seen a few Valeni in my life, and none had anything like that."

Sloane nodded. "It was wild. Who *are* the Valeni?"

"They are the natives of the continent. They are a collective of telv, orkun, and raithe who were never conquered by the Loreni. They retreated from the Old Empire to the Val Forests, and defend them to this day from any outsiders," Stefan interjected.

"Only a few Val Forests have ever been conquered. It is said that Eona herself provides for the Valeni in their forest homes, and they have become her guardians in return. Most who venture into the forests do not return," Gisele said.

"How many are there?"

Gisele shrugged. "Many. There are five such forests in the Sovereign Cities region alone. Four in Avira. Even two in Lymtoria. Western Ikios was the most populated region of the Old Empire."

Sloane shivered. "Tiberius saw many of those areas that had high concentrations of mana in the forest. The monsters were animals adversely affected by mana . . ."

"What are you saying, Sloane?" Stefan asked.

Who knows how much they were changed, and how much more they will be just by living close to those mana . . . wells.

"The Valeni . . . I think they may have been affected as well."

Ressa looked up at the approaching cavalry as it slowed to a stop and the captain dismounted. The remaining men very deliberately found other things to look at—that is, until her second ordered them to assist in the collection duties. *Our deceased will be treated with dignity and respect,* she thought.

Captain Mor'rek glanced hesitantly around the scene as he approached her. She heard the man take a deep breath before coming to a stop, going down on one knee, and lowering his head.

"Commander, I have failed Vlaredia. I accept any punishment you deem necessary," he said.

Good. He accepted responsibility. As soon as she reached the scene, she had sent a rider with orders for the light cavalry squad to make their way here with all due haste. The rider then continued to Goosebourne and General Razane as she awaited the man in front of her.

"Stand up, Captain," Ressa ordered. "Look around. What do you see?"

"Death and destruction. It looks like an army assaulted this location."

"Yes. This would have happened to you as well. *If* you had provoked them."

The man looked surprised and glanced around. She gave him a moment to process the scene around them. There was nothing but rubble where the tower had once stood. The campsite was essentially gone. The storage shed had been destroyed. Her team had set up a collection point where they attempted to sort through the remains of thirty-one of the soldiers who had been stationed here. *That was going to take a lot more time. Some are just . . . parts.*

"What can you tell me about a tanned woman with curly brown hair, Captain?"

The man tilted his head and squinted. "There was one woman who had hair like that, a baroness. Her name was Lady Reinhart. She wore a cloak, however, so I could only see what peeked out from the sides."

Ressa nodded. "Lady Reinhart. Tell me about her."

"She was very confident and a bit overbearing. The baroness said that she had business in Avira. When questioned, she stated they would be traveling through Rosale."

"You said she wore a cloak? Did you not ask her to remove it?"

"I did. However, her cousin, Lady d'Argin of Blightwych, joined the conversation and objected. They had five knights, the two ladies—Lady d'Argin was well armed—and two guards. Both guards also looked professional. I did not feel confident in forcing any issue."

Ressa pointedly looked at where the watchtower once stood. "It is well that you did not."

She paused, considering what the man had related. She knew of Blightwych's royal family. She knew of the families for every kingdom. Lady d'Argin was not well known, but she was in the line of succession for the throne. *Sixth, if I remember correctly.* She was also a knight of a small order, mainly due to her friendship with the woman who had formed it. One notable thing about the noblewoman though . . . she had no baroness cousin from a House Reinhart.

Ressa wasn't sure of what to make of that, but there was seemingly something more there. The sole survivor of this attack had described what he had seen. The man had been returning from patrol when he saw the action. From what she was told, the entire event was chaotic. He wasn't sure what happened, only that their archers were firing on the caravan and a woman with a crossbow fired back, killing two men. Then as the commander of the Vlaredian forces finally made up his mind and organized his troops to attack the small group, the curly-haired woman—Lady Reinhart—used magic and obliterated the tower *and* all but one of the men stationed there.

There is no reason to be on this road if they were traveling to Rosale. The only place this road goes to is—Ressa's eyes widened. The caravan wasn't traveling to the coastal kingdom to the south. *Why? Are they attempting to warn the Sovereigns? That doesn't make sense, they hadn't been anywhere near Goosebourne.* The scene around her worried her, though. If one woman could do this, what feats could her nation's actual enemies perform?

I cannot allow her to assist the Sovereigns.

She turned back to the captain, who had been waiting patiently. "Captain Mor'rek, my team and I will be leaving immediately. You and your men are to take control of this scene until the general sends adequate forces to relieve you. Once you are relieved, you will pass a message along to the general from me, along with a full report."

The man saluted. "What is the message, Commander?"

"I have found a target and will be tracking it. The potential for threat against Vlaredia is high. Target has already spilled Vlaredian blood and could single-handedly tilt any battle against us. Please inform your cousin of my initial destination."

She felt her magic flow through her body as her determination rose. That woman was a problem. One that would need to be handled carefully.

Captain Mor'rek nodded. "Understood. Where are you heading, Commander?"

Ressa's eyes narrowed. "Marketbol. Pass on that I would like to extend an invitation for the general to join me as soon as possible."

CHAPTER FIVE

PREPARATIONS

Gwyn took a deep breath as she put the quill down next to her notebook. She smiled and looked up at Mister Branigan, who nodded his head and walked over to her. The old sun elf picked up the notebook and examined her work, the man nodding along as his eyes scanned over the essay.

"This is well done, Miss Gwyn. However, I would suggest you read Stanza's *Treatise on Political Relations*. It would give you more insight into inter-house politics."

She nodded once, and he continued, "Now, let us delve into proper etiquette when meeting fellow royals. You have improved much since we have worked together. When we arrive in Avira, it will only be a matter of time before you are required to meet the Crown and the family."

Gwyn narrowed her eyes. "Do I *have* to? The crown prince seems like a jerk," she said.

The professor gave her a sad smile. "Trust me, I understand, Miss Gwyn. Those of your station have to meet with people they do not like quite often. That is the way of things. You must learn to wage a war of words. They will be doing the same thing with you."

She groaned. "It's always talk, talk, talk." Raising her hands, one turned icy as she called a mist of frost from it, while the other hand lit up in flame. "It's so much easier to just use magic."

Mister Branigan chuckled and her fire reflected in his kind eyes. "I imagine it is, for you at least. Now, understanding how to address others is pivotal," he began, his tone shifting to one of earnest instruction. "When interacting with fellow nobles in an informal context, it is customary to use 'lord' or 'lady,' followed by their first name. This signifies a level of camaraderie or familiarity, yet still respects their noble status."

He paused, ensuring Gwyn was following along. "For example, if you were to meet the countess Lady Racine's husband, you would address him as Lord Alec, which is informal. However, in formal settings or during your first meeting, you should use their full title and house name, as you would with Count Telford. This demonstrates both respect and awareness of their rank and peerage."

Gwyn listened, trying to absorb the information, but she knew that no matter how much he tried to teach her, she probably would never get all of this noble etiquette stuff. There were so many different rules and situations that called for different things. Every little word mattered; every time you talked to someone, even how you addressed them changed based on where you were or how you were speaking to them. She gritted her teeth.

Fake it till you make it, Gwyn.

Mister Branigan's gaze became more intense, underscoring the importance of what he was about to say next.

"As a princess, you do indeed hold a high rank, yet it is imperative to remember that the twins, the prince and princess of Avira, being of the ruling realm, will be considered your social superiors in Avira. This doesn't mean much in practice, but it is important to remember."

Gwyn nodded as she tried to follow along. It was *so* much. "And what of other kingdoms' royals? Do you think I'll meet them?" she inquired, her mind working through the various scenarios she might face.

"In those cases, respect their rank as your equals in terms of royal blood, but always remember, the context of Avira might change the dynamics slightly. Their specific titles can vary, and understanding these will be crucial, especially in international diplomacy or gatherings where multiple royal families converge. You are a separate case, due to your background. Always have one of your retainers on hand to help you navigate official business. Avira's politics are not kind. I have a few books you should go over to ensure you know all of the nuances. I will test your knowledge before we leave."

Wait, maybe Roz can help. Gwyn let out a slow breath, the weight of her responsibilities and the intricacies of noble interactions settling on her. It was a far cry from the straightforwardness of casting magic, but she knew it was important to these people, even if it wasn't to her at all. "Thank you, Mister Branigan," she said, attempting to make him see that she'd try. Not that she really wanted to, but she at least owed it to those who had helped her so far. "I will study and be ready."

The old sun elf smiled, pleased with her resolve. "I have no doubt you will excel, Princess. You have the makings of a great leader, one who will navigate the complexities of nobility with grace and acumen."

Gwyn smiled.

"How are your magic tests with Miss Rolfe going?"

Her practicing with his wife had been going great. She'd already learned a few new spells in the last month. After spending so much time with her fire, she knew she had to try more elements. Now she could do several spells with her ice magic, and one of the first things she had tried was making a snowman.

Just like in Frozen*!* It just stank that she ended up with only three big ice balls. She giggled. "Sorry, I was remembering something from home." She took a deep breath. Remembering home always tasted bittersweet. She missed it so much.

But she forced a smile as if nothing bothered her. "I remembered a movie about a princess who had ice magic too. She was so cool. *Elsa* didn't have fire magic, though. I'm . . ." She looked at her frozen hand and let her magic dissipate. "*Cooler.*"

The sun elf groaned. "Is your mother fond of these puns you make?"

Gwyn tilted her head and adopted a lopsided smile. "Where do you think I got it from?"

Mister Branigan just shook his head, but the mirth in his features was evident. Gwyn went back to how her time with Professor Maya went. "My practice has been really good. I think Miss Rolfe is really getting the hang of it. She's been so helpful in helping me learn new things. There's a new type of magic she wants to practice. She is also asking a ton of questions about magic and stories from home. She's trying to make sense of it all, I think. Just between you and me, I think she has some magic too. I can see it moving around as she's thinking. Kind of like you."

The man, who was taking a few notes while she spoke, suddenly jerked up in shock. "Excuse me? Say that again, Miss Gwyn?"

She squinted her eyes. "The magic you use. It's all blue, but it's weird and isn't like the magic I do. I've tried to use my magic as you do. Miss Rolfe's magic is close to yours too. Hers is yellow and blue. Your blue is a bit deeper, though, maybe because she has two? Well . . . wait, I have four and those are about the same as yours. Yeah, I have no idea. Something else to talk to Miss Rolfe about!"

Mister Branigan's mouth opened and closed a few times. "I-I think that may be all for today, Miss Gwyn. We will resume tomorrow. Please read the first twenty pages of this book as well." He moved a book from the side over to her, and then stood. "Now, if you will excuse me."

Gwyn raised a brow as the man hastily retreated from the room. She shrugged as she turned and looked at Sabina, who had been reading a book as she sat by the fireplace. *Do you think he didn't realize he has been using magic this whole time?* Gwyn sent.

Sabina snorted. *Probably not. I didn't realize it at first, either. I suspect that with magic that works on your mind, it simply feels different . . . until it doesn't.*

I guess so. I remember him using it when we were learning about languages. Your magic is so cool. I wish I could talk to others like this.

Sabina turned and looked at her. "Do you want to?"

"What do you mean?" Gwyn thought and said at the same time.

Sabina winced. "Ouch."

Gwyn gave her an apologetic look. "Sorry, I struggle to switch between the two. Which I bet is confusing for you."

"It is no bother. We will practice. I *may* be able to use magic to let you talk to someone else," she said.

Gwyn narrowed her eyes. "I am not sure, Sabina."

Sabina tilted her head. "Why not?"

Gwyn considered how to reply and took a deep breath. *I think this should stay quiet for now. The colors all feel like they have different uhhh . . . meanings? No . . . that's not right . . .*

Sabina furrowed her brows. *Concepts?*

Exactly! The colors have different concepts. My blue is different from my red. Then my black is different. It's what you have. I don't think black can do that. It feels more . . .

The mind mage's face dropped. *Evil? Insidious?*

Gwyn quickly shook her head. *No! It simply feels like it is meant to . . . affect things. Not, uhhh ... ugh, why are words hard? Facilitate! I don't think black can connect things and* facilitate *a conversation. You can use it because you are able to read my thoughts.*

Sabina nodded slowly. *That makes sense. Did you think of all that yourself?*

Gwyn nodded. *For the most part. Miss Rolfe and I have a lot of talks about magic. She's really good at helping figure out what it* does. *I think if you had blue magic, it would work differently. It seems to be more the concept that would be required.*

Gwyn chuckled as she remembered something else from home. *A blue mind mage would be like a Wi-Fi router! Just sit there and connect with everyone. Now to find someone who has perfect memory from Earth and they can transmit movies straight to the brain!*

Don't get too ahead of yourself, Gwyn, Sabina thought with a laugh. *That makes sense, though. Thank you.* The knight quickly looked out of the window. *Ready to go? We need to meet up with Lady Roslyn.*

Gwyn's mood suddenly got a lot better, and she couldn't reel in her thoughts before her excitement leaked through her connection with Sabina. "Oops! Sorry."

Sabina stood up and reached for her. Gwyn went over and hugged her knight. The woman pulled her tight as she said, "It's quite alright, Gwyn. I enjoy your excitement. You've been practicing on getting your [**Mental Fortress**]?"

"Yes, it's really tough, but I think that's because I don't have mind magic. I have been working on a different way to do it. I'll figure it out," she said with surety. She knew she could do it. It was simply a matter of time.

Gwyn led the way out of the room, nodding to the guards who stood outside. They had been assigned to Sabina full time and had been told privately about Sabina's magic. Siveril and Theran had worked out a way to limit the number of people who knew about each person's magic. They had decided to assign guards to the knights instead of Gwyn; those guards would then protect Gwyn when their knight was with her. It was a roundabout way of doing it, but it also allowed the knights to practice with specific guards who could be trained to work with that magic.

As it stood now, each of her knights had a team of four guards assigned to them. The remainder of the House Guard worked around the manor and filled in wherever required. The three teams were considered the elite of the house. They were *very* good at what they did. Theran and Taenya had trained them extensively.

Her head knight had been training so much since her duel. However, now she was actually meeting with Mister Onas about the magical stuff he had found. They were trying to work out a deal with someone to get a shipment in before she had to leave for the Royal Academy. Mister Onas had assured her she would have at least something.

Gwyn's face broke into a beaming smile as she and Sabina made their leisurely way through the market. It was indeed a vibrant day, the air thick with the smells of exotic spices and the sounds of haggling vendors and enthusiastic buyers. The four guards who provided escort were not just protectors but also symbols, their appearance alone ensuring that the crowd parted like the sea for them. While her guards didn't have full, shiny armor like her knights, they still looked really good.

Both the men and women wore armor on their left shoulder that had a dragon on it. The shoulder harness had a large circular clasp with her house's crest on it. A vambrace protected the forearm of the hand that carried the spear. The other hand carried a shield on which was painted a beautifully menacing dragon, and which was reinforced with metal that had a small cutout for them to rest their spear on.

The guards' clothing was made of a heavy piece of fabric that looked like a quilt with metal buttons that dropped down a little below their waist. Over they wore a sleeveless blue coat that had silver trim. Their helm covered everything except the front of their faces, but there was a way to attach a facepiece if it was needed. It was engraved with pretty designs and had an edge that went from their temple to a point at the top of their heads where it formed into a shallow cone. They wore regular pants, just with a thicker piece of fabric and cuisses covering their thighs. Also, their boots had grieves attached to the front to protect their shins.

Basically, they looked amazing, Gwyn thought, and when they had one of her knights around them, everyone knew to back away. Taenya and Siveril had done well and put in a large order with Mr. Onas after a lot of meetings. It was clear that they knew how to make a statement with something as simple as appearances.

Gwyn noticed Evocati Khalan first. Roslyn's Paladin of Alos guardian stood out with his gleaming red armor and spotless white tabard. The golden sun centered on the sun elf's chest glimmered in the midday light. The Church of the Celestials had promised a paladin to Gwyn as well, but she and her knights did not wish to cozy up to them quite yet. Siveril had worked hard to build up the influence of their house; they needed to stand on their own now.

The option is there, though. Evocati Amari seemed so serious.

Roslyn's two knights stood behind her friend with their backs to Gwyn as she and Sabina approached. Gwyn could just make out the high elf as she looked at some items on a table.

Gwyn's lips curled into a mischievous smile, her finger pressed to them in a silent plea for complicity as Evocati Khalan's eyes met hers across the bustling market space. Understanding her unspoken request, Khalan could not suppress the amusement in his eyes, his seasoned warrior's demeanor breaking momentarily as he signaled subtly to the accompanying knights. As they turned their heads and saw her, the female knight's face lit up as she realized what Gwyn wanted to do.

With the stealth of a cat, Gwyn advanced toward Roslyn. Her arms spread wide, poised for the impending surprise, and with a dancer's grace, she closed the distance, springing forward to ensnare Roslyn in a joyful ambush. The contact was light, yet it elicited a sharp, surprised yelp from Roslyn, who spun around, her expression a blend of shock and mild indignation.

"Hey there, Roslyn!" Gwyn exclaimed, her laughter ringing clear and bright.

Roslyn's initial scowl softened as she beheld Gwyn's delighted face, but her gaze soon shifted accusatorily toward her knights as the realization of her protectors' betrayal hit her.

"*Greetings*, Princess Gwyneth," she intoned formally, yet it was tinged with a growing smile. "What an *unexpected* pleasure." She shot another scowl at her escort.

Gwyn responded with a playful snort, brushing aside the formalities. "Don't use your noble voice on me, Roz. We gonna shop or what?"

Resignation mixed with amusement in Roslyn's sigh as she scanned their surroundings, the vibrant array of goods momentarily forgotten in the wake of Gwyn's spirited greeting.

"Fine. You win. How are you today, Gwyn?"

"Better now! Whatcha looking at?" She peered over her friend's shoulder down at the table, noticing the wide-eyed vendor, who looked as if he didn't know what to say. An older woman who sat off to the side just sat with a big grin. Gwyn winked at her, which just elicited a fit of giggles from the woman.

Gwyn shivered as she felt Roslyn's exaggerated sigh brush her neck. The ducal heiress nudged Gwyn away gently and looked up at her. "I was waiting for you and noticed these beautiful pieces here," she said.

The man regained composure and bowed slightly. "Thank you for your kind words, my lady."

Roslyn smiled at the vendor and nodded. Gwyn looked down and saw various styles of jewelry made from metal and pretty stones. They reminded her of stuff people made and sold at markets and festivals back home in Italy. She went to pick up an earring that looked pretty, but hesitated.

"May I?"

The man smiled and bowed. "Of course, Your . . . Highness."

She smiled as she picked up the pretty earring that had a blue spherical stone as big as her thumbnail dangling from a short silver chain. The little orb swirled and glowed. Gwyn gasped and nearly dropped the earring but regained her composure and lifted it up to the man.

"What is this?" she asked.

"The earrings are made from the chest stones of a couple of squirrels, Your Highness. They say they're magical. It seems the rumors were true!"

The old woman stood and approached, reaching out for the earring. Gwyn handed it to her and looked up as the woman spoke.

"They would be absolutely beautiful with your house colors, if you don't mind me saying, Princess."

Gwyn looked at the jewelry in the woman's hand, then down and scanned the table. "Do you have any more like this? Small cores? Preferably in red?"

"*Cores?* I like that name. Yes, I do, actually. One moment."

The woman walked to a chest, out of which she pulled a small box. She checked its contents, nodding, and returned to the table. She showed Gwyn a pair of earrings that also had small cores but were red. Gwyn smiled and glanced at Roslyn, who looked confused. "I'll take both pairs, please!"

The woman smiled. "Thank you, Your Highness!"

The man nodded and stepped forward. "Now, these are fairly priced—"

"I can handle the cost negotiations for Her Highness," Sabina interrupted.

Gwyn grabbed the box with the red earrings. She turned toward Roslyn and smiled. "Here! These will be really pretty on you." She really liked Roslyn's piercings. The high elf had five small silver loops that were evenly spaced up the length of each long narrow ear.

Roslyn's eyes widened, but she accepted the box. "For—for me? For what occasion?"

Gwyn tilted her head. "Because you're my friend, silly." She reached over and held up one of the earrings next to the bottom piercing on Roslyn's ear. She nodded with a smile. "Yup, it's gonna look great!" She leaned in close and whispered, "Plus, it may help you use magic. We'll have to go to our practice yard."

Roslyn's mouth opened slightly, but then she closed it and nodded quickly.

Gwyn was happy. She couldn't wait to hopefully help her friend learn magic. *It would be so cool to have someone else my age with magic!*

Sabina quickly finished the transaction for the earrings and turned around, holding a box with Gwyn's. "All done, Your Highness."

"Perfect." Gwyn looped her arm through Roslyn's. "Come along, Lady Roz! More shopping!"

"We're just here to purchase things for the Academy, Gwyn."

Gwyn clicked her tongue at her friend. "And that's *shopping*. Let's go!"

Roslyn's resulting sigh was definitely dramatic.

With their newly acquired earrings safely tucked away, Gwyn and Roslyn continued their stroll through the market, scanning the various stalls for items they might need at the Academy. The market was alive with vibrant colors and bustling activity, merchants calling out their wares, and shoppers haggling for the best prices. Despite the chaos, Gwyn felt a sense of excitement about going to the Royal Academy—especially if she'd have Roz there.

Their list was practical: writing supplies, clothes, and a selection of books that had been recommended by Mister Branigan. Gwyn insisted on picking up some extra ink pots, fascinated by the array of colors available, while Roslyn was more interested in finding the right kind of parchment that wouldn't smudge or tear easily.

As they moved from one stall to the next, Gwyn's keen eye caught sight of a beautifully crafted quill, its feather dyed a deep, iridescent blue with a gorgeously engraved silver nub. Without hesitation, she purchased it, imagining the smooth flow of ink as she penned her notes and letters. Roslyn, on the other hand, chose a more understated yet equally elegant dark wooden quill, appreciating its sturdy feel.

Their supplies gathered, Gwyn declared it was time for a treat, guiding Roslyn to a quaint bakery nestled at the edge of the market. Its inviting aroma reminded Gwyn of a *pasticceria* back in Italy, where she used to indulge in her favorite pastries. She shared stories of the delicate flavors and textures, her eyes lighting up with fond memories.

They settled at a small table outside the bakery, and Gwyn excitedly ordered an assortment of pastries for them to try, each one a work of art, with flaky crusts and sweet fillings.

When their tea arrived, Gwyn was quick to add a generous dollop of honey to hers, savoring the sweet, comforting flavor. Roslyn, however, patiently waited. Gwyn observed this with curiosity, filing away the detail that Roslyn preferred her tea at a milder temperature.

The conversation flowed easily as they sampled their pastries, which elicited murmurs of approval. Between bites, Roslyn asked Gwyn about her home, her family, and the places she missed most. Gwyn's expression grew wistful as she spoke of Italy, describing the bustling streets, the rolling countryside, and the warmth of her family's embrace.

As the reality set in that she might never return to Earth, a shadow crossed Gwyn's face, her smile faltering. Sensing her friend's change in mood, Roslyn reached out, placing a comforting hand over Gwyn's.

"It sounds like a lovely place," she said softly, "and I'm sure it misses you just as much as you miss it."

Gwyn managed a small smile, grateful for Roslyn's empathy. "I really do miss it," she replied, "but I'm starting to think being here isn't so bad."

CHAPTER SIX

INTIMIDATION

Lady Ilyana Trenlore, adorned in attire befitting her status, strode purposefully alongside Ser Taenya toward Onas Fenren's business. She had been tasked with acting as the knight's assistant while they prepared to leave for the capital.

Though a part of her yearned to remain close to the princess, ensuring her comfort and safety, Lady Ilyana recognized the opportunity at hand—a chance to fortify her standing within the house and to carve out a more influential role for herself.

The princess herself was at the market with her friend, Lady Roslyn. It had irked Ilyana slightly that she and the ladies-in-waiting hadn't been able to foster a closer relationship with Princess Gwyn at first. She had come to realize that there was no way such a relationship would hamper her own influence within the house. After all, the association with Lady Roslyn, a figure of significant stature as the future heiress to the Duchy of Tiloral, was an invaluable alliance for any aspiring princess.

It seemed that the princess, while not inconsiderate, had trouble relating to her two older ladies-in-waiting. It was to be expected, Ilyana knew, since she was a few years older than her. More and more, her interactions with the terran were relegated to formal situations. *That* did irk her. She *wanted* to maintain a closer relationship with the girl from another world. She had such an aura about her. Never mind the actual aura that seemed like a blizzard that the girl had learned to cast just this past week.

Ilyana shivered as she remembered how cold the training field had become. *I wish I could cast magic. Oh, the things I could do.*

She could be casting spells side by side with Gwyn as they fought against scantily clad barbarians. Flaming balls of fire would rain down around them as Ilyana cast lightning from her fingertips. She'd swing her sword, clashing against their enemies with fervor. She smiled as she imagined the barbarians charging them with massive swords and axes with nothing but a loin cloth covering their—

"Lady Ilyana. We are here."

She jerked from her reverie and lifted a hand to her face as she felt her cheeks redden. "My apologies, Ser Taenya."

The knight scrutinized her with a raised brow, but then just shook her head and opened the front doors for her. Ilyana nodded her thanks and walked in. The inside was as she remembered it, and it always amazed her how well off the Fenrens were. They were not the largest merchant house within the duchy, but they were within the top five wealthiest.

The Fenrens also had connections throughout the duchy and in the surrounding nations. As far as Ilyana was aware, that the patriarch had staked his merchant house to the princess had been the deciding factor in her father's decision to pledge her to the rising house. He now only had to look at the soon-to-be viscount of Larton to realize he had decided well. She was sure there was more to it but her parents did not discuss such things with her. *Or anything, really.*

Indeed, Lord Iemes had both the Fenrens and the princess to thank for his rising station. She had heard rumors of all that the baron had invested into the house and agreed that such political gambling had paid itself tenfold. House Reinhart's gains from the Telford fiasco alone spoke to that.

The man himself was waiting for them as they entered the lobby. The shrewd businessman was dressed impeccably in a bright blue tunic that seemed to be made of silk. He looked more like a noble than a commoner, a fact that constantly warred with her sense of self. *When does the nobility no longer matter if even the commoners can gain more wealth and influence than us?*

"Taenya! Welcome, my friend," Onas Fenren said.

"Hello, Onas. How are you?" Taenya asked, adopting a kind tone and an affable smile.

"I am well!" He grinned. "What brings you here, today? With Lady Ilyana, as well, I see."

Taenya smirked. "You know why I am here, Onas. Have you managed to fill the list Siveril sent?"

"Yes, of course. You know me. Also, it's good you're here now. I expected you later," he said.

Taenya tilted her head. "We were in the area," she said slowly. "Why?"

"I have to meet with someone about the other item we were hoping to obtain. You joining me will help," he explained.

The knight straightened. "Do they have it?"

Onas nodded. "Yes, and he is asking for an obscene amount of coin. Your joining will help me negotiate from a better position. Lady Ilyana will just be icing on the cake."

Ser Taenya sighed before giving the merchant a curt nod. "Fine. Let's get this over with."

"Good!"

"I'm not your intimidator anymore, Onas . . ."

"Yeah, yeah. Now you're the princess's intimidator. *Everyone* has heard about your duel."

Ilyana's eyes widened. *That* duel was still the talk of the house. The knight had literally challenged a marquess in a duel to the death. She then went and killed his only heir by cutting off his head *and* managed to incinerate a guard with a magical item the princess had given her. Since then, the house guards remained on alert for any reprisals. Ilyana wasn't even allowed to go anywhere without a guard attending her.

It was only a bit unnerving.

Taenya emerged from the House Reinhart carriage in the port district with Ilyana in tow. Onas's new head guard stood next to another guard off to the side and waited for her and Lady Ilyana. Wailant was a sun elf Taenya knew; he had been with Onas's family and company for many years. The only reason Taenya had gained the position over him many years ago was that she was more willing to travel with Onas on his annual route.

Former yearly route. His wife shut that down so quick.

The guards kept sneaking peeks at her when they thought she wasn't looking. While she wasn't wearing her full armor, she *was* wearing enough to protect herself in case of attack. She basically wore the same thing the other house guards wore, except she didn't wear gear with the expectation of using a spear and shield. She did wear her sword and shield, though. Her pauldrons were exquisitely decorated with the dragons of the house as well.

I am certainly glad they aren't real. Despite the objections of a certain princess.

"Ser Taenya," Wailant said, nodding at her as she and Ilyana joined the group. She nodded before glancing back, satisfied as the two house guards stepped from the sides of the carriage and neatly fell into step behind them. The guard who had acted as the driver and one other guard remained behind with the carriage.

She looked over at Onas and narrowed her eyes. "Where are we going, Onas?"

"Just down here. There is a warehouse that sells temporary space to merchants from Maireharbora. He is meeting us there." He turned and started walking down an alley, his head guard moving behind him. Taenya gestured with her head to her people and followed along. The port district was right next to the merchant district of the city and was filled with warehouses and other storage facilities next to the riverfront.

Ilyana looked around before leaning close to Taenya. "Ser Taenya, is this . . . legal?" she whispered.

Taenya turned, her brow raised. "Yes, of course it is. Why wouldn't it be?"

"This all seems really . . . shady."

Taenya snorted. "It's fine. These types of deals are common. Especially with rare merchandise. It's always a big production and merchants tend to bring the biggest, baddest guard they can to try and intimidate the other."

"Are—are we going to have to fight?"

Remembering what the girl liked to do in her free time, Taenya said, "Lady Ilyana, I do believe you have been reading those books a bit much."

Ilyana's eyes went wide and she mumbled under her breath, "I thought I kept it secret."

Shaking her head, Taenya followed the merchant as they made their way through a second alleyway. It wasn't much farther before they reached a particularly dilapidated warehouse.

"Onas . . ."

The man turned slightly and shrugged. "It's fine. The man already had to spend money to travel all the way here. It's likely a coin-saving measure."

Taenya sighed.

The building wasn't quite falling apart but it definitely had seen better days. There was a pair of double doors that looked like they would fall off of their hinges at the slightest gust, as did the cockeyed wooden awning that covered the entryway. The roof was made of thatch about two years past needing replacement. The only thing that looked serviceable were the large double doors at the end of the path from the street to the side for wagons.

Wailant walked up and banged on the door three times before stepping back, hand resting on his sword's pommel. Three heartbeats later, the door opened and a big orkun stepped out.

"What?"

"We're here to see Stoval. He's expecting us," Onas said.

The man's gaze flicked over Onas and his guards before pausing on Taenya and her group. His eyes widened fractionally before his face set into a scowl.

"Who's this?"

Taenya stepped forward. "I am Ser Taenya Shavyre of House Reinhart. Onas is one of my liege's retainers. I am here to ensure any deal made is done honorably," she stated.

The man's eyes narrowed further as he looked her over. Finally, he nodded, before turning and opening the door. Wailant ordered the rest of Onas's guards to remain outside, and after a gesture, one of Taenya's joined them. The group followed the orkun into the warehouse, and Taenya was surprised by how organized it was. The structure was by no means better inside than out, but the operation of those who utilized it was not as shoddy as the building.

The guard led them to the area in the back right of the warehouse. There seemed to be four different merchant groups set up inside. Five more guards stood around several crates and a single wagon. A flamboyant moon elf in a colorful hat and long coat that fell below his knees stood with his hands on his hips. The guard who had led them in walked over and spoke in the man's ear for a moment, which caused the merchant to scowl.

"Onas Fenren," he said. "This is not what we agreed upon. You did not mention anything about a noble house," he said.

"Stoval, friend. Surely you know better. When the house has an interest in something, they pursue it. She will not interfere with our business unless you give her cause. This is all above board, so of course, that wouldn't happen. Right?"

The man hesitated and glanced at Taenya. She smirked slightly. He scrunched his brows together but then sighed.

"Yes. Of course, of course. You know how it is. People tend to try and change deals last minute."

"Oh, trust me. I am well aware. Do you have what you promised?"

"I do, over here," Stoval said, gesturing to the side where an elaborate wooden chest was set up. Gold embellishments and hardware shone against its glossy exterior. The moon elf pulled a key out of his coat and opened a lock on the front of the chest. He paused, glanced at Onas one more time, then opened the lid and ceremoniously reached in. He pulled out a small box with a similar glossy sheen. He turned and walked to a table set up next to the crates and set the box down.

Onas and Taenya approached the table and Stoval opened the box, revealing a silver ring. A solitary diamond sat flush with the band. On either side of the diamond, four symbols in a language she had never seen emitted a soft blue light, which proved one thing . . . *This is going to be ridiculously expensive.*

Onas reached down to pick up the ring, but the box was shut by the moon elf just before he was able to touch it.

"No. You may only look," Stoval said.

"That isn't how this works, Stoval. We already signed an agreement."

"It is with this, Mr. Fenren. Pay the new fee, and you may touch it all you like."

He gave a new price, one that made Onas choke. Even Taenya had to school her expression. Onas immediately complained about how it was ten times the amount they'd already agreed to.

The man picked up the box, held it protectively against his chest, and narrowed his eyes. "This is *one of a kind* in Avira. I have the supply and there is *plenty* of demand."

Onas recovered from his initial shock and fired back. "I *know* you did not purchase the ring for that much. We already made an agreement and I have the documents. Attempting to extort me for more is illegal. That *is* against the law."

The merchant's guards all stepped forward and placed their hands on their weapons. Stoval raised a hand, chuckling. "You can claim whatever you wish. The fact is, you are not getting this *magical* ring without paying. Circumstances have changed. I do not *have* to sell to you. So, are you attempting to steal from me? Because anything less than what I am charging is theft."

Onas scowled and crossed his arms. "You will *never* sell another thing in the duchy again," he sneered.

"You—"

Taenya sighed exaggeratedly, causing the moon elf to pause and look at her. She placed a hand on Onas's shoulder and gently pulled him back. *Time to take a page from Gwyn's book.* She focused and channeled magic into her fist, causing her hand to glow with a red mist. She was sure her eyes were shining as well as she slammed the glowing gauntlet onto the table with her **[Empowered Strike]**. The table shattered beneath her hit, causing everyone around to jump back in surprise. Taenya raised her hand and pointed at the merchant.

"I told your guard that I was here to ensure any deal remained honorable. Let me see the ring."

The moon elf's guards started to draw their blades but Taenya channeled more magic and drew her blade and had it against the nearest guard's neck before any of them managed to pull theirs more than halfway. She narrowed her eyes and swept her gaze over the guards.

"Do not."

Taenya slowly withdrew her sword and then returned it to its scabbard. With one more pointed look at the guards, she reached out her hand to the moon elf. Stoval's eyes were wide and he was shaking, but he dropped the box into her palm.

She nodded at him. "Thank you." She opened the box and pulled out the ring. Examining it, Taenya frowned when she realized it would be too big. Setting it back into the box, she took off a gauntlet and handed it to Onas. Taenya picked the ring back up and slipped it onto her index finger, wiggling the oversized ring around as it settled onto the digit. She felt movement and her breath hitched when the ring slowly shrank until it fit perfectly.

Taenya glanced up with slightly widened eyes at Stoval and Onas, who were both transfixed. The moon elf didn't say anything but had a noticeable scowl on his face.

Onas searched her face questioningly. "Do you feel anything?"

She shrugged but then tried channeling magic *into* the ring and gasped when she felt a surge of magic rushing to her. It suddenly felt as if her ability to use magic were stronger.

"Taenya . . ."

She looked up at Onas. "What?"

"Your eyes."

She squinted and gestured for him to continue.

"They're . . . glowing red."

She looked back down and let go of her magic, feeling the connection dissipate to nothing again. She looked over at the moon elf's guards, and they satisfyingly took a collective step back. She smirked at the fearful expressions on their faces.

With a nod, she took the ring off, placed it back in the box, and then looked up at Stoval. "We will take it." She turned to Onas. "How much were you prepared to give him?"

He told her a much more reasonable price, and Stoval opened his mouth, but Taenya raised a hand. Without looking at Onas, she said, "Pay him double, Onas. We'll take it." She narrowed her eyes at the moon elf. "Unless you have an objection?"

"No. No, I do not," he replied contemptuously.

"Good. Take the money and leave the city. We will not bring up you attempting to break a signed purchase agreement without cause. You will not attempt to defraud anyone in Strathmore again. Her Highness will appreciate the business."

Stoval's eyes widened. "H-Her Highness?"

"Did you not do your research before attempting to swindle Fenren Trading House? They have pledged fealty to Her Highness, Princess Gwyneth of House Reinhart."

The moon elf paled.

She handed the box to Onas and stepped back as the merchants finalized the sale. The scowl on Stoval's face said enough. His guards stared at her warily, but the merchant himself looked as if he would stab Onas at any minute.

"Do not do anything stupid. If you do, you will not like the response that House Reinhart will bring down upon you," Taenya warned.

He turned his scowl on her as he ground his teeth together. "I will not forget this."

"Good. Maybe next time you enter into business *outside of the city,* you won't try to extort a client."

The man clenched his fists, but he did not say anything further. Still, Taenya made sure to keep an eye on the guards and moon elf as they left.

When they emerged from the warehouse, Onas handed the box to one of his guards, who put it into a chest.

"Shall we go show Gwyn?" Onas asked.

Taenya smiled. "Let's do that." She glanced at Ilyana, who had been quiet this far. "You alright, Lady Ilyana?"

The girl nodded and spoke excitedly. "The look on the guards' faces when you started glowing and yanked your sword out and . . . swish!" she said, moving her hand as she acted out the motions. "Right to the man's neck. They were so intimidated. It was amazing!"

Onas chuckled at the girl's enthusiasm, but Taenya just shook her head. "I think you may have been reading a bit too many of *those* types of books, Lady Ilyana."

The girl flushed brightly and jerked her head to face straight ahead.

Taenya chuckled. She glanced at the small chest one of the guards held. *Gwyn's going to love the ring, incidental intimidation notwithstanding.*

* * *

Under the soft glow of the evening lamps, Ilyana found solace in the comforting embrace of her plush couch and the captivating world of her latest book. The day's events had left her feeling a mixture of exhaustion and exhilaration, and she had been looking forward to a quiet evening lost in the pages of her next adventure. Outside her room, she heard small footsteps stop near her door. A silken ribbon marked her progress as she reluctantly set the book aside, sensing the interruption before the knock even echoed through her chamber.

As the door creaked open, Ilyana was taken aback to find Aleanora standing there, her presence unexpected. The girl's light-brown hair was pulled up and tied into a messy bun, and she was still in her evening gown. She looked into the room.

"Lady Ilyana," Aleanora greeted her, almost hesitantly.

"Nora, to what do I owe this late visit?" Ilyana's tone was courteous, and despite their earlier ceasefire in their rivalry, her mind raced with potential reasons for this intrusion.

Aleanora's gaze flickered down the hallway. "May I come in?" she asked, a hint of vulnerability in her voice that softened Ilyana's resolve.

With a graceful motion, Ilyana stepped aside, allowing Aleanora to enter the sanctuary of her room. As the younger lady-in-waiting made a beeline for the couch, Ilyana's heart skipped a beat. She rushed forward just as Aleanora moved the pillow and picked up what she'd hidden beneath it.

Snatching the book before Nora could fully grasp its contents, Ilyana felt a blush creep up her cheeks, and stumbled over her words in a rare display of fluster.

"I-I uh . . ."

Nora's expression softened, her earlier urgency giving way to a moment of understanding.

"I don't care what you read, Ilyana," she reassured, her voice gentle. "I came . . . well, I came to see if you were truly alright. Today's events were the talk of the manor, and I couldn't help but worry."

The air in the room shifted as Ilyana allowed herself to sit on the couch and sink back into the cushions, the weight of the day visibly settling on her shoulders.

"Yes, it was quite the day," she admitted, her guard lowering as she confided in her fellow lady-in-waiting. "I am managing, thank you." She felt a smirk tug at the corner of her mouth. "Honestly? I found it exhilarating. I want to go on more outings with Ser Taenya if that is what comes of it."

Aleanora's eyes widened and her mouth opened slightly. "R-really?"

Ilyana nodded.

The ensuing silence settled awkwardly until Aleanora's next words broke the quiet. "I've been thinking lately . . ."

Ilyana couldn't resist the quip. "That can't be good."

To her surprise, Nora laughed—a genuine, warm sound that echoed softly in the chamber. "Fair enough," she conceded with a smile.

"I'm sorry . . . please, tell me."

Aleanora looked away, biting her lip as if thinking of what to say. When she spoke, it was quietly. "I've been thinking about our role. Instead of chasing Princess Gwyn's favor, which remains elusive despite our efforts, we might consider a more strategic approach to strengthen our positions," she proposed.

Ilyana regarded her with skepticism. This was a girl whose mother was a viscountess, one who sought to increase her house's influence and status. Aleanora had been doing nothing else but trying to position herself to be someone the princess would elevate. Still, curiosity won over. She gestured for her peer to continue, prompting, "Go on."

Aleanora leaned in, her voice dropping to a conspiratorial whisper. "We have an opportunity to anchor ourselves more firmly within the house's structure by assisting in areas that lack noble oversight. There's a gap between the knights' martial prowess and the everyday management of our house, a space where we could become indispensable. Ser Siveril is taking on a lot, and I do not doubt that the princess will reward his efforts. He is doing the work of a noble, but *for now* he is just a knight. That leaves the three of us as the only nobles within the house itself."

Ilyana's interest was piqued as she absorbed Nora's suggestion, the wheels in her mind beginning to turn. "And what, precisely, do you have in mind for yourself?" she inquired. "Or all of us."

"I've observed how Siveril operates, the finesse with which he navigates the intricacies of house politics and estate management," Nora explained. "He was a key advisor to the duke. I believe I could learn a great deal under his guidance, assisting him and perhaps even taking on some responsibilities related to managing our house's assets. And there's Friedrich—he's been learning, but still he's just a knight. I think I could offer substantial support there. The princess could use a noble to help administer everything.

"As for you and Lorrena? I think you'd know better than I what you're good at. You're already going to be attending the Royal Academy. Lorrena as well. But she is still young, and I believe her to be more a typical lady-in-waiting and confidante for our princess. I don't think she will stay long term. I know we're all *supposed* to be returning to our houses, but I am finding that I may not want to."

Ilyana's brows rose at that. It was customary for a lady-in-waiting to spend time within a royal house, but then to be released from the royal's service after a set period of time. They would return to their family with added experience, status, and connections, making them much more of a suitable prospect for potential partners. To stay beyond that service was essentially breaking free of your former house completely. It wasn't common, but it did happen. It tied you even more closely to your liege, and instead of your family having control over your potential marriage or path, your liege would take on that role.

She couldn't imagine Gwyn wanting that responsibility. Gwyn was a free spirit. She was fiery and strong. Intelligent. Basically, she was everything Ilyana didn't expect a princess to be, and she had to say she admired it. Perhaps it was being away from her mother, but Gwyn had this fierce desire to control her own future in a way that Ilyana had never even considered possible.

The idea of integrating deeper into House Reinhart and with Gwyneth resonated with Ilyana, sparking a flurry of possibilities in her own mind. When Nora turned the question back on her, asking what role might pique her interest, Ilyana's thoughts naturally drifted to the scene she had witnessed earlier that day. She recalled the commanding presence of Ser Taenya, how the knight had deftly handled a potentially volatile situation with a mix of strength and cunning.

A slow, appreciative smile spread across Ilyana's face as she found her answer. "I think I do know where I could be most useful," she began, her voice imbued with newfound resolve. "Today, I watched Ser Taenya deal with a merchant who thought he could swindle us, as well as some guards who were less than cooperative. The respect she commanded . . . it was inspiring."

Ilyana's eyes sparkled with ambition as she continued. "I want to learn how to wield that kind of authority, that much . . . *intimidation* to ensure that our house is treated with the respect it deserves. I may not have Taenya's martial skills, but I believe I can cultivate a similar presence and acumen in negotiations and conflict resolution. I can learn strategy. I know it is not typically a lady's place, but I think it is something I want to focus on at the Academy."

Aleanora listened intently, nodding in approval. "That sounds difficult, but I will support you. If we both succeed in these new roles, we could significantly bolster our standing within the house—and perhaps even gain the recognition and influence we've been striving for."

Yes, Ilyana thought. *Mother and Father will be forced to recognize me.*

"We'll need to work together if we're going to help the princess."

"Just tell me what you need," Nora agreed. "We'll let the princess intimidate everyone while we keep everything running in the background."

Ilyana smiled and held out her hand. Nora grasped it firmly, surprising Ilyana with the sincerity in both the gesture and in the features on her face. "To House Reinhart."

Nora's lips turned into a fierce smile. "May Relena have mercy on our enemies."

CHAPTER SEVEN

STRENGTH COMES IN MANY FORMS

Have you heard from Friedrich?" Gwyn inquired as she turned to Sabina. The elf gently shook her head. "Not since last time. But I'm aware they reached Drakensburg without issue. Niles managed to secure some additional provisions, and their departure from there happened immediately after they sent the message."

Gwyn acknowledged the update with a thoughtful nod. "Hopefully we hear something else soon. What do we have to do today?"

"You have nothing on your agenda today, Your Highness," came the poised reply from Emma, who had been following a step behind.

Sabina offered a casual shrug. "Siveril made sure everyone knew you were preparing to leave for the Academy. We still have a few weeks, so that is why we are doing everything needed this week. Get ready for a flurry of last-minute engagements in the days to come."

A sense of disquiet settled over Gwyn as she absorbed this information, her gaze dropping to the floor while they navigated the corridors of the manor. "Oh. No studies either?"

"Mister Branigan and Miss Rolfe are currently organizing the materials you'll need at the Academy," Emma, Gwyn's handmaiden, replied. "They're also devoting extra time to assist Lady Lorrena with her preparation for the entrance examinations."

Gwyn nodded again. She knew Lorrena was struggling with learning everything needed before the Academy would accept her. She was glad they were giving her more help. Siveril and the girl's family were adamant about ensuring Lorrena was able to attend, as her majordomo had insisted that having a retainer join her there was expected. Everything had become almost too much for Gwyn, and she often recalled how immature she had been and the lies she told that had caused so much craziness after she first arrived.

It is just so difficult doing this whole princess thing. At least it's not pretending anymore . . . I really do know how to act now.

As they entered the main hall, the sight of Siveril engaged in a serious discussion with Taenya and Onas captured Gwyn's attention. A small, mysterious box on the table seemed to be the focus of their conversation, though the details escaped her from this distance.

It was then that Gwyn noticed Ilyana, standing somewhat apart from the group, her posture indicative of someone not directly involved but keenly observant. Catching sight of Gwyn, Ilyana approached with a graceful wave and a respectful curtsy, her hands clasped before her.

"Greetings, Your Highness! It is a pleasure to see you today!"

Returning the gesture with a warm albeit slightly amused smile, Gwyn couldn't resist teasing, "You see me every day, Ilyana! What are you guys up to?"

Ilyana stepped next to her and leaned closer. "We . . . I mean, Ser Taenya and Mister Fenren, got you a present!"

Gwyn smiled. Of the three, Ilyana tried really hard to be her friend. It was sad that it felt . . . fake. She didn't think the girl was trying to take advantage of her or anything, it just seemed that Ilyana did not know how to be friends with someone almost six years younger. It made her act in a way she thought Gwyn would *want* her to act. The reality was, Gwyn just wanted the older girl to be herself. In fact, it was the biggest problem with all of her ladies-in-waiting, or the crew, as she'd come to call them. They were stuck performing to the expectations of their parents and how they thought they should act around a *princess*.

Meanwhile, Gwyn just wanted them to be her friends.

"What did you get me?" She lowered her voice slightly. "Don't worry, I won't tell!" she said conspiratorially.

Ilyana hesitated. "Uh. I—"

Gwyn giggled. She reached out, touching Ilyana gently on her arm. "It's okay, I'm only teasing. Come on, let's go see what they have to say. They're acting all serious."

"Oh . . . about that."

Gwyn sharpened her gaze on the high elf's face. "What happened?" she prodded.

"Nothing . . . *bad?*"

Gwyn pressed, but it was clear Ilyana did not want to say.

"Okay, come on. I'll get Taenya to tell me."

With a light-hearted resolve and Ilyana in tow, Gwyn approached the group, her presence initially unnoticed due to the intensity of their conversation. It wasn't until she spoke that they became aware of her approach.

"Hey, everyone, what's got all of you acting super serious?"

Taenya, caught off guard, flinched at the sound of Gwyn's voice, her surprise evident as she quickly recovered her composure. She shot a pointed look at Sabina.

"You could have warned me," she chided.

"Could have. This was more fun," Sabina said.

Gwyn loved the way her two "aunts" had been acting since Taenya's duel. Something had changed between them, and she could tell they were closer because of it. She suspected that it had something to do with Sabina's magic. Turning to Sabina with a curious tilt of her head, Gwyn inquired mentally, *You two talk like you and I do, don't you?*

The woman smirked. *Indeed, we do. It's all thanks to the confidence boost you gave me, Gwyn. Without your encouragement, I doubt I'd have found the courage to explore my abilities.*

In response, Gwyn playfully jabbed Sabina in the arm. *Don't mention it, Auntie.*

Sabina rolled her eyes. *Have you told Taenya about that yet?*

Nope! Have you?

No, I thought you would.

Well, aren't you two . . . like, together, now?

Sabina's eyes went wide, and Taenya raised a brow and looked between the both of them.

"Ahem. You two can have your secret messages later."

Gwyn looked at Sabina and giggled because her eyes were still wide. "Sorry, Taenya. Whatcha guys got there?" she asked innocently, quickly glancing at Ilyana and winking. Her lady-in-waiting just shook her head with a smirk.

Taenya sighed, and Onas looked at them all with an amused expression.

"Remember when we spoke of getting you a magical item, Your Highness?" he asked.

Gwyn nodded.

"Well, with Taenya's timely assistance, we were able to purchase one," Onas said. He reached over and picked up the box.

Gwyn looked expectantly at the small, glossy wooden box and mentally guessed what it was. *Bit obvious.* She was proved right a moment later when he opened it and she saw the large ring inside. It was pretty and silver with a diamond that was set into the band. *Looks like something from my world,* Gwyn thought. None of the rings she had seen here had a gem like that. It seemed everyone wanted to show off as big of a gem as possible instead of almost hiding it in the band. *Actually, that's pretty similar to Earth, as well. They weren't common.*

What looked genuinely pretty, though, were the four little symbols on the band. They were blue and glowing softly.

Do they expect me to wear that? Uh . . . is it a ring for my big toe? She glanced between the ring, her hand, and the adults around her and struggled with what to say.

Surely they know, right?

Taenya, sensing Gwyn's momentary uncertainty, offered a reassuring chuckle before gently extracting the ring from its resting place. "Extend your hand, and trust me," she encouraged, her voice imbued with warmth and assurance.

Gwyn furrowed her brow but did as she was told. Her knight slid the ring onto her index finger, and she gasped as she felt a small surge of magic signal a connection between the ring and herself. The magic in the ring seemed to flow into her as if it knew her and her magic connected with it excitedly. A sudden rush expanded throughout her body as her connection to the magic in the air around her expanded. Gwyn looked down at the ring and cried out in surprise as the ring *shrank* to fit her finger. "It's shrinking!"

Taenya laughed. "It's resizing itself to fit you!"

"That's so cool! Wait . . . you knew this would happen. You coulda told me," she said, her eyes narrowing at the woman, who held a smug smile.

"That's what you and Sabina get for startling me!"

"Hey! *She* did that, I just walked up. Aren't you a knight who should be aware of her surroundings?"

Taenya gasped exaggeratedly. "Hey now! I will have you know that—"

Siveril cleared his throat. "Ser Taenya, it seems that your duel has raised your confidence as of late. Please remember how to act when not in private."

Gwyn narrowed her eyes but noticed Siveril looking at Onas. "Don't worry, Siveril. Mister Onas is part of the family too. He won't tell anyone how we act in the house. Right, Mister Onas?"

The merchant elf adopted a serious expression and bowed his head. "Of course not, Your Highness. I am honored you think so highly of me. I would not betray that trust."

Gwyn smiled and looked at Siveril. The man seemed to scrutinize Onas searchingly, but he finally nodded. "Thank you, Mister Fenren."

Taenya shrugged slightly, just enough so Gwyn would see and Siveril would miss it as he looked at her finger.

"How does the ring feel, Your Highness?"

She flexed her hand and probed at the ring with her magic. It quickly answered her and filled her with magic, but it seemed as if the ring didn't need any prodding to heed her call. With that in mind, Gwyn channeled magic normally and the ring automatically connected with it and helped pull even more into her. It felt as if any magic she used would be stronger and more controllable.

"It feels great, actually. It's really comfortable, and I think it's going to make all of my magic stronger! I can try some of the new stuff I have been wanting to do, now. Probably. Oh! I can try to do some of those magics like you, Taenya! The ones where it makes me stronger. Or—"

Sabina chuckled from behind her. "Slow down, Your Highness. Let's not get too carried away. We'll make time for your training."

Gwyn sighed. "You're right. I'm just excited to be as strong as you two."

Taenya chuckled. "Strength comes in many forms, Your Highness. You'll get there."

Gwyn nodded, smiling as she looked at Taenya and Onas. "Thank you both for the ring. I really appreciate it."

Onas returned her smile and reached out a hand. "May I?" he asked, gesturing to the ring.

Gwyn shrugged and took it off of her finger. She noticed that the ring remained her size. Onas turned it over and showed her the inside. There were more tiny gemstones hidden in the inner ring of the band. Four, to be exact, with three on the top and one on the bottom.

"There is more in here. These gems help what the makers call *mana* to connect with you. The little opal here at the bottom is what does it. At the top we have . . ." He glanced down at the piece of paper in his other hand. "The blue sapphire is what allows it to do what it does, and how it tells the mana what you want it to do. The amethyst helps you use the ring for the shaping of mana, and the ruby allows your ring to *use* the mana it connects with. The diamond *amplifies* everything the ring does for you."

He pointed to a small marking inside the band. "Finally, on the side here, is the maker's mark. The Farum Merchant Company made this. I am trying to connect with them further. I think our house would do very well if we were able to secure sole rights to import their products into Avira."

Gwyn nodded. Truthfully, she had started to tune him out after he'd explained what the different gems did. It sounded like when Mom explained how her different gadgets had worked, like her watch. It was cool to look at the inside of the watch, but usually, everything seemed to go blurry, and she grew more tired as Mom described each little chip. *I wish she was here to explain this, though. I would listen to everything.*

"That's really interesting, Mister Onas. Thank you," Gwyn said as he handed the ring back to her. She slid it back on her finger and sighed as the connection was established. *I don't think I ever want to take this off.*

Onas nodded and backed away. They all seemed to look at her expectantly.

"Um, thank you so much, everyone. I am excited to see what we can do with all of these. Between Ser Taenya and Ser Sabina, I think getting more magic items will be just what the house needs. It would also be good for us to be the only ones to bring these things to the kingdom." She looked at Siveril, who nodded slowly.

"I agree," he said. "This is a good venture for the house if we can manage it. I will write up something for you, Onas, and you can enter House Reinhart into a contract with this Farum Merchant Company if possible. Avira is a large market—surely they would want easy access through its only port. I will also send a letter to the duke. I think we can obtain a deal for it. Use it to sweeten any deal with the owners."

The house is going to be in a good spot for when we find Mom.

Onas tilted his head in thought. "That should work. I will leave *that* in my pocket, just in case. I have just the person for it."

Gwyn tilted her head as she remembered something. "Roz's mom lives there, right? I can ask her to talk to her for us?"

Siveril smiled. "It's alright, we'll make it work. You and Lady Roslyn just focus on your studies. No need to bring politics into your friendship at your age."

Gwyn nodded slowly. She hated politics. Roz always acted like she enjoyed it, though. *Maybe I should ask her how she really feels about all of this noble business.*

"Good evening, Maris." Emma extended a warm greeting to the telv guard stationed by the entrance to Princess Gwyn's quarters. Maris, with her imposing stature and keen eyes, was an integral member of the four guards dubbed The Wynvers, personally selected by Ser Sabina for their dedication and prowess. This unique team, comprising three women and a man, shared an uncommon bond, having undergone rigorous training sessions shrouded in secrecy under the knight's vigilant guidance.

Emma knew it was because of Ser Sabina's magic, and they had been sworn to secrecy as to what it entailed. But Emma knew this too. She was always with the princess; she could see the magic in the way the knight acted. *Ser Sabina had used it when we first met.* She shivered involuntarily, remembering the feeling she had at the time. She had won the woman's begrudging respect since then, and the knight had won hers.

"Evening, Miss Emma. How fares your night?" Maris inquired, her voice carrying a note of genuine interest.

"I'm a touch weary, I must confess. The preparations for our departure have been rather all-consuming," Emma replied, her thoughts momentarily wandering to the lists and plans that had occupied her days and nights.

"Aye, I know the feeling well. My belongings are all sorted and ready. Ser Sabina has been pushing us hard, making sure we're prepared for what lies ahead. It won't be long now, just a few more weeks. I heard that Ser Taenya's team has come back to the manor exhausted almost daily. Ser Taenya has been running them all ragged, from what I've heard."

Emma nodded as the woman gossiped about Ser Taenya's team of guards. The Drakyyds had named their group after the large reptile that roamed and hunted in the forests near the woodland regions in the west. She recalled that Gwyn had said it looked like a dragon without wings. Ser Sabina's group was named after the small flying reptile that they thought was sufficiently similar to the dragon that adorned the house crest. *I wonder if they know exactly how large the princess has described a dragon as being.*

Emma tilted her head as Maris finished talking about her fellow guards. "Is that why Ser Sabina has been staying with Her Highness more often?" Emma asked. "I thought it was something else."

Maris nodded. "Yes, Ser Taenya has been very busy practicing with her team. The only ones who have gotten rest are the Apcerosi."

Ser Theran's guards had chosen a large reptile called the apceros for their emblem. The animal was not native to this region of Ikios and could be found only in the deserts or dry regions of the continent, where it was used as a beast of burden. The large beast had a hardened, shield-like back and its tail looked similar to a mace. The same mace that those guards had tried to use as their main weapons . . . until Ser Theran shut that down and admonished them for leaning too hard into the image. Now she saw them with halberds similar to those the Paladins of Alos used.

Emma refocused on the guardswoman as the telv continued, "Ser Theran continues to strengthen the defense of the house, but his guards don't have as much training to do to acclimate to the *unique attributes* of our leaders."

Emma could understand that, and it was likely the reason for the guards having so much time to come up with antics. Sers Taenya and Sabina both had magic, while Ser Theran did not. She knew that the lady knights were working with their guard teams in a way that took advantage of that magic. She could only imagine what those with Ser Sabina had to go through. Emma shivered again.

Catching Emma's momentary shiver, Maris reassured her, "It's not as daunting as you might think, Emma. We take pride in our role as the princess's guardians—her silent watchers in the shadows."

Just then, the faint sound of movement from within Princess Gwyn's chambers caught their attention. Maris, sensing something unseen, shared a knowing look with Emma.

"I believe Her Highness is ready for you," she intimated, her voice imbued with the weight of their shared responsibility.

With a composed nod, Emma straightened her posture, the brief exchange serving as a reminder of her pivotal role in the princess's life. As Maris gently pushed open one of the grand double doors, Emma cast a final glance at the dedicated "shadow guards," their unwavering commitment inspiring a newfound determination within her.

Emma entered Princess Gwyn's chamber to find it transformed into a miniature winter landscape, the result of yet another of Gwyn's ambitious attempts at mastering her magic. Ice formations, reminiscent of a frost-covered cavern, adorned the room, surrounding the red-faced young princess, who stood at the center with clenched fists, a mixture of determination and frustration etched across her youthful features.

With a gentle sigh that misted in the air, Emma called for assistance. "Guard Maris?" she inquired, her voice echoing softly in the chilled room.

Maris cautiously peered inside, her eyes widening in astonishment at the icy spectacle before her. "Yes, Miss Emma?" she responded, her tone laced with awe.

"Could you fetch Ser Sabina, please? I believe her expertise might be needed here," Emma said, her gaze drifting back to Gwyn, who seemed to be battling a tempest of emotions.

"Right away, Miss Emma," Maris replied with a nod, her steps quickening as she departed on her mission.

Turning her attention to Gwyn, Emma proposed a pause in the young royal's efforts. "Your Highness, perhaps a short respite is in order. How about some tea to chase away the chill? It appears we've been graced with an early winter," she jested lightly, hoping to ease the tension. "Someone must have left a window open."

Gwyn tilted her head and then looked up at her slowly. Emma smirked at her joke as the girl glanced around, groaning as she did. "I almost had it, Emma. I am *so* close!" the princess said.

"And what exactly are you striving to achieve, Your Highness?"

"Dream-me was able to turn everything frozen in a flash! I tried it a different way, and that's how I made my **[Aura of Winter]**. That wasn't right, though. I *need* something like, uh . . . **[Flash Freeze]**, but I can't get it," she bemoaned.

Emma was certainly not the one with whom to discuss the finer points of magic. It was utterly beyond her. She wished Ms. Rolfe was here—that woman had done miracles with the young royal. Still, she had to say *something*.

"Maybe, Your Highness, this dream was not a preview of your current abilities but a hint of what you might achieve with time and practice. There could be foundational skills you need to master first."

Gwyn's demeanor brightened at the suggestion. "That makes sense! It's like the games back home. I have to level up! I'm not high enough to get that spell yet. But that sounds a bit silly . . ."

"It's not silly, Princess. You are just relating it to what you know. It's like when you practice your sword with Ser Theran. He made you do all of those stances and movements before even touching a sword, correct?"

The realization dawned on Gwyn and her eyes widened. "You're right! He called it fundamentals. I don't have the fundamentals of ice magic yet. You're so smart, Emma. Thank you!"

The girl was always so sweet. She hoped that never changed. Emma smiled and stepped aside as she heard Ser Sabina enter behind her. *This is going to be a pain to clean up.*

Ser Sabina's low, urgent tones with Gwyn didn't escape Emma's notice as she began her task, moving books and valuables to safer ground. Emma's role had never been to instruct or reprimand the princess for the magical experiments that sometimes went awry; that was a boundary she respected, even as she wished for the knight to gently guide Gwyn toward more suitable venues for her practice.

Catching a fleeting look of remorse on Gwyn's face, Emma felt a twinge of empathy for the young girl. Such incidents were part of the learning process, yet they came with their set of challenges—not least of which was cleaning up afterward.

She had barely moved some books when she heard noises from outside. Emma peeked up at Ser Sabina, who had frozen stiller than the spikes of ice around them. After a moment, the knight's eyes shot wide.

"We're under attack." Her swift glance encompassed Emma and the princess, a silent vow of protection before she hastened to the doorway. "Maris! We're under attack! Warn the others! I have the princess!"

Emma looked at her princess even as her hand slid down her dress to the dagger she had hidden on her leg. She glanced at Ser Sabina, whose face wore a look of determination.

"Sabina, what's happening? Is everyone else safe?" Gwyn's voice trembled, a stark contrast to her usual confidence. The vulnerability in her eyes struck Emma deeply, reinforcing the gravity of the situation they faced.

Sabina kept her focus on the door. Emma saw Gwyn nod, but the woman hadn't said anything. She attributed it to the knight's magic.

Before Emma could offer words of reassurance, Ser Sabina's commanding voice cut through the tension. "Emma, stay close to Gwyn. Protect her with everything you have," she ordered, her gaze locked on the doorway, anticipating the imminent threat.

Emma nodded, her resolve solidifying. "We're here, Your Highness. You're not alone," she assured the girl.

Gwyn reached out, her hand gripping Emma's. "I'm scared, Emma. I don't want anyone to get hurt because of me," she whispered, her eyes searching Emma's for comfort.

Emma offered a reassuring squeeze in return, her protective instincts intertwining with a deep affection for the young princess. "We'll get through this together. You're strong, Gwyn, stronger than you know. And I'll be right here with you," she promised.

She turned toward the door as she heard the first shouts in the distance. *They are in the manor.*

As the attackers grew louder, signaling their approach, Emma positioned herself between Gwyn and the door, her dagger hidden in her hand, ready to defend them both. The anticipation of the confrontation heightened the tension in the air.

Emma saw movement and instinctively jumped to protect the princess. Reacting on instinct, she propelled Gwyn to the side, positioning her body as a shield between the princess and their assailant. The movement was fluid, driven by an adrenaline-fueled need to protect at all costs.

The impact was swift and sharp—a sudden, piercing sensation that stole Emma's breath away. She looked down, seeing a rod coming from her side, just below her breasts. A soft, disbelieving "Oh" escaped her lips as the magnitude of her injury became clear. Emma's legs faltered, her strength fading as she succumbed to the gravity of her wound.

As she collapsed, the room around her seemed to blur, her thoughts consumed by concern for Gwyn's safety. Emma's only regret was the possibility of leaving the princess unprotected.

CHAPTER EIGHT

HOW INNOCENCE DIES

As Gwyn regained her footing, the world around her seemed distant, sounds echoing as if underwater. It was then her gaze fell on Emma, sprawled motionless on the floor where she had pushed Gwyn out of harm's path. The sight of the bolt embedded deeply in Emma's side beneath her ribs sent a shock of disbelief through Gwyn's heart. Emma's breaths were shallow and labored, her eyes flickering with panic before locking onto Gwyn's with an urgent clarity.

Ignoring the sound of Sabina and the attackers fighting behind her, Gwyn rushed to Emma's side, falling to her knees to clutch her hand. "No, no, no . . . Emma? What can I do, tell me," she pleaded, voice trembling with desperation.

Tears welled in Emma's eyes as she struggled to maintain her grip on Gwyn's hand, her breaths becoming more erratic. She attempted to speak, a mere exhale escaping her lips before her gaze stilled and her hand slackened in Gwyn's grasp.

"Emma?" Gwyn shook her, denial lacing her voice. "Emma! Wake up. It's going to be okay. Please." A grunt from behind her took her attention, and she turned to see Sabina narrowly dodge a sword swipe. The reality of the situation crashed down on her as she stumbled backward, her vision constricting as darkness crept along its edges.

No, not again . . . Gwyn felt empty as she took in the sight before her. Emma wasn't moving, and her chest didn't rise and fall as it should. Her handmaiden's body was still, and blood pooled around her from the wound on her side. *We were just talking. Everything was fine.*

Grief and burning rage began to build inside her, threatening to overwhelm her senses. She looked up at Sabina, who was fighting two elves, and they were forcing her backward, one step after another. One of the two had a quiver hanging from his belt with bolts in them. The other had none.

Him.

Gwyn focused and called on the blue magic to try to shut down almost every emotion within her. It did not work as intended. However, instead of sadness and rage, cold fury and determination took over where the fire had sought to consume her. She had failed. *Again.* Another one of her family was dead, and she didn't stop it.

Him.

Gwyn demanded her magic come to her, the colorless magic all around them. She reached out and felt it constrict around the elf that had killed her family. She closed her fist, and then, with a thought, **[Altered]** the mana around him so that it grabbed and threw him away from Sabina. Her knight would handle the other. *This one must die.*

Gwyn walked toward the elf she'd thrown. "You," she snarled. Her hold over the blue magic faltered. She felt the fire licking her skin as her eye sockets became nothing more than a route for the flame to escape the inferno raging within her. Her eyes *were* fire and everything she saw was tinted in red. She focused and used her **[Mana Sight]**, her vision taking on a new hue as all of the mana around them came into focus. *Yes. The ring makers were right. This is what it is.*

The killer rose and lifted his sword. Sabina called out in impotent fury from where she fought the other guard, unable to push the elf back.

The attacker in front of Gwyn narrowed his eyes. "It is nothing personal, Princess. Your knight started a war. We are here to finish it." His voice quivered, and he hesitated. That was his last mistake.

"It's personal for me." She lifted her hand. *Him.* "*Burn.*"

Her magic rushed at her order and her **[Pillar of Flame]** instantly ignited on him. The flame was white with a tinge of black at its edges, and it engulfed the elf. She poured more and more mana into the pillar, not letting it go.

The man screamed. Oh, how he screamed. A primal howl of pain that died out within seconds, but Gwyn didn't stop. When she did let go of the magic, a molten mass of metal and a charred form collapsed to the ground. She turned, regaining control over the blue magic. The other attacker was already on the defensive as he held his sword up and kept his front focused on both Sabina and Gwyn.

She looked at Sabina. "You have magic. Finish this."

Her knight's eyes widened slightly. *Gwyn . . .*

Kill him, Sabina. Now, she ordered mentally.

Sabina narrowed her eyes but nodded and focused on the man. The elf started backing away, but then Gwyn saw his eyes go wide and then suddenly glaze over as he froze in place. Slowly, the man released his sword, and it clattered to the ground. Sabina gave Gwyn a questioning look, to which Gwyn nodded once. Sabina's eyes turned black as they reflected the knight's mana. The man's hand shook fiercely, but he reached down with jerking movements and withdrew a dagger from a sheath on his belt. He fought it the entire way, but the outcome had been determined as soon as Sabina committed.

Gwyn didn't look away as the man brought the blade over and down into the hole in his chest plate where his neck protruded. She didn't look away as he plunged it to the hilt and collapsed.

Even with eyes as black as an abyss, Sabina peered at her with a look of concern.

Gwyn ignored it. "We need to make sure everything else is okay."

To her credit, Sabina didn't press, but the knight did take a deep breath as she seemed to war with her thoughts. Gwyn kept her blue magic moving throughout her mind, shutting down any chance of the situation catching up to her.

Sabina knelt next to Emma, feeling at her neck and mouth before she glanced at Gwyn and subtly shook her head, eyes clearing as she did. Gwyn took a deep breath and let her magic settle throughout her body.

I am frozen. My emotions are ice. Now is the time to protect my family. She took one last look at Emma's still body. She could let it all crash into her later.

Turning toward Sabina, she resorted to thoughts instead of speech. *Let's go. Lead the way. I will protect us.*

Sabina nodded hesitantly. *We will need to move quickly.*

The two of them exited the room and moved down the hall. They found Maris near the stairs. The woman was also dead, but the bodies of two more attackers lay next to her. Gwyn looked up at Sabina, whose eyes were already black again. Her hands clenched her sword tightly. *They will all burn.*

They continued down the stairs, hearing shouts and fighting throughout the house. Guards and staff lay dead down the stairs. *How? How did they do this?*

I do not know. I didn't feel anything until it was too late. I wasn't focused on my magic, and they moved quickly, overrunning everything as soon as they committed. My . . . range didn't catch them until they were already entering the manor. I am sorry, Princess.

Do not be sorry.

They moved toward the great hall, and a crash resounded to their right. Sabina lifted her sword and a man and woman burst through a doorway. Gwyn saw a flash of mana inside and threw up an **[Ice Wall]**. It was a weak thing that barely covered the entrance to the door, but it was enough to stop the bolt that slammed into it.

The wall collapsed almost immediately, and Sabina called out to the two. "Get out of the way! Hurry!"

They quickly moved behind Sabina and Gwyn, huddling together.

Sabina glanced at Gwyn. *Three men. Two crossbows.*

Can you?

Not without excessive focus. It takes a lot out of me. I can distract them. Can you—no. I will...

Distract them, Sabina. I promise I won't hesitate. Our people are dying.

Sabina seemed to war with herself, but she nodded. *Be ready. As soon as you hear them yelling.*

Gwyn channeled mana and got ready to move. Orbs of fire formed over her shoulders. Her hands burst into flames, and she nodded at Sabina. The guard tilted her head and squinted her eyes in concentration

Gwyn heard the scream of surprise from within. The thwack of a crossbow firing. She entered the room and launched her [**Fireballs**] at where she thought the men would be. Three of the four missed, but a scream of pain told her one she had sent had hit home. Gwyn lifted her hands and forced fire to launch out in a [**Gout of Flame**]. She sprayed the fire left and right as she slowly walked further into the room.

She barely had the presence of mind to jump backward as a form came barreling at her from the right. A man crashed into the wall but quickly lashed out with a sword that narrowly missed her. Her eyes widened, and she almost let her blue mana drop as her focus was nearly torn away. Gwyn did the only thing she could think of and dug deep into the frozen rage within her. She shaped it into the same spell that she had given to Taenya to protect herself, letting it loose.

A [**Blast Wave**] exploded from her and consumed everything within five paces of her with white flames of incinerating fury. The man fell, his screams turning to pained whimpers as he quickly succumbed.

Gwyn turned and looked at the last man alive in the room. The telv quickly dropped his sword and raised his hands. His eyes were wide with fear as he scrambled backward.

"No. No no no . . . *Please!*"

"*Burn,*" said Gwyn.

Sabina stood impatiently as she waited to move into the room. The heat was unbearable, and she knew that it would not discriminate in whom it consumed. She let the emotions throughout the manor fill her, feeling guards and servants alike fighting their attackers. Many had died, but House Reinhart was not over-run yet. Sabina went on alert the moment she felt the slight crack forming in the ice that held Gwyn's emotions at bay.

The shrill shriek coming from the room caused her to raise her blade. But she relaxed as a look through the door let her see all of the flames were pulled from the walls and furniture back into Gwyn's outstretched hand.

Sabina glanced back at the two servants who remained huddled together in fear. "Lock yourself into a room. I believe the upstairs is clear. *Be careful.* Run if you have to." They quickly nodded and left.

Gwyn emerged, and Sabina's [**Detect Emotions**] showed . . . *nothing.* Gwyn was completely blank to her senses, and it scared Sabina. She scrutinized the princess, who was moving back into place behind her, but saw nothing except calm determination. She reached out mentally to her.

Stay close.

Gwyn stumbled slightly but nodded, the stress of too much mana use getting to her. *I will.*

Sabina moved quietly but deliberately through the manor as they made their way to the great hall. She felt four people entering through the front door just up ahead and moved her sword into position.

Four.

Gwyn's [**Fireballs**] formed over her shoulders, and she looked around, her gaze settling on a guardswoman who lay slumped against the wall with a bolt protruding from her neck. The princess moved over and closed the woman's eyes, but then drew the woman's dagger from its sheath. She turned and nodded at Sabina.

Ready.

Sabina narrowed her eyes. *Magic. Not dagger. Understood?*

Gwyn scowled at her for a moment but then acquiesced, dropping the blade to the floor.

Sabina turned and made her way toward the four she sensed, flattening her back against the wall. She moved her sword slowly to the edge and used the mirrored finish to try to see around the corner without exposing herself. She wasn't able to see much, but she caught sight of two men looking away from her.

With swift movements, she moved her sword to her left hand and drew a throwing knife. Taking a deep breath, she stepped around the corner and threw the blade at the first man she saw. Another man jerked in surprise and shouted out in warning but wasn't quick enough. The blade flew through the air and embedded itself just behind her target's ear.

Sabina brought up her blade, but then immediately jumped back around the corner, pushing Gwyn away as she did. Not even a heartbeat later, two bolts came flying past the corner, punching into the wall behind her. Sabina gently probed at their minds and used [**Conjure Hallucinations**]. Her magic caused the remaining attackers to see two house guards rushing at them from around the corner. In *her* sight, she saw two shadowy forms with swords and shields charge the remaining three men.

Sabina surged from around the corner and raised her sword. All of the attackers assaulted the apparitions and were thrown off guard when their attacks simply passed through the air. One of the men stumbled with the momentum of his swing.

The spell collapsed immediately, but then Sabina was there. She swung and caught the stumbling man at the weak point where his breastplate overlapped with his cuisses. A gap just large enough for her blade had opened up, and she quickly took advantage.

Her sword bit deep, and she knew the man was done even as she yanked back to move toward the next two. Both of them shouted for aid, and she had enough presence of mind to [**Detect Emotions**], and feel two more presences coming in the door. Sabina raised her sword and stepped back as two large knights entered. Each held a longsword and settled into stances as they confidently moved toward her.

Shit. Gwyn. Her charge had been using a lot of magic, and she wasn't sure how much more the girl could handle. She had to get her away.

One of the knights lifted his visor and gestured behind her. "Give us the terran, and all of the death ends. You need not die for an outsider. The only two who must die are the princess and the knight who killed Lord Nicolas."

"You'll not have her, you bastard. You chose the wrong house to attack, and your lord will die like his son," Sabina sneered.

The knight frowned but set his visor back into position. "Very well then. We will purge this entire house."

Sabina felt another presence approach and settled into a stance. *Be ready,* she warned Gwyn. *I will need your fire. Hit the first to approach me with all you have, unless you see a crossbow. Those need to die first.*

Gwyn moved out from around the corner, her hands alight with a fluttering flame. *Understood.*

Sabina narrowed her eyes. *She's reaching her breaking point. The strain is getting to her as it does me. Just one more fight. You can do this, Sabina.*

With a deep breath, the knight stepped aside to give Gwyn room to cast her spells, but then she heard the princess gasp.

Wait!

What is—

A spear flew through the front door behind the two knights and impaled the one who had spoken to her. Someone in silver-and-blue armor came striding through the door with a sword.

Theran?

Theran raised his sword and then launched it at an impossible speed toward the second knight, who was just turning around. The blade seemed to glint with mana as it pierced through the knight's armor as if it were paper.

Sabina took advantage of the shock and rushed forward, bringing her sword up and across one of the guards, who had nothing but a surprised look on his face. She followed up by moving toward the last guard, but the man managed to get his sword and shield up to block her attack. He swung back at her, but she parried and stepped back. She moved to swing at the man again, but Theran appeared behind him, grabbed him by the armor, and threw him to the side. The guard crashed into the wall, his weapons clattering away as he crumpled to the floor.

Theran knelt behind the man, grasping at his neck and head as he did. The guard struggled, punching and batting at the elf's armor and helm, but Theran was able to position his hands where he wanted. With a quick, final motion, he snapped the man's neck.

Letting the body fall, he picked up his sword, turning to her and Gwyn. He removed his helm and saluted. "I was training and came as soon as I could. Are you injured?"

"We're fine, Theran. I'm happy to see you," Gwyn said.

Using [**Detect Emotions**], Sabina felt more presences approaching, and focused on the distinct surge of <<*Anger*>> and <<*Determination*>>. She gestured to Theran and warned, "More coming. I can't tell if they're hostile, but they're angry. Prepare yourself."

Gwyn's hands reignited into flame, and Theran turned and lifted his blade.

Sabina sighed in relief as she heard a familiar voice call out.

"House Reinhart! We're coming in!"

Taenya and a paladin entered, followed by Siveril and what seemed like all of the remaining guards. Taenya's eyes widened but then seemed to sag in relief as she saw Gwyn. Her sword fell to her side, blood dripping from the blade onto the floor as she exhaled deeply.

"Your Highness, Sabina, you're both safe. Are you injured?"

Gwyn said nothing, so Sabina shook her head. "Her Highness and I are not injured. Emma saved the princess, and one of my guards died, and I do not know where the rest are. I have no idea if the house is secure, but for now, we are alive."

She narrowed her eyes as the paladin with Taenya removed her helmet. Sabina had seen the sun elf before. "What are *you* doing here?" she asked.

The paladin ignored her and bowed to Gwyn. "Your Highness. The church could not ignore this attack. I was already nearby and decided to assist."

Sabina narrowed her eyes again. "You were spying."

The sun elf gestured at herself. "Hard to spy when you stand out so much. We have been watching the manor since Her Highness met with the archpriestess. Yet even my small team was surprised by the ferocity of this assault."

The paladin—Amari, Sabina recalled—then saluted. "I am here to protect Her Highness. I sent my team to the temple. A full contingent should be coming soon. We will help you secure the grounds," she stated with finality.

"We will speak of this later. For now, guardsmen: teams of four, secure the manor. Theran, stay with the paladin," Taenya ordered.

Sabina gasped and clutched her chest as she felt a storm of emotions surge from behind her. Gwyn had let go of whatever magic was keeping her feelings contained. She turned and saw her ward collapse to her knees as she broke down in sobs. Sabina rushed to her side.

It's alright. You're safe. We're safe.

Taenya walked into the office with two of her guards behind her. Theran was already there, along with the paladin, Evocati Amari. Siveril was at the ducal palace with Sabina meeting with the duke.

While that left Gwyn without a knight at her side, she had ten guards upstairs protecting her: the other two of Taenya's guards and all four of Theran's, along with four others from the house. The remaining members of Sabina's team had all been found as Theran cleared the manor after the attack. The missing three were found surrounded by eight dead attackers from the marquess Angwin. One of the guards was dead, and one more had died of his wounds later that night. The last was still recuperating from her wounds, but the surgeon had hopes that she would be on her feet within the week. The guard was adamant that she would be ready in time for the trip to Avira.

The attack itself had claimed many lives, and not just of the guards. It seemed that the attackers had killed indiscriminately, and almost forty percent of the house had died either by a blade or bolt. None of them had expected such a response from the marquess, and it had caught them completely off guard. They had been outnumbered by the attackers twofold, and that was including the servants.

The servants didn't go down without a fight, though. And they suffered the most.
"What can you tell me?"

Theran shook his head. "We are as secure as we can be." He gestured to the paladin. "With the paladins here, it is a sufficient deterrent for anyone who thinks they can attack. This show of force cannot be good for us, however."

"I do not care about appearances right now. Evocati, how long are your forces able to remain on the grounds?"

The sun elf glanced toward the window. "I can justify a presence until the duke acts. After that, it becomes an Aviran issue. *I* would be able to remain, but if there is no active threat to an Honored One, the rest cannot stay."

Taenya jerked in surprise. "An *Honored One?* When did this occur?"

"Her Holiness decreed it this morning. Lady Roslyn had already been recognized. The archpriestess recognized Princess Gwyneth officially, which is what authorizes her protection to this level."

Taenya sighed and looked at Theran. "We need to move up the timetable. One week, then we make for Avira. Whatever guarantees Siveril gets from the duchy will not be enough. The marquess doesn't have influence within the capital, and the princess will be safe at the Academy. The Polite War is forbidden upon its grounds."

"We can have people ready by then. Ser Sabina . . ." He glanced at the paladin.

Evocati Amari sighed. "I know of Ser Sabina. Not fully, but I know enough. Her Holiness has ordered our silence on the matter. You can trust us."

Taenya narrowed her eyes. "How?"

The paladin tilted her head. "How . . . what?"

"How do you know?"

"I—I cannot say."

Taenya shook her head. "If you cannot trust us, then we cannot trust you. You will not be coming with us."

Amari's eyes shot open wider. "I have been ordered—"

"No. Unless Her Highness overrides me, you are not coming. Not to mention that you are not conspicuous at all in that armor."

"Your armor and sigil are widely known at this point as well, Ser Taenya. You too will stand out."

Taenya scoffed. "I do believe that red—"

Theran looked askance at her denials. "Taenya. You may need her. It's just her, not all of them. More protection for Her Highness is a good thing. By just being near, Evocati Amari may dissuade someone from attacking. No one wishes to go against the Church."

Taenya narrowed her eyes, but with a sigh, she relented. "Fine. You will answer to me in absence of any direct orders from Her Highness. I will not have you get in the way."

Amari smirked. "That is no problem. The Paladins of Alos only chafe at taking orders from those we do not respect. After what we've seen of you? You have it."

"And don't start kissing my ass. That won't make me like you," Taenya said.

The smirk fell, but the paladin nodded. "Understood."

"Now, please excuse me. I have a traumatized princess to tend to."

Both nodded to her before she turned and walked out.

Taenya took a deep breath as she reached the door to Gwyn's suites. She paused, placing a hand on the door frame and leaning into it. She closed her eyes, ignoring the concerned guards near her.

She thought back to Sabina's explanation of what had happened in Gwyn's rooms before they were attacked and what Gwyn had ordered her to do. While Taenya may dislike it, the attack was within the conditions she had set with Sabina for the use of her powers in such a way. Yet it seemed that it had disturbed even the elven knight to use her magic in such a fashion.

Gwyn had gone through much since arriving on Eona, and she had nevertheless maintained a level of innocence and hope that was admirable. After this, Taenya had to trade duties with Sabina. The mind mage hadn't been able to withstand the feelings coming from the princess. Sabina confided her suspicion that her connection with the girl had made her too susceptible to any overwhelming emotions that were emitted. Since then, Sabina had described it as a dark storm, an emotional tempest filled with grief, guilt, and rage.

"Ser Taenya? Are you alright?" one of her personal guards asked.

She nodded once, then turned the handle and entered the room.

I just hope that happy, kind girl is still in there somewhere.

CHAPTER NINE

THE SOVEREIGN CITIES

After their tense encounter with the Valeni, the caravan proceeded with caution, journeying at a deliberate pace. Gisele, prioritizing safety, opted for early stops each evening, selecting only locations that offered strategic defense. Although these precautions ultimately proved unnecessary, Sloane couldn't help but feel relieved they had taken such measures.

Something about the encounter with the Valeni lingered in Sloane's mind, igniting a cascade of questions. The enigmatic nature of mana, the evolving abilities among people, and a particular fascination with the Valeni's captivating cat-like eyes—these reflections consumed her thoughts.

As they ventured beyond the edge of the forest, the terrain gradually transitioned from rolling hills to burgeoning signs of civilization. Their path weaved through quaint hamlets, run-down villages, and alongside farmland, which made her feel better about their *Oregon Trail*–esque adventure thus far.

Finally approaching Marketbol, Sloane shielded her eyes against the brilliant sunlight, her gaze drawn to the city's splendor. Unlike any she had witnessed before, Marketbol flaunted its affluence unabashedly. Its walls shimmered like pearl under the sun, adorned with vivid red accents and matching rooftops that hinted at the wealth within. Gold-trimmed roofs added to Marketbol's majestic palette, creating a mesmerizing visual tapestry.

A strangely out-of-place butte not far inside the wall hosted the most fantastical building she'd seen yet. Atop the verdant, tree-dotted hill, the vast building spanned the peak, complete with an expansive terrace that seemed to defy gravity. Its design, reminiscent of ancient Nordic architecture, featured nested roofs and bold angular overhangs that captivated Sloane's imagination.

On the opposite end of the city, isolated from the rocky prominence, rested what could only be described as the palace. Set upon a sprawling grassy hill, it commanded attention, completing the picturesque landscape that Sloane now found herself in.

As they got closer, she noticed a few peculiar landmarks. "Hey, what are those buildings?" she asked Stefan, who was sitting next to her on the wagon's driving bench.

He shifted so he could squint and look in the distance, shielding his eyes from the sun with his hand. "Ahh, that building there by itself on Market Rise is the Banking Guild's headquarters. The bigger palatial structure on Bol Hill is the city's Hall of Governance."

"Really? That's where they get the name Marketbol? It's a market, on Bol Hill? Wow," she said drolly.

Stefan chuckled. "Indeed, there have been proposals to change its name in the past, but the locals have steadfastly refused, clinging to tradition."

Sloane nodded as he spoke. She could understand it. It was their home, and some people loved their cities deeply, faults and all. Looking at the structure on the cliff, she imagined how difficult it would be to go up any stairs to it. She mused aloud, "I can imagine getting up to the headquarters is a pain."

"Actually, scholars and workers from the Eastern Reaches engineered a brilliant system of lifts." Stefan's gaze wandered as he searched the landscape, then pointed. "Ah, there. You can observe it now," he said, indicating the structure.

Narrowing her eyes against the distance, Sloane was surprised as she discerned a platform being descended from the terrace.

"Huh. An elevator."

Stefan glanced at her but did not reply.

Reflecting on Marketbol's appearance, she added, "The city is undoubtedly beautiful. Though it appears as though the cost of living would be high. Everything seems so . . . meticulously planned."

"It is. Elodie would know more, though. If she says we have enough to purchase a location for a center, we do."

Together, Sloane and Elodie had devised a strategy to secure a property as near as possible to the Scholars' Quarter. It seemed that the city had a fairly important school that was specialized and focused on merchants, economics, and trade skills—a perfect breeding ground for the professionals and experts they aimed to recruit for the Reinhart Center.

In-depth conversations with Adaega further solidified Sloane's decision; Adaega's comprehensive vision for the project resonated deeply. The trio, along with Ernald, had spent countless evenings discussing the Reinhart Center's direction. Positioned in Marketbol, the center would delve into the study of materials, their properties in conjunction with mana, and practical applications. Adaega had also persuaded Sloane to remain vigilant during her journey to Avira for additional opportunities, ideally to establish a sister center dedicated to magical studies. These establishments promised not only a consistent revenue stream for her house but also significant influence and opportunities for networking within the region. Elodie was wholeheartedly on board, confident that the Romaris family would eagerly support any profitable endeavor.

Thinking of profit, Sloane sighed. She and Elodie had finished the rune card terminal with the help of her smith, Koren, and she was ready to test it as soon as they reached the city. Elodie had explained the importance of setting everything up properly, and an especially important thing they needed was at the suggestion of her uncle—they had to get a lawyer.

"I trust her judgment," Sloane said aloud to Stefan. "First on our agenda is to seek out this Baker individual Giallo told me to find so I can deliver his message, followed by securing one of these esquires for the house."

Stefan gave her the side-eye. "Can we settle into an inn, first? A bath would be nice."

She paused. They had been on the road for roughly eight weeks, with only intermittent stops. The only cleaning they'd been able to do was with stream water and wooden tubs in a couple of villages that had been *freezing*. The group was tired and worn out from the travels. Relaxing for the rest of the day would be a smart decision.

"That's probably a good idea," she agreed.

As Stefan turned his attention back to the road, Sloane seized the moment for a discreet self-check, camouflaging a quick sniff under the pretense of surveying their surroundings. The immediate regret and the effort to suppress a recoil betrayed the necessity of Stefan's suggestion.

He was talking about a bath for himself . . . right?

Sloane navigated the streets flanked by Nemura on her right and Deryk on her left. Their destination, Drury Lane, loomed ahead. The bath she had indulged in earlier, albeit brief and less luxurious than she'd desired, had washed away the grime of travel, leaving her feeling rejuvenated. Stefan's suggestion to prioritize cleanliness had indeed been wise. *Good looking out, buddy.*

Approaching a congregated group, Sloane prepared to sidestep the assembly, but a swift glance from one of the elves within the group prompted their hurried parting, allowing her easy passage. Her initial surprise quickly faded as she considered her companions: her polished appearance coupled with the formidable presence of a knight and a guard by her side was bound to command attention.

In fact, it quickly became apparent that their presence warranted a certain level of deference, as passersby instinctively cleared a path for them. This observation cemented Sloane's understanding of the influence their small party wielded simply by walking together.

Marketbol was beautiful and immaculate. The streets bustled with activity yet retained an air of tranquility. Public spaces were alive with individuals enjoying the serene beauty of gardens, parks, and the gentle sounds of flowing fountains. Artistic statues lent elegance, while the city's inhabitants, engaging in leisure or commerce, added a vibrant pulse to the serene landscape.

There even appeared to be individuals dedicated to maintaining the cleanliness of the streets and alleys. It was so refreshing to see it all. The safety, the prosperity . . . Sloane wanted this for when she found her daughter.

She could see her breath as she walked, but the dryness of the day kept any chance of snow away. The season was shifting to winter, and everyone was bundled up for warmth, but that didn't keep the little ones indoors. Children ran around and played various games. Around a small plaza, an elf boy kicked what looked like a leather ball away from a girl, and Sloane smiled as the telv girl ran hard to catch up to him. Other boys and girls jumped up and down, calling out for him to pass.

I bet Gwyn would love to play soccer.

Sloane considered Adaega and her prior request to find somewhere safe. *This will be a good home for her.*

Sloane smiled as she noticed a group of people lounging in a park they were passing. An older telv couple was sitting on a blanket, a little basket filled with what looked like lunch and snacks. A wine bottle sat between the two and the man was placing grapes and cheeses onto a plate while the woman read a book. The woman said something as she turned a page, and the man chuckled. Sloane couldn't help but giggle as she watched him pluck a grape from his plate and place it into the woman's open mouth.

It was so domestic and so . . . cute.

Deryk's gentle nudge brought her attention back to their path, directing her gaze across the street. After allowing a few carriages to rumble by, they crossed over to a bustling street alive with an array of shops: produce vendors, a butcher, and a delightful variety of bakeries, each with its specialty, from fresh bread to delectable pastries.

A sign caught Sloane's eye, prompting a smile at its straightforwardness: Baking Company. A name that couldn't be more on the nose if it tried. *Zero effort guys. Come on.*

Nemura's amused huff was audible as they stepped into the spartan bakery. The interior was stark, devoid of any embellishment, with a counter dominating the space and a large stone oven tucked in the corner. Beside it, a door led to another room, guarded by a man perched on a stool by the counter. To the left, shelves brimming with an array of breads spanned the wall, some loaves edging toward a charred appearance.

The worker, a lithe raithe with ash-colored skin and storm-cloud-colored eyes half hidden beneath shoulder-length black hair, looked up. His attire was unassuming, mirroring his air of ennui. Upon noticing the visitors, his expression shifted from indifference to surprise, his mouth agape, as if the very concept of customers was a novelty to him.

Sloane greeted him with a wave and approached the counter. "Good afternoon! Are you the *Baker?*"

Deryk groaned behind her.

The raithe stared at her and replied, "No, milady, I am not the baker. May I be of assistance to you?"

Sloane shook her head sadly. "I'm afraid not directly. I was hoping to discuss a potentially large order with the baker directly to see if it's feasible."

The man nodded along as she spoke. "A-a large order? How large, milady?"

She nearly froze. *I haven't gotten that far yet!* "Um, well . . ." She trailed off, turning to Nemura for support. "Nemura, what would you estimate our order size to be?"

Nemura's gaze sharpened. "We're looking at providing for at least one hundred people, perhaps more," she specified.

The raithe inhaled sharply. "I see! Allow me to fetch the baker immediately." He began to move toward the back room but paused, a sudden thought occurring to him. "And when would you need this order?"

Offering a reassuring smile, Sloane said, "As soon as you can manage. It's a rather significant order."

Acknowledging her urgency, the attendant's eyes grew even wider. "Understood! Thank you, milady!" With that, he hurried off to the back.

Both Nemura and Deryk exchanged glances with Sloane, their expressions a mix of amusement and exasperation. She shrugged.

"What? He seemed to take the request seriously."

Nemura shook her head. "You are about as subtle as a rockslide."

Sloane sniffed. "Thank you."

Their attention shifted as the raithe returned, this time accompanied by a moon elf who immediately took measure of the trio with a critical eye. His twilight-blue eyes narrowed as he surveyed the scene before directing his employee.

"Go tidy up the back. I'll handle this."

The raithe looked between Sloane and his boss, a flicker of uncertainty crossing his face, before resigning with a quiet, "Alright, boss."

After the raithe departed, the elf folded his arms across his chest. "You're not here to buy bread."

Sloane raised a brow. "Why not? Your bread looks delicious."

The man scoffed. "No one comes here to buy the bread. It's shit. All of that is made by my apprentice, and I don't have the heart to tell him he'll never make it as a baker. If they want the good stuff, they know how to order it. Now, what do you really want?"

"Can you make . . . *muffins?*"

He scowled. *"What?"*

Sloane guessed he wouldn't appreciate her jokes any longer. The way Nemura and Deryk shifted their stances confirmed it.

"Never mind. You are the *Baker?*" she asked, ensuring to emphasize the name.

His eyes narrowed. He hesitated slightly but then gestured around. "That is why you are here. What is it to you?" He shifted his arms.

"I was asked to tell you: 'Vlaredia moves for the Malduhr Pass.' But that no longer matters."

The man froze. "Who told you that?"

"We recently had business with the Academy in Thirdghyll."

The Baker brought one hand up to his chin in thought. "You have my attention." He turned and yelled into the back, "Oi! You're done for the day. Head home. Now."

A voice responded and the apprentice emerged. He gathered his belongings quickly and cast curious looks at the trio as he exited, leaving an air of unanswered questions lingering.

The Baker walked to the front door, flipped the small sign in the window, and latched the door shut. When he turned around, it was almost as if he had become another person.

His stance, his posture, the way his muscles relaxed all seemed different. Sloane found it disconcerting.

"Who are you, and why does that message no longer matter?" the Baker asked.

Sloane inhaled deeply. "I am Lady Sloane Reinhart. I worked with a man named Giallo on a . . . project. Can you verify your affiliation with the Academy?"

The man nodded. He walked to the counter and reached underneath, bringing out a very familiar hat, but of a different color.

"Does the name Giallo have special meaning to you?" he asked.

She nodded. "It means 'yellow' in a language I know."

"I am Cerulean. His hat would have been like this, but yellow. I can give no other confirmation that you would understand. However, if that is not enough, I suggest only giving me easily verifiable information. Which was the intent of the message you gave. No secrets."

She nodded. That made sense. Sloane wasn't a spy, and as Nemura had said, she didn't quite have the skill set for it. "Thirdghyll has fallen. Monsters attacked it. Goosebourne has fallen. Vlaredia has taken control of it."

Cerulean's eyes widened and he opened his mouth to speak, but she held up a hand. "Vlaredia is just north of the Agenval Forest," she said. "We wiped out a watchtower that was set up, but they are definitely moving south with a large army."

When Sloane didn't continue, Cerulean spoke. "The monsters from Valesbeck made it to the city? What of the people?"

Sloane scowled. While she wasn't sure if the man knew of the plan, she was still bitter about it. She was just happy she had been able to facilitate the evacuation of the number she had. She gestured to Nemura.

"I am Nemura, formerly a senior guardswoman of the Thirdghyll Guard. I was released from my service to join Lady Reinhart's house and assist in spreading the message. There were many survivors from the guilds as well as most of the guard garrison of East Fort, including their families. The fort was able to hold out for several days, but they had to retreat to Vilstaf. We saw no survivors from the nobility. We are not aware of what happened to the count. However, we have reason to believe he was ambushed as he attempted to escape a battle in which his personal guard was decimated by monsters."

Cerulean nodded. "And the army? You suspect it is coming here?"

Deryk raised his hand slightly, and everyone turned to face him. "I am Ser Deryk of Blightwych. The Vlaredians made no indications of moving toward Westaren. Their forces were clearly moving to secure the south and seem to be setting up Goosebourne as a secure point from which to launch attacks into this region of the cities."

Cerulean sighed. "That is not good news. Lady Reinhart, do you have any pressing business to attend to?"

"I have some business, yes."

"I would like to request that you join me in meeting with the city's leadership, and include any of your retainers who could give pertinent information. Marketbol sent its army east a while ago. They should be near the next city by now."

Deryk tilted his head. "Laudenwych? That's over one hundred and fifty kilometers from here."

Cerulean nodded. "Yes. They're heading to the front. Every city in the region has sent its armies. Valecan, Laudenwych, Wardenshirst, and Marketbol. There are fears that the Vlaredians will take the border city of Constanden before they can be reinforced. The closest city, Valecan, sent its armies to attempt to relieve the sieged army. Laudenwych sent its armies to reinforce the Valecani army. The remaining armies are being sent north to reinforce Sacksburn to hold the plains west of the Farum Mountains. However, if the Vlaredians made it through the pass, they will have attacked Sacksburn and possibly even taken it already."

Sloan felt overwhelmed by all of the location names. She would definitely need to get someone to show her a map back at the inn. She knew the region only very broadly. North of them was the Agenval Forest, and east was a lake just below the southern edge of a long mountain range. The pass the army had gone through was the only way through the mountains without going all the way south and around. East of the mountain range was a large plains area that ended at another, smaller mountain range, where Reanny and her brother were from. Beyond that lay a valley, where the city that was fighting sat closest to the Empire. She knew there was a large town with a massive fort in a narrow opening between the mountains east of them, with another of the Val Forests to the east of *that. Shit, man, so much stuff is* east. *Absolutely need a map.*

Sloane sighed. "So, basically, you have an army on the way here, and you have no army to defend yourself with?" she asked.

Cerulean nodded. "It is the Sovereigns that do not, but you are correct. We need to meet with the leadership and pass this information on. There may be time for them to get word to the nearby Cities. Then all we can do is hope an army can make it here in time."

Deryk looked at Sloane. "We should get Ser Gisele and Ser Ismeld."

Sloane nodded. "Agreed." *I certainly do not want to explain this alone.*

She turned back to the moon elf. "Okay, Cerulean. We'll go with you. I have a vested interest in this city remaining safe. Let's see what we can do."

The man let out a hesitant chuckle. "That is, if they listen to us. I *am* a spy, after all."

"Oh . . . yeah. There is that."

He smiled. "Don't worry. They won't throw us into the dungeon or anything. I hope."

She looked around at the bakery. *I have a feeling they already know he's a spy.*

Mariel's footsteps echoed softly against the polished stone floors as she exited the chapel nestled within the Temple of the Celestials. The weight of her future responsibilities as a priestess of Tenera pressed heavily on her shoulders, each session with the elders adding another layer to her understanding—and her apprehension. Gripping her notebook, she navigated through the temple's sacred halls, her mind focused on her lessons for the day.

But as she crossed the threshold into the dormitories, the ambient chatter dimmed, replaced by a palpable tension. Mariel couldn't help but notice the whispers that seemed to ripple through the air, each syllable laced with judgment. The glances thrown her way were far from subtle, filled with a mix of curiosity and disdain. It was becoming increasingly clear that her recent endeavors, especially her interactions with Praetor Shalas, were not going unnoticed by her peers.

The girls, once her companions in faith and study, had grown distant, their camaraderie eroded by a sea of whispered rumors and unfounded accusations. The closer Mariel grew to her sacred duties, and particularly to Praetor Shalas, the more isolated she felt. It was as if her dedication to her calling and the mentorship she received had set her apart, marking her as a target for envy and speculation.

They were jealous, the praetor had said. It was normal for young girls to experience it, and Mariel should rise above it. She had potential.

All Mariel felt was darkness.

She prayed nightly to Tenera for guidance, to help her. But the roiling black inside of her begged to be released. She wouldn't let it be.

Mariel pressed on, her resolve firm despite the cold reception and turmoil within. The path of a priestess had never promised to be easy, she reminded herself. It was a road paved with sacrifice, discipline, and, often, loneliness. Loneliness was all she knew—ever since her family had given her to the Church. Yet the whispers and sidelong looks stung more than she cared to admit. They served as a constant reminder that her place within the temple, and among her fellow acolytes, was precarious, subject to the shifting sands of opinion and rumor.

The week was nearly up, and she couldn't wait until she could go out in the city. To get away from all of the people who made fun of the shy, mumbling girl getting extra training from the lead paladin.

Not that they were allowed to know it was because of her gifts. On that, the high priest and praetor Shalas had both sworn her to secrecy.

Mariel reached her chamber, a small, austere room that offered a modicum of privacy and solace that she shared with two others. Luckily, both of the girls were out. Closing the door behind her, she allowed herself a moment to breathe, to let the mask of stoicism slip. The notebook, filled with her notes, thoughts, and dreams, felt heavier in her hands.

Later, as she lay in bed, her roommates both sleeping, she found herself gazing out the window, her eyes lifting to the celestial dance of the Sister Moons. It was nights like this when she was able to push aside the loneliness. As long as the sister goddesses shined down upon her, she knew she wasn't truly alone.

Not really.

She wiped a tear from her cheek and rolled over.

In the quiet of the night, she touched upon the darkness she kept locked within her, allowing just a sliver to seep out. In this moment of vulnerability, she offered her prayers to Tenera. She yearned for the day when she would feel acknowledged, integrated into a community larger than herself. She sent her prayers soaring for the parents who had abandoned her, hoping for reconciliation or understanding. And with a heart heavy with longing, she beseeched the darkness to dissipate, to release its grip on her soul.

CHAPTER TEN

BEARER OF BAD NEWS

The return to the inn—and the subsequent gathering of those eager to visit the Hall of Governance—had been more expedient than Sloane had anticipated. Ernald's determination to remain in Marketbol had solidified after a meaningful conversation in which he vowed to protect the members of her house, thereby enabling Stefan to accompany them. Seizing the opportunity, Elodie had orchestrated a sightseeing excursion for the entire household, incorporating a strategic review of potential locations for the Reinhart Center. This plan would streamline the selection process, making it easier for Sloane to evaluate and decide.

Their passage through the city was facilitated by two spacious carriages arranged by Cerulean. The interior of Sloane's carriage boasted a luxurious design—a wraparound bench upholstered in plush, burgundy fabric. Cerulean positioned himself opposite Sloane, while Stefan and Nemura sat beside her, with the tall telv woman facing the door. The second carriage carried the knights and Tiberius, whom Sloane had managed to keep hidden from Cerulean's notice until now.

"This could go any number of ways. General Irileth should be in the Hall—I just need to secure a meeting with him," mused Cerulean, his attire a sharp all-black ensemble accented by a cerulean hat, reminiscent of the outfit Giallo had worn back in Thirdghyll. Yet his anxious demeanor betrayed nothing of the confident facade he had once displayed.

"You know, your bakery isn't exactly subtle," Sloane deadpanned. "It practically screams 'this business is a front.' I'd be supremely surprised if they don't realize who you are. Allow me to take the lead. That way, if they somehow fail to recognize you, you can still maintain your cover."

Cerulean reclined slightly. "I would appreciate whatever discretion you can provide. But what is your plan for securing an audience?"

With a confident smirk, Sloane glanced at Stefan. "We'll do it live."

Stefan shifted uneasily in his seat, a look of confusion spreading across his face. "What exactly does that mean?"

"Don't worry," Sloane replied with a playful glint in her eye. "I'm just going to be the bearer of bad news."

Nemura turned to look out the window. "We're here."

Sloane smiled. "Let's do this. Time for me to earn my keep—and pretend that everything I do is perfectly normal." She added, "Please, watch me. I don't think this will tire me out, but just in case . . . catch me if I fall over."

The large woman tilted her head. "What is 'this'?"

With a knowing smile, Sloane allowed her mana to surge toward her eyes. She felt that familiar rush of energy as she directed it precisely where she intended. Gazing into a carriage mirror, she watched as her eyes ignited with a vibrant blue glow, and a fine mist spiraled from their corners. It was a subtle spectacle, yet she knew it would require effort to maintain for hours.

Nemura raised a brow but nodded.

Caught off guard by the display, Cerulean could only stare, wide-eyed. Amused by his reaction, Sloane confidently opened the carriage door and stepped out into the bustling streets. "Remember, this is perfectly normal."

Exiting the carriage with Nemura and Stefan close behind, Sloane took in the scene: the knights were already strategically positioned outside, and Tiberius, who was perched on Ismeld's shoulder, scrutinized her with keen interest before going still. A soft chuckle escaped her at the sight.

Cerulean, still bewildered, squinted at her. "What?"

"Nothing at all," she responded, shaking her head lightly.

In one fluid motion, Sloane beckoned to Tiberius. The falcon soared from Ismeld's shoulder, executing a graceful arc in the air before landing lightly on Sloane's shoulder. The act drew astonished gasps and murmurs from the gathering crowd. A guard at the entrance dashed inside, presumably to report the unusual sight.

Cerulean seemed to reconsider his earlier assumptions.

"Alright, fall in, and let's go. Ser Gisele, if you please," Sloane instructed.

Nodding, Gisele stepped to the forefront and guided their group into the Hall of Governance. Sloane trailed closely behind the orkun knight, her gaze roaming the grand surroundings. The stationed guards could not hide their astonishment, their eyes fixed on Tiberius and the soft glow emanating from Sloane's eyes. Discreet murmurs and exchanged glances confirmed that her visual effects were drawing the intended attention.

Upon reaching the entrance, they were greeted by guards and a telv official clad in a finely crafted tunic in a vibrant red with gold trim that complemented his dark-brown trousers and leather boots. Sloane appreciated the unmistakable style; the people here clearly had a distinct and unwavering aesthetic.

"G-greetings. Welcome to the Hall of Governance. Do you have an appointment, or may I assist you in some other way today?" the official inquired, his voice betraying a hint of uncertainty.

Sloane decided to overlook that he had omitted his own introduction. As Gisele subtly stepped aside, Sloane took the opportunity to introduce herself. The official's reaction to her luminous, misty eyes—a mixture of shock and fascination—gave her a brief advantage.

"I am the baroness Lady Reinhart of Blightwych, here on business from Westaren regarding the Banking Guild and other guilds collectively. Moreover, I bear urgent news for General Irileth and the council—a matter of grave importance."

Momentarily disconcerted by her commanding presence and the unexpected nature of her visit, the telv official struggled to compose himself. After a brief pause, he managed to muster a controlled yet apprehensive tone.

"Do you possess an appointment?" he asked, his voice slightly strained.

Sloane sighed. "How could I possibly have an appointment? As I stated upon arrival, I bring critical information. Such time-sensitive knowledge precludes scheduling. I am sure the general, at the very least, will appreciate my warning. After all, your city's safety depends on it."

At that moment, Tiberius let out a metallic screech, emphasizing her point and causing the official to jerk backward in surprise.

"Uh. Right," he muttered, his eyes darting around before settling on a nearby guard. "You, come with us. The baroness requires an escort to the council chambers immediately."

Sloane tilted her head. "Is the council in session? Will the general be present? It is *vital* that the general attend."

Gesturing briskly toward the grand entrance, the official began leading them into the heart of the building. "Indeed, milady. The general is present. I truly hope the urgency of your message justifies this interruption," he replied, a note of snark in his tone.

"Rest assured, it does."

Catching Cerulean's eye, Sloane offered him a reassuring nod, a silent acknowledgment of both their smooth progress and a hint of triumph at having made it through the door. Cerulean, in turn, bowed respectfully and discreetly stowed his hat in a satchel. She had a fleeting thought: *He'd better not try anything, or I'll kill him myself.*

As they hastened through the opulent halls, Sloane found herself nearly jogging to match the brisk pace of the telv official. One guard hurriedly maintained position, half walking, half running, while a contingent formed a rear escort. Their procession finally halted before a set of intricately carved wooden doors, adorned with gold filigree and trimmed in the city's signature red.

The official conferred briefly with the guards stationed at the doors, then signaled for the party to wait.

In the interim, Sloane and her companions were respectfully asked to relinquish their weapons. Their escorts assured them that the arms would be returned after the meeting, preserving the protocol of safety without compromising the dignity of the knights.

They moved through the grand opened doors into the council chamber. Immediately, Sloane's eyes were drawn to the center of the room, where an imposing circular table stood surrounded by seven exquisitely crafted chairs, each adorned with gold trim and red tufted fabric.

Every chair was occupied by either a telv or high elf, except for one sun elf woman. Their extravagant robes and jewelry, combined with their dignified expressions, radiated authority and age. The sun elf, notably, appeared closest to Sloane's age. An elderly telv man in gold-finished armor stood beside the table; his ceremonial breastplate featured two meticulously engraved birds of prey. His eyes were fixed on the falcon resting on Sloane's shoulder in a silent, intriguing acknowledgment that did not go unnoticed.

The official who had escorted them positioned himself before a crest painted on the chamber floor, presumably the city's emblem, and bowed his head in respectful greeting to the council. "Honored council," he intoned, "I present to you the baroness Lady Reinhart of Blightwych, bearer of urgent news from Thirdghyll."

Stepping aside, he gestured for Sloane to advance. Acknowledging his cue, she confidently approached the crest and positioned herself as directed.

"Good afternoon," she began, her voice clear and composed. "I am Lady Sloane Reinhart. If it isn't obvious, I am not one of the many peoples of your world. I am a terran. Now, I wanted to point this out because I wish to note that I am not an agent of any government. I care little for your politics or maneuvers insofar as they do not interfere with my immediate interests." She paused, letting her words settle over the assembled council.

After a moment of silence, Sloane cast a brief, reassuring glance toward Nemura before refocusing on the council. "Thirdghyll has fallen and has been decimated by what I can only describe as monsters. The few survivors have retreated to a nearby town, where Guildmaster Romaris is stabilizing conditions for the guilds. However, that is not the purpose of my visit."

Uneasy whispers rippled through the council as the general's gaze sharpened. "Then, Lady Reinhart, what brings you to us?" he asked, concern edging his tone.

"The Vlaredian Empire has seized control of Goosebourne and is now consolidating forces to move south," Sloane declared.

The revelation triggered immediate chaos; council members voiced shock and disbelief in a cacophony of overlapping exclamations. Sloane waited patiently for the turmoil to subside. An elderly high elf finally restored order, striking the table with a commanding thud. Grateful for the interruption, Sloane acknowledged him with a nod.

The elder, his hair a distinguished gray, spoke on behalf of the council. "Lady

Sloane, we appreciate this information," he stated, earning nods from his colleagues. "What evidence can you provide to support these claims?"

"I have seen it," she affirmed. Channeling her mana to strengthen her bond with Tiberius, she signaled subtly. In response, Tiberius soared across the chamber, his cry echoing off the walls before he gracefully landed on the center of the table, capturing the council's attention.

One of the council members, the sun elf woman, leaned forward. "What is that?"

Sloane stepped forward. "This is Tiberius—an experimental scout golem that I constructed. I am . . ." She paused, remembering her conversation with Maud and Gisele. "I suppose you could call me an artificer; I use the mana introduced by the Flash to create magical items. Tiberius here is one such example." She lifted her hand and showed off her watch. "I am able to connect with him as he flies and see what he sees. I was able to see the Vlaredian army as it entered Goosebourne. I saw the forces moving from it and heading south."

She gestured to Gisele, who joined her. "Ser Gisele, the Knight-Captain of the Order of Haven's Hope, can elaborate further."

"Greetings, council members of Marketbol," Gisele said, saluting the gold-armored telv. "General Irileth."

"Welcome, Ser Gisele, to Marketbol. Please," the old elf councilman said, gesturing for her to continue.

"Our caravan was forced to avoid eight patrols of six or more. Near the Agenval Forest, we were intercepted by a large light cavalry scout force, but we passed through unhindered. Our attempt to avoid conflict with the Vlaredians lasted until we reached a hastily constructed watchtower just before the forest, where we were attacked by a garrison of thirty-two. Lady Reinhart had to use her magic to protect the caravan. After neutralizing the watchtower threat, we moved here as swiftly as possible. Tiberius was then employed to scout, and we observed roughly five thousand troops moving from Goosebourne—which, by our estimate, is merely a fifth of the remaining forces in the city."

Several gasps filled the room. Sloane noted the general grinding his teeth. "General Irileth, my purpose in Marketbol is to establish relations with the Banking Guild and to acquire property for my house. I have a vested interest in this city's prosperity and safety. Moreover, I have been informed by sources from Westaren that your defenses may be lacking. They intimated that prompt communication of this information might enable you to seek aid from nearby cities. While I am not a soldier, I am willing to assist in defending our mutual interests."

The general narrowed his eyes. "I have heard reports of you terrans, and how you are from another land. Were you perhaps a military leader among your people?"

Sloane shook her head in confusion. Before she could respond, he continued,

"I know my duties, Lady Reinhart. I do not require you to remind me. After all, you are not a soldier. We will call on you if your aid is needed."

Sloane nodded, internally cringing. "Very well." *Let the soldier do the soldiering, Sloane.*

The sun elf at the table tilted her head. "What *are* your interests in Marketbol?"

"I'm not sure this is the appropriate forum," Sloane replied, "but since I am already here, allow me to say that I have a reference from Guildmaster Romaris regarding a business venture involving the entire Banking Guild. I also have plans for a venture specific to my house—I intend to purchase property for that purpose."

An elderly high elf chuckled softly. "Then you shall require a meeting with me, Lady Reinhart. I am Grandmaster Markus of the Banking Guild."

Sloane raised an eyebrow. "Oh. Well, do you have any availability in your schedule?" she asked, smiling.

"I believe we can arrange something, my lady. It is the least I can do in thanks for your warning us of the threat." Glancing around, he added, "I also believe General Irileth has much to attend to, so I propose we adjourn this meeting to let him resume his duties." The council members nodded.

"Thank you, Lady Reinhart," said a high elf. "We will be in touch. Perhaps you could join us for a meal soon. If you will excuse us."

Sloane nodded in acknowledgment. "Thank you." She lifted her hand, and Tiberius left the table, returning to her shoulder promptly.

The sun elf councilwoman raised a hand. "Lady Reinhart, one last thing. I would very much like to learn more about your golem. Please leave your contact details and your current residence with the adjutant. We shall reach out."

Bowing her head, Sloane replied, "I will." She turned and followed the group out of the room. Stefan conferred with the telv official to pass on the requested details. Once outside the Hall, Sloane sighed and allowed her constant mana channeling to subside.

Nemura stepped up beside her and whispered, "How are you feeling?"

Sloane rolled her shoulders. "I feel good. That wasn't nearly as bad as I expected." *Rather anticlimactic, to be honest,* she thought.

It wasn't long before they returned to the inn. Cerulean had thanked her for not revealing his cover—and she was surprised that the matter hadn't been raised again.

"You needed help, huh?" Gisele asked Sloane.

Sloane laughed softly. "I expected a bit more pushback, to be honest. You all provided moral support—although I think the general appreciated your report more than mine."

"Well, you did play into your role quite well," Gisele said with a shake of her head.

Sloane raised an eyebrow. "What do you mean?" She maneuvered around a server setting down mugs on a large table where other knights sat. She chose two empty chairs at the end, and they sat.

"You acted like a noble who came in and made demands outside of their experience. The general looked like he was about to pop a vein."

Sloane winced. "I just wanted to . . ." She sighed. "Yeah, that wasn't a good look. But he doesn't need to like me—just ensure our people here remain safe."

Gisele shrugged. "I agree. Although, I hope you understand they'll want to see what you can do in case the city comes under siege. You did offer to help."

With a groan, Sloane buried her head in her hands. "Shit. I didn't think that through. It's fine. We'll deal with it if it comes to it."

Gisele patted her shoulder. "I'm sure you'll do just fine."

Sloane had a thought that had been bugging her since the meeting. She glanced around at those present. "Why didn't anyone even acknowledge Cerulean?"

Deryk and Ernald laughed from across the table.

"Why would they?" Gisele asked from beside her.

Sloane squinted. "Isn't it obvious?"

They must have noticed her confusion, so Ernald elaborated, "Deryk, do you want to tell her, or shall I?"

Deryk motioned for him to continue. The sun elf sat up straighter, as though about to reveal a long-held secret. "I've been holding this in ever since we couldn't say anything in Thirdghyll. The Westari Order of Secrets—yes, that ominous *Academy*—they're considered a joke."

Her eyes widened in surprise. "What?"

Deryk sighed. "They are *excellent* assassins—among the best on the continent—but when it comes to espionage, their spycraft is laughable. No one takes them seriously."

Ernald leaned forward. His head blocked out Deryk's, forcing the orkun to cut off mid-speech. Sloane heard him sigh again. The sun elf took over. "And at some point, one of the Westari kings thought it was a great idea to have his not-so-secret-but-effective order of assassins run his nation's espionage apparatus. For a reason that escapes me, that has held true for half a century. To literally everyone but them, their spycraft is a joke," he said.

"Or perhaps that's exactly what they want everyone to believe," Sloane suggested drolly.

Gisele huffed. "No, that would make sense if true, but the reality is, no one wants to tell them. Places like the bakery are allowed and almost welcomed because it highlights where the Order of Secrets bases its operations. The Sovereigns learned from their mistakes and use that to feed them misinformation. It's a balancing act because they really are good assassins. They're just probably the worst spies of, well, anywhere."

Sloane hummed thoughtfully. "So, we don't need to interact with them anymore?"

The knight-captain shook her head. "No, not at all. If they need anything, they'll come to us."

Sounds like something out of a bad spy comedy. Sloane shrugged and looked at her companions. "What should we do now?

"We should probably get back to training," Gisele suggested.

Sloane nodded. "Yeah . . . we should. First—"

An elf man interrupted as he arrived at their table. "Lady Reinhart, Grandmaster Markus requests your presence tomorrow at the tenth bell. He will receive you at his office."

Sloane glanced at Gisele, who shrugged. "Huh. That was quick." Turning back to the man, she said, "I will be there with my retainer. Thank you."

The man nodded and turned, nearly colliding with another woman waiting nearby. After a brief exchange—a subtle connection passing between them—the telv woman moved aside and allowed him to pass. She looked at Sloane.

"Lady Reinhart, I, too, request a meeting. Lady Emerys asks to see you at your earliest convenience—perhaps after midday tomorrow, so you can refresh yourself after your meeting with the grandmaster."

Sloane squinted at her and then turned to Gisele. "Who is Lady Emerys?"

The woman raised a brow. "She is a member of the council? Lady Emerys expressed a desire to discuss your . . . uhhh . . . your bird?"

"Oh! Yes, I would be happy to meet with her. Thank you."

The woman bowed her head and proceeded to give her instructions on how and where to meet the sun elf council member. After she left, Sloane pointedly looked around before leaning toward Gisele.

"So . . . who *is* Lady Emerys?"

"Her house is one of the original founders of the city, along with the Banking Guild. That affiliation guarantees her a permanent seat on the ruling council."

Sloane nodded. "See anyone else ready to pop up and invite me to another meeting?" she asked softly.

Gisele scanned their surroundings. "Nope."

Sloane sighed. "Good. I don't want to go to any more meetings."

"Better you than me."

Sloane raised an eyebrow before her lips curved upward.

Gisele leaned away. She shook her head, pointing at Sloane. "Don't you dare even ask—I'm not going. I'll make you take Ismeld."

"But Giselllllle, it'll be fun!" Sloane sang out. She tried to put an arm around Gisele's shoulders, but the knight ducked under it.

"I swear to Alos, woman. Don't make me. I know where you sleep."

"Don't tease me with a good time, Gisele."

Gisele jabbed Sloane hard in the ribs.

"Ow! Damn it, Gisele!" Sloane said, rubbing at her side. *That's going to be a bruise by morning.*

Gisele scowled. "You want to start?"

Sloane remembered how long the knight had held a grudge against the guys. Raising her hands in surrender, she said, "Alright, alright. Point made. You're too good at holding grudges."

Gisele nodded. "I appreciate the compliment."

CHAPTER ELEVEN

EXPANDING OPERATIONS

W elcome, Lady Reinhart. Please, right this way. We have reserved the lift for your use," a high elf announced as Sloane arrived at the Banking Guild headquarters.

Sloane looked up. The headquarters sat atop a three-hundred-and-fifty-meter butte, accessible only by a large lift. A spiraling staircase also led to the top. *You won't catch my ass walking up there. That's a 'nah' from me*, Sloane thought.

The lift emerged from a base building, heavily guarded. Security here was tighter than anywhere she'd been. Sloane was relieved she'd only brought along Stefan and Elodie—apparently, they wouldn't allow more than one guard to accompany her.

"Thank you," Sloane said to the high elf. "That wasn't necessary. I am sure you are very busy."

The woman blinked. "Nevertheless, the grandmaster has ordered it, so we must comply."

Sloane nodded. "These are my retainers—"

"Yes, Miss Romaris and Mister Stranca. We were expecting them as well. Here we are, my lady."

Sloane raised a brow. "Well, then."

They stepped onto the lift, which was spacious enough for twenty to thirty people. Sloane moved to a corner so she could gaze out through the glass as the lift jerked to life and began its ascent. Marketbol looked completely different from anything she had seen or heard of on Earth. It seemed as if every detail had been coordinated and planned to an insane degree, and it surprised her to see how well maintained it was. Everywhere she looked, it completely defied all expectations. *If this is what this world has to offer, I need to protect it. A place to fall back on when I find Gwyn.*

"Beautiful, isn't it?" Elodie remarked from beside her.

Sloane's eyes remained fixed on the view: the rolling plains in the distance, the gleaming white-and-gold towers set into the wall, as the two towers that sat beyond it—it all was picturesque. "It certainly is. But why would your uncle ever want to leave here?"

Elodie laughed. "I've often wondered that myself. He never would have risen to his position without venturing out, though I always cherished our returns here."

Sloane peeked at the woman, who was also glued to the view outside the glass. "I never asked, do you have family here?"

Elodie smiled. "I do. Some distant relatives. My uncle took me in after my parents died in a fire when I was young—he felt it was his duty. Unfortunately, his commitments to the guilds left little time for family, so most of my upbringing was entrusted to a nanny he hired. He even paid for my education here in Marketbol. I attended the economics school and was among the top students. It was only natural that I join him."

"I can understand that," Sloane replied.

The remainder of the ride passed in comfortable silence until the lift settled onto a terrace above. The high elf attendant smiled as the gate opened.

"Please, this way, milady."

Sloane and her retainers followed her through the headquarters. Sloane was surprised by the paucity of regular people; everyone seemed engrossed in work. "It doesn't seem very busy," she said.

"Oh, that's because this is where decisions for the whole Banking Guild are made. Routine business is handled elsewhere in the city," Elodie explained.

The assistant nodded with a smile. "Quite right, Ms. Romaris. Here we are. Grandmaster Markus will join you momentarily."

After thanking the attendant, Sloane entered a room dominated by a large table and expansive glass windows spanning nearly one entire wall. A tall-backed chair was framed by a breathtaking panoramic vista of the city and its Hall of Governance, and across the table sat three other chairs, facing the view. *I imagine this would be pretty intimidating to most.* While the view was certainly something, she'd had the opportunity to see similar views on Earth in various meetings.

Sloane took the center seat as several attendants approached, placing a glass of water garnished with what appeared to be thin slices of lime before each of them. Once they were left to their solitude, Elodie retrieved a satchel of documents and spread them neatly on the table. Stefan brought forth the case containing the runecard and its terminal.

Sloane sipped her water. She cracked her knuckles, folded her hands, and rested them on the table.

A few minutes later, the door opened and the old elf from the council meeting entered. Sloane rose.

"Grandmaster Markus, thank you for having us."

The man smiled and extended his hand. "Please, just Markus, my lady."

Sloane grasped his hand; his handshake was surprisingly firm. "As long as you call me Sloane."

"Wonderful! I see you have Ms. Elodie with you, so I assume you come highly recommended by my dear friend Lanthil."

Elodie produced a sealed, rolled letter. "My uncle wrote this personally to the guild council. I—I hadn't expected to meet with you directly."

Markus chuckled as he broke the seal on the letter. "For the warning you gave, I could do no less."

"Will the city be able to get aid in time?"

"We aren't sure. General Irileth sent out riders the moment we finished the meeting. We also sent scouts toward Agenval. I suspect he will also ask to meet with you," he said.

Sloane nodded. "I will ensure I am available for a meeting."

The old man grunted softly before scanning the letter. He raised an eyebrow and looked at the case Stefan had placed on the table. "Hmm."

Sloane tilted her head, but let the man take his time.

With a subtle nod, he placed the letter down and tapped it once. "May I see it?" He extended his hand.

Sloane nodded at Stefan. The raithe rose, circled the table, opened the case, and laid out its contents for the grandmaster.

Markus gently picked up the runecard, examining it, humming to himself as he did. Sloane smiled and started explaining how the items worked, showing off the functionality of the runecard. The old elf nodded along as he watched with rapt attention, allowing her to explain everything before sitting back. He crossed his arms and stared down at the items in front of him.

"Do you know why the Banking Guild has the influence it does, Lady Reinhart? Why more often than not we are the ones in each region and district that run guild affairs?"

Sloane shook her head. "Honestly, no. I assumed it was due to superior logistics or personnel—or perhaps because you control most of the money."

He smiled. "That is a very logical supposition—those certainly help. However, one could say that the Merchant's Guild has a better handle on logistics. It is, after all, a core part of their profession. Holding the money has less to do with it than you'd think. That *cannot* affect anything we do. As soon as it looks like we are holding an entity's money hostage, we lose credibility. That is one aspect that, by its very nature, *will* remain neutral. Even in this war against the Empire, we will not freeze Vlaredian assets."

Sloane blinked. "That—that is very commendable. I cannot say that nations in my world would remain so neutral even in the face of such threats."

"Oh, we aren't entirely neutral. We are simply able to segregate that aspect of our business. We do more than hold everyone's money. But the reason we hold such influence is that we pride ourselves on reacting to trends quicker than any other guild. We have to. Trends can make or break an economy, and the economies of the nations that reside on Ikios are more fragile than most would have you believe."

"I think I understand. Your adaptability is what makes you valuable, and you've trained your people to be as well. That *is* an ideal leadership trait. It also explains Guildmaster Romaris's ability to react quickly to the knowledge of the monster swarm."

Markus nodded with a smile. "Precisely. Lanthil makes an old man proud. I expect great things from him. He will gain a not insignificant amount of influence and credit within the Guild from this. I agree with him that this is something that will change everything for not only the Guild, but for the entire region. I do have one question, however."

Sloane tilted her head. "Yes?"

"I have heard reports of terrans and the many different origins of them. How advanced is this concept you have created?"

Sloane squinted. *When were credit cards invented? The seventies? Shit, I don't know.*

"Admittedly, Markus, I do not remember. They were so ubiquitous that I never really thought about it. I have an idea of when it was, but it may be incorrect. The *implementation* of this concept in my world was based on different materials and factors that cannot be easily replicated here. Mana and magic make that unnecessary, however. The cards we used in my world were from a society hundreds of years more advanced than your own, but that fact won't matter for much longer."

The grandmaster took a deep breath. "Why is that?"

"Because mana and magic change *everything*. Here, we will be able to achieve feats my world could only dream of. I intend to make the most of it," Sloane stated.

Markus nodded. "I think Lanthil was right about you. Alright, Sloane. Let's discuss how to change the world."

"Thank you for meeting with me, Lady Reinhart," Lady Emerys said as they strolled through the sun elf's garden terrace overlooking the city. The young leader of one of the city's preeminent houses seemed genuinely interested in what Sloane could bring.

"Of course, I wouldn't want to pass up a chance to show off my friend here."

Tiberius chirped from where he sat on her shoulder, giving her a skeptical look. *Or at least I assume it's a skeptical look. His eyes don't blink. Maybe I can create a—no. Focus, Sloane.*

Emerys chuckled softly into her hand. "Do you get distracted often with thoughts of work?"

The mechanical falcon let out a pointed screech that made Sloane narrow her eyes.

"Shush, you traitor," she deadpanned to her bird.

Emerys exchanged amused glances between Sloane and Tiberius. "Fascinating. I would love to discuss these 'golems' and other uses for them, if you would. Or anything else you believe would be worthwhile."

Sloane smiled. "Allow me to tell you about the Reinhart Center."

Two weeks had passed since Sloane's meeting with the Banking Guild—a period filled with planning, restless nights, and fleeting moments of hope that the grand designs set in motion might one day bear fruit. Not to mention many discussions of what to do in their search for Gwyneth. Cristole and Deryk had been working together to gather information, but thus far their efforts had proved futile.

One chilly afternoon, Sloan and Stefan strolled down a polished cobblestone street in one of the more affluent areas near the center of the city. Stefan had settled well into his new role as one of her primary guards. The raithe looked professional now clad in fitted black armor with accents in Reinhart blue. Runic etchings on his breastplate and gauntlets glowed softly, drawing awe-filled stares from all of those they passed. His dark blue cloak completed the look. Sloane knew he relished the not-so-subtle attention he received. She recalled the delight on his face when he first tried the two enchanted daggers she had provided.

She enjoyed taking in the sights as they walked. They saw the Marketbol School of Economics, where Elodie had studied. Sloane was confused at first, as the walking paths seemed empty beyond its open gate, but Stefan helpfully mentioned that the school was likely on break due to an upcoming city holiday.

The two of them wandered for a while longer, soaking in the sights, until Stefan's voice broke the reverie. "Look, there's the tea shop where we're meeting Elodie and Adaega."

Intrigued, Sloane quickened her pace until they reached the quaint shop. Its exterior was charming—a modest storefront set behind a small outdoor seating area. The building itself had large, arched windows framed by ivy clinging to ornate wrought iron. As they pushed open the door, a soft bell attached to the frame announced their entry, and the rich, comforting scene of pastries and steeped tea immediately enveloped them.

Inside, the shop was a haven of warmth and refinement. One wall was lined with shelves laden with hand-painted ceramic jars holding what Sloane presumed was an array of teas. The counter, polished to a high shine, bore a handwritten menu boasting "the finest teas from across the central plains" alongside a few exotic varieties of which Stefan helpfully noted the rarity. The murmur of quiet conversation came from a handful of tables within the room as a few staff moved to help the customers.

A telv woman behind the counter greeted Sloane with a friendly smile. "Welcome to Silken Leaves. May I help you find your preferred tea today? We also have a few specials that just arrived."

Sloane took a moment to absorb the surroundings, then replied thoughtfully, "I haven't tried many teas here. My favorite is unavailable—it's a bergamot and black tea blend."

The woman frowned. "I am unsure what bergamot is, but if you describe the flavor, I may be able to provide an alternative."

At Sloane's description of Earl Grey tea, the telv woman's eyes lit up in understanding. "Ah, that sounds like a blend popular in the Lehelia queendom called Morning Veil. Unfortunately, we do not carry it in stock. However, may I suggest something a bit unique to our region? We have a local blend called Sunlit Meridian. It carries a similar robustness but with an added note of wild citrus and a hint of floral honey. Many of our regulars swear by it."

Intrigued, Sloane nodded. "That sounds interesting. Would it be possible to sample it at a table? I'm meeting two companions soon, and I'd like to enjoy it while we wait."

"Certainly," the telv woman replied. "Please, choose a table, and I'll have it brought out for you shortly."

Sloane turned to Stefan, a slight smile playing on her lips. "I think I'll sit outside for a bit and watch the world go by. I enjoy a bit of people-watching—it always helps clear my head before meeting with friends."

Stefan nodded, following her as she made her way to a small outdoor seating area. The space was inviting, set in a sheltered nook with wrought iron chairs and small tables under a pergola draped with the same flowering vines that framed the windows. Sloane settled into a chair, the ambient chatter and soft clink of cups blending into a comforting background melody.

A few minutes later, the door opened and the telv woman reappeared, balancing a tray. "Here you are, milady," she said softly, setting a cup and pastry in front of Sloane. "I'll pour your tea, and I've also included a small pastry I thought you may enjoy, at no charge. It has an apricot filling that is quite good, if I say so myself."

She carefully poured the steaming tea from the teapot into Sloane's cup, filling it with a gentle cascade that released fragrant wisps into the cool air. Sloane lifted the cup with a gracious nod.

"Thank you," she replied, taking a careful sip of the hot, aromatic brew. The flavors instantly hit her tastebuds and she closed her eyes in bliss. "It's lovely."

The pastry that reminded her of *sfogliatelle* from southern Italy. She bit into the flakey, buttery pastry, which instantly brought a relaxed smile to her face. She thanked the woman again, complimenting the items before the telv stepped away.

It wasn't long before a familiar voice cut through the mellow atmosphere. "Lady Reinhart?"

Seeing Elodie and Adaega approaching, Sloane turned away from the pastry she was enjoying and waved with a smile. "Elodie, Adaega! Please, join me," she called, gesturing to the vacant seats.

Stefan inclined his head and stepped aside to let the two women pass. Elodie smiled and greeted him before she and Adaega sat with Sloane.

Stefan lingered, ensuring they had space while also keeping watch for any onlookers. Sloane winked and nodded toward a pair of women at a nearby table who were casting curious glances in his direction. He scoffed lightly, smirking before turning his focus back to their surroundings. Sloane laughed softly.

Adaega smiled. "Sloane, we have some news!"

Elodie nodded and pulled out a stack of yellow-tinted paper, the stuff made of materials that were uncommon to Sloane. The elf placed them on the table and looked up at her. "Just you and Stefan?"

Sloane shrugged. "Ernald and Nemura went to recruit guards for the house and the Center." Glancing at Elodie, she added, "I assumed you knew."

Elodie's eyes lit up in realization as she snapped her fingers. "Oh, that *was* going to be today. I got so caught up in going through all of our options these last few days, that I forgot. *That's* why Ernald wasn't with us today."

Adaega nodded. "He did say he'd be busy. I, too, was excited about potential locations for the Center and forgot to ask his plans."

A crisp breeze rose suddenly and Sloane pulled her cloak a little tighter around her. Satisfied, she picked up the steaming mug to warm her ungloved hands.

"So, what news do you two ladies have?" Sloane sipped her tea, the warm liquid soothing her throat.

Elodie's eyes went wide. "Lady Reinhart, I am not—"

Sloane held up a hand to stop her financial advisor. "Sorry, I meant 'women.' 'Ladies' is a holdover from my world and normal interactions there. I'll be more conscientious. Please, continue."

The elven woman relaxed and glanced down at the stack of papers. "We have narrowed down to a handful of locations for the Center. Three seem to be the most promising, but I didn't want to leave out options since you may see something we missed."

Sloane raised an eyebrow. "I am sure your thoughts are spot on."

"We evaluated all our requirements and eliminated eleven facilities. Since we're just starting, we wanted a location that could also accommodate your rune-card business. Two of the three ideal locations work for that purpose. The third fits your original requirements perfectly, but isn't ideal for the other business," Adaega explained.

"They are all within budget, though the third would push us slightly *over* due to needing another site for the Reinhart Runic Company. I have four options for that. Lastly, I have a small location in mind for the 'customer relations' concept for the Merchant's Quarter," Elodie added.

Sloane nodded. "Show me what you have."

*   *   *

Thwack. Thwack. Thwack.

Ressa turned just as three arrows slammed into Mathias, the youngest member of her team. The telv grunted, took two steps while trying to raise his sword, but then let out a final gasp, collapsing.

"To the left! Shields! Shields!" Ressa called out, pulling her shield up just in time to feel the thumps of two more arrows pound into it.

We need to end this and get away from the forest.

She pulled in magic from the air around them. It filled her, strengthened her. Ressa turned her head, seeing one of the Valeni archers moving from behind the trees. She slammed her sword down into the ground and then used her **[Fracture World]** spell around them. Reality itself seemed to crack as her yellow magic took hold. The Valeni cried out and stumbled in fear as her illusion held up, creating an area where her yellow magic would be stronger. She lifted her hand and pointed at the four archers that had flanked them. She cast her **[Create Illusion]** spell to form a mass of shimmering, translucent arrows. Then, pulling at the blue and yellow magic pouring into her, she cast **[Alter Conjuration]** to make her illusions *real*. With a flick of her wrist, the objects flew out. Ending any further threat from the archers.

She grabbed the hilt of her sword, yanked the blade from the ground, and turned, seeing the rest of her men finishing off the remainder of the Valeni attackers.

Ressa surveyed the area, ensuring no more Valeni remained nearby. Satisfied that they were finally alone, she walked over to the team. Her second, Alexi, stood over one of the Valeni, while the medic closed Mathias's eyes. The telv caught her eye and shook his head. "I'm sorry, Commander. He's dead."

She sighed. "Alexi, the scouts should be this far soon. Choose two and stay back until they get here. Ensure his body is treated with dignity."

"Understood, Commander. Here, you should look at this," he said, concern lacing his voice.

She walked over and looked down at the Valeni. Ressa narrowed her eyes and bent next to the Valeni telv. Lifting his eyelid, she was startled by the appearance of the man's eye, then confirmed the other was the same. "Are they all like this?"

A cursory check confirmed that all of them had similar features. Their eyes were feline, and their nails were longer and sharpened almost into claws. "What does it mean, Commander?"

She shrugged. "I am unsure. Have the scouts take the bodies as well. The army will want to know."

"Understood, I will—"

"*Commander!*"

They looked up at where one of the men had rolled over one of the Valeni. "You need to see this!"

What followed defied everything she thought she knew.

"*What* is that, Algor?" She asked her team's medic as the team all stood around looking down at the . . . rear of the body.

The telv shook his head, stumbling over his words for a moment. "I—it's a tail."

She sighed, looking down at the furred tail connected to the Valeni's lower back and what seemed like fur going up the man's spine. "I know *that* much, but why is it connected to a telv?"

His eyes were wide, and he shrugged. "I have *no* idea, Commander. I have never seen anything like this."

"Alexi, it is even more important that the army gets these bodies. If the Flash caused this somehow, we need to know. We also need to know *how* it occurred." She raised her voice, ensuring every one of her team could hear her. "Everyone, we are nearly to the plains. From now on, I am Ressa. No more ranks. We cannot be found out by the Sovereigns. Is that understood?"

A smattering of *yeses* and *yes, ma'ams* satisfied her that the group had heard her. It would not do if they slipped up and got caught. *That will be a fight I do not wish to be in.*

With a nod, she sheathed her sword and strode back to her horse. Her people would settle matters here; it was time to get to Marketbol.

CHAPTER TWELVE

OPEN HOUSE

Sloane and Nemura arrived at the first potential property feeling both curious and hopeful. From what Elodie had briefed her on the location, it seemed promising, but experience had taught Sloane not to raise her expectations prematurely.

"Thank you for seeing us, Ser . . ."

"Ser Luven, milady," the middle-aged telv knight replied warmly, offering a polite bow. "It was quite fortuitous that your retainer contacted our house when she did. I had just returned to the city."

Elodie and Adaega stood patiently nearby, offering reassuring smiles as Sloane joined them with Nemura. Ser Luven appeared to be a kind, helpful man, impeccably dressed in attire befitting his administrative role within the city. According to Elodie, he held a minor position within Marketbol's governance structure and had been extremely courteous in their earlier interactions.

Sloane smiled. "Fortunate timing, indeed."

Ser Luven gestured toward the building as they all approached it. "This building has a storied past within Marketbol. Allow me to show you around and explain its features."

Sloane remembered that it had originally been a noble estate converted for governmental use, then later put up for sale again. That raised a few mental flags. *Sounds like something may be wrong with it*, she thought.

The knight guided them through an impressive wrought iron gate into a courtyard filled with neatly trimmed hedges, vibrant flower beds, and a pristine stone walkway. The soothing trickle of a fountain in the courtyard provided an inviting ambiance as they approached the main structure.

The building itself was nice to look at. It adhered to the city's aesthetic with its white stone exterior and red shingled roof with gold-painted trim along the edges. Sloane thought that if it were made of wood instead of stone it would definitely give Scandinavian vibes, with its tiered overhanging roofs and centered arched entrances. It did have a golden spire that she'd noticed on many buildings in the city. Sloane wondered what it denoted.

Her curiosity got the better of her. "Ser Luven, what's the purpose of those spires on buildings throughout the city?"

The knight glanced upward. "An old lord had a vision of adding uniformity and distinction to buildings associated with governance or significant civic functions, so he pushed the council into commissioning these golden spires. Paid for by citizens of Marketbol, might I add. Now they've become purely decorative, yet people associate them with authority and importance. You'll find a few of the more prominent houses use them now for that reason."

"Interesting," Sloane replied thoughtfully, her curiosity momentarily satisfied.

They walked into the building, and Sloane was taken aback by the wide-open entryway that expanded into a lobby. There was a stairwell off to the right side, with doors to the left, while the rear of the lobby sported a set of double doors.

Sloane studied the layout, slightly perplexed. "This was built as an estate?"

"Yes," said Elodie. "The city council modified the structure to better fit administrative functions. Those double doors lead to a large chamber, likely for meetings or similar gatherings."

"What was the purpose of this building before it was put up for sale?" Adaega asked.

"It was the old Banking Guild's headquarters. I remember coming here when I was younger."

"Is that really considered governmental?" Sloane asked. Elodie and Ser Luven both chuckled.

"For Marketbol, yes," Elodie clarified. "The city itself owes its existence to the Banking Guild. The Guild's grandmaster even holds a seat on the ruling council, as you know. In fact, it's the only permanent seat."

The knight smiled. "The current location of the Banking Guild took a decade to construct. It was a very in-depth process. I dare say it is a memorable landmark of our city now."

"Interesting," Sloane said.

Ser Luven began guiding them through the premises, explaining the various rooms and modifications. Over the next hour, he answered questions and elaborated on how certain spaces had previously been used.

Adaega, however, thought that the central district's regulations would make industrial work impossible. Sloane agreed, and in the end they had to pass on the location. She had to admit that while it wouldn't work well for the Center, its former role as a guild's headquarters had her thinking about something else for it.

The next two hours passed swiftly as the group met with an esquire representing the owner of a property in the Scholar's Quarter. The neighborhood itself was vibrant and scholarly, characterized by grand buildings dedicated to Marketbol's renowned economics school. Wide pathways, shaded by carefully manicured trees, connected ten structures of varying size and purpose, creating an inviting, campus-like atmosphere.

As the esquire guided them through the property, Sloane took careful note of its details. The central building featured towering windows that allowed sunlight to illuminate spacious offices and halls, ideal for lectures or seminars. Beyond that, smaller structures scattered about seemed well suited to house the laboratories, offices, or workshops—even a dormitory—that her team would need. The bonus was that all of this was surrounded by a three-meter-tall wall that included five squat towers, one at each corner and one opposite the main gate.

Sloan wasn't sure why this particular campus had such added security, but she wouldn't complain. It would keep her people safe.

What caught her attention most was the former workshop area: a sturdy, stone-built structure at the rear of the campus. Once clearly a foundry used for teaching, it had fallen into mild disrepair, yet the massive workspace, complete with a high ceiling and sturdy foundations, held immense potential for manufacturing and experimentation. She could already envision her runecard production taking shape within these walls.

The school administration, however, had reservations about hosting significant commercial enterprises within the quarter. The gentleman representing the school—polite, articulate, yet clearly cautious—emphasized their reluctance to allow the space to be overtaken by purely profit-driven endeavors.

Adaega stepped in smoothly, engaging in thoughtful dialogue about shared-use arrangements. She proposed scenarios where students could directly benefit from internships, shared research opportunities, or even potential apprenticeships within the Reinhart Center. Adaega's well-structured argument began to visibly ease the man's apprehension.

Sensing an opening, Sloane carefully outlined the vision for the Reinhart Center, emphasizing its research-oriented goals, particularly its focus on mana and its potential economic applications. She reassured him the intention was to collaborate closely with the academic community, not overshadow it.

The esquire expressed openness to Adaega's proposals of shared usage, especially if students and faculty could directly benefit.

"It's perfect in many ways," Sloane admitted to Elodie as they later walked toward their next appointment. "But we may need to secure a separate space for the business side of things. The school clearly wants to keep commercial activities limited, and we need those capabilities to grow effectively. Then there's the price."

Elodie nodded, offering a reassuring smile. "Indeed. But their openness to cooperation is encouraging. Perhaps we can leverage the council to put in a word for us."

Sloane sighed lightly but agreed, her mind already forming plans. Despite the setback, possibilities were beginning to take shape—and for now, that would be enough.

When they arrived at the final location in the Merchant's Quarter, Sloane could see its appeal. A large building sat nestled in a long row of merchant head-quarters and guilds. The structure bore the marks of its former life as a guild location, reliefs subtly reflecting the business of the former proprietors.

"Adaega? Could you start looking around, please?" Sloane asked. "I need to talk to Elodie for a moment."

Adaega approached the high elf who was guiding their tour, initiating an earnest conversation with her about the details of the property. Sloane gently pulled Elodie aside.

Elodie tilted her head as she looked up at Sloane. "Milady?"

"I have a question. If you don't know, it's fine, but . . . how exactly does someone create a new guild here?"

The sun elf's brows furrowed thoughtfully. "As far as I know, any profession can create a guild. There would need to be enough members of that profession to require it, though. I believe the founder would need ratification and admittance into the guilds as a whole. That just seems logical."

Sloane nodded thoughtfully. "And do you know how many members a new guild would need before it's even considered?"

Elodie gave a slight shrug. "Truthfully, no. There hasn't been a new guild established within my lifetime, and the existing ones are quite entrenched."

"Interesting. Alright, something for later. It's a bit ambitious anyway—probably best as a long-term goal rather than a near-future plan."

Elodie seemed confused for a moment, but then her eyes opened wide. "You mean to start an Artificer's Guild?"

Sloane shrugged. "If we can find other artificers? Why not? I am sure we can get Reanny involved. This is more long term, though." She glanced at the entrance to the building. "Let's go see what Adaega thinks of this place, yeah?"

Elodie nodded quickly, but Sloane could tell the cogs were turning in the woman's head. "Come on, let's catch up with Adaega. She seems to be getting all her questions answered."

Nemura placed a hand on Sloan's shoulder as they walked toward the building, and bent down to whisper into her ear. "It is a good plan, milady. However, we shouldn't do it here in Marketbol. Wait until we reach somewhere more neutral with fewer competing interests."

Sloane nodded slightly. "Good thinking. We'll discuss it in private later."

Adaega did not seem happy when they reached her.

"Is something wrong, Miss Merbaker?" Sloane asked carefully.

Adaega sighed deeply. "This location will not work. The documents stated there would be space for a foundry. It's in the basement. There's poor ventilation and no way to cool it. Koren would be miserable. Alchemy facilities are abysmal as well. We would need a separate location for both. It's large like we want, but it is more office than research space."

Sloane glanced at Elodie. "Is this too large for the other business?"

Elodie looked around before nodding. "Yes. It will be some time before we need something larger. The product will be made elsewhere and then moved to us for final touches and etching."

Sloane exhaled slowly, nodding thoughtfully as she absorbed their concerns. She turned to the woman guiding them, giving her an apologetic smile. "I appreciate your time, but it appears this property won't meet our immediate needs. It's lovely, just not right for what we require now."

As they departed the property, Sloane glanced back, her mind churning with possibilities despite the immediate disappointment.

"Well, that settles it," she said decisively, turning to her companions. "We'll need to reconsider and possibly widen our search. At least take this one and the first location off the list. We can put the campus into the 'maybe' pile."

Elodie smiled faintly. "Agreed. I'll see what else is available within our time frame. Perhaps something closer to the industrial district would suit our needs better."

Sloane nodded appreciatively at both women. "Great. Let's go debrief at the inn. We'll find the perfect place; I'm not too worried."

Back at the inn, Sloane felt exhaustion creeping into her bones. She stifled a yawn and Adaega chuckled softly.

"I hope we aren't boring you too much, Sloane."

Sloane shook her head, giving an apologetic smile to the two women seated with her. "Not at all, I'm just a bit tired. So, have you two come to a decision?"

Elodie nodded. "After looking at the other options . . . and careful consideration, we really think the location in the Scholar's Quarter remains our best choice. It's the only one that will allow us to have a dedicated site for Koren. Having a separate building for the alchemists is a good thing as well. The only concern is having to deal with the Marketbol School of Economics."

Adaega shook her head dismissively. "That won't pose an issue. I agree entirely—the location is perfect. But there's one significant concern we haven't yet addressed."

Sloane raised a brow. "What's that?"

"You are currently the only one who makes the runecards work. We have no one else with . . ." She looked down at her notes. "The Artifice domain for their magic."

Sloane sighed, realization dawning. "And that makes the entire business reliant on my presence—but I can't stay here indefinitely."

Adaega nodded. "Precisely."

Sloane swore.

"Don't worry. I think that will be a fun project for Ernald and me to undertake."

Sloane tilted her head in confusion. "What do you mean?"

"We will find someone. Give us a couple of weeks, I know you want to move on as quickly as possible, but . . ."

Sloane shook her head. "We need to get everyone settled into the Center. Elodie, can you work on purchasing the scholar's location? Also decide on the runecard location. You will be running it, so I trust you. And there's the Vlaredian army to worry about. I should meet with the general."

Nemura, who had quietly been poking at a bowl of greens, interrupted carefully. "Lady Reinhart. I don't think that is a good idea. You recall how he reacted when you offered suggestions the first time."

"You're right, Nemura. Could you meet with him instead?"

Adaega and Elodie observed their conversation, choosing to remain silent.

Nemura narrowed her eyes but eventually nodded. "Fine. I will meet him. Will you please take Stefan with you?"

"He should stay with the others. Speaking of, how goes recruiting guards?"

"Ernald has narrowed down the potential recruits to twenty, with two senior guards. He expects to have everything finalized and prospects chosen within the week."

"Good. We will meet with them once he has selected the team. They can take over security for our people then, and we can slowly transition everyone to the Center."

"We will be ready. I can work with Koren and Rel about moving the wagons to the Center after Elodie finalizes the purchase. Then I can start searching for staff," Adaega added.

"Good."

Elodie looked up from her notes. "I will also make the other purchases, although I believe those locations will not be used at first. They will sit dormant for some time. Is that acceptable?"

Sloane considered. Was it worth it to get them now? Probably not. It would be a while before they got set up here enough to need them.

"Let's wait until we can actually utilize them," she said. "As long as you are able to find somewhere as soon as they are needed. I should be able to assist anyone Adaega and Ernald find in setting up the initial batch of cards. We only need one thousand within the year for the test run that Grandmaster Markus wishes to do."

Elodie made notes. "Will the house require a manor or some type of residence for you in the city? I apologize, I did not consider that."

Sloane shook her head. "No, I don't think we should waste money on that. I think it'll be a while before I can return. Ensure everyone in the house can have somewhere to live. If this is where I choose to settle after finding Gwyn, I'll find something then."

She sighed. There was so much to do and she wasn't sure how she was going to fit it all in. She was surprised by how calm and unconcerned she felt by the prospect of an army approaching Marketbol and wondered if it had to do with her growing ability with mana. No one else she'd seen yet had been able to cast spells like her. *Am I becoming overconfident? Well, I still can't fight worth a shit. Maybe I should start training again. All it will take is someone with magic and the ability to fight and I'll be screwed.*

She watched Nemura stretch and yawn, her muscularity defined. *She will definitely kick my ass in training. Gisele will kick my butt for the fun of it . . . the guys think I'm fragile . . . Maybe I can wait to start training until after we leave. This place is safe enough for me to focus on my work.*

Elodie and Adaega stood after finalizing details and last-minute needs.

"Elodie? A moment?" asked Sloane, standing.

"Yes, my lady?"

Sloane took a deep breath and lowered her voice, standing close. "How can we afford all of this? I've been letting you handle it, mainly because I'm still not used to the value of things here . . . but even I know that there is no way we have enough funds to purchase prime real estate within a major city, let alone an entire campus. What aren't you telling me?"

The woman nodded. "I understand your hesitation. However, I have been accounting for everything most diligently. Both Grandmaster Markus and Lady Emerys sent along recommendations to use for the school. It helped lower the price significantly. That said, yes, it was still too much for what you had available. Uncle Lanthil foresaw this. As part of his deal to support you and invest in you, he gave me access to a considerable line of accounting. Further, the grandmaster authorized an advance from the Banking Guild to offset costs related to establishing the runecard business. That will go toward the estimated value of the several structures on the campus that will contribute to that business directly.

"The Farum siblings, as you are aware, have been expanding their business. Not to mention your profits from the Smithing Guild. That is another venture I will be expanding here for the house. If you are able to establish another venture here, that would be most beneficial. Perhaps something else with your runes? Either way, once the route from Vilstaf opens up, we will be on the path to being fine. I am certain."

Sloane nodded. *It's like getting business and government loans. That's all. Just need to pay them back and we'll be fine.*

"Okay. I trust you, Elodie. Just please make sure we are not becoming beholden to anyone politically by doing this."

The guardswoman smiled. "We will not. The Romaris family is fully on your side. Uncle believes working with you will be a beneficial relationship. He wishes to remain close for the foreseeable future, and locking you into unfavorable deals would not foster an advantageous association. As a reminder, my joining your house is part of a continued commitment to see your influence and prosperity rise. For doing so also helps my uncle."

"Thank you, Elodie." Sloan returned to the table and sat down. Nemura gave her a considering look. She had surely overheard her conversation with the sun elf.

Soon Sloane would actually own something in this world and her connection to Earth was steadily falling further and further away. Her thoughts moved to her daughter as she sat there silently, brooding over what Gwyn could be doing.

After settling in Marketbol, one of the first things Sloane had done was make inquiries about any terrans, even merely sightings. Surprisingly, there were many but not many had been right in the city. It seemed as if no matter where she went, she was just missing other humans. A large group of them had formed up and decided to join the Marketbol army; they had left several weeks prior as the force moved east to reinforce the Sovereigns under attack there. Another group had left as well, not desiring to be in a "nation" at war. When she inquired as to where the group was going, her informant mentioned a kingdom named Rosale.

Sloane had heard of Rosale and knew it would be one of her stops on the way to Avira. She wondered if she would see any of the humans there. Leaving Adaega behind, ostensibly in Ernald's care, she would be leaving the only other human she knew. While she had come to consider the knights her friends and companions, it wasn't the same. Maybe it was that connection to home. Even if Adaega's Earth was different, she was still relatively used to many of the same things Sloane was—if only seventy years behind her. She could discuss a lot more commonalities with Adaega than with the knights. It was refreshing and, if she was being honest, comforting.

Sloane sighed.

"Everything alright?" Nemura asked.

Sloane nodded. "Just thinking. There's so much to do. So many places to search. I keep second-guessing myself about whether or not I'm doing this right. Whether my priorities aren't misplaced."

Nemura glanced over Sloane's shoulder, focusing on something behind her. Sloane turned and saw Maud looking at her with concern.

"How do you always find me when I'm feeling this way?" Sloane asked.

Maud smiled and came and sat at the table with her.

Nemura glanced between the two of them and stood. "I am not good at these talks. I will go and try to gain an audience with the general." She rested her hand on Sloane's shoulder. "That said, Sloane? You're doing the right thing. You have a goal, one that takes you through many key locations. This allows us to get as much information as possible about Gwyn from as many places as possible. Your decision to set up the Center and the other business is sound. You need funds, but you need to also be taken seriously. With enough influence, you'll be able to deal with other parties better. We're here to help you, but you are helping yourself at the same time. I respect that, and I am sure others will as well. If you keep beating yourself up, it will make everything much more difficult. You have a plan. Stick to it."

Sloane patted her guardswoman's hand in thanks. "That was quite the little speech. For what it's worth, you're pretty good at it."

Nemura huffed a laugh. "I will let you know what the general says if I can even meet with him."

"Thank you."

Nemura nodded at Maud. "Ser Maud, I leave her in your care."

Maud smiled. "Don't worry about her, Nemura. We're gonna have some fun."

Sloane turned and looked at the redheaded telv after her guardswoman left. "So, what's up?"

"Ismeld is off handling some business for the Order, but the rest of us were about to go grab some drinks at a tavern down the way. Would you like to join us?"

Sloane leaned back in her chair, balancing it on the rear two legs, as she considered. "You know what? Sure. Let's go. Everyone else is busy, and I have nothing else to do until tomorrow at the earliest."

Maud smiled and clapped her hands. "Perfect! We haven't had a chance to chat over ale in a while! You can tell me some more about your Earth stuff. I vaguely recall you saying something about a treat called gelato."

Sloane snorted as she stood. "Girl, it's time I told you about a delectable and divine dessert we need in our life right now. I can't remember if I've asked, but do you know what chocolate is?"

Maud shook her head, and Sloane followed the knight out of the inn.

"Oh no. You're telling me this world doesn't have chocolate?"

"No? What is it?"

Sloane smiled. "Let's get an ale, because we have so much to talk about."

They walked down the sidewalk toward the tavern, moving through the evening crowd. The sun was slowly going down earlier as the seasons changed, and already, workers were lighting the oil lamps that lined the street. They talked about different types of desserts they enjoyed. Maud pointed out the tavern's sign and Sloane caught sight of Cristole standing outside, waiting. He waved, and Sloane was about to return the gesture but hesitated as she noticed an orkun woman across the street. She seemed to be watching Sloane intently, but when she noticed Sloane's gaze, she turned her head and started talking to a telv man standing with her.

"Sloane, you came!" Cristole said.

Sloane jerked her head back around. "Yeah! Maud told me she'd buy me an ale if I told her all about something called chocolate that we have on Earth."

Cristole tilted his head. "Chocolate? We have that here too. It's made from cacao, correct?"

Sloane's and Maud's eyes widened. "Yes! That's it!" Sloane said excitedly.

Maud looked confused. "We do? What?"

"Yes, it's a luxury food from Zhaoloka."

Maud groaned. "Of course it is."

Sloane perked up, remembering that Zhaoloka was an island nation off the coast of the continent to the southwest. She would be taking a ship from Swanbrook to Avira along the southern coast. "Oh?" she said. "Will my ship stop in Zhaoloka, you think?"

Cristole looked at her with sympathy and shook his head. "No. They are fiercely xenophobic and completely isolationist. I am afraid that you may never get that chocolate."

"W-what? Never?" she stammered. *So, more than a business empire, I need a real empire. After all, there is chocolate in the offing.*

Maud patted Sloane on the back. "Come on, Sloane. Let's get you that drink."

Sloane sighed. "I think I may need more than one."

CHAPTER THIRTEEN

EXPLOSIVE INTRODUCTION

In the chaotic years immediately following the Flash, the battles that first tested the mettle of early mages were as remarkable for their ineptitude as they were for their novelty. Combatants often fumbled through spells mid-fight, functioning on instinct rather than proper knowledge of the three forms of casting.

These situations were wrought with both great advancements and deadly incidents that were as likely to harm friend as foe.

Early records rely on eyewitness accounts or nostalgic recollections from mages later in their years. Scholars, warriors, and leaders of that time alike found themselves learning not merely tactics, but the very nature of magic and mana itself.

Early Arcane Conflicts: Lessons from the Aftermath, 251 SA

Even in the early evening, the tavern was already filled with lively chatter and hearty laughter, creating an inviting, albeit loud, atmosphere. The diverse patrons included many telv, several orkun and raithe, and even a handful of dwarves.

Spotting the other two knights, Sloane grinned. Gisele sat with her back to the bustling room, while Deryk faced her across the table situated beside the wall, near a hallway leading toward the back of the tavern.

Unable to resist, Sloane quickly stepped past Cristole, leaning over and wrapping her arms playfully around Gisele. Lowering her voice theatrically, she whispered into the knight's ear, "Hey there. What's a pretty girl like you doing in a place like this? Come around here often?"

Gisele snorted, shaking her head slightly. "Really, Sloane? Sit your rear down."

Laughing, Sloane slid into the chair next to her. "My *rear?*" she teased.

Cristole sat opposite Gisele, raising an eyebrow as Sloane shot him a mischievous wink. The high elf chuckled softly, shaking his head in good-natured amusement.

A playful jab from Gisele's elbow caught Sloane's ribs. "Behave," the knight warned, failing to hide a smile.

Maud giggled, settling comfortably into the seat next to Sloane. "You two are adorable."

"You hear that, Gisele?" Sloane nudged her friend's shoulder again with a broad smile. "We're *adorable*."

Gisele groaned dramatically, rolling her eyes. "You're insufferable."

"Oh, come on, you love me," Sloane teased lightly, nudging her once more.

Cristole smiled warmly. "You're in high spirits today, Sloane."

Maud shot her a knowing glance, but Sloane gave her a pointed look. *Don't you dare out me.*

She refocused on Cristole, keeping her tone light. "I am! We found a great location for the Center, and Elodie, Adaega, and Nemura are finalizing all the details for the house. Things are finally falling into place."

Maud kept her lips sealed.

Gisele nodded approvingly. "That's excellent news. Ernald is close to selecting your guards?"

"Yes, according to Nemura. I plan to meet with him soon. It feels like I keep getting pulled in a thousand directions lately, but I'm glad you all invited me out tonight."

With a gruff nod, Deryk pushed a large mug toward her. "Here."

"Thanks!" She eagerly took a generous swig, immediately coughing and sputtering slightly at the drink's strength. "Shit, that's strong."

Deryk shrugged nonchalantly. "It's what I always drink."

Cristole chuckled, taking a careful sip of his own ale. "We avoid whatever Deryk orders for exactly that reason."

Sloane nodded with mock seriousness. "Yeah, I can see why. This stuff will put hair on my chest."

Cristole suddenly choked, coughing as ale spilled from his nose. "*What* did you say?"

The entire table erupted in laughter, drawing curious glances from nearby patrons. Sloane leaned back, thoroughly enjoying the easy camaraderie of her friends.

"Wait, so you're telling me your gelato is that easy to make?" Maud asked, clearly intrigued by Sloane's description of the process and all of the different flavors of gelato she enjoyed.

Sloane gave Maud a thumbs up, taking another swig of her ale. "Yup! The only problem is, it needs to be frozen. Which is probably a large issue around here."

"I could see that. I take it this was a luxury item for your world?" Cristole asked.

"No, it was quite common. There were small businesses that sold only gelato, in different flavors and styles. It was quite cheap too, at least where I lived. Cheap enough that it was reasonable to assume anyone could afford it, no matter their station in life. We had appliances called freezers that would keep everything inside frozen. So you would freeze your ingredients, work with them, then put them back in the freezer. Almost everyone had one," she explained.

"Wait!" Maud interjected excitedly. "I bet we could do that now!"

Sloane raised an eyebrow, curious, but Gisele voiced the question first. "How? We have ice sellers, but they're mostly limited to bringing ice down from mountain regions to the cities near their base."

Maud shook her head fervently. "No! Think bigger." She leaned forward, eyes sparkling with enthusiasm. "Magic!"

Gisele frowned slightly. "Magic?"

"We haven't seen magic like that, Maud," Cristole added.

Which was true: none of the magic they'd seen had been 'elemental'—if Sloane had to classify it based on the fantasy she knew. But that didn't mean it wasn't possible. *I would be surprised if it wasn't, actually.*

"We could. It seems quite likely a possibility. Fire? Water? Stone? Air? Magic seems rare, despite initial suggestions otherwise, but I do not doubt that there is magic that can manipulate the core elements," Deryk added.

Sloane groaned and pointed at the man. "First off, yes, I was wrong about the magic thing. I was still trying to figure everything out and got excited by a new discovery. Second, your idea of what constitutes an element is way off." *Although maybe that changes with the introduction of magic . . .*

Deryk crossed his arms and leaned back in his chair. "How?"

"Well, there's this thing called the periodic table of—"

Before Sloane could elaborate, a door down the hallway was abruptly thrown open, drawing everyone's attention. The noisy clatter of boots and murmured voices announced the arrival of several newcomers, who entered with the unmistakable air of authority and purpose.

As the group noisily walked toward the bar, Sloane caught sight of an orkun woman slinking in from behind them with a telv man. The sight of her made Sloane widen her eyes in surprise. *It's the same woman from across the street.*

Her features were striking—a prominent scar slashed down her face, starting just below her eye and ending at her jawline. She sported rough, practical armor and held a confident stance. Her dark hair was styled asymmetrically, longer on the right and closely cropped on the left, a bold choice that reminded Sloane of modern trends back on Earth.

Nice to see people with edgy haircuts here too! Maybe one day . . .

The man with her also sported a scar going down his face. He too held a professional demeanor despite the varying quality of armor that he wore. *Mercenaries?*

Sloane's eyes lingered curiously on the mercenaries, especially the intriguing orkun woman, until Maud gently tapped her shoulder, breaking her reverie.

"Sloane? You still with us?"

Sloane blinked and quickly refocused on the group around the table, offering an apologetic smile. "Sorry, yeah. Just got distracted."

"Clearly. Anything interesting?" Gisele asked.

"Just people-watching," Sloane replied evasively, taking another cautious sip of the potent ale.

The group continued their cheerful conversation, drifting through lighter topics—favorite foods, amusing anecdotes from past journeys, and playful teasing about swordplay practice. The atmosphere around the table grew warm and comfortable, a welcome reprieve from the constant pressure of recent days.

Soon, the warmth of the tavern was joined by the melodic sounds of instruments drifting from a corner of the room. Sloane turned her head, noticing a duo preparing to play. A sun elf man tuned a stringed instrument, and moments later, a young telv woman stood beside him, poised to sing.

The musician strummed a few introductory notes, and the woman's voice rose clear and vibrant, blending harmoniously with the tune. Sloane felt her spirits lifting instantly. Around them, patrons quickly joined in, their voices uniting in a joyful chorus that echoed through the tavern.

Sloane laughed as Gisele and Maud playfully stumbled over the lyrics, their voices competing in comedic discord. Cristole shook his head, feigning embarrassment. Maud giggled and nudged Sloane, encouraging her to join in. As the music swelled, Sloane couldn't help but oblige. She belted out the catchy chorus and laughed.

For the first time in what felt like forever, she allowed herself to fully relax, the weight of responsibility easing. Her heart still twinged with guilt for enjoying herself when she didn't even know where Gwyn was, but she reminded herself firmly that moments like these were essential—they were small anchors to help her hold on to her sanity in a world filled with chaos and uncertainty; otherwise, she'd fret herself into despair.

Eventually, the song reached a vibrant crescendo and faded into cheerful applause. Sloane leaned back with a satisfied sigh, feeling lighter than she had in weeks.

Just as they were about to leave, Deryk leaned forward, his voice low. "Hold on a moment. Don't look around too obviously, but there's someone paying a little too much attention to us. By the entrance."

Gisele's expression immediately sharpened. "Are you sure?"

"Positive," Deryk confirmed. "They're being discreet, but not discreet enough."

Sloane felt a knot form in her stomach. Her eyes darted toward the bar for just a heartbeat, but nothing seemed amiss. Still, the knights' instincts hadn't steered her wrong before. "Who do you think they are?"

Cristole shook his head subtly. "Too soon to tell, but we shouldn't take any chances."

Deryk gestured toward a rear hallway. "There's another exit at the back, through the kitchens. I suggest we use it."

Gisele nodded. "Good thinking. Better safe than sorry."

"I'll lead the way." Cristole stood, adjusting his sword belt. "Maud, keep close to Sloane."

Sloane glanced briefly around the room one more time, her eyes unconsciously seeking the pale-green skin of the intriguing orkun woman, but she was nowhere to be seen. *That's odd. When did she leave?*

There was a man at the bar, cloaked in plain attire, his posture a bit too rigid to appear casual. He avoided her gaze with deliberate intent.

Gisele placed a steadying hand on her arm, guiding her forward. "Come. Eyes ahead."

Sloane nodded, forcing herself to trust the knights. Following Cristole's lead, they moved quietly toward the hallway at the back and made their way carefully through the bustling kitchen, ignoring curious glances from cooks and serving staff, until they finally emerged into the chill of an empty back street.

The cold air felt sharp after the warmth of the tavern, and Sloane shivered lightly, glancing around as adrenaline sharpened her senses.

Deryk scanned the area carefully before nodding.

The alley was dimly lit, shadows clinging to the corners where lamplight couldn't reach. They moved quietly but purposefully, until suddenly, a woman's voice sliced through the silence, sharp and commanding. "Sloane Reinhart?"

Before anyone could stop her, Sloane blurted out, "What? Who's there?" She heard the distinct twang of a crossbow firing.

In the next instant, Gisele's crimson shield shimmered into existence, intercepting the bolt mere inches from Sloane's chest. The projectile clattered harmlessly to the ground.

Chaos erupted as figures surged from the shadows, converging upon them. Blades gleamed in the sparse light, and Sloane's heart raced as her companions swiftly readied themselves to face the attack. She moved to draw her blade as she saw the same orkun woman from before.

"You!" she shouted, but the woman simply narrowed her eyes as she advanced.

Gisele grabbed a discarded wooden crate and hurled it at the orkun woman, who raised an arm just in time to shield herself. It splintered upon impact, forcing a grunt from the mercenary.

The telv and two other mercenaries pressed forward, blades slicing the air toward Deryk. He swiftly stepped back, maneuvering around broken cobblestones and scattered refuse to avoid the attacks. Cristole joined him, blade flashing in the dim moonlight.

From deeper in the alley, two more mercenaries advanced, kicking aside empty crates and debris. Maud quickly seized a rusted metal bucket and hurled it at one of them. The bucket struck the orkun man squarely, causing him to stagger and almost fall. Charging forward, Maud swung her mace forcefully against the man's shield. He stumbled back, slipping on the slick stones, and dropped to one knee.

Without missing a beat, Maud pivoted, her mace swinging in a tight arc at the second man. The blow glanced off his raised shield with a resonant clang, but Maud pressed her advantage, following up with a relentless overhead strike. He grunted, his defense faltering as he stumbled backward, nearly tripping over an overturned barrel.

Gisele navigated around Sloane to aid Maud, sword gleaming menacingly. Sloane drew mana into her palm, focusing intensely.

She raised her hand to cast a **[Flashbang]** spell just as the world, for only a moment, lost all sound . . . and shattered.

Ressa cast her **[Fracture World]** spell, fracturing the alleyway into an illusion filled with cracked reflections, as if mirrors had shattered around them.

The sudden shift startled the terran woman and kept her from finishing her spell, her attention scattered momentarily by the warped world around her. Unfortunately, the knights accompanying the woman seemed unfazed.

Ressa looked anxiously at the mouth of the alley, aware that the clanging of blades would soon summon unwanted city guards and onlookers.

Time was slipping away. She had to incapacitate or eliminate the terran swiftly—before the woman's magic became a larger threat.

The female orkun knight moved away from the redheaded telv and pivoted sharply, swinging at Ressa. Quickly raising her shield, Ressa deflected the strike and countered with a fierce, unrelenting assault. She forced the knight back, pressing her against the rough stone wall. But the woman parried skillfully, lunging back at Ressa with a thrust that scraped harshly against her shield. Seizing the opening, Ressa knocked the blade aside and delivered a swift kick to the knight's knee, buckling her stance.

"Alexi!" she called out, needing him to take over against the orkun woman.

He moved in quickly, stepping past a broken cart and overturned crates. As Alexi engaged the orkun knight, Ressa quickly turned her attention to the redheaded telv, who, impossibly, had managed to seize one of her men's shields and was now easily holding both men off.

The telv woman pushed forward with surprising strength, driving one attacker into a stone wall. He stumbled, narrowly avoiding falling onto the broken remnants of pottery that littered the alley.

Cursing under her breath, Ressa turned her attention back to the terran woman, who had recovered from her distraction and was looking at Ressa's spell curiously. *Amateur. Pay attention to the fight and your allies.*

The terran's eyes flickered dangerously as she drew upon her magic once again. She brought her sword up and the blade glowed blue with runes. *Oh, shit.*

The terran plunged the sword into Ressa's spell, and immediately the illusionary cracks wavered around her. Then, with a burst of blue mana, the illusion shattered completely.

Ressa barely had time to dodge as the terran hurled a crackling purple orb. It sailed past her, striking the alley's brick wall and erupting into magical sparks that scattered harmlessly across the cobblestones.

She turned her focus entirely to the human woman, who was readying another spell. She concentrated quickly; her **[Create Illusion]** made a whisper of yellow magic that coalesced into an illusion of spectral arrows appearing in the air in front of her fingertips. Her immediate use of **[Alter Conjuration]** allowed the arrows to solidify into actual objects.

Ressa gestured with her sword and launched arrows at the terran, but a large, shimmering wall of red energy formed and stopped her conjured attack dead. The arrows fell to the ground in a clatter, and she looked up at the orkun woman in anger.

The big orkun knight to the left kicked out at Ressa's man and connected with his chest, sending him tumbling.

Alexi took advantage of the orkun woman's spellcasting to push her back. The big orkun stepped in to assist the shield caster. However, Alexi's aggressive attacks distracted the woman enough for her spell to fail and collapse.

Taking advantage of the moment, Ressa snarled as she focused on conjuring individual arrows rather than barrages of them, using that to fire at the terran at a steadier rate.

Sloane grunted as she threw herself sideways, narrowly evading the magic arrows streaking toward her. The arrows slammed into a stack of old crates behind her, splintering the wood with concussive force. *Too close.*

"Who the hell are you people?!" Sloane shouted in anger. She had no idea what they wanted or why they were attacking; she just knew that they had to find a way to stop them or retreat.

Her heart pounded as she regained her footing on the uneven cobblestones, eyes scanning the dimly lit alleyway. Movement to her side caught her attention.

Cristole was busy fighting two men and seemed to be struggling.

In an attempt to help, Sloane swung her sword at the man closest to her. She tightened her grip around the hilt of her sword, runes flaring brightly along its blade as she lunged forward. Her swing arced toward the attacker, who spun quickly to face her, his shield raised defensively at the last second.

The impact of her enchanted blade sent a shock up her arm, her teeth grinding together at the jarring collision. The man hissed and was forced off balance, allowing her to bring her hand up and cast a **[Mana Bolt]**. Unfortunately, he turned his stumble into a roll and dodged it.

Sloane fired again, but the man evaded. She cried out in frustration and channeled deeper, forming four [**Mana Bolts**] around her. She raised her hand, already drawing mana into her palm, ready to unleash her attack—

"Name's Ressa, and this is for those you killed, bitch."

But the voice, far too close, and a flash of movement caught Sloane's attention too late. A fist flew toward her face, and her desperate attempt to block it failed. Pain exploded through her jaw as bone fractured with a sickening crack. Her vision went white as she toppled backward, the world spinning violently around her.

Instinctively, she released the mana she'd gathered, blindly firing her magical bolts into the air. The explosions resonated dully in her ringing ears as tears filled her eyes, blurring her surroundings into indistinct shapes and shadows. Ineffectively, she cried out as she felt more pain drill through her shoulder. Sloane hit the ground hard, feeling the brutal scrape of stone against her skin. Panic and pain surged within her, confusion clouding her mind.

Ressa stood cautiously from behind the shattered remains of a crate, splinters of wood scattered around her feet. Her chest heaved with exertion. She'd managed a solid strike against the terran, breaking the woman's jaw, but the uncontrolled barrage of magic had forced her to dive hastily for cover.

Time is running out. Someone will have heard us by now. A cry on her left forced her to refocus on the fight, while the terran staggered to her feet in a daze.

Ressa's men were struggling, barely holding their own against the knights. An unwelcome surprise, to be sure. She'd failed to consider how skilled these Blighters could be. The high elf knight was pushing two of her men back, and she had to stop him before they gave him an opening. She raised her hand and quickly cast her illusion spell, melding it seamlessly into an arrow with [**Alter Conjuration**]. It streaked forward, slamming into the knight's side, causing him to stagger. *Good, that's one down.*

His surprise caused him to almost miss the attack coming from one of her men, but he still managed to parry it. He stumbled backward, reached down, and ripped out the arrow with a yell. Ressa narrowed her eyes, wishing that creating more complicated arrows with barbs or the like wasn't so intensive for her magic.

Ressa was about to cast more when a green glow surrounded the man, and a flare of green erupted from the point her arrow had pierced, and she watched the wound close in front of her eyes. The high elf scowled before launching another attack on her men.

Ressa instantly locked onto the telv woman, whose green eyes glowed brightly. The healer. *We underestimated her.* The telv's weapon also emitted a bright green light from an orb set inside of the head. Ressa snarled as she cast her [**Conjure Object**] spell to send shards of metal at the woman. The redhead swore, but she yanked up her stolen shield just in time to stop the spell.

Deciding quickly, Ressa summoned more mana, ready to end this drawn-out fight decisively. *Let's see you stop this.* Raising her hand, she began to cast.

Gisele scanned the alley, assessing the rapidly deteriorating situation.

Sloane was already down. Her jaw hung at an unnatural angle—clearly broken. An arrow jutted from just below her shoulder, and her arm hung uselessly at her side. Sloane's gaze drifted unfocused, her movements sluggish as she turned in place. She was all but out of the fight. *She's not a fighter. She wasn't made for this.*

Maud was proving her worth today. Cristole had taken a hit, but Maud had managed to heal him—though even now, she was being pushed back, forced onto the defensive by the relentless assault of two mercenaries. With Maud locked in combat, she couldn't get to Sloane. *We need to finish this and get her some healing.*

Deryk was locked in combat with the telv swordsman, the duel too evenly matched to predict an outcome. Outnumbered and now without Sloane's magic, they were at a severe disadvantage.

Still, if we can hold them off until the guards arrive, we should be fine. There's no way this much ruckus won't bring them running. Someone must have gone for help.

But Gisele couldn't count on that. She and Maud weren't like Sloane or this Ressa woman—they couldn't wield magic offensively. And their opponents were far too good at keeping them off balance, disrupting their spellwork.

These people were not what they appeared. Definitely not mercenaries. She'd caught the magic-wielder saying something about people Sloane had killed.

Shit. Vlaredian soldiers. That changed things. If she wanted to turn the tide, she needed to keep them off balance.

Cristole was faltering against his two opponents, struggling to keep up despite Maud's earlier healing. He wasn't at full strength. Gisele clenched her jaw, raised a hand, and cast her [**Protective Barrier**], separating one of the mercenaries from her lover.

The soldier's eyes widened as he swung his sword at the translucent shield. The blade bounced off harmlessly.

Gisele's attention snapped back to Ressa just as the woman lifted her hand, mana coalescing at her fingertips, preparing another spell.

No, you don't.

Gisele lunged, closing the distance before Ressa could release her magic. She crashed into the orkun caster, wrenching a startled yelp from her as they slammed into the alley wall.

Gisele's sword clattered from her grip, but she didn't care. She had the advantage now. Seizing Ressa by the front of her armor, she drove her into the rough brick again. A satisfying *thud* accompanied the impact as the woman's head snapped back. Ressa cried out and started to slide downward, dazed.

Not giving her a chance to recover, Gisele punched her hard in the ribs, growling in frustration as her fist met hardened leather. The hit barely registered. She swung again, aiming for Ressa's head, but the soldier reacted faster than expected. She dropped lower, avoiding the strike entirely.

Gisele's knuckles slammed into the unyielding brick wall. Sharp pain flared up her hand, and she barely had a moment to register it before Ressa struck, ramming her fist into the side of Gisele's knee. Her leg buckled, but she used the momentum to drop her weight onto Ressa's extended leg, forcing a sharp cry from the soldier. *Got you.*

But the position was unstable. Gisele shifted to regain her footing, inadvertently giving Ressa the opening she needed. The smaller orkun lashed out with a slow left-handed swing. Gisele batted it away contemptuously. *She's slowing. I have her.*

Ressa slammed into her side, knocking the wind from her. Gisele staggered—not from pain but sheer surprise. Both of them swung with wild, desperate energy, each struggling to regain their footing. Neither had the upper hand. In the end, they broke apart, scrambling backward to put distance between them.

Gisele breathed heavily, chest rising and falling with exertion. Ressa, by contrast, looked barely fazed.

Without warning, the woman launched herself forward. Gisele cursed and tried to raise her hands. She was too slow. A fist connected with her face, and her vision went white. Still, she fought to raise her guard, tried to prepare for the next attack. Through the haze of pain, her vision cleared just enough to meet Ressa's gaze—calm, confident, utterly in control.

Gisele didn't see the next blow coming. Pain exploded through her jaw—again. Ressa had just driven an uppercut into an already fractured bone.

But she wasn't done. The soldier grabbed Gisele by the shoulders before she could recover and smashed their heads together. Ressa let her go.

Dazed and reeling, Gisele stumbled backward. Her limbs felt leaden, her thoughts sluggish. She tried to lift her hands in defense, but she was moving too slowly. *I should have used a damn barrier.*

Then, suddenly, a blinding flash erupted in front of her.

Sloane was *pissed*. That *bitch* broke her jaw.

Ressa staggered back, shielding her eyes as she tried to retreat down the alleyway, still reeling from Sloane's **[Flashbang]** to the face. *Should've put more into it*, Sloane thought. The spell had been weak—barely more than a quick burst of light.

Sloane's pain was nearly unbearable; she wasn't going to last much longer. She was running on pure adrenaline and hate. But at least Ressa wasn't pummeling Gisele anymore.

She forced herself to take stock of her condition. Her left arm hung useless at her side. *Broken? Dislocated?* It didn't matter—she couldn't use it. Every breath, every slight movement sent waves of agony through her body. She couldn't function like this.

Drawing in a ragged breath, she channeled mana through every fiber of her being. The familiar rush filled her veins like a shot of pure adrenaline, a momentary relief from the relentless pain.

Her vision tinged blue as mana vented from her eyes in wispy trails, the sensation as natural as breathing. With sharp **[Focus]**, she filtered through the glow, forcing her sight to clear. The searing agony dulled into something tolerable, just enough to move—to fight. Barely a heartbeat after casting her **[Flashbang]**, she scanned the scene.

Deryk was still engaged with the telv mercenary, parrying a brutal strike. Instead of countering with his blade, he lunged forward and grabbed the man. In one fluid motion, he lifted the mercenary clean off the ground and spun, hurling him down the alley like a discarded ragdoll.

The orkun knight caught Sloane's eye and nodded before rushing toward Gisele and dragging her back to safety.

Good. One less thing to worry about.

Sloane raised her working hand and cast two more **[Flashbangs]**, targeting the men harassing Maud and Cristole. Both groups recoiled, crying out in shock. But they recovered quickly, retreating with precision and reforming into a defensive line within the narrow alley. The three with shields locked them together, forming a protective wall for the casters behind them.

Sloane's gaze snapped back to Ressa. Rage twisted inside her, raw and blinding. *She's just one more person between me and finding Gwyn.*

Her hand trembled as she raised it, pushing past the fresh wave of pain. She screamed as she forced more mana through her battered body, her veins burning under the strain. *Not much longer. Just hold on a little longer.*

Ressa's unfocused eyes widened as if she felt Sloane gathering her power, as if she sensed the raw, unfiltered mana twisting into form in front of her.

Sloane locked eyes with the orkun woman.

Then, with a scream, she channeled her rage into her **[Arcane Barrage]**.

Ressa felt the air grow thick—heavy, charged.

Then, something shifted.

Her connection to the blue magic flickered as it was pulled toward the terran, siphoning from the very air around them.

She didn't think. She *acted*. With a sharp gesture, she cast one spell after another, first forming a thick, translucent wall of energy, then solidifying it into stone.

A heartbeat later, a force slammed into the barrier with such ferocity that the alley trembled beneath her feet.

Ressa's blurred vision swept to take in her men. Alexi, barely more than a shadowed figure in her sight, was already pushing himself up from where the orkun knight had thrown him.

Then the second hit landed.

Her stomach lurched as she saw the wall shake more than it should have.

"Move back! Now!" she barked.

A crack rang out—sharp, final.

Ressa's breath hitched. She threw up another wall and retreated, moving backward as more of the terran's attacks slammed into her defenses. She felt the first wall collapse, the mana tether severing violently as the rubble caved in.

Then came the next barrage, striking the fresh barriers one after another in a relentless cascade, each explosion roaring through the alley like a siege engine hammering against a fortress.

She's holding back.

The realization settled like ice in her veins. Even now, the terran was *restraining herself.* If the aftermath of the watchtower was anything to go by, she could be unleashing far worse.

Somewhere in the distance, she heard shouting—not in the direction of the terran and the Blighters. Ressa gritted her teeth, hastily raising another wall just as the exterior stone behind her exploded outward, sending debris raining into the alley. Her second wall cracked under the force, then shattered. Her shield and sword clattered to the ground as she lifted her hands, her spell returning to her like a long-lost instinct.

The air around them shifted. Reality warped.

[Fracture World].

Sound dulled, distorted, and cracked like splintered glass. The weight of her magic pressed down on her bones, but she welcomed it, *needed* it to hold back the terran's onslaught.

Ressa conjured another barrier. Not a moment too soon. The next explosion rocked the buildings around them; a window shattered. More debris. More dust. Screams. They needed to get away.

Another attack. Then another.

She had fought in wars. She had seen battles, sieges, and destruction. But *this*—this felt different. This felt like standing inside a city under siege, where the walls shook with every distant crash, each impact bringing them closer to inevitable ruin.

Is this how the men at the watchtower felt? No. *They didn't have a chance.* The terran killed them all with *one* spell.

Ressa forced more mana into her workings, pouring everything into reinforcing her conjured stone. The sound of the battle dulled in her ears. The dust choked the air, thick and stifling. Blood trickled from her nose, but she ignored it. The only thing that mattered was holding the line.

Then—

A final explosion.

Silence.

She didn't lower the barrier immediately, waiting, listening. The air was thick with tension.

Her men still stood, fear plain on their faces. The ones with shields pressed together in a tight formation. The orkun who lacked one huddled close to another. One of her telv men had stepped in front of him, shielding him with his own body.

It's over. Ressa exhaled, slow and controlled. "Be ready. I'm dropping it." She bent down, retrieved her shield and sword, and adjusted her stance.

With a deep breath, she raised a hand and cast **[Create Illusion]**, summoning a dozen ethereal arrows to hover above her. Then she reached out, connected with her own magic, and dispelled the conjured wall.

The energy fractured, dissolving into yellow mist. Ressa squinted into the darkness, peering past the settling dust, through the scattered rubble. She saw nothing.

Her men inched forward cautiously, eyes darting, scanning every shadow.

"They're gone," Ressa said, exhaling slowly. The exhaustion hit her then, creeping in at the edges of her consciousness. She had burned through a staggering amount of magic, and she knew that as soon as the battle fervor faded, she'd collapse. She'd sleep like the dead and wake up hungrier than she had in weeks.

"Ressa, we should go," Alexi muttered.

She clenched her jaw. The terran was strong. Capable. But she wasn't a fighter. If it hadn't been for the knights, Ressa would have captured or eliminated her. She had surprised the woman with her magic, but even if the terran understood more about her abilities now, that didn't change the outcome of a real battle. Ressa had been trained for this.

Still . . . she turned the battle over in her mind, analyzing every decision. *What could we have done differently?* They had outnumbered the knights, surprised them even. And still, they had failed to gain a decisive advantage. *We underestimated them. They're veterans too.*

"Commander."

Ressa blinked, pulled from her thoughts by Alexi's urgent tone.

"We need to go. The guards will be here soon."

She took one last glance down the alley. *Next time.* Turning to her team, she nodded. "Let's go. We need to lay low. We'll create more opportunities soon."

CHAPTER FOURTEEN

CHANGE OF PLANS

Sloane jerked back into consciousness, pain ripping through her shoulder as something tore free. A primal instinct to scream only made it worse, her broken jaw grinding together in excruciating protest. Panic surged, her mind fogged with disoriented terror. She blinked, vision blurred, her eyes darting frantically around the softly lit room. Nothing made sense for a moment, but then she caught sight of the battered nightstand, the familiar quilt bunched at the end of her bed, and at last, Gisele's concerned face leaning over her.

Only then did Sloane realize she was back in her room at the inn.

The orkun spoke softly, her voice steady, grounding. Then, the pain returned in full force. Sloane whimpered as Gisele carefully pulled the arrow free, her breath catching as fresh agony radiated from the wound. *How the fuck did that woman even create that?*

A second face appeared: Maud. Without hesitation, the redhead pressed a glowing hand to Sloane's shoulder, letting warm green mana flood into her. The sensation was almost unbearable. Her flesh crawled as it knit itself back together, muscles shifting unnaturally, bones grinding into alignment. Her shoulder writhed beneath her skin, nerves screaming as they were forcefully mended. A final pulse of magic. A sharp tug of something inside of her shoulder. Then relief. Sloane barely had time to register it before Maud shifted focus, moving to heal her jaw.

The itch started first—a maddening, deep sensation like something slithering beneath her skin. Sloane clenched her teeth, refusing to cry out, but she tightened her grip on Gisele's hand as Maud's magic forced the fracture back into place. The final snap of bone resetting nearly made her pass out again.

"Breathe," Gisele murmured, her voice firm but reassuring. "She's almost done. You're doing so good, Sloane."

Sloane nodded slightly, letting the mana flow through her, soothing the raw pain in its wake. The ache dulled, and eventually, the healer finished, her magic fading into a lingering warmth.

As soon as her jaw was functional, Sloane turned her head, tracking Maud as the telv moved toward Cristole.

"W-what the fuck was that?" she rasped, her jaw still stiff.

"Empire's Fist," Deryk said flatly, as if that explained everything.

"We don't know if they're Empire's Fist," Gisele snapped, her voice sharp. She sighed, rubbing a hand through her hair. "Sorry. I do suspect that they were Vlaredian."

"Only thing that makes sense," Deryk replied, unmoved by her irritation.

Sloane exhaled through her nose, pressing a hand against her still-sensitive shoulder. "I don't know what the hell that is, but that's not what I was asking," she ground out, wiping the tear streaks from her face.

Gisele cast a glance at Cristole, concern flickering in her eyes. He gave a slight nod, and after a deep breath, Gisele turned back to Sloane, offering her a damp cloth. "I have no idea what that magic was."

Sloane sighed, wiping at her face and dabbing at the dried blood on her shoulder. "Her magic . . . it was illusions." She paused, her fingers pressing against the place where the arrow had struck. "But she could make them real." She dropped the now red cloth into Gisele's waiting hand, voice lowering. "That arrow is real."

Cristole, still leaning against a wall, nodded grimly. His face remained tense, a hand hovering protectively over his side. Maud stood beside him, her magic still working, likely tending to deeper wounds—injuries battlefield healing alone hadn't fully mended.

Gisele stared down at the arrow on the floor. "You two are lucky that woman's magic used a bodkin arrowhead." She narrowed her gaze on Cristole. "Especially you. Ripping it out mid-fight?"

Cristole grimaced. "I knew I had Maud's support."

Maud's magic flickered and faded as she finished healing him. Then, without hesitation, she punched him in the shoulder. "I was fighting two people, you ass. Healing your idiotic ass nearly got me turned into a pincushion. Never pull an arrow out without me right there." She glared at him. "You had no way of knowing if the head was barbed."

Deryk gave her an approving nod. "You fought well today, Maud. You keep your trophy?"

Maud smirked, gesturing toward the shield leaning against the wall near the door. "Of course. They tried to hide it with some paint, but this is definitely a well-made Vlaredian shield. It'll go well with my collection."

Gisele nudged the arrow with her boot, her expression dark with contemplation. She looked up, scanning the group. "This is magic, right? Can she feel where this is somehow?"

Sloane reached down and picked it up. Channeling mana into her eyes, she activated [**Mana Sight**], watching as the object glowed a dull yellow in her vision. The entire arrow wasn't just imbued with mana—it *was* mana. Frowning, she returned it to the floor and grabbed her sword. With a sharp swing, she brought the blade down on the shaft. The |**Spell-Piercing**| rune flared as the blade met the conjured wood. The arrow dissolved into swirling golden mist.

Sloane exhaled. "I think it's safe to say yes."

Gisele looked at Deryk. He met her gaze and nodded.

Without hesitation, Gisele fired off orders. "We need to relocate. Change inns. Tonight. And we need to warn the guard." She took a steadying breath before turning back to Sloane. "Work with your guards and Ernald. Your house needs to be on full alert. If it *is* the Fist operating within the city, we all need to be constantly prepared."

Sloane nodded. "I'll talk with Nemura now." She rubbed her jaw absently before glancing around once more. The others had already burst into motion, moving with purpose.

Without another word, she turned and left the room.

"You are not going anywhere without me again. You realize this, right?" Nemura said, her tone leaving no room for argument.

Sloane sighed. "Yeah, I figured you'd say that." She ran a hand over her face, still feeling a phantom ache from her injuries. "It was rough, Nemura."

Her mechanical falcon screeched.

"Yes, yes. You too, Tiberius."

The bird let out a softer chirp before resuming its watch over the door. Even *he* was on edge. Unfortunately, he was just a scout, *not* a fighter. Sloane frowned. *Maybe that's something I need to work on. A design for the future—something to keep both Gwyn and me safe.*

Nemura narrowed her eyes and leaned down in front of her. "We're also going to work on your fighting. And your ability to react in a fight." Her voice hardened. "You stand still too much. You're lucky to be alive."

Before Sloane could respond, Nemura plucked a cloth from the table and dipped it into Sloane's glass of water.

"Hey!"

Ignoring the protest, Nemura grabbed Sloane's chin and tilted her head, examining her closely. "Maud missed a spot. Hold still."

With a gentleness that didn't match her usual demeanor, Nemura brushed Sloane's hair aside and dabbed at her temple. The damp cloth stung against the raw skin. Sloane winced.

"Don't be a lamb. This isn't bad."

She shot Nemura a glare but let out a resigned sigh when she caught sight of the pink-tinged cloth.

The telv pulled back, her expression unreadable. "You *do* realize none of the guards Ernald has been working with will be able to fight the Empire's Fist?"

Sloane frowned. "No? I'm not even sure what they *are*."

Nemura nodded, as if she expected that answer. "The Empire's Fist is an elite force within the Vlaredian military that answers directly to the empress. We—*they* are some of the best fighters in the region." Her voice turned grave. "If they *were* the Fist, we need to prepare. They won't give up easily."

Sloane tilted her head slightly. She hadn't missed the way Nemura had phrased that.

"*We?*"

Nemura exhaled slowly, something unreadable flickering in her eyes. "I was once a member," she admitted. "Before I was discharged. I left the Empire for the only place that would likely accept me—Thirdghyll." She hesitated, biting her lip before meeting Sloane's gaze. "I would ask you to keep this between us, if possible." Then, more firmly, she added, "I swore a vow. You have my allegiance, milady."

Sloane's eyes widened slightly. "Is this going to be a problem?" she asked carefully. "Fighting your former countrymen?"

Nemura's gaze sharpened, unwavering. "The only problem will be if they attempt to harm you again." Her voice dropped to something cold. Final. "Because *I will end them.*"

"Nemura, if—"

The telv lifted her chin, moving in closer. "I left for a reason," she said evenly, "but I'm not ready to discuss it." Her sharp gaze softened slightly. "You accepted me without question and have given me nothing but respect. I will give you the same courtesy. Please continue that."

Sloane held her gaze for a moment before nodding slowly. "I understand."

Nemura returned the nod, then stepped back, straightening to her full two-meter height. Something about her stance suggested she was still wrestling with unspoken thoughts, so Sloane shifted the conversation.

"Did you speak with the general?"

"Yes," Nemura said, crossing her arms. "He said he would meet with you if needed. But he gave me nothing on his messengers."

Sloane sighed. "Alright. Let's find Ernald and move everyone to a new inn."

Nemura tilted her head. "You know, we *could* move everyone to the Center."

Sloane hesitated, considering it.

"It won't be as comfortable," Nemura admitted, "but we can set up the dormitory while we work on the rest. With everyone there—and with its walls—we'd be in a far more defensible position."

It *would* work. The Center would be functional sooner, and they wouldn't have to keep relocating every time trouble found them. No cozy-inn comforts, but that was a small price to pay for stability.

Sloane exhaled, making her decision. "Okay. I'll talk to Elodie and Adaega."

* * *

"Damn it!" A sharp crack echoed through the room as Ressa's fist met the wall. Her knuckles ached, but she barely felt it over the sheer frustration burning in her chest. The plan had gone completely *tits up* almost immediately.

It had taken them *hours* of carefully moving through the city, dodging guards, and keeping to the shadows before they finally found somewhere to lie low. Some clever use of her magic, and now they had privacy.

"We can fix this . . ." Alexi said, but his tone betrayed his doubt.

Her second-in-command was *pissed*. The orkun knight had bested him in front of the entire team, and the humiliation still burned. He wanted a rematch as much as the rest of them.

"I just—she—ugh!" She clenched her fists. "She killed our people. And with no effort. They didn't have a chance. No way to fight back. No way to stop it." Her jaw tightened. "Just . . . gone." Ressa closed her eyes and took a deep, steadying breath. "I need to be stronger." *Can we even fix this? The entire damn city knows we're here now.*

Her people exchanged glances, but she knew it was clear that they were at a severe disadvantage now that they knew it was their one magic-wielder against the other group's three. With one of those being able to magically heal injuries . . . it made things significantly more difficult.

She exhaled sharply. "The plan to capture or eliminate her failed. The knights will report this—hell, the guard will know by now. We've lost the element of surprise. I should never have let my emotions get the better of me when I spoke to her. I'll take responsibility for that."

"Commander, *stop*." Alexi's voice was firm, cutting through her self-recrimination. "We cannot change the past. We have to focus on what happens next. What's the plan?"

Ressa sighed. *What's the plan?* Everything had gone wrong since they got these damn orders from the empress. First the watchtower—and that still pissed her off. Then the Valeni who killed Mathias. Now her failure in handling Reinhart. She glanced around at her team. They stood quietly, waiting. Alexi was steering her back on course. Unprofessional, she knew, but all she felt was disappointment. And anger. *You vented. It's over. Move on.*

Sloane Reinhart had wiped out so many of their people—like it was *nothing*. And now they potentially had to contend with the entire city watching for them. *We have to change tactics.*

She needed to speak to the general. The terran was too entrenched now. The guard would be on high alert—any direct strike would be damn near impossible.

Ressa straightened. "We pivot." Her voice was clear, decisive. "We support the army. Since the plan is a siege, anything we can do to shorten it, the better."

The others listened intently, hanging on her words.

"First, we disappear. We focus on *targets of opportunity*. Keep the terran *paranoid* and the knights chasing shadows. But more than that, we look for ways to weaken the city itself. We need to determine what support, if any, Sloane Reinhart is providing to Marketbol. Even if we can't kill her, even if our attacks fail, as long as we remain free, we can *contribute* to the war effort." Her gaze hardened. "We will reassess how to approach the terran . . . later."

Alexi scanned the dimly lit room. "How do we avoid capture until the army arrives?"

Ressa took a slow breath, exhaling through her nose. She had an idea. And it was *risky*. But it would work. "I have a plan for that," she said.

It had been two and a half weeks since the Vlaredian attack, and neither the knights nor the city guard had seen any sign of them. General Irileth had put his forces on alert, but it seemed the Empire's Fist had vanished into thin air.

As time passed, it became clear that the general was shifting focus to matters he deemed more pressing.

Elodie had finalized the purchase of the Center, and Ernald had finished selecting members of her new House Guard—coincidentally on the same day as the tavern attack. Meeting the guards afterward had gone well, and it was a relief to learn that two of the senior guardsmen were former officers in Marketbol's army. Ernald had no doubt about their ability to work together.

Sloane took in her surroundings as she walked up to the Reinhart Center's campus. Workers bustled about, hauling newly purchased furniture and equipment into the buildings. They paid her no mind as she passed the visitor center—soon to be used for screening guests before they were allowed entry with an escort, of course—and made her way toward the main entrance.

A guard stationed at the door nodded in acknowledgment and pushed it open for her.

The reception area was spacious, with several desks arranged for directing visitors to the appropriate offices. The receptionists would also handle appointments for those working at the Center.

As soon as she stepped inside, Sloane paused and took a deep breath. Tiberius shifted on her shoulder, his talons tightening slightly against her coat.

"Are you okay? You look exhausted."

Sloane turned to see Adaega standing beside her, concern in her gaze. She forced a smile, nodding. "I'm fine. It's just . . . it'll take time for everyone to adjust. Now that so many people live here, they're relying on me. It's more stressful than I expected, but it'll be worth it."

Adaega gave her a knowing look. "It has been busy. But we have it well in hand." She crossed her arms. "The esquire, Nadia, is working on a contract to recruit a scribe. If we get him, I'll have more details for you."

"Nadia? Have I met her yet?" Sloane asked, trying to recall. The past two weeks had been a blur of new names and faces, and they were all starting to blend together.

"Yes, Stefan's sister."

"Oh! Right." Sloane snapped her fingers. "The big sister who treats our *scary, roguish Blade* like she still has to look after him."

Adaega laughed. "That's the one. She's a lovely woman. I need to set up another meeting between you two, but with everything going on, we keep missing each other."

"I know. I'm sorry." Sloane sighed. "With everything that's happened, I've thrown myself into work. I've been pulled in a dozen different directions."

Adaega waved a hand dismissively. "We *understand*. But remember—you have a team now. If you need something, that's literally why we're here." She jerked a thumb toward one of the offices. "For now . . . are you ready for the meeting?"

Sloane nodded and let Adaega lead the way. She waved to the guardsman standing outside and motioned for him to follow.

Inside, the room was sparsely furnished. A few tables and chairs had been pushed together to create a larger space for everyone to gather. Near the fireplace, Nemura stood deep in conversation with General Irileth, another elf Sloane didn't recognize, and Gisele.

Across the room, Ernald and one of his senior guards—a telv—were speaking with two other telv officers from the army, neither of whom Sloane had met before. None of the other knights were present. She knew they were elsewhere, working to ensure the Vlaredians didn't catch them off guard.

The guard who had accompanied Sloane took a position outside the door, standing watch to prevent interruptions—or eavesdropping. Sloane scanned the room and held back a sigh.

Adaega stepped forward at her nod. "General Irileth, officers of the Marketbol Army, I apologize for the lack of amenities, but please, have a seat so we can discuss the purpose of your visit."

The general turned to his men and nodded. One by one, they took their seats, the general settling in the center chair—directly across from the spot marked with a small nameplate indicating where Sloane should sit.

She smiled. "General, now that we're all here, what can House Reinhart do for you?"

General Irileth, clad in his golden armor, studied her. The gray-haired telv gave no indication of discomfort, though Sloane had to wonder if he ever wore anything else.

"Lady Reinhart," he said, his sharp eyes flicking over her. "I notice your eyes are no longer filled with magical mist."

She shrugged. "I needed to make sure I wasn't dismissed." A pause. "I don't regret it."

The general smirked. "I don't believe you should. It certainly worked," he admitted, though there was a rueful edge to his tone. He leaned back in his chair and exhaled slowly. "I would appreciate it if what we discuss does not leave this room."

Sloane glanced around at her people—Nemura, Gisele, Ernald, Adaega—knowing none of them would breathe a word of whatever came next. Still, she offered reassurance.

"The nearest city, Mogagale, is calling its bannermen to arms," the general said, his voice grave. "*Now*. That is a slow process. As such, they will not be here in time."

Sloane stiffened. That meant something serious. Something imminent. But she had to ask. "Here in time for what?"

Irileth's gaze met hers. "Scouts report that the Empire's army will soon be on the move," he said, his words heavy. "The council requests that you make good on your word, for we will have to hold out until our reinforcements can arrive."

Silence. Tension thickened the air. Sloane looked around the room, taking in the tight expressions, the rigid shoulders. Even Gisele, usually composed, met her eyes and gave a slow, measured nod. She turned back to the general, thoughts racing. What could she do? Where could she best apply herself?

Irileth waited, his scrutiny unwavering but patient. His subordinates mirrored his stillness, their expressions unreadable as they awaited her response.

Sloane inhaled deeply, then leaned forward, resting her hands on the table. "Let me tell you a bit about our capabilities. Then, General, you can tell us how we can help."

At her words, Irileth nodded. Immediately, his men reached for scrolls, notebooks, and a map, unfurling them across the table.

It's time to work.

CHAPTER FIFTEEN

SECURING ADVANTAGES

*"The difference between a spell and a revolution is whether or not
you can mass-produce it."*

—Sloane Reinhart

Another four weeks had passed since preparations for the Vlaredian Empire's army had begun. Scouts now reported that the enemy force would arrive within the week—though not without complications. The army had attempted to bypass the Agenval Forest and, in doing so, had been attacked.

Those Valeni give no shits.

The assault itself hadn't inflicted significant damage, but it *had* forced the Vlaredians to reroute, delaying their advance by an entire week. Forced westward, they were now slogging through the hills—a delay made even worse by a storm that had turned their path into a sea of mud.

Tiberius had been flying almost nonstop for that entire time, dispatching detailed statuses of the incoming forces. Every time Sloane relayed another setback, the army's morale soared.

Unfortunately, that excitement had been dulled when another message arrived—one reporting that the *other* Sovereign army had also been delayed. Not due to battle. Not even due to terrain. Weather had prevented them from mustering at all.

The city had been so dismissive of the Empire's aggression that it had been caught completely off guard. The only standing forces Marketbol had were its city guard. Despite the approaching army, General Irileth and his men didn't seem nearly as concerned as she felt they should be. Marketbol was about to come under siege.

Yes, preparations were constant. But there was an air of complacency—one that was starting to affect Sloane as well. *I keep catching myself slipping into it too.* The only thing keeping her on edge was the fact that no one had seen or heard from Ressa or her soldiers.

Nemura remained a near constant presence, always reminding Sloane not to let her guard down. The former Fist was convinced that Ressa and her team were simply waiting—hunting for targets of opportunity that could put the Empire's forces in a more advantageous position once they arrived.

At Nemura's insistence, Sloane had relayed concerns to the army that Ressa's team might attempt to sabotage food supplies in some way.

All this kept her both physically and mentally busy as she moved from one planning session to the next. As she walked outside, she looked up, catching sight of Tiberius as the falcon circled overhead, keeping watch.

Nemura and a group of guards had just escorted her from yet another meeting—this one with Lady Emerys. The woman had wanted to discuss the possibility of designing golems to be used as scouts for the army.

Sloane had promised to look into it. *If I can even remember how I did it*, she'd thought. She would spend some free time developing blueprints and instructions that she would leave with Adaega. Sloane seriously doubted she had the time to set up a manufacturing arm for golems.

They reached the gates of the Reinhart Center just in time for her next meeting. Four guards at the entrance saluted as she and Nemura approached, quickly moving to unlock the gate and let them through.

Sloane stepped into the courtyard and took a moment to observe the ongoing work. All around her, staff hired by Elodie and Adaega moved with purpose, attending to their various tasks. Their storage warehouse—and many of the other facilities—were filled to the brim with dry goods and barrels of clean water, all in preparation for the siege.

Guards from both her house and the city patrolled the grounds, several nodding in acknowledgment as they passed. From here, she could hear the steady hammering from the forge at the rear of the campus—a sure sign that Koren and his two new apprentices were hard at work, preparing weapons and armor for enchanting.

"Sloane, behind you," Nemura warned from her right.

She turned just in time to see more people and supplies approaching the gate. A wagon loaded with crates of silden ferns rolled past. The alchemy hall was its destination, where Rel and Kemmy were busy producing large quantities of enchanting ink.

That was why she was here—to enchant equipment for the Marketbol. Stretching, she let out a yawn and caught sight of her director of the Reinhart Center approaching.

"Every time I see you, you look exhausted," Adaega said.

Nemura coughed, giving Sloane a pointed look. "She's been working *nonstop*. I had to force her to sleep. You wouldn't believe how long it took to convince her that sleeping on a cot in a workshop wasn't proper for a baroness."

Adaega frowned. "I suppose part of that is my fault, with how much work has been coming in." She hesitated, then sighed. "Admittedly, I'm not used to working with nobility."

Sloane waved a hand dismissively. "If it makes you feel any better, I'm *still* not used to how nobility works here."

Adaega nodded sagely. "Shall we?"

Sloane gestured toward the main building. "After you, Director."

Following Adaega inside, Sloane couldn't help but be amazed by how much progress had been made in just one day. The place was running like a well-oiled machine, every person working with precision to provide support to the city's defenders.

A *proper* house. She felt an unexpected swell of pride for what they had built, even if it was still new. Elodie and Adaega were exceptional at their jobs, and Sloane wished she had the time to do more to help them. But time was something they didn't have. With the Vlaredians marching toward them, there was no telling what would happen when the siege began. And if they couldn't break free of Marketbol in time . . .

Swanbrook before winter . . . Is that even possible anymore?

"Sloane."

"Hmm? Oh, sorry."

Adaega shook her head but didn't seem surprised. By now, those closest to Sloane were well aware of how easily she got lost in her thoughts. "In here."

The office where she had previously met with General Irileth and his commanders had been rearranged. The tables had been shifted, and chairs were now arranged in front of the fireplace. Bookshelves lined the walls, filled with volumes that practically called to her. Sloane wished she had the time to sit and read.

A young telv sat behind one of the tables, his posture rigid. He looked no older than seventeen or eighteen, with dark-brown hair and sharp, vibrant hazel eyes. His face was clean-shaven, his expression unreadable. At their entrance, he stood.

Adaega greeted him first. "Hello, Orthan. This is Lady Sloane Reinhart."

Orthan gave a stiff nod but said nothing.

Sloane glanced at Adaega, who sighed, crossing her arms. She tried again. "Good afternoon, Orthan. Would you like to introduce yourself?"

The boy's face twitched slightly before he stepped forward. He bowed formally from the waist and straightened. "My name is Orthan Barat. I am the second son of Lord Amil Barat and the youngest person on this continent to be considered a master scribe. My father is a former member of the Ruling Council, and my brother is currently training to become a paladin. When he finishes, I will be next in line for House Barat."

Sloane raised a brow. "What is a master scribe?"

Orthan's eyes narrowed, his expression twisting as if she'd just asked whether water was wet. Before he could answer, Adaega let out a soft sigh and stepped in.

"It means his ability to create official records and documents is highly skilled and well regarded. He can speak and write in all of the major languages. More importantly, it means he could be called upon to work in official ceremonies between heads of state and nations."

Sloane tilted her head. "So . . . you can write well?"

The boy looked offended. "There is more to a scribe than simply writing, Lady Reinhart." His voice was clipped, his tone strained. "A scribe creates works meant to withstand the test of time. A master scribe pens documents intended to last for centuries, scrutinized by scholars long after we are gone."

Sloane frowned. Something about his speech felt off. His words sounded rehearsed—like he was reading from a script rather than speaking naturally. Odd, considering he was nobility. Shouldn't he already be comfortable speaking to others?

She waited, giving him space to continue.

"My father has been searching for a way for me to gain experience and assistance with my . . . abilities."

Sloane looked to Adaega for clarification.

Adaega merely shrugged. "Orthan has an attunement to blue mana and an Artifice affinity. With a little work, I believe he'll be able to take over the assistant rune scribe position."

Sloane narrowed her eyes. "Assistant rune scribe?"

Adaega stepped closer, rising onto her toes to whisper in Sloane's ear. Sloane tilted her head slightly to make it easier for the shorter woman.

"His father's house is in decline," Adaega murmured. "They're looking to tie their fortunes to yours—through some process that would make them subordinate to House Reinhart. The boy will work for us until it's time for him to take over his house."

Sloane raised a brow. "There's a lot to unpack there, Adaega. What exactly does it mean for them to tie their house to mine?"

Adaega shrugged. "Ernald tried to explain it to me, but the best I got was that they would pledge their house to yours. Your house would have authority over them, but apparently there's more nuance, since you're technically the same rank. In the end, I'm not entirely sure. That might be a question better suited for Nadia or one of the knights."

Sooo . . . kind of like a subsidiary? It was confusing—definitely something she needed more clarification on. "This doesn't seem ideal," she admitted. "Can we be sure he won't become a competitor when he leaves?"

Adaega sighed. "Trust me, I know. It'll have to do for now. We're still searching for someone else. But we do have a contract that should protect us from the worst of your concerns." She paused. "That said, we really need to figure out what this arrangement between houses actually means."

Sloane exhaled slowly. *This world is so damn confusing.* She turned to Orthan. "I look forward to seeing what you can do."

The boy nodded, returning to his seat. He pulled out a book, flipping it open without another word.

Adaega shook her head but gave a small smile. "It'll take some work, but trust me . . . he's a genius."

Sloane and Nemura followed Adaega to the Center's auditorium, the second-largest building on campus. Several small classrooms in the building were already being converted into research spaces, but the real focus was its massive auditorium and hall. Designed with flexibility in mind, it could easily be reconfigured to host galas and large events—an idea that made Adaega particularly excited.

The moment they stepped inside, Sloane took in the hive of activity. Smiths from the Smithing Guild and soldiers from the city moved with purpose, preparing materials and bringing in even more supplies.

The sloped floor's seating had been removed entirely and replaced with workbenches and quilts where spears, bows, shields, and all manner of weapons were being readied for the city's defense. Jewelers had been brought in to etch runes into the weapons. There were far too many for Sloane to inscribe herself.

The city had been relentless in securing resources. Hundreds of hunters and soldiers had been sent into the countryside to track and kill whatever beasts they could find. The meat would help sustain the population during the siege, but more importantly, the cores they harvested would be critical to the enchantments Sloane was working on.

To her dismay, the city had also expedited the execution of criminals to obtain their cores as well. She didn't know how to feel about that. On one hand, the value of those cores had been paid out to the families of the criminals' victims, meant as restitution. On the other . . . *it still feels wrong.* At least, that's what she told herself.

Maud, though, had taken it especially hard. Since the announcement, she had been spending more and more time at the local temple, offering her healing services and assisting the church in their work with the city's masses.

Sloane had been surprised by how readily the church had accepted her help. The appreciation they showed the knight was genuine.

Sloane's gaze drifted toward the center of the hall and landed on the enchanting table, a recent addition built specifically for empowering runes. Forged from steel, the table's surface was engraved with intricate runes, its design both functional and elegant. At each corner, blue mana cores had been inlaid, allowing her to draw mana directly from them by placing her hands on two designated points.

The table had been the brainchild of Koren and a team of city scholars. They had provided the concept; she had made it a reality—with the house smith's assistance, of course.

Settling into the chair, Sloane took a slow, measured breath as she scanned the hall, watching the ongoing work.

One of the city's officers approached her. "Lady Reinhart, we have tested the various rune combinations you suggested," the high elf woman reported. "I'd like to share our findings."

Sloane gestured for her to continue. "Please, what have your people found?"

The officer pulled out a notebook and flipped it open. "Based on our tests, we believe the ballista bolts should use the |Arcane Explosion| runework. While we agree with your initial assessment of its efficacy, we have found that the magic's burst—combined with the bolt's impact—would be strong enough to critically damage the walls of a siege tower."

She paused before adding, "Additionally, pairing this with the |Lighten| rune would allow our ballistae to outrange anything the Vlaredians can field. We would also like the |Strengthen| rune applied to the ballistae themselves."

Sloane lifted a hand. "One note: |Lighten| alone won't achieve the effect you want."

The officer stilled, listening intently.

"You'll need at least two additional runic chains. First, we want to |Strengthen| the bolts—more force means more kinetic energy on impact. We're also going to cheat standard physics a bit by using mana to enhance propulsion." Sloane leaned forward, tapping a finger against the table. "We'll need a |Speed| rune linked to a detection trigger—something like |Detect: Momentum| then |Increase: Speed|. That way, the enchantment activates the moment the bolt is fired."

The officer nodded, though she looked as if she was still processing the information.

"Now, the last part is *critical*," Sloane continued. "A lighter bolt will struggle with penetration. To counter this, we'll use |Detect: Impact| then |Amplify: Mass| on the bolt head. That way, the moment it strikes the target, the enchantment negates the |Lighten| effect and increases the density of the bolt head.

"Combine that with the |Spell: Arcane Explosion|—which we'll also tie to a detection rune—and you maximize damage. Plus, the explosion will destroy the bolt itself, preventing the enemy from recovering our runework."

She exhaled. "Now, all of this means the bolt will require *a lot* of mana draw, which could affect the final design. Also, since ballistae are made of wood, enchanting them might be problematic. We may need to adjust the approach, but let's start here."

The officer's brow furrowed as she absorbed Sloane's barrage of information. After a moment, she nodded.

"The . . . *physics* behind the enchants is outside our expertise," she admitted. "However, we anticipated the difficulty of enchanting wood, especially given the complexity of these runes. To address that, we've had our woodworkers inlay a green mana core into each siege engine." She glanced at her notes. "We believe a |Renew: Wood| runic chain would be beneficial in case the ballistae sustain damage."

Sloane's eyes lit up. "Oh! That's actually a great idea." She had to admit: despite the looming siege, despite the stress of preparing for war, she enjoyed this part.

During the initial meetings with the city's military experts, Sloane had given a brief primer on how runes and runic chains functioned, explaining the logic behind their construction, how mana flow dictated their effectiveness, and how various detection triggers could be used to optimize enchantments.

The back-and-forth brainstorming sessions that came next had been some of the most engaging, invigorating discussions she'd had since arriving in this world. The officers, siege engineers, and scholars of Marketbol had challenged her ideas, proposing alterations and refinements to make their defenses more efficient, practical, and sustainable under siege conditions. While she was able to provide the most effective solution *most* of the time—providing a huge boost to her ego—there were suggestions reflecting scenarios or processes she hadn't considered.

Sloane thrived in that space—the puzzle-solving, the collaborative innovation. What was the best way to fortify ballistae with enchantments while balancing mana draw? How could they ensure arcane defenses wouldn't interfere with mundane defenses? Could runes be adapted for the city's existing weapons and armor, or would they need to start from scratch?

They had debated, adjusted, tested, and iterated, working together to push magical enhancements to their limits. For the first time in weeks, Sloane had felt a flicker of something beyond survival. It wasn't just about defending Marketbol. It was about building something better.

She turned to Nemura. "Can you get me some wood?"

Nemura arched a brow. "Would you like a rod? And how big do you like it?"

Sloane smirked. "Doesn't matter—the bigger, the better, so I can practice the work."

Nemura laughed, shaking her head as she walked away.

Sloane glanced up at the officer. The woman was very deliberately staring into her notebook, refusing to meet her gaze.

Nemura returned, carrying a fifteen-kilo ballista bolt as if it were nothing more than a twig. The high elf officer arched a brow as Nemura dropped the two-meter-long bolt onto the table with a loud thud.

Sloane gave her a look. Nemura smirked. Shaking her head, Sloane turned her attention back to the work at hand.

The soldiers had the right idea, but their runic chain wasn't going to cut it. It had no way of detecting damage, which was a crucial flaw. However, choosing **|Renew|** over **|Repair|** or **|Alter|** was actually an inspired decision.

The bolt would serve as the perfect test piece—far easier to work with than an entire siege engine. Grabbing her inscribing pen, Sloane got to work, modifying the runework so that it would actually repair damage to the wood itself. She channeled her blue mana, focusing as she etched:

|Detect: (Durability: <DAMAGED>)| then **|Draw: (Power)** as **(Mana: Green)|** then **|Renew: (Element: Wood)|** then **|Amplify|**

Satisfied, she considered where to place the green mana core. *Well . . . this is a test.* She grabbed the metal head of the bolt and, using her mana, cast [**Alter**] at it.

The tip collapsed inward under her control, reshaping itself as she rounded out a small indentation. Carefully, she placed the green core into position and, with another pulse of mana, solidified it into place.

Sloane smiled. *Now that's a staff worthy of a half-giant druid.* With the core integrated, she quickly adjusted the mana conduits to ensure everything connected properly.

Nemura and the city officer stood by, observing her work.

"Now, we need to break this," Sloane said to her guardswoman.

Nemura nodded, already moving. She placed the staff-sized bolt on the ground, then drew her sword.

Sloane watched as Nemura channeled her mana, the blade faintly glowing red as her mana-infused ability took hold. After a brief pause, the guardswoman swung.

A resounding crack echoed through the hall, drawing the attention of everyone nearby. Sloane stared at the bolt, now neatly split in half. She waited.

The green core pulsed—a steady, rhythmic light—before the energy rushed down the conduits and spread through the wood. Within five seconds, the wood stitched itself back together, seamlessly fusing along the break.

"Perfect." Sloane exhaled, nodding in satisfaction. "I'll use this runic chain on the ballistae. I think there are a few other enchantments I can add to enhance the power and efficiency of the siege engines themselves." She looked at the officer. "After all, the ballistae are more important than the individual bolts when it comes to transferring kinetic energy."

The soldier stood there, wide-eyed, before furiously scribbling notes in her book.

Sloane smirked. Glancing down at the meter-long bolt, she turned to her guard. "Okay, Nemura. The rod's all yours. Feel free to test it in private." She winked.

Before she could react, a sudden slap on her back nearly sent her lurching forward. Nemura's booming laughter filled the hall.

Shaking her head, Sloane couldn't help herself—she laughed, too. The tension that had been building for weeks finally cracked, if only for a moment.

Not much longer until we're in yet another fight for survival. Have to take the good moments when they come.

CHAPTER SIXTEEN

NOT A GOODBYE

Gwyn stepped out of the temple, her magic keeping her emotions locked away. To her right, Taenya walked in her gleaming silver armor, every inch the ceremonial knight, her presence a silent declaration of House Reinhart's strength. To her left, Paladin Amari matched her stride, the woman's scarlet armor reflecting the midday sun. Somewhere behind them, Sabina and Theran moved through the gathered crowd, ensuring her people were safe.

The church had provided a private setting for the ceremony, and Siveril had made certain that every family member of those lost, along with any member of the house who wished to pay their respects, could attend. It was the third funeral Gwyn had ever gone to. And they did not get any easier.

She had to sit in the front—seen, but not intrusive. Look solemn, but not too broken. Be present, but allow space for the grieving. The families needed to see that she cared, that their loss mattered to her. It was a delicate, exhausting balance, one she was still learning to master.

Nineteen. Nineteen people of her house had died in the attack. It did not matter who they were: guards, staff . . . Emma. The thought made her stomach twist. It made her furious. And the worst part? There was nothing they could do except wait.

This doesn't happen at home.

At least they would be leaving soon. Preparations were complete, and she had one last thing to do before their departure—say goodbye to Roslyn.

Plans had changed. Roslyn's grandfather had altered her travel route, making it impossible for them to journey together. When Gwyn had asked Siveril if she could go with her friend, he had simply said, *You cannot.* No further explanation. No compromise.

That meant she wouldn't see Roslyn until they both reached the capital. After winter.

She clenched her jaw. Having her friend along would have helped. Would have given her something else to focus on. Now, all she had was the waiting. At least her ladies-in-waiting would be with her. *I can't wait to leave this city.*

A guard held the carriage door open for her, offering his hand. She took it without thinking, stepping up into the carriage. As she placed one foot inside, she glanced back at her escorts. Taenya met her eyes and gave her a nod before turning to mount her horse, where another guard held the reins.

Amari saluted, then pivoted and strode back toward the temple. Unlike Khalan, the paladin wasn't bound to her side at all times. She would return to the manor later.

The carriage door shut, sealing her inside. Alone, Gwyn sank into the seat, her shoulders curling inward as she let her **[Frozen Heart]** thaw. A sharp, shuddering breath escaped her, and then the emotions crashed over her all at once. That was the price of using the spell for too long—every emotion she had suppressed hit like a tidal wave the moment the spell was ended.

Only this time, there were no more tears left to cry. Only the inferno remained. And all it wanted was to consume.

Gwyn stepped into Roslyn's wing of the ducal palace, nodding in thanks to the guards who had guided her. By now, she had come so often that it felt refreshingly normal—no fanfare, no formalities, just a routine visit.

The duke had granted her permission to come and go as she pleased, which meant she could skip all the ceremony and stuffy noble customs that usually came with visiting someone of Roslyn's station. That suited her just fine.

But when she stepped into the sitting room, Roslyn was nowhere to be found. That was surprising. Usually, her friend could be found curled up in some nook or nestled into a couch, nose buried in a book.

"Roz? Where ya at?" she called out.

"Here! Ahh—!!"

The startled cry to her left made Gwyn whip around, instinct kicking in before she even processed what was happening.

Time seemed to slow as Roslyn slipped, tumbling from the ladder attached to the towering bookcase along the wall. Gwyn reached for the white mana around her, pulling it to her with an effortless click in her mind and forcing it to catch Roslyn.

The **[Telekinesis]** spell surged through her, filling her with energy just as she wrapped the magic around her falling friend.

Roslyn's descent slowed, then stopped entirely. She hovered just a few handspans above the wooden floor. For a moment, there was only silence. Then Roslyn looked at Gwyn, then down at the ground and screamed.

The shrill noise made Gwyn jolt in surprise, her concentration slipping. *Oh no—*

With a dull thud, Roslyn hit the floor. "Ow!"

Guards rushed in, Khalan and Roslyn's lady knight close behind. "My lady!" the knight cried, hurrying to her charge.

"I am fine! I am not hurt! I was just startled," Roslyn reassured them, rolling onto her stomach and pushing herself up.

Gwyn gave her a weak smile. "Are you sure? You landed on your butt pretty hard there at the end."

Roslyn waved off the hands reaching to help her, brushing herself off before planting her hands on her hips. "That is only because you dropped me!"

Khalan and the Tiloral knight exchanged baffled glances, their eyes darting between the two girls.

"Well, it's not my fault you screamed after I saved you," Gwyn shot back, throwing her hands up. "Who does that?"

"It happened so fast! I barely even realized I was falling until you caught me! I wasn't even aware you could do that! And why did you do it so high?"

The female knight's eyes widened at Roslyn's words, clearly catching the implication.

"My lady—"

"I didn't know you were there! Would you rather I let you fall all the way?" Gwyn huffed, crossing her arms.

"No! But—ugh, ow!" Roslyn sighed, rubbing her lower back. She walked up to Gwyn, ignoring everyone around them, and took a deep breath, her tone softening. "Thank you for catching me. And I apologize for startling you . . . though I believe my rear has paid the price for screaming."

Gwyn snorted, grabbing her into a hug. "I'm just glad you're okay."

"You caught her?" Khalan asked, his voice tinged with disbelief.

Roslyn turned, keeping one of Gwyn's arms wrapped securely around her. "She did! I was startled when she entered the room, and fell from the top of the ladder."

The paladin's gaze shifted to the towering bookshelf, then to Gwyn. "How . . . ?"

Gwyn sighed. "I used white mana . . . like I did during the attack . . . and made a new spell."

Khalan stared at her, unblinking. "You *made* a spell . . . just like that?"

She shrugged. "Yeah?"

The sun elf exhaled sharply and shook his head. "Is Evocati Amari with you today?"

"Nope. Taenya and Siveril are talking to the duke, my guards are out front, and I think Amari's coming by the manor tonight." She gave another casual shrug.

Khalan glanced upward in thought, then exchanged a look with Roslyn's knight—a pained, reluctant one. The woman gave him a small nod, which seemed to be all the permission he needed to take his leave.

"Would you like some tea, my lady?" Roslyn's knight asked her charge.

Roslyn glanced at Gwyn, who gave her a quick nod. Gwyn remembered her conversation with the archpriestess—it was the polite thing to do. And, well . . . she *was* a little thirsty.

"Please, thank you," Roslyn said.

With the tension settled and Roslyn safe, the guards returned to their former positions, though one guardswoman remained inside by the door.

"My lady, I will check on the status of our departure while you have your tea. I will return shortly," Roslyn's knight said before stepping out, murmuring something to one of the servants as she left.

Gwyn glanced around the now nearly empty room. "So . . ."

Roslyn huffed a small laugh. "Indeed."

"You leave today?"

"Yes. We were supposed to leave this morning, but you had—"

"I know." Gwyn took a deep breath, looking at her friend. "Roslyn?"

"Yes, Gwyn?"

"It gets better, right?" she asked quietly. "It isn't always like this?"

Roslyn wrapped her arms around her again. "Even if it doesn't, I'll be here for you." She hesitated for a moment, then added in a whisper, "I have a secret to tell you."

Gwyn wiped her eyes and pulled back just enough to meet Roslyn's gaze. *Seems I still have some tears left after all . . .* "What is it?"

Roslyn's voice dropped even lower. "I have Ser Roderick performing a task for me. Well, for *you.*"

Gwyn squinted at her, mind racing. *He's doing something for me?* "What is he doing?"

The high elf leaned in. "He's looking for your mother. Discreetly."

Gwyn's breath hitched, her chest tightening as she fought down the wave of emotion surging through her. Without thinking, she pulled Roslyn into a fierce hug, grinning at the small *oof* of surprise from her friend.

"Thank you, Roz," she murmured.

"Of course," Roslyn said warmly. "What are friends for?"

"Finding your missing parent, obviously," Gwyn quipped, huffing an airy chuckle.

Roslyn grinned, looking quite pleased with herself. "Precisely."

A servant entered the room carrying a silver platter, the delicate clinking of porcelain the only sound as he carefully set the tea service on the small table by the window. The faint aroma of steeping leaves filled the air, warm and soothing.

The girls took their seats, settling into the quiet comfort of the moment. Gwyn's gaze drifted outside. The changing seasons had always fascinated her—how the leaves transformed from vibrant greens to fiery reds and deep golds before finally falling, surrendering to winter's approach. As if on cue, she watched a lone brown leaf detach from its branch and spiral gently to the ground. She smiled. There was something reassuring about the predictability of nature.

The servant poured their tea, adjusting the cups to their preferred tastes before stepping back with a polite bow. Both girls murmured their thanks, waiting for the liquid to cool before taking their first sips.

"Now," Roslyn began, breaking the silence, "I remembered what you said about Mr. Fenren's search. Ser Roderick is using the house's contacts to look in places we may have more access to. He says there may be some difficulty because of the war."

Gwyn frowned. *War?* No one in her house had mentioned anything about a war. Or maybe she had forgotten? "What war?" she asked, trying to recall any relevant discussions.

Roslyn waved it off like it was just another noble inconvenience. "The Empire of Vlaredia invaded the Sovereign Cities. The fighting has escalated into a full-scale war."

Gwyn's breath hitched. "But my mom might be in the Sovereign Cities!"

Roslyn hesitated before responding, her voice calm, measured. "Gwyn, as a terran, your mother wouldn't be a citizen of any of the cities. And if, by some chance, she arrived in the Empire itself, she wouldn't be in one there either. If she's anything like you—"

"She'll be right in the middle of every possible bad thing and will have to constantly fight off horrible people who are trying to hurt her! Roz, this isn't making me feel better!"

Her mind spiraled, images flashing too fast to process. The battles, the threats, the constant danger. If her mother had been thrown into this world like she had . . . *She doesn't even have a house to protect her! She's not a queen! I lied!*

Gwyn's breathing turned shallow, her vision blurring at the edges. *She's alone. She's alone. She's—*

"Gwyn?" Roslyn's hands found hers, squeezing tightly. "Gwyn. Breathe."

She did. One sharp inhale. Another.

"Your mother is going to be fine," Roslyn continued, her grip steady. "I have faith. Every time I've gone to the temple, I've prayed to Alos for her safety."

Gwyn nodded numbly, swallowing hard past the lump in her throat. "It's just . . . so hard, Roz. People don't know that we don't even know where she is."

Roslyn gave her hand another reassuring squeeze before letting go. "I know. But we'll keep it a secret, and we'll help you." She smiled, soft and full of quiet determination. "Cenphine has blessed you with family, and I feel like you're the sister I never had. We'll help you find your family."

Gwyn should have felt comforted by that. Should have felt warmth at Roslyn's words. Instead, a strange disappointment settled in her chest.

"Cenphine?" she asked weakly.

Roslyn tilted her head. "The goddess of family."

Maybe I should go pray to her? She sighed. *Oh. We probably won't have time to stop by the Temple of the Stars before we leave.* Gwyn let out a slow breath. "Thank you, Roslyn."

Roslyn beamed as she lifted her teacup, bringing it cautiously to her lips. The quiet slurping noise made Gwyn smile. Her friend winced, setting the cup back down with a soft clink. *She's finally starting to feel comfortable enough around me to actually do that.* Before, Roslyn had always insisted on waiting until her tea was nearly cold, claiming it was improper to make such noises when testing the temperature. But Gwyn had long since learned exactly how long the tea needed to cool before it was just right for her friend.

Roslyn leaned in, lowering her voice to a whisper. "So, I have been practicing. I can feel the magic . . ."

Gwyn sucked in a sharp breath. "You—" She caught herself and shot a glance toward the guard standing by the door. Then, lowering her own voice, she leaned in closer. "You can *feel* mana? Can you use it yet?"

"Not yet . . . but I can feel it." A determined spark flashed in Roslyn's golden eyes. "I will learn magic like you. And then we will stand side by side against the world if we have to."

Gwyn's stomach twirled like a ballerina onstage. A bright, fluttery feeling filled her chest, bubbling up like excitement and warmth all at once.

She loved spending time with Roslyn—it made her happy. Truly happy. Her best friend. The one person she trusted completely. She found herself grinning as she watched Roslyn absently slide a fingertip along the rim of the saucer beneath her teacup, lost in thought.

"We'll have to find somewhere to practice when we're both in the capital together," Gwyn murmured.

Roslyn straightened with a nod, her usual noble poise returning in full force. "Yes! I will find an adequate training location while I await your arrival."

Gwyn chuckled, knowing full well that Roslyn wouldn't just find a *suitable* location—she would spend *far too much* time meticulously selecting the *perfect* one. The thought filled her with an odd sense of contentment. "I can't wait."

Her gaze flickered to the tea sitting between them, steam curling lazily from the surface. She gestured toward Roslyn's cup. "Your tea's ready."

Roslyn squinted, skeptical. "Really?"

Without hesitation, she lifted the cup and took a sip. The moment the warmth touched her tongue, her expression brightened, her whole face lighting up.

"Perfect!"

Perfect.

Gwyn stood quietly off to the side, waiting outside the ducal palace as Roslyn spoke with her grandfather, the Duke of Tiloral. Siveril and Taenya stood beside her, their presence solid and reassuring, while her four guards took up position behind her, spears and shields at the ready.

The midday sun gleamed off the polished armor of Taenya's Drakyyds, their perfectly coordinated stance making them look even more impressive. The wingless dragon—drake?—that served as their emblem shimmered under the light, catching every golden reflection. It made Gwyn absurdly happy. The level of detail Taenya and Theran had put into ensuring her house looked fabulous was nothing short of perfection.

She turned her head, looking up at Siveril. "So, what did you guys talk to the duke about?"

The old high elf glanced down at her, his serious expression telling her probably more than he intended. "With your permission, I feel it would be better to discuss it at the manor, Your Highness."

Gwyn sighed. "I understand. Is it going to delay us leaving?"

He shook his head. "No. You will be able to leave on time. This concerns . . . wider and future interests."

Gwyn nodded but didn't press further—because at that moment, Roslyn finished her conversation and turned toward her. The blond elf smiled the moment she spotted Gwyn, waving eagerly before making her way over. Gwyn caught the affectionate look the duke gave his granddaughter behind her back and felt warmth bloom in her chest. *They are such good people.*

The thought barely had time to settle before Roslyn reached her and all but crushed her in a tight hug.

"Gwyn! I'm going to miss you. I hate goodbyes."

Gwyn chuckled, gently prying herself away just enough to hold Roslyn's arms and meet her violet eyes. "I'll be leaving soon, and then we'll see each other in the capital. It's like my mom always said, 'This isn't goodbye, it's see you later.'" She squeezed her friend's arms. "Plus, you have to get everything ready for when I get there!"

Wait! I remember something else! "Oh! And get with Friedrich! Mister Niles should have a place for us to live in the city by the time you arrive—since you're going the quick way now. You can work with Friedrich to help with whatever you need."

Roslyn glanced back at one of her knights, who gave a small nod of approval. "I'll do that. Thank you, Gwyn."

Gwyn hesitated, her voice quieter. "I wish I could go with you."

Roslyn nodded quickly. "I do too! But Grandfather—" She turned toward her knight as if looking for confirmation. "Maybe?"

The woman's expression was firm but kind. "I'm sorry, milady. The duke and the king of Dirn Loduhr were quite adamant that only you and your immediate retainers be allowed passage. Her Highness definitely does not apply."

Roslyn deflated slightly. The knight gave her a small smile. "But you will see her soon—at the beginning of spring."

Roslyn sniffled. "I can't wait until you arrive." She looked like she wanted to say more but didn't. A tear slipped down her cheek.

Gwyn reached out, catching it with her fingertips before pulling her friend into another hug. She whispered into her ear, "Hey. Hey. None of that. We'll be back together soon, like the best of friends. And then we'll stand side by side and face down the Royal Academy. Together. Deal?"

Roslyn pulled back to meet her gaze. "Deal," she said softly, "but not friends. Sisters."

Something tugged inside Gwyn's chest, an emotion she couldn't quite place. Her lip twitched. *Sisters fight, don't they?* She thought of Taenya and Sabina and their occasional bickering. *I don't think I want that . . . but I don't want to be just friends, either.*

She closed her eyes, breathing in deeply. *Why is this so confusing?* When she opened them, Roslyn gave her a sad smile.

Gwyn tried to blink away the sudden sting behind her own eyes, but Roslyn reached up first, cupping her cheek and wiping away the tear with her thumb. Her hand lingered just long enough for Gwyn to instinctively lean into it, warmth spreading across her skin. It was a feeling she couldn't ever remember having before. And she never wanted it to go away. She pulled Roslyn in for one last hug.

"I'll see you soon, Roz."

As they separated, Gwyn took a steadying breath, pushing past the bitter-sweet weight in her chest. She held out a hand. "Come on. Let's get you to your carriage."

Taenya waited, giving her princess the privacy she deserved as Gwyn walked hand in hand with Lady Roslyn to the carriage. The girl's knight stood dutifully by, while the other was nowhere in sight, but Taenya knew he would likely rejoin them before their departure. The man had sought a private meeting with her the past week, asking pointed questions about Gwyn's mother. *Gwyn has a good friend if she's willing to push her retainers that far to assist.*

Across the courtyard, the paladin Khalan caught her eye and dipped his head in acknowledgment. She exhaled slowly. *I will have to work with him again in the future.* She had little patience for religious zeal, and the Paladins of Alos often carried themselves with a self-righteousness that set her teeth on edge. *To be fair, Khalan and Amari don't seem that way. Perhaps that was by design.*

"You need to learn to work with the paladins," Siveril murmured beside her, as if hearing her thoughts. The older knight's gaze was fixed on the princess as she said her goodbyes to the Tiloral heiress.

Taenya nodded, suppressing the flicker of irritation. She had hoped the capital would provide some respite while Gwyn attended the Royal Academy, but politics never truly rested.

"I am aware," she replied evenly. "I'll discuss the particulars with Evocati Amari tonight."

Siveril's gaze flicked toward the duke before responding. "Good. You need to leave soon. We cannot give the Angwins time to prepare or catch wind of your plans."

Taenya crossed her arms, her eyes narrowing slightly. "And what of our own preparations?"

The knights of the house had discussed options the night prior. Taenya was disappointed that she would not be a part of what was to happen.

Siveril's expression remained unreadable, but there was a sharpness in his voice when he replied, "The message will be sent before we depart."

She didn't need him to elaborate. The Angwins had struck first, but they would learn soon enough that House Reinhart was not a house that merely endured attacks—it also answered them. Hard.

"It won't be subtle," she said, more statement than question.

Siveril shook his head. "It can't be. If we're to establish ourselves, there must be no question that attacking us comes at a cost."

Taenya exhaled through her nose, tension winding through her shoulders. She wasn't one for needless bloodshed, but justice—no, *retribution*—was necessary. If they let the attack go unanswered, it would invite more. The strike would be measured but decisive. Good. Let the Angwins learn what it meant to cross them.

"And what about the news from the duke?" she asked.

"That . . . is more long term."

Taenya's brow furrowed. "The princess will be in the capital."

Siveril exhaled, a rare trace of unease flickering in his expression. "She wouldn't be the target. Lady Roslyn would. The duke will warn us if he believes he must recall the girl."

The war between the Sovereigns and the Empire was escalating, but threats weren't limited to battlefields. There were those within the kingdom who sought to take advantage of the turmoil, shifting the balance of power in dangerous ways. The duke suspected this was the source of the crown prince's newfound confidence. *If they join the war . . .*

"That doesn't fill me with confidence," she admitted.

"It's why you need to get closer to the paladins," Siveril said, his tone edged with quiet urgency. "I'm not sure how much longer we can afford to entangle ourselves in Aviran politics, especially with the direction they're heading in."

Taenya remained silent, watching as Gwyn hesitated at the carriage steps, her fingers curling before she finally pulled away and gave Lady Roslyn one last wave. The Tiloral heiress stepped inside, disappearing from view, and Gwyn turned back toward them with a sad, fleeting smile.

She's having to grow up so quickly.

CHAPTER SEVENTEEN

SHADOWS OF RETRIBUTION

Mages who delved into the art of assassination quickly realized how uniquely suited their magic was for the task. For years, countermeasures lagged behind their craft, leaving their targets defenseless against illusions, mindweaving, and the veil of shadows.

When no such protections were in place, assassins wielding these magics operated with impunity—silent phantoms who struck unseen and left only death in their wake. At first, the only reliable defense was to employ such mages of one's own, turning the shadows against themselves in an endless dance of unseen warfare.

The Hidden War: Espionage and Assassination
in the Age of Mana, 121 SA

Sabina stood in the dimly lit chamber of the manor, the flickering candlelight casting long shadows along the walls. Across from her, Ser Siveril adjusted the fit of his gloves, his expression unreadable, while Ser Theran leaned back against the heavy wooden desk, arms crossed over his chest.

"Taenya is with the princess?" Sabina asked, though she already knew the answer.

Siveril gave a curt nod. "She is. I made sure of it. Gwyn cannot know about this—now or ever."

Sabina exhaled slowly, her magic brushing outward, a habitual check for any uninvited ears. The only presences in the room were those she expected. Siveril's emotions were of particular interest to her.

<<Resolve, Cold Certainty>>

She could appreciate a pragmatic approach.

Theran, though, frowned slightly. "It *will* be a clean job?"

Sabina met his gaze evenly. "Of course."

There was no hesitation. No uncertainty. House Angwin had crossed the line when they had orchestrated the attack on Gwyn. The house had been hit hard. Nineteen dead. And the blood of their people demanded justice, and justice would be delivered tonight.

"Gwyn must be kept away from this," Siveril reiterated, his voice lower now. "She is young. Even with everything she's been through, she still holds to . . . a certain idealism. It is necessary to protect that while we can."

Sabina tilted her head. "She is not a fool. She will know, eventually."

"Eventually," Theran agreed. "But not now. Not while she is still holding on to something better than this."

Sabina considered that for a moment. *Better than this.* The thought was almost foreign to her now. A child's hope. A noble's luxury. But not hers. Not anymore.

She adjusted the gloves on her fingers, flexing them once before tucking them beneath the sleeves of her darkened coat. "I'll be gone before the third bell. Moreno and Wentham will not see the morning."

Theran nodded. "Taenya will cover for you if needed."

Sabina smirked faintly. "I won't need it. My team will wait in reserve." She turned, fading into the shadows at the edge of the room, her magic twisting the light around her, bending perception until she was nothing more than a passing whisper of air.

Justice would come. And it would wear the veil of the unseen.

Sabina moved like a whisper through the city's shadowed streets, her steps measured, her senses stretched outward. The Angwin manor lay nestled within one of Strathmore's more affluent districts, where wealth insulated its residents from the desperation that clung to the lower quarters like a sickness. Here, the roads were paved with smooth stone, oil lanterns hanging from their posts flickered with their carefully maintained flame, and guards patrolled in measured intervals—not with the weary eyes of overworked soldiers but with the arrogant precision of those who had little to fear.

She let the veil of her magic settle over her as she moved, bending perception, ensuring that any casual glance passed over her without recognition. She wasn't invisible, not exactly—but she was *unnoticed*, an absence rather than a presence. The fewer minds she had to tamper with tonight, the better.

Ahead, in the shadowed alcove of a recessed garden, her team of four waited. Nasha was the first to rise at her approach, straightening from where she had been leaning against the stone. The telv woman was the only surviving member of the original group of Wynvers, the small unit of specialists assigned to her who had defended House Reinhart during the attack.

Nasha's keen hazel eyes flickered over Sabina, noting her arrival with the quiet, professional acknowledgment of a soldier who had seen too much and survived more than she should have.

She was clad in dark leathers reinforced with quieting layers of cloth, her pale skin barely visible under the hood drawn over her short, practical braids. Her sharp, angular features were partially hidden by the hood of her cloak, but Sabina caught the glint of steel at her hip and the steady intensity in her eyes.

"Ser," Nasha murmured, dipping her head in quiet acknowledgment. The others followed suit, their postures tense but prepared.

Those three were less familiar to Sabina, as they were new to the house and her team, but she knew their capabilities. A compact high elf man with a dagger resting loosely against his thigh—Renic, a scout and infiltration expert. Beside him, a broad-shouldered telv woman named Marta, who specialized in brute force when subtlety failed. The last was a raithe woman, Dahlia, a capable duelist who could wield both steel and mana in equal measure.

All had the ability to use magic similar to her own, though not nearly as well or as extensively. That would come in time.

Sabina wasted no time. "Update me."

Nasha stepped forward, her voice low but clear. "We've confirmed both targets are inside. We confirmed Moreno's arrival at dusk, and Wentham has not left since morning. Ser Wentham remains in the manor proper—he rarely strays far from the main hall. Ser Moreno is more active, moving between the guard house and the main building throughout the evening. Security is tight—more than we anticipated. They're expecting retaliation."

Sabina barely resisted the urge to smirk. *Good. They should be afraid.* "How many?" she asked.

"A dozen armed guards between the outer perimeter and the manor itself," Nasha continued. "Patrols rotate in pairs. The grounds are well lit, and they've stationed a few archers on the balconies. They also have dogs. While my senses aren't as fine-tuned as yours, I don't believe I sensed anyone with magic."

Sabina's lip curled slightly. "Anything unusual?"

"A small group of paladins," Nasha said. "We haven't identified them yet, but they aren't interfering, just watching. They've positioned themselves in an empty shop up this street, maybe a hundred, one-fifty meters down. No signs they're making any moves against House Angwin directly, but they're keeping an eye on the estate."

Sabina's magic reached outward, tasting the air for the presence of these interlopers. She could *just* feel them in the noise of all the other people in the area. The paladins were there—faint echoes of mana, static and restrained.

She exhaled slowly. "They won't know we were ever here."

The others exchanged glances. It wasn't bravado. It was a simple fact. Sabina's magic would see to that.

She turned back to Nasha. "Entry points? Still the same as planned?"

"The west side has a gap in patrol coverage, but it's minor," the telv woman replied. "There's a servant's entrance that's used sparingly. You could force it, but you'd risk setting off an alarm. Best approach would be the terrace. It's partially obscured, no direct sightlines from the front, and it leads into the guest wing. Both targets will pass through that area eventually unless they head to their rooms for an early night. They haven't in the three days we've been watching."

Sabina nodded, considering. "Then I'll take the terrace. Silent, quick. No unnecessary engagements. Only move in if you hear signs of alarm."

Renic cleared his throat. "And if we're spotted before?"

Sabina turned her gaze on him, her dark eyes unreadable. "You won't be. There's no reason any of you should be seen, let alone confronted."

Renic hesitated, then nodded.

Sabina gestured to the alley's entrance. "Alright. Stay alert. If something *does* go wrong, I'll make enough noise so that you at least know about it. Now, move to your assigned locations."

The others dispersed, melting into the night, leaving only Nasha at her side. The telv lingered for a beat longer, her voice quieter now.

"Ser Wentham," she said. "He's a coward. He'll run."

Sabina's expression didn't change. "If he somehow is alerted to my presence and runs, do *not* let him get away."

Nasha studied her, then nodded once. And then she was gone, leaving Sabina alone with the night. She took one last breath before slipping into the darkness.

She moved through the shadows like a wraith, her presence concealed beneath layers of illusion and silence. The manor loomed ahead, its pale stone walls illuminated by the glow of lanterns and the soft shimmer of moonlight. Wealth and power clung to the air here, thick and arrogant, but beneath it all lay the subtle undercurrent of fear. *Good.*

She weaved through the outer perimeter, keeping low as she traced the path toward the west side of the manor. The terrace was her goal. A more direct entrance might have been quicker, but it would have risked detection. The terrace, with its half-obscured vantage point and limited line of sight, was a safer option.

Closing her eyes, she reached inward, letting her mana flow through her mind and body. Then, with careful precision, she wove a spell of [**Alter Perception**], wrapping it around herself like a cloak.

The world around her warped, not visibly but in the way she existed within it. To any onlookers, she was nothing—an absence in space, a moment the mind refused to process and therefore instantly forgot. She was not unseen but unnoticed. If someone looked directly at her, their mind would simply insist she wasn't important enough to acknowledge. A shadow in the night. A whisper in the wind.

Satisfied, she moved. Crossing the open space toward the manor, she stepped lightly, avoiding the crunch of gravel and shifting her weight with practiced precision. She passed within feet of one of the patrolling guards, his gaze sweeping right over her without hesitation. He didn't pause. Didn't even blink in her direction.

Sabina smirked. Nearing the outer wall, she slowed. A guard stood at his post, his back straight but his mind sluggish with boredom. He wasn't expecting an attack—just waiting out his shift, oblivious to the danger that had already arrived.

Sabina reached out with her magic, brushing against the surface of his thoughts, feeling his exhaustion, his distracted musings about a warm bed and a waiting lover.

Perfect. She cast a spell and whispered into his mind, her voice slipping past his defenses like silk. **[Suggest]**—*Your patrol route changed. You should check the southern perimeter.*

The suggestion took hold, latching onto the quietest part of his thoughts, reshaping his perception just enough that he didn't question it. He stiffened slightly, then exhaled and turned, his boots crunching softly as he strode away toward the southern wall.

Sabina watched him go, waiting until the sound of his steps faded before she moved. With the guard gone, she pressed against the cool stone of the manor's wall, glancing upward. The terrace was two stories above—reachable, but not without effort. There, a lone archer stood, scanning the grounds with casual disinterest. His bow rested against the terrace railing, his eyes tracking the shifting patrols below.

It was an easy climb, but she couldn't risk him sounding an alarm.

She reached out again, her magic slipping past the layers of his awareness. He was tired—long hours of standing watch, boredom creeping into his thoughts, the warmth of a well-kept manor calling to him. She pushed. **[Sleep]**.

The archer's breathing slowed. His eyelids fluttered, his body swaying slightly. A moment later, he slumped against the railing, sliding down until he sat with his head tilted forward in a deep, unnatural slumber.

Sabina wasted no time. She gathered herself, channeling mana into her limbs, reinforcing her strength as she leapt. Her fingers caught the edge of a carved window ledge. After a quick check of her surroundings, she pulled herself up in fluid, practiced motions, finding footholds where there were none and reaching the terrace in a matter of moments.

At the top, she quietly swung over the railing, landing in a crouch beside the sleeping archer. She checked him briefly—his pulse was steady, his breathing even. He wouldn't wake anytime soon.

With the terrace secured, she turned toward the locked doors leading inside, letting her senses stretch outward.

It was time to begin. The terrace doors were locked, but that was expected. More importantly, she could feel the faint presence of someone in the adjacent room. A single guard, pacing slowly, his thoughts sluggish but alert enough that she couldn't risk unnecessary noise.

Sabina exhaled, focusing. She reached into the man's mind, careful not to push too deep, and used **[Calm Emotions]**. His nervous tension dissipated, his shoulders slackening, his mind settling into a dull sense of ease. He was no longer on edge, no longer actively looking for threats.

Sabina allowed herself the ghost of a smirk. She reached for the lock, her fingers tracing the mechanism before retrieving her lockpicking kit and slipping the tools into the keyhole. With a bit of effort, the tumblers shifted, clicking softly, and the door eased open with barely a sound. She slipped inside, merging with the dimly lit room beyond.

The guard in the office sat down stiffly in a chair as she moved in, her [**Alter Perception**] spell keeping her hidden and the door "closed" to any who would look at it. She stood just inside the doorway, watching as the [**Calm Emotions**] sapped the man's natural vigilance. This man, unlike the archer, would be noticed much sooner, so if anyone woke him, his current state needed to hold up stronger to questioning.

She stepped in closer, her voice slipping into his mind like a lullaby. [**Suggest**]—*You're tired. You've been on shift for far too long. You should rest.*

The man blinked slowly, his mind sluggishly accepting the thought as his own. His shoulder slumped further, his fingers twitching as his body betrayed his exhaustion.

Sabina pushed deeper. *You've done your duty. No one would blame you for resting just a little while.* The worlds settled into the quiet corners of his mind, reinforcing what he already wanted to believe. She reached into his thoughts, sifting through the recent hours, finding the threads of memory tied to his exhaustion. With careful precision, she twisted them with [**Alter Memories**] to nudge reality just enough that it wouldn't unravel.

He *remembered* that his shift had run longer than scheduled. That the captain had told him to stay until morning. That it was perfectly fine for him to close his eyes for just a little while. A slow exhale escaped his lips, his head bobbing slightly as the weight of sleep threatened to take him. She nudged him off of the precipice with [**Sleep**]. His body relaxed completely, his breathing deepening as his mind succumbed to the spell like the archer outside. His head lolled to the side, his arms slack at his sides.

With careful precision, she took hold of him, shifting his body to a more natural position in the chair. He would look as if he had simply dozed off during a long night, nothing out of the ordinary—sleeping on duty withstanding. Even if someone checked on him, they would see only a man worn down by fatigue and discipline him as such, not suspect that someone had subdued him.

First, Moreno.

Sabina kept hidden as she felt out for any patrols or servants walking around. Seeing that the coast was clear, she moved out into the hallway with careful, silent steps against the marble floors. She followed the layout of the manor she had memorized. Moreno was a creature of habit—he had certain places he lingered in the evenings: the kitchens, a study, a private lounge, and lastly, a sitting room where he conducted business even at late hours.

She reached the corridor leading to the sitting room and slowed. Voices. Sabina pressed herself into the shadows just beyond the doorway, allowing the sounds to filter through her heightened awareness.

"I swear it, Ser! I didn't steal anything!" A woman's voice, her emotions <<*Frantic, Desperate*>> to Sabina's senses. The woman was telling the truth.

[**Detect Emotions**] reflected the minds of four people within the room. Based on their thoughts, it was Moreno, two guards, and a maid. One guard was focused on the conversation; the other was filled with worry about other, more personal matters.

"You were seen near the storeroom," the more attentive guard said. "It's not the first time someone's caught you lurking where you don't belong."

"I was only there because the steward sent me to clean—"

"Enough." Ser Moreno cut through the exchange, cool and unimpressed. "Your excuses bore me, girl. I could have you flogged for thievery . . . or I could send you to the Angwin mines. Maybe that would loosen your tongue."

Sabina barely resisted the urge to smirk. *Not tonight, you won't.* She reached into the man's mind, slipping past the edges of his thoughts like water seeping into stone. He was already convinced of the woman's guilt. That would not do.

[**Suggest**]—*Your time isn't worth a petty servant's alleged crime. Let her go.*

There was a beat of silence. Moreno exhaled through his nose. "Fine. You will leave with a warning."

The room stilled, the maid sucking in a breath of disbelief. She felt the uncertainty in the guards' thoughts.

"If I find out you lied," Moreno continued, "the punishment will be severe. Get out of my sight."

The woman didn't hesitate. She curtsied stiffly and all but ran from the room. Sabina shifted subtly to the side as she passed, ensuring she remained unseen.

A moment later, the guard beside Moreno cleared his throat. "Ser, if I may . . . that was unusually lenient of you."

Moreno frowned slightly, rubbing at his temple. "Perhaps. I—" He blinked. "No, you're right, Brant. I wouldn't have done that normally . . ." His mind was catching up to the foreign thought, realizing it didn't quite belong.

Sabina moved before he could question it further. She stepped into the room, her magic weaving into the perception of all three men within. They saw her. But not as herself. To their eyes, she was nothing more than another maid, unassuming and harmless, carrying herself with the demure posture expected of a servant.

Moreno's eyes barely flicked toward her. "What is it?" he asked, irritation still tinging his voice.

Sabina dipped her head slightly. "Apologies, ser. A man claiming to be a creditor is at the gate, asking for Guardsman Brant. He apologizes for the late hour."

The named guard, standing to Moreno's right, straightened immediately. Moreno's brow furrowed, His emotions turned from irritation to anger. That was all the opening Sabina needed. While their focus shifted away, she moved.

[**Alter Perception**] slipped into their thoughts. To them, she remained standing where she was, unmoving as she awaited a response. But in reality, she had already taken silent steps forward as she slid her daggers free from their sheaths with practiced ease.

She was behind the first guard before he even had a chance to breathe in confusion. The steel kissed his throat before he could make a sound. She pressed in, her dagger slicing deep, parting skin and arteries in a single motion. A rush of hot blood spilled out as she wrenched the blade free.

Her [**Alter Perception**] became increasingly complex as she combined it with [**Calm Emotions**] and cast the spell at Moreno.

The second guard turned, eyes widening in alarm. Her magic twisted around him, [**Conjure Hallucinations**] forcing his vision to warp as his mind filled with something other than what was real. He stumbled backward, his breath hitching in panic as he saw an attacker that did not exist, an illusion so vivid his body reacted as if it were real. He swung his fist at empty air; any shout he would have made was choked by confusion.

Sabina used the moment to drive her dagger between his ribs. He let out a ragged gasp, his eyes searching hers for a brief moment as reality reverted just before the strength left his body and his form crumpled to the floor.

Silence settled. Only Moreno remained. Still unaware.

Sabina released the hold on her illusions, allowing herself to step into his reality fully. His breath hitched as he realized something was wrong—his men were down. He turned, hand reaching for the blade at his side.

Sabina's magic lashed out. The panic drained from his face in an instant. The tension in his limbs loosened, his body betraying him as the impulse to fight fled. He *knew* something was wrong as <<*Panic*>> overcame him, but his mind refused to react as it should.

Sabina took a step forward, holding his gaze as she reached into the depths of his consciousness, seizing control of his will.

He stiffened. His mouth opened, but no words came. No screams. No protests. Only her voice. Inside his mind. *House Reinhart sends its regards.* His eyes went wide.

She plunged the dagger into his chest, piercing his heart with a practiced, deliberate twist. He convulsed once, his breath escaping in a final, shuddering exhale. She held on to him as he sank to his knees, then carefully lowered him to the floor, ensuring the death was quiet. Controlled. Effortless. She exhaled, wiping her blade clean against the dead man's tunic before rising to her feet.

One down. One more to go. Before she left the room, she checked the door and found a welcome surprise. There was a key in the lock, one that could be used on both sides of the door. She used it to lock the room behind her as she exited, hopefully ensuring no one would find the bodies until she was long gone.

Sabina slipped deeper into the manor, her steps silent as she navigated corridors toward Ser Wentham's quarters. Her presence remained veiled, her magic wrapping around her like a second skin. The manor was alive with quiet sounds—the distant clatter of dishes being cleaned, the murmured voices of servants, the occasional shuffle of boots on the marble floors.

It didn't take long to find Wentham's room. The door was marked by its subtle embellishments, an understated but clear indication of his rank within the household. A guard stood just outside. As Sabina approached, a servant rounded the corner, walking directly toward her.

Sabina didn't hesitate. The moment before the man would have noticed her, Sabina *wasn't there*. The servant's eyes slid past her, unfocused, never registering the shape in the dim corridor. To the man, the hallway was empty. He passed by without slowing, completely unaware of the shadow that had brushed past him. The guard, still standing at ease outside of the room, saw nothing.

A moment later, Sabina was inside Wentham's quarters. The entry room was warm, the air thick with the scent of wax and parchment. A small desk sat against the far wall, papers stacked neatly, an inkpot and quill beside them. A small bookshelf stood sentinel next to it, filled with tomes that would not be read by their owner again.

In the bedchamber, a chest sat at the foot of the bed, clothing draped over its edges. And there was Wentham himself, moving through the last steps of his nightly routine. He stood before a mirror, undoing the buttons of his vest with slow, methodical fingers. His movements were tired, his expression drawn. He wasn't expecting anything except the promise of a night's rest. He blew out the flame in the bedside lamp. Darkness settled into the room.

Sabina waited with the patience of a predator. She remained perfectly still, watching as Wentham pulled back the covers and slid beneath them, exhaling heavily. His body sank into the mattress, his breathing deep and slow.

She waited longer still, counting the seconds, listening. The steady rhythm of his breath as it eventually slowed, his muscles easing.

Now. Crossing the room in absolute silence, she approached the bed, her magic reaching forward, sinking into his mind.

Wentham twitched slightly as she slipped past the first layer of his thoughts. Surface details were easy—his lingering exhaustion, irritation at the guard rotations, a fleeting thought about an overdue letter. She pushed deeper.

Who gave the order to attack House Reinhart?

His mind supplied the answer with ease. *Lord Angwin.*

His memories were laid out before her. Wentham had been given the directive before Angwin left the city. The assault on House Reinhart had not been a rogue action by subordinates—it had been planned, deliberate.

And Wentham had ensured it would succeed. He had paid off the guard lieutenant overseeing the city watch in that district, ensuring that any call for aid from the Reinhart manor would be delayed. The bribe had been substantial and effective. By the time any response could have arrived, it would have been too late.

Moreno had been the one to handle the logistics—the men, the mercenaries, the precise execution. But Wentham had ensured that when it happened, there would be no repercussions from the city officials. Unless the duke himself intervened, that is.

And they had held enough forces in reserve in case House Reinhart was capable of an attempt at immediate retaliation. Forces that had not even the slightest ability to detect, let alone stop Sabina. The knowledge settled into Sabina's mind like cold steel. All the details. Names. Numbers. She had it all.

The whole thing, despite having failed—in no small part due to magic they could not have foreseen—had been carefully orchestrated. Calculated.

Sabina did not speak. She did not give him the opportunity to wake or struggle. She simply pressed deeper into his mind, locking him in place as her dagger slid from its sheath.

His breath hitched for the barest second, his body twitching against the unseen force holding him still. His eyes fluttered beneath closed lids, his mouth barely parting. He couldn't move. Couldn't cry out. The blade found its mark. Wentham shuddered, his hands managing to clench the sheets, but no sound escaped him.

Slow. Silent. She kept his mind locked as he died so his final moments were spent in mute, helpless stillness. When the last breath left him, she withdrew the blade, grabbed a handkerchief from the bedside table, and wiped it clean. She stepped back.

The job was done. Sabina exhaled slowly, centering herself. She'd done this for Gwyn, to ensure her safety. Without another glance, she turned and retraced her steps, slipping through the manor undetected.

By the time she reached the border of the estate, her team was already positioned in the shadows where she had left them. Nasha met her gaze, the silent question in her eyes. Sabina gave a single nod. Without a word, they melted into the city streets, disappearing into the night.

House Reinhart had sent its message: It did not forgive. And it never forgot.

CHAPTER EIGHTEEN

SAYING FAREWELL

And remember, there will be those in the capital who seek to use their higher status as a snub against you. Or against the princess for having such *low-status* ladies-in-waiting. You are to be the *voice and hand* of royalty.

"The princess has no siblings, which means she is a *crown princess*, even if her nation does not formally use such titles for an heir. Do not forget that. When the crown prince inevitably calls to meet her, your liege will stand as his equal in status, if not in influence. Additionally—"

Nora sighed internally and tuned out her mother's latest lecture. It wasn't anything she hadn't heard before. She knew her mother meant well, but it was *so* tedious to be reminded of duties she had trained for her entire life. How many times could someone reiterate the same expectations?

"... I *still* cannot believe that Her Highness has not chosen you as her principal lady-in-waiting yet. I have spoken to Ser Siveril and expressed my—"

"Mother," Nora cut in, keeping her tone measured. "It is no concern. Gwyn—*Princess* Gwyneth—simply does not ascribe to such a practice. If ever there is a need, I suspect she will do so. But as of now, we do not have enough tasks as it is. Her Highness is still young. As is Lady Lorrena."

Her mother narrowed her eyes slightly. "How well is Lady Lorrena performing? Is she *still* struggling with what is required of her to attend the Royal Academy with Her Highness?"

Nora grimaced. Lorrena *was* struggling. But everyone had taken time to help her. The girl needed to attend the Academy with Her Highness—she was meant to be her retainer there.

The alternative? Finding a retainer among the students already attending. And no one had to tell Nora how *poorly* that would reflect on House Reinhart.

"She is a most *studious* young lady," she replied diplomatically.

Her mother pursed her lips. "I will send word ahead to the capital. While we do not hold much influence there, I *do* have a few contacts we can lean on. Perhaps—"

"Mother. *Please*." Nora exhaled. "We will handle it. Ser Siveril and Taenya have everything well in hand."

Her mother sighed but, for once, relented. "Very well." A pause. Then, far too casually, she added, "Ah, Aleanora, it seems to have slipped my mind, but I was speaking to Ser Siveril, and he mentioned that you were working to attend the Academy yourself in two years, when you turn sixteen."

Nora stiffened.

"I simply do not recall us discussing that previously," her mother mused, her tone far too casual to be *truly* casual.

Nora barely resisted the urge to sigh. *Of course.*

"Will Lady Ilyana be attending this upcoming year?"

Aleanora Olacyne groaned internally. *I cannot wait until we leave.*

The Trenlore family was made up of nine children—three girls and six boys. Even now, Ilyana Trenlore sat in her customary seat, far down the long dining table from her mother and father, as though distance alone determined importance.

She had come for one final dinner, to tell everyone goodbye before departing for the capital. Instead, as the youngest daughter and the third-youngest overall, she was invisible. Her two younger siblings, the twins, were wrapped up in their own conversation, speaking with rapid-fire excitement that excluded anyone else from participating.

Her next eldest brother, a quiet loner who spent more time painting tiny statues of knights and soldiers than interacting with people, simply sat in his chair, picking at his food with disinterest.

Ilyana had been *cursed* with this family. *Being chosen to join Gwyn was the best day of my life*, she thought. She drummed her fingers idly against her leg, her gaze flicking between the fading sunlight streaming through the windows and the polished silverware. She felt *bored*.

She wanted to go back to *her* house—to House Reinhart—where there were people who appreciated her. She could be working on her studies, reading, *doing something useful*. Even spending time with . . . *Nora*.

In House Reinhart, she had the freedom to indulge in her own pursuits without feeling like a ghost at the dinner table. If she wanted privacy, she could find it, without anyone begrudging her for wanting to be alone.

Here? Here she was *stuck* listening to— She glanced up the table, forcing herself to catch the current topic of conversation.

". . . Laura, we *must* discuss the entertainment for your wedding feast!" one of her older brothers was saying, his tone painfully affected. "I saw the most *adorable* fool the other day—truly delightful. I believe I could arrange an introduction."

"Oh? That sounds *wonderful*." Laura, Ilyana's eldest sister, giggled behind her hand. "I have a troupe arriving overmorrow to perform for me. Perhaps your fool could join them for an audition?"

Ilyana barely concealed a snort. Laura was twenty-two and only just now engaged. *Bit of an embarrassment, really.*

Their mother tutted, expression prim as ever. "Laura, you know I am handling everything for your wedding. Entertainment is already arranged."

Probably because you can't afford anything else, Ilyana thought, swallowing the words before they could slip free.

It was always the same. Her siblings spoke as though they were high nobles with vast estates and powerful demesnes. In reality, House Trenlore was a *small* barony, little more than a footnote in the region's hierarchy. Their lands consisted of a single town that was barely more than a village, two actual villages, and a hamlet. Hardly the grand holdings her family pretended to rule.

She let their conversation wash over her, tuning out the inane posturing, the self-important tones, the desperate grasp at importance.

Finally, she'd had enough. She looked down the table at her parents. They were deep in conversation, neither of them sparing her so much as a glance. They hadn't spoken to her once. That decided it. She would leave now. Unfortunately, even *leaving* this family required an unnecessary amount of protocol.

Ilyana lifted a hand, and a servant stepped forward immediately, bowing slightly. "My lady?"

She kept her expression neutral, controlled. "Could you please convey my wishes to the lord and lady?"

The man nodded, waiting for her instruction. "Of course, my lady. What would you like me to pass along?"

Ilyana smoothed a nonexistent wrinkle in her gown. "I believe it is time for me to depart. I must retire for the night. I have a long day of travel ahead of me tomorrow."

The servant tilted his head slightly, a flicker of confusion crossing his face. "May I tell them where you are going, my lady?"

Ilyana froze.

She *must* have misunderstood.

Slowly, controlling her tone, she asked, "Could you repeat yourself?"

The servant's posture stiffened as he seemed to realize his mistake, his thoughts scrambling for correction.

"I . . . I will tell them, milady," he amended quickly, lowering his gaze.

Ilyana exhaled, turning her head away. She watched as the servant strode down to her parents, bowing deeply before murmuring her message. Her mother barely looked up from her conversation with her father, waving a dismissive hand. The exchange lasted only seconds before the servant turned and hurried back toward her.

Ilyana sat a bit straighter, expecting her parents to call upon her. To acknowledge her. Instead, the servant stopped before her and bowed. "Lord and Lady Trenlore express their desire for you to represent House Trenlore well and will see you soon, as they eagerly await a dinner with your new liege. They suggest next week would be an appropriate time for your lady to attend the manor for a repast."

Ilyana gritted her teeth, instantly seething. They had *forgotten*. She clenched her hands beneath the table as heat surged through her chest.

"It is *Her Highness*," she corrected, her voice like frost on steel. "You will use her proper title or you will *not* speak in my presence again. Is that understood?"

The servant paled, eyes widening in terror at the ice in her tone. He scrambled back, muttering apologies, bowing hastily as he all but fled.

Ilyana didn't spare him another thought. She was already rising from her seat, her fury propelling her forward as she strode toward the head of the table. The chatter in the dining hall died instantly, her siblings falling silent at the sudden, unmistakable rage in her steps.

For once, she *relished* the quiet. She came to a halt near the head of the table, just behind her oldest sibling and brother, Ewan. If glares could cause harm, her parents would have instantly frozen as solid as Gwyn's ice magic.

"You *forgot*?" she hissed.

Her father's face turned a deep shade of red, anger flashing in his eyes at her disregard for the house etiquette. *Relena, damn his etiquette.*

"Ilyana," her mother chided gently, a forced smile on her lips. "What has you so *out of sorts*?"

Ilyana turned her glare on the woman. "*Out of sorts*?" she repeated, her voice low and venomous. "Did you *forget* I am a lady-in-waiting to a *princess*? Or are you just *daft*?"

Her father started to rise from his chair. "Now, you—"

"No, *my lord*," she cut in sharply, the title dripping with scorn. "You *knew* I was coming to dinner because I leave for the capital tomorrow. I will not return for *years*. But now?" She let her lips curl into something that wasn't quite a smile. "I *may* not return at all. And as a reminder, *my lord*, you pledged this house's fealty to my liege, and *I* have her ear."

The silence that followed was *delicious*.

"You're *leaving*?" her oldest sister, Laura, asked, finally looking up from her plate.

Ilyana stared at her siblings in disbelief. "Did anyone even *realize* I was *gone*?" she demanded, voice rising. "I am going to attend the *Royal Academy*! I am the *first* in this family to do so, and ALL OF YOU JUST *FORGOT*?"

She felt tears start to form. Her hands shook with the force of her fury, but she refused to let her emotions show beyond that. She would *not* let them see her crack.

"You forget your place, daughter," her father snapped. "How *dare* you speak to your family in this way? You will return to your room, and we will determine your punishment in due time."

Ilyana let out a short, sharp laugh. "Did you simply throw me away at the first house you could in an attempt to gain influence without regard to your duty?" She looked at her mother. "Did you, Mother?"

Her mother let out an exasperated sigh. "Ilyana, you are speaking nonsense. Of course not. You are being silly. Now, *sit down*. You are embarrassing yourself. Our house simply used its good name to assist a small house of no name."

Ilyana's lip curled. "This house is an embarrassment."

Her father slammed his fist against the table. "*Enough!* You will leave this instant, or I will have you *removed*."

"Again, are you *daft*, Father?" she asked, her voice deceptively calm. "I *am* leaving. That is the entire *point* of why I am standing here." Ilyana tilted her head, mockingly thoughtful. "Are you going to dictate my *breathing* as well?" Her voice started to waver with her racing heart. Her confidence, however, soared.

Her father's face darkened further. Veins stood out in his temples as he turned to order the servants to escort her away.

And *that*—that was what finally sent her over the edge. She was being *ignored*. *Again*. Her vision whitened at the edges. She could feel her magic thrumming at the surface of her skin. She barely registered the rush of energy before she snapped.

A pulse of power surged through her as her fist came down on the dining table in a **[Fierce Strike]**. The solid wood cracked from end to end, the force of the blow shattering a leg completely. With a thunderous crash, the heirloom table—a relic of House Trenlore for generations—collapsed onto its broken corner, splintering as eleven full-place settings shattered against the stone floor.

Gasps filled the air. The stunned silence that followed sent a thrill through her. Ilyana slowly straightened, fixing her father with a cold, impassive stare. "You will hear from House Reinhart on your *obligations* to your liege, *Lord Trenlore*," she said smoothly.

The man dared to scoff. "You are no longer a daughter of mine," he spat. "You will be *nothing* without us."

Ilyana blinked. And then she *laughed*—a full, amused, mocking laugh, as if he had just told her the most ridiculous joke in the world. Without another word, she turned. She ignored the gasps, the clamoring of her siblings as they *finally* sought her attention. She didn't even spare them a glance. She moved toward the manor entrance with a grace she had earned, her steps slow and deliberate.

She noticed the way the servants shrank back, the way the guards—her father's *own men*—moved aside, clearing her path. More than one had alarm in their eyes.

She smirked. *They are nothing compared to House Reinhart's guards. Now they are true warriors.*

As Ilyana stepped onto the path leading away from House Trenlore, toward the carriage waiting for her, she inhaled deeply. For the first time in her life, she *truly* felt free. She smiled, feeling as if she could glide and dance all the way to her *real* home.

"Goodbye, Papa!" Lorrena called out as she readied herself to leave home again—this time, for a long while.

Her father laughed warmly as he and her sisters approached from behind. "Oh, my silly Lorrena, this is not goodbye. We will visit you in the capital! We are *so* proud of you for all of your hard work, and you bring honor to our house by attending the Royal Academy."

Lorrena flushed at the unexpected praise, her heart swelling and twisting at once. She loved her time with Princess Gwyn, but she would miss her family more than anything.

She rushed forward one last time and wrapped her arms around her father in a tight embrace. He chuckled as he held her close before she turned and threw herself at her sisters, squeezing them just as fiercely.

Her eldest sister bent down and whispered into her ear, "Mother would be so proud, Lore."

The words struck something deep inside her. She couldn't help it. The tears came. She missed her mother *so much*, and she knew she would miss her family just as terribly once she was gone.

"I love you all *so* much!" she choked out.

Her father and sisters laughed softly, though she could hear the emotion in their voices.

"We love you too, little Lore," her father said, his large, warm hand resting on her shoulder. "Remember, you serve a princess now. Every action you take reflects upon our family. Continue to make us proud, my daughter."

Lorrena trembled. The weight of expectation pressed down upon her, as it always did. Her family was everything; she would not disappoint them. She had worked so hard in her studies. She had to pass the Academy exams. She *would* pass them. Mister Branigan had said it was exceedingly rare for a girl from a small baronial family to gain entrance. But she had to do it. She needed to be at Princess Gwyn's side. Ilyana would be studying at the other part of the Royal Academy, far from them most of the time, so Lorrena was the only one who could remain beside Her Highness. And Princess Gwyn would need her.

Swallowing her emotions, Lorrena stepped away and turned toward the waiting carriage, a House Reinhart guard already stationed beside it. She blinked quickly, forcing away the last of her tears before they could fall.

She would become something worthy. She would not disappoint them. *Just like Mama would have wanted.*

Gwyn was busy writing a letter. For a long time, she had simply gone with the flow, trusting those around her to help determine the best way forward. And they *had* done well. Every person in her house had continually proved how lucky she was to have such incredible people willing to stand by her. But it was time she did something to give back.

Back when she had been thrust into the center of attention at the duke's court—when Count Telford had forced that whole *ordeal*—she had learned something valuable. Even a duke would pay attention to her if he felt obligated. It helped that the duke seemed like a genuinely kind man, especially when she had seen how he interacted with Roslyn. She didn't want to take advantage of that, but there came a time when, in her mother's words, you had to *pony up or shut up.*

Her house had been attacked. Her people had been *killed*. And it had happened *in the duke's city*. In a way that was far too blatant.

So, Gwyn wrote a letter. It wouldn't fix all of the wrongs. But it could help one. And maybe, in time, it would help her, too.

A knock at the door pulled her from her thoughts. "Come in," she called, setting down her quill.

Sabina hadn't been avoiding her, per se, but it was clear the attack had affected the woman. It was something she'd noticed even more after the funeral. Gwyn may have forced her to go too far.

The door opened, revealing one of Sabina's guards, a telv woman, one of the new ones to join her knight's personal group.

"Your Highness, Keston requests an audience," the guard said formally.

Gwyn closed her eyes briefly. The attack. The lifeless stares of her people as they lay in the halls, unmoving. The weight of it all still haunted her dreams. She pushed the thoughts aside. When she opened her eyes, she smiled. "Keston never needs to request an audience," she said lightly. "Tell him to come on in."

The high elf entered, but Gwyn could tell immediately that something was off. He hesitated, lingering near the door. The guard exited and closed the door behind her.

Gwyn tilted her head. "Keston, what's wrong?"

He shifted uncomfortably, weight moving from foot to foot. "Your Highness—"

"*Gwyn*," she corrected instantly.

Keston sighed, rubbing the bridge of his nose. "I'm *trying* to be formal here, Gwyn."

She rolled her eyes and gestured to the chair opposite her. "Sit. We don't *do* formal. You're my *friend*."

His shoulders dropped slightly, and he slumped into the chair. "Fine," he muttered. Then, with an almost sheepish grin, he added, "I have a request. Oh—and I *may* have volunteered to be the one to tell you."

Gwyn leaned forward, raising a brow. *This should be interesting.* "Volunteered? That makes it seem like no one wanted to do it."

Keston chuckled. "I didn't mean it that way. I just used it as an excuse to come talk to you." He scratched the back of his neck before adding, "Onas and his daughter are here, but I wanted to request something of you as my liege . . . because I know what he's here for."

That made her curious. "Okay, now I *really* want to know. Spit it out, Keston. What do you want?"

He took a deep breath. "Onas is here to say his farewells, since you're leaving tomorrow," he started, then pointed to the ring on her right index finger. "He's also here because his daughter, Kerala, is heading to Westaren to find the dwarves who made your ring. I would like to go with her."

Gwyn's eyes widened. "*What?* But . . . what about your training? You're going to become a knight. Isn't that what you wanted?"

Keston hesitated. "Yes." Then, more urgently, "And I *still* do!"

His face twisted with conflict as he exhaled heavily. "It's what Raafe would have wanted. But . . . you're leaving, and so much has happened. Did you know that during the attack, I was with Ser Theran, training? That's why we weren't here. I wasn't here to protect you. And luckily, you didn't need me. Your knights have everything well in hand. But I—" He shook his head. "I feel like I should be doing something right now." He clenched his fists, then relaxed them, taking another deep breath.

"You're the liege of the Fenrens as well, but they're sending only their own guards with Kerala. I think it would be beneficial for you to send someone too. And . . ." He met her eyes. "You need someone who knows you to go with her. Because I can search for your mother on the way. If I find her, I can tell her how to find you."

His jaw tensed and he closed his eyes briefly before opening them again. "Then, when I return, I can resume my training. That is, if you still wish for it."

Gwyn didn't hesitate. She stood, walked over, and wrapped her arms around him in a quick hug. She stepped back and caught his eyes.

"Of *course* I still want it, Keston. But are *you* sure this is what you want?"

Keston had been one of the first people she'd met in this world. A lot of time had passed since then, but he had always been there—always been kind to her. He'd wanted to protect her, especially after Raafe died.

She wanted him to be happy. She remembered their early conversations—back when Raafe was still alive. Becoming a knight had been a dream for Keston. A distant star he never thought he could reach. He had found joy in cooking, something that gave him purpose while traveling. It had been a fun thing they had shared together. He had always been happiest when cooking or when protecting her. As if both were a service to the friend he had lost.

Keston gave her a sad smile. "It's what Raafe would have wanted. And for now, that's good enough for me, Gwyn."

She hated that he was still lost. Maybe this trip would help him find his way back. The thought made her sad, but she nodded.

"In that case," she said, "make sure you get a full set of armor—like Taenya's Drakyyds."

Keston, the former merchant guard turned house guard, blinked at her in confusion. "But . . . I'm not one of them."

She grinned. "No, but it'll be easier to add to. Because you'll need to modify it."

He narrowed his eyes. "Modify?"

She smirked. "Yeah. You'll need to add wings to that little lizard they like."

Keston huffed a laugh. "Gwyn, you *do* realize those aren't little at all, right?"

She giggled. "If you saw how big *dragons* are, you'd think they were."

He shook his head, but she saw the tension ease from his shoulders as a genuine smile broke across his face. Then he stood and bowed. "Thank you, Your Highness."

She inclined her head, matching the formality with a nod of her own. "Thank you, Keston. For being my friend. I hope your trip goes well."

"And yours, Gwyn."

She hesitated, just for a moment, making him pause mid-turn. "Actually," she said, lips curving into something mischievous, "I have one last job for you before you leave."

Gwyn looked back one last time at the manor—the place that had been her home for nearly the entire time she'd been in this world. It had sheltered her, protected her, *given* her so much. And now she was leaving it behind.

It would be a long time before she returned to Strathmore. Maybe that was for the best. The memory of Emma's sacrifice was still too fresh. Her handmaiden had saved her. And now she was gone. Just like Raafe. Two people had died so that she could live. It . . . it didn't feel right. Why was *she* still here when they weren't?

All I want to do is find Mom. Why does this sick world have to be like this? Why does everyone close to me keep getting hurt? Gwyn's eyes burned, welling with unshed tears. *Why did I live? Why did they think I was worth it? I'm just . . . me. Who else will die before this is all over?*

She had nightmares every time she closed her eyes—visions of Emma and Raafe dying, again and again. Standing there, taunting her. Telling her that it should have been her.

Gwyn squeezed her eyes shut, forcing her thoughts into silence. She reached for the spell and used her **[Frozen Heart]**. The spiral ended.

She inhaled deeply, then opened her eyes and forced a small smile as she looked up at Sabina. The knight sat astride her horse, watching from above.

Sabina didn't speak, but Gwyn knew she had seen the momentary break in her composure.

She turned back toward the gathered house members standing outside the carriage. Giving them one final glance, she lifted a hand in a slow, measured wave. Then, without another word, she stepped in.

Inside the carriage, the quiet was almost suffocating. Her three ladies-in-waiting sat in silence, their greetings having been short and subdued. Perhaps it was the early morning, or perhaps they, too, were lost in their own thoughts.

Gwyn sat back, observing them closely. She reached out—not physically, but with her mana—letting it sing in a quiet song to the air around them. She could see the mana around them churning. She couldn't sense emotions like Sabina, but she could sort of get an idea based on how someone's mana moved around them.

Aleanora was clearly excited. The girl thrived on adventure, as if setting out into the unknown was all she had ever wanted.

Ilyana was tense, but there was a determination to her. Something had changed about her. There was a fire in her now, barely restrained. Gwyn made a mental note to talk to her more. She did know that Ilyana had spoken with Siveril for a long time the night before. Maybe it had something to do with that.

Lorrena's sadness wafted through her mana in waves. With the way she clenched her fists, there was clearly some resolve there. But her determination felt different from Ilyana's. It wasn't anger that drove her. It was something else entirely.

Gwyn exhaled slowly, pressing her hands against her lap. "Okay," she said at last, voice breaking the stillness. "Let's do this."

The three girls turned toward her. Each gave a nod. Each nod said something different. Gwyn didn't need magic to understand them. She knew one thing.

When she did return to Strathmore . . . Lord Angwin would burn.

Ser Siveril Norric, majordomo of House Reinhart, made his way toward the parlor of Reinhart Manor, where his expected guest awaited.

The household was quieter than usual. The princess, Sers Taenya and Sabina, and the royal entourage had departed that morning just before daybreak. Their absence was felt.

The first frost of winter had set in, and the caravan needed as much daylight as possible to ensure they reached Drakensburg before travel became treacherous. Timing was everything—a few days' delay could turn the journey into a battle against the elements.

It was unfortunate that Lady Roslyn would not be stopping in Drakensburg herself. She had been meant to originally, but machinations from the crown prince had forced the Duke of Tiloral to take precautions. The public itinerary remained unchanged, and officially, nothing had shifted. But Siveril knew the truth: the ducal heiress would not be taking the expected route. Instead, she would be traveling through Dirn Loduhr, the dwarven city nestled deep in the Loduhr Mountains. A city whose relationship with the kingdom surrounding it had long been . . . strained.

Siveril did not know the particulars of whatever deal had been struck to ensure safe passage, but he could imagine that the price of such transit was very high.

He entered the parlor, his gaze sweeping over his visitor. The old man was dressed in his usual attire—rich but restrained, a deliberate display of understated status, woven in the scarlet and gold of House Tiloral.

The two knights flanking him stepped away as Siveril approached, nodding respectfully before making their way out of the room. The unsaid message was clear. Siveril was favored. Trusted explicitly. He dipped into a perfectly measured bow.

"Your Grace, I did not expect you to come by today."

The Duke of Tiloral smiled as he stood. "You did not expect me to visit *ever*, Siveril," he remarked, a smirk tugging at the corners of his mouth. "Alas, circumstances—and a certain letter—require it."

Siveril did not raise an eyebrow as his princess so often loved to do, but if it were anyone else standing before him, he might have.

"A letter, Your Grace?" he asked evenly.

The duke chuckled. "We are alone, Siveril. You have earned my respect enough to know what that means."

Siveril exhaled, propriety and decades of ingrained deference warring against the duke's casual expectation. Still, he would oblige.

"Of course, Dasron. What business brings you here?"

The duke's eyes crinkled as he silently reveled in his small victory. "One of your guards arrived with correspondence."

That caught Siveril's attention. *Who? And why? Did Taenya . . . ? No, she would have informed me.*

His momentary confusion must have been evident, because the duke let out an amused laugh.

"She's shrewder than you give her credit for, it seems. Your princess penned the letter herself," Dasron said with a shake of his head and a rueful chuckle. "She believes I have been remiss in my duties."

Siveril's eyes widened slightly. *She . . . what?*

"According to her," the duke continued, a note of bemusement in his voice, "and I cannot say that I disagree, the blatant attack on your house could only have occurred if my guard failed in their duty to uphold the peace within the very city that holds the seat of my duchy." His gaze sharpened slightly. "As such, she argues that I should be required to pay reparations to House Reinhart, as compensation to her . . . family and for the people she lost."

Siveril's mind raced. The princess had appealed to responsibility—not just to justice, but to duty. And she had done so in a way that would force the duke to acknowledge the role of his own house in allowing such an attack to happen. A bold move.

"She goes on to state," the duke continued, "that House Reinhart will, of

course, provide their expected compensation to the families of those who per-
ished, but also that *I* should take steps to 'amend the strained relationship with
the one I respect the most.'"

Siveril's thoughts churned. On the one hand, the princess was correct. On the
other, the reality of politics did not allow such things to be so simply addressed.
The duchy was still their most critical ally. A strained relationship here could be
dangerous. And yet . . .

He sighed. "I trust you have investigated the lack of response by the city
guard?" Siveril knew the truth, although it had been gained by Sabina when she
had infiltrated and eliminated her targets within Angwin's manor in the city. But
he could not admit that to the duke, of course.

The duke's expression shifted and became, it seemed to Siveril, predatory. For
the briefest moment, he wondered if he had made a mistake in asking.

"We have found the issue," Dasron said, his voice measured but carrying a
distinct edge. "It seems my son has not been as strict in rooting out corruption
as befits one of House Tiloral. While he did not act directly, his failure to hold
certain individuals accountable allowed this to happen." The duke paused. "That
has been rectified."

Siveril inclined his head. He knew better than to ask how that rectification
had taken place. Clearly, the bribed guardsmen and officials had been found;
hopefully, they hadn't spent any of the money they'd gained. The duke usually
went easier on those who relinquished their ill gains and used such funds to support new initiatives in the city.

The duke continued, "I was awake late into the night, considering how to
approach this." He exhaled, his displeasure evident. "Angwin's attack was not
within the customs of the Polite War. However, he is even more entangled with
the crown prince than I had anticipated. I cannot overtly move against him—he
owes my duchy fealty. But at the same time, I cannot risk escalation with the
Crown by censuring him directly as his liege."

His hands curled into fists before relaxing. "I find myself constrained, my
hands tied in a most frustrating way. Luckily, some loose ends recently found
themselves managed."

He fell silent for a moment. Then, his sharp gaze met Siveril's. The duke
smiled faintly, though there was something almost knowing in his eyes. There
was something in his tone.

And in that moment, Siveril understood. The duke knew they had something to do with what had transpired at Angwin's manor in the dead of night.
And more than that, he approved.

The duke continued as if he hadn't just subtly agreed with the killing of
multiple people in his city. "But that still leaves us with the issue of a noble who
believes himself shielded from a proper response. Your princess, again, has provided a clue as to what path I can take."

Siveril's brow furrowed. He shook his head slowly. "I cannot fathom what she would have requested."

The duke nodded. "She stated that Ser Siveril Norric is an honorable man who should not be 'a mere knight,' and that it appears there is an opportunity to reward his loyalty to the duchy." His lips curled slightly. "It seems that Angwin has made quite the lasting impression on the young royal . . . and not a good one."

Siveril remained still, though his mind worked quickly, analyzing the weight behind those words.

"So," the duke continued, his tone shifting to something almost casual, "I suspect you've heard that old Normen Varence recently passed without an heir. At least, I hope you've heard, since your princess came by this information. As such, his lands have reverted back into the hands of the duchy. And I believe I have come to a decision."

Siveril's eyes widened slightly. But before he could respond, the Duke of Tiloral reached down to retrieve a scroll case from beside his chair. With measured ease, he pulled out the document inside.

"I know you hate being the center of attention when you are the subject of it," the duke said, amusement flickering in his gaze. "So we will keep this informal."

Siveril straightened instinctively.

"The town of Galehaven serves as the seat of a small county," Tiloral explained, "but its location is critical—it lies on a major route into the Kingdom of Meris. I expect you to increase its prosperity, strengthen its infrastructure, and build something there that I can trust to defend the duchy should I call upon it."

He paused, then added, "In fact, given the growing tensions along our borders, I may need to station soldiers within the county. But I cannot afford to oversee every standing force under my banner—not without creating unnecessary burdens." He met Siveril's gaze. "It is far more efficient for those soldiers to be beholden to a house that governs it."

The air in the room shifted. The weight of what was being offered pressed down on Siveril's shoulders.

"Do you believe," the duke continued, voice edged with something knowing, "that your liege would approve of her majordomo becoming a count?" He tilted his head slightly. "Personally, I think it is far more fitting for a royal to have someone of higher station managing her affairs. Angwin was not entirely incorrect in that regard."

A *long* pause. Then: "Where he erred was in disregarding the man—which, to me, is always the more important factor in the end." Tiloral's sharp gaze settled fully on Siveril. "So, what do you say, *Your Lordship?*"

Siveril held his breath. He had never dreamed of rising beyond his station. Had never even sought it. And all it had taken was believing in a young girl from another world.

He straightened, adjusting his coat, and then bowed deeply, a gesture of the utmost respect. "I agree and accept, Your Grace," he said solemnly.

As Siveril rose, he knew exactly what his first act as count would be. There was a wrong that needed to be righted—a debt owed to one of the young ladies in his care.

After that? What came next would not be so polite.

CHAPTER NINETEEN

FINAL STAND

One of the most frequently cited examples of a monsterized species is the drakyyd lizard, due in large part to the terran reaction to its mutated form. According to many of the Displaced, one variant of the monsterized drakyyd bore a striking resemblance to creatures from their own world known as drakes. The name spread quickly, sparking a broader trend of renaming monsterized creatures based on terran terminology. This phenomenon was later reinforced by the discovery that the monsterization process—triggered by high concentrations of ambient mana—had not only transformed existing fauna, but also introduced an almost incalculable number of entirely new species to the world of Eona.

A History of Monsters, 173 SA

House Reinhart was on the move—or more precisely, the entourage and guards escorting Princess Gwyneth were.

They had left Strathmore just before dawn, slipping out of the city quietly. The roads were clear, the early hour and winter's first frost keeping most people indoors. The caravan made steady progress north, crossing the broad Strath River before turning onto the road toward the Naro Pass.

The pass earned its name from its geography: a narrow corridor of land squeezed between the Loduhr Mountains and the ancient Ayeval Forest. It was the most efficient route from the Duchy of Tiloral to the capital, at least for those who wanted to stay within Aviran territory.

The alternative route passed through the dwarven city of Dirn Loduhr via underground tunnels. Gaining permission to travel through dwarven lands was exceedingly rare, especially for citizens of Avira. Relations between the two powers remained tense at best.

Recognizing the importance—and vulnerability—of the pass, the Crown had long ago commissioned a fortress on the duchy's side of the corridor, just before entering the Duchy of Avira.

In recent years, however, the crown prince had diverted funds elsewhere, persuading the king to scale back the royal presence. A token force remained, but ensuring the responsibility for maintaining the castle fell to the Tilorals.

They had accepted the burden happily and had quietly stationed their own troops alongside the diminished royal garrison. Castle Naro now served as a frontline defense, capable of holding off both dwarven incursions—which was unlikely due to the cordial relations between the duchy and Dirn Loduhr—and potential Valeni raids long enough for the duchy to respond.

As the princess's caravan moved along the road, what few travelers there were gave way without hesitation. Two carriages, two wagons, and a mounted escort made it clear that this was a noble party.

Among the riders were two knights skilled in magic, as well as eight members of the specialized guard teams trained for elite assignments.

Ser Taenya Shavyre kept track of every detail. Her responsibilities included managing the three ladies-in-waiting, two scholars, seven servants, twelve regular house guards, and, of course, the princess herself. Fortunately, the guard teams were experienced and reliable. A single instruction to one of the three senior guardsmen ensured that everything—from daily travel to overnight arrangements—was handled without issue.

Evocati Amari had ridden ahead on Church business and was expected to rejoin them near the town of Mardale in a few days. She hadn't shared the specifics of her errand, only that it would be "worth it." Taenya had learned not to ask too many questions when the paladin's tone implied divine interference.

One of the blessings of the Naro route was its infrastructure. Every half day's travel brought them to a village, hamlet, or roadside post where they could rest and resupply. They would reach Mardale the next day. From there, it was another few days to Castle Naro, then nearly a week of slow travel through the pass itself.

Taenya exhaled, watching her breath cloud in the crisp air. There was still a long road ahead. But everything was in motion. And for House Reinhart, that was what mattered most. It would take them another three or four weeks to reach the city of Drakensburg.

They had departed from one of the many villages scattered along the route earlier that morning. The stop had been pleasant—quiet, even—with their group nearly filling the only inn situated in the village's small central plaza. It had given them a rare opportunity to rest, regroup, and plan the coming leg of their journey without the usual rush to break camp at dawn.

Now, the caravan was back on the road. Taenya rode at the front, Sabina at her right. Two scouts were ahead of them, ranging just far enough to give warning if anything lay in wait. The rest of their escort flanked the carriages or followed closely behind the wagons, the formation tight and deliberate.

She cast a glance toward the raven-haired high elf riding beside her. Sabina looked composed—her posture straight, her expression unreadable, but Taenya could tell there was more simmering beneath the surface.

She hadn't been the same since the attack on the manor and subsequent response. It wasn't the violence that had shaken her, Taenya knew. Sabina had always been calm under pressure, effective when others hesitated. But there was something different this time. And that lay in the way she had used her magic. The way she had ended one of the knights. It had disturbed her—cut deeper than she wanted to admit.

Her friend had also told her how she'd used her magic to keep her targets still in her retaliatory strike. While it wasn't as mentally taxing as taking control of her enemy's body and forcing them to kill themselves, it was eating at her. Taenya just didn't know how to help.

"You alright?" Taenya asked softly, her voice just loud enough to be heard over the rhythm of hooves on packed earth.

Sabina nodded, her gaze forward. "I am. Just lost in my thoughts."

"Do you wish to talk about it?"

"Ask me again in Drakensburg."

Taenya nodded once, keeping her voice gentle. *I'm here. Okay?*

The elf's ear twitched ever so slightly. *I know.*

They didn't speak again for some time, letting the hush of the road and the gentle clatter of the caravan fill the space between them.

The clouds above thickened slowly, blotting out more of the sky with every passing mile. A light breeze carried the scent of distant rain, and fog had begun creeping along the distant hills, curling at their edges like fingers stretching toward the road.

Taenya guessed they had a few more hours until they reached the next village. Hopefully, the weather would hold until then. With luck, they'd make it to the inn before the storm broke—and more importantly, avoid travel delays the next day.

She kept herself busy by riding along the length of the caravan, checking in with the guards, servants, and members of the entourage. Everyone seemed in good spirits, if a bit subdued from the early start and gray skies.

They had to pause briefly to let some of the passengers relieve themselves, but the stop was short-lived, and they were soon back in motion.

It wasn't long after when Taenya noticed the first sign of potential trouble. The birds. Circling high above in slow, lazy spirals. She narrowed her eyes, scanning the landscape. There were only a few sparse trees nearby, and the hills ahead rolled gently with no obvious cover. The fog was creeping closer, enough to make visibility difficult farther out, but still—there was nothing visible that posed a threat. Even so, her instincts prickled.

She turned toward one of her Drakyyds—Oren, a solid, experienced telv who had once served in the duchy's standing army. He was one of the three senior guards they'd brought along. Recruiting him had taken effort, but a personal recommendation from the Duke of Tiloral had opened doors.

Duchy soldiers were worth their weight in gold compared to the often under-trained royal army. It was rare to pull talent directly from the duchy's active service, and Taenya knew what it meant that he had chosen to join them.

"Oren," she called, her voice sharp. "Grab someone and scout ahead. Something's off."

The telv followed her gaze toward the circling birds. His expression hardened.

"I see them. We'll find out what's wrong and be back soon."

"Be safe," she said. "If anything seems amiss, you turn around. No risks."

He saluted, then spurred his horse into motion, calling for another guard to follow as he passed.

Taenya turned in the saddle and called to one of the guards riding beside the wagons, instructing her to relay word back. Everyone needed to be on alert.

She glanced at Sabina again, and the high elf met her gaze. *I do not feel anything.*

That helped. Not much, but enough. If Sabina couldn't sense any hostile intent or danger, it meant that whatever was ahead was either distant or subtle.

Still, Taenya didn't like what the presence of that many carrion birds meant.

The caravan continued on at a steady pace. There was no cause to stop—not yet.

But Taenya had learned to trust her instincts. She spotted the returning scouts in the distance and immediately guided her horse forward to intercept them. Sabina stayed at her side, silent but watchful. The two guards rode hard, pulling up with urgency as they reached her.

"Ser Taenya!" one of them called out, his face pale beneath his helm. "There was an attack ahead. A full escort force is . . . they're dead, Knight-Captain. Several wagons, horses, bodies—strewn across the road. It's . . . a slaughter. The path is mostly clear, though."

Taenya's jaw tightened. "Can you tell how long it's been?"

Oren grimaced. "Judging by the state of things, no later than this morning. The bodies are stiff, but not bloated. And the smell . . ." He seemed disturbed. "The carrion birds have been feasting all afternoon."

Taenya gave a short nod and turned to Sabina. "Can you warn the passengers? I want them to remain inside the carriages while we investigate. We'll keep moving, but stop the caravan within sight of the scene—far enough that they aren't exposed to it. I'll take a team forward to assess."

"I'll let them know," Sabina replied quietly. *Be careful, Taenya.*

I will, she thought back. *After all, my early-warning knight has my back.*

Sabina's returning smile was faint—tinged with doubt, as if the words hadn't brought her much comfort. She turned her horse and began riding toward the carriages.

Taenya watched her go for a heartbeat longer, then faced Oren again.

"Sabina's Wynvers will stay close to the carriages. Get the rest of the Drakyyds and take half of the remaining guards. We move ahead now."

It didn't take long to reach the site. But nothing Oren had said prepared her for what lay before them.

Carnage. Two wagons, ruined as if smashed by siege weapons, lay across the road. One was a blackened husk, the other splintered and half-buried in churned mud and ash. Bodies lay everywhere. Scorch marks stained the dirt surrounding the blackened corpses of fallen guards. Arrows jutted from broken shields and splintered cart walls. Blood pooled in the depressions of the road.

Taenya dismounted, handing her reins to a waiting guard. Her boots crunched over the scorched gravel as she approached the wreckage, her eyes scanning for identifying marks, any hint of a banner or insignia.

Faint cinders still smoldered beneath the collapsed frame of the burned wagon. The second wagon appeared to have been the site of a desperate last stand.

Six bodies lay in a defensive ring around a seventh, their broken shields forming a crude wall, their swords and spears scattered.

She glanced at the Drakyyd beside her, a sharp-eyed elven woman. With a nod, they approached together. Taenya crouched next to one of the fallen men. His armor was torn open across the chest—deep, ragged gouges cleaved through steel. Claws.

The elven guard gasped.

Taenya turned to her. "What is it?"

"Ser Taenya . . . come look. Is this . . . ?"

Taenya stood and followed her over to the central body, the one the others had died protecting.

The armor was elaborate. Silver chased with green and yellow trim, now dulled by dirt and dried blood. The plating was dented and cracked, the helm pierced and twisted. Wind tugged at the shredded remnants of a tabard.

Three holes in the chest—large enough for a fist—had been punched clean through the breastplate. A slow death. Painful. Relena had claimed him.

Taenya narrowed her eyes. "Who is it?" She didn't recognize the armor or the colors.

The guard didn't answer. Instead, she stepped forward and ripped the helmet off with a rough motion, tossing it aside like an insult.

The revealed face answered Taenya's question. Gaunt. Pale. Twisted in death. The man who had started a sequence of events that had ended with Taenya dueling the son of Lord Angwin and the manor being attacked in return. The scars along his cheek and exposed arm confirmed it. He'd been burned at court by a furious princess who had seen through his lies.

The man who had tried to bind Gwyn in an illegal marriage. A manipulator who had craved power and was willing to sacrifice anyone to obtain it. A monster in noble's clothing. Count Agrond Telford lay dead.

And not a single part of her mourned him. Taenya stood still, taking it all in. Now that the initial shock had passed, the scene was coming into focus—too clearly. This had been an ambush. A force positioned here to intercept *them.*

And by the look of it, they might have succeeded: Taenya wasn't certain House Reinhart would have survived that battle, at least not unscathed and intact. It would have depended on whether or not they'd caught Gwyn unaware. She wasn't invincible.

Dozens of bodies lay scattered and broken, torn apart by fire and steel. Whatever had laid waste to this force had done so with utter, merciless devastation. Fire had ravaged the scene of battle, and whoever or whatever had inadvertently assisted House Reinhart was nowhere to be seen. *I'm not even sure I want to know what could do this.*

And then, of course, she heard it. A sound that gripped her spine and froze it. Far off in the distance, a massive roar echoed across the hills. It was raw and primal. Furious. A cry that seemed to shake the very ground she stood on.

Taenya's eyes widened as the sound faded into the thickening fog. The guard beside her had already drawn her steel spear and brought up her shield, tension radiating from her frame.

"We need to get back. *Now.*"

The woman nodded, and together they jogged back toward the rest of the advance party.

The other guards were already alert, their spears angled and heads swiveling as they scanned the misty hills.

Senior Guardsman Oren jogged forward, his voice steady despite the tension in his shoulders. "Ser Taenya! It came from the northwest."

She opened her mouth to respond, but another voice interrupted her.

"Taenya!"

Taenya turned, brows rising, heart tightening.

"Taenya! Did you hear that?!"

Gwyn was running toward her. The young princess was dressed for the cold in a high-collared wool coat of deep blue, buttoned neatly down the front and cinched at the waist with a black belt bearing House Reinhart's silver sigil. Silver thread shimmered along the seams of the coat in a pattern of dancing flame, catching the pale light as she ran. Her simple but finely made leather boots were practical, warm, and well fitted.

Taenya's heart dropped. "*Gwyn?* What are you doing out here?" she asked sharply, eyes immediately darting to Sabina beside her. "This is *not* a scene appropriate for a young girl."

She insisted. You know how she can be.

Taenya shot her friend a glare that promised they were not done with this conversation.

"Taenya, be nice to Sabina. *I* made her let me come," Gwyn said, hands on her hips. "What *happened* here? Did you *hear* that sound?"

Grinding her teeth, Taenya forced down the swell of frustration. "An attack," she answered, gesturing toward the carnage. "It looks like . . . something attacked the group here. And I suspect they were meant for us."

Gwyn's eyes narrowed. She turned, scanning the scene as her expression hardened. "Who were they?"

"Count Telford's men."

The princess nodded once. "*Good.*"

Taenya blinked. But before she could respond, another roar split the air. Closer this time. And with it came something else—pain. The sound echoed with rage, but also . . . suffering. She spun toward the northwest, her grip tightening on her sword hilt.

"I think you should return to the carriage, Your Highness," she said, tone firm but controlled.

Predictably, Gwyn did not agree. "I'm fine. Do you see *those* wagons?" she pointed toward the ruined convoy. "Staying inside didn't help them. I can help more out here—especially with my magic."

Taenya raised a hand to object, but Gwyn cut her off before she could utter a word.

"You *know* I'm right, Taenya. Come on. Let's go."

The knight squinted. "Go *where*?"

"Toward the sound," Gwyn replied, as if it were the most obvious thing in the world.

Taenya's eyes widened in disbelief just as another roar—louder than the last—ripped through the air. This time, it was unmistakable. Something out there was hurting.

"No. That is not a good idea whatsoever."

Gwyn sighed. "Taenya, either we go now while we know where the noise is coming from, or we let it surprise us—like it did Telford. I think going in prepared is the better option."

It stung that the girl had a point. Taenya didn't like it—not one bit—but that didn't change the reality of the situation. Gwyn was only ten. And it was Taenya's job to keep her safe. But over and over, the girl had proved that her magic was not just useful—it was indispensable. She had saved lives when she swept through the manor like a flaming Hand of Alos. Taenya didn't even know what temperature was required to burn a man to ash in seconds, but Gwyn had done it.

She still remembered watching the girl sleep for an entire day afterward, her body utterly spent. Magical exhaustion from drawing too much mana too quickly. It wasn't sustainable. It was something Taenya had resolved to study further once they reached the capital—right after they found a proper house physician. One who could be trusted not only with the health of nobility, but with *magic* . . . and with secrets.

She let out a long breath. Gwyn wasn't going to back down, and Taenya knew it. Despite her misgivings, it might be safer to have the girl with her than to leave her behind.

"Fine," she relented at last. "You stay close. If it gets bad, we run. Whatever this is, it took out dozens of men."

Gwyn gave a casual shrug. "So did I."

Taenya shot her a flat look.

Gwyn rolled her eyes. "Understood," she said, though the fire beginning to leak from the corners of her eyes betrayed her excitement.

Taenya turned to the others. "House guards, hold position and remain with the carriages. Wynvers and Drakyyds, you're with me. Stay tight. We're looking for something big and clearly capable of taking on an entire unit—and, from the looks of it, *winning*."

They rode cautiously, following the edge of the fog, until the source came into view. Taenya slowed. The group followed her lead.

What lay ahead sent a chill through her bones. A vast, cone-shaped swath of blackened land stretched out before them—easily thirty meters wide at its farthest point. The earth was charred and scorched, smoking slightly where embers still clung to life. Trees had been felled or reduced to twisted husks.

At the center of the devastation were two figures. One was the crumpled body of a knight in battered armor, lying beside a horse that had fallen hard and hadn't moved since. The other was a massive beast.

Shaped like a drakyyd but much larger, the monster lay on the ground, yet its shoulders rose higher than Taenya's head as she sat on her horse. A crown of curved, brutal-looking horns sprouted from the top of its skull. It looked at them, its long and angular head slowly turning on a thick, sinewy neck. A small horn jutted from the tip of its snout, and its pained eyes were red and burning. *Just like Gwyn's.* The creature's deep scarlet scales shimmered like forged steel, each one overlapping like plates of armor. Sharp, jagged spikes ran down its spine, giving it a menacing silhouette even in its stillness. Its tail, long and muscular, ended in a horrible diamond-shaped spike that looked capable of smashing stone.

The drakyyd raised its head slowly, then unleashed a thunderous roar in their direction. The sound rumbled through the ground beneath Taenya's boots, but the beast made no move to advance. It remained curled where it lay, and then she saw why.

A lance—long, thick, and cruelly barbed—pierced deep into its side. The shaft quivered slightly with each ragged breath the creature took, the weapon clearly lodged beyond the reach of both its massive, taloned feet and its snapping maw.

With a pained snarl, the monster reared its head back and unleashed a gout of flame. It fell short by nearly ten meters, but even from that distance, Taenya felt the heat wash over them, dry, blistering, and oppressive, like standing at the edge of a desert forge.

The creature roared again, its pain unmistakable this time. The sound was lower, trembling. A sound of agony. It laid its head back down and closed its eyes. For a moment, Taenya thought it might die right then and there.

She heard a sudden gasp and turned. Gwyn. The princess was staring at the wounded creature, her expression unreadable.

Taenya's heart lurched as Gwyn jumped down from the horse and moved toward the monster with determined steps.

Sabina, caught off guard, reached out to grab her but missed, nearly falling from the saddle as she scrambled to keep herself upright.

"Gwyn!" Sabina called out.

The girl did not stop. Taenya jumped down immediately, her boots slamming into the earth as she broke into a run.

The monster's eyes snapped open. It let out a deafening roar, this one full of rage. The sound shattered the relative stillness, and the horses panicked, rearing and crying out in fear. Guards were thrown from their mounts, hitting the ground hard.

Taenya turned to the two senior guardsmen from the Wynvers and Drakyyds. "Check the fallen! I'll get her!"

She turned just in time to see Gwyn break into a jog.

No. Taenya's eyes went wide. "Gwyn! No, come back!"

The girl didn't even glance back. Flames burst around her, curling and dancing as if the air itself recognized her command. Her body glowed with an aura of mana, and Taenya could see the fire sparking at her fingertips, trailing in her wake.

The drakyyd's eyes locked onto her. They widened—ever so slightly. It inhaled.

"No! Gwyn!" Taenya yelled.

The beast unleashed its fury. A massive jet of fire roared from its throat, engulfing the ground before it in a blinding column of flame.

Gwyn vanished into the inferno.

Taenya's breath caught. *Please . . . no.*

Gwyn reached deep into the red mana, pulling it to her with instinctive ease as the drake bellowed its fury toward her. The fire was immense—hotter and more forceful than anything she had ever faced. But mana sang to her. She raised her hand, letting her **[Fire Shield]** bloom into existence. The translucent blaze flared to life around her just as the drake's deep-crimson fire slammed into it.

Her orange flames met its red—and she pulled. The torrent of fire curved, wrapping around her shield before bending inward. The inferno didn't harm her. It became hers.

The drake was wounded. A long, cruel lance pierced its side, just out of reach of its claws and snapping jaws. And Gwyn's heart ached. It was just trying to protect itself. Unlike a dragon, the poor thing had no wings to fly away. It couldn't escape. The evil men had trapped, cornered, and hurt it.

She had to help. She stepped forward, ignoring Taenya's distant shouts. If she turned back now, she knew the knight would lock her in the carriage for the rest of the journey. *I have to do this.*

The drake lifted its head slightly, wary now. Its massive red eyes locked onto her with suspicion, glowing with something deeper than primal rage—awareness.

Gwyn raised a hand, still engulfed in flickering flames. "It's okay. I'm a friend. I won't hurt you."

The beast let out another breath of fire—but this time, she caught it effortlessly, folding it into her shield as if she were welcoming it home.

The flames held strength, but their connection to the mana was weak. The drake's fire was born of its body, not its will. It could create fire, but only barely sang to the red mana that gifted such flame. Impressive, considering the raw force of it. But vulnerable to those who could truly wield magic—to those who could sing.

She absorbed the last of the fire into her shield and paused. Something was different. The flame merging with hers felt . . . strange. Her own fire was bright, wild—mundane in the way a campfire was. But the drake's fire—it carried a kind of majesty, a resonance that made her skin prickle. It felt . . . *regal.*

As is fitting, she thought. Dropping her shield, Gwyn whispered, "You're gorgeous. Your fire is powerful . . . strong."

The drake growled in response, a low, cautious rumble.

She took another step closer. "If only you had a better connection to the mana. It was almost enough, wasn't it?"

She was only a few paces away now. Still, the drake didn't strike. Instead, it coiled its tail tighter around itself, watching her with wary eyes. It reminded her of a wounded cat—prideful, dangerous, and far too intelligent.

"It's okay. I won't hurt you," she said again, softer this time. She glanced over her shoulder at the battlefield—the blackened corpse of the knight who had fought to the end. His once-silver armor was soot-stained and melted in places, his body a grim monument to the price of ambition.

He had fought valiantly, but he'd followed the wrong man. Gwyn didn't know who he was, but she knew what kind of person he must have been. People could be understood by those they served.

She turned back to the drake. "I'm sorry he hurt you."

The beast let out a deep rumble, lowering its head again and closing its eyes.

Gwyn gave a quiet, sad chuckle. "You can't just pretend I'm not here, you know."

One eye cracked open. The drake slowly turned its head away. Gwyn laughed softly and took another step, reaching out a hand to touch it. It snapped its head back, nipping at her.

Gwyn yelped, yanking her hand away. "Hey!" She narrowed her eyes, lips pursing in mock offense. Pulling from her memory of the drake's fire, she shaped a small burst of flame to mimic it. The fire flowed from her palm in a soft wave, tinged with the same deep red hue, and rippled across the drake's snout.

The beast jerked its head back, blinking in surprise. Then it huffed and returned fire—a small, almost playful puff that rolled toward her.

Gwyn laughed, catching the fire and letting it dance around her hand. She pulled it inward, claiming it with her will. That familiar rush filled her, but this time, the mana responded *differently*. It sang. Red mana surged into her unbidden, wrapping around her like a cloak. Something inside her shifted. She raised her hand and summoned flame. It came immediately—no delay, no resistance. Not orange, not wild. This fire was deep red, threaded through with golden lines. It was beautiful.

And then she heard it. A sound, soft and melodic, like distant chimes stirred by wind. It resonated through the air, through the mana itself, and into her very soul.

Everywhere. Nowhere. She thought she was imagining it, until she saw the drake stir. It lifted its head, eyes searching the air.

It heard it too.

Gwyn jerked her head around, searching for the source of the chime-like sound, and spotted Taenya in the distance. Her telv knight stood rigid in the saddle, scanning the area as if she, too, had heard the ethereal melody.

Their eyes met. Taenya pointed at her, alarm flaring across her face. Gwyn raised a hand to wave. But Taenya's eyes went wide, and her arm shot forward in a sudden gesture.

Gwyn felt a shove from behind. "Ah!" she yelped as she toppled forward, landing face-first in the sooty dirt and grass. Startled, she rolled onto her back, coughing as she looked up at the massive drake looming over her. It pulled its head back slightly, until its enormous maw was no longer directly above her.

It looked . . . smug. Pained, but smug. *That jerk pushed me over!* Gwyn sighed, brushing soot off her sleeves as she climbed to her feet. "That wasn't nice."

The drake let out a low, pained sound and turned its head. Its gaze had shifted downward, toward the massive wound in its side and the lance.

"Do you . . . want help?" Gwyn asked gently.

With a rumbling growl, the beast shifted, twisting with effort. It moved its head slowly toward its curled tail, groaning as it strained.

Gwyn circled around, trying to see what had drawn its attention, and froze. Nestled in the scorched dirt, partially hidden beneath the drake's tail, was another form. Another drake. But smaller . . . and motionless.

This creature was the same deep crimson, almost black with a red sheen, and roughly the size of a large dog, like a Great Dane.

The massive drake nudged it gently with its snout, urging it to move. It didn't. The mother looked back at Gwyn, eyes full of something that pierced right through her.

Pain. Hope. Loss.

Gwyn's breath caught. Her chest tightened and tears prickled at her eyes.

"You were just . . . protecting your baby."

A soft, sorrowful sound escaped the drake's throat as it rested its head atop the unmoving form of her youngling.

Gwyn took a step closer, but the drake growled in warning.

"Stop," Gwyn said, holding up her hands. "I'm trying to help."

The beast narrowed its eyes at her, but after a long pause, it shifted slightly, granting her access.

Gwyn slowly but deliberately moved closer. She activated her [**Mana Sight**] and the arcane energy of the world bloomed into vibrant color across her vision. Red mana clung to the small drake, pulsing weakly. At the same time, green mana curled beneath the ground around it.

Gwyn glanced to the side and spotted Taenya approaching cautiously. The knight's crimson aura shimmered as if strengthening her body, preparing for anything.

Gwyn knelt beside the baby drake. There was no movement. She reached out and peered closer. A red core still flickered in its chest, small and faint. But it was disconnected, floating untethered. It was lifeless.

The sob escaped Gwyn before she could stop it. She rushed to the mother's side and pressed herself against her massive, scaled head, wrapping her arms around her in an awkward hug.

"I'm so sorry," she whispered. "Those awful men did this to you."

The drake rumbled softly, the vibration deep enough to hum in her bones. She turned slightly, resting her head down again. One eye opened—slit-pupiled and feline—and fixed on Gwyn with quiet sorrow. She pulled back gently. Then, slowly, deliberately, she brought her head forward again. This time, she tilted to the side and leaned in, closing her eyes.

Gwyn reached out. She pressed her hand and forehead against the beast's scaled brow. "You beat them," she whispered.

The drake huffed, and the air around them shimmered with heat—confirmation, pride. It hadn't been in question. Only whether she would survive.

Gwyn stepped back slightly as the drake slumped further into the dirt, her breathing growing more labored. She looked up at Gwyn with heavy, pained eyes. A soft whimper escaped her throat.

Gwyn placed her hand gently on the mother drake's snout, tears trailing silently down her cheeks. "I'm right here," she murmured. "I won't leave you."

Even when she felt Taenya's hand settle gently on her shoulder, Gwyn stayed where she was—kneeling beside the drake, her hand resting on the creature's fading warmth.

Resolving not to leave the mother's side, she inched closer, pressing her palm lightly against the creature's massive snout. The drake turned her head with effort and laid it down beside her youngling. She gave Gwyn a final look—one filled with quiet resignation, perhaps even gratitude—before letting out a pained breath and closing her eyes.

She did not move again, her head resting beside her baby's still form, her gaze forever fixed on the offspring she had failed to save.

Gwyn's heart shattered. She collapsed to her knees, sobbing into her hands.

Taenya moved closer and wrapped her arms around her from behind, pulling her gently into a warm, protective embrace. They sat like that for what felt like hours. Time seemed to slow, the world dimming around them.

Eventually, Gwyn tilted her tear-streaked face upward and looked at her adoptive aunt. "Why is this world so cruel?"

Taenya gazed down at her, her expression soft with sorrow. "We have not yet learned the true value of a life," she said gently. "But that's why Eona needs people like you, to guide it into a future none of us could have imagined. You and other terrans, like your mother, have lived better lives, seen better ways. Listening to your stories and dreams gives me hope. You're better, Gwyn. Stronger. No matter what has happened, you've endured. Don't give up on us yet."

Gwyn sniffed and nodded, her voice small. "It's just so *hard*. There are so many bad people, Taenya."

Taenya offered her a sad smile. "I like to think there are good people too." She looked at the drake. "And not just people. Good beings. You have a heart of gold, Gwyn. No one else I know would've rushed into the arms of a dying monster to comfort it in its final moments."

"She was just a mother," Gwyn whispered, "trying to protect her baby." Her lip trembled. "When I looked at her, I saw Mom. I can't imagine what she's feeling. Do you think she's okay?"

Taenya took a deep breath. "If she's anything like you, then your mother hasn't stopped searching. And she won't. Not until she finds you."

Gwyn looked back at the drake's body, quiet for a long moment. "Taenya?"

"Yes?"

Gwyn hesitated, then asked in a steady voice, "What will people do when they find her?" She gestured toward the drake with a tilt of her head.

Taenya paused.

"Well—"

"Tell me the truth," Gwyn said, her voice firm despite the emotion wavering beneath it.

Taenya met her gaze and answered honestly. "They'll harvest her for her parts. Study her. Figure out what made her so powerful—and how to kill others like her more effectively."

Gwyn's breath hitched. She turned back to the drake, her heart aching again. There was no way they could bury her. She was far too large—at least the size of one of those old Earth delivery vans. But maybe . . .

"She was a protector," Gwyn murmured. "Trying to shield her baby from monsters." She paused, then looked back at Taenya. "Can we bury her baby? And . . . I think we should take her core. And maybe her scales too. They'd be useful, right?"

Taenya's eyes softened. "Of course. I'll gather the guards. We'll bury the little one with full respect. But are you sure about the core?"

Gwyn nodded slowly. "Yes. I think I carry her fire now. It feels right. The core shouldn't be left for someone else to take. It should be used—by us. For something good." She touched the small mana core dangling from her earring.

"These help my magic. In stories from my world, there were people like me. Mages and wizards of great power. And they all had something in common."

Taenya tilted her head, thoughtful. "What's that?"

"A staff. And a drake's core will make it stronger than anything else around."

She looked back at the drake and whispered, "Then, when I use fire against people like this, it'll be like you're helping me. And all the evil will *burn*. Just like you did to them here."

She reached out one last time, laying her hand gently on the drake's snout, just behind its horn.

"Thank you," she whispered. Then, with a deep breath, she stood.

As Taenya called for the guards to begin their solemn task, Gwyn turned and walked away, her steps slow, her shoulders heavy.

Sabina was waiting. She offered a hand and helped Gwyn back onto the horse. Without a word, they turned and began the quiet ride back to the caravan.

Gwyn glanced back over her shoulder, watching as the guards carefully moved the baby drake's body. The mother lay where she had fallen, massive, majestic, and still. It was a sorrowful end to what should have been a different story, Gwyn thought. A mother protecting her young. A quiet life far from men and their greed. But it had been ruined by one who cared only for power.

Thank you, Gwyn thought, *for taking care of that evil man for me. I wish I had been here sooner. Maybe we could have helped you. Maybe we could have been friends.*

She felt Sabina shift slightly. The older woman reached back and gave her leg a gentle squeeze. Gwyn smiled and leaned forward, wrapping her arms around Sabina's back in a tight hug.

I hope you're okay. I'm sorry I pushed you.

I will be alright, came the soft, steady reply. *It has just taken time to reconcile my feelings after everything I've had to do. I do not blame you. I would do it again if it meant protecting you. It's just difficult on my mind.*

Gwyn hugged her tighter. *Then I'll protect you too.*

A quiet mental nudge followed. Warm. Steady. It made Gwyn smile. She turned her gaze forward again, blinking against the cold breeze that rushed over them. She was ready to continue the journey. Sad and yet grateful that she had been there for the drake in its final moments. That it hadn't died alone. She hoped—*truly* hoped—that she had given it even a sliver of peace before the end.

But the encounter had shown her something more. Something *important*. If drakes walked this land . . . then dragons *must* exist somewhere out there.

And I'm going to find them. Gwyn looked down at her hand, where the fire still lived beneath her skin—warmer, deeper than before.

When that day comes, when I've mastered my flame, nothing will ever be able to harm my family again.

CHAPTER TWENTY

WAR AT DUSK

Tiberius landed beside Sloane, his metal talons clicking sharply against the stone. She stood atop the ramparts of Marketbol's outer walls, staring into the distance, trying to visualize how it would look when the enemy finally arrived.

The army was close now. She had worked closely with the city to use her golem scout to track the approaching forces, and her assistance had been well received. With the Vlaredian threat near, Marketbol's leadership had grown wary of sending scouts out too far. Only a few teams remained beyond the walls, their focus shifted to tracking enemy supply movements rather than engaging directly.

Sloane glanced at the army commander standing with her. The high elf's posture was resolute, but subtle tells in his expression betrayed his tension. *Understandable*, she thought. Marketbol prided itself on its defenses, but when faced with the reality of an opposing army, one's confidence could only stretch so far—especially when the city's own standing army had all but vanished.

She exhaled heavily through her nose. "It looks like their rear force has caught up. The army now numbers closer to ten thousand—not counting their support personnel and followers." She hesitated before adding, "I'm reluctant to send Tiberius any farther out. I'd rather keep him close." She met the commander's eyes. "They've also moved past the point you mentioned."

The man sighed, nodding. "If they're past the fork, then it's likely they'll arrive by nightfall." He closed the notebook he had been writing in. "I'll relay the report. Will you be attending the meeting, milady?"

Sloane looked at Nemura, who gave her a curt nod.

"We will," Sloane confirmed.

The commander saluted, murmured his thanks for her assistance, and made his way back toward the command post.

Sloane turned her attention north, scanning the path the enemy would take. Her mind drifted, turning over everything that had led to this moment. It felt like no matter where she went, some new calamity reared its head. Every step forward only pulled her into *another* conflict, *another* desperate attempt to keep her footing. She had to keep getting stronger. She had to keep making contacts. And . . . *Where the hell is that woman?*

Still no word on Ressa or the Empire's Fist, which had been supposedly operating inside the city. Not even hints. *Could they have left?* For the second time, she considered the disturbing possibility that they had help in remaining hidden. The thought unsettled her, but more than that, she knew she wasn't ready to fight Ressa again. Her training with Nemura over the past month had made that abundantly clear. The gap between them wasn't just wide, it was a chasm.

As a former Fist, Nemura had a unique insight into their tactics. The biggest wild card was magic—how Ressa and her people had integrated it into their combat strategy. Whatever the case, Sloane *knew* she wasn't at their level. Nemura had put her through the ringer, training her five nights a week until she was nothing but exhausted, bruised, and barely standing. Just last night, Nemura had given her an assessment of her progress. Apparently, after four weeks of grueling training that had made every backbreaking college workout she'd ever done seem like child's play, Nemura had deemed her "no longer a lamb facing a lion." Was she now a sheep facing a lion?

She wanted to improve. She had thought her fencing experience would help, but even Stefan had laughed at that idea. Her two guards had very different approaches to fighting than Gisele and the knights, which only added to her frustration.

Finally, after one particularly bad sparring session, Nemura had clapped her on the shoulder and told her to stop trying to become a master swordswoman. "Focus on your magic and stay behind me," the guardswoman had said.

Sloane had huffed at the time, but then thought, *She's definitely the tank of the group. It makes sense. I guess the spellblade life isn't for me.* She turned and sighed. "Have you heard anything?"

Nemura didn't even have to ask what she meant. They'd had this conversation *many* times before. The telv shook her head. "Nothing."

Sloane sighed again.

"They'll show themselves soon," Nemura said.

"How do you know?"

The guardswoman's expression darkened. "Because it's what *I* would do." Her voice was calm, but there was steel behind it. "Knowing my army was approaching, I'd be looking for ways to weaken the city before the assault. Her priorities changed the moment she realized the fight wasn't as easy as she'd expected."

Sloane scowled. "Sure *seemed* easy for them."

"No one died." Nemura's tone was matter-of-fact. "You were the most injured, but only because they were focused on you. I have to admit, the knights were better trained than I initially thought."

Sloane glanced sideways at her. "Have you heard of her before?"

Nemura shrugged. "Ressa is a common name. It's been a long time since I was in the Empire. I won't know for sure until she makes her move"—her eyes hardened—"and I'm there to *stop her.*"

Sloane exhaled, shaking her head. "I'm glad one of us is confident."

Nemura didn't hesitate. "Just make sure to use as much magic as possible if multiple people come after us." She folded her arms. "After the meeting, I'm having Stefan stay with you as well. The Center will be fine with Ser Ernald and the guards."

Sloane gave her a flat look. "Didn't *you* say that the guards wouldn't be able to stop them?"

Nemura turned to her fully, expression unwavering. "They wouldn't," she admitted. "But having Stefan here will ensure *we* can." Her voice brooked no argument.

"From this point forward," she continued, "everyone wears armor and weapons. And you?" She met Sloane's eyes. "You should *never* be without guards."

Sloane inhaled deeply, glancing back toward the horizon.

Why is the waiting so much worse?

Gisele and Ismeld joined them as they made their way toward the Hall of War—the headquarters of the Marketbol Army and the central meeting place for all of the commanders defending the city.

Sloane still wasn't entirely sure what had changed General Irileth's mind about including her, but she suspected it had something to do with the work she had put into fortifying the city's defenses.

The improvements to the ballistae would likely prove critical in anti-siege warfare, and with those in place, there wasn't much left to do except wait—and hope that reinforcements would arrive in time to lift the siege. *Because we're stuck here without them.*

Sloane and the two female knights stepped into the crowded chamber, while Nemura and Stefan remained just outside.

Ismeld had accompanied Stefan back from the Center and had reported that it was now fully locked down, with armed guards on high alert. The remaining knights had gathered just outside the Hall in a nearby park and were geared up and ready.

Inside, Sloane and the knights entered a large, circular chamber with wooden bleachers curving around the outer walls. The design gave the space a natural amphitheater feel, ensuring that all present could see the center of the room.

An adjutant quickly approached and guided them toward their assigned seats near the back. After a respectful incline of his head, he departed without another word.

Sloane settled into her seat and assessed the room, gauging the atmosphere. To her surprise, the air was calm. There was no frantic whispering, no signs of anxiety or unease. She, on the other hand, had to press her hands against her legs to stop herself from bouncing them anxiously.

To distract herself, she looked down at the center of the chamber. There, an intricately crafted table stood—a map table, but unlike anything she had seen. The inner table was a large, circular display, its surface a perfectly detailed wood carving of the surrounding region and Marketbol itself. The craftsmanship looked flawless, as if the entire relief map had been seamlessly embedded into the table's surface rather than placed atop it.

A walking space encircled this central table, where three young officers stood holding long poles. It took her a moment to realize what they were for. *They're here to move the figurines.* Scattered across the map, small figurines marked various units and locations—a living representation of the current battlefield state.

Surrounding the main map table, a second, much narrower table encircled the room, leaving a single gap for access. Seven designated seats lined this outer table. But only four were prepared for use. *The others must be with the army that left*, Sloane thought.

Before she could dwell on it, movement at the entrance caught her eye. Gisele leaned in, whispering just loud enough for her to hear. "When the general enters, make sure to stand."

Sloane nodded slightly. A moment later, two soldiers in gleaming gold armor stepped in, moving to either side of the doorway. Then, a third soldier entered and announced the commanding party.

As General Irileth strode into the room, flanked by three other figures in elaborate armor, Sloane followed the lead of those around her, standing alongside the rest of the room.

The three officers accompanying Irileth were veterans, that much was clear—two telv men and one high elf woman, all nearly as old as the general himself. Each carried themselves with a quiet confidence, their expressions unreadable as they took their seats.

Irileth nodded once, a silent invitation for everyone to sit once more. For a moment, he simply surveyed the chamber, his sharp gaze sweeping over every face. Eventually, he nodded to himself, then looked down at the map table. He crossed his hands behind his back.

"Scouts have confirmed: the Vlaredian army will arrive tonight." The general's voice was firm and steady, carrying easily through the hall. The words hung heavily in the air. "The war against the Empire, the one we expected to be fought far from our lands, will instead be fought at Marketbol's gates."

Sloane saw his jaw tighten as he paused to let the news sink in. Then he continued. "Our army is gone. They left two months ago to support our fellow Sovereigns, believing the front lines lay elsewhere. So the Empire has outmaneuvered us. But it does not matter. With the timely expertise and assistance of a new citizen of our fine city . . ." His gaze found hers, and for the briefest moment, Sloane saw a smirk tug at the corner of his lips. ". . . we have improved our ability to hold out against the approaching army, and hold we shall."

His tone brooked no uncertainty. "Even now, Birith marshals Its forces to relieve us. But until they arrive, it falls to us to ensure that Marketbol remains standing."

The general's gaze swept across the assembled officers, commanders, and strategists. "Our city is a bastion of the plains." His voice was iron. "And we will not fall."

A tense silence followed. He gestured to one of the men at the outer ring table. "Commander Varka," he said, his tone shifting, "please go over the initial plan."

The telv man stood, and Sloane couldn't help but take note of his odd appearance: a scruffy, long beard contrasted sharply with his completely bald head. *Not the look I expected for a military commander.*

"Brothers and sisters, Alos himself smiles upon us!" Varka's voice carried easily through the chamber, rich with authority and fervor. Sloane stiffened.

"Erbium, as well, has blessed this city by sending one who could only be his pillar. The god of crafting has aided us through sanctified weapons of war—tools that will turn the tide in our favor!"

Sloane glanced at Ismeld, catching the same conflicted expression she felt mirrored on the knight's face. She grimaced and leaned close to Gisele. "I thought we were in a military briefing, not a sermon," she whispered.

Gisele kept her face forward as she murmured, "Stop squirming. He'll get to the point eventually."

Varka continued, his voice rising with conviction. "Now, these weapons are *key*! We must take the Imperials by surprise for the greatest effect. We will allow them to establish their positions, to fortify, to believe they are secure—and *then*, we will let loose our arcane wrath!"

A cheer rippled through part of the crowd. Sloane clenched her jaw. This was not going in a good direction. Agnostic and not particularly religious herself, she didn't want to be a supporter of some religious war. The way the man was talking brought to mind the effects of religious extremism in her own world. While this man was probably not pushing for something to that effect and was hopefully just pumping up morale, she couldn't help but draw some comparisons. This society wasn't as modern as she thought, after all.

"The fury of the guilds will be upon them! And all of it—every strike, every spell—will fall under the watchful gaze of Erbium himself!"

Sloane watched General Irileth, trying to gauge his reaction. The man's expression remained impassive, not giving anything away.

It was probably best that she kept her opinions to herself. Or she could likely discuss the religious aspects with Gisele, talk about some of the stuff her own world went through. Her friend wouldn't judge her.

The commander pressed forward, diving into tactical details, outlining the broader strategy the city would employ once the Imperials arrived.

Sloane forced herself to listen, absorbing the key points and hoping Ismeld and Gisele would explain it more later. When he finally finished, another telv commander stood and gave formal thanks for the zealous explanation.

The next speaker was far more measured. He spoke about the long-term strategy for the siege, breaking down what would be expected of each squad, team, and division. His words held weight, but it was clear that they would need to adapt as the situation unfolded.

Good. At least someone is thinking flexibly.

Then came the assignments. Squad leaders, garrison commanders, siege teams—each given their roles and positions. And then—

"Sloane Reinhart."

She sat straighter, listening as the commander outlined her role. She would be stationed on the walls, specifically facing where the enemy army would be concentrated. A team of soldiers would support her, along with her own two guards, ensuring she had protection while she worked.

The knights, meanwhile, would be patrolling key locations throughout the city, guarding against the ever-present threat of Vlaredian elites still lurking somewhere within Marketbol.

That assignment, at least, made perfect sense. But *hers*? Sloane frowned. This was a sharp reversal from the general's earlier stance. He had seemed hesitant to involve her too deeply, but now? *I can almost see the council's hand in this.* Was this political? Was she being used as some kind of statement? She turned toward Gisele again.

"Psst, what do you—"

The knight barely spared her a glance and cut her off with a sharp look. Then, after a brief pause, she murmured under her breath, "You are the bait."

Sloane froze. Gisele's expression didn't change. "It's the only thing that makes sense," she added, her voice low.

Sloane slowly leaned back in her chair, her stomach twisting. *Fuck.*

Sloane stood on the wall with Nemura, staring out into the fading light of evening. It was almost time. The Vlaredian army was advancing, hoping to use the waning daylight as cover to position themselves for the attack. The city was already locked down. Soldiers stood at the ready, siege weapons loaded, archers in position. Her job was to help ensure the main gate did not fall in the opening fight.

The city's military leaders wanted this to turn into a siege. They had no forces to attempt a breakout, no standing army to challenge the Imperial formation head-on. All they could do was force the attackers into a stalemate—one that would drag on. And if that happened . . .

Sloane exhaled. *If the siege lasts too long . . . food shortages, fuel shortages—it won't just be the soldiers paying the price. It'll be the city's people.* She pushed the thought away and turned to Tiberius, perched atop a custom stand, his metallic frame still.

For now, the golem falcon was in standby mode, his sensors trained on the enemy forces. Through her |**Golem Sight**|, connected to her watch, she could tap into his vision—a more advanced reconnaissance tool than the city had ever had access to before. Better yet, by displaying his vision on the watch's screen, she didn't have to waste time explaining what she saw—the officers could see the troop movements in real time. A huge advantage.

Still, even with that, the air was heavy with tension. The soldiers along the wall moved with honed efficiency, following sharp orders barked down the line. Sloane watched teams rush to their positions, loading the ballistae with the enchanted bolts she had worked on for weeks.

They had adapted the original plan, adjusting their designs based on time constraints. The bolts themselves had been enchanted—but not nearly to the extent she had originally envisioned. There simply wasn't enough time. Instead, they had reinforced them and incorporated a series of runic chains that allowed the ballistae to manipulate the bolts in-flight.

But the real innovation was in the siege engines themselves. She and the city's engineers had developed a way for the ballistae to channel power into the bolts before firing. With preset runes, operators could select between piercing bolts and explosive ones, adjusting for different battlefield needs. They had even implemented minor enchantments on the cocking mechanisms, reducing reload times by half. This wasn't just a siege weapon anymore. It was a game-changer.

And in the future, there was even more potential with blueprints for a magazine-fed system to increase rate of fire. *Not that any of that matters if we don't survive tonight.*

Around her, siege crews repositioned their weapons, finalizing their preparations. Sloane and Nemura were left relatively alone, positioned near one of the primary ballista emplacements at the front.

Her artillery spell, while useful in theory, had nowhere near the range that the city's siege weapons provided. If the Imperials somehow negated their advantage, then she would be called up to—Sloane resisted a groan—*as that zealous commander put it, "rain Alos's Fury upon them."*

Beside her, Nemura shifted, eyes scanning the horizon. "It's time," the telv warrior said, voice low. "The ballistae teams are nearly prepared." Her scaled plate armor gleamed faintly in the dimming light, the vambrace on her right arm catching the glow of the city's torches. Over her leather vest, a red shawl concealed a layer of chainmail, while her greaves, the same burnt gold color, completed the look. Her war hammer rested at her side, positioned for a quick draw, and her shield sat securely on her back. Every inch of her screamed readiness.

Sloane nodded. This had to work. Because if the city's defenses failed, Marketbol wouldn't just be under siege. It would fall.

A distant shout pierced the night. Sloane jerked her head around just as the first ballista fired. A thunderous crack split the air, followed by a chain of hasty commands down the wall. More ballistae fired, their bolts streaking into the distance. Explosions of purple arcane energy lit up the darkening sky.

Sloane's stomach dropped. *The trap was sprung too soon.* Shouts of disbelief and alarm rang out even as more siege weapons discharged. Sloane rushed to the edge of the wall, gripping the stone parapet as she looked over. Her breath caught.

The Vlaredians had *shield mages.* Six crackling blue barriers, varying in size, flickered against the night, shielding key sections of the army as they attempted to retreat out of range.

She scanned the battlefield. The city's premature strike had ripped through the front lines, leaving scores of soldiers dead, their bodies blasted apart. A gap in the shield formation revealed where a lucky hit had eliminated one of the mages.

How did they find shield mages so quickly? Her mind raced.

Ressa. They had her. *Of course* they had her. That meant they already understood the value of mages. And if they understood that, their first priority would be protecting their forces from exactly what she had done to the watchtower weeks ago.

Sloane activated [**Mana Sight**], her eyes flashing as she traced the mana flow across the battlefield. She quickly pinpointed the shield mages, isolating their mana signatures. She found no offensive casters. Finding mages was difficult enough, but finding ones capable of offense and defense while spreading them across multiple war fronts? That was nearly impossible. Even so . . . *seven mages, gathered here?* Sloane exhaled sharply. *Impressive.*

One of the ballistae fired, its massive bolt streaking through the night. Sloane's eyes flicked to the runes, watching as the penetration enchantment activated. The projectile sliced through one of the enemy's magical barriers, breaching the shield in a flash of blue energy before slamming into a group of men attempting to retreat.

A direct hit, but not the kind she wished she could have achieved. She had wanted to imbue the bolts with both the penetration spell and the explosive spell. Had that bolt detonated after impact, it would have obliterated the entire pocket of retreating soldiers. Still . . . breaking through the shields forced the Imperials to move faster.

Sloane exhaled sharply, forcing down frustration. Her heart thundered in her ears with the sounds of distant shouts and cracking ballista bolts echoing off Marketbol's stone walls. She took a cautious step forward, eyes locked onto the nearest siege emplacement to ensure it remained operational.

She hadn't gone two steps before Nemura yanked her back hard. "Look out!"

A whisper-thin whistle pierced the air, a silver streak flashing past where she'd just stood. Her stomach twisted. That had been meant for her.

THE FIST STRIKES

Sloane's instincts took over. She threw her hand up and cast two [**Flashbang**] spells, lobbing them in the direction the arrow had come from. The sudden bursts of light lit up the adjacent rooftops, revealing movement in the city behind them.

Her vision blurred as Nemura practically threw herself in front of her, shield raised high. A quick white sheen flashed over the shield as two more arrows shattered against it.

It's too dark, I can't even see the . . . wait. She used her [**Mage Sight**] and yellow mana flared in her vision. More conjured arrows. She tried calling out a warning, but she was too late.

Another flurry of arrows sliced the air in a brutal hail, pelting the guards around her. A group of Marketbol soldiers dropped instantly, pierced through by shafts of radiant mana. Screams followed, swiftly drowned by shouts of alarm.

She barely had time to process before two black-armored soldiers stormed up the wall's steps, swords drawn. Eight more soldiers swiftly ascended the stairs behind them. The two leading figures halted for just a moment—a familiar, smaller orkun woman and a towering telv man whose helm reflected the distant torchlight ominously.

There was a blur of silver as throwing knives materialized midair and flew toward her. Sloane flinched, but Nemura didn't even budge. Her shield shimmered with that same quick white flash, and every one of the daggers stopped dead.

Nemura rolled her neck, the motion casual, but Sloane saw the tightness in her stance, the readiness for a real fight. "Sloane," she said, her voice calm but full of intent, "any chance of one of your siege blasts?"

Sloane's hand twitched. She shook her head. "Not here. Too damaging. I'm limited to bolts."

Nemura barely reacted, nodding once. Sloane glanced to her right, seeing a group of Marketbol soldiers standing with them, shields raised, short spears at the ready. Her heart hammered in her chest as she drew her sword, its runes flaring to life.

"Take the siege weapons!" a woman's voice commanded, voice ringing through the chaos. "Move! We'll hold these ones off!" *Ressa.*

The Vlaredian squad surged toward the nearest ballista, weapons flashing in the firelight as they clashed with the Marketbol soldiers defending the fortifications. Two of the Marketbol soldiers broke rank and rushed forward, moving to engage the Imperial soldiers.

Sloane barely had time to register the motion before more conjured arrows appeared. They ripped through both men, finding every weak point in their armor with surgical precision. The two soldiers staggered, then fell. Her heart clenched at the sight, but she couldn't dwell on it.

Nemura barely hesitated. "Sloane! Stop them!" she barked, already rushing Ressa with a soldier at her side.

Sloane whipped around, spotting the Imperial soldiers darting through the chaos, already engaging the defenders in their way. She lifted her hand, mana surging, and fired two **[Mana Bolts]** toward the enemy soldiers racing for the nearest ballista.

Before impact, two metal shields materialized in midair, shimmering yellow. Ressa. The bolts deflected instantly. One bolt struck a barrel of oil, the resulting explosion igniting the night with a flash of searing heat. The second bolt careened toward two soldiers battling the telv Fist. With a burst of energy, it slammed into one. His body collapsed against the wall, spear falling from his grip.

The telv seized the advantage instantly, blade flashing as he cut down both soldiers with ruthless precision. His dark eyes locked onto Sloane next, and without hesitation, he charged.

Sloane barely had time to react. The telv rushed forward, and she reflexively cast a **[Flashbang]**, but he anticipated her move. He raised his shield, the burst of light deflecting harmlessly off its polished surface.

She whirled, lifting her sword just in time to block his opening strike, the force jarring her arm. She gritted her teeth, pushing back, adjusting her stance as he pressed the attack. The telv soldier advanced relentlessly, his blade a blur as he drove her backward, every ringing clash of steel reverberating through her bones.

Behind her, she heard Nemura's battle with Ressa—the ring of steel, the clash of shields, the grunts of exertion. Then: a sickening squelch followed by a male's grunt of pain. Sloane wanted to look, but she couldn't afford to.

She ducked a savage swing, retaliating with a swift thrust of her own that scraped harmlessly off the man's shield. The man lunged, forcing her onto the defensive, his sword slicing dangerously close. She sidestepped, ducked under another swing, and lashed out with a quick thrust—he parried, responding with a sharp kick that caught her in the side, sending her stumbling.

Her breath hitched, pain flaring along her ribs. She recovered fast, lifting her buckler, but her opponent was already pressing forward again.

Her mind raced. She wouldn't win this fight by outmatching him in skill. She needed a burst of magic. Mana surged to her fingertips, and she hurled a [**Mana Bolt**] point-blank.

The man dodged, but the bolt clipped his shoulder, sending him staggering to the side with a curse.

Sloane pressed the advantage, swinging her sword downward, the runed blade flashing bright. He blocked, but she followed up with another [**Flashbang**]. He managed to keep his shield in front of his eyes, merely jerking his head side to side from the sound.

Nearby, defenders struggled to repel the charging enemy soldiers. Shouts of desperation mixed with cries of pain as the Vlaredians fought toward the ballista. Sloane heard Nemura grunt in pain, her attention briefly flicking to see Ressa delivering a swift, fatal strike to the already injured soldier. Nemura roared in fury as she pressed the attack anew.

Focus, Sloane! She snapped her eyes back just in time to dodge a killing blow aimed at her chest. The telv pressed, exploiting every mistake, every hesitation, each strike precise and relentless. She caught his next swing on her shield, the impact rattling painfully through her arm, sending tremors of agony into her wrist.

Heart pounding, she stumbled backward, her foot catching on a fallen soldier's leg. She nearly tripped, barely managing to catch herself as she frantically raised her sword. Without thinking, she fired two more desperate [**Mana Bolts**].

Sloane's bolts went wide, one smashing into a barrel, sending debris flying, the other bursting against a distant defensive tower. *Damn it!*

The chaos of battle was overwhelming—the noise, the shouting, the distant explosions of artillery strikes. It was all she could do to keep her focus before the telv swordsman was again upon her.

He swung but she caught the blow on her shield. She stumbled, nearly losing her footing as his blade came down again. The soldier forced her backward, every strike rattling painfully through her wrist.

Gritting her teeth, she remembered Nemura's constant drills, the bruises and late nights of training. With a surge of resolve, Sloane lowered herself into the stance Nemura had hammered into her bones, shifting her weight to let the attacker commit fully to his next strike.

When he swung again, runes flared on the backside of her shield to dissipate the shock as she caught his strike head-on. With a grunt of exertion, she shoved the Vlaredian away, then snapped a kick to his knee, causing him to buckle. Pivoting swiftly, she slashed at his exposed flank, runes glowing as her blade bit into armor. The force staggered him, but his defense was swift, and he countered with a brutal backhand blow.

Sloane almost lost her footing as the hit sent her reeling. She spat blood and lifted her sword and shield. The man hesitated, sizing her up. He probably didn't expect her to fight as well as she had been thus far. Another impact rocked the wall nearby, sending bits of stone and burning debris flying across the rampart. Heat washed over her side, and she reflexively flinched away. The enemy's siege engines had clearly begun returning fire, and the city's defenders shouted urgent orders in the distance rushing to reload their enchanted ballistae.

Across the rampart, the fight intensified around the ballista. Defenders had rallied, managing to corner the Vlaredian squad, shields and spears pressing forward in a tightening circle. Yet Sloane could sense desperation in the enemy soldiers' movements, a reckless determination driving them onward.

In that brief moment of distraction, the telv mercenary lunged. Sloane stumbled backward, barely raising her buckler in time to deflect the blow aimed at her head. The force reverberated through her arm, pain jolting through her wrist.

He swung again, this time lower, aiming to get below her smaller shield. Sloane desperately hopped back, losing her balance but managing to fire an awkward **[Mana Bolt]** as she fell. It burst on the ground, knocking him off his feet. It was enough for her to scramble to her feet.

Sloane heard Nemura grunt in pain again. Without thinking, she turned and launched a **[Mana Bolt]** toward Ressa, but the orkun conjured a wall that absorbed the blast. The stone exploded outward, quickly turned to glittering yellow motes of mana before it could endanger its caster.

"Focus on your fight!" Nemura barked.

Sloane spun back around, pulse racing, just in time to see the telv soldier lunging again. Reacting instinctively, she drew deeply on her mana and hurled two rapid-fire **[Mana Bolts]**. The soldier ducked the first, but the second clipped the side of his shield, knocking him off balance with a satisfying clang.

Seizing the advantage, she surged forward, pouring mana into her sword as the runes glowed bright. Her strike smashed into his shield, denting it, and driving him backward. Yet he quickly retaliated, throwing a swift, desperate swing that Sloane barely parried. Her muscles burned from exertion, the weight of battle draining her rapidly.

Gritting her teeth, she cast another bolt point-blank, hitting the telv squarely in the chest. He flew backward, crying out as his armor buckled beneath the magical impact. She settled herself and snap-fired another **[Mana Bolt]** that caught the man's shield just right, and at the perfect moment, as he was standing up. His arm jerked awkwardly in a satisfying snap.

With a shout, Sloane conjured two rapid-fire **[Mana Bolts]** and slammed into his chest. The telv roared in agony, collapsing, his weapon skittering away.

Victory surged briefly as an enraged scream erupted from Ressa. Sloane felt grim satisfaction, until another volley of conjured arrows appeared, aimed directly at her. Nemura shouted a warning, and without thinking, Sloane drew deeply on her reserves, a fierce shout tearing from her throat as she unleashed an [**Arcane Explosion**] directly in front of herself.

The blast tore through the incoming arrows, splintering them mid-flight. Wood fragments showered down, stinging her exposed skin, forcing her to duck behind her buckler. As the burst dissipated, she staggered upright, ears ringing, vision blurred.

In that instant of distraction, Nemura surged forward, hammer connecting fiercely with Ressa's shield, sending the smaller orkun sprawling backward. Nemura struck again and Ressa hurtled over the rampart's edge.

Heart racing, Sloane lurched forward and peered over the wall just as Nemura shouted in frustration. Ten meters below, impossibly, Ressa lay on an enormous pile of soft, conjured pillows, and began to roll gracefully back onto her feet.

Oh, you have got to be kidding! Fury surged through Sloane as she cast another pair of [**Mana Bolts**], launching them toward the retreating figure. The first missed, exploding harmlessly against a stone wall, but the second clipped the mage's shoulder, briefly staggering her.

Before Sloane could finish Ressa off, another explosion shook the wall. A burning projectile slammed into the stone just a dozen meters away, showering the area with flaming debris and sending defenders sprawling. Screams echoed around her, blending with shouted orders and the distant thunder of siege engines.

Nemura yanked Sloane back from the edge in time to avoid more conjured arrows. "Keep your head down!"

Sloane cursed, rage rising, but she had no time to dwell. She spun toward the ballista just as a defender's triumphant shout announced they had cornered the squad. Spears raised, shields locked tight, the defenders prepared the killing blow.

Before they could close in, one of the Vlaredian soldiers tore a heavy sack from his back, hurling it desperately toward the siege weapon. Sloane's eyes widened, realization dawning a heartbeat too late.

Another soldier, bloodied but defiant, yanked a flaming torch off the wall. Then, in a moment that slowed Sloane's world, the man flung it through the air toward the sack.

"Get back!" she screamed, her voice lost in the chaos.

The sack erupted violently, an inferno tearing through the ballista and the surrounding defenders. Flames surged skyward with the blinding burst of fire and splintered wood, shockwaves knocking survivors to the ground. A deafening silence fell over the wall, broken only by the crackling flames and distant shouts.

Sloane staggered, vision swimming, heart hammering violently. Smoke and embers drifted through the air, harsh and stinging. The wall lay strewn with broken bodies and shattered defenses, but they hadn't lost. *It could have been much worse.*

She raised her head slowly, meeting Nemura's gaze.

"I will kill that woman," Nemura said.

Sloane gritted her teeth. "I should've just destroyed the whole damn block."

Nemura shook her head grimly. "Normally, I'd agree, but you'd have taken innocent lives along with her. You did the right thing."

Sloane stared at the city, feeling a sickening sense of unease. "How many more tricks do they have?"

Nemura gripped her shoulder, armor scraping metal against metal. "Whatever comes next, we'll handle it together."

Even amid the chaos, Sloane drew strength from those words, but deep down, she knew their situation was about to get much worse.

"Milady Reinhart!"

Sloane turned. Several soldiers were standing around the man she had hit with her spells.

"This one is still alive!"

Sloane looked at Nemura, who narrowed her eyes. "It is time we got some answers," Sloane said, sheathing her sword and attaching the sling back to her buckler so she could slip it over her shoulder.

The guardswoman nodded. "I could not agree more."

Sloane looked up just as more explosions sounded in the distance. She flinched as hurried footsteps pounded up the stairs behind them, and her heart lurched—were more of Ressa's soldiers coming? She spun, hand raised defensively, only to see Marketbol soldiers rushing onto the wall. A young telv woman in armor halted in front of her, snapping off a hasty salute.

"My lady! The gate has been attacked—we need you to repair it immediately!"

Sloane shared a tense glance with Nemura. "The rest of the Fist must have attacked elsewhere," she murmured, before addressing the soldiers standing anxiously nearby. "Lead the way. And hurry."

Nemura didn't hesitate. "Stay behind me, Sloane."

Sloane quickly sent a mental pulse to Tiberius. Her golem's chest lit with a familiar blue glow as he swiftly turned his head, metal eyes tracking her. With a shrill cry, the falcon spread his wings and glided gracefully to her shoulder.

Together, they hurried down from the ramparts, soldiers forming a protective ring around them as they raced toward the main gate.

Chaos met them when they arrived. Smoke filled the air, acrid and choking. Civilians rushed back and forth, buckets of water sloshing as they fought desperately to douse small fires. Bodies lay scattered across the stones—Marketbol soldiers mixed with a few black-armored Vlaredians. The metallic scent of blood lingered heavily, adding to the grim atmosphere.

Sloane caught a flash of red hair as Maud hurried from one fallen soldier to another, green mana glowing faintly as she healed the wounded. Cristole and Deryk sat among the wounded, both slowly sipping water.

Ismeld approached quickly, looking harried and tense. "Sloane! Nemura! You're both alright?"

"We are," Sloane replied. "Ressa attacked us. Nemura knocked her off the wall."

Ismeld's eyes went wide. "Did you kill her?"

Nemura growled. "That woman, Commander Ressa Ka'ai, managed to cast a spell to conjure *pillows* that cushioned her fall, then got up and fled. We did capture her partner, though."

I've never heard anyone speak of pillows with such disdain before.

"What happened here?" Sloane asked.

Ismeld exhaled sharply. "The rest of the Fist and a squad of regulars attacked the gate directly. They almost broke through—got way too close. We took casualties but managed to drive them off. Deryk and Cristole were injured, but still"—she gestured toward the massive wooden doors—"you really need to see if you can fix this before we speak further."

Sloane nodded grimly, following the knight to the gate. Her heart sank when she saw the damage up close. The huge wooden doors, thick and heavily reinforced with steel bands, were cracked and warped. Their massive iron hinges strained dangerously, twisted from whatever blows the enemy had inflicted.

"Oh shit," she muttered, immediately stepping closer. Without waiting, she activated her **[Mana Sight]**, scanning the damage as carefully as possible. Her stomach dropped—one or two more solid hits and the doors would collapse entirely.

Turning to a nearby soldier, she shouted urgently, "I need a ladder! Hurry—I have to reach those hinges!"

The man nodded, sprinting off to gather assistance. In the meantime, Sloane got to work on the lower hinges. Kneeling, she rapidly inscribed the runes for **|Strengthen|** and a runic chain that would **|Repair|** the hinges upon damage.

A ladder was brought and set up, and she quickly finished her work, taking the time to inscribe **|Renew|**-based runic chains into the wood of the door that would allow minor repairs as needed. Sharpened by urgency, she moved her hands swiftly and precisely.

After inscribing the final runic chain, she paused, sweat beading on her forehead. Soldiers were nervously watching her work and the tension in the air was palpable. Channeling her mana, she empowered each rune, feeling the magical connections solidify and take hold. The metal glowed softly for a moment before fading as the enchantment set in place.

Satisfied, she climbed back down, legs shaky from adrenaline. "It's done," she said, stepping back to examine her work critically. "It won't win any craftsmanship awards, but it'll hold the gate together a while longer."

An officer was standing behind her, arms crossed. "How long, do you think?"

She sighed. "Honestly? A few good hits more than normal. More than we'd have had otherwise."

The man nodded, his expression tense but determined. "It'll have to do. Thank you, milady."

Ismeld placed a gentle hand on Sloane's shoulder. "I think they have this under control now."

Nemura frowned deeply, her gaze scanning the devastation around them. "What exactly happened here? How did they get close enough to cause this much damage?"

The high elf knight glanced around, her expression darkening as she took in the lingering chaos. Soldiers moved swiftly, some hauling away wounded, others forming defensive lines to guard the gate. "The Vlaredians infiltrated the gate plaza under disguise. They brought explosives and something that set fire to nearly everything in its path," Ismeld explained grimly. "When they realized their deception had been discovered, they acted quickly."

She gestured toward the gate. "The initial blast nearly breached the gate itself, but Gisele managed to put up a protective barrier in time. Most of the damage you repaired was from what she couldn't block. After the first explosion, they ignited a barrel filled with some alchemical mixture that spewed a burning liquid everywhere. Gisele threw up another barrier—barely holding it back—while we engaged the attackers."

Nemura narrowed her eyes. "Where are the Vlaredians now?"

Ismeld sighed, looking at the scattered bodies on the ground. "Gone. After Gisele contained the flames, we held the gate while some soldiers chased the saboteurs through the alleys." She frowned. "Those men unfortunately didn't get far. Archers cut them down from hiding."

Sloane followed her gaze, taking in the still-smoking devastation, the blackened stones, the bloodstains. "Ressa came straight here after she escaped us," she murmured softly.

Nemura growled. "She brought Alexi Zil'vost, her loyal lapdog. Of course she did."

Ismeld crossed her arms, nodding gravely. "These people aren't going to stop. The Empire's Fist completely outclasses the city's forces. Marketbol's true army is elsewhere, fighting battles that no longer matter. We can't be everywhere at once, and these saboteurs will inevitably strike wherever we're weakest."

"I'm beginning to see that," Sloane replied, unease knotting her stomach. The situation had gone from tense to desperate in mere moments.

"Lady Reinhart?" a familiar voice called, pulling her attention away.

Sloane turned swiftly, nearly jumping as she saw General Irileth standing a short distance away, his face grim and shadowed in the flickering torchlight.

"My apologies, General," she said quickly, inclining her head respectfully. "I didn't see you."

He raised a hand in dismissal and approached. Ismeld and Nemura straightened, visibly attentive, their earlier frustration set aside.

"No apology needed," Irileth said tiredly, glancing around at the chaos.

"General, why are you out here in the open?" Ismeld asked. "With no guards, at that?"

"I ordered my guards to assist with the injured and recover those who had died."

"Do you need something from us, General?" Sloane asked.

The old telv's armor was smeared with soot, and there was a deep weariness etched into his features. He looked as if the weight of the city's defense had aged him another decade in one evening. "I overheard your conversation, and I fear you're correct, Lady Knight. Our remaining forces are spread thin, and we cannot withstand continuous sabotage from within."

He met Sloane's gaze directly, sincerity evident. "Still, your quick actions tonight prevented a complete disaster. For that, you have my gratitude. If the gate had fallen, the enemy would already be inside our walls."

Sloane exhaled slowly, shoulders slumping slightly with relief. "So, the overall plan still holds?"

Irileth gave a stiff nod. "Yes. Our initial defense was successful enough. The Vlaredians have withdrawn to reassess. Despite the magic they used to defend against our ballistae, they've taken significant losses, and they're unlikely to risk another direct approach tonight. I have already ordered increased patrols through the city; we'll find these saboteurs."

Nemura's voice cut through the air, skeptical. "You think they've gone back into hiding?"

Irileth looked at her, his expression unreadable. "Most likely. They struck hard but failed. Ressa is no fool; she won't risk further exposure until she sees another clear advantage."

Nemura sighed, her jaw clenching. "She'll find one eventually."

The general's eyes narrowed thoughtfully. "Then we'll be ready."

Ismeld shifted her stance, tension radiating from every line of her body. "General, has there been any news from Barith?"

The creases in Irileth's face seemed to deepen even more. For a long moment, silence stretched painfully as he considered how to answer.

Finally, the telv exhaled slowly. "No. We've heard nothing. The messengers we sent have not returned, and our scouts have seen no sign of reinforcements."

Sloane swallowed, a chill sliding down her spine. She'd expected bad news, but not complete silence. "Nothing at all?"

Irileth's voice softened, revealing the barest hint of uncertainty. "Nothing. We're alone, at least for now."

Sloane took a slow, steadying breath. *Shit.*

CHAPTER TWENTY-TWO

SHIFTING TACTICS

Sloane paced the Center's conference room in frustration, turning abruptly toward the nervous sun elf soldier. "Where the fuck is she? You've searched practically every building door-to-door—how can you still not have found her? Don't you have the man I disabled held prisoner?"

The soldier visibly flinched at her tone, his gaze darting anxiously between her and Nemura. Before he could respond, Nemura stepped forward, arms crossed, voice cold. "Exactly. He should've been under heavy guard. Explain."

The man swallowed. "The prisoner . . . escaped, Senior Guardswoman."

Gisele's head snapped toward him, eyes blazing in disbelief. "What?" She jabbed an accusing finger at him. "He was an enemy saboteur—a combatant captured in your own city. How exactly did you let him slip through your fingers?"

The soldier stiffened, mouth working silently, clearly trying to muster an explanation. Before he could speak, a telv officer stepped forward confidently, shoulders squared, her face taut with controlled urgency. "My lady," she began respectfully, eyes locked on Sloane. "While I understand your frustration, we're under siege. Our resources are stretched. I apologize, but we cannot prioritize your demands over protecting the rest of the city."

Nemura started to interject, irritation flaring on her face, but Sloane raised a calming hand. "Nemura, it's fine. She's right." She exhaled, pressing a hand against her forehead, forcing herself to remain calm. "As long as security at the campus remains strong—it's vital to our defensive efforts—then the rest takes precedence."

The telv woman nodded gratefully, clearly relieved to avoid further conflict. "We will continue securing the Center as promised. Additionally, we're reallocating what forces we can back into the city to maintain order, especially around critical locations."

Nemura's eyes narrowed. "Be cautious with that. They'll exploit any gap in your coverage to strike again. If your patrols encounter the Empire's Fist, do not engage without overwhelming numbers—particularly if the mage is present. She's the most dangerous."

The officer nodded solemnly. "Understood, Senior Guardswoman."

Sloane rubbed her forehead, frustration mounting. Her thoughts raced, replaying every moment they'd encountered Ressa's strange magic and the conjured walls, arrows, and even daggers. She suddenly went still, eyes widening. "Wait," she murmured softly, realization dawning. "Ressa . . ."

Gisele leaned closer, catching her tone. "What was that, Sloane?"

"Her magic," Sloane said louder, turning urgently toward the group. "Ressa's magic is illusion-based, right? She created solid walls in the alley from nothing. I bet she's hiding right now—creating barriers, false walls from thin air."

The gathered soldiers exchanged wary glances, shifting uneasily. Sloane turned to the telv officer, her voice firm and urgent. "She's hiding them in plain sight. They might have a wagon—or a house—something mundane and easily overlooked. She conjures walls inside, blocking your patrols from finding them. If she can summon weapons and shields instantly, why not furniture or partitions? I'd bet every gold coin I have that's exactly how they're doing it."

The woman's eyes widened in alarm. "You believe her magic can do something that . . . extensive?"

"Absolutely," Nemura insisted. "It's precisely what I'd do if I had her magic, or someone under me with similar capabilities. She could have a mobile hideout, disguised as simple cargo, right beneath our noses. Small variations are what you need to look for. Doors that seem slightly off, walls thicker than they should be, rooms smaller than their exterior suggests—those will be your clues."

The telv officer swallowed, clearly startled by the implications. She quickly nodded, then gestured to the soldier at her side. "Relay this immediately. Have our patrols double-check anything suspicious. No one engages without backup—especially if there's even a hint of magic involved."

The soldier saluted and rushed off without hesitation, urgency fueling his steps. After a few more questions and updates, the officer also left them, promising to try to keep them updated as time allows.

Sloane nodded, watching as the telv officer exited the room. As soon as the door shut behind her, Gisele turned to Ernald, her tone firm. "You'll need to warn the House Guard. Their patrols alone won't be enough."

Nemura nodded, arms crossed. "No. While I wouldn't bet on an attack here, I won't rule it out, either. Ressa is shrewd—she's already shown she's willing to wait as long as necessary for an opening."

Ernald ran a hand through his hair, looking weary. "I'll speak with Adaega and Elodie about hiring more guards."

Sloane tilted her head. "Do you think that's even possible right now? The city's stretched thin."

The sun elf knight sighed. "Probably not. With the city calling up the militia, I doubt it. But it doesn't hurt to try, right? The Guard's been running themselves ragged since the first attack. If we don't get more people on shifts soon, they'll be too exhausted to fight if something does happen."

She considered it for a moment before nodding. "I trust you. Take care of our people, Ernald."

"I will, Sloane. I swear it."

Sloane turned to the remaining two women. "What now?"

Gisele sighed, rubbing the back of her neck. "Now? We settle in. Keep working on whatever we can to improve our odds."

Nemura nodded. "Sieges aren't glamorous. Once the initial chaos settles, they become a waiting game. The Vlaredians are building a fortified camp, so they're planning for a long haul. I assume their supply line through Goosebourne is safe now."

Sloane frowned, crossing her arms. "Sounds exactly like how sieges worked in my world—except the Vlaredians have shield mages. That changes the game entirely." She paused, brow furrowing. "And the Valeni . . . their involvement still bothers me. I thought you said it was rare for them to attack."

Gisele looked at Nemura and gestured for her to explain.

"Historically, the Valeni have remained in their forests. The occasional raid or skirmish happens, usually younger warriors testing themselves—it's almost a rite of passage. But a coordinated attack? That was a surprise.

"What typically happens is predictable. Travelers might encounter a Valeni scouting party. If they establish superiority, the Valeni leader either backs down or presses the attack. If they choose to fight, it becomes a battle of survival.

"Most of the time, avoiding casualties on either side prevents long-term retaliation. If you subdue the Valeni without killing them, their unseen observers—the ones you don't notice—might let you pass unchallenged. But that doesn't mean it ends there. Those same Valeni might attack other travelers later to reclaim their pride. That's why your choice not to kill them was the right one. You established dominance with your magic without provoking future reprisals."

Sloane absorbed the information, recalling her past encounters with the Valeni.

"So, you think the surprise attack against the Vlaredians was a mistake?"

Nemura nodded. "At least, I hope so. The Valeni are changing, just like everything else. And if your theory about mana concentration is correct, then we may be facing yet another newly empowered race. The difference between them and your people is that the Valeni have already secured their lands. They aren't scrambling to survive—they're adapting to something new."

Sloane exhaled. "That's a lot of good information. Thank you." She sighed, glancing toward the window. "I guess we'll see what the future holds."

The moment of reflection passed, and she shifted gears. "What are you two going to do now?"

Gisele shrugged. "I'm going to train." She smirked, glancing at Nemura. "Want to join?"

The telv woman considered. "I'll need to work out a schedule with Stefan and Ernald, but yes. I also want guardsmen with you whenever you leave the campus, Sloane."

Sloane nodded. "That's fair. Thank you, Nemura." She ran a hand through her hair, feeling the weight of everything settling on her shoulders. "I have a few projects to focus on, so I'll be staying put for now. I still need to set up the backend of the runecard system and get our new scribe ready to start working on them."

Gisele grinned. "I can't wait to see what you create when you're stuck and bored. Last time, you built a metal falcon."

Sloane groaned. "Don't even get me started on that. I still don't fully understand what I did that night." She hesitated, then muttered, "That tea—"

"Clearly reacts strangely with terrans," Nemura interjected. "Or at least, some terran variations. Different substances have unexpected effects on different races. I'd be careful."

Gisele blinked. "I have to admit, I never even considered that."

Sloane let out a dramatic sigh. "That's information that would've been very useful earlier in my arrival."

The orkun knight shrugged unapologetically. "It's rare. But now you know." She turned to Nemura. "I should update the others. Should I expect to see you at the training pad later?"

Nemura nodded. "Yes. I'll be there."

Gisele turned back to Sloane, her smirk softening into something more serious. "Nothing is going to happen for a while. But be prepared—when something does happen, it'll be fast, and it'll be bad." She exhaled. "You're building a valuable relationship with Marketbol. If we survive this siege intact, it will serve you for years to come."

Sloane pressed her lips together, nodding slowly.

"Focus on your projects," Gisele continued. "Let us and the army handle defending the city and our people."

Sloane inhaled deeply, rolling her shoulders before giving both women a firm nod. "You're right. Let's get settled and get some work done."

The air in General Razane's command tent was thick with the smell of sweat, damp earth, and smoldering embers from the brazier in the corner. Ressa stood before the war table, hands clasped behind her back, chin lifted, meeting the general's steely gaze.

She had faced death, defeat, and disaster before, but failure still curdled in her stomach like spoiled wine. And this was her second failure against Sloane Reinhart.

She inhaled slowly, forcing down the anger simmering beneath her skin. "The gate strike failed, General," she reported crisply. "Nine dead, five wounded. The survivors include the rest of my team. They barely escaped. The Blighter knights with Reinhart responded too quickly and their magic was too much."

General Razane, a tall, broad-shouldered telv man with hard eyes and scarred hands, leaned against the war table, fingers drumming once before stopping. "And your mission on the walls?"

Ressa clenched her jaw. "Reinhart was there. One of my men and I engaged the terran and the soldiers with her to give the sappers a chance to reach their objectives. I thought I could handle her, but one of our own was there—a former Lieutenant Nemura Kho'lin, who had left the Empire after her discharge. The woman was skilled and at the end . . . threw me off the battlements before I could finish it. I didn't get a chance to see the effect of the squad I sent after a ballista."

Razane's golden eyes narrowed. "One was destroyed and that greatly relieved pressure on our forces as we pulled back. So that much was a success. I presume the soldiers died with it or were captured. The gate failure is unfortunate, but we would not have made it to the gate in any significant numbers due to the surprise the defenders gave us." He paused briefly. "Kho'lin . . . I recall hearing that name. In a positive way, as well. It appears she no longer holds her homeland in high regard since her discharge. You said you were *thrown?*"

Ressa barely resisted the urge to grind her teeth. "Yes, General," she admitted. "I survived thanks to a prepared escape. It appears the terran has been getting training, likely from Kho'lin. Worse still, one of my men was captured."

Silence hung over the tent. Ressa continued quickly. "We recovered him before he was interrogated, but it was too close. The city guard is getting better at tracking us. We won't be able to move through unnoticed forever."

Razane folded his arms, the fabric of his cloak shifting as he considered the report. "So," he said slowly, "not only did you fail to eliminate Reinhart, but Marketbol now knows you're active within the city?"

Ressa forced herself not to react. "Yes, General."

Another tense pause. Ressa pressed on, desperate to shift focus before the general dismissed her outright. "If I may . . . We need to change tactics. Our biggest problem isn't just Reinhart—it's the city's magic. Our soldiers are outmatched. Even with the shield casters, our siege tactics are outdated. Every day that passes, Reinhart and her people make the city harder to break."

Razane's expression didn't shift, but his fingers tapped idly against the war table again. "Go on."

Ressa exhaled and stepped closer, pointing at a map of Marketbol. "Sloane Reinhart has turned her 'Center' into a war engine. She's producing enchanted weapons, magical ballistae, and fortifications that are reinforcing the walls faster than we can break them." She met Razane's eyes. "The siege will take until spring at this rate—longer if we can't overcome the ballistae."

The general scowled. "We don't have that much time."

"Then we eliminate the Reinhart Center."

Razane studied her.

"It's feeding the city its greatest advantage," Ressa continued. "We can't touch the walls—not when this woman keeps reinforcing them. I saw the report when we returned. We lost half our first siege teams before we even reached striking range. One of the shield casters was nearly killed and will be out for at least a month, minus a leg. But if we destroy the Center, they'll lose their ability to magically power their defenses. They'll have to fight a normal siege again."

The general leaned over the map, tracing the layout of the city with one clawed finger. "And you're certain you have a way in and out?"

"For now."

Razane's gaze snapped up, sharp. "For now?"

Ressa lifted her chin. "The route we've been using is still intact, but it won't last much longer. The city guard is doubling their searches. We'll get one, maybe two more chances before they find it."

Razane huffed, clearly irritated. "Then we make it count." He straightened, considering his options. "You are aware that the city is waiting for reinforcements from Barith, yes?"

Ressa nodded.

"Then I want you to slow them down. Head south. Eliminate any scouts or forward detachments from Barith before they can reach Marketbol. That will give the city a false sense of security if you do not strike again anytime soon."

Ressa felt a wicked grin tug at her lips. "Yes, General."

Razane studied the map one last time and nodded. "After that, return to Marketbol. Plan your attack on the Center. However, you are not to sacrifice you and your men to accomplish it. If you find yourself unable to complete the mission, pull out without giving away your ingress point."

He went to his writing desk, grabbed a sealed report, and handed it to a waiting courier. "Send this to the empress."

Ressa arched her brow. "What's in the report?"

Razane's lips curled slightly. "I'm requesting more magic-wielders. And I'm informing Her Majesty just how effective magical weapons and wielders have been during this siege. Both the good and the bad, since they were used to devastating effect against our forces." He turned back to Ressa, eyes burning with expectation. "If we are to win this war, the Empire must evolve."

Ressa saluted sharply. "I'll work with the magic-wielders you have in the army. See what we can come up with."

Razane smirked. "See that you do."

The night air was thick with the scent of burning wood and ash, the distant echoes of marching boots a constant reminder that the enemy lurked just beyond the walls.

Inside Marketbol, life continued—grim, tense, and desperate. Supply lines tightened. Food rations shrank. The people waited for relief, knowing it might not come.

Sloane threw herself into her work, expanding the runecard system, developing new defensive enchantments, and working with the city's military and engineers to maintain their arcane weaponry. She slept in short bursts, her hands always stained with ink and mana, exhaustion creeping in with every day that passed.

The Reinhart Center became a hub of constant activity, its forge burning through the night, soldiers and artisans working side by side to reinforce the city's defenses. But with every improvement they made, the Vlaredians adapted.

Scouts reported enemy siege engines being constructed, more shield mages spotted among the ranks. The Imperials were learning.

Sloane sat at her desk, scrolls and diagrams spread around her, exhaustion tugging at her limbs as she studied the newest reports.

The war was shifting. And soon, something was going to break.

Sloane pressed her fingers against her temples, willing the headache away as she read over yet another request for materials. In the weeks since the siege had begun, the Reinhart Center had become the heart of Marketbol's defense, and the demand for magical enhancements had only grown more frantic since the last Vlaredian attack.

Sleep had become a luxury she couldn't afford.

The constant churn of the forge, the relentless etching of runes being inscribed, and the hum of mana-infused projects in progress never ceased. The Center had evolved into more than just an academic facility—it was a war factory, churning out enchanted weapons, armor, and siege modifications at an exhausting pace.

They'd even started researching creating golems there.

Sloane pushed the scroll aside and rubbed her eyes. "Elodie," she called, her voice hoarse from disuse.

The sun elf woman, who had become something of a second-in-command, barely looked up from the logistics board she was working on. "Yes?"

"How bad is it?"

Elodie finally sighed, setting her quill down. "It's getting harder to meet demand. The ballistae modifications are working, but we're running low on enchantment-grade materials. The burnout we found in certain materials is eating through our supply of silden ink. We'll need to start salvaging metal from other sources soon."

Sloane frowned. "Like what?"

Elodie hesitated. "Deconstructing parts of the city's decorative metalwork. Old railings, abandoned structures. Anything not critical."

Sloane exhaled sharply. They were cannibalizing the city's infrastructure to keep fighting.

"We need to find another source," she muttered. "I'll work on alternatives."

Before Elodie could respond, the doors to the workshop burst open, revealing a dust-covered Adaega.

"They're attacking the walls again," the Reinhart Center director announced breathlessly. "This time the eastern side of the city. Gisele and the knights are responding."

Gisele wiped sweat from her brow, fingers brushing against the soot and blood smeared across her cheek. The air was thick with the acrid scent of burning pitch and the heavy iron tang of spilled blood.

The attack had been repelled, but it had been too damn close for comfort.

She stepped over the cooling corpse of a Vlaredian soldier, her grip tightening around her sword hilt. The fight had been fast, brutal, and relentless—small-scale, but clearly meant to test Marketbol's defenses on the opposite side of where their camp sat.

The enemy wasn't just attacking the gates anymore. They were searching for weaknesses, patterns in response times—an opening. They were using their shield mages to help attack single areas. It allowed them to get to the walls, and even destroy one ballista with one soldier managing to light an alchemical device that exploded next to it.

Gisele scanned the scattered bodies—a mix of imperial soldiers and Marketbol defenders—before her eyes settled on Ismeld, who was speaking with a group of weary-looking soldiers.

As Gisele approached, the high elf knight glanced up, her face set in a hard line. "We need to start assuming these are distraction attacks. They're testing us."

Gisele nodded, rolling her stiff shoulders. "Agreed. That means we have to start setting up our own counter-traps."

"Are you suggesting ambushes?"

"Yes. They expect us to respond predictably. We give them false patterns, then when they think they've found a gap, we crush them."

Ismeld's lips twitched slightly in approval. "A bit ruthless for a knight? Whatever would our old knight-commander say?"

Gisele smirked. "He'd be proud. My aim is to defend the city. Not play fair. Just like the old man taught us."

The high elf nodded. "I'll speak with the city guard captains about organizing rotating ambush teams. If they're going to keep sending scouts, we'll make sure fewer return."

Gisele exhaled, nodding. "Good. Now, what's the casualty count?"

Ismeld's expression darkened. "Seven dead, five wounded. Maud is tending to them now."

"We're bleeding out slowly." She hated it. The waiting, the attrition, the slow drain of lives while the enemy sat outside the walls, tightening the noose.

If something didn't change soon . . . Marketbol would break.

CHAPTER TWENTY-THREE

HOLDING STEADY

Gisele pulled her cloak tighter around her armor, exhaling into the frigid night air. The cold had settled over Marketbol in full force, coating the city's streets with a thin layer of frost. Their boots crunched lightly on the frozen ground as she and Nemura walked through the near-empty streets, heading back to the Reinhart Center after finishing their patrols.

The city had been eerily quiet for the past two weeks. No raids, no sabotage, no direct assaults from the Vlaredians. The enemy had gone silent, pulling back into their fortified siege camps, content to wait out the city's suffering.

Gisele hated this uneasy stillness more than the battles. She exhaled sharply, her breath misting. "It's quiet," she muttered.

Nemura, walking beside her with a hand resting lightly on the hilt of her war hammer, gave a short nod. "Increased shifts on the walls the past few days."

They were just two blocks from the Reinhart Center when the bell tolled. A low, deep chime that reverberated through the city—a sound of alarm, a warning of attack. Gisele's heart clenched. Nemura's head snapped up.

A deafening boom shook the night, a distant fireball bursting against the sky. For a split second, everything was silent. Then came the shouting, the heavy pounding of boots against stone as Marketbol's defenders rushed toward the north wall.

Gisele and Nemura exchanged a single glance—no hesitation, no words. They ran. When they arrived at the north wall, chaos had already taken hold.

Flames licked at the battlements, casting long shadows over the exhausted soldiers struggling to man the defenses. Fifteen-to-twenty-meter-tall siege weapons loomed in the distance, behemoth constructs of war, launching massive containers that exploded in a bath of flame and also rocks weighing more than two men. The air reeked of burning oil. The firelit night made the thick winter frost steam where the flames consumed it.

Gisele's stomach twisted as she scanned the battlements. Already, two of the city's enchanted ballistae were destroyed, their wooden frames cracked and burning. That brought their total losses to six since the siege began. They had started with twenty-two and managed to rebuild only three so far. They were running out of time.

Gisele grabbed the nearest officer, her voice sharp. "Where's the commander? Who's in charge here?"

The panicked soldier turned. Blood was smeared across his face and his armor was singed. "Commander Halem is dead! Major Vasril is leading now—he's at the center of the wall, trying to get the remaining ballistae firing!"

Another explosion rocked the night, and one of the flaming containers smashed into a tower, perfectly aimed at one of the slits, allowing the fire to splash inside. The screams of burning soldiers cut through the cold air, sending a chill deeper than the winter winds ever could.

Nemura cursed viciously, yanking her war hammer free. "We need to stop those siege engines before they break the walls apart."

Gisele didn't hesitate. "We get to the major, now."

They pushed forward, dodging through stumbling soldiers, vaulting over collapsed barricades, and pressing toward Major Vasril, who was barking out orders.

The sun elven officer had his hands braced against a siege map, his face a mask of grim determination. His officers were frantically calling out orders to reinforce the wall, but the repeated impacts from the enemy trebuchets were disrupting the movements all along the battlements.

"We're out of penetrator bolts! The ballistae aren't doing shit against those shields!" someone shouted.

"We need to take out the siege weapons now!" another soldier yelled.

"Get a runner to the western wall, we need more penetrator bolts before this section of the wall falls!" the major shouted to one of his soldiers, shoving the man to get him moving.

Gisele's eyes narrowed as she looked out past the battlements. The remaining ballistae were still firing, but every shot that hit the enemy siege engines was being stopped by shimmering magical barriers. One of them seemed to flicker with the last hit.

There. She turned to the nearest group of officers. "Listen up! We need to take out those shield mages. Forget the siege engines—target anyone casting! Aim for the center of that left shield. Have all of the ballistae focus their fire on it!"

One of the officers hesitated. "Are you sure that'll work? Nothing is getting through."

Gisele's grip tightened on her sword. "If we don't, we're fucked. Trust me, it's weakened."

That got their attention. The order spread quickly and engineers switched targets, ignoring the siege weapons and instead focusing on the mages protecting them. The next volley flew true. Large, enchanted bolts rained down on the shield caster who powered the leftmost shield.

The shield flickered, then shattered. One more bolt landed right where the mage was standing and exploded.

The nearest ballista launched a massive enchanted bolt, striking the unprotected siege engine, exploding against it, and sending shrapnel into those around it. With one of the Imperial war machines destroyed, the city's defenders roared.

Gisele bared her teeth, turning to Nemura. "We keep doing this until they break."

Nemura gave a savage nod. "Finally. A fight worth having."

The battle was far from over. The siege engines still loomed, their crews scrambling to reinforce them. The Imperials had magic, numbers, and momentum.

But Marketbol had something else: desperation. And desperation made for dangerous enemies.

The flickering lantern cast jagged shadows across the abandoned storehouse, barely illuminating the faces gathered around Ressa. Her team moved like ghosts, their breathing shallow, their gazes wary, their weapons within reach. Marketbol had grown dangerous.

A light knock at the hidden door set everyone on edge. Ressa's hand drifted to the sword at her waist, but the patterned rhythm of the knock told her it was one of her own.

Joren, one of their scouts, slipped inside, his breath ragged. "We've got a problem," he said immediately.

Ressa narrowed her eyes. "What kind of problem?"

Joren ran a hand through his sweat-dampened hair, glancing at the rest of the team before settling his gaze on her. "The city guard knows where we are."

Silence snapped through the room. Ressa's blood went cold. "Explain," she demanded, her voice like iron.

Joren nodded quickly. "A patrol near the outer market—two of them were talking about increased searches. Said they had direct orders to check the area around the South Quarter, focusing on abandoned buildings." He swallowed. "They know we're in the city. They know we're nearby."

The entire group tensed, hands shifting toward weapons.

"So much for lying low," Alexi muttered.

Ressa's mind raced. The Reinhart Center attack was already a risk, but now? Impossible. They'd never make it out alive. Her jaw tightened as a new plan formed in her mind. They could still make someone bleed.

"The Center attack is scrapped," she said, eyes sweeping the room. "We're not hitting Reinhart tonight."

Some of her team exhaled in relief, others stiffened, their frustration visible.

"But we're not leaving empty-handed," she added, voice low and dangerous. "We're going to make the Guard hurt."

A slow, sharp grin spread across Alexi's face. "Oh? That sounds promising."

Ressa smirked. "We're giving them something to chase."

She grabbed a chalked piece of charcoal from a supply pack and tossed it to Joren. "We're going to leave clues, just enough to make them think they're closing in."

Alexi snorted. "And when they do?"

Ressa's smirk turned razor-sharp. "We'll be waiting." She turned toward the back of the hideout, where a trapdoor led deeper beneath the city. "The catacombs."

Her words hung heavily in the air. Then Alexi exhaled, his grin turning more predatory. "A perfect place for an ambush."

Ressa nodded. "We draw them in, let them think they have us cornered. Then, we shut the door behind them."

Joren ran a hand over his face, taking a slow breath. "So we're hunting the hunters now?"

Ressa drew her dagger, flipping it once before tucking it back into its sheath. "We always were."

Weeks had passed, and Sloane had settled into a grueling routine. The Vlaredians had received reinforcements, bolstering their ranks and allowing them to construct a second fortified camp, one that effectively cut off any hope of reinforcements reaching Marketbol. The city had long anticipated the siege tightening, but watching the enemy encircle them like a noose still sent a chill through Sloane that had nothing to do with the bitter winter.

There had been discussions about countering the Imperial camps directly. Ideas were thrown around such astrebuchets enchanted with runes, magical projectiles that could shatter fortifications from afar. But the city's leadership hesitated. They feared Ressa and her saboteurs would immediately prioritize those weapons, and given the destruction they'd already caused, Sloane wasn't entirely sure she disagreed.

Ressa's team had made only one appearance since the failed attack on the walls—but when they did, they left devastation in their wake.

One sharp-eyed officer had managed to pick up a clue, leading the search efforts to the city's sewers and catacombs. The underground network had expanded so much over the years that even Marketbol's current officials had no accurate maps of its full layout.

Still, the officer—the same telv woman who had met with Sloane weeks prior—had organized an ambush, taking a large force of soldiers to flush them out.

Instead, the Vlaredians were waiting; they knew the attack was coming. They turned the ambush into a slaughter. Eighteen dead and six wounded. And not a single casualty on Ressa's team.

Only then did Marketbol's leaders finally take the infiltration threat seriously. Curfews were implemented. Checkpoints were erected throughout the city. The militia was called up and placed on permanent street patrols, trudging through the cold and snow at all hours.

Nemura had been furious. She spent hours railing against the city's arrogance, seething at how long it had taken them to act. And Sloane understood the frustration. Marketbol wasn't just fighting an external siege, they were trying to survive a protracted war within their own walls. And they were floundering. Sloane didn't know if they would last long enough for reinforcements to arrive.

Her efforts with Tiberius had paid off and she had finally spotted the first scouts from Barith to the south. At least, she thought they were scouts. After she reported it, the city's army had given her a missive for Tiberius to deliver, but the scouts had fled at first sight. That was not a good sign.

When she later overheard General Irileth cursing nonstop about the incompetence of allied scouts, she found it deeply ironic. Marketbol's fate hinged on the reinforcements from Barith. And they might not even be able to reach them.

So Sloane barely stopped working. Figuring out other uses for her watch, designing new grenade types, and coming up with new ways to enchant equipment were just a small portion of what she focused on.

The days blurred together in a constant cycle of experimentation. Her most recent failure had been attempting to communicate through mana, a project she had been obsessed with for the past week.

Unfortunately, she simply didn't have the right magical affinity to make it work. So, instead, she fell back on what she knew best. Which was why she was currently buried in notes, working with Orthan Barat on a way to streamline the fabrication process for runecards.

Sloane barely looked up from the runecard prototypes scattered across her worktable when Orthan Barat spoke.

"Lady Reinhart, I want to have stamps made," the young scribe said with his usual straightforwardness.

Sloane glanced at him, quirking a brow. "Of course, Orthan. What type of—"

"Could you please commission a stamp for each rune you know of, in at least five different sizes?" he interrupted, his voice crisp and his response fully prepared. "Additionally, I request a complete explanation of the runes and their functions. I will write a reference manual for scribes."

Sloane leaned back, eyeing him with growing approval. The kid was thinking ahead.

"That's a great idea," she admitted. Then, a thought struck her. "Could you also put together a travel version of the manual for me? Something with all known runes, with room to add more as we discover them?"

Orthan frowned in thought, drumming his fingers lightly against his leg. After a few seconds, he nodded. "That is a task I can accomplish."

"Fantastic!" Sloane grinned, already considering what material the manual should be made of. "Maybe we could make it out of—"

"I will handle the details," Orthan cut in smoothly, already shifting his focus. "For the runecards, the stamps will allow me to produce the cards more efficiently."

Sloane opened her mouth to respond but then froze, a sudden realization hitting her like a bolt of lightning. "No . . . we can do better than that."

Orthan looked up. "Better?"

Sloane tapped her fingers excitedly against the table. "What if we didn't just use individual rune stamps? What if we designed a full-scale mana-powered press?" Orthan blinked, but she was already rolling forward. "We build a machine that runs on mana. Instead of stamping runes one at a time, we create a single large stamp that matches the exact size of a runecard. The machine presses the entire sequence in one go, leaving only the name field blank to be filled later."

A sharp gasp came from the doorway. Sloane turned to see Adaega standing there, eyes wide with realization.

"You mean to start an industrial revolution using mana as the power source?" The Reinhart Center's director stared at her with something between awe and trepidation. "What about electricity?"

Sloane barely had time to react before Orthan, still playing catch-up, asked, "Electricity?"

Sloane shot him a small grin. "It's a form of energy that comes from the existence of charged particles, either statically or dynamically."

He furrowed his brow, clearly intrigued. Before he could ask, Adaega cut in smoothly, smiling at the boy's curiosity. "I'll show you later, Orthan. We can run a few small experiments to demonstrate it."

Sloane chuckled at his mildly disappointed look, then turned back to Adaega to address her earlier question. "Mana is the better option right now. We don't have the infrastructure to use electricity, but mana is abundant and easily manipulated. The more I work with these runecards, the more I realize . . ." She exhaled. ". . . I bit off more than I can chew."

Adaega lifted an eyebrow. "You finally admit it?"

Sloane shot her a flat look, then sighed. "We're working at a much earlier technological level than what I'm used to. The gulf between our civilizations is wider than I realized."

"Mana will allow us to traverse that gulf?" Orthan asked, his voice steady but thoughtful.

Sloane nodded. "Yes. In many ways, it will. We're at the cusp of something huge, and I mean to ride the wave before anyone else realizes what's happening."

She glanced at the frosted windows, where the distant smoke of enemy campfires lingered on the horizon. "This will put us in a position of power," she continued. "I won't say *safe*—not with an army sitting outside the city—"

"Or the soldiers actively targeting you," Adaega helpfully added.

Sloane sighed again, rubbing her temple. "Yes. That too."

Adaega smirked. "Good. Just making sure you remember the constant threat of death hanging over you."

Sloane waved her off. "The point is, I can get this started, but we need to scale back our initial goals."

Adaega nodded. "Elodie will be thrilled. She's been saying the same thing for weeks."

Sloane glanced at her curiously. "She still wants to focus on the nobility and merchants first, right?"

Adaega nodded again. "Yes. That'll significantly reduce the number of rune-cards we need." She turned to Orthan. "Can you start drawing designs that Koren and his smiths can use for the runecard stamp plates? You already have the prototypes that Lady Reinhart has been working with."

The boy straightened, nodding. "Yes, Miss Adaega." He gathered his satchel and notebook and began scribbling down ideas as he walked toward the door.

Sloane watched him go, an amused smile twitching at her lips. "Alright, let's go meet with Koren and go over the press. I know he's been working on a way to speed up the production of the runecards."

The two women gathered their things and stepped out into the cold after-noon, their boots crunching through the snow covering the stone pathways. As they crossed the Reinhart Center's campus, the faint clang of hammers against metal echoed from Smithing Hall, a constant backdrop to the facility's relentless production.

Upon entering the hall, they were immediately greeted by a young orkun man, one of Koren's assistants, who had taken up the role of receptionist and general task manager. He sat at the front desk, diligently organizing ledgers, but the moment he noticed them, he quickly stood, offering a respectful bow.

"Lady Reinhart, Miss Adaega! Welcome. Are you looking for Mister Koren?" He straightened, his expression attentive. "He's currently inside the foundry. Should I retrieve him?"

Sloane chuckled. "Adaega and I will go to him. I'm sure you're busy."

"It's no problem, milady. I can—"

"Relax," Adaega interjected with a small smile. "The baroness and I can walk there ourselves. You should return to your duties. Lady Reinhart doesn't require people to drop everything for her at a moment's notice."

Sloane smiled at Adaega's gentle admonishment and turned back to the assis-tant. "She's right, but I do appreciate your willingness to help."

The young man bowed deeper. "Thank you, milady."

They continued on, making their way through the bustling complex. They approached the foundry, where a group of house guards stood stationed out-side, alongside a city soldier keeping watch. The presence of guards around the foundry had increased over the past weeks—a necessary measure considering the increasing number of sabotage attempts within the city.

The soldier at the entrance took half a step forward, as if about to challenge them, but then recognition flickered across his face. He quickly stepped aside.

One of her guards chuckled. "Welcome, milady. Koren's been busy today. I think he'll welcome the distraction."

Sloane smirked. "I may be giving him an even bigger headache."

Another guard let out a gruff laugh. "Thanks for the warning, milady. In that case, I think we'll be asking to be relieved for the next few hours."

Adaega shook her head at their antics, but Sloane laughed. "It won't be that bad." Then, with a conspiratorial grin, she added, "But it will help us make money."

The foundry was alive with movement. Workers weaved through the sea of glowing furnaces and hammering stations. Blacksmiths, metalworkers, and rune engravers worked side by side, the air thick with heat and smoke, the glow of molten metal casting shadows across soot-stained walls.

Since the siege began, Sloane had allowed the city's armorers and craftsmen to rent use of the foundry, ensuring that Marketbol's forces remained equipped.

The arrangement had become one of the Center's major revenue streams. Weapons and armor were forged, repaired, and enchanted, a near constant process that left no shortage of work for those in the trade.

Adaega had once informed her that, aside from two larger forges elsewhere in Marketbol, their foundry was one of the largest facilities in the city. Even so, demand had risen to the point where space was becoming an issue.

It was said that the city's leadership had purchased nearly every last store of metal within Marketbol, emptying warehouses regardless of previous agreements with merchants. Sloane had no doubt that desperation was beginning to set in.

Amid the movement, Koren spotted them and approached, wiping blackened hands against his apron. "Lady Reinhart," he greeted, his voice deep and even. "Good day to you." He dipped his head toward Adaega. "Miss Adaega. What can I do for you?"

Sloane smiled. "I have a project I want to go over with you."

The smith inhaled slowly, surveying the busy foundry before giving a curt nod. "Come on, let's step over here."

He led them to a smaller workstation—a table set off to the side, partially cleared of tools and scrap metal. One of his apprentices must have noticed the meeting forming, as the young man hurried over, bringing paper and a quill.

Koren leaned forward, forearms resting on the table, and looked between them expectantly. "Alright. I'm listening."

Sloane didn't hesitate. "You've been working on a way to quickly produce the runecards, correct?"

He nodded. "Yes, my lady. We've been casting metal molds and pouring the material in, then letting them cool. At the moment, we can produce about twenty cards per batch."

Adaega immediately gestured for the apprentice, taking the quill and jotting down notes. Sloane needed to find a better way to take notes herself, something more efficient than parchment and ink.

"That's a good start," she continued, refocusing. "Right now, Orthan is designing a series of stamps for you to fabricate. Each card will then be fed into a machine that will stamp the runes onto them."

Koren's brow furrowed slightly. "Are you talking about something similar to a coin press?"

Sloane's eyes lit up. "Sort of, but with some key differences."

Koren leaned in, intrigued.

Sloane gestured animatedly as she explained. "Instead of hammers or levers, we're going to power it with mana. The operator will place the blank cards into a slot, tighten them down, and press a switch. The press will activate, stamping the full rune sequence instantly."

Koren nodded slowly, absorbing her words. "A controlled, mana-powered mechanism . . ."

"Exactly."

Koren's apprentice ran and grabbed more paper as Sloane and Koren bounced ideas back and forth. By the end of the discussion, they had the foundation of a working prototype. Adaega left behind detailed notes, ensuring Koren had everything he needed to start fabricating the necessary components.

Sloane leaned over the prototype to the runecard backend, exhaustion pressing against her skull. They were eight weeks into the siege, and the wear was beginning to show. People were short-tempered. The knights were stretched thin. The soldiers patrolling the streets looked like ghosts—pale, hollow-eyed, surviving on sheer willpower and rationed meals. And food was running low. Marketbol's reserves were still holding, but if the siege stretched longer than expected, famine would do what swords couldn't.

The Center was still functional, still producing weapons, but Sloane was too aware of how thinly stretched everything had become.

They were making just enough enchanted bolts to keep the ballistae relevant. Just enough runic repairs to keep the gates intact. Just enough weapons to equip new recruits. But soon, just enough wouldn't be enough anymore.

Adaega approached, looking more exhausted than usual. "Scouts from Barith should be close by now," she murmured. "If they break through, we'll finally have reinforcements."

Sloane nodded, gripping the edge of the worktable to steady herself. "If."

That "if" felt bigger than the walls surrounding the city. Her eyes flickered with mana light, her mind already moving to the next problem. If they were going to survive this siege, they needed to come up with a plan to attack the army. Something the Vlaredians wouldn't expect. If no one else was coming up with a solution, she'd just have to figure one out herself.

* * *

The low murmur of voices filled the temple's great hall, punctuated by the scraping of wooden bowls and the soft footsteps of weary acolytes moving between the gathered citizens. Mariel wiped her hands on a cloth, stepping away from the long tables where she had been helping distribute food.

The city's rations weren't exactly low, but the temple was doing its part to ensure that none would starve by helping ration and serve it fairly. The people who came for aid were tired, gaunt, and haunted, but they still muttered thanks as they took the bowls she and the others passed out.

As she stepped back, stretching her stiff fingers, a soft voice called her name. "Mariel."

She turned to see the temple's high priest, his face displaying an easy kindness despite the heavy exhaustion behind his eyes.

"Would you deliver a message for me?"

She inclined her head immediately. "Of course, High Priest."

He handed her a sealed note, the wax still cooling. "Take this to Praetor Shalas. She should be in the medical tent in the garden."

Mariel nodded, tucking the message into the folds of her robe before heading toward the temple's rear courtyard.

The garden, once a place of serenity and prayer, had been transformed into a field hospital. The massive canvas tent that had been erected housed the injured, its interior crowded with makeshift cots and tables. The air inside smelled of herbs, sweat, and sickness, a thick mixture of life clinging desperately to itself.

Mariel stepped inside and hesitated, taking in the sight before her. A red-headed telv woman knelt beside an older man, her hands glowing faintly green as she healed his broken bone.

The knight. The foreign healer. Someone who had caused quite the stir among the faithful. Many had openly prayed their thanks to the gods for sending someone so obviously blessed by their will.

The older man sighed in relief as the light faded and he slowly moved and flexed his leg. The woman smiled at him as she squeezed his shoulder, murmuring something that caused him to chuckle, and then moved on to her next patient.

Mariel's gaze shifted to Praetor Shalas, who stood near the priestess overseeing the medical ward. The two women were speaking in low voices with equally grim expressions. Mariel straightened and made her way toward them.

Shalas noticed her approach and excused herself from the conversation, meeting Mariel a few steps away. "Mariel." Her tone was firm but not unkind.

"The high priest sent me," Mariel said, bowing her head slightly as she extended the sealed message.

Shalas took the letter, breaking the wax with her thumb and skimming the contents. Her expression remained neutral, but after a moment, she tilted her head down slightly and whispered, "You should stay away from the medical tent—especially after the last incident."

Mariel's stomach tightened, but she simply nodded. "Understood, Praetor."

Shalas gave her a small nod before stepping away, already moving toward the priestess again.

Mariel turned and walked back toward the temple, her steps slow as she let the words sink in. The incident Shalas had referred to had been an accident. Hadn't it? Mariel swallowed hard, her hands clenching slightly in the folds of her robe. She hadn't meant to do anything wrong, and luckily only Praetor Shalas knew she was at fault. It was just a momentary slip after seeing someone she respected dead. Anyone would be emotional in such a situation.

She shivered, pulling her cloak tighter around herself as she reached the quieter halls of the temple. She had been so careful to keep the darkness inside, to lock it away, to never let it take hold. But it was still there. And every day, she feared it would slip through her grasp again.

Mariel quickened her pace, heading toward her quarters. She needed to pray. Tenera would give her comfort and guidance. She needed to be certain it wouldn't happen again. Because if she lost control . . . she wasn't sure she'd ever get it back.

Sloane headed toward a waiting carriage after a busy day of work at the Center. And she still had house duties to accomplish—paperwork to fill out and reports to read from House Barat, which had pledged itself to her banner in a small ceremony during which Ismeld and Gisele stood by as witnesses.

Stefan and four house guards stood nearby, prepared for the trip. Tiberius was perched comfortably on Stefan's shoulder, chirping a greeting as Sloane approached.

"How are you, Stefan?" she asked, noting the fatigue in his stance.

The rogue smirked, but it was laced with exhaustion. "I'm sore. I swear Nemura does this on purpose—it's like she has a personal vendetta against me."

Sloane tilted her head. "What exactly is 'this'?"

He let out a dramatic sigh. "Kicking my ass during spars."

She laughed, shaking her head. "You'll get her eventually. Remind me to tell you about the 'rogue' archetype from my world's stories. It might give you an edge as you develop more mana abilities."

His brows rose. "I'll take literally anything that helps me beat her just once."

Sloane grinned. "You know Nemura only pushes you because she respects you, right?"

"Tell that to my bruised ribs."

She smirked. "So to speak."

He frowned. "What does that—"

But Sloane, laughing, had already turned away. She extended her arm, allowing Tiberius to transfer from Stefan's shoulder to her own before she climbed into the carriage as the guards secured the doors. The siege wasn't slowing down. And neither was she.

The ride through the Upper Quarter was slow and methodical, as was usual for this part of the city. Nemura and several guards had escorted her from the small manor the city had gifted her after the initial Vlaredian assault had been repelled, an acknowledgment of her contributions to the city's defenses.

The Upper Quarter was where the social and political elites of Marketbol resided. The council's decision to grant it to her hadn't been just about gratitude. It was an investment, a move to cement a relationship with House Reinhart, one that would persist long after the siege ended.

Being granted citizenship had been completely unexpected, and while it gave many benefits that not all people living within enjoyed, it was still second to citizens who owned land within the city. It was somewhat rectified by her owning the Center, but there was still fuss over her having an actual domicile, not just a place of business.

Nemura had convinced Sloane to stay at the Reinhart Center, insisting it was easier to protect. But Ismeld and Gisele had pushed her to use the manor as a location for personal meetings—a way to separate house business from that of the Center's. The city had even spared a handful of guards specifically for her protection, not that they were particularly necessary. The Upper Quarter was already one of the most heavily patrolled areas in Marketbol.

With her newfound status, nearly every door was open to her. She had priority access to resources. If not for the siege, her house's advancement would have been unimpeded. Sloane intended to cultivate that influence—to ensure House Reinhart became a force within the city long after the war ended. But first, they had to survive it.

The carriage rumbled forward, moving steadily through the cold streets. Sloane sat back, lost in thought, until a commotion ahead snapped her focus. She leaned toward the window, squinting to see through the crowd gathering in the distance.

A low murmur filled the air, the sounds of discussion, prayers, and chanting rising as they approached. She banged her fist against the carriage wall. A small window slid open, and Stefan's face appeared, his expression mildly annoyed.

"What's going on ahead?" she asked.

"Something at the temple," he said, craning his neck to look. "It shouldn't take long."

Sloane narrowed her eyes. She'd heard plenty about Marketbol's religion from the knights but had never experienced it firsthand. She knew Maud visited the temple regularly, using her magic to help heal the wounded.

Despite her initial worries when she'd first arrived in this world, the Church hadn't tried to coerce her into service, nor had it demanded anything from her. If anything, it had been grateful. It clashed with every expectation she'd had.

You know . . . no time like the present, she thought now.

"Stefan," she called. "Let's check it out."

His eyes widened slightly. "Are . . . you sure?"

Sloane smirked. "Yes. It's about time I learned more. We have the evening free."

He sighed heavily. "Alright. I'll have the driver park. Then we'll go."

Sloane nodded, settling back as the carriage jerked to a halt.

The cold air bit at her skin as she stepped down, Tiberius shifting on her shoulder. The crowd was thick, and as Stefan and two of the guards worked to clear a path, she caught sight of the temple's entrance.

The temple was an imposing structure, adorned with intricate carvings depicting figures of wisdom and battle, a testament to both the divine and the mortal struggles of the world. Several priests stood at the temple steps, speaking to the gathered crowd in calm, authoritative voices.

As they neared the entrance, a high elf clad in ceremonial robes stepped forward to intercept them. Her piercing silver eyes took them in quickly before she dipped her head slightly in greeting.

"May I help you, my lady?"

Stefan stepped aside, his expectant look practically saying, *This was your idea—go on, then.*

Sloane cleared her throat, smiling politely. "Hi! I'm Lady Sloane Reinhart. If it's not obvious, I'm a terran." She chuckled nervously before continuing. "I was hoping to learn more about the temple, especially since I'll be here for a while. A friend of mine comes here regularly to help with healing."

Recognition flashed in the woman's expression before she smiled warmly. "Ah, Ser Maud." She clasped her hands together. "She has been an absolute blessing to our efforts. Of course, please—right this way. I would be honored to introduce you to the high priest."

Sloane nodded. "Lovely! Thank you." She fell into step behind the priestess.

Stefan sighed quietly beside her. "I hope you're ready for this," he muttered under his breath.

Sloane smirked. "Sounds like you aren't. That crowd seems to be enjoying whatever's happening."

The raithe hesitated, then shrugged. "That's fair." He cast a glance toward the priests. "They're just . . . too stuffy for my tastes."

Sloane grinned. "Then this should be entertaining." She looked around, taking in the intricate architecture, the glow of ever-burning sconces, and the hushed reverence that filled the air.

Perhaps this would be more interesting than she'd thought.

CHAPTER TWENTY-FOUR

EVERY STEP COUNTS

Contrary to the assumptions of many among the Displaced, immediately following the Flash, the Church was exceptionally supportive of research into mana and its various applications. Indeed, numerous early breakthroughs were either pioneered by the Church or discovered concurrently alongside other early innovators. In fact, much of the terminology we use today can be traced back to only a small handful of influential individuals—some of whom were members of the Church itself.

It could be argued that the race toward dominance in this new era began before most even realized it had started. And a race it most certainly was—one the Church leveraged skillfully, positioning itself as a dominant yet impartial organization that oversaw innovation and established regulatory standards. This approach ensured the Church faced minimal opposition from the many nations of Eona.

A History of Mana, 184 SA

Sloane and Stefan followed the priestess into the temple, their footsteps echoing softly against the polished stone. They'd barely entered when guards in pristine white gambesons stepped decisively into their path, hands resting purposefully on their weapons.

Sloane halted abruptly, eyebrows rising in surprise. Before she could question them, a voice—level and stern—resonated clearly from behind the guards.

"Priestess, you know we cannot permit so many armed guests inside at this time."

Stefan let out an audible gasp beside her, drawing Sloane's attention sharply toward the approaching figure. A stunning sun elf walked confidently toward them, the warm lamplight illuminating her dark skin and accentuating the rich crimson of her polished plate armor. Over the armor she wore a pristine white tabard, intricately embroidered in gold thread with delicate patterns that framed a prominent, geometric sun emblem emblazoned just below her chest. A massive kite shield rested comfortably on her back. On her right hip hung a flanged mace, and a dagger lay sheathed on the left.

Sloane's eyes flickered to the dagger's placement. *Huh, she's probably left-handed.*

The priestess recovered quickly, smiling graciously. "Oh, Praetor. My sincere apologies—you're absolutely correct."

Praetor? What a strange name . . .

The sun elf's sharp gaze swept over Sloane and her guards, her expression unreadable. "I am Praetor Shalas," she said firmly. "Your house guards must remain here, at the entrance, with our temple guard. Your personal guard"—she nodded pointedly at Stefan—"may stay at your side. However, your weapons are to remain sheathed at all times, Blade."

Stefan, much to Sloane's astonishment, immediately straightened into a crisp salute, bowing his head respectfully. "Of course, Praetor."

Sloane's jaw dropped as she shot a shocked look at Stefan. Just moments earlier, he'd been grumbling about how stuffy and overly serious the church was. *The hell just happened?*

Praetor Shalas's lips curled upward slightly as she clearly noticed Sloane's reaction. She returned her attention to the priestess. "I'll escort Lady Reinhart from here, priestess. Thank you."

The high elf blinked, clearly caught off guard for a brief instant, before quickly regaining her composure. "As you wish, Praetor." She turned back to Sloane, offering a polite bow. "Lady Reinhart, it was truly a pleasure to meet you. Please pass along my warm regards to Ser Maud."

"I will do that," Sloane assured her. The priestess inclined her head again before swiftly retreating toward the entrance. Something about the exchange felt . . . peculiar.

"You wear your curiosity and confusion rather openly," Praetor Shalas remarked calmly, a hint of amusement entering her voice. "That certainly appears to be a trait common to all terrans."

Sloane shifted her gaze back to the imposing woman, taking a moment to study her more closely. Shalas appeared to be about her own age, yet carried herself with a confidence and poise Sloane had yet to master herself.

"I imagine it's about as common among terrans as it is among any other race," Sloane replied diplomatically.

"Hmm." The praetor's ambiguous response lingered in the air between them. She gestured down the wide temple aisle, signaling them to follow. Without another word, she began walking deeper into the sanctuary.

Sloane quickly moved to match Shalas's pace, and Stefan fell quietly in step behind her. As they walked along the temple's outer aisle, Sloane felt a sudden pang of familiarity. The layout reminded her vividly of cathedrals she'd visited in France—especially the Amiens Cathedral. Tall pillars of pure white marble rose gracefully on either side, supporting vaulted ceilings that seemed to stretch upward forever. Vines twisted gently around the columns, their lush greenery contrasting beautifully with the stark marble, bringing unexpected warmth and life to the sacred space.

A series of roof lanterns lining the vaulted ceiling allowed sunlight to cascade down, illuminating the interior in a warm, natural glow. The soft, golden light lent the temple a serene atmosphere, calming in stark contrast to the siege raging beyond the walls.

"Your temple is lovely," Sloane remarked quietly, genuinely impressed.

The praetor nodded, a minimal, indifferent sound escaping her lips.

They exited what Sloane assumed was the main worship hall intended for lay visitors, and entered a quieter rear section reserved exclusively for clergy. Here, clusters of priests and priestesses stood in hushed conversation, their voices carrying softly, like whispers brushing against stone.

Sloane instinctively lowered her voice to match the reverent quiet as she glanced at her escort. "Are we meeting the high priest?"

Praetor Shalas tilted her head slightly but once again made no verbal reply. They continued down a narrow corridor, approaching a set of heavy wooden doors. Beside them stood another sun elf, clad in ornate red armor similar to what Shalas wore, though his was notably plainer, perhaps denoting lower rank or status within the order. With a silent nod, the guard gestured to the room beyond, indicating that they were expected to enter.

Sloane let out a small, frustrated sigh, casting a pointed glance toward Shalas. "You really don't communicate well. Is that a common trait among members of your order?"

Behind her, Stefan made a quiet choking sound, startled by her boldness. A soft, breathy chuckle escaped from the praetor.

"I imagine it's as common as in any other profession," Shalas answered dryly.

Sloane huffed out an amused breath, stepping past the woman and entering the indicated chamber. *Cheeky bitch.*

The medium-sized chamber seemed to have served previously as a small chapel, though all furniture had been removed for its new purpose. The only remaining object, in the center of the room, was a solitary pedestal holding an impressively large crystal ball that glittered faintly in the natural sunlight streaming from above.

Sloane halted mid-step, staring at the crystal suspiciously. "Well, this isn't ominous or anything . . ." she murmured under her breath.

"I imagine it could appear that way. Good. I am satisfied."

Sloane groaned quietly, shaking her head in mild exasperation. "Can we get the other priestess back, please? She was much livelier."

"Sloane!" Stefan whispered sharply from behind her, clearly alarmed. She ignored him completely.

Praetor Shalas turned to face her. Her expression was serious, intense, as if this moment were a test. "Tell me, Lady Reinhart, why have you come here today?"

Sloane met the woman's gaze evenly. They were alone now—just her, Stefan, and the enigmatic sun elf—and she sensed that straightforwardness would be more respected than subtlety. *Fine. Directness it is.*

"I saw the crowd gathered outside and became curious," she admitted honestly. "The fact that your temple seems completely unfazed by the arrival of magic—particularly my friend's healing abilities—also piques my interest. Frankly, I expected a much different reaction from any religious institution here. I suspect your calm acceptance means you have discovered magic within your own ranks. If that's true, I'd like to learn what knowledge you possess, and I'm prepared to exchange my own knowledge in trade."

Praetor Shalas narrowed her eyes slightly, reassessing Sloane with a sharp, critical gaze. The silence stretched between them as the woman considered her carefully, weighing some internal decision before finally nodding once.

"Fair enough," the praetor said. "You are not like the other terrans I have met."

Surprise broke through Sloane's carefully composed exterior before she could stop it. "You have met other terrans?"

The praetor's eyes widened slightly in mild amusement. "That is precisely what I said. It appears you wear your emotions openly, as one might wear clothes. You will need to school your expressions more carefully if you hope to survive within the level of society you have entered."

Sloane swallowed lightly, a flush of embarrassment rising at the woman's blunt critique. "I'll take that under advisement."

"See that you do," Shalas said calmly. Her eyes held a subtle glint, something resembling approval or perhaps respect. "But yes, I have encountered other terrans before. Many, in fact."

Sloane took a deep breath, hesitating. *Should I ask?* Her eyes searched Praetor Shalas's unreadable expression, weighing the risk of revealing too much against her desperate need for answers. She'd made numerous mistakes in her interactions since arriving in this world—trust given too readily, secrets revealed at the wrong moment—and yet this was a chance to find clarity. *I have to try.*

"Have you . . . have you met or seen any children?" she finally asked, her voice softer than she'd intended, tinged with fragile hope.

The sun elf cocked her head slightly, dark eyes narrowing just a fraction, as if reading deeper into Sloane's soul. For a brief, unsettling moment, Sloane wondered if the woman truly could peer into her mind; perhaps some magic granted her insight.

"I have," Shalas said carefully. Her voice softened with unexpected empathy. "But I suspect none of the children I've encountered are the one you seek."

Sloane swallowed, heart tightening painfully in her chest. "How do you know?"

"None bore even the faintest resemblance to you." Shalas regarded her thoughtfully, analyzing her reaction. "Your tone isn't one of idle curiosity. You're searching for someone deeply connected to you. Your own child, perhaps?" She paused, eyes narrowing slightly. "You seem too old to be searching for a sibling, so—a son, then?"

Sloane winced involuntarily, feeling as if the praetor's words had peeled away an armor she'd carefully erected around herself. She shook her head slowly. "No. A daughter."

Shalas's expression softened further, and her voice grew gentle, understanding. "I'm sorry. Among those I've met, there were two young girls—but both were siblings, accompanied by an older relative. A grandfather, if I recall correctly."

The fragile thread of hope Sloane had desperately held on to snapped. She couldn't stop herself—the weight crashed through her, and a small, anguished sob escaped her lips. Her shoulders slumped, and suddenly, the praetor was there, steadying her with firm yet gentle hands on her arms.

Leaning close, Shalas dropped her voice to a comforting whisper, compassionate and firm. "Alos will protect her until you are reunited, I'm certain of this. You hold your strength with grace; do not falter now. I know not of your terran gods, but Alos sees no difference among his followers. His radiance touches all races equally. Still, I'm not here to convert you, merely to assure you that in time you might come to see the value in Him and His pantheon's guidance."

Sloane took a shaky breath, gathering her composure, and nodded slowly. "Thank you. I . . . apologize. I didn't mean to come here burdened with personal matters. I came for other reasons."

The praetor nodded in acknowledgment. "Yes. You came for magic."

"Yes. I've learned so much since arriving in your world, and yet . . ." Sloane hesitated, uncertain how best to proceed. She forced herself to stand straighter, reclaiming some of the authority she'd momentarily lost. "I'm not entirely sure where to start. Is there someone here with whom I might sit down and share findings, exchange knowledge?"

A faint smile curled the corners of the elf's lips. "I suspect I know precisely how to begin. Please, join me." She gestured meaningfully toward the pedestal bearing the crystal ball at the center of the room.

Sloane's brow furrowed slightly in uncertainty, but she stepped forward nonetheless, curiosity overriding hesitation. "Um . . . alright."

She approached cautiously, feeling an odd sense of anticipation as she stood beside the pedestal. Suddenly, Shalas turned her head to the side, her hand resting deliberately on the hilt of her mace.

"She's in position," Shalas called clearly, her voice echoing slightly in the chamber. "We're ready."

Sloane immediately tensed, head snapping around in alarm. Reflexively, her hands shot upward, mana surging into her fingertips, forming two rapidly charging [**Mana Bolts**]. She took a swift, defensive step back as the door opened abruptly, admitting a high elf in elaborate ceremonial robes.

Shalas raised an eyebrow at her display, gripping the haft of her mace tightly—but she made no move toward hostility. "I did not realize you were so easily startled, Lady Reinhart. Please, dismiss your spells."

With a scowl firmly directed at the woman, Sloane lowered her hands, allowing the bolts to dissipate harmlessly back into mana. Frustration surged through her at the praetor's casual dismissal. "I cannot believe you're unaware of what's happening within your own city walls right now, Praetor Shalas," she sneered sharply. "I've been ambushed twice already by a Vlaredian mage and her soldiers."

The praetor arched a delicate eyebrow, clearly unimpressed. "I assure you, I'm well aware. I merely assumed you possessed greater control of your reactions. That was my mistake." Her voice dripped with exaggerated patience. "In the future, I shall ensure the wind announces its presence clearly, lest it frighten you into reducing our city to ash."

Sloane's scowl deepened, her mind churning. Moments ago, Shalas had shown genuine compassion when she'd spoken about Gwyn. "You're deliberately provoking me. Why? We don't even know each other. What have I done to earn your hostility?"

The praetor opened her mouth to respond, but before she could speak, the high elf priest who'd joined them earlier interrupted.

"Terrans," he said coldly, like an accusation. He narrowed his eyes at Sloane, particularly at the mechanical falcon perched calmly on her shoulder. "Your people have descended upon our world like an unpredictable storm, each one certain that they alone can reshape our society for the better."

Sloane bristled, shoulders tightening. "I haven't done anything that wasn't welcomed by the people of this world."

Shalas again began to interject, but the priest cut her off with a sharp gesture, continuing firmly, "Oh, of course. What reasonable person could resist such honeyed promises of improvement? Your actions may appear benign—perhaps you even truly seek to help—but let us not pretend your motives are entirely altruistic. You seek something for yourself, as all terrans do. And before you protest, I do not fault you. Your people are hardly alone in this, and you are far from the worst of your kind."

His voice dropped lower, almost pained, as if recalling memories he would rather forget. "Do you know why the Vlaredian army now threatens our city? How they came to be here?" He took a measured breath. "A terran collaborated with the dwarves of Dheg Malduhr. He promised them powerful new *technology*—a weapon fueled by what you now call mana. By magic. That city, Dheg Malduhr, is now gone. Destroyed utterly in a single terrible blast that tore apart an entire mountain."

Sloane gasped audibly, eyes widening in horror as her hand rose instinctively to cover her mouth. *No. He couldn't have . . . Someone designed a magical nuke?*

The priest's penetrating gaze bored into her. "I can see by your reaction that you may know exactly what transpired. That, Lady Reinhart, is precisely the issue. Terrans before you have come with promises and grand ideas, yet have only brought death and devastation upon innocents. The Church learned this from one of our own—a priest who survived that catastrophe. Because of this, the temple leadership within the Sovereign Cities has sent an urgent request, and we now await a Decree from Her Holiness, the Archpriestess. A Decree to forbid the use of all terran-designed weapons henceforth."

Sloane exhaled slowly, suddenly realizing she'd been holding her breath tightly in her chest. "Good," she said firmly.

"W-what?" Praetor Shalas blurted out, her surprise evident. Sloane felt a small surge of satisfaction at finally seeing the elf woman caught off guard. *Serves you right.*

"I said *good*," Sloane repeated with greater emphasis, meeting Shalas's startled gaze steadily. "I know precisely what weapons my people can create. Honestly, I still don't fully understand why you call us 'terran,' but every explanation I consider frightens me. If there truly are terrans here who come from a more advanced civilization than my own, then the potential for devastation is horrifying. You speak of one destroyed city? My people had tens of thousands of such weapons—each capable of annihilating entire cities instantly, enough to obliterate all civilization worldwide many times over." Her voice faltered slightly, eyes shadowed by the weight of that revelation. "I would never want your people to live under that constant threat, where one man's whim could end life as you know it."

Behind her, she heard a small gasp of shock—likely Stefan, absorbing the knowledge she had just openly shared. Good. He needed to understand the stakes. Her speech may have used a bit of hyperbole, but if it helped get the point across, then so be it.

Sloane took a steadying breath and continued, her gaze resolute. "I have indeed crafted weapons, but only to defend myself and those around me. And even those are far less destructive than magic itself. The power of mana offers so many alternatives beyond mere destruction. Take Tiberius here," she said, glancing affectionately at the golem perched calmly on her shoulder. "Creation is what interests me—not devastation."

As if in response, the metallic bird let out a small, resonant screech, sounding almost musical but with an unmistakably mechanical undertone.

"I truly wish to establish positive relationships," Sloane said, choosing her words carefully. "You both understand why. My goal—my only goal—is to find my daughter. Making enemies will only complicate that search. Of course, that ship has already sailed with the Vlaredians. So, forgive me, but I won't share her name. If she arrived within the Empire, I won't risk them learning about our connection."

Praetor Shalas inclined her head solemnly, her tone softening. "It would be utterly unconscionable for me or anyone of my order to use a child against you. Such an act would go against every belief I hold sacred. Whatever reservations the high priest and I hold regarding your people, you can trust at least that much."

Sloane dipped her head slightly in acknowledgment, grateful despite lingering caution. "Thank you."

The high priest took a deep breath, visibly reassessing her. "You genuinely seek to help us, rather than harm?"

"I understand my track record may not be as clear-cut as I would like," she admitted earnestly, "but yes, that is my intention. I have people here whom I care for deeply, and only one of them is another terran. I wish to protect them, regardless of where they're from. As I mentioned before, my intention is to build lasting relationships and find the resources to fund what could become a search lasting weeks, months, or even years. I'll go wherever necessary to find my daughter, but I cannot do that if I am destitute."

The praetor glanced toward the high priest and gave a subtle nod. "She speaks the truth."

Sloane's eyes widened in surprise. Quickly, she activated her [**Mana Sight**], sensing the gentle pulse of magic fading around Shalas. "Did you just cast a truth spell? A lie detection spell?"

The sun elf sighed deeply, looking faintly amused. "You truly are a scholar, Lady Reinhart, to your very bones. Yes, I used a spell designed to discern the veracity of your words. It's precisely why I have been provoking you—one's true character often emerges under pressure."

Dropping the sight spell with an irritated huff, Sloane scowled at her openly. She gestured toward the large yellow orb that sat atop the pedestal in the room's center. "And what exactly is this, then?"

The high priest stepped forward, his demeanor growing serious yet hopeful. "While you've made considerable strides in uncovering the truths about this new age we find ourselves in, Lady Reinhart, you're hardly alone in your pursuit. This room represents the first step toward something far greater—something that will become a cornerstone of our future society."

Sloane cocked her head, curious, and beside her, Praetor Shalas chuckled softly. "I doubt I even needed magic to read that reaction."

Sloane raised an eyebrow sharply. "Careful. Just because you've managed to break my guard doesn't mean I'm afraid of you."

Shalas's expression shifted suddenly, her gaze sharpening dangerously, like a blade finally unsheathed. "I am a Paladin of Alos," she said, her voice deep and powerful, carrying an unyielding edge. "I rose to the rank of praetor by spilling the blood of those who threatened innocents. Compared to me, the Empire's Fist are little more than mewling cubs, desperately trying to live in our shadow. Do not mistake my current demeanor for weakness, Lady Reinhart. If you ever seek to harm me or anyone innocent, I assure you: I will cut you down before you cast your first spell, no matter how powerful you believe it to be."

Sloane smirked defiantly, refusing to back down. "Seems you can be provoked just as easily, Praetor."

Shalas scowled sharply, jaw tightening, but the high priest let out an amused, hearty laugh. "You two can settle this over a pint of ale after we conclude here."

The praetor sputtered indignantly, and Sloane scoffed, turning toward the high priest with surprise. "Wait—members of your church are allowed to drink?"

The high priest smiled warmly. "Whyever would we not be?"

Sloane considered it briefly, then shrugged. "Huh. Fair enough. Please, continue. You were about to tell us about the room."

With a slight nod, his voice composed, he said, "As I was saying, Lady Reinhart, this room represents the beginning of something entirely new—something profound and deeply significant. We have named it a Ceremony of Paths, and it shall be conducted exclusively by specially trained priests and priestesses. Utilizing this orb, combined with our emerging magical abilities, we can discern what changes mana has bestowed upon an individual, as ordained by the divine will of the gods. This revelation can provide us with insights into a person's strengths, affinities, and latent talents. We intend to use this knowledge to guide the people of Eona, helping them discover their rightful place in this changed world—to give direction and purpose to those who might otherwise feel lost or unfulfilled. Our hope is that—"

Sloane's breath caught, excitement flooding through her. "Holy shit. You can read my status."

A gratifying look of utter confusion crossed the faces of both the high priest and the praetor. The priest paused, blinking in bewilderment. "You . . . understand what we're attempting here?"

She quickly gathered her thoughts, adrenaline sharpening her focus. "If I'm correctly translating all your religious jargon, then yes. You're intending to use magic to read or reveal information about me as it specifically relates to mana and whatever new abilities or changes occurred following the Flash."

The priest glanced cautiously at Shalas, who seemed equally surprised, then nodded slowly. "Yes, Lady Reinhart. That's essentially correct." His gaze shifted slightly as he considered the interruption, clearly having lost some of the practiced rhythm of his carefully rehearsed speech.

Sloane offered him an apologetic, slightly sheepish smile. "So . . . should we start, then?"

The priest drew a calming breath, regaining his composure. "Yes. Yes, of course. Please approach the orb. Place your hands on either side, where the runic markings are engraved. I will place my own hands opposite yours."

Sloane stepped carefully up to the pedestal, finally taking a closer look at the orb resting upon it. Her eyes widened in surprise as she noticed the subtle golden-yellow swirling deep within its crystalline depths. *Impossible . . .* A sudden surge of excitement rose within her chest.

"This is a core! Where in the hell did you find one this large?" she blurted. The core before her was enormous, easily the size of her head.

Praetor Shalas's expression shifted into smug satisfaction, pride evident in the slight lift of her chin. "My paladins and I hunted down a massive beast in the mountains south of Marketbol. It had preyed upon several surrounding villages, terrorizing innocents. Though dangerous, the creature was slow, predictable. After a difficult battle, we recovered this orb from within its corpse."

Sloane shook her head in disbelief, quickly explaining, "These orbs are known as mana cores. We all have one—every living creature does. Animals, people, even the monstrous beasts twisted by excessive mana. Your mana core is what links you to mana and allows you to channel it into magic. I never suspected that one could be this size."

The high priest absorbed her words with interest, his eyes thoughtful. "Your core . . . yes, now that I know what to look for, I can see it clearly within you. Thank you for providing this information freely, Lady Reinhart. It will help greatly."

She arched an eyebrow, muttering dryly under her breath, "I've given away quite a bit of free information since arriving here."

Shalas's scowl returned instantly, her amusement fading into something sterner. Sloane held back the impulse to roll her eyes. *God, I simply don't understand this woman.* Looking back pointedly at the enormous core, Sloane refocused on the immediate task. "May I?"

The high priest nodded solemnly, positioning his hands on the runic markings opposite hers. Taking a steadying breath, Sloane activated her **[Mana Sight]** and carefully placed her palms on the indicated spots atop the massive mana core. The instant the high priest mirrored her actions, Praetor Shalas moved briskly to a nearby shelf, retrieving a wooden plank, a rolled-up scroll, and a quill. Returning swiftly, she set herself up beside them, ready to document the event.

"Ready, High Priest," she announced quietly.

The high priest's eyes drifted closed, and a moment later, Sloane felt a subtle but distinct surge of mana flow outward from the orb, gently washing over her before retreating back into the crystal sphere. Glancing downward in astonishment, she saw the orb's core shift from its swirling yellow to a pure, brilliant white, then ripple outward into a mesmerizing swirl of vivid colors, glowing faintly beneath their fingertips.

The high priest opened his eyes slowly, and an expression of unguarded surprise crossed his features as he absorbed the unfolding revelation.

"Praetor, record this," he instructed, voice thick with awe. "Attunement: Blue, Red, and Yellow."

A strangled noise escaped the normally composed paladin. From the corner of her eye, Sloane saw Shalas's eyes were wide. Sloane bit back a small smile, refocusing as the high priest's voice deepened, his eyes glowing faintly yellow and becoming unfocused.

Shalas hastily began writing, her quill scratching rapidly as the high priest dictated the information revealed by the ceremony.

Sloane Reinhart
"The Enchantress"
Terran
Path: Enchanter (Innovator)
Steps: 41
Core Quality: Exceptional
Affinity: Artifice, Alteration, Evocation
Attunement: Blue, Red, Yellow
Alignment: Mental
Key Attribute: Control

Praetor Shalas gasped audibly, though her hand never paused from its frantic transcribing. Moments later, the glow faded from the priest's eyes, and he blinked, regaining awareness. Sloane's mind reeled, momentarily stunned. *Steps? Forty-one? Wait . . . does that mean . . . holy shit. I'm level forty-one?*

The high priest exhaled slowly, turning toward the paladin. "Did you record everything accurately, Praetor?"

Sloane raised an eyebrow in surprise. *He doesn't remember?*

Shalas nodded slightly, voice subdued. "Yes, High Priest. Her steps . . . they're significantly higher than anyone we've tested thus far. There's also a new detail listed: Core quality."

He glanced thoughtfully at Sloane. "Core quality . . . Fascinating. Perhaps the added depth of insight comes from the information Lady Reinhart has already provided. Remind me, Praetor, what was her step count again?"

Sloane felt a thrill of excitement. *Interesting. The more aware he becomes of how the system operates, the more details he's able to perceive? I wonder just how far that can go . . .* Unable to suppress her amusement, she allowed herself a small, satisfied smile. *Exceptional, huh? Aw, shucks. Thank you, System, you sweet thing.*

The praetor cleared her throat softly, clearly uncomfortable. "Forty-one, High Priest."

The man's brows lifted slightly as he turned to Sloane, regarding her with a new appreciation. "Indeed, that is considerably higher than anyone else we've examined thus far." His gaze slid back to Shalas, curiosity evident. "Remind me, Praetor, what step were you on?"

"Twenty-eight, High Priest," Shalas murmured quietly, almost inaudible, eyes briefly downcast.

Sloane fought back a smug grin.

The priest crossed his arms thoughtfully. "Hmm," he mused.

Curiosity quickly overcame Sloane's momentary satisfaction, and she turned toward the priest. "Why do you call them steps?" she asked.

The priest looked at her with an expression she imagined one might use when instructing a curious child. "Because," he explained patiently, "they represent the key steps taken along your life's path, guiding you toward fulfilling the purpose that the gods have ordained for you. Each step symbolizes a significant advancement, a clearer understanding of your true self, your true purpose in our new, mana-touched world. This is but an excerpt in your life's story."

Sloane winced slightly, muttering under her breath, "But they're levels." She couldn't quite suppress her disappointment at the Church's choice of wording.

Praetor Shalas's expression darkened immediately, her scowl returning in full force. "The gods have granted us this extraordinary gift," she declared with quiet conviction, as though chastising a stubborn student. "They seek to elevate every soul on Eona, to bestow upon them a measure of true power. The steps are a reflection of how far you have ascended toward the heavens."

A switch flipped somewhere deep inside Sloane, and suddenly an irresistible urge to needle the woman overcame her. She tilted her head with feigned innocence. "Ah, so they're like steps on the staircase to power?"

"Yes, precisely," the praetor said curtly, her tone rigid and controlled. "I see you're beginning to grasp our perspective."

Sloane nodded sagely, deliberately contemplative. "These upward steps . . . if only there were another, clearer word to describe the sensation of progress we feel—like reaching a new . . ." She snapped her fingers theatrically, as though struggling to remember. "It's on the tip of my tongue."

Shalas's gaze hardened, clearly unamused.

Unfazed, Sloane continued with exaggerated thoughtfulness. "I mean, why climb a staircase to begin with? Surely we're aiming to reach a higher . . . hmm. I swear, there must be a better word for this." She glanced theatrically toward Stefan, who stood rigidly behind her, eyes flicking anxiously between the two women. "Help me out here, Stefan. What would you call that? A new floor? No, that sounds silly . . ."

Stefan's face grew pale, his mouth opening and closing in reluctance to engage with the growing tension in the room.

"Leave," Praetor Shalas said abruptly, eyes flashing with barely restrained fury.

Sloane turned slowly back toward the paladin, smiling sweetly. "I'm sorry, what was that, Praetor Twenty-Eight?"

The praetor took a tense step forward, fists clenching and unclenching rhythmically at her sides. "You—"

"Doesn't feel very good, does it?" Sloane interrupted sharply, dropping her amused facade. "Perhaps in the future, you'll reconsider being an asshole just to provoke an honest reaction."

She paused, an intriguing thought suddenly striking her, distracting her from the praetor's escalating anger.

The high priest exhaled slowly, stepping in diplomatically. "Lady Reinhart, please. Praetor Shalas, perhaps you—"

"Wait," Sloane interrupted, eyes alight with sudden curiosity. "Could we perform this ceremony on my guard?"

Stefan immediately began coughing violently, eyes bulging slightly at the unexpected suggestion. Shalas looked as if she were on the verge of an aneurysm.

The high priest cleared his throat cautiously, glancing uncertainly between the two women. "Very well, Lady Reinhart. If you would please step forward, Mister . . ."

"Stefan," the raithe guard choked out nervously, stepping hesitantly toward the pedestal. "Stefan, High Priest."

Sloane gave him a hearty slap on the back, eliciting a startled cough. "Come on, buddy, no need to be shy. This is a rare opportunity we might not get again anytime soon."

Stefan swallowed visibly but nodded his understanding, approaching the pedestal and placing his hands on the indicated markings. The high priest mirrored him, and Sloane calmly stepped back beside Praetor Shalas. Feeling particularly petty, she shifted slightly closer, deliberately invading the sun elf's personal space. The soft grinding of Shalas's teeth was like music to her ears.

The massive core shifted again beneath the men's palms, swirling rapidly until it settled into an inky, shadowy black, signifying Stefan's raithe attunement. The high priest's eyes grew distant, glowing faintly once more as he began reciting what Sloane assumed was a simplified form of Stefan's status sheet. Praetor Shalas quickly transcribed the details onto her scroll.

Sloane watched closely. *No matter how benign or routine this information might seem, that paper is coming with us when we leave.*

Stefan Stranca
"The Blade"
Raithe
Path: Infiltrator (Rogue)
Steps: 22
Core Quality: Vulgar
Alignment: Physical
Key Attribute: Capability

Control and Capability. Two out of three . . . but only level twenty-two? Sloane suppressed a sigh. *Come on, Stefan, no wonder Nemura's still kicking your ass. Those are rookie numbers.*

The high priest's eyes cleared, awareness returning as the magic faded away. Stefan stared wide-eyed, glancing back and forth between the paladin and Sloane, clearly uncertain about what he'd just witnessed.

"Did you find that informative, Stefan?" Sloane asked lightly, trying to mask her mild disappointment.

He nodded rapidly, visibly flustered. "Yes, my lady. Very."

She sighed internally. *Shit. I'm going to have to talk with him about how this isn't some divine revelation, aren't I?* Another moment passed and she shook her head subtly, dismissing the thought. *No. I really shouldn't get involved with religion. Let him believe what he wants. Safer for everyone.*

Turning to the high elf, Sloane inclined her head respectfully. "I sincerely appreciate the knowledge you've provided us, High Priest. This ceremony has been enlightening. If you wouldn't mind, I would prefer to keep the record Praetor Shalas wrote down."

He raised an eyebrow curiously, and she took the opportunity to elaborate further. "If you'll indulge me, I'd like to share something important from my world—a concept called privacy protection. Despite how Praetor Shalas and I may have interacted thus far, I genuinely believe you both to be honorable individuals. If your church intends to regularly perform this ceremony, it's critical that you understand the sensitivity and value of the information you'll uncover. This knowledge will be worth more than gold—potentially more dangerous than possessing a queen's most scandalous secrets. The details revealed in this ceremony will provide intimate knowledge of people's greatest vulnerabilities, strengths, and secrets. It must remain neutral, protected, and separate from any external power or influence."

Praetor Shalas seemed to put aside their recent antagonism, her expression turning grave. "Can you elaborate further, Lady Reinhart?"

Sloane nodded appreciatively. *At least she can set her pride aside when it matters.* She continued carefully, "High Priest, I don't expect you to answer directly, but I suspect your current level—or steps, forgive me—is probably similar to either Stefan or Praetor Shalas."

He considered her carefully, then gave a reluctant nod. "Indeed, it is."

She pressed onward, her voice cautious but clear. "I suspect that as you become more accustomed to using this spell, and as you advance further in steps"—she glanced pointedly at Shalas, who coughed quietly in mild irritation—"you'll eventually uncover even more detailed information about a person's abilities, strengths, and weaknesses. Imagine having access to the exact spells or capabilities of anyone you examine. Such information could easily be weaponized, potentially placing a target upon you or the priests who know it. What if, for instance, one of your priests learned sensitive details about a prince or princess who later ascended to a throne? What lengths might they go to in order to purge all who know their intimate secrets?"

Praetor Shalas's eyes widened in shock, clearly grasping the enormous implications of what Sloane described.

"That is extremely valuable insight, Lady Reinhart," the paladin admitted softly, her voice now full of seriousness and respect.

"I agree wholeheartedly," the high priest interjected swiftly, regaining his composure. "I will immediately consult with Her Holiness, the Archpriestess. We will establish a dedicated order within the Church, one tasked specifically with safeguarding this information. The Church must remain a neutral haven in troubled times, open to all who seek aid. We cannot fulfill the Celestials' will if we become corrupted by such knowledge." He offered a deep, respectful bow. "Thank you for your counsel, Lady Reinhart. It's amusing, isn't it? How obvious something can seem once pointed out clearly."

Sloane smiled slightly, nodding. "In my world, we have a saying—or rather, something similar—that hindsight is always perfectly clear. Essentially, things become obvious only after the fact. Perhaps it's wiser to approach anything new by imagining all the ways it could go wrong rather than focusing solely on the one way it might go right."

The high priest inclined his head thoughtfully. "Wise words indeed, my lady."

Looks like that annual personally identifiable information training from work finally came in handy, Sloane admitted privately.

Praetor Shalas cleared her throat softly, stepping forward. "High Priest, forgive me, but your next meeting approaches. Perhaps Lady Reinhart could schedule another time to continue discussing magic and related matters?"

Oh? Now you want to play nice? Sloane suppressed a smirk.

The high priest nodded quickly. "Ah, yes, Lady Reinhart. Thank you again for coming. I sincerely hope you'll return. I believe we can continue our discussions on magic in a more open forum next time—an exchange that would benefit both your interests and our mission. I hope, in time, you'll see that the Church truly seeks to do good in this changing world. Until then, I wish you safety and good fortune."

He gently took the written document from Shalas, carefully rolled it up, and offered it to Sloane. Accepting it gratefully, she gave him a warm, respectful smile.

"Thank you, High Priest. I very much look forward to our next meeting."

Stefan began turning toward the door, but as the high priest departed, Sloane couldn't resist one final dig at the paladin.

"So, Praetor Shalas?" she asked sweetly, her tone deliberately saccharine.

The sun elf turned slowly to face her, expression carefully blank. "Yes, Lady Reinhart?"

"Are you still up for that ale?"

Shalas's eyes narrowed slightly, tension flickering across her features. After a brief pause, she huffed dismissively. "Not on your life."

Sloane grinned openly, triumphant. *Knew you were still a cheeky bitch.*

CHAPTER TWENTY-FIVE

RESTLESS THOUGHTS

The soft rhythm of the wheels beneath her lulled Gwyn into a stupor. Wrapped in a woolen blanket and leaning into the corner of the carriage, she was teetering on the edge of sleep and dreaming of the mountains of Italy.

Her mother's voice carried over the crunch of snow beneath boots: "Come on, Gwynnie! You're not going to catch up if you keep stopping!"

Gwyn, barely seven, huffed dramatically as she trudged through the ankle-deep powder, her scarf fluttering behind her.

"I'm trying!" she called out, cheeks red, breath misting in the cold air.

Her mother stood a few meters ahead, a bright smile on her face, her own coat dusted with snow. She held a thermos in one hand, and with her other, she waved the girl forward.

The mountains towered behind them, their snow-capped peaks gleaming under the winter sun. Around them, pine trees stood like silent sentinels, their branches heavy with frost.

"I brought the good stuff," her mother said, wiggling the thermos.

Gwyn's eyes lit up. "Cinnamon cocoa?"

"The very same."

With a giggle, Gwyn broke into a slow, awkward run. Her mother knelt down, catching her in a warm hug as she crashed into her. They both laughed, the sound echoing through the trees.

They sat together on a wide rock, sipping cocoa and watching the slow descent of snowflakes. Her mother tucked Gwyn's hood tighter and brushed a few flakes from her eyelashes.

"You know," her mother said softly, "these are the kind of days I'll remember forever."

Gwyn leaned into her. "Me too, Mommy."

"I hope that wherever you are when you get big, you always find time to stop and relax. Even if the world's spinning fast."

Gwyn smiled. "When I'm big, I'll have to live by myself. Promise you won't forget me?"

Her mother's laugh was tender. "Forget you? Never. You're my whole world, Gwynnie."

A gentle hand on her shoulder stirred her.

"Your Highness?"

Gwyn blinked, the warmth of the cocoa fading as reality returned. She looked up into Ilyana's soft expression.

"We're here," Ilyana said. "The village has a tavern with rooms. Come on."

Rubbing her eyes, Gwyn nodded and pulled herself up, clutching the blanket close. The cold had seeped into the carriage, but the memory of her mother kept her warm.

The village was quiet, tucked between low hills and wrapped in fog. The tavern was small but clean, with a bright fire roaring in the hearth. A handful of villagers sat near the far wall, casting curious glances as Gwyn and her group entered.

Sabina and Taenya spoke briefly with the tavernkeeper, securing three rooms—one for Gwyn and her ladies, another for the knights, and a third shared by the tutors.

Later, once warm food had been served and the others had retreated to their rooms, Gwyn sat cross-legged on a pile of pillows in the room she shared with her ladies-in-waiting. Lorrena sat near the window, gently plucking the strings of her viol, the soft melody winding through the room like a lullaby. Ilyana was seated at the small desk, her brow furrowed as she wrote in her journal, the feathered tip of her quill twitching now and then as she paused to think.

Aleanora, the second-oldest of the three girls, sat nearby brushing out her long auburn hair. She was quietly humming along with Lore's tune.

Gwyn really missed Roslyn at times like this. It was always so easy to talk to her. The two of them would stay up late and have long chats about anything and everything. Roz really was her absolute best friend.

She found herself often feeling awkward and detached when she was alone with her ladies-in-waiting. Even though they tried really hard to make her feel at ease, and she felt like they were becoming more like friends finally, she missed the familiarity and ease of conversation she had with Roz. Roslyn was a friend who didn't have to worry about saying the wrong thing. Someone whom she could trust with all of her secrets. Still, she knew Roz would be nudging her and jerking her head toward Nora in this situation, trying to get her to open up.

Gwyn let out a quiet sigh and asked, "Did, uh, did you ever go on trips like this when you were younger?"

Aleanora blinked, then smiled. "Not like this, no. However, my family went to the lake every summer. Although my mother hated it, we'd fish, swim, and have these ridiculous singing contests. My little brother thought he could out-sing the birds."

Gwyn huffed a laugh. "Did he win?"

"Absolutely not."

They both laughed.

And just like that, Gwyn knew Roz would have shot her a smug look of victory. She fell into an easy yet largely superficial conversation with Nora. It was nice, even though it still felt a bit lacking.

"Was it difficult growing up as the only girl in your family?" Gwyn asked.

Aleanora shrugged. "I simultaneously had a lot of pressure to be perfect and less expectation of responsibility. I'm the third child, but the only girl. My father was always pretty lenient with me and my brothers, so I think my mother started to be harder on me to overcompensate. I ended up being the one my brothers would come to when they messed up and didn't want Mother to find out. She can be quite strict. She works me fairly hard at times, so being here with you is a bit of a relief in that regard. And I get more responsibility, which is an added benefit."

"What do you want to do after the Academy?" Gwyn asked. She caught Ilyana sneaking a glance over at them, clearly listening in.

Aleanora exhaled softly. "Honestly? I don't know. The things Ser Norric does would be something I'd enjoy. He does so much, and for someone of my station, it would be a perfect role. Unfortunately, being the only daughter limits my options. My mother's probably arranging suitors right now. Wouldn't surprise me if I have to start meeting them while we're in the capital."

"Ugh." Gwyn frowned. *That sounds awful. Boys are just . . . gross.*

From her spot at the desk, Ilyana looked up with a smirk. "Well, there are a lot more boys to choose from in Reme. The Academy alone is filled with them. I can help if you want."

Gwyn was confused for a moment then realized Ilyana was talking about the capital. It was odd to hear it by its actual name rather than just "the capital." Avirans certainly believed their kingdom was the center of everything. Aleanora blinked. "You'd . . . help me with that?"

Ilyana nodded, twirling her quill. "Sure. If you're going to be forced into meeting potential matches, might as well know what you're getting into. Besides, someone has to keep you from settling for a boring one."

That was one thing that Gwyn was *not* looking forward to when they reached the capital. Her tutor had told her that many young nobles often travel to Reme solely to attend social events to find matches.

Gwyn had no interest in that.

She also worried about people trying to steal her time with Roslyn. Aleanora had told her before that the heir of a duchy was someone everyone had their eye on. She hated how just the thought of it made her tummy twist.

Aleanora chuckled. "Then I'd like that. Thank you, Ilyana." Before she could say more, a knock came at the door. She jumped up and rushed to answer it.

The door creaked open, and Gwyn's tutor, Maya Rolfe, peeked her head in. "Your Highness? Are you still awake?"

"Yes, Miss Rolfe, we're just relaxing."

"Wonderful! Would you like to convene the Research Club?"

Gwyn's eyes brightened. "Yes, please!"

She scrambled to her feet and went to the small nightstand, pulling her well-worn leatherbound journal from its spot. Tucked between its pages were small scraps of paper, dried petals, and little notes of things she wanted to tell her mom.

Clutching the journal to her chest, she turned back to Aleanora. "Save me a pillow?"

"Always."

Gwyn followed her tutor down to the firelit common room, ready to explore more mysteries of magic. The tavern was quieter now. Most of the villagers had left, and the fire burned low. They settled at a small corner table away from the hearth.

Gwyn dropped into the chair with her journal and grinned, the pretense of formality gone between the two of them. "What are we researching tonight?"

Maya returned the grin, already opening a leather case filled with chalk, parchment, and a tiny vial of glowing ink. "You. Specifically, your fire."

"My fire?"

Maya leaned forward, her tone equal parts excitement and curiosity. "Gwyn, the red-gold fire you've used is fascinating. It doesn't appear to react like any fire I've seen."

Gwyn nodded. "Maybe because it's magical. I get the feeling it's related to dragons—which I think is what that drakyyd had started to turn into, but without wings. Like a drake. I remember from my stories that they're the non-flying version of dragons."

Maya tapped her quill against her notes. "But here's the thing—no one on Eona really knows what a 'dragon' is. There are drakyyds, sure, beasts the size of a big hound, dangerous but known. And wynvers, the little flying reptiles that like to curl up by fires to stay warm. I suspect that the mana around us is changing these creatures somehow. However, that leaves more questions."

Gwyn was intrigued. "Like what?"

"*How* is it changing them? Why isn't it affecting *people*? And if it is, what is it doing to us or them? Drakyyds are forest dwellers, so that leads me to believe the large one you encountered ventured from the Ayeval Forest. *What* is happening inside of the forest to make such a creature? If mana is twisting the animals that we know and turning them into things even your world believed fictional, then what else can we expect? I realize you have a fantastical vision of what dragons are based on your stories, but I fear what a real dragon would be like and how dangerous it would be. Look at the damage that . . . drake did before it was subdued."

"But she was just defending herself and her baby!" Gwyn protested.

"I can agree with you on that, but that doesn't mean she wouldn't have preyed on livestock or attacked people if she or her baby got hungry. A predator that large has a large food requirement."

Gwyn pursed her lips. "Okay, I can see that. Still, she felt smarter than just a simple animal. It was like she understood me."

"I would be really interested to observe an interaction with another one day, if it could be made safe."

Gwyn smiled. "Me too."

Maya tapped her quill against her notes. "Now, back to your magic. What if your interaction with that large drake somehow resonated with your mana and changed it? We need to explore the difference. Your fire isn't just hot—it's intense. Commanding."

"I like that." Gwyn flipped her journal open and scribbled: *Draconic fire = commanding, rare, influenced by positive dragon meeting and sharing fire?*

"But while we're exploring fire," Maya added with a sly smile, "I want you to focus the next week on your white mana. You already used it once when you helped Roslyn float after she slipped."

Gwyn smiled proudly. "She would've hit the ground so hard. It just felt . . . right."

"That's what makes it important. I don't want you to rely only on fire. It's powerful, sure—great for fighting or lighting campfires like you've been doing lately."

Gwyn snorted. "Hey, it's really good for that. I'm the official portable torch."

Maya laughed. "Exactly. But you're more than that, Gwyn. Your magic has *so* much potential to make daily life easier. Think about it. How can your magic improve both your life and the lives of others around you?"

Gwyn scribbled eagerly: *Focus for the week: white magic. Use magic for daily tasks. More utility, less burny.*

Maya nodded. "Mine's more . . . analytical. It helps me understand patterns, connections. It's logic. Intuition powered by structure."

"So, yours is like . . . *insight.*"

"Exactly."

Gwyn wrote: *Maya: Blue = Insight / Structure?*

Their theory came together slowly: that each color of magic had an underlying *concept*—a theme that governed its behavior, limits, and maybe even intent. Not just power, but purpose. For it to work, you needed to fit your view of what you wanted magic to accomplish together with its concept. Like how Gwyn's red mana controlled her fire, but it wasn't *just* about fire. It was about her anger and desire for making things right. For protecting her people.

When they took a break, Maya leaned back and said, "Since we're getting closer to the Naro Pass, and I brought up the Ayeval Forest, I wanted to tell you a bit about the Valeni. I know you've been asking."

Gwyn perked up. "Yes, please!" She hesitated a moment. "Why don't people know more about the Valeni? It seems like no one really talks about them. Not even in the history books I've been studying."

Maya nodded slowly, her expression growing more serious. "That's because we don't know much. The Valeni keep to themselves. Their political structure is a mystery to most and each Forest is its own entity. Imagine them as separate countries. What little we do know comes from fragmented texts—mostly from old Loreni records."

She continued, "The Valeni are descendants of an empire that existed on Ikios long before the Loreni crossed the sea and began settling here. Those texts describe how the empire was already in decline when it came into conflict with the Loreni, who were extremely warlike during that time. The Valeni were deeply connected with nature, and as the colonization period neared its end, many of them retreated into the forests, where they already had towns and villages nestled among the massive trees. They vanished into those woods and never really came back out—at least, not in any organized political way."

Gwyn scribbled in her journal: *Valeni = descendants of ancient empire. Forest retreat. Deep connection with nature. Loreni conflict = collapse. Elves were the bad guys?*

Maya smiled at the summary. "That connection with the forests? It runs deep. And they've had generations to make them nearly impenetrable to outsiders."

Then she picked up where she left off. "There are four Val Forests in Aviran lands. Each of them could be a kingdom on its own—massive, ancient, and full of hidden towns and even cities. The Valeni live in them. The Ayeval Forest is the most open; they keep to themselves but are the most likely to trade with individuals. Independent observations have noted that they've built relationships with the Mistval Valeni and the dwarves of Dirn Loduhr."

"Wait, but wouldn't that mean crossing Aviran land? The Naro Pass that we're about to go through?"

Maya nodded. "Exactly. Some believe there's a massive tunnel under the pass that the dwarves dug centuries ago, but there's no real evidence. Just rumors."

Gwyn scribbled that down immediately. "What about the others?"

"The biggest is the Aerinval Forest. It's nearly a kingdom in size and population. It's also the one Avira fears most."

Gwyn's eyes widened.

Maya went on, her tone quieting. "Avira tried to invade. Twice. Once they sent an army of twenty thousand. The Valeni wiped them out. Another time, a king demanded they give up rights to their forest. When they refused, he threatened to burn it down."

"What happened?"

"They sent back his envoy's head, raided a castle, and killed the king and his son. A distant cousin had to take the throne."

Gwyn blinked. "Whoa."

Maya nodded solemnly. "The subsequent kings have never tried again." She stretched and looked out the window, where the twin moonlight filtered in. "We should call it for tonight. It's getting late, and tomorrow when we stop for the night, you'll have the grump working with you."

Gwyn giggled. Maya's relationship with her husband, Mister Branigan, was fun. She closed her journal and hugged it to her chest. "Thanks, Maya."

"Anytime. Sleep well, Gwyn."

Gwyn climbed the stairs silently, careful not to wake anyone in the quiet tavern. The door to her room creaked slightly as she opened it and slipped inside. One of the two beds was already occupied—Lorrena curled beneath the covers, her breathing deep and even. Ilyana sat upright at the edge of that same bed, speaking softly across the room to Aleanora, who lay in the bed she'd be sharing with Gwyn. Both girls looked up as she entered.

"Hey, Gwyn," Ilyana whispered with a warm smile.

"Welcome back," Nora added, brushing her hair back from her face.

Ilyana stood. "Do you need help getting ready for bed?"

Gwyn shook her head, setting her journal on the nearby nightstand. "Thanks, but I've got it."

She changed quickly and quietly, slipping into the soft nightshirt she'd brought with her, then padded over to the bed and climbed in beside Aleanora.

"Good night," she whispered.

"Night, Gwyn," the girls replied together.

She lay on her back, facing the ceiling, eyes fluttering closed as her thoughts wandered. She imagined swirling lights of mana—blue, red, black, and yellow—all blending together like the night sky. Then the shapes began to shift, forming wings. A massive, gleaming dragon soared through her imagination, its scales glowing like embers.

In her mind, she sat astride it, flying high above a field, laughing as a crowd of noble boys shouted up at her, all of them chasing after her with rings and flowers. Gwyn clung to the dragon's horns and urged it higher.

"Gross," she mumbled sleepily.

Then she drifted off, soaring on the back of her imagined dragon, far beyond the reach of anyone who might try to catch her.

Taenya sat on the edge of her bed, slowly running a whetstone down the length of her sword. The motion was familiar, grounding, but her thoughts were far from calm. The quiet of the tavern settled around her like a blanket as the warmth of the fire flickered in the small hearth.

A soft knock came at her door. She placed the sword gently across her lap and rose to answer. Maya was standing there, her expression thoughtful but warm.

"Gwyn just went to bed," Maya said.

Taenya stepped aside and gestured her in. "Thank you for checking in on her. She's been carrying more than she lets on."

Maya nodded as she entered. "I enjoy our lessons and research together. She's handling it well. Better than anyone could expect. Her magic is progressing quickly—maybe too quickly. There will be a time when her magic outpaces her maturity. I fear it may have already: there are times when her emotions seem to be all over the place, and others when it's almost like she has none. I'm having her focus on magic that brings more positive improvements to her life. She's more than just fire, and I want her to know that. I don't want her to drown in all that anger I know she's hiding inside."

Taenya leaned against the wall, arms folded, her gaze distant. "She's more than any of us were at her age. And I agree. I also worry about how fast she's being forced to grow. It's not just about when her magic outpaces her maturity. How do we guide her when she's already stronger than anyone else in a room? She's not just magically strong, she's stronger than any girl her age has any right to be. She's growing like a weed. It won't be long before she's my height. How do we keep her grounded when she has such power in her hands?"

Maya tilted her head. "By caring about her and supporting her. Letting her see that her feelings are valid and giving her safe ways to express herself. She has good people around her. Especially you."

Taenya gave a quiet, appreciative smile but said nothing.

After a moment, Maya asked, "And what about your magic? You haven't said much about it lately. I know things have been . . . tumultuous since the attack on the manor, but you need to stop ignoring it, Taenya," she said gently but firmly. "Magic isn't something you can shelve until you're ready—it's already part of you. And if you keep letting it go unshaped, it'll start shaping you."

"I know. But I have so much to—"

"Taenya, magic left untended isn't harmless. You have to stop bottling it up like it's an inconvenience. It's part of who you are now. You have to learn how to control it or you risk being unable to help your charge. You asked how you guide her? You'll have to first strengthen your own magic. You don't have to be able to summon fire from the gods to smite your enemies, you just need to be proficient enough in your own magic to be able to stay at her side as *she* does."

Taenya hesitated. "It's complicated. We talked about it briefly, but I feel spirits sometimes. Animal spirits. It's like they're right *there*. When the drakyyd died, the feeling was the strongest. It was like . . . it left something behind, and I could reach out and touch it. I don't know what it means. It affects other things too, like my connection to my weapons and armor that we talked about . . . it's grown. I feel them like they're parts of me."

Maya nodded slowly, clearly fascinated. "That sounds like something you should explore. That sense of connection? It's not just instinct. That's mana, Taenya. Maybe your magic isn't just summoning mana creations that resemble animals but actually connecting with spirits and summoning those. You've said you always feel it strongest when you get this feeling of protection. It's like what Gwyn and I were talking about: magic needs to relate to concepts. Yours reflects a guardian's bond. A need to protect."

Taenya looked down at her hand, flexing her fingers. "I can feel it now, at the edge of everything. Like the spirits are waiting for me to call them."

"Then you should," Maya said gently. "Who knows what else you might be able to do if you understand the full extent of that bond."

Taenya nodded, her voice quieter. "I will. I promise."

"Good." Maya's tone softened even more. "Also, I really do think you're doing a good job. With Gwyn."

The knight let out a breath and sat on the bed. "I don't know if I am. She's walking into politics too soon. I fear what the Academy will be like. What the court will demand from her. And now there is the fact that the crown prince is guiding Angwin's actions. If that's true and the royal family is turning against Tiloral—against House Reinhart—then everything changes."

Maya frowned, her brow creased. "It's a dangerous path. But Gwyn is building her own identity. She's strong. And she has House Reinhart's strength behind her. And yours."

Taenya didn't reply immediately, but the words did soothe something in her. They talked a little longer, sharing quiet speculation about how Gwyn might be received in Reme, especially among the nobility, how the students would react to her being a terran, and how her magic would be seen, until Maya finally excused herself for the night.

Left alone, Taenya walked over and sat by the window, watching the light of the twin moons mix their yellow and silver light to create shadows across the floor. The warmth of Maya's words still lingered, but they couldn't drown out the thoughts that crept in from the corners of her mind.

She propped one leg up on the wooden chair beneath her, arms folded across her chest as she stared at the stars outside. The window pane fogged slightly with her breath. This quiet—this peace—was rare, and she knew it was temporary. Every kilometer they traveled brought them closer to the capital. Closer to danger. They'd already avoided an ambush by Count Telford; what else was waiting for them?

Gwyn was growing into something fierce. Magic and titles aside, she had a sharp mind and even sharper instincts. Taenya was proud of her, but pride was a double-edged sword. The more Gwyn grew into her role, the more real it all became—the threats, the responsibilities, the scrutiny. And Taenya was the shield.

She reached for the leather satchel beside her bed and pulled free the half-written letter. The parchment crackled softly in the quiet, the words staring up at her with an unfinished plea. Her family was still in Meris. She hadn't seen them since her knighting. They didn't even know what she'd become—not really.

They didn't know she had killed a noble's heir. That she had drawn steel against a marquess's guards. That she had stood as the blade of a princess.

Her eyes moved across the ink, then down to the blank bottom half of the page. She sighed. *No. Not tonight.*

She folded it again, this time more carefully, and slid it away. Instead, she turned her focus inward. She rested her hand on her knees, closing her eyes as she sought the rhythm she'd found during practice. The cadence of breath and blood.

The red mana came easily—eagerly, even. It responded to her like a loyal hound, curling around her heart and threading through her limbs. She breathed it in deeply.

But it wasn't just her mana. She could feel her sword, leaning against the far wall. She didn't need to see it to know it was there. She could feel the straight edge of the steel, the slight imperfections in the grip, the quiet strength in its weight.

Her armor, too. Each piece hung nearby, but she could feel them like phantom limbs. The greaves that braced her legs. The pauldrons that shielded her shoulders. They weren't just tools. They represented the oaths she had made. Extensions of the role she had stepped into.

And there—just beyond that awareness—something more.

She didn't know what it was. Not exactly. But it had been there since the day they had found the site of the ambush. Like a sleeping presence. A watchful silence. Waiting.

She reached for it—not physically, but through the weave of red mana inside her. It stirred, almost with irritation, in response. Faint, but undeniable. Like she was disturbing its rest.

"I hear you," she whispered.

There was no answer. But the sensation remained. She opened her eyes. Her heartbeat was steady. Her breath calm.

The duel played in her mind like a worn-out melody. The blood. The silence after the killing blow. The weight of it had never left her. She had done what needed to be done. Everyone told her that. Siveril had said as much. But it hadn't *solved* anything. If anything, it had made things worse.

They had been cornered. Angwin had maneuvered them into a no-win situation. The duel had been the only exit, but it painted a larger target on Gwyn's back. On all of them.

Taenya hated politics. This so-called Polite War, the Great Game. She hated games played with people's lives. But she was part of it now. She had become a player whether she wanted to be or not.

And it made her wonder: Was she guiding Gwyn toward strength? Or pushing her into something she might never come back from? Was she . . . a good protector? Or just a sharp sword?

She rose slowly, letting her hands brush along the hilt of her blade as she passed it. It pulsed gently beneath her fingers, steady, like a heartbeat.

She paused, turning her palm upward. Mana stirred. And with it, those connections. Her sword. Her armor. The invisible weight of duty.

And in the corner of her awareness . . . the presence waited.

She didn't reach further. She knew Maya was right in that she needed to practice. But not tonight. Soon. Soon she would need to. One day, she would call on them. And when she did, she would be ready.

She extinguished the lamp and climbed into bed. Tomorrow would come quickly.

The darkness wrapped around her, not like a threat, but a quiet shield. After all, the night was Sabina's domain, and she trusted her friend. Between the two of them, Gwyn had the protection of both the light and dark.

CHAPTER TWENTY-SIX

AVOIDING DELAYS

Taenya."

The telv knight stirred beneath the blankets, groaning softly as the familiar voice pulled her from sleep.

"Taenya. *Wake up*," the voice hissed, closer this time. She blinked her eyes open to find Sabina's face mere inches from her own. Taenya groaned and flopped an arm over her eyes. "What is it, Sabina?"

"Get up."

Lifting her head, she squinted past Sabina toward the window. Nothing. Just the deep darkness of night pressing against the glass.

"Why? It's still the middle of the night. And why are you in my room?"

Sabina didn't flinch. "I have a bad feeling." Her voice was low, serious. "I think . . . we need to leave. Soon."

That snapped the last of the sleep from Taenya's mind. She pushed herself upright, her senses sharpening. "What's wrong?"

Sabina stood from her crouched position beside the bed and crossed the room to the small table where the oil lamp sat. She struck the flint, and a soft glow spread across the chamber. Shadows danced along the walls as she turned the flame up.

"I don't know," the high elf said, turning to face her. Her expression was composed, but her tone held weight. "I just have this feeling. Something is *off*. We shouldn't be here when the sun rises."

Taenya studied her for a moment. Sabina's instincts had never failed them, not once. Whether it was paranoia, premonition, or something deeper rooted in her magic, it didn't matter.

She nodded. "Alright. Even if it's nothing, we can make good time on the road."

Sabina gave a short nod, already turning to leave.

"Let's get everyone up," Taenya said, swinging her legs over the edge of the bed and reaching for her boots. "Do you want to deal with a grumpy princess, or should I?"

Sabina sniffed, not even looking back. "I'd rather not be the bad guy tonight. So, by all means, please enjoy."

Taenya rolled her eyes, smirking faintly. "Fine. Wake Oren and have him get the guards ready. You handle the rest of the entourage."

As Sabina disappeared into the hallway, Taenya reached for her armor and sword belt, shifting into the mindset of a commander. She threw on her cloak after getting her armor on, then, remembering her talk with Maya, drew some mana into herself and pulsed it.

The armor faintly glowed and physically shifted until it was fitted just right.

Taenya yawned behind her hand holding the reins. Astride her horse, she swept her gaze slowly across the caravan. The first rays of sunlight were beginning to crest the horizon, casting golden hues over the road ahead. They had already been traveling for at least a bell or two.

The guards were quiet but alert, their posture reflecting the steady rhythm of trained readiness. The only sounds were the occasional snort of a horse, the soft clink of tack, or the distant, tentative song of birds awakening to the day.

The carriages moved smoothly along the road, their passengers mostly still asleep. Taenya could see that the curtains on Gwyn's carriage were drawn, but faint flashes of light shimmered intermittently behind the fabric.

Practicing again, she thought with a weary smile. Nearly every moment Gwyn wasn't fulfilling duties, she had her nose buried in a book or was working on her magic—sometimes both. And more often than not, it was both at once. *That just seems unsafe*, Taenya mused dryly.

Ahead, Sabina rode with her usual air of intense focus, the lingering effects of the previous night's unease still clinging to her. The familiar thrum of the high elf's magic shimmered faintly around her, subtle but unmistakable to Taenya's senses. Gwyn suggested it could be mana based, similar to her sight, but more of a feeling for Taenya.

Two Wynvers rode alongside Sabina, flanking her in silence like shadows that breathed. Sabina had jerked her head several times, reacting to distant whispers only she could hear. Each time, she'd scanned the terrain, eyes sharp, before forcing herself to refocus.

Taenya had asked about it the first time. Sabina had waved her off, telling her she would alert the group at the first sign of trouble. Taenya didn't push.

The attack on the manor had left a mark on all of them, but for Sabina, the inability to sense it in time had carved a deeper wound.

They rode in silence, the wheels of the wagons humming along the well-worn path. As the sun climbed higher, the stillness lifted. Light conversation sparked among the guards and servants, the early hush of travel replaced by the soft murmur of voices.

Not long after, they stopped to eat. Breakfast was a simple porridge, prepared by one of the house servants. It was filling, but nothing remarkable—certainly not what one would expect for a royal meal.

Still, Gwyn had treated it like a feast. She'd eaten with gusto, praising the servant's efforts and thanking them with genuine warmth. Taenya had only smiled knowingly. The girl acted as if she were *starving*, and Taenya had no doubt why. Gwyn's relentless training had shifted in focus over the past week. Less spectacle. More control. And now with the direction Maya had given her the previous night, it was as if the girl had taken it as a challenge she needed to win.

And it drained her in a different way. The princess had confided that focusing on finesse and discipline was somehow even more frustrating than unleashing great, roaring spells.

Taenya could relate. It wasn't just Maya pushing her to take her own training more seriously. Gwyn had taken to dropping subtle hints—or not-so-subtle challenges—whenever the opportunity arose. She found herself occasionally rising to the bait. *I can't let a child constantly outdo me*, she thought with a faint smirk. *Even if she is a magical prodigy.*

They were currently on their way to the final town before entering the Naro Pass—Mardale. A quiet little place nestled at the foot of the mountains, known more for its proximity to the pass than anything else. It was also where Taenya expected them to reunite with Evocati Amari.

Turning her head at the sound of hoofbeats, Taenya saw Oren as he rode up beside her. The experienced telv guard's expression was composed, but there was a thoughtful weight behind his eyes.

"Ser Taenya, I'd like to request we use the spare time we've gained to rest an extra day in Mardale," he said. "We've made good progress, and I believe it would be prudent for everyone to be at their best before we enter the pass."

Taenya considered it. They'd made good time over the past stretch of road, thanks to early starts and light traffic. Despite the rough terrain and stops along the way, they had gained nearly two full days of travel. Using one of those days to rest before entering the Naro Pass wasn't just practical—it was smart.

She nodded. "I agree. While I doubt we'll face an incursion, it never hurts to be prepared."

Oren shifted slightly in his saddle, glancing toward the hazy silhouette of the mountains in the distance. "It's not just the Valeni I'm worried about, ser. Some of the guards and I were discussing it this morning. We think the entrance to the pass may be the most likely place to—"

"To arms!"

The shout came sharp and sudden. Taenya's head snapped toward the voice.

Sabina. The high elf was already turning in her saddle, her posture rigid and alert. Her eyes, filled with alarm, had turned pitch black and glowed faintly with power.

Taenya's heartbeat quickened, and she put her hand on her sword. She turned back to Oren without missing a beat. "It seems the pass was too obvious. Get archers onto the carriages—tell them to tie themselves down."

Oren nodded once, sharply. "Understood," he replied. He wheeled his horse around and began calling out orders.

Sabina was approaching fast. Taenya guided her mount toward her. "What is it?" she asked.

"Riders," Sabina said tightly. "Distant road. I count at least twenty."

"Where?" Taenya asked, scanning the dim morning haze. The light was still soft, the sun barely above the horizon. "Do you sense hostile intent?"

Sabina's brow furrowed. "Something's . . . off. They're coming from behind that hill rise—any moment now."

Taenya followed her gaze. Sure enough, a group of riders trotted into view, emerging from behind a distant hill along a parallel road. They rode in organized ranks. And there were far more than twenty. "Closer to forty," Taenya muttered.

The riders hadn't spotted them yet—the caravan remained partly shielded by trees and terrain—but it was only a matter of time. The guards were already reacting, moving efficiently to defensive positions, arming themselves without needing to be told twice.

Taenya's mind worked quickly. The duchy wasn't relocating soldiers. At least, not without informing House Reinhart. And cavalry forces didn't move without reason.

She turned and signaled for the caravan to slow its pace, lowering her voice as she passed orders. "Keep movement quiet. As quiet as we can manage."

It was a stretch. Carriages, wagons, horses—they were anything but quiet. Still, perhaps they could delay detection, maybe even slip away unnoticed if the riders weren't looking for them specifically. She doubted it. Even as she gave the order, she knew it was likely futile.

The riders, now just over half a kilometer away, slowed.

Keep going. Ignore us . . .

But they didn't. Taenya watched as several of them peeled off from the formation, angling their horses toward the caravan. Several riders stopped entirely, then began adjusting their course—riding directly toward them across the open field.

She straightened in her saddle and called out to the guards, her voice clear and commanding. "Prepare yourselves!" Her eyes swept over the four archers tied down atop the carriages. She noted the shields they had set up—angled just right to offer protection without obstructing their aim. Good.

Oren's voice rang out behind her. "Do not fire unless you hear me or Ser Taenya give the command! This could still be nothing!"

Taenya nodded at the order. As much as her instincts screamed that this was something, discipline had to be maintained.

The last thing House Reinhart needed was for one of their archers to loose an arrow at an innocent man-at-arms simply because they looked threatening.

Still, the riders didn't slow. The full column—at least forty strong—turned as one and began charging over the grassy field that separated them from the caravan.

The morning light hadn't fully broken yet, so the details were hard to make out. But their armor was uniform enough to suggest organization, though it lacked the bulk of proper full plate. At least they weren't knights.

"Let's move!" Taenya barked, spurring her horse forward.

The caravan jolted to life. The carriages and wagons picked up speed, bouncing violently over the uneven road. She heard a startled shriek from one of the carriages and grimaced.

Hold together. She kept her gaze locked on the approaching riders and drew her shield from its place beside her saddle.

Oren must have seen the motion, because his voice followed immediately. "Shields up!" The guards reacted swiftly, pulling their shields into position and adjusting formation.

Then, just as expected, several of the oncoming riders reached for bows.

"Arrows! Cover!" Taenya shouted.

A dozen guards shifted behind shields or cover points. The four archers atop the carriages ducked lower behind their defenses.

Taenya tracked the first volley . . . and blinked. The arrows missed. All of them. Poorly aimed, their arcs wide or falling short. Another volley followed. It too scattered uselessly across the space between the two forces. *What in the goddess's name . . . ?*

"Return fire!" the senior guardsman called. The four atop the carriages rose smoothly and loosed their arrows, joined by the six mounted bowmen at the rear. While their bows weren't designed for mounted warfare, the closing distance helped compensate for lack of precision.

Ten arrows flew. Five struck targets. Only one found more than armor or shield. A horse went down hard, crashing into the dirt with a strangled whinny as the arrow punched into its shoulder. The rider tumbled forward in a spray of dust and hooves.

One down, Taenya thought grimly, as she brought up her shield again. She heard a voice yelling at the riders, and almost immediately the group shifted as one, pulling away from their headlong charge and instead repositioning to run parallel to the caravan—but at a much greater distance. Taenya narrowed her eyes.

A tense, drawn-out exchange of arrows ensued. Her archers fired five volleys in total, and only two more of the enemy's riders were struck. In contrast, the enemy continued to fire sporadically, their arrows falling short or wide. A waste.

"Cease fire!" she shouted, lifting a hand to signal the order. The riders still loosed occasional shots, but they kept their distance, refusing to close in. It was clear now—they weren't attempting to break the caravan. They were *herding* them.

Taenya turned sharply in the saddle. *Sabina! Can you hear me?*

The response came swiftly. *Yes! What is it?*

I need you to read their minds. What are they thinking?

Sabina called out to her Wynvers, pulling them into a tighter formation. Taenya couldn't see her, but it didn't take long for her friend to answer.

They're corralling us! Sabina's voice rang through their link. *We're heading straight into a larger force—right ahead of us.*

Shit.

What should we do? Sabina asked mentally.

How far?

There was a pause. When Sabina replied again, her tone was alarmed. *We're almost there. We need to stop or turn back now! They know about Gwyn's fire.*

Taenya's eyes went wide. She turned to look ahead, squinting into the early morning fog.

The road ahead was quiet. Too quiet. A thin veil of mist hung low over the grassy fields, the kind that would've seemed peaceful on any other day. Most townspeople wouldn't even be at work yet. The world was still waking up.

So how had this force prepared so quickly?

How did they know? she asked, the question tight in her chest. *Our travel plans weren't public.*

These ones don't, Sabina replied. *They were simply told to meet with a force today—meant to ride down anyone who tried to flee. They didn't expect us. They're adapting to what they've stumbled into.*

Bastards. *Gwyn . . .*

Should we have her assist? Sabina asked gently.

No. We shouldn't rely on a child to fight our battles. If it comes to it, I don't doubt she'll fight, but this is our duty, not hers.

Taenya steeled herself and turned, standing slightly in her stirrups. "Slow! Prepare to stop the caravan!" she bellowed. "Wagons to the front, form a shield in front of the carriages!"

The guards snapped into motion at her command, the practiced efficiency of House Reinhart's training kicking in.

They had minutes at most. And Taenya would use every one of them. They needed to establish a defensible position. If she could force the riders into a proper fight—on her terms—they might just win. After that, who knew? But they couldn't outrun them. Not with the carriages. Not with the wagons. And Taenya didn't want to involve Gwyn—not again. The girl was *always* fighting battles no child her age should ever face. No. This would be handled by her. By the guards. Gwyn deserved to be a child for at least a little longer.

If she could just get the riders off their horses, they'd stand a better chance. But a spear line would only hold so long. Arrows would pick them off. Or worse, the enemy could encircle them completely. And if they lit their arrows . . . targeted the carriages . . . *Shit. I know what I have to do.*

Sabina, she sent, keeping her thoughts steady and firm. *Get to Gwyn. You're the last wall. We've discussed this. Do you remember her code word?* She felt the familiar flicker of discomfort.

I do.

She turned to Oren, voice sharp and unwavering. "Circle! Now! All guardsmen: prepare to defend Her Highness!"

The wagons came to an abrupt halt. Guards sprang into action, forming up between the approaching riders and the heart of the caravan.

The enemy clearly hadn't expected them to stop and hold. The riders were forced to loop around, swinging wide in order to reposition.

Taenya galloped forward, placing herself between the two front wagons, which had been angled to form partial cover for the carriages behind.

"Drivers—protect the carriages! Archers, *volley!*"

The Reinhart archers didn't hesitate. Arrows were loosed in quick succession, whistling through the air toward the riders.

Taenya turned briefly to scan the carriages. The four drivers and their assistants had already disembarked, falling into a tight shield wall in front of the royal carriage. *Good.*

But then came return fire. And it wasn't aimed at them. Her eyes widened. *The horses.*

"Protect the horses!" she shouted.

Twenty arrows came first. Then twenty more. Her guards scrambled to interpose their shields, raising them high in hopes of intercepting the deadly hail. It wasn't enough. Five arrows struck true.

Screams filled the air as horses went down, kicking and thrashing in pain. Riders crashed to the ground, some stunned, others already scrambling to check on their fallen mounts.

Oren and a pair of guards leapt into action, protecting the horses while the archers continued their exchange of fire from atop the wagons and along the flanks.

Why aren't they committing?

Taenya! Sabina's voice slammed into her thoughts. *The army is coming!*

Taenya turned and her heart sank. From within the fog, a battle line emerged. Rows of marching soldiers, their shields gleaming faintly in the light. Spears. Banners. There were hundreds.

They've been keeping us pinned. She turned slowly, taking in the stunned expressions on her guards' faces. They saw it too now.

Oren looked at her, his voice low but steady. "Ser Taenya—your orders? Should we charge the riders?"

Her gaze flicked between the riders and the looming army drawing ever closer. She clenched her jaw and closed her eyes and listened.

The hiss of arrows cut through the air, each volley followed by her men's urgent shouts as they tried to track and call out where they would land. Oren had to shout for them to stop—too many voices overlapping, confusion threatening to create fatal mistakes. Her archers needed focus, not chaos. They returned to calling targets instead, each shout clear and precise.

Taenya reached inward, drawing deep from the well of mana she'd been quietly nurturing, the magic she'd trained only sporadically, and even more rarely in secret alongside her team.

One of the archers called out for another bundle of arrows.

What surprised her most wasn't desperation—it was the lack of it. There was no panic in her guards' voices, no fear. If anything, they were growing more determined, galvanized by the overwhelming odds rather than cowed by them. They knew what they faced, and they stood ready to meet it.

The spell she had worked to refine—one born from discipline, strengthened by the events of the past days—was ready. The encounter with the drake had changed something in her. Deepened it.

Her Drakyyds sensed what she was about to do and immediately moved to support her, forming up around her like the wall they were trained to be. She placed her hands at her sides, grounding herself as the magic built, the energy thrumming beneath her skin. She didn't hear the roar of mana so much as feel it—a growl in her bones.

As the tension reached its peak, she lifted her hands and gave shape to her intent. A cloud of thick, red mist burst from the ground, rising and swirling outward as her [**Summon Animal Spirit**] spell took form. The haze rippled with mana, pulsing like a heartbeat.

After thinking it over, she had learned the spell had two paths. The first allowed her to conjure a creature of raw mana, an echo of a beast with no true spirit. It obeyed her entirely, born of her will.

The enemy riders hesitated, their arrows ceasing as they stared at the forming mist. One of their commanders—a man with a sword raised high—began shouting orders, his voice echoing across the field.

She ignored him. Her Drakyyds held their line, shields up and steady, bracing in front of her as a protective wall. She kept her focus on the spell, channeling everything into the mist. The mana churned like a storm, heavy and volatile.

But this time, the spell wasn't taking the first path. It was reaching deeper, toward that connection that had worried her. Now she realized what it was really doing. And it was so simple. The second form of the spell sought something real—a spirit nearby, one that had recently fallen within her reach.

It required consent. A contract. Connection. She felt the pull, the thrum of resistance as the spell latched onto something just beyond the veil. That *connection* surged—and with it, a challenge. The spirit didn't want to be summoned.

She realized then: whatever it was, it was powerful. Too powerful. This wouldn't be a simple summoning; it would be a battle of wills. And once the spirit was brought forth, she wouldn't be able to hold it long. It would take *everything* she had just to keep it tethered.

The mist surged as she slammed her will into the connection, pouring her strength into the bond, shaping her desire into words her heart could barely contain. *You will answer to me.*

The spirit pushed back. She felt it, its anger, pride, and its refusal to be commanded. It didn't yield. It never had.

Still, she pressed harder. *You are a protector*, she sent through the bond. *Help me protect the one I am sworn to.*

The response was a rumbling growl that vibrated through the mist and through her soul. The horses nearby reared in panic and several guards startled, though Oren quickly barked orders, keeping control. He moved the uninjured mounts behind the formation, while riders dismounted and fell into a spear wall, forming up in practiced cohesion.

Taenya closed her eyes, sweat beading on her brow. The spirit was close. It had not submitted— but it was *listening*. And she knew what, or rather *who*, the spirit was. It was no surprise that she would not bow. But she would stand beside her.

A bellowing roar that was deep and guttural erupted from within the swirling, still-growing red mist. One of the senior guardsmen shouted a warning—arrows incoming, all focused on the cloud.

Fools, Taenya thought. They didn't understand what they were provoking. *Give us your aid*, she sent, her will threaded through the mana. *Answer me.*

The spirit resisted. She was angry. She just wanted rest. A wave of bitterness rolled over her—resentment as heavy as stone.

Taenya gritted her teeth. The spirit had been wronged. It had died violently. Those it cared for had been slaughtered, and now the world called it back, demanding more. She did not *want* to return.

Arrows continued to rain down into the mist, piercing nothing but air and rage. Her guards took advantage of the enemy's distraction and returned fire with precision. Shouts echoed across the field, sharp with confusion and panic.

But Taenya didn't look back. She couldn't. Her focus was locked on the summoning, the spiraling tug-of-war between her will and the spirit's fury. *Please*, she begged silently, pouring everything she had into the spell. *We need you. They will die if you do not come.* She reached deeper, tapping into her core, feeling it pulse like a second heartbeat. Pain bloomed across her chest, radiating outward in sharp spikes. She gasped, then screamed as mana surged through her, searing along her nerves like fire. She did not stop.

Gwyn needs me.

She pushed everything she was into the bond. *Protect the one who holds your fire*, she whispered into the connection. *Protect her from the allies of those who harmed you. Who killed your child. Let this battle be your vengeance. Once they are gone, or we escape, you can return to your rest. I swear it.*

For a long moment, there was nothing but strain and silence—then, a sorrowful howl. The world around her paused. The mist stilled, hovering in the air like breath caught in a lung. And then a roar shattered the quiet. Primal. Furious. The sound rattled through her bones and echoed in the very fabric of the mana surrounding them. The red magic flared so brightly that Taenya had to raise her arm to shield her eyes.

A surge of power rushed through her body and she felt something *click* inside of her.

When the light finally dimmed, the mist began to coalesce. And from it emerged the spirit. A red drakyyd took shape, massive, translucent but not ethereal. It was a being forged from mana, from fury and memory and bound duty. It was not a ghost. It was a *force*. The drakyyd towered as tall as the wagons, her regal presence matched only by her lethal grace. The light of the red mana shimmered through her scales, making her seem half-submerged in flame.

The creature turned her head toward her, the blazing eyes meeting her own. There was a question in the drakyyd's gaze.

Taenya answered with steel in her voice, her mind sharp as a blade: *Them. We do not have much time. They seek to delay us—to let others kill us. They fear us. Destroy them.*

The spirit needed no more. With a roar that cracked the air, she charged. The enemy riders reacted too slowly. They tried to scatter, to pull away from the now-solidified threat, but it was too late. The drake crossed the open field in three massive strides.

She slammed into a mounted rider, and though she was no longer made of flesh and bone, the hit struck with devastating force. Horse and rider flew through the air, torn from the battlefield like scraps of parchment in a storm.

Riders scattered in all directions, but they weren't broken. Those wielding bows loosed arrow after arrow into the red spirit. Others brandished spears and lashed out whenever they passed too close.

Taenya felt every impact as if they were raindrops striking her skin, the steady rhythm of pain dulled but present. Her connection to the *Draconic Spirit* gave her more than control: it gave her *awareness*. And with each strike, she felt the bond strain.

It was like watching a deadly game unfold. The riders circled the spirit, peppering it with attacks from all sides, trying to wear it down or confuse it. The drakyyd responded with fluid, ferocious movement, lunging, leaping, and swiping at anything within reach.

In less than fifteen seconds, five riders were taken down. But Taenya could feel it slipping. The size of the spirit was simply too much. Every other summoning she had tried before had been manageable—small creatures with no spirit, most no larger than a hunting cat. But this was a force. And it was draining her rapidly.

Oren, ever perceptive, saw her faltering in the saddle and immediately shouted, "Increase fire!"

The archers responded without hesitation. Taenya watched through blurred vision as several more horses went down. And the drake, sensing her weakening grip, glanced her way.

Their eyes met. And the spirit roared. She reared up, then lowered herself in a coiled crouch before launching into the air in a single, bone-rattling leap. She crashed into a tight cluster of five riders, scattering horse and man alike in a chaos of movement and earth. Another leap. A swipe of her tail. Three more fell.

"Target the horses!" shouted her senior guardsman. "Force them to ground!"

The archers adjusted their aim again, arrows now flying toward legs, shoulders, flanks. Horse after horse collapsed or bucked wildly, throwing their riders. The drake pressed the advantage, tearing through the broken formation.

But Taenya was fading. She tried to hold the connection—clinging to it with everything she had—pulling more and more mana into herself. But the strain was too much. She lasted nearly another thirty seconds. Then the world tilted.

She sagged in the saddle. Two of her Drakyyds reached up just in time to catch her as she began to fall, cradling her with practiced ease and dragging her behind the front lines.

Taenya! Sabina's voice rang sharply through her mind, tight with fear. Her vision swam as she looked across the field. The riders were regrouping, many now dismounted and charging toward the carriages. She spotted Sabina, and behind her, Gwyn.

The girl was being held back by one of the guards, her wide blue eyes locked on Taenya. She was afraid. Taenya's chest tightened and her breath hitched. She couldn't move. The darkness was pulling at her, and she couldn't resist. But she had one thing left.

One word. The word Gwyn had taught them. The one she swore would never be used lightly. The one that would tell Sabina to do whatever it took. Taenya screamed it into the link with everything she had left.

Pandora!

As her consciousness slipped and the weight of overexertion took her, the last thing she saw was the sky above them, darkening unnaturally. Blotting out light like ink poured into water.

And then: nothing.

CHAPTER TWENTY-SEVEN

PANDORA

Captain Gerard led the light cavalry force now struggling to contain what should have been an easy target—the princess's caravan.

They had stumbled upon the group by sheer luck, and at first, it had seemed like a gift from the gods. An isolated royal caravan, lightly defended, far from any support. An opportunity that could not be ignored.

But now, after the ferocious resistance and the unexpected use of magic, Gerard knew that their luck had soured. They needed something decisive. They had to break the enemy now or not at all.

He had originally intended to force the caravan into the waiting arms of the larger force positioned ahead, where the girl and her protectors would be overwhelmed by sheer numbers.

That opportunity was gone. The enemy had stopped and dug in, refusing to flee. Worse, they had met his charge with force. Arrows had thinned his ranks. Then the enemy knight had summoned some monstrous magical beast—larger than a carriage, red and terrible—and it had torn through his cavalry before it finally collapsed.

He had been warned about the princess's fire, about her flame. But no one had told him about a knight who could summon spirits of rage and death.

Now, his unit was fractured. Half his men were dismounted. A quarter were either dead or too injured to fight. And the enemy archers were cutting down horses like they were straw targets.

They had to act. Now. If they gave the caravan even a moment's reprieve, it would be their undoing. Gerard clenched his jaw, frustration bubbling beneath his calm surface. They couldn't afford to hesitate. They had to strike hard and fast.

He paused, suddenly aware that something was wrong. The morning sky . . . it was dimming. He looked up, furrowing his brow. Not clouds. Not fog. Just . . . darkness. Spreading like ink across paper.

His men were shifting uneasily, muttering to each other. The light was fading. The sky turned black. Gerard's heart dropped. *A third magic user?*

No one had warned him about the other two, and now he and his men were paying for it. They needed to act immediately.

"Attack!" he roared, raising his blade high.

His dismounted men surged forward, weapons drawn, rushing the defensive line. He turned his horse, circling briefly to assess his remaining forces, then kicked it into a full gallop toward the heart of the caravan.

But then it hit. A black mist erupted from the knight who stood next to whom he suspected was the princess. Whatever the mist was, it wasn't smoke. It wasn't shadows. It was *abyss*.

It poured from her like water spilling from a shattered vessel, consuming everything in its path. Gerard's shout caught in his throat.

The mist grew so fast, he couldn't even warn his men. It swallowed the field, the wagons, the sky. His eyes widened in disbelief as every horse in his line suddenly reared in a panic, screaming as if the void itself were clawing at their minds. His own horse bucked violently beneath him, hooves skidding across the earth.

Then it turned, and the saddle failed him. Gerard reached out instinctively, grasping for reins, for anything. But there was only air. He tumbled from the saddle and the ground met him hard. His sword flew from his hand. Pain exploded in his ribs as he struck the earth, the breath ripped from his lungs. He groaned, rolling quickly to the side just as his panicked horse reared and thundered past him. Hooves pounded the earth, missing him by inches.

All around him, horses whinnied in terror, shrieks so primal and raw they sent shivers down his spine. The animals flailed, twisted, and bolted in every direction, desperate to escape the suffocating blackness that now surrounded them. From his position on the ground, Gerard watched helplessly as two of his men were crushed beneath the chaos of the stampede.

Pain lanced through his side as he forced himself upright, his breath catching. The sharp ache told him what he already suspected: at least one rib was broken.

Staggering forward, he spotted his sword half-buried in the churned-up dirt. He stooped to retrieve it, wincing as the motion sent another wave of pain through his torso. He scanned the battlefield as he straightened, locking onto the familiar shape of his shield a few paces away. He stumbled over, snatched it up, and strapped it to his arm with shaking hands.

Then he looked up, and his world narrowed. His ears filled with a piercing ring, muffling the sounds around him. Everything went hazy, as though he were underwater.

Instinctively, he reached up and rubbed at one ear, trying to shake it off. His voice came out muted as he tried to call out, "Form up!" But it was as if no one heard him.

Others were reacting the same way—some clutching their ears, others shouting into the void with panic on their faces.

And then, the whispers began. Low. Sinister. Unnatural. The hissing came next, slithering through the air like smoke through a crack in a door. Shapes emerged in the thick, black mist—figures made of shifting shadows.

Gerard froze as the creatures took form. Damned creatures that Relena should have cast into the underworld. Twisted mockeries of Loreni, each one clad in black, smoke-like armor that shimmered with shifting edges. From their skulls sprouted a crown of jagged horns, and in their clawed hands they gripped blades and shields that looked real—solid and deadly.

Their forms shimmered like heat over stone, never still. Almost as though they were only half in the world, flickering between planes. But their eyes glowed like coals, and their presence was very real.

Gerard opened his mouth to issue a command, but again his voice seemed swallowed by the oppressive silence. *No. Not silence.*

The whispers. They pressed in on all sides, deafening in their own way.

He waved his arm violently, motioning to his people. "Attack! Focus on the demons!" he yelled, trying to break through the magical haze.

A few turned toward him, their expressions confused, but they saw his gesture and nodded. That was all the time they had.

The creatures' mouths opened far too wide, splitting in ways that should have been impossible, revealing rows of jagged, obsidian-like teeth. With a piercing, collective screech, the demons surged forward. They moved as if they were guided by one mind, a single wave of violence—fast, efficient, merciless.

The first lines of Gerard's soldiers barely had time to react before the demons crashed into them. Swords clashed. Shields buckled. A demon swung a heavy mace down toward Gerard, and he barely raised his shield in time. The impact rocked him, his knees nearly giving out as the force echoed up his arm and into his spine. The muffled sound didn't match the blow's power. He staggered, gritting his teeth, and forced himself upright.

To his right, one of the female high elves from his unit turned to speak, but her voice came out thin and distant, as though smothered by the hissing whispers surrounding them. Gerard couldn't hear her. Could barely hear anything anymore, except the unnatural sounds of battle that now raged around him.

The black-haired woman called out again, her mouth forming words he could barely understand. He gave her a confused look, but she only shook her head in frustration and darted forward, slipping into the fray with fluid precision.

Gerard quickly adjusted, shifting into a practiced rhythm beside the clearly trained soldier. Together, they launched at the nearest demon, his shield deflecting its strike while her blade found an opening.

The demon shrieked as their coordinated assault overwhelmed it, and in a moment, it collapsed into a swirl of black mist, dissolving as if it had never existed. Gerard stood blinking, chest heaving, the surreal nature of the battle gnawing at the edge of his focus. He turned to the woman, trying to make out her voice as she spoke again.

"Good job! There are more. I'll get these," she said, already pivoting toward another group of demons.

Something about her speech caught him. Her lips moved slightly out of sync with her words, as though the sound and motion didn't quite belong together. He shook his head, trying to banish the growing sense of wrongness. *We need to finish this before these demons start affecting our minds.* He took a moment to glance across the battlefield, trying to gauge the flow of combat. Not far from him, four of his soldiers had begun pressing the offensive. He watched with genuine surprise—and no small amount of admiration—as they tore into the demons with brutal efficiency.

A woman led the charge, swinging her blade with reckless abandon, cutting through shadows like she had been born for it. A high elf man and a raithe . . . His vision blurred. Gerard shook his head and looked back at the . . . *No, I meant high elf woman.*

The two flanked the lead woman, cutting through anything she missed. Their movements were smooth and measured, each blow calculated. They fanned out, drawing several of the enemy away from their allies. The last of the four, a telv woman, moved with a deliberate grace. Her strikes were precise, her focus razor-sharp as she weaved between other squads, lending aid to those already locked in battle.

Gerard narrowed his eyes. *That kind of discipline under pressure . . . I need to remember those four.*

"They have their fight in hand," came a voice nearby. "Focus on those around you!"

The words rang clearly this time. The sounds of battle rushed in around him again, as if someone had turned the world's volume back up. Steel clanged. Voices shouted. The pounding of footsteps and the roars of the demons crashed into his ears all at once.

He gasped and turned to the high elf soldier who had just spoken. "Was that you?"

She gave him a slightly frustrated look. "What?"

He opened his mouth to respond, but then his eyes went wide.

A shadow loomed behind her.

"Look out!" Gerard shouted.

She turned just in time, catching the demon's strike on the flat of her blade. Another surged toward one of the nearby soldiers. She reacted with startling speed, her form blurring as she launched into a counterattack, her blade a silver arc of motion.

Gerard found his own target and charged it. He swung, but the demon twisted, ducking beneath the strike and lashing out in return. Gerard grunted, catching the counter with the rim of his shield. The impact jarred his arm, but he twisted with it, using the momentum to shove the creature back. It stumbled, off balance. He didn't hesitate. He lashed out his sword in a tight, brutal arc, catching the demon across its exposed side. The shadow gave a strangled hiss as its form unraveled into mist.

Gerard caught a glimpse of the high elf woman nearby taking a hit to her arm. The blow looked solid; it should have broken bone, maybe even severed the limb entirely. But she barely flinched. She shrugged it off and retaliated with brutal efficiency, her blade slicing clean through the demon that had struck her.

She's not even wearing steel, he thought, eyes narrowing. *That blow should've cleaved her arm off. Maybe she dodged it just in time?*

Before he could make sense of it, another of his soldiers stumbled, shoved off balance by a lunging demon. The creature raised its sword to strike.

Gerard reacted without thinking, driving himself forward to push the man out of the way. Agony tore through his side as his injured ribs screamed in protest. He stumbled, and for a heartbeat, he could do nothing but watch.

The demon's blade came down hard, slamming into the soldier's shoulder. The man cried out in pain and crumpled to the ground.

Gritting his teeth, Gerard surged forward. He batted the demon's sword aside and drove his blade toward its side. It snarled, tried to parry, but missed. His strike sank deep, and the thing let out a guttural hiss as it collapsed into mist.

Gerard barely had time to recover before another came charging at him—larger, faster. It roared as it closed the distance. He sidestepped at the last moment, twisting his body to avoid the brunt of the charge. He swung his sword in a tight arc, cleaving through its neck. The head separated cleanly, and the demon dissolved into shadow like the rest.

There are so many . . . Panting, Gerard turned to check on the injured soldier, only to find the space empty. He swept his eyes over the battlefield, heart hammering. *Where—?*

A few paces away, another demon crouched low to the ground, clutching at its shoulder and hissing in pain. Gerard's brow furrowed. *Wait . . . I stabbed it in the side, not the shoulder.*

"Don't just *stare* at it!" the high elf woman barked. "Kill it before it kills another one of us!"

Even as she spoke, she took a second to sweep her long black hair into a ponytail, her sharp eyes already searching for her next target.

It stung—to be called out again. *Twice* in the same fight. But she was right. He stepped forward and drove his sword down, silencing the wounded demon as it too dissolved into vapor. Behind him, another shout. He turned in time to see one of his telv soldiers struggling, locked in a frantic duel with a demon and casting him desperate glances for help.

It felt as if for every demon they killed, another emerged from the mist to take its place. They were being worn down, piece by piece.

"Another—your right!"

The warning cut through the noise, and he reacted just in time. His shield snapped up, catching the blow meant for his ribs. A parry, then a quick sidestep. The follow-up swing missed him by inches. Gerard countered, driving his blade into the demon's stomach. With a final screech, it evaporated like all the rest.

Gerard turned to assist the telv who had been steadily driven back, just in time to see a demon slip in behind him. "Behind you!" he shouted.

"Captain! There are too—" The soldier's words were cut off as a blade burst through his back. His body went rigid before crumpling to the ground.

Without hesitation, the black-haired high elf woman beside Gerard surged forward. She grabbed the demon by the chin, twisted its head, and exposed its neck, driving her blade deep and ending it in a single, brutal motion.

Gerard started to turn away, but something tugged at his instincts. He narrowed his eyes, glancing back. She was already moving to intercept another demon, her fluid stride betraying no hesitation.

But something was . . . off. *Hadn't she been wearing something different a moment ago?*

Before he could puzzle it out, she turned her head toward him and pointed through the fog. "We have to get through the mist."

Gerard didn't question it. He looked around at his scattered unit. "Form up!" he bellowed. "We have to push through this mist. Protect each other!"

Another demon lunged. Gerard snarled, catching the strike with the rim of his shield and twisting it away before slashing down in reply. The creature dissolved in a familiar cloud of black mist.

He could barely keep track of his own footing, let alone monitor the rest of the battlefield. The demons were pressing harder now, their strikes more frequent, more coordinated. They were trying to keep the soldiers scattered—isolated. But that aggression came at a cost.

Overreaching, the demons began to leave gaps. Gerard's soldiers, battered and weary though they were, recognized the shift and responded with vicious resolve.

With the high elf still at his side, her movements swift and deadly, they began pushing the tide back. What few men remained gathered into a wedge behind him, carving their way forward step by step.

Then, through the thinning mist, Gerard saw them. Two shapes. A small one, slight of frame, and a taller one beside it. *The princess.* "There!" he barked, pointing with his sword.

The high elf turned her head, her voice dropping into a low snarl. "There she is. Get her."

"We almost have them! Push forward!" Gerard shouted, rallying those still on their feet. He surged ahead, cleaving through another demon as he drove forward with renewed purpose. The high elf matched him stride for stride, their blades flashing to keep his flanks protected.

As they closed the distance, the shapes resolved more clearly—the knight with the black eyes, and the girl behind her. The knight's gaze met his, widening in alarm. She said something, her voice tight with fear, but Gerard didn't hear it. Didn't care. They had to strike now, before the princess could unleash whatever magic they'd been warned about.

The knight raised her hands in what appeared to be surrender. He didn't buy it. *Her magic's still active. It's a trick.* With a swift lunge, he drove his blade forward, piercing her unarmored abdomen. She gasped and fell without resistance.

One threat down. He turned his eyes on the princess. *Kill her!* The thought thundered through his mind, and he didn't hesitate. He brought his sword down toward the screaming girl—

"I got her!" Gerard roared, raising his blade high. "Take the rest! We've won!"

His voice echoed across the battlefield. The black-haired elf beside him raised her sword in salute, her face beaming with satisfaction. She glanced around, pride in her expression.

Gerard felt it too. They had done it. The princess was dead. And with her, House Reinhart's defiance. *Lord Angwin will reward us well,* he thought. *A princely reward . . .* Victory had never tasted so sweet.

He turned and looked down at the knight as she lay sprawled across the earth, her final breath fading into the air. A twisted mix of fear and surprise was etched into her expression, frozen there like a grotesque mask.

The mist around him began to thin, curling away in wisps as if retreating. The demons, too, vanished—each one dissolving into black clouds that evaporated on the wind, leaving behind no trace of their existence.

Gerard stared at the fading darkness with grim satisfaction. *Demonic magic,* he thought. *This house was steeped in pure evil.* But now they were gone. Purged. He had done what had to be done. The death of a child—of a princess—was regrettable, but their sins had demanded it.

He closed his eyes and whispered a quick prayer to Relena, Goddess of Death. "May you pass judgment on their wicked souls."

As if in response, the morning light returned in full, breaking through the gloom like a blade through cloth. Sunlight poured across the battlefield, illuminating the blood-streaked ground.

Relief washed over him. The demonic summoner's dark magic had died with her. He tilted his head back slightly, letting the wind rush across his face, the sensation like a balm. A moment of peace. A moment of triumph. They had won.

House Reinhart—the traitors who had struck down his liege's son, the monsters who'd dared to wield forbidden magics—was no more. The girl who burned loyal nobles with fire, the knight who had killed Lord Nicolas . . . *Where is she?* Her head would be mounted on a pike.

Gerard opened his eyes and froze. *What? No . . .*

The field in front of him had changed. His soldiers, the men and women of his command, were strewn across the ground. Not fallen enemies. *His own.*

The caravan stood in the distance—untouched, intact—as if he had turned his back to it completely. Confusion twisted through him like a blade.

And then he saw her. The princess—alive. She stood beside the knight who had fallen from her horse earlier, who was very much on her feet. The high elf summoner, the black-eyed demon-witch, was nowhere to be seen.

He spun around and stopped cold. The bodies of the two he had just killed lay nearby, but they weren't the knight and the girl. They were his soldiers. One was the unit's surgeon, a stab wound in her gut. The other had fallen forward, blood staining his armor where the woman had been trying to dress a wound.

Gerard's breath caught. He turned again, his eyes sweeping across the battlefield. It was nothing but chaos and scattered corpses. His people . . . it was as if they'd fought *each other*. His mind blanked, scrambling for logic that didn't exist. *It isn't possible.*

You did this. You killed your own men. Betrayed them. The voice slithered into his thoughts, cold and cruel. Mocking. It didn't come from without. It came from *within.* From *everywhere.*

How? The demons . . . I killed the demons . . . We won . . .

His chest heaved, panic rising.

You were quite skilled as you slaughtered them with such fervor, the voice whispered. *It's too bad you serve such an evil man.*

A wave of revulsion slammed into him, so strong it felt like a physical blow. His stomach twisted, and fear surged alongside nausea.

"No . . . no, no, no."

"*Yes,*" came a voice from his left.

He turned, eyes wide. The high elf woman. Standing before him as calmly as if the battle had never happened. He tried to lift his sword. His body obeyed slowly, sluggishly. Too slow.

The blade pierced through his chest before he could raise his own. Gerard gasped, pain blooming like fire across his ribs. Still, he tried to strike back.

But then her form shifted. The black mist curled around her, and the illusion peeled away. Not a soldier. Not a woman. The demon summoner. Her eyes were endless pools of inky black, bottomless and cold. His gaze flicked past her, movement drawing his eye.

The four he had seen earlier—those eerie, efficient fighters—strode through the battlefield like disciples of death. They moved among the fallen, blades in hand, finishing off any soldier who so much as twitched. Each bore a single pauldron engraved with a wynver gleaming in the renewed light.

Executioners.

He returned his gaze to the woman holding him fast, her sword still embedded in his chest. "How?" he croaked.

She didn't speak. She only looked down.

He followed her gaze. His breath stopped. Beneath his feet was no longer solid ground, but a pit. A swirling void of pure black. Within it, countless hands reached upward —twisted forms, clawing souls—dragging, yearning. Terror overtook him.

"Relena, save me!" he screamed. The woman yanked her blade free. His sword dropped from numb fingers.

Captain Gerard fell—

Into the abyss.

Sabina turned away, letting the cavalry captain crumple to the ground behind her. With a steady breath, she released the spell, the final threads of her hallucination magic unraveling into the wind. She wiped the blood that had been trickling down from her nose, a symptom of overexerting herself with her magic.

Her Wynvers rose from where they had waited in readiness and snapped into crisp salutes. Sabina gladly returned the gesture. They had performed flawlessly. Silent, deadly, and efficient. She could not have asked for more. And for once, she allowed herself to feel pride, in them and in herself. A small, tired smile crept onto her lips as she lifted her hand and studied the ring Gwyn had lent her.

Its faint glow shimmered softly, the runes along the edge still warm with residual mana. It had helped stabilize her power, amplify her reach, and stretch her hallucinations further than ever before. Even still, it had almost not been enough. She lowered her hand and turned toward the waiting carriage.

Taenya stood there, one hand resting on the frame, the other gently supporting the small girl beside her. But Gwyn wasn't waiting.

She ran forward the moment she saw Sabina, arms outstretched. Sabina blinked, caught by surprise, just before the girl flung her arms around her in a tight hug.

"You're okay!" Gwyn said, her voice thick with emotion. "That was so scary, Sabina."

Sabina stiffened instinctively, shame and fear overriding her previous high. But she didn't pull away.

"I was scared that you'd get hurt," Gwyn whispered. "There were so many of them, and it was just you five."

Sabina closed her eyes for a moment. *She was worried. For me.*

Taenya stepped up beside them, her tone quiet but steady. "You did well. I am proud of you."

Sabina turned, reaching out to clasp the knight's forearm. Their eyes met, and for the briefest moment, she felt Taenya's usually guarded emotions bleeding through the cracks.

<<Exhaustion>>

<<Relief>>

<<Pride>>

<<Worry>>

<<Determination>>

Sabina dipped her head, the hint of a smile touching her lips. "Thank you."

Taenya sighed, casting a glance toward the remaining guards gathering nearby, forming ranks, checking the wounded. Sabina gently pulled back from Gwyn and looked around as well.

The battlefield might be theirs for now, but the fight wasn't over. "We still have the army," she said, voice low. "It's still coming."

"If we head back toward Strathmore, we should be able to outrun them," Taenya added, her voice laced with uncertainty despite the plan.

"No."

The single word cut through the moment like a blade. Sabina and Taenya both looked at her in surprise. Gwyn's face was set. Her eyes, so often bright with curiosity or warmth, were hard.

"No?" Taenya repeated, slipping into formality, mindful of the many ears around them. "What do you mean, Your Highness?"

Gwyn stepped forward, straightening as she turned to address the circle of guards, soldiers, and survivors surrounding them. She took a steadying breath and pointed toward the distant line of soldiers still forming in the hazy light.

"No more." Her voice rang with command. "They've attacked us twice now. They think they can walk away from it, that they can do whatever they want." She turned slowly, her gaze sweeping across the group. "In my world, actions have consequences. And here?" She placed her hand over her heart. "Our people—members of our *family*—have been killed. And they will not stop until we are dead." She pointed at the group, voice rising. "Until *all* of you are dead. But I am *done* running."

The silence that followed was heavy. Taenya stepped forward, her voice soft. "Your Highness . . . Gwyn . . . we can't fight that army. We don't have the numbers. Not nearly enough."

Gwyn's eyes didn't waver. "You two . . . my wonderful knights. You've both pushed yourselves. You've shown them what magic can do." She turned to Taenya, her voice softening. "Taenya, you are our sword. Our shield. Our defender."

Sabina straightened as the young girl turned her gaze from the telv knight and fixed it on her.

"Sabina," Gwyn said, voice calm and clear, "you are the darkest night. The shadows that protect us, even in the day."

The princess turned, her small frame facing the guards gathered nearby. "All of you. You are brave. You've overcome every obstacle placed before us. Every time we've fought, it's been against greater numbers—and still, you stood. You are the best House Guard anyone could ever ask for, and I am proud . . . so proud that you've chosen to stand with me."

Her voice held steady, but the emotion behind it resonated. "That drake we found . . . she was a mother. She died trying to protect her baby. Her *family*. And those people"—her voice sharpened—"killed her. They killed her child. And still, she fought to her last breath. She didn't die quietly. She took Count Telford and all of his men with her."

Gwyn's hands clenched at her sides. "I want to find my mom. I miss her every single day. But I can't—*we* can't—keep moving forward if we're constantly being hunted by evil men. This is where we make our stand. Like that drake, we will destroy anyone who tries to harm our family."

She paused, her voice trembling not with fear, but fury. "I don't want to die. I don't want any of you to die. But I am sick and tired of this Polite War." She pointed at the distant army, now more visible as the morning fog continued to lift.

"They think they can win. That they can break us. Do you know why they keep sending people?" She looked between Taenya and Sabina. "Because they're scared."

Gwyn took a breath, then continued, her voice gathering strength. "Taenya. Sabina. We've all used our magic, but not together. I know you're tired. You've both given so much. But we can't rest—not now. And there's nowhere left to run." She stepped forward, eyes shining. "We end it now." She punctuated her words with a sharp, decisive gesture toward the field.

Oren and the other guards exchanged glances, then looked back at the princess. And as one, they dropped to a knee. The senior telv guardsman raised his voice, clear and proud.

"Your Highness . . . *my princess* . . . we are with you. We are yours to command."

Sabina looked at Taenya. The knight met her gaze and gave a slow nod. A tear traced down Taenya's cheek.

She's afraid. Not for herself, but for Gwyn.

Gwyn looked between her two knights. "Sabina? Bring back the night."

Sabina dipped her head. "Of course."

Gwyn turned to Taenya. "Taenya, I need something that will make them pause. Can you bring her back again?"

Taenya's jaw tightened. She hesitated—just for a breath—then nodded. "Not for long," she said, voice low. "But yes. I think I can." She turned to Oren. "I'll need to be watched. Closely. I . . . don't know how it'll affect me."

Sabina looked down at the ring on her finger. She took a slow, steady breath, then slipped it off and held it out. "Gwyn . . . you'll need this."

The girl's eyes lit up with gratitude as she took the ring and slid it back onto her hand.

Oren stepped forward again. "What would you have of your Guard, Your Highness?"

"First," Gwyn said, "we get the wagons and carriages back into formation. I want our people safe. I'm sure Sabina can feel how scared they are. They have been locked in there since all of this started."

Sabina nodded silently, the overwhelming emotions coming from within the carriages confirming Gwyn's intuition.

"After that?" Gwyn continued, lifting her chin. "All any of you have to do is cover me."

Sabina heard Taenya's faint, sharp inhale behind her. "What are you going to do?" she asked.

Gwyn looked back at the field, her expression hardening. "It's time Lord Angwin learns what it means to strike at House Reinhart. That army?" she said, pointing ahead once more. She raised her other hand, a clenched fist engulfed in deep red fire laced with golden streaks. "It will be the first to burn."

CHAPTER TWENTY-EIGHT

POINTS WELL MADE

It took far too many battlefields and far too many corpses before the armies of the continent understood a simple truth: clumping thousands of soldiers together wasn't a show of strength against a mage—it was an invitation to be annihilated.

At first, generals dismissed the idea that a single spellcaster could change the course of battle. They were wrong. The scorched plains outside of Drakensburg, the ash-covered trenches of Derenhold—these battles became grim testaments to that folly. But the second lesson came just as hard: it was not enough to avoid presenting a target. One needed mages of their own. Ones capable of shielding their forces, of countering fire with frost, shadow with light.

Only after those brutal campaigns did the doctrine change: never bunch undefended, never underestimate, and never march without your own mage.

A Treatise on the Arcane's Effect on Wars: Vol. II, 212 SA

Gwyn stared at the army arrayed against them, her fury simmering just beneath the surface. They advanced slowly, confidently—each step heavy with the weight of assumed victory. As if the destruction of their forward force had been meaningless. As if their numbers alone guaranteed success. It was the same arrogant certainty she had seen in Count Telford in the duke's court. The belief in their own superiority, not questioned but accepted as absolute truth.

It grated at her. The entire system was broken. And she knew it needed to be torn down.

Taenya had once told her that she could be the change this world needed, but Gwyn still didn't see how. All she saw now was a path paved in fire and ruin. Maybe that was what her knight had meant—that the system needed to burn, so something better could rise from the ashes. That, Gwyn could do. But first she would make a point. Starting now.

A strong feeling of déjà vu swept over her. She looked to her right. Taenya stood in her armor, helm in place, visor down. The dragon etched on her shoulders was unmistakable. Just as in Gwyn's dreams.

To her left, Sabina stood tall and silent. Her armor matched Taenya's in cut and purpose, though the helm had been crafted to accommodate her pointed elf ears. No army stood at their back. No cavalry waited for a signal. Only twenty guards and two knights surrounded her.

Ahead of them, over two hundred soldiers of House Angwin marched toward their position. And yet her people stood firm. They had faith in her. She would not fail them.

There would be no great army to shield her while she cast. No phoenixes of fire to rise on her command. There would be no last-minute negotiations, no time for diplomacy or words. When the soldiers crossed into her range, she would strike.

She just needed Taenya and Sabina to make them pause. After that, it would be all on her.

Taenya took a deep breath. She knew she should be resting since her mind was frayed, stretched thin like a bowstring pulled too tight. Her connection to the mana felt taut, dangerously close to snapping if she tried to pull from it too hard or too fast.

Still, she thought, *I have to do this. Just enough to give Gwyn the opening. Enough to make them hesitate.*

For the first time, she felt a sharp pang of jealousy toward Sabina and Gwyn. Their magic felt so natural, so strong. Their connections to mana were like flowing rivers, steady and deep. Hers was more like threading a needle through a shifting current.

She knew the reason. She'd spent enough time studying the nuances of her own magic to understand. Taenya wasn't a *pure* magic user. Yes, she could cast spells, summon spirits, and manipulate mana, but she could also use it physically, in ways similar to Theran. Magic affected the people of House Reinhart in three distinct ways: there were pure casters like Sabina and Gwyn, physical enhancers like Theran, and then there was her. She stood at the intersection of both. It was both a blessing and a curse.

In the duel against Marquess Angwin's son, she had used mana to augment her speed and power—just as Theran would have. And now, she summoned spirits and cast a form of magic like a mage. But because her abilities were divided, she would never reach the same level of raw power as someone who was purely one or the other.

She was versatile—adaptable. But sometimes, she wished she could conjure the towering illusions Sabina could create, or ignite the battlefield with a single thought like Gwyn.

Still, she reminded herself, *I have a role to play. And I will not fail her.*

One advantage Taenya had come to appreciate was how Sabina's magic affected her less than it did others. It wasn't that she didn't trust her friend—it was a relief, really. If Sabina's mind-altering magic had less of a hold over her, it meant other mind mages would likely struggle to manipulate her as well. Perhaps it was a result of her own more mental connection to mana, the way her abilities threaded between the physical and the arcane.

Whatever the reason, Taenya could feel her strength growing with every surge of mana she channeled. Each time she pushed herself to the edge, her grip on her magic became a little steadier. A little sharper.

The enemy was close now, almost within range. Just a little farther. She reached inward, searching for her link to the *Draconic Spirit*. She was there, burning bright. The spirit's presence was strong, eager, restless. This time, she wanted out. Wanted vengeance. She hungered for the soldiers of House Angwin.

One last time, she promised the spirit silently. *Then you may rest*. The mana around her responded. A low rumble vibrated through the air. With the previous casting, the spell had been changed. It was exactly what she needed now, and one that made it even easier to cast than before.

Taenya raised her hands and began casting [**Summon Draconic Spirit**]. Red mana surged through her, flowing like molten fire to a point just in front of their defensive line. The guards didn't so much as flinch as mist rose from the ground, thick and crimson, and a deafening roar erupted from within it—the unmistakable cry of the drakyyd returning.

The spell reached the point where it no longer needed her direct shaping. With a strained breath, Taenya lowered her hands. The summoning was complete. Now, it was just a matter of feeding the spirit mana through her core—tenuous though that connection was. The spirit would remain for as long as she could keep her tethered.

Taenya winced. It was already starting to drain her.

It didn't take long before her summoning spell began to solidify, the contest of wills barely a whisper this time. The spirit had already accepted the bond, drawn in through both oath and contract. There was no resistance—only anticipation.

With a flash of red mana, the *Draconic Spirit* burst forth from the mist with a thunderous roar, its scaled form coalescing in front of their line. Emotion radiated from the creature; she was fierce, protective, ready. She had felt Gwyn's fire and recognized her. She turned her massive head and bowed toward the girl in a gesture both regal and reverent.

Gwyn smiled, her expression calm as she returned the nod.

The spirit's roar was still echoing through the air when a surge of black mist poured from Sabina's position. It rushed outward in all directions, swallowing the light as the sky turned dark overhead. Her friend had joined the fight, adding her own power to the growing tide.

And then Taenya saw it: what they'd all been waiting for. The ripple. A shift in the enemy's formation. Subtle at first, but unmistakable.

The line of approaching soldiers had stopped—they were hesitating of their own accord.

It was time.

Even through the building tension, Gwyn could just barely make out the shouts of officers calling orders as day turned to night. The battlefield darkened under Sabina's mist, and the *Draconic Spirit* surged forward with a thunderous roar. Shields were raised. Spears dropped into formation. It was all exactly as she wanted.

Gwyn reached inward, feeling her connection to the mana sing in response. She pulled at it, shaping her intent into spellform. She closed her eyes, listening—*feeling*.

The mana was alive. It hummed, vibrated with potential, but it had no direction. It reached for her, and she answered with a gentle nudge. Gwyn sang her own desire, putting her intent into her spell. She needed the soldiers to hesitate just a moment longer.

Her [**Aura of Winter**] was designed to center on herself—at least, that was how it had functioned during her practice sessions. But today, she needed something broader. A force more like Sabina's [**Obfuscating Mist**], but hers would be cold. Icy. Commanding.

Gwyn felt her connection to mana deepen as it began to understand what she was asking of it. Frost crawled across her hands. She raised them, and the mana surged up her arms, heavy and dense, as if she were lifting iron.

The air around her dropped several degrees in an instant, her breath crystalizing in front of her face. She directed the spell outward, drawing on an image: waves crashing upon a rocky shore. She imagined each crest rolling over itself in a freezing torrent.

The mana began to comply, shifting, answering her vision. She knew she had strength in her connection, but forcing too much mana into a spell could leave her drained and defenseless. Like Taenya after she pushed past her limits. It was a concept she'd studied carefully—one mana itself seemed eager to teach.

Her connection to the mana was like a rubber band: slack when untouched, but tense and volatile the more she pulled. Push too far, and it could snap back—painfully—or worse, break entirely. That break was what had happened to Taenya.

Prolonged overuse had other dangers. Mana sickness, mana exhaustion—terms Miss Rolfe used with clinical precision. It seemed her knights would be attending lessons soon, whether they liked it or not.

That can come later, she reminded herself. *Focus.* Gwyn took a deep breath. Frost spilled from her lips. She pulled her fists in close—then *pushed*.

A [**Wave of Frost**] exploded outward from her, a glacial surge that began just ahead of the *Draconic Spirit*. It spread wide enough to engulf the entire front of the enemy formation.

Ahead of her, she saw sweat streaking down Taenya's temple. Her knight was already straining from the summoning. "Now, Taenya!" Gwyn shouted.

There was no verbal response from the knight, but the drakyyd reacted immediately. With a sudden roar, she launched herself forward, using the cresting frost wave as cover. She moved as if she could see through both the frost and Sabina's black mist. And as she neared the enemy line, she did not slow. She leapt, soaring over the spears of the front line, and crashed down into the heart of the enemy formation.

Gwyn smirked and turned her focus to the flanks, even as the *Draconic Spirit* rampaged through the heart of the enemy formation. She pulled at her favored mana—red, wild and fierce—and felt the air around her heat instantly. Her eyes burned with fire, and the sensation filled her with glee. She imagined how she must look: radiant, terrifying, untouchable.

The draconic flame churned inside her like a storm, and she loosed her next spell with confidence, casting [**Pillar of Flame**] at both wings of the enemy's line simultaneously. Twin columns of red and gold fire erupted skyward, swallowing soldiers in an instant. The enemy's formation scattered, and chaos spread like wildfire.

The center, caught between panic and pain, continued to battle the drakyyd, though Gwyn could tell the spirit's time was nearly done. Taenya's pale, sweating face was proof enough. A moment later, the massive spirit collapsed into mist, its roar fading into the charged air.

Without hesitation, Gwyn summoned as many [**Fireballs**] as she could. She flung them into the disoriented ranks, hurling them one after another as soldiers tried to retreat from the fading spirit. Scarlet explosions rocked the battlefield, lighting up the front lines. Screams rang out as bodies fell in smoldering heaps.

But Gwyn wasn't finished. Two more [**Pillars of Flame**] roared into existence, consuming the battered remnants still attempting to regroup at the center. A third pillar followed, aimed directly at a cluster of archers trying to reform. Their uniforms—cheap, light, hastily thrown together—ignited almost instantly.

The sheer force of the flame sent nearby soldiers scrambling to help their burning comrades. Gwyn turned her attention elsewhere, scanning for the next target.

A shout echoed from within the enemy ranks—an order, a desperate one—and with it, what remained of their discipline collapsed. The army surged forward in a ragged charge.

But it was already too late. Gwyn and Taenya had thinned their numbers significantly. What cohort remained was broken, panicked, and bleeding.

Gwyn called to the mana again, thinking of her earlier spell. The [**Wave of Frost**] had stalled them. She wondered what would happen if she shaped red mana into the same form. She pulled harder. The connection tensed—tight, resistant—but she pushed through. Compressing the spell's shape, she narrowed its path and released a new spell: **[Inferno Wave]**.

It wasn't as wide as the frost, and it moved slower, but its impact was immediate. The charge faltered, then halted entirely, as men screamed and scattered. The wave of fire rolled over the rear lines, engulfing those too slow to run.

They have called for a retreat. Sabina's voice echoed in her mind calmly.

Gwyn watched as the flames caught fleeing soldiers, and satisfaction bloomed in her chest. She was about to turn, ready to address her people, when the sound of horns cut through the air.

Her breath caught. "Sabina? What is that?" she asked quickly, unable to keep the concern from her voice.

Taenya looked up, visibly swaying on her feet. "I don't see anything," she murmured.

Sabina's eyes closed. The black mist that still hung across the field collapsed, vanishing as if it had never been, and the light of day returned in full.

Gwyn blinked against the sun, then gasped. "*More* people?"

A massive group on horseback thundered into view, charging directly toward the remnants of the army. From her vantage point, Gwyn could see they numbered nearly three-quarters the size of what was left of the foot soldiers. And they weren't slowing down.

"Look at their armor!" Senior Guardsman Oren called out.

Gwyn squinted, trying to make out the fast-moving figures closing in on the rear of the enemy. Her eyes widened as the gleam of crimson plate caught the light. She heard Taenya suck in a breath beside her.

"It's the Paladins of Alos," the knight said, almost in disbelief. "It seems Amari got tired of waiting on us."

The remnants of Angwin's army scrambled to reform, but their retreat had already broken any cohesion. Panic had splintered their formation. They had no time to properly respond.

The paladins, clad in brilliant scarlet armor, smashed into the rear of the army with devastating force. It was a level of violence even Gwyn's spells hadn't matched. One that was brutal, disciplined, and completely overwhelming.

Entire lines of soldiers were crushed beneath hooves before a single paladin even swung a blade. What had been a rout became a massacre. Within five minutes, the battlefield was quiet again. More than two hundred of Angwin's soldiers lay dead, and not a single paladin had been injured.

Taenya exhaled slowly, her eyes still on the mounted figures cutting through the last of the resistance. She glanced at Sabina. "It seems we should be nicer to Amari."

Gwyn gave a short, hesitant laugh. The sight was . . . disturbing. Efficient and righteous, yes, but still unnerving. "You'd better be, after this."

Sabina nodded solemnly. "Let's get to the carriages and wagons. We should meet up with her."

Gwyn looked back once more, letting her gaze linger over the battlefield. Smoke still drifted in curling wisps. The air was warm, heavy with the scent of ash and blood.

She turned. Her people needed her. It was time to check on them.

Sabina looked around and let out a quiet sigh of relief as she spotted the entrance to the inn they would be staying at during their time in Drakensburg. They were still far from the capital, but this city was a common stop for nobles on the road, and the inn itself was known as one of the finest in the region. Its clientele often included titled travelers and merchant lords alike.

Aleanora's mother did well, Sabina thought, allowing herself a moment of appreciation.

As they approached, Paladin Amari gave her a curious look and arched a brow before stepping around her to enter. Two of Sabina's Wynvers followed close behind, slipping into position just as ordered. They would remain near Gwyn, assisting her while she got settled and ensuring her safety during the transition.

Sabina had a dozen tasks waiting for her. But in that moment, all she could do was stand there, staring at the doorway.

A hand touched her shoulder, and the familiar lack of emotional noise told her who it was.

"You going to stand there or go in?" Taenya asked, her tone light.

"I-I am going in," Sabina replied, though her feet didn't move. When she did try, Taenya gently pulled her back, stepping close. A shiver ran down Sabina's spine at the proximity.

"Are you alright?" her friend whispered, concern threaded through her voice.

Sabina nodded slowly. *I am. Just relieved to be here.* She paused. *Will the capital really be safer?*

Taenya considered her words before answering, her reply brushing through Sabina's thoughts like a steady wind. *If it isn't, we'll face it together. We just need to look after that girl.*

The thought made Sabina sigh again. "You're right. This is going to be a long winter, isn't it?"

Taenya gave her shoulder a reassuring squeeze, then pulled her into a side-hug. "It'll only feel long if you snore."

Sabina squinted. "What do you mean?"

Taenya chuckled. "Did I forget to mention? You and I are sharing a room."

Sabina groaned. "You're the one who snores." *This is going to be a long wait until the Festival of Love.*

As if reading her mind, Taenya laughed again. "It's not that long, Sabina. The Festival of the Hearth begins soon. I think Gwyn will enjoy it."

The Festival of the Hearth marked the middle of winter, while the Festival of Love celebrated its end and the arrival of spring. It was also around then that mothers learned about the pregnancies conceived over the cold winter nights.

Sabina nodded, grateful for the brief moment of levity. They would spend the winter here—safer within the city walls rather than risking the dangers of travel during the season of snowstorms and ice-slick roads. It was the prudent choice. The right choice.

I hope so, she thought. *She definitely could use something to take her mind off—*

Her eyes widened slightly. An idea had just come to her—one that might help not only Gwyn, but also others like her. *Taenya? I think I have something to discuss with you during our time here. In secret. I could use your help.*

Taenya paused mid-step, then turned to meet her eyes. Sabina must have looked more serious than she intended, because Taenya reached out, took her hand, and gave it a firm squeeze.

"I will always have your back, my friend."

Sabina smiled, warmth blossoming in her chest. It felt good to have people who cared.

Gwyn sat on her bed, knees pulled tight to her chest. Tears streaked her cheeks as she rocked herself slowly, arms wrapped around her legs.

I'm sorry, Mom. I had to. They were going to hurt us. I'm sorry.

The tears came again. It felt like no matter what they did, someone was always trying to hurt them and trying to use her. And though no one in their group had died this time, a few guards had been injured. Nothing too serious, they said. They'd been *lucky*. She felt herself growing stronger with each battle, each spell, each new challenge, but it still didn't feel like it was enough. *People know what I can do now.* Each new enemy seemed more prepared than the last. All it would take is one adult—someone trained, powerful, and cruel—and she wouldn't be able to protect her people. Not Sabina, not Taenya, not even the guards. She was still just a kid. Her magic wouldn't be enough one day, and when that day came, everyone she loved would die.

And it will be my fault.

They were stuck here in this unfamiliar city for over forty days while they waited out the winter, and she hated it. She hated the way everything was always decided for her. Where to go, what to do, how to act. *Why can't I just be older? I wish I wasn't so . . . small.*

Gwyn squeezed her eyes shut as more tears slid down her face. *Mom could be out there right now, and I wouldn't know. I can't help her, and I feel like I need to.*

What if she's . . . dead?

Gwyn rotated the ring on her finger slowly as she rocked herself in silence, trying to stay calm. Trying *not* to use her magic.

I wish I had proof. Anything. Just knowing her mother was alive would be enough. But she couldn't even go look for her. She had to go to school. A *stupid* academy where she wouldn't be allowed to see Sabina or Taenya except on week-ends. Lorrena would be there, yes, but that was it. Ilyana would be in the older students' school, but that was too far for regular visits. Close enough to feel her presence, but not close enough to reach. Aleanora would be working with Taenya while studying with Maya and Mister Branigan. It was all just horrible.

Then, a name drifted through her mind, and with it, the tension in her chest eased. *Roslyn. She'll be there.* Gwyn took a deep breath. That one thought made everything feel just a little better. Roslyn, her best friend, would be there at the academy with her. Someone she could talk to, who wouldn't judge her, whose shoulder she could cry on.

I miss you, Roslyn. I'll be there soon. She sniffled and wiped her face, clearing away the tears and snot with the sleeve of her nightgown. Then she pulled at her mana, letting **[Frozen Heart]** settle over her mind and emotions like a soft, icy veil. The aching subsided. The chaos in her chest quieted.

Gwyn stood and put her smile back on. She just needed to be strong a little while longer. She could fake it until she made it. Just a little while longer.

For a moment, her spell seemed to . . . stutter.

Mommy? Please hurry.

Roslyn sat up as a knock sounded on the carriage door and Ser Roderick leaned his head in. "My lady, we have arrived."

She nodded, brushing the front of her dress smooth and tugging her cloak tighter around her shoulders as a cold breeze slipped through the narrow open-ing. "Thank you, Ser Roderick."

The knight dipped his head and stepped away. Roslyn shivered and pulled the thick blanket beside her over her legs.

After leaving the dwarven Under-Nation of Dirn Loduhr, they had contin-ued with barely any pause, the biting wind and icy roads doing little to slow them as they pushed onward toward the capital. The caravan was well-supplied, boasting numerous carriages and wagons filled with provisions. Still, she couldn't help but note the number of guards accompanying them—far more than she'd ever traveled with before.

Why so many? I never needed this many going to Maireharbora . . .

The cold had been relentless. They had traveled straight through the Festival of the Hearth, not stopping for winter rest, and made remarkably good time considering the conditions. The guards lit countless campfires at night to keep everyone warm, and her own tent had relied heavily on heated ovens and thick furs. Without them, she might've frozen where she lay.

Her thoughts turned inward. *I wish Gwyn was here . . . I wonder what she's doing right now.* She sighed softly. *Probably something better than this.*

The carriage shifted and lurched forward again, slowly passing beneath the high arch of the city gate. Roslyn leaned closer to the window, her breath catching at the sight. Towering walls gave way to the grand structure of the South Gate, a massive entry point into the capital city.

Her eyes remained fixed on the scene outside as they entered the heart of Veradon. This gate led directly toward the Old Town and the Vermeil Highland, where the ducal estates were nestled like jewels among snow-draped trees. Beyond them lay the palace and the royal administrative heart of the kingdom.

Few people were out in the cold morning, but those who were moved purposefully. Street sweepers shoveled snow from the wide boulevards, clearing paths with practiced rhythm. The city, even half-asleep, was clean, orderly, and immense.

I wonder how Gwyn is doing in Drakensburg. Roslyn smiled faintly. *I hope her journey was more peaceful—and warmer—than mine.* She snorted softly to herself. *Of course it was warmer. She can control fire!*

Her fingers moved unconsciously to the earring in her ear—Gwyn's gift. She smiled again, this time more deeply, feeling a flicker of warmth despite the cold.

Drawing the curtains closed, she leaned back as the carriage rolled through the gates of the Tiloral estate. Palatial and dignified, it stood second only to the Crown's holdings within the capital. The approach was lined with perfectly maintained hedges and wide stone paths, everything in its place.

As the carriage came to its final stop, Roslyn stood and moved toward the door. It opened before her hand reached the handle, and Ser Roderick stood waiting, offering a steadying hand. Ser Janine bowed respectfully as Roslyn stepped down, her boots crunching softly in the snow.

Her paladin protector, Evocati Khalan, stood nearby, speaking with a knight dressed in armor that looked very familiar. The human man's meticulously groomed mustache confirmed her suspicion—it was the same knight she remembered from her visit to Gwyn's manor.

Roslyn stepped forward and offered a polite dip of her head. "Sir Friedrich, is it?"

The man gave a formal bow and smiled as he straightened, his mustache lifting with the expression. "It is, milady. Sir Friedrich von Boden—formerly of the Holy Roman Empire, and now proudly sworn to House Reinhart in this new world. Her Highness asked that I meet you upon your arrival."

His accent was thick but precise, and Roslyn found it endearing. She recalled Gwyn telling her that Friedrich had learned Common after arriving on Eona. He'd clearly come far in that time.

Roslyn giggled. "That's funny. She told me to find you once I got here."

Friedrich chuckled. "She is fond of you, it seems." His gaze drifted to her assembled entourage—Khalan, Roderick, Janine, and the full escort of guards. "You are well protected, my lady. Still, Princess Gwyn wished for me to accompany you, if you would allow it."

Both Khalan and Ser Roderick looked as if they were about to object, their expressions tight with protective instinct. But Roslyn smiled before they could speak.

"I would love for you to join me until my friend arrives, Sir Friedrich."

The knight nodded with a small, respectful smile, then turned to Ser Roderick. "I will follow your lead, Ser Roderick."

Ser Roderick gave him an appreciative nod in return, clearly recognizing both the man's experience and intent.

Roslyn took a brief moment to study Friedrich's armor more closely—the craftsmanship, the polished surface, the understated, purposeful design. Her gaze flicked back to her own knights, to Roderick and Janine. She sighed softly. *They really do have better-looking armor than ours.*

Not that she would ever tell Gwyn that.

CHAPTER TWENTY-NINE

STONES IN THE SNOW

Drakensburg smelled of woodsmoke, roasted nuts, and pine. Gwyn walked at a steady pace, her wool-lined cloak wrapped tightly around her shoulders as snowflakes drifted lazily through the winter air. The stone streets—worn smooth by centuries of passage, bordered by old stone buildings and timber-fronted shops dusted with white—had been swept clean by the locals.

The city had a quiet dignity to it. No grandeur or towering spires like Strathmore. No dramatic ocean cliffs or harbors like the stories Roslyn told her of Maireharbora. Drakensburg was more grounded. Rooted. This was a city built by farmers and craftsmen, nestled on fertile plains and framed by the shadows of two distant Val Forests and the icy slopes of the Dirn Mountains. It felt like a place that could outlast empires simply by existing.

Gwyn breathed it in deeply. She liked it here. People were out in surprising numbers for such a cold morning. Wrapped in furs and scarves, they bustled about their errands—trading goods, chatting on stoops, checking the winter vegetables stacked outside a grocer's stall. It wasn't lively in the way cities sometimes were. It was *busy*. Purposeful.

Amari walked a short distance behind her, watchful but unintrusive. The paladin's crimson cloak caught the light as she moved, drawing a few glances from passersby. But most eyes slid off Gwyn easily enough. She was dressed like any minor noble might be—modest, functional, and with no tiara in sight. Plus, Aleanora had helped do up her hair how she wanted, in a way that covered her ears.

She peered into the window of a little shop advertising winter pastries, then crossed the street to admire a row of hand-carved toys stacked in a stall. Her fingers hovered over a small wooden fox before she moved on.

As she passed a side lane, she heard a sound that made her stop. Laughter—sharp, cruel, the kind that hit her like a slap. She turned her head slightly.

Down the narrow lane, five boys in finely tailored winter coats had cornered a girl. Gwyn couldn't hear every word, but the tone was unmistakable: their teasing was meant to wound. The girl clutched a box tightly to her chest, her cheeks red from cold and humiliation.

Gwyn narrowed her eyes and took a step forward but stopped short. A boy—maybe their age, maybe younger—had stepped into the circle at the same time. His clothes were rough, his boots scuffed and clearly repaired more than once. His voice rang clear even from where Gwyn stood.

"Leave her alone."

The noble boys turned in unison, their posturing now aimed at him.

"Oh, look. Her mudwalker came to fetch her."

"Shouldn't you be sweeping stables, not talking to your betters?"

"Shouldn't you be kissing each other's arses at some party in your father's fancy house?" the boy snapped.

One of them laughed, loud and ugly. "Oh, you're going to get it now, trash."

Another reached out, but the girl grabbed the boy's arm and together they bolted. Within seconds, the two of them had vanished into the winding alleys behind a row of buildings.

The noble boys sneered and dispersed, muttering to each other with amused disdain.

Gwyn stood still for a beat, watching them go. She exhaled quietly. "Well," she murmured. "*That* was interesting."

Amari raised a brow but didn't speak.

Gwyn's lips curled into a thoughtful smile. "Let's follow them. Just casually."

Amari sighed but fell into step behind her. They weren't hard to follow. The pair had fled through a narrow corridor between buildings and emerged on the far side of the street. Now, they were walking briskly through one of Drakensburg's smaller market squares. It was less crowded than the one near the city center, but still lively, with rows of stalls clustered between squat stone buildings, selling everything from dried meats and herbal teas to secondhand scarves and quilts.

Gwyn stayed at a distance, weaving through the foot traffic with the ease of someone who had learned how not to be noticed, thanks to Sabina's lessons. Amari shadowed her in silence, keeping her distance too and drawing looks with her crimson apparel, drawing attention away from Gwyn.

The two Gwyn followed didn't notice. The girl was speaking quickly, her hands moving as she talked, clearly still upset. The boy was listening intently, nodding every so often, but Gwyn noticed the way he kept rubbing his shoulder, probably smarting from when one of the noble boys had shoved him.

They stopped at a produce stand, and Gwyn decided that was her moment. She took a breath and stepped forward—just a little too close—letting her shoulder brush the boy's as if by accident.

"Oh! I'm so sorry," she said, pulling back and offering a polite smile. "I wasn't watching where I was going."

The boy blinked, clearly startled, but managed a quick smile. "It's alright."

The girl's expression was a different story. Her blue eyes narrowed slightly and she stiffened, stepping closer to him, almost like she was guarding him.

Gwyn pretended not to notice. "You were very brave, by the way," she said, looking at the boy. "Back there, in the alley."

The boy's face turned red. "You saw that?"

"I was nearby," Gwyn said with a small nod. "You did the right thing."

The girl crossed her arms, clearly still uncertain about this stranger inserting herself into their conversation.

Gwyn smiled at her too, though she made sure it wasn't smug. "Sorry if I'm intruding. I just thought . . . well, not many people would've stepped in like that."

She looked the girl over, happy to see she hadn't been physically harmed. "I'm not fond of bullies. So I wanted to make sure you were, you know, alright."

The boy looked at the girl as if for permission to speak. When she gave the faintest of nods, he turned back to Gwyn. "They've been doing it for weeks."

So it's a pattern, Gwyn thought. *Typical.*

"I'm Gareth," the boy added. "And this is . . . um, Thalia."

The girl gave the faintest of nods.

"I'm Gwyn," she offered.

Thalia's eyes flicked over her again, clearly not buying the casual act. "Just Gwyn?"

"Just Gwyn." She grinned.

Gareth, for his part, looked completely charmed. But Gwyn kept her focus on Thalia. She found something interesting about the girl, who couldn't have been more than a year or two older than Gwyn, even if they were the same height. *Maybe it was the way she looked at the boy when he wasn't looking?* There was something in that look.

"What are you doing in this part of the city?" he asked. "You don't sound like you're from here."

"Visiting for the winter," Gwyn replied smoothly. "Thought I'd get to know the city. It's lovely."

"It's cold," Thalia muttered, then quickly added, "but I guess it has its charm."

Gwyn let out a soft laugh. "I agree with that. Back home we would travel to the mountains that were *really* cold." She shook her head as she thought about the trips. A strand of hair fell over her face, and she tucked the lock behind her ear without thinking.

The boy gasped loudly. "You're one of them . . . uhh . . ."

"Terrans," the girl added helpfully.

Gwyn smiled and nodded. "I am!"

That seemed to draw in Gareth even more. Gwyn could tell Thalia was attempting to feign disinterest, but despite being clearly annoyed by Gareth's overly friendly manner, she asked pointed questions that betrayed her curiosity. *Or maybe to get me to focus on her instead of Gareth.*

They spoke for a few more minutes, Gwyn asking harmless questions—where to find the best sweets, where the nearest bookshop was, and if there were any other local shops worth going to. Gareth answered most of them eagerly. Thalia remained cool, but Gwyn could see the way her eyes tracked everything. She wasn't rude. Just wary.

Eventually, Thalia checked the angle of the sun and tugged Gareth gently by the sleeve. "We should go."

"Oh," Gareth said, clearly reluctant. "Yeah. Right."

"It was nice meeting you," Gwyn said.

"You too," Gareth replied, giving her a smile that might have melted snow if not for the wind. Thalia only nodded.

As they walked away, Gwyn watched them for a moment, her smile fading into something more thoughtful.

"She's protective," Amari said quietly behind her. "Sharp. She doesn't trust you."

"She's right not to," Gwyn replied softly. "I wasn't exactly honest."

"You never lied."

"No," Gwyn said. "But I didn't tell the truth either."

They walked to the bookshop Gareth had mentioned and Gwyn pushed the door open. A little bell jingled overhead. The warmth hit her the moment she stepped inside.

The bookshop was a narrow, two-story building with gently slanted walls. Books were piled high on every surface, and an herbal smell—lavender and old parchment—made Gwyn sigh with contentment. It was the kind of place that made you never want to leave.

A small fire crackled in the hearth across from the counter, and bookshelves leaned just a little too much under the weight of their contents. A small mezzanine sat above the entrance with more books visible through a wooden railing, and a sliding ladder stood off to one side. It was quiet, save for the turning of pages as the bookseller perused a volume.

Behind the front counter stood a high elf man with silvery-blond hair pulled back into a simple ponytail, a soft green waistcoat over a high-collared shirt, and something that made her pause . . . glasses. She couldn't recall seeing anyone else in this world wearing a pair before. These were intricate brass-rimmed spectacles, adorned with delicate scrollwork and tiny floral engravings that gleamed faintly in the sunlight streaming in through the window.

She'd need to ask Mister Branigan or Maya about that.

"Welcome," the bookseller said, his voice low and polite. "Come in, come in. Please, take your time. Let the shelves speak first. They usually know what you're looking for before you do."

Gwyn smiled at that. "I like that."

Amari stayed near the door, removing her gloves and warming her hands by the fire as Gwyn wandered between the shelves. The titles were mostly in the Ikiosan trade script, with the occasional spine flourished with Loreni script tucked in between. Fiction and history, poetry and philosophical musings—rows upon rows of everything she loved.

She stopped at a shelf labeled *Folk and Fable* and ran a gloved finger along the spines. Her eyes landed on a weathered volume bound in green cloth: *The Oak and the Flame.*

"That one," the bookseller said, stepping around the counter. "A local favorite. Legend from the old forest villages. It's about a flame spirit and a tree guardian who learn they cannot protect their land alone. They have to trust one another."

Gwyn pulled it free and opened to the first page. The ink was hand-pressed, the script elegant.

"I love stories like this," she said softly. "My mother used to read them to me when I was little. Where I'm from, there are so many examples."

The bookseller's brows lifted with curiosity. "Ah, yes. You are a terran, aren't you?"

She nodded without looking up. "I am."

"If you don't mind me asking . . . do stories from your world often line up with ours? Or is it all wildly different?"

Gwyn turned the page, smiling faintly. "There are differences. Surface things. Names. Settings. But the heart of them—what they're really about—that's where it feels familiar."

"Can you give me an example?"

She closed the book and hugged it to her chest for a moment. "There's one my mother read to me: *The Fox and the Grapes.* It's about a fox that wants to eat some grapes hanging from a vine, but he can't reach them. After trying again and again, he finally gives up and walks away, saying they were probably sour anyway."

The bookseller's brow furrowed thoughtfully. "So, he convinces himself they were never worth it."

"Exactly," she said. "But it's not about grapes. It's about pride—pretending you didn't want something just because you couldn't have it. It also teaches a lesson about the dangers of envy and the importance of contentment. I've read stories here that feel the same, even if the characters are different. No foxes, no grapes—but the heart of the story's still there."

The bookseller's expression softened. "Yes, I think the truth of things tends to survive, even if the details change."

"I like that." Gwyn followed the bookseller back to the counter with the book. "Here, I'll take it."

The man nodded, carefully wrapping it in a paper sleeve and tying it with twine. "For what it's worth, miss . . . I think the world always needs people who remember its stories."

Gwyn passed over a few coins and accepted the package with both hands. "And I think it needs more people like you to keep them alive. I'm here for the winter, so until next time." She turned toward the door, heart a little lighter.

"Well?" Amari asked, when they were back out in the crisp afternoon air.

Gwyn held up the cloth-wrapped book with a small grin. "I think I made a friend."

"He did seem pretty interested in what you had to say."

"He was just curious," Gwyn said as they started down the stone-paved street. "I'd be too if someone from another world showed up in my shop and started comparing my favorite books to stories from their home." Amari dipped her head, conceding the point.

They walked on in companionable silence. Around them, the quieter side streets of Drakensburg buzzed softly with the activity of early evening. Market stalls were being closed and windows shuttered. The snow had started to melt earlier in the day, and now the streets were edged with slush that crunched under their boots.

Gwyn glanced toward a cluster of old townhouses on the next block. "Drakensburg's really growing on me," she said.

"It has a kind of charm," Amari agreed. "Less pageantry than Strathmore. More grit."

"That, and the bookshops are way better. We'll have to look around for more. That'll be our goal for the winter: check out every single bookstore in the city."

Gwyn clutched the book closer to her chest as they turned down the next lane. The sun cast long golden beams between the rooftops. The cold didn't bite as sharply now, and her spirits felt lifted after the bookseller's curiosity and respect.

"I want to find something sweet," Gwyn said suddenly. "That walk left me starving. I think we passed a pastry stall two streets over, near that linen shop with the bright orange shutters?"

Amari arched an eyebrow. "Already hungry again?"

Gwyn smiled without apology. "It's thinking food. Besides, I've decided that no one's allowed to think hard about stories that are similar between two worlds on an empty stomach."

They reached the end of the lane, just where it opened onto a broader street. Gwyn slowed, her gaze flicking across the crowd. People milled about—merchants packing up, bundled shoppers hurrying home, a courier darting between them. Then, a flash of movement caught her eye.

Two boys, familiar silhouettes wrapped in expensive winter cloaks, moved briskly down the opposite side of the street. They were walking fast, whispering between themselves with furtive glances over their shoulders.

Gwyn's brow furrowed. "Those two—Amari, those are some of the boys from earlier. The ones that were bullying Gareth and Thalia."

Amari turned her head slightly to follow Gwyn's line of sight, her expression sharpening.

"They look like they're heading somewhere in a hurry," Gwyn said, pulse quickening. "I don't like it."

"I'll keep up," Amari said calmly. "Don't worry about me."

Gwyn nodded once, and they both quickened their pace.

The boys turned the corner into a wide plaza bustling with late-day foot traffic. Gwyn picked up speed, weaving between market stalls and families dragging bundled children in tow.

When they reached the open space, they stopped near a statue of some long-forgotten hero and scanned the crowd. "Do you see them?" Gwyn asked.

Amari was already looking. "No. They vanished."

"Great," Gwyn muttered, twisting around. "They were just here. I saw them cut between those two carts." She quickly slipped around a peddler's display of wool scarves and turned sharply down a side street she would have sworn she saw one of the boys disappear into. The noise of the plaza fell behind them as they passed into a quieter lane, lined with narrow shops and shuttered cafés.

Their boots splashed faintly through patches of slush. A cat darted across the street, spooked by their sudden presence. Gwyn slowed. Her breath fogged as she scanned every doorway, every alley mouth. Nothing.

They turned onto another street. Then another. After several more minutes of hurried walking, Amari's voice came from just behind her.

"It's been nearly a quarter bell, Gwyn. If they were up to something, they're long gone."

Gwyn stopped, exhaling sharply through her nose. She looked around again at the empty corners and disinterested faces of a few passersby.

"I just . . . I don't want something else to happen," she said quietly.

Amari placed a hand gently on her shoulder. "If they're planning anything, we'll hear of it. They're not smart enough to stay subtle for long."

Gwyn nodded reluctantly, casting one last glance over her shoulder.

"Alright," she murmured. "Let's head back."

They turned another corner, the evening sun casting the city in pale gold. It was then that Gwyn heard a sharp sound, something like a yelp or scuffle, echoing from the alley just ahead. She froze. Amari stopped beside her.

The noise came again. A grunt. Raised voices. Gwyn's heart sank. She already knew what she was hearing. Her gaze snapped to the side alley. Amari didn't need to ask. The two exchanged a look—wordless and immediate. They ran.

The alley narrowed quickly, framed on either side by leaning timber buildings with crooked shutters and snow-dampened awnings. Faint light spilled in from the street, casting long shadows that twitched with movement. Gwyn's boots slipped slightly in the wet slush as she rushed in, Amari just behind her, one hand already resting on the pommel of her sword.

* * *

Thalia had never liked Janus Ordell. Pompous, preening, and so smugly sure of his own importance, the boy was everything she couldn't stand in society's upper circles. He treated servants like furniture, dismissed anyone from lesser families as irrelevant, and carried himself like the gods themselves had personally appointed him heir to the city. The funny part was, he wasn't even from the city. His family only came to Drakensburg each winter to get away from the little town they lorded over.

His father, Lord Ordell, had been trying to worm his way into the viscount's favor for years. That the viscount was her uncle made him believe the best way was through her father, despite the fact that he and his brother only spoke when absolutely necessary. Just recently, at her uncle's ball to celebrate the Festival of the Hearth, he'd suggested to her father a potential marriage arrangement—some nonsense about uniting their households and "securing a promising future."

The very idea made her stomach turn. Her father hadn't said yes, but he hadn't exactly said no either. Not yet. Her father was too nice for that. And ambitious. But at least not to the point where he'd sacrifice her.

She would never tie herself to someone like Janus. Not even for influence. Not even for duty. And especially not when he surrounded himself with those bootlicking little sycophants—boys who fed his ego and followed him like dogs, laughing at his every cruel joke.

Even if she didn't like Gareth—and she *did*, even if she hadn't admitted it out loud—she would never choose Janus. And yet, here she was. Cornered in an alley, Gareth at her side, and Janus and his pack blocking the way.

Thalia looked at the boys in front of them. She was trying to wedge herself between Gareth and Janus, but one of the other boys grabbed her arm and yanked her back.

"Let her go!" Gareth shouted, surging forward—only to be met with a sharp kick that dropped him hard to one knee.

The tall boy turned on her, his polished boots crunching on the frostbitten cobbles. His face twisted in a sneer, nostrils flaring.

"Him?" Janus spat, jabbing a finger toward Gareth. "You chose *him*?"

Thalia didn't flinch. Her arm ached where she'd been yanked, and her heart pounded in her chest, but her voice was steady.

"You think you can just dismiss me and my father," Janus went on, "and walk away? You embarrassed me in front of everyone. You *humiliated* me."

Thalia narrowed her eyes. "Whether Gareth were here or not, I would never choose you," she snapped.

He stepped toward her, looming. "And now you're going to learn what happens when you forget your place—"

Crack. Her hand flew out before she even thought about it. The slap rang out in the alley like a thunderclap. Janus's head snapped to the side. For a heartbeat, he stood there stunned, blinking at nothing, mouth hanging open. Then his face twisted with fury.

"You little—" he snarled, shoving her with both hands.

Thalia gasped as she stumbled backward, but Gareth caught her around the shoulders, steadying her before she hit the ground.

She regained her footing, trembling. Her eyes burned. Her jaw clenched. Rage was hotter than fear now. She stepped forward again, teeth bared. "You don't get to treat people like this—!"

Janus didn't answer. He turned, striding to the other side of the alley. He bent to pick up a jagged stone from the frost-streaked ground. Thalia's heart lurched.

"First I'll deal with *him*," Janus said, his voice tight with seeming mania. "Then we'll see if you still want to slap me." He raised his arm.

Thalia didn't think. "No!" she shouted, lunging forward. "Don't you *dare*—"

She didn't see the throw—only the motion, the blur of his hand, and then the terrible sound that followed. White light exploded in her vision. Pain bloomed across her forehead like fire. Her knees buckled. The alley spun. She fell, the world turning to ice beneath her.

Somewhere nearby, Gareth screamed her name.

Then everything went still.

The voices sharpened—teenage boys jeering, a girl who sounded like Thalia shouting, her voice cracking with panic.

Gwyn's boots skidded on a patch of slush, her heart already racing. Five boys loomed in the alley, dressed in coats far too fine for where they stood. Their silks and embossed leather looked garishly out of place among the dirt and frost-streaked brick. In the center of their loose circle stood Gareth, his arms raised defensively, chest heaving. His face was flushed, eyes burning with helpless frustration.

Next to him stood Thalia, her braid half-unraveled, her cheeks flushed with cold and rage as she shouted something Gwyn couldn't make out, trying to move toward the tall boy.

Gwyn didn't stop to think. She raised a hand, her eyes locking onto the tall boy just as he bent, snatched up a jagged stone, and drew his arm back.

"No!" Gwyn shouted, her palm flaring with magic. She reached out with [Telekinesis], willing the spell to grab the stone mid-flight. But she was too slow. The spell didn't lock in time.

Crack. The stone struck Thalia squarely in the forehead. She let out a startled cry and collapsed instantly, legs folding underneath her. Blood blossomed from the center of her brow and ran down her temple as her body crumpled to the frozen ground. Her head hit the cobblestones with a sickening thud.

Gareth shouted her name.

"Enough!" Mana jumped from Gwyn as heads turned.

Amari was already surging past, crimson plate catching the last light. "Check the girl!" she barked, sprinting ahead.

Gwyn raced after her, heading for Thalia.

The boys froze for a moment before all five of them stepped back.

"A paladin," one of them whispered.

The leader's face drained of color. "Run." He spun around—just in time for Amari to reach out and seize him by the front of his coat.

She yanked him off the ground with one hand and drove him into the nearest wall with a solid *thud*. Snow fell from the eaves above. His feet dangled a good handspan above the cobblestone. The other boys froze.

Gareth had dropped beside Thalia, his voice shaking as he cradled her face. "Thalia—Thalia, say something."

Gwyn knelt next to him, her heart pounding. "Let me see."

Gareth jerked back, his eyes wild and wary. Then he recognized her.

She stiffened, protective and uncertain all at once. "She needs a healer."

Thalia blinked, eyelids fluttering. Her voice was faint. "S'fine . . ."

"No, it's not," Gwyn said gently, looking over the wound. Just a gnarly gash that didn't look like it needed stitches. What concerned Gwyn was how hard her head had hit the ground. "But with some rest, you'll be okay."

Thalia groaned faintly.

"Unhand me!" the tall boy barked, his voice high with outrage. "My father is a baron, Lord Ordell! If you so much as touch me again—"

"You've given me your name," Amari interrupted, her voice as cold and smooth as a river stone. She tilted her head. "How helpful." She let him dangle another moment, eyes narrowing. "Drakensburg's guards will be quite interested to hear about a baron's son and his friends attacking a child in an alley. Especially when there's a paladin as a witness."

The tall boy's mouth opened, but Amari gave the wall another *thump* with his body. "Try running," she said flatly. "I'll be happy to add 'resisting' to your list."

She released him, and he crumpled to the ground, too stunned to move.

"Amari," Gwyn said quietly, kneeling beside Thalia. She looked up, meeting the paladin's gaze. "Let me take her home."

Amari gave a small nod, then turned to the other boys. "Stay right here."

They didn't move a muscle.

"I've got her," Gwyn said. "Gareth, help me get her up."

Together, they lifted her, one arm each. Thalia was only half-conscious, her steps slow and unsteady.

"Are you all right to walk, Tal?" Gareth asked, his voice filled with concern as he helped Gwyn steady her.

Thalia gave a weak nod, though her eyes were glassy. She tried to take a step and nearly crumpled, and Gwyn shook her head.

"I'll carry her."

Gareth opened his mouth to object, but Gwyn slipped her arms beneath Thalia's knees and back and lifted her cleanly from the ground. Thalia let out a soft sound of protest, but she let her head rest against Gwyn's shoulder, too dazed to argue.

Either she's really light . . . or I've gotten a lot stronger.

Behind them, Amari's voice snapped through the alley like a blade. "Gwyn, I'll hand them off to the city watch. Do not get into any fights or cause trouble. Meet me at the inn."

"I will be fine." Gwyn met her eyes. "Don't let him weasel out of it."

Amari's lips twitched. "Wouldn't dream of it."

As Gwyn turned to carry Thalia out of the alley, Gareth trailing at her side, Amari's voice rang out once more.

"You," the paladin barked at one of the stunned boys. "Run to the nearest watch post. Tell them a paladin has detained several noble sons on charges of assault and unlawful restraint. Then *bring them back here.*" When the boy hesitated, she added, *"Now."* He ran.

Gwyn held Thalia close as they made their way out of the alley and into the fading evening light. Gareth kept pace beside her, glancing nervously at the girl in her arms.

"She okay?" he asked softly.

"She will be," Gwyn said. "We just need to get her home."

They passed from the bustle of the market district into a quieter, more affluent neighborhood. The noise of the streets faded behind them, replaced by the crunch of their boots on snow-frosted stone and the distant call of someone lighting lanterns. Neatly trimmed hedges bordered walkways, and tall houses with polished windows stood back from the road in quiet elegance.

Eventually, they reached a cream-colored home, stately and tall, with ivy climbing its front and warm light spilling from its windows. A pair of stone planters flanked the broad front steps.

As they approached, the door burst open. A woman stood there, her apron catching in the breeze. "Thalia!" she gasped, hands lifting to her mouth. She hurried down the steps. "Oh gods, what happened?"

"She and Gareth were attacked," Gwyn said, keeping her voice steady. "A group of boys threw a stone. It hit her here." She gestured gently toward the girl's brow. The wound on Thalia's forehead had stopped bleeding, but blood still streaked the side of her face, dried now into the edge of her jawline.

The woman's face went pale. "Oh, stars." She immediately stepped forward, reaching to touch Thalia's cheek with trembling fingers. "Bring her inside—quickly."

Gwyn nodded and climbed the steps, and Gareth held the door open for them both.

The entry hall was warmly lit and elegantly appointed. A polished floor runner stretched across the marble tiles, and portraits hung in neat rows along the wall. The air smelled faintly of lavender oil and cedar. The maid directed them toward a sitting room with plush seating and a low table set for tea. She gestured to a velvet chaise. "Lay her down here."

Gwyn lowered Thalia gently onto the cushions. The girl stirred, eyelids fluttering, her lips parting in a soft sound of pain. The woman disappeared for a moment, then returned swiftly with a basin and clean cloths.

Thalia hissed as the maid began cleaning the wound with practiced care. "It's alright, darling," she murmured, voice gentle. "It's not too deep."

Gwyn stayed nearby, her hands clasped in front of her, uncertain whether to leave or wait. She watched as Gareth knelt beside the chaise, brushing a hand through Thalia's tangled hair. His brows were drawn together, his expression tight with guilt.

"What happened?" the maid asked quietly, dabbing at the wound again. "Who did this?"

Thalia winced, then muttered, "It was Janus. And the others."

"That baron's son?" the maid asked, frowning.

Thalia nodded. "Those boys . . . they've been bothering us for weeks. They caught up with us after we left the market. I told Gareth not to stop, but they surrounded us in an alley. I tried to reason with them, but they wouldn't listen. I guess they were especially upset after he stood up to him earlier when they were harassing me. Then they started pushing him. I couldn't let him get hurt."

"And then?" the woman prompted, her tone still low, but with a sharp edge that hadn't been there before.

"We couldn't get away." Thalia's voice wavered. "There were too many of them. I—I didn't know what to do."

The woman's mouth tightened into a thin line. "Relena damned brats." She didn't raise her voice, but the bitterness laced into her words was sharp. She sighed, her demeanor softening. She gently threaded her fingers through Thalia's hair. "I'm just glad you're safe now."

"They might've hurt her worse," Gareth said, voice low, "but then . . . *she* showed up." He turned his head to look at Gwyn.

The maid's eyes followed his gaze. "And you are?"

"Gwyn," she said softly. "I was nearby. We heard shouting. My companion and I stepped in.

"She had a paladin with her," Thalia added, her tone still wary but threaded with something else now—gratitude, maybe. "The moment they saw her armor, they froze."

"The paladin slammed and held Janus against a wall," Gareth explained.

The maid pursed her lips but didn't argue. "Good. Maybe that'll teach the little beast."

Thalia's eyes slipped closed. She let out a quiet sigh, leaning into the cushions as the maid wiped the last trace of blood from her brow.

"She'll be alright?" Gareth asked.

"She'll have a nasty bruise, but yes. She's lucky. And she's strong." Gareth's shoulders sagged with relief. The maid looked at Gwyn again. "Thank you. For helping her."

Gwyn dipped her head. "I couldn't just walk away."

"Well, I'm glad you didn't. The city could use more folk like you."

There was a long pause as the woman returned her attention to Thalia, quietly giving her another once-over with a soft expression.

Gareth sat back slightly, his gaze never leaving Thalia's face. She blinked her eyes open again and slowly turned to meet Gwyn's. Thalia gave her a single nod. Firm. Not quite warm, but no longer cold. That was enough.

"I should go," Gwyn said, glancing toward the doorway. "I'm glad you're safe."

The maid folded the cloth and set it aside before she rose and moved to open the front door for her. "If you're ever near this part of town again, do stop by. I'll see that Thalia's father knows."

Gwyn smiled faintly. "Thank you. I hope she feels better soon." She met Thalia's eyes for a moment. Without another word, she stepped back and slipped out the door into the cold evening, the door latching gently behind her. The sky outside was slipping into dusk, and her breath fogged as she exhaled. The streets had grown quieter, the shadows stretching long. She started down the path toward the main road where the inn was, her boots crunching softly against the snow-covered stone.

She'd remember those boys. They'd better hope Amari handled the situation.

CHAPTER THIRTY

DRESS REHEARSAL

Their time in Drakensburg passed quickly, and soon they found themselves halfway through the season. The midpoint was marked by Winter's Fest, a holiday of light and revelry—one the city took quite seriously. It was a time of celebration, tradition, and, apparently, an annual party hosted by the city's viscount, Lord Roth.

Gwyn sat inside a carriage, dressed in far too many layers of fine silk and lace, clutching her hands tightly in her lap as they made their way toward the viscount's manor.

"I'm not sure I can do this, Taenya," she muttered. "You know I'm terrible at these kinds of things. All the acting. All the princessing."

Taenya, seated across from her, offered a small, amused smile. "You'll be fine, Gwyn. This is good practice before we reach Reme. The balls there are far more cutthroat. Drakensburg is positively tame by comparison."

"You're *not* helping," Gwyn mumbled, eyes narrowing.

"I'm helping more than you think. Sabina is just a thought away, and Aleanora will be at your side the entire time."

Gwyn glanced at her sharply. "Why can't *you* stay with me?"

"Because then it wouldn't be good practice."

Gwyn groaned, resisting the urge to fling herself sideways across the bench in despair. The girls had spent forever getting her ready—twisting her hair into careful braids, applying just the right touch of color to her lips and cheeks—and she didn't want to ruin it all with a tantrum.

Amari, perched beside the driver outside the carriage, chuckled loud enough for the sound to carry in. "Taenya's right. This is the perfect setting for you to practice socializing. I'll be speaking with the high priestess tonight, since, thankfully, I hate these things."

Gwyn sighed heavily. "Even *she* gets out of the talking."

Taenya shook her head, her eyes dancing with amusement. "Think of it as . . . dress rehearsal."

Outside, the first snowflakes of the evening drifted lazily from the sky, swirling in the crisp air as the carriage slowed to a halt. Lord Roth's manor stood before them, grand and stately, its arched windows aglow with golden candlelight. Laughter and music spilled faintly from the open doors as carriages lined the curved approach.

Taenya exited, and Gwyn took her offered hand and stepped down with practiced grace, the chill kissing her cheeks. Her boots sank slightly into the small layer of snow on the stone drive as she looked up at the facade of the sprawling manor, then toward the gathered guests already making their way inside in glittering clusters.

Her stomach fluttered. She straightened her shoulders and took a steadying breath. *Okay. Practice. Just pretend it's practice.*

Behind her, Amari stepped down from the carriage in crimson finery topped by a white capelet trimmed in gold. Even without her usual armor, the sun elf still managed to look regal, commanding attention as effortlessly as breathing.

Snow crunched underfoot as Gwyn walked with quiet poise in her sapphire-blue gown. Silver embroidery traced delicate patterns along the hem and sleeves, shimmering faintly beneath the golden glow of the lantern-lit courtyard.

The grand space before the manor looked like something out of a painting—stone walkways fanned outward from the central drive, each lined with evergreen trees trimmed in silver ribbon and delicate glass baubles. Ice-sculpted ornaments sparkled between the snowbanks. Gentle music drifted from within the manor, soft strings and lilting flutes weaving through the hum of conversation and laughter.

The second carriage rolled in behind theirs, and Ilyana, Aleanora, and Lorrena descended from it one by one. Their elegant gowns were bejeweled and subtly layered. In shades of pearl and pale blue, with silver thread glinting through their shawls and delicate hairpins nestled into their carefully styled hair, her ladies-in-waiting clustered around Gwyn like petals to a bloom—not cloying, but constant.

Sabina joined them, moving to Taenya's side. Both represented the house colors in deep blue tunics accented with silver, and wore their hair neatly pinned up.

Taenya said something, but Sabina didn't react. The high elf was laser focused on the manor in front of them, probably getting a feel for the emotions.

This house feels like it could be a fun place to live, Gwyn sent privately to her. *Don't you think? I wonder what it would take . . .*

Sabina stiffened, her eyes flicking around the manor grounds. *You're joking . . . right?* came the immediate reply, sharp with alarm. Gwyn could feel the pulse of panic that followed. She smirked, but didn't respond.

A steward greeted them with a polished bow and guided them through the open entrance. They passed a cluster of finely dressed nobles murmuring quietly and others trickling in and out of the grand hall. Gwyn kept her head high, her posture graceful and composed, even as the knot in her stomach pulled tighter.

They were led to a pair of twin doors that opened to reveal the ballroom. Gwyn's breath caught as she stepped into the room. She was so entranced by the sight that she almost missed the steward announcing her.

The ballroom glowed with light and life. The space stretched wide and tall, and the ceiling was framed in ornamental woodwork and painted panels. In the center of the vaulted ceiling was a dome of glass that offered a perfect view of the twin moons peeking through scattered clouds. Chandeliers hung from above, their crystals faintly aglow with actual *magic* and casting flickers of prismatic light across the polished stone floor. Gwyn made a mental note to find out everything about those crystals.

Long tables laden with sweet and savory delicacies lined the room, and the scents of sugar, spice, and roasted meats wafted through the air. Near the hearth, a small group of musicians played with practiced ease, their notes drifting warm and bright through the room.

The crowd shimmered in silks and satins, in velvets and brocades dyed in every shade of winter—stormy grays, deep blues, snowy whites.

Heads turned as Gwyn and her companions entered. The conversation quieted as guests took in the unfamiliar group. Or, rather, took *her* in. A princess not from the capital. Not from any local house. Invited, yes, but very clearly an outsider. She felt their curiosity settle on her like a shawl of snow, delicate and cold.

Sabina moved closer. "The rest of us are going to mingle," she told Taenya softly. "Catch up after you meet the host?" The knight-captain gave a slight nod.

Sabina looked at Gwyn, her voice settling in her mind. *I won't be far from you. Reach out if you need me or Taenya.*

"I will."

Sabina gave a faint smile and touched her arm gently. *Good luck, Gwynnie,* she sent before she stepped away with Amari. The paladin nodded to Gwyn before walking with Sabina toward the city's high priestess. Obviously hungry themselves, Ilyana took Lorrena by the arm, stating they were going to ensure the food was up to Gwyn's standards.

Taenya and Nora stayed behind. Gwyn's lady-in-waiting fell into step beside her. "I'll be staying with you, of course," she said reassuringly. "Besides, I rather enjoy watching people try to figure out who you are, and why a terran girl is *so* important."

That earned a quiet laugh from Gwyn, who clasped her hands in front of her as they slowly moseyed through the room. Her eyes followed Aleanora's gaze toward a pair of older nobles discussing something near a side alcove. They paused their conversation and all but stared at the two girls as they passed.

"I recognize them from Strathmore," said Taenya quietly. "That's Lady

Deren. She's got family holdings near the lake. And the man she's with? That's Ser Velan. He's the former captain of the city watch—retired now, but still carries significant weight with the guard. He and I have met several times to discuss potential security concerns. Going to him is a bit more discreet than heading directly to the watch." A moment later, she nodded toward a heavyset man walking toward the nobles. "And that's Lord Therrien. He owns most of the barley harvest west of here. Our duchy purchases a significant sum of it."

Gwyn took it all in as they continued moving slowly through the room. Merchants wearing their finest discussing tariffs near the wine table. Visiting minor nobles exchanging pleasantries with local elites. Even a few younger heirs nervously attempting conversation with someone of greater status. All of it a carefully orchestrated dance of politics that Nora helped her navigate.

She really would be wasted as fodder for an arranged marriage, Gwyn thought. Around them, the ballroom shimmered with motion—dresses rustling like whispers, soft music weaving between conversations, and the muted clink of crystal against silver as guests sipped wine and nibbled at tiny confections from trays carried by liveried servants.

Then, a ripple stirred through the crowd. A cluster of nobles entered at the far end of the room, announced one by one with crisp clarity. The viscount Roth was at their head, flanked by a few of the more prominent city lords and ladies—figures Aleanora quickly identified in a low murmur as members of the region's oldest houses, those whose names were etched into the early histories of Drakensburg.

The viscount himself was not what Gwyn expected. Lord Roth was shorter and leaner, with silver-shot black hair slicked neatly back and a finely tailored doublet of emerald green with understated gold trim. His smile was practiced—warm without being kind, smooth without sincerity. People leaned in when he spoke. Laughed when he laughed. Gwyn could feel the force of his personality stretching across the ballroom like a net of silk threads.

Taenya leaned in again. "There he is. Let's go."

Gwyn nodded once, smoothing her gloves as she turned to lead the way with Taenya and Aleanora a step behind. She focused on keeping her posture perfect, her expression a calm mask of polite interest.

Those around them moved away slightly to give them space, but Gwyn still had to force herself to ignore the obvious eavesdropping. Lord Roth spotted them quickly, his smile brightening as he stepped forward with open arms.

"Ah," he said, voice mellow and measured, "our honored guests from House Reinhart. Princess Gwyneth, it is a pleasure to welcome you to my home. The stories barely do you justice."

Gwyn dipped into a shallow curtsy, her movements smooth despite the tightness in her chest. "You're very kind, Lord Roth. Thank you for including us."

"Of course, of course. Drakensburg is all the richer for your presence," he said smoothly. "I trust your accommodations have been satisfactory? I insisted on only the finest for you and your attendants."

"They've been lovely," Gwyn replied, careful to match his tone. "We're grateful for the hospitality."

He inclined his head, eyes gleaming with something too sharp to be mere charm. "If there's anything at all you require, you need only ask. A city's duty is to serve its guests . . . especially those who may be future allies."

Taenya stepped in subtly, her smile a touch tight. "We'll be sure to keep that in mind."

"Of course," the viscount said again. "I must circulate, but please enjoy the evening." With another bow, he turned and transitioned to a different group of nobles.

Gwyn let out a slow breath.

"Thoughts?" Taenya asked quietly after they stepped away.

"He reminds me of people my mom would talk about," Gwyn muttered. "Someone who tries to act all nice and helpful but is really trying to get something. But he also seems smart."

"Both accurate," Taenya said with a small smirk. "He didn't get where he is by being a fool. We likely won't see him again, but just be careful if he comes to you when I'm not around. He'll want something."

"I know," Gwyn murmured.

Taenya looked over her shoulder. "I'm going to find Sabina. She's lurking near the musicians, keeping an eye out. You'll be fine."

Gwyn gave a small nod, watching her go. The knot in her chest tightened again.

Aleanora glanced at her, expression softening. "You don't have to do this alone, you know."

"I know," Gwyn said quietly. She was so nervous, she just—she closed her eyes for a moment and inhaled deeply. She needed to stop worrying so much. After all, she had magic. Mana sang through her core.

She cast **[Frozen Heart],** letting it wrap around her like frost on glass. The effect was instant. Her nerves dulled. The tension in her shoulders melted. Her heartbeat slowed into a steady, calm rhythm.

She opened her eyes. Magic really was the answer to her problems. She turned toward Aleanora, a smile curling her lips. "Let's do this." They weaved through the room, walking slowly and luckily avoiding interactions. She saw her other two ladies-in-waiting gravitate toward them, moving like planets around their sun.

Her good luck, though, eventually seemed to come to an end. More guests began to notice her.

Nora leaned in. "There's a girl quite interested in you across the room. She's constantly looking this way."

Gwyn followed her gaze. Thalia was staring directly at her. She was dressed in a slate-blue gown with a high collar and matching gloves. Her posture was perfect, her hair pinned in soft curls. But her expression was wide-eyed. She was mid-sip from a crystal flute, frozen in place.

Gwyn gave the barest nod. "That's Thalia."

Nora arched a brow. "The girl you helped?"

"Mm-hmm." She tugged gently at Nora's arm. "I want to talk to her."

They angled slowly toward the girl's side of the ballroom. But just before they could reach her, they were intercepted by two high elves, a man and woman, who stepped forward with polished smiles. Their attire quietly proclaimed wealth and taste. The man wore a layered ensemble of dark plum and navy silks, and his high collar was pinned with a jeweled clasp in the shape of a falcon. The woman's gown, with silver thread embroidered into winding vines along her sleeves and hem, shimmered faintly under the chandelier light.

Gwyn could tell immediately—by their confident bearing, the subtle way they surveyed the room, and the practiced ease of their smiles—that they were either nobles or merchants of significant influence. Their faint laugh lines and touches of silver at their temples suggested they were perhaps close in age to her mother.

Aleanora reacted swiftly and with grace. "Princess Gwyneth," she said, her voice poised and polished, "may I present Master Elenvir and Mistress Danessa. They own the Danner Consortium—focused on construction and supply, if I recall correctly."

Gwyn withdrew her arm from Aleanora's and folded her hands neatly in front of her, offering a respectful nod. "A pleasure to meet you both."

Her introduction drew a quiet ripple of attention from those nearby, but the pair handled it with effortless composure.

"The pleasure is ours, Your Highness," Mistress Danessa said, her voice warm, eyes alight with curiosity. "To my knowledge, royalty has never graced this little gathering of ours. Certainly not royalty from Avira."

Gwyn smiled. "It's my first time in Drakensburg. The city has a quiet beauty to it—especially in the snow."

"Then we hope it's the first of many visits," Master Elenvir added with a nod, his tone respectful without being deferential.

They spoke for a few minutes—polite exchanges about the event, the musicians, and the charming touches of the decor. Danessa and Elenvir wove in a detail that made Aleanora glance at Gwyn with interest.

"You're responsible for the crystals in the chandeliers?" Gwyn asked, eyebrows lifting slightly. "They're resonating with magic."

Danessa let out a musical laugh behind her hand. "Indeed! A rather serendipitous discovery. One of our artisans experienced a blessing shortly after the . . . *event*, and he found he could manipulate the crystal veins within a specific geode cache. The result was . . . well, what you see above."

"That's incredible," Nora murmured beside Gwyn, eyes fixed on the delicate crystals refracting shifting hues overhead. "Are you planning to sell them beyond Drakensburg?"

"The supply is limited at present," Elenvir replied. "But yes, that is our hope. This ball serves, in part, as a demonstration. If the demand is strong, we may expand production—though for now, Drakensburg will remain our focus."

"And you're also in construction?" Gwyn prompted, tilting her head.

The pair nodded in tandem. "We specialize in large-scale civic and institutional work," Danessa said, clearly pleased by the question. "We oversaw the recent expansion and renovation of the temple near the central square."

"My great-grandfather, in fact, helped direct the architectural planning for the castle's upper tier and the newer walls of the city, many decades ago," Elenvir added, a hint of pride in his voice.

"I've visited both during my walks through the city," Gwyn said sincerely. "They're lovely spaces. I especially enjoyed the stained glass at the temple."

Mistress Danessa dipped her head. "We are honored to hear that, Your Highness."

"If you ever require assistance for projects within Drakensburg or the surrounding region," Elenvir said, "the Consortium would be eager to assist, be it for construction or interior work."

Gwyn nodded thoughtfully. "I'll certainly keep that in mind."

As the pair moved on, Gwyn turned back toward where Thalia had been. But the girl wasn't there. She swept the crowd and found her only a few paces away, standing just behind a group of chatting nobles. Thalia's posture was composed—shoulders straight, hands folded neatly at her waist. But her expression betrayed her. Her eyes, wide and fixed on Gwyn, were filled with something that looked an awful lot like realization. Not fear or awe, but that silent, startled moment when everything clicks into place.

Gwyn's lips parted slightly. *I see what Nora means. It's fun seeing that moment people realize who she really is.*

Standing at Thalia's side was a man Gwyn had not seen before but recognized instantly. The resemblance was too strong to miss. He was tall, with a noble's bearing and the kind of presence that made people lean in when he spoke. His dark hair was silvering at the temples, framing a sharply cut face lined just enough to hint at experience rather than age. But it was the eyes that cinched it—that deep blue was very distinctive. It had to be her father.

The magistrate was engaged in conversation with a small knot of well-dressed men, their laughter and smiles too eager by half. They hung on his words as though every phrase might contain the answer to their ambitions. *I can see the resemblance to his brother,* Gwyn thought, recalling Lord Roth's carefully measured warmth and effortless charm. *They were both born to live in the public eye.*

Sabina, Gwyn reached out mentally, her tone smooth and quiet behind the words. *Could you send Taenya over? I'd like her beside me when I speak with Magistrate Roth. Just in case he wants to make a deal or something.*

There was a beat of silence, then a faint pulse of affirmation. *Of course. She's just over by the western arch with a local vintner. She'll be there shortly.*

Gwyn didn't glance around to check—she didn't need to. She trusted Sabina. She trusted Taenya even more.

Sure enough, less than a minute later, Taenya emerged from the crowd with a graceful ease that belied her readiness. She appeared regal in her uniform, with her hair pinned up. Her posture wasn't overprotective or threatening. Just . . . present.

Thalia tugged gently at her father's sleeve, a subtle motion that was not lost on Gwyn. He followed Thalia's gaze and met Gwyn's eyes. He said something to the group, and whatever it was, the men responded with polite nods and shallow bows as he excused himself. Then, with Thalia at his side, he walked directly toward Gwyn. He moved with the effortless poise of someone used to attention—but not someone who craved it. His steps were unhurried, deliberate. Thalia's expression was tightly composed now, though Gwyn could still see the remnants of confusion lingering behind her careful mask.

Gwyn squared her shoulders, letting the mask of royal poise slide into place. She felt Aleanora shift beside her, stepping just a bit closer, her posture attentive but non-intrusive.

This should be interesting, said Taenya.

"Magistrate Roth is approaching," Gwyn murmured under her breath as she faced the knight. "I thought it best you were here for this."

Taenya dipped her head just slightly. "Understood, and I agree."

Roth offered a polite bow—not too deep, but respectful—and met Gwyn's gaze directly.

"Your Highness," he said smoothly. "I regret that I've not had the pleasure of making your acquaintance until now. Magistrate Caedin Roth, at your service."

Gwyn inclined her head, the gesture subtly matched to his. "Magistrate Roth. It's an honor."

He smiled in a way that seemed genuinely pleasant. "The honor is mine, Princess. Your visit has stirred quite a bit of interest. It's rare that royalty passes through our city—many tend to take routes that go around us. Drakensburg hasn't seen a long-term guest of your station in some time, if ever. And certainly not one who's left such a memorable impression." He said it without edge, without implication, but Gwyn heard it nonetheless.

There's a lot of people not fond of the royalty here.

She returned the smile with just enough of an edge to match. "I hope that impression has been a better one than what you're used to."

Roth's eyes crinkled at the corners. "Oh, it has. More than you know." He paused, then gestured toward Thalia beside him. "My daughter, I believe, has already had the privilege."

Thalia lowered her head slightly in a quiet curtsy. "Your Highness."

Gwyn dipped her head in return. "It's good to see you again, Thalia."

Thalia's gaze flickered—surprised, maybe, or just unsure how to take the warmth—but she nodded again. "I . . . I thought you were a priestess," she admitted, glancing between Gwyn and the imposing figure of Amari across the room. "Because of the paladin. I never imagined . . ."

Taenya chuckled lightly. "A priestess? Oh, Eona forgive me, but that is rather amusing." She quickly sobered and dipped her head in apology. "Forgive me, Your Highness. No offense meant."

Gwyn smirked at the overly professional tone. "None taken."

Roth's smile grew slightly. "It would be an easy mistake to make, especially if the fantastical rumors trickling up from the south are true."

"Unfortunately, they are," Taenya said, her tone serious.

"Well, I hope that Drakensburg proves a safer harbor than what you've experienced thus far," Roth said, voice quiet and sincere. "I can only imagine the shock you must've felt. Being a terran, and already faced with such hostilities . . ." He glanced at his daughter, his expression tightening with subtle disapproval. "Though the extent of our hostilities, it seems, are limited to wintering brats who resort to bullying and assault when they do not get their way."

"I'm just happy that Thalia and Gareth are alright," Gwyn replied sincerely.

Beside her, Thalia stiffened ever so slightly at the mention of her friend, a small flicker in her composed demeanor, but her father didn't miss a beat. Magistrate Roth's eyes briefly flicked to his daughter in quiet amusement.

"Of course," he said smoothly. "I had a rather enlightening conversation with young Gareth not long ago. His concern for Thalia's well-being was . . . heartfelt. And his protectiveness, I must admit, is most assuring. A boy with both a sense of loyalty and a spine—something we're increasingly short on these days."

Gwyn smiled faintly at that, unsure whether the man's comment was a subtle endorsement or merely a dry observation. Thalia, however, looked down and busied herself with the clasp of her glove, cheeks faintly pink.

"Was the boy who attacked Thalia punished?" Gwyn asked, her voice quiet but firm.

Magistrate Roth's smile thinned ever so slightly. "Insofar as the law could reach him, yes," he replied. He didn't elaborate further, though his tone carried a note of . . . not quite satisfaction, Gwyn thought, but something close. A carefully measured message, perhaps, to anyone listening.

"Of course, such actions are never sufficient," he added softly, "when weighed against what might have happened. But we must work with the tools we have."

Thalia's shoulders had relaxed somewhat, though she still kept her eyes averted. Gwyn glanced at her, then back at Roth.

"Still," he said, returning his gaze to Gwyn, "we're fortunate. And I'm grateful, for what your paladin companion did and what you chose to do."

Gwyn met his eyes squarely. "So am I."

Roth folded his hands behind his back. "If I may, Princess. This city . . . remembers kindness. And it remembers strength. You've shown both. If ever there is something I—or Drakensburg itself—can do for you, you need only ask."

Gwyn let the silence hang for half a breath. Let the weight of it settle.

"Thank you," she said softly. "I sincerely appreciate that."

The magistrate inclined his head, his expression unreadable for a moment longer before softening into something more measured. "I hope you enjoy my brother's celebration, Your Highness. You've more than earned it."

He and Thalia stepped away, only to be met with others eager to speak with him, and the hum of the ballroom swallowed his absence.

Gwyn exhaled slowly. She was free again, if only briefly.

Taenya rested a hand on her shoulder. "Well done."

More people waited. More names she would have to remember, more smiles she would need to fake. It didn't matter who they were or what they wanted. None of it ever did. This was her role now. The politics. The power. The endless smiling. Just one more part of being a princess. She hated it. And if this was only just a dress rehearsal for the capital . . .

Gwyn rubbed at her temple. She would kill to have some healing magic because a headache was quickly forming. It didn't help that Winter's Fest was not a quiet affair.

Music curled through the air like ribbons—fast, bright songs that made feet itch to move, and then slower ones that turned the floor into a sea of swaying elegance. People laughed more easily as the evening wore on, cheeks flushed from drink or dance or both.

Gwyn Reinhart, however, was not one of them. Though she smiled, though she curtsied and spoke when spoken to, there was a part of her that never quite loosened. Too many eyes tracked her movements. Too many names she didn't yet know whispered around her in low tones. Every introduction came with unspoken expectations. Every compliment was barbed with curiosity.

She'd done well enough so far—Taenya had said so. Even Aleanora had looked quietly pleased. But it was still exhausting. She had no idea how Roslyn could do this so easily.

So, when the moment came—when the tempo of the music changed and conversation drifted toward the long banquet tables—Gwyn took the opportunity and slipped away, her breath fogging slightly as she passed through a quiet hall and into the cool hush of one of the side parlors, a modestly lit room with a pair of open glass doors leading onto a quiet terrace. Frost clung to the balustrades outside, and the air beyond was crisp and still.

She stood near the edge of the room, nursing a cup of spiced cider that wasn't really appealing, when she noticed a familiar silhouette step through the open archway. Thalia.

She paused when she spotted Gwyn, and for a second, her eyes flicked toward the door as if considering retreat. Instead, she inhaled once and approached.

"You know, I really did think you were a priestess," Thalia said by way of greeting, her voice quiet but clear. "The day you found us. With that paladin at your side and the way you spoke . . . I assumed you were from the temples. I don't know why I didn't consider that it would be strange for a terran to be a priestess so soon."

Gwyn gave a soft, amused huff. "I've been working with the Church a lot, but nope, not a priestess."

"Also, I was wrong," Thalia admitted, stepping beside her. Her eyes flicked to the crowd behind them, then back to Gwyn. "I owe you an apology."

Gwyn turned slightly. "You don't."

"I do," Thalia insisted. "I was . . . rude. Suspicious. And cold."

"You were cautious. And protective." Gwyn smiled gently. "I'm not unfamiliar with that feeling."

Thalia looked away, then reached up to brush a strand of hair behind her ear. "Still. I was wrong about you. Thank you for what you did. I know I thanked you before, but it wasn't enough."

"You really don't have to—"

"I do." Her voice was firmer now. "You didn't just help me. You didn't have to stay. You didn't have to check on Gareth or follow those boys to where they'd cornered us or carry me through the city. But you did."

Gwyn hesitated. "I've been in situations where everything's not normal. I know how much it means when someone shows up anyway."

Thalia's gaze softened. "He still talks about you, you know."

"Gareth?"

A nod. "He wanted to come tonight, but . . ." She gave a small, rueful shrug. "It's not really a space for people like him."

Gwyn bit her tongue. *That's a problem for later.* "I hope he's well," she said instead. "And you, of course."

"He is." Thalia smiled faintly. She touched her eyebrow where her pink wound had started to scar. "He says it gives me character."

They shared a quiet laugh. A beat passed.

"Can I ask you something?" Gwyn said. Thalia nodded.

"How did you know?" Gwyn asked. "That you liked him?"

Thalia blinked. "Gareth?"

Gwyn gave a sheepish smile. "I just . . . I saw the way you looked at him. And you knew what to say. You didn't hesitate."

Thalia looked down at her gloved hands. "I guess I just realized I wanted to be around him all the time. That I missed him when he wasn't nearby. And that when things got hard, he was the first person I thought about." She looked up, eyes clear. "There's no one else who makes me feel like that."

Gwyn was quiet for a moment, her gaze drifting back out to the snow-dusted terrace.

Thalia studied her face. "Is there someone like that for you?"

"I'm . . . not sure," she admitted. It was all so confusing.

Thalia nodded. Then, gently, she reached out and squeezed Gwyn's arm. "You'll get there. You're still young."

"I don't feel so young anymore . . ." Gwyn whispered, almost to herself.

Thalia either didn't hear or thankfully chose not to reply. They stood like that for a while, not speaking, letting the quiet hum of the distant ballroom and the hush of falling snow fill the silence between them.

Eventually, Thalia pulled her hand away. "I should get back. Father will be wondering where I've gone."

Gwyn nodded. "Thank you for coming to speak to me."

Thalia hesitated at the entrance. "We may not see each other again before you leave for the capital."

Gwyn smiled softly. "I'm here until spring. We'll see each other, I promise."

Thalia returned a warm smile. "I'd like that." She turned and vanished back into the hall. Gwyn stood alone for a moment longer, then turned to follow.

Back in the ballroom, the music had shifted to a gentle instrumental, a piece with lilting strings and the occasional delicate trill of a flute. Guests mingled near the hearths and along the periphery of the dance floor, where a few pairs were dancing gracefully.

Gwyn wandered through a few groups with deliberate ease. She wasn't actively eavesdropping, but that didn't mean she wasn't listening.

". . . well, the baron was livid, of course," said a tall woman with silver-streaked hair and a fur-trimmed shawl. "Had to pay restitution to the magistrate and the city directly. I heard it was no small sum."

"That boy should've been thrown in the cells," muttered her companion, a stocky man with a wine glass clutched in both hands. "But instead they're just sending him home with his tail between his legs. Typical."

"He's lucky the paladin didn't press for formal charges. You can't bribe the faith," the woman replied. "Still, I imagine the viscount wanted him gone more than punished. Drakensburg doesn't like problems that linger."

"That whole family's a problem," the man huffed. "Wintering here like they belong. Just because you hold a title in the east doesn't make you our equal."

Gwyn passed by slowly, keeping her eyes forward, her expression serene. But her ears caught every word. She reached one of the refreshment tables, plucked a delicate tart off a silver tray, and popped it into her mouth.

Janus Ordell had avoided imprisonment. Of course he had. A fine. A public embarrassment. A swift and quiet exit from the city. It was still far less than he deserved.

She leaned slightly against the table, watching as couples twirled across the dance floor. Laughter and music filled the space again, warming it like a hearth. She clenched her hands slightly at her sides.

There was power in titles. Enough to protect even the violent and cruel, so long as they were born with the right name. She glanced to her left, where Aleanora stood just behind her, scanning the crowd. Gwyn gave the girl a soft nudge with her elbow.

"Go enjoy yourself," she murmured. "I'll be fine."

Nora hesitated, then gave her a firm look. "Only if you promise to call me over if someone tries to talk to you about 'being an exotic outsider' again."

"I solemnly swear," Gwyn replied with mock gravity.

The older girl rolled her eyes and turned away, disappearing into the crowd with surprising grace.

From the corner of her eye, Gwyn caught sight of Amari. The woman stood against one of the pillars at the far end of the room, expression stoic, arms crossed. Sabina wasn't far either, shadowed near the entrance to the hall, scanning faces with that careful stillness of hers. Even Taenya was close, currently guiding Lorrena toward the dessert table with a proud smile.

Not everyone gets away with cruelty. Gwyn thought. Not forever. She would remember Janus, or at least the type he represented. She would remember the way he had laughed before throwing that stone. The way his father had tried to sweep it under a rug built from coin and reputation. And she'd remember that, even in a world ruled by politics and etiquette, justice didn't always come from courts. Sometimes, it came from memory. And from power. Hers was still growing.

The music shifted to another, slightly livelier tune as Gwyn stood at the edge of the ballroom near one of the towering windows. She was sipping from a delicate glass of what tasted like sparkling grape juice when she caught movement nearby.

A telv noble girl, likely no older than fifteen, with thick chestnut curls pinned with a silver comb, was making her way hesitantly toward a small group of boys clustered near one of the marble pillars. Her elegant, though not ostentatious, gown was a lovely pale green, and the way she moved made it clear that someone had coached her for this moment. Each step was carefully measured. Each breath was shallow.

Gwyn watched as the girl stopped before the group and, with a small curtsy, asked one of the boys—taller than the others, with his chest puffed out like a rooster—if he would honor her with a dance.

The boy didn't even bother pretending to consider it. A few of the others laughed, low and cruel, and one of them leaned in to whisper something behind his hand. The tall boy smirked, gave a mock bow to the girl, and turned deliberately away, dragging the entire group with him. They drifted across the floor like a tide, leaving the girl standing alone in their wake.

Gwyn's stomach turned. She watched the telv girl blink rapidly, her lips pressing into a tight line as she turned away and tried to disappear into the crowd.

Not tonight. Gwyn crossed the floor with purpose, the layers of her gown whispering with each step. The girl had paused near one of the tall floral arrangements that marked the edge of the dance floor, and was pretending to examine the blossoms while clearly trying to collect herself.

Gwyn stopped a few feet away and offered a warm smile. "Hi," she said gently. "I'm Gwyn."

The girl's head snapped toward her so fast, Gwyn thought she might stumble. "Y-your Highness!" she stammered, bowing awkwardly. "I—I didn't realize—can I help you with something?"

Gwyn's smile widened. "Actually, I was wondering if you might grant me a dance."

The girl froze, her mouth opening and closing. "Me?"

"You," Gwyn confirmed. "It would be an honor."

A few heads nearby turned at the declaration, but Gwyn ignored them. The girl looked at the group of boys, then back at Gwyn, still visibly caught between disbelief and panic.

"Please?" Gwyn added, offering her hand.

The telv girl took it hesitantly, her fingers trembling slightly as Gwyn led her onto the floor. As they joined the other couples, the musicians flowed seamlessly into a light waltz.

"I'm sorry if this is too much," Gwyn said quietly as they found their rhythm. "I just couldn't let what happened a moment ago stand. Those boys were awful."

Just proving that boys are indeed gross.

The girl shook her head quickly. "No! I mean, thank you. It's just . . . my mother and aunt insisted I try. They said I had to be brave and speak to them. That it would reflect well on our family."

Gwyn frowned. "Well, they were wrong. You're lovely, and anyone would be lucky to dance with you. And if they can't see that, they're not worth your time."

The girl's lips quivered, but then a small, genuine smile broke through. "Thank you. That is very kind of you."

Gwyn smiled back. "So what's your name?"

"Lia," the girl replied, her voice steadier now.

"Well, Lia," Gwyn said, spinning them gently through the next step, "for tonight, I declare that you're off duty from impressing anyone. You're here to enjoy yourself. And maybe make some of those boys jealous in the process."

Lia giggled at that, the sound bright and unguarded. "I think you've already taken care of that."

They danced another full turn, moving easily now, as if they'd been dancing together all evening. By the time the music slowed, Lia's face was flushed, her smile unforced.

As they stepped apart, Lia began to bow again, but Gwyn caught her gently in a hug instead. The girl stiffened for half a second, then melted into it.

When they parted, Gwyn gave her a reassuring squeeze on the arm and whispered, "You're great. Don't let anyone define your worth. Least of all gross boys with too much hair oil and who think far too highly of themselves."

Lia let out another laugh, and this time it held no hesitation. "I won't. Thank you . . . Your Highness."

Gwyn winked. "Just Gwyn tonight."

As she stepped back into the flow of the ballroom, Gwyn caught Sabina's gaze from across the floor. The knight's expression was unreadable, but the warmth in her eyes was enough.

It wasn't long before the music began to slow and soften, as though even the orchestra could sense the night's momentum waning. The lights of the ballroom dimmed gently, casting the ice-laced decorations in warmer hues. Everything had taken on a gentler edge, as if preparing to be remembered rather than lived.

Gwyn found herself mid-conversation with an over-eager noble boy who'd managed to corner her with questions about being a terran princess. She smiled politely, nodding in all the right places, but her eyes darted subtly in search of an escape.

She didn't need to look far. A familiar hand touched her elbow. "Apologies," Ilyana said smoothly, her voice pitched just right to cut through the moment. "I'm stealing her for a dance."

The boy blinked, a little disappointed, but Gwyn shot him a gracious smile and allowed herself to be led away with a grateful breath. Once they were at the edge of the floor, Gwyn turned to her lady-in-waiting. "You're the best."

Ilyana smirked as they began to move with the tempo. "It was getting painful. I could feel Sabina getting twitchy from across the room."

Gwyn laughed, letting the last of the tension slide from her shoulders. "He just kept going. I didn't think it was possible to explain just how different everything is and how, no, I do not want to see your family's library."

"Oh, sweet Gwyn," Ilyana said with a wink. "That's just code for getting some alone time."

They danced easily together, not worrying about precision. "You've handled the night fairly well," Ilyana added. "You're getting good at this."

Gwyn tilted her head. "At dancing?"

"At being . . . you. The version of you that the world expects to see."

Gwyn didn't answer right away. She turned slightly as they spun, catching sight of the others. Nora was seated with a pair of local girls around her age, all three leaning in with laughter in their eyes as they whispered over a shared plate of candied nuts. Lorrena, meanwhile, was dancing slowly and carefully with a kind-faced noble boy. They weren't speaking much, but they didn't seem to need to. Lorrena's smile said enough.

"They've grown so much," Gwyn murmured.

"So have you," Ilyana said quietly. Then, with a cheeky grin: "Though I'm still prettier."

Gwyn laughed aloud as the music came to a soft close. "Debatable, Blondie."

They stepped away from the floor, parting with a small curtsy. Gwyn made her way toward the edge of the room where Sabina stood with Amari, each holding a drink, their expressions ever watchful, though slightly more relaxed than earlier in the evening.

"You're . . . glowing," Sabina said to Gwyn.

"I danced twice, helped a girl find some confidence, and only got cornered once. I'm calling that a win."

"Hmm, you seem more confident than when we entered," Sabina said softly. Her voice was warm. "A season ago, you would've run from a party like this."

"A season ago, I didn't know how to do any of this," Gwyn said. "It's still hard. But it's not impossible. Not anymore."

Sabina didn't seem convinced but remained quiet.

Gwyn looked out over the ballroom, at the guests laughing, snow drifting just outside the tall windows, the smell of pine and spiced wine in the air. "I think I'm starting to understand why all of this matters. Not the dresses or the music or the butt kissing, but the way people remember how you make them feel. What you stand for. What you protect."

Sabina nodded. "Good. Because they're starting to see it too."

Gwyn glanced toward the ballroom doors, where Magistrate Roth was speaking with another noble, Thalia at his side. They shared a look, and both gave her a nod before stepping out into the cool night air. Gwyn watched them go, her thoughts turning over slowly.

It wouldn't be long now until they left for the capital. Drakensburg had shown her that safety wasn't guaranteed, not even for people trying to do the right thing. And that power alone wasn't enough, but with the right people, with care and attention and strength, it could be built. One day, she would need that. A place of her own. A home where her people would never be afraid—not of nobles, or war, or cruelty in an alley. Maybe that place wasn't as far away as she'd thought.

A few minutes later, Taenya arrived at her side. "The carriage is ready."

Gwyn nodded. She turned once more, letting her gaze sweep the room—this warm, glittering space full of possibility. Then she walked out with her guard and her ladies, the night air cold and clean on her cheeks. She stepped into the waiting carriage, the door closing softly behind her.

They still had a while until spring and Reme. Plenty of time to visit every bookstore. She had to create memories because it would be years before they returned—but when that day came, she hoped to leave as deep an impression on the city as it had left on her.

CHAPTER THIRTY-ONE

PRACTICAL DISCOVERIES

For centuries, the traditional calendar of Ikios—rooted in the divine cycle of the Four and the turning of the seasons—served its people with quiet consistency. It needed little change in an age where life moved with the rhythms of planting and prayer.

But with the arrival of the Displaced and the dawn of magic, the world shifted. Industry no longer followed the sun; it followed mana, steel, and spellcraft. Trade demanded precision, factories demanded schedules, and the old ways—while still sacred—proved ill-suited for a modernizing age.

In 89 SA, after mounting pressure from prominent houses, merchant guilds, and academic circles, the Church of the Celestials convened a historic conference in Strathmore. For three contentious weeks, voices were raised, tempers flared, and no consensus seemed possible. Yet, with persistence—and no small amount of divine patience—a new structure slowly took shape.

Timelines were realigned. Traditions were preserved where they could be, modernized where they could not. The year of the Flash—when mana emerged and the Displaced arrived—was designated as Year 0. From that moment forward, history would be measured in the terms of magic's arrival, marking the Second Age of Eona.

The Age of Magic.

Mana and Industry: The Early Contemporary Era, 522 SA

Weeks passed—so many that, back on Earth, it would have been months. Alas, Eona's calendar provided no specificity to conveniently track the passage of time beyond the four seasonal references. Winter gradually gave way to spring, but the city remained stubbornly trapped in a siege with no resolution in sight.

Yet even with the new growth budding in the gardens and the scent of thawing soil in the air, the city of Marketbol remained a prisoner. No longer surrounded by fire and steel, but by a slow, steady strangulation.

The siege had shifted. Gone was the press of constant violence; instead, it became a grinding game of attrition. The Vlaredian army rarely launched anything beyond occasional probing skirmishes, just enough to keep the defenders on edge. They never committed their shield mages to anything serious, and Sloane understood why. Those casters were precious, likely difficult to replace, and the enemy was choosing to wait the city out instead.

And they could afford to. A city this large would eventually collapse under its own weight. Not from cannon fire or fireballs, but from hunger, exhaustion, and despair. Even the wealthiest citizens had been forced to reduce their standards of living, rationing and strict resource management applying to all strata of society. The outer neighborhoods were hit the hardest, their stores of food and firewood running dangerously low as winter waned.

The promised reinforcements from Barith remained maddeningly absent. Occasionally, scouts bearing their banners were sighted on the horizon, but they vanished just as quickly. City leadership continued to offer reasons for the delay—harsh snows, impassable roads, internal disputes—all plausible lies, spoken in soothing tones meant to pacify.

"It's all under control."

"They're coming."

"We need only endure a little longer."

Sloane didn't believe a word of it. She had spent much of the long season buried in her work. Her time was split between the Reinhart Center, her small Upper Quarter manor, and the rare official meetings she couldn't avoid. Mercifully, Ressa's attacks had been few and far between, though each had sent ripples through the fragile calm of the city.

The first was a strike on a supply depot, one holding materiel for the army—a tactical, if predictable, target. It also kept Sloane working longer hours since the Center had to put extra effort into replacing what they could.

The second was far more unsettling. A strike deep in the Central Quarter, near enough to her new home to set the entire neighborhood on edge. The target had been a seemingly mundane government building, and whatever had been within it remained classified.

But the third . . . the third was different. A Merchant Guild warehouse, filled with luxury goods and food stockpiled for the aristocracy, was completely destroyed—not looted, not repurposed. Destroyed. And yet, somehow, the food was never found among the ruins. Instead, it miraculously reappeared in the poorest district of Marketbol, handed out in alleyways and communal kitchens with no explanation. A pointed message, clear as day.

Gisele and Nemura had both been as confused by the action as the military leaders. That the Vlaredians were deliberately avoiding actions that harmed the common folk didn't quite make sense. But Sloane guessed they were trying to turn the populace against the city's leadership.

Nemura said that it was a complete departure from what she knew of Vlaredian war doctrine, but she couldn't rule it out.

Sloane's own efforts to root out Ressa had led nowhere. The idea to inspect buildings for false walls or conjured passages had turned up nothing. Ressa vanished when she wished, and no number of clever suggestions or exhaustive patrols had managed to pin her down. The mystery gnawed at Sloane.

She exhaled slowly, trying to clear her thoughts as she returned her focus inward. **[Meditation]**—a spell she'd developed over the winter—had become one of her most useful tools. It calmed her, rebalanced her after heavy magic use, and gave her clarity. It also demanded a certain emotional stillness. If she let her frustration spike too high, the spell would shatter like glass.

She focused, drawing in steady breaths as she let herself drift into that quiet inner place. Her near constant reliance on mana—combined with similar feedback from her team and the alchemists—had led to two major discoveries. But before those breakthroughs, there had been many small revelations, tiny fragments of understanding that slowly began to coalesce into something larger. Something powerful. And if the war wasn't going to end soon, they would need every single advantage they could muster.

Most of her house had taken up her and the Church's offer to undergo the Ceremony of Paths, and the results had been . . . enlightening. From the soldiers and guards to artisans and staff, each had learned something intrinsic about themselves—something once invisible, now made tangible. Their key attributes.

Ernald, in true fashion, had jokingly dubbed them "the Three Cs," and the name had stuck among the guards and staff alike. Capability, Constitution, and Control. It was neat and simple. Almost too perfect. And yet the more Sloane explored it, the more those old frameworks from her world—the ones built into RPG systems and character sheets—started to feel like useful models again. She'd begun filtering every new discovery through that lens, guiding their research as if she were building systems in a game.

Their early research had confirmed that every person had all three attributes, but one always stood above the rest. This primary attribute reflected the essence of their path, their calling in the world.

Capability shaped physical and magical aptitude. Those with high Capability were stronger, faster, more agile. But it wasn't just physical. Magic users with higher Capability also showed signs of more raw power—not necessarily in how often they could cast, but how potent their spells were when they did. Sloane had long suspected her own spells changed subtly in strength based on need, but this attribute helped clarify that it wasn't just instinct—it was measurable. Or at least observable.

Constitution altered the body itself. The resilience of one's skin, how much physical abuse a body could endure before breaking, and even susceptibility to disease all correlated to Constitution. Maud and the alchemists had noted that those with a stronger level of Constitution rarely fell ill, even during the long winter months. It also influenced stamina, in two forms: physical, as expected, and something less tangible: mental stamina.

That second form had taken some time to understand. Maud had helped her realize that mental stamina linked directly to how long someone could cast magic without faltering. It wasn't about power but endurance. The migraines Sloane suffered after prolonged spellwork had made that painfully clear. It was the reason she'd worked so hard to develop her [**Meditation**] spell—a spell to restore herself faster. The relief it provided had confirmed the theory.

Sloane paused her writing, a new idea forming. *What if our core acts like a spigot? The higher the quality, the stronger the flow of mana it can handle, thus the more mana that gets absorbed into our bodies and affects it in the three ways. So, pulling too much mana through your core is what strains your body. Could there be such a thing as mana poisoning? Overdrawn reserves leading to permanent damage?* It was something to test—carefully.

The third attribute, Control, was hers, the defining trait that had shaped her path from the moment she'd touched mana. It influenced the body, yes, but more than that, it governed precision, perception, and finesse. Fine motor control, reflexive adjustments, an almost intuitive understanding of one's limits and surroundings. Among the few confirmed mages within her circle, Control also played a critical role in efficiency—less mana wasted, tighter spellcasting, cleaner results.

Sloane wished there were more magic users to test with. The sample size of mages was still too small, but what they did know pointed to clear patterns.

The first thing she'd done after learning all this was consult her watch. It didn't give her precise numbers, but it gave her enough of an idea. From that, she'd discerned that her Control was affecting her body significantly more than her other two stats. Her Capability was around two-thirds the strength of her Control. Her Constitution, barely a third. That ratio, however, did not hold for others. Whatever shaped the attributes—path, purpose, core quality—it wasn't that simple.

They had learned the most from those aligned to physical paths. The larger sample size let them identify patterns and correlations more reliably. From that, they'd begun to understand that a person's path shaped which attributes would grow most swiftly, while core quality governed the depth of that growth and how potent those attributes might become. She was sure there was a way to measure the effect of those attributes and quantify how much a person gained each step. Like stats each level grants in a game.

Sloane couldn't help but note the similarity to another familiar system: rarity. That's what it felt like. Core quality wasn't just a trait but also a tier, and likely a gatekeeper to advancement. *Perhaps,* she mused, *rarity determines how efficiently the attributes affect your body.* It would explain the disparities in growth. Which meant, if the numerical stat theory held up, the higher the rarity, the more you gained per step.

They'd cataloged three known core qualities: Common, Uncommon, and Rare. Sloane, it turned out, was the only person they'd discovered with a Rare core.

Only six others within her house and their allied knights held Uncommon cores. Of those, only Nemura and Ismeld were frontline fighters. The others were far more diverse.

Kemmy, the sharp-minded alchemist, held an Uncommon artisan-aligned core. Two were house guards, one of whom had shown signs of strong leadership potential, possibly influenced by his purpose. The final one was an administrator Elodie had recently hired to manage their growing runecard business. That telv had a bureaucrat-aligned purpose, which prompted Sloane to ask Adaega to begin compiling a list of house personnel and their declared purposes. To her surprise—and mild amusement—Adaega had already done it.

Among the members of Sloane's house, the diversity of roles had become more evident as they continued to map out the traits revealed during the Ceremony of Paths. They had leaders, bureaucrats, artisans, laborers, fighters, two rogues, a healer, and, of course, an innovator—herself. Sloane suspected there were more roles—more purposes—hidden among their people, but those revelations would come in time.

Their ongoing testing, especially among the guards, had produced some fascinating results. When they compared individuals of the same step and similar purpose, they found their attribute values—Capability, Constitution, and Control—were remarkably consistent. Not identical, but close enough to make general comparisons and controlled testing viable.

But then they widened the sample. They began testing individuals with similar purposes but at different steps. What they discovered was nothing short of groundbreaking. Attributes affected people differently. For example, two people with similar Capability scores might not produce the same results. A person who had been physically stronger before the rise of mana would still likely hold that edge—unless the other person's level difference was large enough to close or overcome the gap. In short, mana-enhanced attributes built atop the foundation of the person, not in place of it.

They proved this with a particularly frustrating test. Sloane, fully aware she was at a much higher step than Deryk, and that her core quality was two full ranks above his, had been confident that her raw stats would now surpass his. She and Koren, their smith, had arranged a weight-lifting test with carefully crafted tools to measure the differences. And Deryk had wiped the floor with her. Sure, she could lift more than she had ever dreamed possible on Earth, but he could lift much more.

That was when the breakthrough came. They began testing others, like Maud and Gisele, and it became increasingly clear that alignment—a person's internal resonance with mana—had a massive impact on how attributes manifested. For example, a person with a physical alignment would see physical benefits from higher attributes, while those with a mental alignment would experience cognitive or magical enhancements.

Perhaps alignment was simply a way to define how a person infused mana into their body—that is, if that's what was happening. *Ah, how I wish I had a better understanding of biology at times like these. There's so much more to learn, so much knowledge to refine as more data gets discovered.*

As it turned out, Gisele had a hybrid alignment, and their working theory was that her attributes contributed equally to both her physical and magical abilities. She was the bridge between their more extreme cases.

So despite Deryk's lower step and core quality, his physical alignment made his Capability attribute far more *functionally impactful* than hers.

It wasn't enough to know your attributes. It was about how your purpose, path, core quality, and alignment all interacted, and that was a level of complexity Sloane hadn't accounted for at first. But she found it utterly fascinating: a massive mana-centric body system working in tandem with the physical one.

A sudden knock echoed through her office, breaking her concentration. She opened her eyes just as her **[Meditation]** spell faded gently into the background, like a stream of mana retreating back into stillness.

The door cracked open and a young telv woman—Adaega's most recently assigned assistant—peeked her head in.

"My apologies for disturbing you, m'lady," she said, voice soft and respectful.

Sloane gave a small smile as she pushed herself off the floor and stood. Her body felt lighter, her mana flow steadied and refreshed. "It's no bother. What can I do for you?"

"Your meeting with Alchemist Kemilla is scheduled to begin shortly."

Sloane blinked, then turned to glance out the wide arched window beside her desk. The sky had shifted again, a pale spring light casting long shadows. *Huh. More time passed than I thought.* Judging by the sun's position, she had been meditating for four full bells, if not more.

"I'll be right there. Give me a moment to clean up."

"Of course, m'lady," the assistant said with a bow, and she disappeared from the doorway.

Sloane looked around her study, then crossed to where her cloak hung neatly from a wall hook. Though the worst of winter's chill had passed, the air outside could still bite at you if you weren't dressed properly. She fastened the cloak over her shoulders, collected her notes, and headed out.

"Lady Sloane! Welcome, welcome. We're ready for you in the back," Rel called out the moment she stepped into the Alchemy Hall.

Sloane nodded politely to the young high elf man stationed at the front desk before following Rel through a set of double doors. Beyond them, the quiet of the entry hall gave way to a controlled chaos—the living heart of the alchemical operations.

The space pulsed with activity. Tables were lined with beakers, alchemical glassware, notes, and mana-inscribed equipment. Scents of herbs, minerals, and distilled components mingled in the air, pungent and sharp on the nose.

Kemmy, ever the whirlwind of energy, moved between stations, barking out precise instructions to the gathered alchemists and apprentices. Sloane spotted one group preparing batches of what appeared to be enchanting ink, the mixture glowing faintly under layered sigils. Nearby, another team worked with a complex distillation rig—thin glass tubing connecting a boiling flask to a larger collection jar, vapor condensing along its curve.

"Kem! Lady Sloane's here," Rel announced as they entered.

"Thanks, Rel," Sloane said with a warm smile. The orkun woman gave a nod. She was still adjusting to working with the broader team of alchemists. For all her sociability on campus, she maintained a surprisingly solitary work ethic, usually keeping close only to her partner, Kemmy.

From across the room, the raithe woman perked up, glancing over from where she was tending one of the gently bubbling setups. The beaker in front of her shimmered with vapor, its contents a clear liquid that steamed slightly in the cold spring air.

Is she distilling water?

Kemmy stripped off her thick protective gloves and strode over, her dark eyes bright with excitement.

"Lady Sloane! Perfect timing, really," she said, her tone brimming with pride.

Sloane returned the grin. "What are you working on? I noticed your apprentices are back on enchanting ink production. And . . . distilling water?"

The raithe practically lit up, her whole body buzzing with barely contained enthusiasm. "Yes! The ink batches are running smoothly now, thanks to the consistent silden fern supply from the greenhouses you helped the city establish. But this"—she gestured grandly toward the setup—"this is something far more exciting."

Rel, lingering nearby, let out a dramatic sigh.

Kemmy didn't miss a beat. "We're refining an elixir that Rel discovered—accidentally, I might add. We're experimenting with the process to make it more potent and reliable."

Sloane drew her brows together in curiosity. "Accidentally discovered? What happened?"

Rel rubbed the back of her neck, visibly sheepish. "I was working on a basic tonic, something for fatigue. I was exhausted, working late, and I grabbed the wrong canisters when filtering the water. Instead of crushed stone and sand, I used a blend of crushed crystals that had been infused with mana."

Sloane's eyes widened. "Wait, what happened?"

Kemmy laughed softly, clearly enjoying the retelling. "It created a weak tonic with some unexpected effects. We started testing and—"

"Wait! You drank it?" Sloane interrupted, turning a concerned look on Rel.

The orkun woman waved her off, as if this were entirely normal. "Yes, yes. We've tested this sort of thing before. It didn't show any toxicity. We were careful."

Sloane's mouth fell open slightly. *You were careful?* The words echoed in her head like a warning bell. *They're drinking experimental mana-infused solutions with no modern safety protocols.*

Of course, no regulatory framework existed yet. Safety regulations—things she had taken for granted on Earth—were still decades, if not centuries, from being formalized here. She could already see Adaega's face when she brought this up. Another item for the poor woman's ever-growing to-do list: implement safety standards across the Reinhart Center.

Sloane exhaled softly, pinching the bridge of her nose. "Alright. I'm afraid to ask, but . . . what happened after she drank it?"

"It gave me energy!" Rel said brightly. "Not a lot, but enough that I felt like I could keep working. I wasn't as tired."

Sloane blinked. *So . . . they've made an energy drink? A mana-based caffeine substitute?*

Kemmy was nodding enthusiastically beside her. "Exactly. And we ran more tests. You remember our earlier discussions about stamina—how mana seems to influence it?"

"Yes . . ." Sloane said slowly, already trying to connect the implications.

"This tonic replenishes stamina," Kemmy said, her tone charged with excitement. "And we've already made two different versions using different ingredient combinations. We also tested different types of mana-infused crystals. The key is that the crushed crystals must be pre-infused with mana from specific sources. We're using different cores to do the infusion. Now we've got a supply of crushed crystals aligned with every known mana type. But the most effective for this tonic seem to be green and blue."

Sloane considered the implications, trying to frame it in terms of the systems she'd been learning. Unfortunately, this was veering into chemistry and botany—more subjects that weren't her strong suits. She could keep up in theory, but the specifics were best left to the experts. Fortunately, she trusted her people.

Kemmy led her to a nearby workbench, where a telv alchemist was methodically pouring freshly distilled water through a shimmering blue filter made of crushed stone. Beneath the filter sat a large glass jar filled with vibrant herbs and Altered plant matter.

"Here," Kemmy said, gesturing. "These plants have been grown in soil saturated with mana, just like the ferns we use for the enchanting ink. It's the same basic principle: infused soil, controlled conditions, directed growth."

Sloane leaned over to get a better look. The glow from the blue stone filter gave the workspace a strange luminescence. "Who's been handling the cultivation work? I don't remember assigning an herbalist."

Kemmy didn't pause. "You didn't. I asked Miss Adaega to hire one after the first greenhouse was erected. He's been cultivating our stock of magical plants for some time now, and also collaborating with the city to improve agricultural techniques. He's the one who took your initial idea—mixing powdered mana crystals into soil and infusing them with mana using green cores—and turned it into a working process."

Sloane raised her brows. "I thought that was you."

Kemmy smiled, unbothered. "It *was*, at first. But once we brought in a specialist, we started refining the approach. He and I worked together, taking your concept and expanding it. We experimented with various plant types. Some respond incredibly well to mana saturation, while others don't show any noticeable effect. But we're learning." She turned back to the workbench and pointed. "Watch."

The telv alchemist mixed the heated, distilled water with the jar of plants. As he stirred, the liquid began to glow, a soft green shimmer that intensified the longer it steeped. After several minutes, he lifted the jar with gloved hands and poured it through a funnel and fine strainer, filling a small glass bottle. Once done, he moved to the next prepped bottle in a line.

Kemmy pulled on a fresh glove and picked up the first finished vial. She held it up to the light. The liquid pulsed softly, as if it had a heartbeat.

"Now," she said with a grin, "we use a bit of magic . . ."

Sloane watched closely. She knew Kemmy was one of the few people in the house who had both a mental alignment and an Uncommon core quality. Her attunement was green, and her domains were Artifice and Abjuration—a potent combination for alchemy, especially when crafting stable, mana-reactive substances.

Rel, for her part, had a Common core quality, but also carried a mental alignment. She was attuned to green mana as well, though her domain was Alteration, just as suited to experimentation and refinement.

Sloane watched with fascination as Kemmy's eyes took on a faint luminescent tinge, a subtle green light flickering in their depths. Her fingertips shimmered too, glowing faintly the same color as she cradled the bottle in her hands. The liquid inside responded almost immediately—it began to swirl, then brightened, casting a glow that reminded Sloane of a blue glow stick in the dark.

Once the mixture settled, Kemmy placed the now vibrant vial back into the wooden rack with obvious satisfaction. Her smile stretched wide across her face, and Sloane couldn't help but grin in response.

"So that's it?" she asked, gesturing to the vial. "What exactly did you do with your magic?"

Kemmy nodded, practically vibrating with excitement. "That's it! We've discovered that magical alchemical substances do work on their own, but if we guide them—if we use our mana to align and empower the mixture—they not only stabilize better but also become far more potent. Think of it as sealing the intent into the concoction."

Rel added, "It also extends shelf life—well, so far. We'll see how it holds after a few weeks in storage."

"Would you care to test it?" Kemmy asked, holding up the bottle like a trophy.

Sloane glanced between her two alchemists, amusement flickering behind her eyes. *Why does it always feel like I'm the guinea pig in these scenarios?* Still, curiosity tugged at her. *Ah, what the hell.*

"This blue one—this is the mental stamina elixir?" she confirmed.

Kemmy nodded again, clearly eager. "It is. Designed to replenish mental focus and spellcasting endurance after burnout."

Sloane took a measured breath. "Well, I'll need to burn through a good chunk of mana first. And that might not be wise in here."

Rel chuckled knowingly. "We figured. Come on—we had Koren set up a dedicated testing area for you."

"What?" Sloane blinked. "When did that happen?"

The two women laughed and beckoned her to follow. With a resigned sigh and the usual mix of anticipation and trepidation, she trailed after them out the back of the Alchemy Hall.

CHAPTER THIRTY-TWO

SURPRISE DEMONSTRATIONS

"If they ask if it was safe, just smile and nod, alright?"

—Kemilla Bratianu, Alchemist of House Reinhart

Sloane followed Kemmy and Rel down a path along the perimeter wall of the campus. As they rounded the corner, approaching the Guard Hall, Sloane noticed that a grove of trees had been recently cleared.

Nestled near the outer wall was a new stone pad, cleanly constructed and etched with fresh markings. A solid stone wall had been erected along the far edge, standing about five meters high and about six wide. Lines had been painted across the floor at precise intervals, and a series of small obelisks—each about a meter tall—were placed neatly in a grid formation, one meter apart, along the edges of the pad leading up to the wall.

Sloane stopped in her tracks and turned to Kemmy, her brow raised. "What exactly is this?"

The raithe smiled proudly. "A magic-test range. Built with you in mind. You should be able to safely cast just about any spell you have at that wall without worrying about collateral damage."

She gestured toward the wall. "Adaega even had Orthan practice some of his enchantments on it. He inscribed several rune chains meant to absorb and disperse mana. The director figured it would be a good test for other, more commercial uses, as well."

Sloane perked up, genuinely impressed. *So that's what Adaega meant when she mentioned Orthan had been working on a special project.*

Curiosity sparked, she stepped up onto the stone pad. Her boots echoed against the smoothed surface. She passed over a painted circle near the center of the platform, its purpose unclear but likely connected to spell measurement. She made a mental note to ask.

Approaching the wall, she stopped to study the intricate reinforcement. Steel bands, spaced half a meter apart, wrapped horizontally along the stone face. Along each band, runes had been etched with a steady, practiced hand.

Immediately, she recognized a few: |**Strengthen**|, |**Resist**|, and—her favorite—a newly theorized enchantment: |**Spell-Resist**|.

She had only recently begun testing its practical application. If it worked as intended, it would reduce the effects of spell-based impact on armor and structures. A critical development for outfitting knights, especially when facing arcane casters. Though it still wouldn't do much against conjured physical objects like the ones Ressa favored, it would be highly effective against pure mana attacks—the kind Sloane specialized in. Ironically, it might be the perfect defense *against her.*

She smiled wryly. *Well, if you can't counter them, become the benchmark.*

"What do you think?" The voice came from her right, light and filled with satisfaction. Sloane turned to see Adaega approaching with a small entourage—and not just any group. Flanking her were all the key figures from Sloane's house and knightly retinue, their expressions subtle but undoubtedly expectant. Behind them, another cluster of figures caught her eye—General Irileth and several high-ranking officers of the Marketbol army whom she recognized from meetings or strategy briefings. Beyond them even, a smaller, more refined group made their way into view: city council members, adorned in their formal robes, looking far too smug for a casual walk through campus.

They were all watching her. Sloane narrowed her eyes and crossed her arms. "This feels suspicious."

Adaega laughed, the sound warm and familiar. "We all planned this. It's the official unveiling. This is your fully operational spell-testing range. It cost a small fortune in materials, but I believe it will prove well worth the investment." She glanced back toward the crowd and smiled proudly. "And I am especially proud of the work young Orthan put into it."

The telv boy straightened at the praise. "Thank you, Miss Adaega." He turned to Sloane and dipped his head. "Lady Reinhart, I hope it meets your expectations."

Sloane chuckled. "Considering I didn't know it was even being built, I'd say I didn't have any expectations." That drew a round of laughter from those around her, easing the formality.

"You should see what it can do!" Gisele cut in excitedly. "The obelisks in particular! I want to take the concept and build something similar back home."

Sloane examined the small stone obelisks she'd initially dismissed as simple markers. Now that she was closer, she saw that the pillars, nearly a meter tall, had embedded runework. Curious, she squatted next to one, tracing the designs with her eyes. There were two runes she recognized followed by one she didn't. She looked up, brow raised.

"You used |**Store: (Spell)**|?" she asked Orthan. "But . . . I don't recognize the second rune."

"I did, Lady Reinhart," Orthan replied. "Ser Gisele provided the initial spell we stored."

Sloane's eyes widened in realization. "Wait. There's a mana crystal in here?" Looking closer, she noted the faint shimmer of a red mana core fitted seamlessly into the structure.

Adaega nodded. "Yes. Each obelisk is powered by a dedicated core. This is more than a simple test range—it's a prototype. A potential new system for city-wide defense using enchantment and runic triggers. It's also a demonstration of our team's ability to design and execute complex magical systems without your direct oversight." She smiled. "But of course, you're the only one who can truly test it."

A wave of giddiness rose in Sloane's chest. She looked around again—not just at the setup, but at the people. They weren't just here for a demonstration. They were here for her.

Adaega gestured toward a small pedestal just off to the side of the platform. "That's the central control mechanism. Would you like to do the honors?"

Sloane shook her head and smiled. "No. Orthan? Come here."

The young telv's eyes lit up with excitement. He stepped forward and studied the pedestal for a moment before pressing a rune-etched button marked with |**Trigger**|.

Immediately, the entire testing pad thrummed with energy. A low hum filled the air as the obelisks flared red, and the rear wall lit with soft blue light. Two shimmering walls of red energy erupted on either side of the platform, stretching from floor to sky. They snapped into place with a sharp crack of magic, stabilizing at the same height as the massive stone wall at the far end.

The crowd collectively gasped. Sloane stepped back, stunned by both the sight and the sheer execution. This wasn't just a clever enchantment. It was a new form of mana-based infrastructure. Something she hadn't even fully envisioned yet. And her people had built it without her.

Her thoughts spun with refinements she could make: additional runes, modifications to the spell-storing logic, material efficiency. But none of that was the point. This was their work, their idea—their victory. It wasn't about perfection but about proving they could stand on their own; they could carry her vision forward, even when she wasn't there. When she left—when she finally left to search for Gwyn—they would be ready.

Her throat tightened. She swallowed hard and turned to look at the crowd. Their expressions were everything, filled with pride, admiration, and hope. Adaega stood just ahead, her smile radiant.

"Was this your doing, Adaega?" Sloane asked, her voice soft but full of appreciation.

She didn't miss the moment—Ernald squeezed Adaega's hand before straightening his posture, pride clear on his face. Sloane's heart warmed. The two had officially entered a relationship not long ago, and watching them together never failed to bring her a quiet joy. She still remembered the day they'd told everyone.

Adaega had practically glowed for hours afterward, and the smile on Ernald's face had been equally telling.

Naturally, Sloane and Ismeld had given the poor sun elf no end of grief for it. Especially when it came out that Adaega had been the one to finally make the first move, after weeks of Ernald completely missing the signs. *You go, girl.*

As if on cue, Nadia and Elodie stepped up behind Adaega. Elodie placed a supportive hand on her shoulder. The three of them had become nearly inseparable. Whether they were organizing the Center's operations, collaborating on recruitment efforts, or just enjoying a rare moment of calm, the bond between them was unmistakable. A quiet strength, woven through friendship.

Adaega nodded in answer to Sloane's question. "Yes, Lady Reinhart. After we gathered the data on all house members, I began searching for a way to truly showcase what the Reinhart Center and its people could do. This project became a collaboration across every division. Each person contributed their talents and perspectives, and what you see here is the result of their combined effort."

"Speech!" someone called from the crowd. Sloane didn't need to look to know who it was, but she turned and narrowed her eyes playfully at the source. "Gisele, you rascal. You know I hate public speaking."

A chorus of chuckles met her glare, and Gisele threw up her hands in mock surrender.

Sloane faced the gathering crowd. "This is truly impressive," she began, her voice steady. "I am amazed at how polished and well-executed this entire system is. And let's not ignore the fact that you managed to pull this off in between all the other projects I've been pestering you about."

A wave of laughter rippled through the group like sunlight. She took a breath. "When I first imagined the Reinhart Center, I envisioned a place where like-minded individuals could gather to raise the quality of life for all—here in Marketbol, and one day beyond it. A place where curiosity is not only encouraged but rewarded. A place of learning and experimentation, where the mystery of mana could be explored without fear."

As she spoke, more members of House Reinhart approached and gathered around her, forming a semi-circle on the testing platform.

"A refuge for other terrans like Adaega and me," she continued, her tone warming. "But also a beacon—a place where friends could come together and forge something greater than any one of us could achieve alone. A place where the extraordinary isn't just studied—it's made."

A smattering of applause rose from the crowd, then hushed again as she lifted her hand and scanned the people she had come to rely on and care for. She felt the presence of those she'd come to know and find friendship in, yet would have to soon leave behind—Ernald, Adaega, Elodie, Rel, Kemmy, Orthan, Koren, and more.

"My greatest fear since arriving here has always been about what I leave behind. You all know . . . my time in Marketbol isn't permanent. I have a journey ahead of me, one that will take me far from this city, and far from all of you."

A quiet settled over the crowd, heavy but not grim.

"And yet," she continued, voice steady, "in such a short time, this Center has grown from a simple idea into a living institute of growth, learning, and innovation. It has become a place of purpose and progress. And that is because of each and every one of you."

She turned her gaze back to Adaega and Elodie. "With Adaega Merbaker and Elodie Romaris leading here, House Reinhart and its Center are in capable hands. Never forget that this"—she gestured to the range, the people, the enchanted walls glowing faintly—"was made possible not by me alone but by all of you."

Sloane's words were met with a wave of enthusiastic applause. She paused, breathing in the energy of the gathered crowd, letting the moment settle around her like a warm cloak. She saw the glimmer of emotion on Adaega's face, the quiet pride in Orthan's posture, the clenched jaw of Elodie trying very hard not to tear up. And for the first time in what felt like months, Sloane allowed herself to believe: *When I leave . . . they'll be okay. They'll thrive.*

She swept her gaze across the assembly—her people, her friends, her allies. With quiet conviction, she continued: "To those of House Reinhart and to all who support what we've built here—thank you. To the city's leadership, who took a chance on a vision not yet realized, I hope you now see the potential of what lies ahead. You placed your faith in a few women who dreamed of something more. This . . ."—she gestured around them—"is only the beginning." Her voice gained strength with every word. "And I, for one, cannot wait for the world to see what House Reinhart has in store." She crossed her hands over her heart. "Everyone, from the bottom of my heart . . . thank you." She bowed her head in heartfelt gratitude.

A beat of silence passed before there came another burst of applause, louder this time. But before it could build too far, Sloane raised her hands with a playful grin, and the crowd quieted once more.

"Now," she said, voice laced with anticipation, "who wants to see how well this actually works?"

A cheer rang out as she turned smoothly on her heel and faced the wall. With a practiced flick of her wrist, Sloane snap-fired a **[Mana Bolt]**. The orb of purple energy hissed through the air before colliding with the stone wall. It exploded in a brilliant burst of light, the impact resonating across the field. The wall shimmered as veins of blue energy spread out from the point of impact—proof that the enchantments were active and flawless. No damage. Not even a crack. She smirked with satisfaction. *Nice.*

Gathering her mana, Sloane extended a hand and cast an **[Arcane Barrage]**. A series of sharp, humming blasts launched from her palm, striking the wall in rapid succession. She swept her hand sideways, curving the final bolts toward one of the red energy shields, sending a cascade of sparks and rippling feedback across its surface.

Laughter bubbled up from her throat. Behind her, cheering erupted again.

Let's see how much this thing can really take. With renewed determination, she pushed further. A series of [**Mana Bolts**] spun into existence over her shoulders. One by one, she launched them at varying angles, some straight into the wall, others to test the shielding. Each impact was met with resistance, the defenses holding steady against the growing onslaught.

After nearly half a bell of continuous spellcasting, her body began to protest. Her limbs grew heavier, her core sluggish. She could feel the mana strain, the pull on her internal pathways, the sharp edge of overexertion beginning to press against her senses. But the crowd was still with her, watching, riveted.

A gentle tap on her shoulder brought her out of her haze. She turned her head, breathing hard, and found Kemmy standing beside her. A beat later, Rel and Adaega flanked them, subtly stepping in to block her from the crowd's line of sight.

"Lady Reinhart," Kemmy whispered, offering a folded cloth.

Sloane frowned, confused, until she dabbed her nose and saw the stains of red. "Did anyone—"

"No," Kemmy said softly. "Here. Drink this." She handed Sloane a small bottle.

The elixir. In all the excitement of the unveiling and spellcasting, she had completely forgotten about it. And now, standing here drained and bloodied from overuse, it was suddenly clear: *That's why Kemmy had worked so hard to finish it in time for today. Well played, Kemmy.*

Sloane uncorked the bottle and raised it to her lips, downing it like a shot of alcohol. The liquid was bitter, herbal, with a thick texture that reminded her of cough syrup. But as unpleasant as it was, the effect was nearly immediate. Warmth bloomed within her chest, spreading outward like heated balm sinking into sore muscles. The tension in her limbs eased. The ache in her core lightened. The pressure on her mind lifted.

She reached for her mana again and blinked in surprise. *No strain. No resistance. No exhaustion.* The elixir hadn't just dulled the fatigue. It had restored her. The weight on her shoulders seemed to disappear as her core flowed with steady, balanced energy once more.

She looked down at the bottle in her hand, then back at Kemmy, her expression full of awe. "This . . ." she whispered. "This changes everything."

With a burst of laughter, Sloane threw her arms around the petite raithe standing beside her. Kemmy yelped in surprise as Sloane lifted her off the ground in a sudden, joyful spin. The cheers behind them faded into a blur of color and motion as the moment pulsed with warmth.

Rel, eyes wide, raised her hands in mock surrender as Sloane carefully set Kemmy back on her feet. Still chuckling, she turned to face the crowd, her smile broad and unrestrained, her chest light with exhilaration. She knew she looked ridiculous, but she didn't care.

"Wonders never cease within House Reinhart," Sloane said, her voice lifting over the gathering with confident warmth. "I know many of you already know them, but for those who don't, allow me to introduce Kemilla Bratianu and Rel Sha'rak."

She motioned for both women to join her, and they stepped up. Kemmy's cheeks flushed, and Rel maintained her composed calm, though Sloane didn't miss the pride behind her sharp eyes.

"Kemmy," Sloane said, "is the department head of our Alchemy Hall. She oversees all the Center's work in alchemy and, now, herbalism. And together, these two incredible women were the ones who discovered the formula for enchanting ink. The same ink that now empowers the city's defenses. The very ink used in the runes protecting these walls. This city."

A ripple of surprise and awe moved through the crowd, followed by murmurs of approval. General Irileth took a step forward, recognizing the significance of what was being revealed. Sloane caught his eye, then turned her attention fully back to the audience.

"Mana," she said, letting the word linger, "affects all of us in different ways. Physically. Mentally. Every action we take, every spell we cast or ability we use—it draws on our stamina, one way or another. But what if we could recover that stamina?"

She turned slightly toward Rel, who held up a second bottle. "These two," Sloane said, gesturing between Kemmy and Rel, "have discovered and developed elixirs that do just that. One for physical stamina, the other for mental stamina. Just moments ago, I was nearing magical exhaustion from casting. Some of you here"—her gaze swept across a few knights in the front row—"have seen me reach my limits before. But this time, I drank one of these elixirs. And it worked. It reversed that fatigue."

Her tone grew passionate, her eyes gleaming. "Now imagine our soldiers, up on the walls, fighting for days as the Vlaredians try to breach the city. What if they had access to these elixirs? They would still tire, yes—but they'd retain the ability to cast, to fight, to endure. Longer than the enemy ever could."

Another wave of excitement swept the crowd—this time louder, voices rising in animated speculation. Sloane pressed forward, seizing the momentum.

"And what if that was only the beginning? Ser Maud uses her magic every day at the temple to heal the wounded, but what if that same healing could be channeled into a potion? What if a simple elixir could seal a wound, mend a bone, or halt a fever?"

She looked at the city council members, then the military officers, then back to her people. "What if doctors, apothecaries, and field medics didn't have to pray for a miracle? What if healing was something we could bottle, mass-produce, and deliver to anyone who needed it? Imagine the world we could build with such advancements."

I'll, uh . . . leave the naming conventions to the alchemists. That's their territory.

The audience fell into a moment of stunned silence. And then the cheering began, followed by a growing surge of questions and excitement rippling outward like a wave.

Beside her, she heard Kemmy whisper, just loud enough for her to catch: "Is that really possible?"

"If mana allows Ser Maud to heal grievous wounds with a few whispered words and a prayer's focus . . . then yes," answered Sloane. "I absolutely believe it's possible. With alchemy." *Even if—especially if—I'm just pulling all of this from fantasy stories back home.*

Rel exhaled slowly beside her, her mask of calm slipping for just a moment as the weight of what they'd committed to became real. "This is going to be a lot of work."

Kemmy gave a small, gleeful laugh. "I can't wait."

Sloane turned to them both, her smile returning full force. "I can't either."

And for the first time in a long while, it truly felt like the future was within reach.

CHAPTER THIRTY-THREE

FOR EVERYTHING ELSE

I t was late on a summer night, the kind that clung to the skin with lingering warmth and silence too deep to trust. The Vlaredian army had launched another of its predictable, ill-fated probing attacks, meant to test the reflexes of the city's defenders. They weren't serious assaults—just enough to keep the enemy on edge.

The siege had dragged on for several seasons now, and the command group still hadn't figured out how to counter the terran's infernal enchanted ballistae. The magic-infused weapons devastated any attempt to use their own mages offensively. Worse, concentrated fire from the city's enchanted emplacements had overwhelmed the shield mages in the past. They couldn't afford to lose more.

Reports of Sovereign forces amassing to the south were becoming more frequent. General Razane was worried—Ressa could see it in his tightened orders and increasingly cautious deployments. Scouts estimated a decent-sized army just a few weeks out, and if it closed the distance, withdrawal might become their only option.

If the army pulled back, she would need to reassess the entire mission and figure out how to proceed without their backing. Sabotage and subversion without external pressure was far riskier.

She had already suspected that after the Marketbol campaign, she and her team would be moved to information gathering rather than focusing on aggressive operations.

"Wait," she whispered, holding up a hand. "Let the patrol pass."

As one, her team dropped low, pressing themselves into the shadows where the moonlight couldn't find them. The quiet shuffle of gear and boots dulled against the packed earth and stone. Overhead, soldiers strolled the ramparts with all the urgency of routine.

Every patrol at this hour ran the same route. Every ten minutes, on the mark.

These soldiers are so predictable. They'd memorized the patterns weeks ago—shifts in timing, watch rotations, slack points in coverage. The chaos her team had sown inside the city had forced the Marketbol army to split its focus, maintaining constant street patrols and quelling civilian unrest. The food shortages, rationing, forced curfews, and closed taverns had done the rest.

Small riots flared up almost daily. And while the unrest helped the army operate in the shadows, it also stretched them thin. Only the walls facing the Vlaredian camp remained properly manned. *Useful. But also limiting.*

The actions of her team to redistribute supplies the affluent had hoarded to the poor had started a protest that had forced the city to reposition enough soldiers away from the wall. The army had been able to launch an attack and destroy one more ballista with that distraction. It was a war of attrition, after all.

Some of the younger rank and file of the Vlaredian army had grumbled about why they hadn't just poisoned the city's water supply. General Razane ensured his officers shut down such talk. They would compose themselves and fight honorably. Unnecessarily targeting civilians would do them no favors in the many fights ahead after Marketbol.

As always, Ressa used the lull in movement to run through their objectives and rehearse contingencies. Her mind was a blade, honed on years of experience and narrow success.

A soft fluttering whistle sounded—three short bursts.

Clear. She nodded. "Quiet. Move out."

The group rose and slipped along the base of the outer wall, silent as smoke. Another twenty meters brought them to a spot only they knew.

Ressa took the lead, reaching out and brushing her fingers across the stone. A trace of lingering mana shimmered at her touch. She raised her other hand and cast **[Dispel Conjuration]**.

A faint golden mist bloomed into existence, swirling once before it dissipated, revealing a narrow tunnel where there had been only solid wall. It had once been a tunnel a pair of smugglers were using to sneak in illicit goods. She and her team had found and followed them late one night. Of course, they had eliminated any potential issues and repurposed the tunnel for their own objectives.

They'd now used this entrance half a dozen times, maintaining it with a precision and care its former users had not. Ressa's magic lasted only a few days before fading naturally, and she had to reapply it regularly to keep the hidden entrance active.

That they hadn't been discovered yet was frankly surprising. She could only assume the groups searching for them hadn't been able to search everywhere for signs of magic. It was a trick she'd recently learned from one of the shield casters. **[Mana Sight]** was a powerful tool, one that could help the defenders pinpoint their entrance very easily. It was just another reason they had to be constantly on guard.

She waved her team forward. One by one, they slipped into the tunnel like ghosts. She followed last, then paused and turned, casting **[Create Illusion]** followed by [**Alter Conjuration**]. The stone wall shimmered back into place, seamless and whole.

From deeper in the tunnel, the soft scrape of boots echoed as her team climbed into the small, storage-like building built directly against the wall. The forgotten warehouse used by a minor merchant company, then by the deceased smugglers, was now hollow and half abandoned thanks to the siege.

Inside, Ressa conjured another illusion, removing a piece of the ceiling and replacing it with a basic ladder of stone and wood. They climbed into the narrow crawl space between roof and ceiling, their makeshift hideaway for the next day or two.

She sealed the gap behind them, then finally allowed herself to breathe. *We may need to relocate soon.* She took in the cramped space. The team was already moving into practiced positions—two on watch, the rest settling in quietly. They had enough food and water to last them two days, maybe more if they rationed tightly.

Alexi approached and handed her a blanket. Ressa took it with a nod and settled herself into the corner, placing her satchel and weapons within reach. The blanket rustled softly as she spread it out, then tucked herself in as best she could in the confined space. And finally, in the rare stillness, her mind wandered.

Ressa and her team had spent the better part of the siege waging a quiet war of sabotage—starting small fires and eliminating scouts and advanced forces from the south. All around becoming whispers in the dark. Every strike was a message. Every disappearance, a warning. And all of it aimed toward one goal: to disrupt the city and draw out the terran.

She was lucky that the empress understood the magnitude of the obstacle Lady Reinhart presented. Had the broader war not been progressing so favorably elsewhere, Ressa was certain the pressure to resolve this situation—to eliminate the terran outright—would have been far more intense. As it stood, they'd at least succeeded in keeping Reinhart bottled up in Marketbol.

She'd heard the rumors and engaged in small talk with some of the army's officers. The rest of the warfront was advancing. Vlaredian forces in the east had maneuvered south with precision, outflanking Sovereign reinforcements and seizing the city of Valecan, where they had shattered an unprepared army from the plains. Even now, the bulk of the Empire's strength pushed toward Earthenwilde, a strategic bastion at the edge of the central plains, where they would likely clash with the final major concentration of Sovereign troops.

Even though her position within the Empire's elite forces afforded her access to intelligence few others were privy to, Ressa wasn't *in the know*. Operational security ensured that she would not know anything more than what the public could know. With her mission regularly taking her behind enemy lines, the risk of capture meant that her team should not have information that could be used as a weapon against the Empire.

She knew the limits of the war effort—the political balancing act required to keep so many enemies at bay. They could not overextend. A considerable portion of their troops had already been redirected toward the Kingdom of Avira, the Empire's other major rival, where tensions simmered on a fragile border.

Ressa didn't know the full details of what was happening in the west, but word had spread of a naval campaign already underway—another army sailing to strike the Sovereigns by sea. It was a bold move. And one that carried its own risks.

But what concerned her most wasn't victory on individual fronts. It was whether the Empire could maintain its momentum. Wars fought on too many fronts had broken stronger empires than theirs.

In her opinion, the Empire needed to expand quickly, make their point with decisive victories, and then consolidate. Every new territory brought new challenges—resistance, governance, supply—and if they were drawn into a prolonged war, she wasn't certain the Empire's internal stability could endure.

But if the Marketbol siege held, and if the eastern legions reached them in time, then the Empire would be in an excellent position. They could dictate terms. The Sovereigns' strength had always lain in their southern cities, and if they fell . . . well, the rest would follow.

A few days passed before her next move. Her team struck again—another warehouse sabotaged, more materiel destroyed, more doubt sown. Observations were gathered on the Reinhart Center—entries and exits, guard rotations, construction patterns.

And when they left the city under the cover of darkness once again, slipping through the same hidden entrance they'd used countless times, the operation was clean. Silent. A complete success.

No one saw a thing.

Sloane passed four guards on her way inside, two of them wearing the Banking Guild's blue tabards, a recent addition to the Center's security detail. She stepped into the Runic Hall, her private refuge in an increasingly public life.

This was her sanctuary. Her forge of thought and craft. A place where, for a few hours at least, the noise of the world could be reduced to the delicate scratch of ink against parchment and the quiet pull of mana through conduit lines.

The building had once been a temple to Erbium, the dwarven God of Crafting. Since the campus's reopening, the dwarves had moved to a newer, grander location across the city, leaving this one quiet and vacant until she repurposed it. Now, the old temple stood reborn—a future home for dozens of enchanters, runecrafters, and artificers. It was one of her proudest transformations.

As she stepped into the vaulted central chamber, the warm scent of aged stone and fresh ink greeted her. She spotted Orthan seated at a long table near the front, hunched over a fresh sheet of parchment.

Sloane paused to observe. The young telv seemed deeply focused. His tools were arranged with obsessive care: quills and pens in a neat row from smallest to largest, two inkwells angled just so at the corner of the table, a stack of custom-made parchment sitting perfectly to his left. A single sheet sat in front of him as he carefully inked what she instantly recognized as a [**Mana Bolt**] spell scroll.

They'd discussed this project weeks ago, an experiment in combining metal filament with parchment to create functional, single-use spell scrolls. Orthan had insisted on doing the initial trial himself, and now, watching him work, Sloane could see why.

She activated her [**Mana Sight**], her gaze sharpening. His runes weren't just aesthetic; they were intricately layered to help the scroll retain mana stability. The enchanting ink flowed cleanly, reacting to his touch. A secondary spell dried the ink the moment he lifted his pen.

He's getting faster, she thought. *And more precise.*

He was just finishing the last stroke when she finally spoke. "Orthan—"

"Do not interrupt," he said without looking up.

She blinked, caught off guard, and watched as he finished the rune, cleaned the pen tip with a cloth on his right, and returned it to its proper place. Only then did he turn to face her.

"Lady Reinhart," he said with a formal nod. "I've completed the first spell scroll."

She smiled. "I see that. How long did this one take you?"

Orthan glanced at the scroll, then around the room as if reading the light. "Approximately four bells."

Sloane hummed thoughtfully. "That would make them expensive to produce if each takes that long. Maybe—"

"A moment," he interrupted again, reaching for a second blank sheet of parchment. He placed it beside the completed scroll and hovered his hands over both. Mana flowed through him in a clean stream of blue light. A faint glow pulsed from the completed scroll and passed into the blank sheet.

In seconds, an exact copy appeared.

Sloane raised her eyebrows. "I forgot you could do that."

He nodded. "It doesn't work with the runecards, and I can only do it once per day. So this is likely the first time you've seen it."

"Still," she said, studying the scrolls, "Adaega mentioned the ability." She gestured toward the duplicate. "May I?"

He handed it over without hesitation. Sloane examined it with [**Mana Sight**] engaged. She picked up the original for comparison. No difference. The runes were identical. Even the flow of enchanting ink was indistinguishable. *Even if only once a day, this is an incredibly potent skill.*

"Orthan," she said, "tomorrow, could you make another copy and ask Miss Kemmy to analyze the ink? I'd like to confirm it's the same material down to the composition."

"Yes, Lady Reinhart," he said with a sharp nod. His eyes flicked toward her belt. "What are you working on today?"

She smiled. Orthan's curiosity always intensified whenever she was working on something new. The boy practically radiated fascination with runes and everything they could accomplish. His only frustration—one she knew weighed heavily on him—was his inability to alter materials like she could. Without her affinity for Alteration, he was limited to the traditional methods of etching and engraving runes directly into metal, wood, or stone. It was a limitation she hoped to remove before she left the city.

In her spare time, she'd begun a new project: two true enchanting pens, each embedded with gems and designed to cast spells themselves. If the concept worked, these tools would let enchanters inscribe runes onto any material, bypassing the need for manual carving altogether. Someday soon, one of them would belong to Orthan.

"I'm finishing the runecard database for the Banking Guild," she said, making her way toward her main workbench. "I finally received something I've been waiting on."

Orthan leapt to his feet, eager as ever, and followed at her heels. They passed one of the Guild guards stationed near the wall—a precaution due to the delivery—and she exchanged a respectful nod with the armored man.

She spotted the sealed box on the table and opened it. Inside lay five softball-sized blue mana cores, each glowing faintly with stored power. Nestled beneath them, secured in a second, heavily padded compartment, was a massive black diamond, accompanied by an array of precisely cut gemstones—sapphires, topaz, pink sapphires, and others. The black diamond, easily over five hundred carats, sparkled ominously in the lamplight. It was a staggering display of wealth. On Earth, this would've been priceless. Here, it was valuable, yes, but abundant enough to be used practically.

Sloane inhaled deeply, steadying herself. To her left, a pedestal frame stood open, its inner components exposed. The polished casing had been peeled back, revealing her progress—precisely fitted conduits, embedded runic plates, and calibrated enchantment lines. Behind it sat the prototype model, a more utilitarian version that had already proved functional and could manage data well enough for a small provincial town. But this new pedestal was the primary node, the final version of what she'd been prototyping for so long. It was the central database, the hub that would eventually control the entire runecard system across regions.

She grabbed her notebook from her satchel and flipped to the relevant page. Dozens of scribbled notes, diagrams, and runic formulas covered the paper. She had chosen a pedestal design intentionally; it was a familiar shape, something that would feel authoritative yet approachable to the world she was helping shape.

With Orthan watching silently beside her and the Banking Guild guard keeping a respectful distance, Sloane pulled up her stool and got to work.

As always, when dealing with complex runecraft, she referred back to the most invaluable magical artifact she possessed—her watch. Using it as both inspiration and schematic, she had devised a network of interconnected systems that would allow input, storage, display, and manipulation of user data within the runecard system.

She carefully slotted the topaz, sapphire, and small pink sapphire into channels of inscribed silver beneath a polished glass panel. The display would be powered by its own mana crystal, supplemented by one of the dedicated blue cores.

That display panel alone contained an entire series of runic chains, meticulously constructed to pull and present specific information from the database—account balances, histories, permissions, and more. Each client would carry their personal runecard, but the Guild itself would hold management cards that could override and access broader system functions.

Below the display sat the part she was most proud of: the keyboard, a sprawling panel of characters—letters, numerals, and unique symbols—each connected to an assigned input function. It was the world's first functional keyboard, rune-etched and hand-built from scratch. It had taken weeks of collaboration with Orthan to determine the most efficient layout. Together, they had developed a localized version of QWERTY, optimizing the order of the alphabet to match natural speech and writing rhythms.

Naturally, the boy had immediately asked her to build him a typewriter next. And she would. Of course she would. But first . . . this.

The management card would serve as the key interface between the user and the pedestal. Inserted into the slot beside the display, it allowed authorized Guild staff to select and manage individual accounts. A card tray sat just beneath the screen, flanked by a set of small, precisely arranged matching gemstones. These acted as a conduit, syncing the card's embedded data with the pedestal's systems.

All of this comprised the upper assembly, but it was only part of the whole.

Sloane exhaled slowly and turned to the heart of the system. Carefully, she slotted in the oversized sapphires, diamonds, and other support gems into the main circuit board. With practiced strokes, she etched the final set of runes: |Intent|, |Knowledge|, and |Calculate|—the core logic that would drive the pedestal's decision-making and data handling. Then she positioned the board alongside the massive black diamond she'd installed earlier—the primary storage gem, the component that would house the entirety of the system's data.

Then came the final step. Opening a recessed panel near the pedestal's base, Sloane reached into a padded case and pulled out a mana crystal the size of her hand. A crystal cut for stability and power—not volatile, not flashy, but steady. She pressed it into the slot, and a faint click signaled the bracket had locked into place.

Immediately, the pedestal hummed to life, a low, comforting vibration resonating through the stone floor beneath her feet. Runes ignited across its frame in waves of cool light. The display flared with a swirl of mana before fading into an idle state—a polished black surface waiting for input. The keyboard, newly installed, glowed with soft blue characters and sigils.

Sloane stepped back, her heart thudding with anticipation. She grinned. *Finally.* Turning, she gestured to the Guild guard standing nearby. "It's ready."

The man straightened and gave a respectful nod. "Please give me one moment, Lady Reinhart." He moved briskly to the entrance and exchanged quiet words with the guards stationed outside. Returning, he informed her that the test item and representatives would be en route shortly.

While she waited on the representatives to arrive, Sloane went to her workbench to prepare the support terminals that would eventually accompany the system at every Guild branch. There were two devices: the first was designed for viewing and managing existing accounts, while the second was built for creating and imprinting new runecards.

The imprinting device was a compact steel box with two trays, one for blank cards, the other for newly created ones. At its center sat a smooth hemisphere of polished opal, embedded with faint runic lines.

The terminal interface, meanwhile, resembled an oversized calculator. It featured a display panel and an array of input keys, each labeled with symbols and numbers for adjusting values, verifying identities, and executing account operations. She had done several design iterations before landing on this final, sleek version.

Sloane adjusted the placement of the terminals, dimly aware of Orthan beside her. Looking up, she caught the smallest twitch of amusement in his otherwise even expression.

"I can see that you are excited, Lady Reinhart," he said, his tone flat but knowing.

She laughed softly and nodded. "I am. This project has taken months, and now it's finally done. All that remains is testing it and then training the Banking Guild's staff. What do you think of it?"

Orthan studied the pedestal for a long moment before replying. "It is . . . an interesting tool. I look forward to seeing what other objects you design."

Her smile deepened. "Thank you, Orthan. And I can't wait to see more of your work. The spell-testing platform? It's been marvelous."

He fidgeted, looking down. Praise still made him uncomfortable. "I simply contributed," he murmured.

Sloane shook her head. "Your contributions were pivotal. Don't sell yourself short."

He gave a respectful nod—just a small motion, but meaningful.

She smiled again, then turned back to her workbench, tidying her space as she waited for their next guests. The hum of the pedestal behind her was steady and warm, like the pulse of something alive and waiting.

Soon, she thought, *we'll see just what this system is truly capable of.*

Twenty minutes later, a group of five Banking Guild representatives and two additional guards arrived at the Runic Hall. At the front of the group stood a well-dressed high elf, who offered a polite bow.

"Lady Reinhart," he greeted. "We've brought the current records of an account the grandmaster has selected for today's test."

Sloane clasped her hands together in front of her and smiled. "Wonderful. What House Reinhart specializes in—what you're witnessing here—is something we've started calling manatech: a fusion of magical systems and physical mechanisms designed to create an entirely new class of technology."

She gestured toward the workbench behind her. "Here, you'll see every device necessary to establish a full runecard system within the Banking Guild's Marketbol branch."

One of the attendants, a sharp-looking telv woman, began taking notes immediately. Sloane continued, standing beside the two terminal devices. "We've also created detailed schematics so that members of House Reinhart can construct additional devices as needed to support the Guild's network. Each branch should have at least one of each, though for larger branches, I recommend having multiple terminals, especially these," she said, motioning to the viewing and input consoles.

"However," she added with emphasis, "you will only ever need one pedestal per location. This is important. I'll personally oversee the setup of the first system here in Marketbol. Just ensure that each pedestal remains within seventy-five meters of its terminals. That distance is the limit of their current communication range. Within that radius, the terminals can pull and update data from the pedestal's database."

She glanced back at the pedestal, the soft blue glow of its core pulsing gently within. "The pedestals utilize blue mana cores for strength and enhanced mana connectivity. That also enables one of the most exciting features—inter-pedestal communication. Each pedestal can connect with others. The range, as we've found, is functionally unlimited as long as a mana-rich environment exists between them."

She watched as a few of the officials exchanged looks of surprise and intrigue. This wireless communication, powered through intent-based connection via mana, had been one of her most significant accidental discoveries. She hadn't expected it. Not at first. But in hindsight, it made sense. Mana was everywhere, and with the right runic guidance—and intent—it could form a sort of invisible web. A core in the pedestal was solely dedicated to managing this data transmission between connected devices.

"Now, terminals themselves don't use mana cores," she said, drawing their attention back. "Without them, they can't transmit intent beyond a limited range. But pedestals can, and that's how the system remains synced."

She didn't go into all the details—like how she was already working on a more ambitious version of the concept: The Archive. That would come later, once she had the main network established and could figure out a method to build stable connections without expensive blue cores. She and Adaega were still developing it, but the dream was there: a continent-spanning information network, built on intent, mana, and connection.

Maybe after I find Gwyn. Once we've had time to settle somewhere . . . If she couldn't make progress on the journey, she'd return to it after.

Once she'd explained the devices, their functions, and the best strategies for implementation, it was time for the real test. One of the Banking Guild guards stepped forward and opened a small reinforced chest. Inside, nestled atop a velvet lining, was a sealed scroll.

The elf beside her unrolled it carefully and held it up for her to see. It displayed the details of an active guild account: her own.

Sloane looked up at the high elf official, brow slightly furrowed. "You intend for me to use *my* account? Is that not a bit . . . unorthodox?"

"Please don't worry, Lady Reinhart," the elf replied smoothly. "We're all here simply to observe the demonstration, and the grandmaster has the utmost confidence in your integrity. If you would, please walk us through the process—setting up a new card, performing a withdrawal, and closing an account. Then I'll repeat each step myself. We'll conclude by establishing a new account, which is when we'll stop using yours."

Sloane looked down at the scroll in his hands, frowning. "This . . . seems incorrect." She turned away. "Orthan," she called gently to the young telv. "Could you retrieve Elodie for me?"

He straightened quickly. "At once, Lady Reinhart."

"I assure you, my lady," the high elf said, "this is the most up-to-date information we have regarding your account."

She gave a small shrug. "I believe you. Still, I'd feel more confident having the person who manages House Reinhart's finances present. I should've thought to include her earlier."

The man dipped his head politely. "Of course. Your caution is understandable. And no apologies are necessary—you're providing a tremendous service to the Guild."

She arched a brow. "The Banking Guild *is* paying me for this."

"Indeed," he said with a soft smile. "Quite handsomely, if I may say so."

A few minutes later, Elodie entered the hall, Adaega at her side.

"Lady Reinhart, you sent for me?" Elodie asked, notebook already in hand.

"Yes. Could you please verify this account information?" Sloane gestured toward the scroll the elf held.

Elodie glanced at Adaega with a look that sparked Sloane's suspicion and lifted the ledger she'd been carrying. She gave Adaega a triumphant grin. *They had a bet.* From the looks of it, Elodie had won.

"Certainly, milady." Elodie stepped closer, scanning the contents of the scroll with a sharp eye. Her brow furrowed, and she flipped through several pages of her notebook before stopping midway. Then, with a raised brow, she looked directly at the high elf.

"This number is incorrect. Where are all of these extra funds coming from?" *Wait. Extra?*

Before either of them could respond, a telv aide leaned in and whispered something into the elf's ear. The man nodded once, then turned back toward them with a calm expression.

"The grandmaster authorized the release of additional funds to your account as a reward for completing the first batch of deliverables tied to the runecard system." He paused as the aide whispered again. "We've also been informed that you now have a sufficient quantity of cards available?"

Sloane gave a cautious nod. "Yes. We have enough for five hundred active accounts, and more in production."

Elodie, meanwhile, was still scanning her records, her expression a blend of irritation and mild astonishment. "I have the payment milestone recorded here but this still doesn't line up. You're over the projected amount."

The high elf inclined his head. "Your records are, of course, correct. The grandmaster considers the overage a bonus, in recognition of your house continuing this work under siege conditions."

Sloane blinked. *Hazard pay.* That was unexpectedly generous.

She placed a hand on Elodie's forearm, applying gentle pressure. The woman gave her a tight nod and closed her ledger, though a faint frown still lingered on her face.

She's probably just frustrated she didn't already know. She's used to knowing everything before I do. "Thank you," Sloane said to her quietly, then turned her attention back to the assembled group. "Now, let's begin."

She walked over to the issuing terminal and opened two small boxes on the workbench. "First, you take two cards," she said, holding them up. "One from the stack of management cards, and one from the customer batch. You place them in their corresponding slots on the terminal, then press this rune here." She tapped a small glowing symbol on the device. "This starts the synchronization process. When the light flashes four times, the customer card is ready."

The terminal pulsed softly, then the card glowed once, twice . . . four times.

"Now," she continued, "have the member place their hand on the sensor—the opal hemisphere here. The system will read their mana signature. You'll feel a small pull of energy."

Sloane demonstrated, placing her hand atop the smooth stone. A slight, familiar rush passed through her as the system registered her signature. A second later, the terminal flashed twice, confirming the imprint.

She smiled, lifting her hand. "That's it. Their card is now ready. From here, you can embed a gemstone based on their membership tier and stamp their name and nation of origin onto the card."

She handed her freshly imprinted runecard to Elodie and picked up the documentation from the bench. The group moved as one toward the pedestal, circling it with interest.

"Next," Sloane said, "you take the management card and insert it here."

She slid the card into the pedestal's slot. It was met with a series of light pulses, then a steady blue glow. The screen flared to life with a swirl of blue mana, then cleared to display a clean interface. As it recognized the card's connection to a new account, it began prompting the user for information.

Sloane turned to the telv woman who'd been diligently taking notes. "Please, would you mind assisting with this part? Since this is my account, I'd like to guide you through it personally. It'll help ease my mind."

The high elf official nodded and gestured for the telv to proceed. She stepped forward, gazing down at the keyboard and glowing display.

"It's asking for the member's name," she said.

Sloane nodded. "Yes. What you're looking at is something we call a keyboard. Just press each key to input the letters of the name, like so." She guided the woman through entering the letters in Common, slowly at first, but the telv adapted quickly, pecking away as each new prompt appeared. When she reached the end of the input sequence, Sloane showed her the confirmation key, and they continued through the required information—contact codes, account tier, identification marks. Once the data was finalized, the pedestal gave a short series of flashes before emitting a soft chime.

Sloane carefully removed the card and handed it back. "This card is now fully initialized. You'd then stamp it with relevant info—name, origin, and membership level—and store it securely. This particular card will mark my account as originating in Marketbol."

She turned back to the group, her voice gaining energy. "Now, here's a very important part: if I travel to another city—say, Swanbrook—and their pedestal doesn't have my account information, my runecard will prompt their system to pull it from the Marketbol database."

She led them to the second terminal. "This terminal," she said, "is for teller stations. You'll want one of these at every customer-facing desk. A staff member would request the member's card, insert it into the slot, then ask the member to place their hand over the sensor for identity verification."

She placed her card into the reader and demonstrated. "Once the system confirms the match, it will display the account information. The teller can then perform minor account functions using these buttons—numeric inputs and function keys. You can add or remove funds, add authorized users, or update member details."

Sloane pressed a few keys, pulling up a new prompt. "For example, I'm going to add Miss Elodie Romaris here as an authorized user. She'll be able to act on behalf of House Reinhart using this card—or even *without* it—since the pedestal now recognizes her as part of the account."

The pedestal gave a soft pulse of light as the system updated. "This change will now propagate to every pedestal connected to the network," Sloane explained. "Rather than constantly updating every single terminal across the Banking Guild, we only need to update each pedestal. They, in turn, will synchronize across the system."

She looked up and grinned. "So, every time I access my funds in Swanbrook, my account syncs and stores to my card. When Elodie updates our account here in Marketbol, that data is pulled down into the network and reflected everywhere else. Instant, secure, and accurate." She rested her hand on the pedestal, the faint hum of mana echoing beneath her fingertips. *For everything else . . . there's Runecard.*

Sloane pointed to a second card slotted discreetly into the side of the pedestal, just beneath the keyboard. "This right here is critical. It's the security card slot. Each authorized staff member will be issued a personalized card—keyed to their mana signature. Without one of these inserted, the pedestal won't function."

She met the Banking Guild officials' eyes, her tone firm. "You'll generate these directly from the pedestal when you set it up. For now, this card is temporary and will be destroyed after we issue the official one to your branch manager."

The high elf inclined his head respectfully. "This is incredibly well-thought-out, Lady Reinhart. Thank you. Would it be possible to run through the process a few more times? We've brought several accounts for testing."

"Of course!" Sloane said, nodding. "We can go through it for everyone you'd like. Once we're done, I'll head over and help your team get everything set up."

The telv woman with the notebook raised her hand slightly. "Lady Reinhart, how many teller terminals are currently available?"

Sloane glanced upward in thought, tallying the figures in her mind. "We've completed fifteen so far. I believe the branch here in Marketbol has . . . twenty teller stations?"

"Yes, Lady Reinhart," the woman confirmed.

"Then fifteen will do for now," the high elf replied smoothly.

With that, Sloane moved into full teaching mode. She walked each person through the steps again—setup, authentication, and basic account management—answering questions patiently and clearly. As the demonstrations concluded, a new team of guards arrived to begin transporting the equipment to the Guild's main office.

Before they left, Sloane handed the high elf a bound notebook. "This contains everything Orthan and I wrote down—an instruction manual for each system. If your staff gets stuck, it should cover every use case."

The elf accepted it with both hands, bowing his head slightly. "Thank you again, Lady Reinhart. When should we expect you at the branch?"

"Give me a few—"

One of House Reinhart's senior guardsmen, Gregor, rushed into the Runic Hall, breathless and flushed. "My lady! Your presence is requested—urgently." Everyone turned to look at the man, whose chest was heaving.

Sloane held up a calming hand. "Catch your breath."

He nodded and straightened. Sloane glanced at the high elf, then sighed softly. "It seems I must apologize again. I don't know when I'll be able to meet with you personally, but I'll arrange for support."

Adaega stepped forward before the elf could speak. "Lady Reinhart, Elodie and I can go with the Guild's people. You've shown me the test version. I know how it all works. And now we have the manual too."

Sloane gave her a grateful look. "Are you sure?"

Elodie nodded in agreement. "We've got this. Don't worry."

"Very well." Sloane exhaled and looked at the high elf. "I'll leave the rest in their care. If you need anything, just reach out to me directly."

A round of acknowledgments and thanks followed as Adaega and Elodie turned their attention to coordinating with the Guild staff.

Sloane stepped aside with Gregor, guiding him a few paces away for privacy. Her voice dropped. "Alright, you've caught your breath. What's going on?"

Gregor nodded, more composed now. "A moon elf named Cerulean showed up. He's currently speaking with Ser Ernald. I was ordered to find you immediately. He says he has vital information."

Sloane's expression sharpened. Gregor hesitated just a moment longer, then leaned in and whispered, "He says he's found the Vlaredian woman."

Her heart slammed in her chest. *Finally.*

CHAPTER THIRTY-FOUR

OUTMANEUVERED

Gregor left Sloane at the entrance to the meeting room, to return to his post. She went in and was unsurprised to find the usual suspects gathered. Gisele and Nemura stood alert, while Stefan leaned against a wall near the window, arms crossed. At the far end of the room, in front of the cold fireplace, was Cerulean, the moon elf spy. He stood with that infuriating calmness he always wore, like he already knew the end of the story and simply hadn't decided when to tell it.

Everyone seemed poised, the air tense with anticipation. Sloane could feel it immediately—this wasn't a social visit.

Gisele spotted her first and gave a short nod. "Sloane—good, you're here. Now we can begin."

Sloane nodded back, stepping further into the room and letting the door close behind her. She directed her gaze at the moon elf. "Cerulean, welcome. I was told you have information for us?"

The elf inclined his head smoothly. "I do. During one of my usual late-night strolls—you know, as one does in times of war—"

"After curfew? Hmm," Nemura muttered.

Cerulean ignored her, his eyes on Sloane. "—I came across a rather curious sight. A group of soldiers slipping out of an otherwise empty warehouse. It caught my attention. Naturally, as a concerned citizen of this besieged city, I thought it prudent to investigate—"

Sloane cut him off with a sigh. "Cerulean, please. Save us the dramatics."

He gave her a flat look, letting the silence stretch just long enough to be mildly irritating. "Fine," he said at last. "Yes, your elusive Vlaredian Fist has a way through the wall. Or they're holing up in that warehouse. Based on its placement along the wall, I'd bet on the former. I do recall an alleged smuggler who may have used a tunnel in the area."

Without further preamble, he pulled a scroll from inside his coat and walked over to the table at the center of the room. Unrolling it, he revealed a detailed map of the city, complete with markings and several circles drawn in red ink.

Sloane stepped forward, eyes scanning the contents, then groaned, lifting a hand to cover her face.

"Cerulean," she muttered, exasperated. "You're not *supposed* to show evidence of your clandestine work to people outside your organization. This is literally a spy's map." She gestured at the map. "Are these *patrol routes*? You're showing us *every* place you've been watching."

Cerulean looked unbothered, though his brow twitched in annoyance. "You're not a city official, Lady Reinhart. You have a Westari in your service. You owe no loyalty to Marketbol—at least none that precludes sharing a few red circles."

"That's not the point!" she snapped, then immediately shook her head. "You know what? Never mind. Where is the warehouse?"

With a smug flick of his fingers, he tapped a spot on the map just along the northern stretch of the outer wall. "Here."

Gisele and Nemura leaned in, scrutinizing the location. After a moment, they both nodded.

"We've got it," Nemura said calmly, her tone diplomatic. "Thank you, Cerulean. Your assistance in this matter is appreciated."

The moon elf straightened, the barest glimmer of satisfaction on his face. "Then I'll take my leave." He started to leave but paused just beside Sloane. He leaned in slightly, voice low and cool.

"I know what they say about us, Lady Reinhart. But we do try to do our duty. We train from childhood to be killers, not spies. We're given our new name only after we're told that gathering information now serves our country better than a Blade ever could."

Sloane met his eyes without flinching. "Then your government has failed you, Cerulean. If your enemies, or even the cities you operate in, had any sense, they'd have already taken you into custody."

He gave a small, humorless laugh. "Perhaps. But we're not quite as inept as we pretend to be. You think we want this role? The few of us who are good at it are taken from the one we were meant for. Most of the time, it's easier to learn from the dead than to chase whispers. But there is one thing you should know: we are never truly alone in the city we operate within."

He stepped back, offering a final parting glance. "Good luck in your hunt, Lady Reinhart. It sounds . . . tantalizingly full of challenges."

And without waiting for dismissal, he swept from the room with the same dramatic flair that always seemed to follow him.

Sloane let out a breath and turned to the others. "So," she said, "what now?"

Nemura folded her arms, her gaze hard. "Now we wait for the right moment to strike. Ser Deryk, will you accompany me to observe the location?"

He nodded once. "Of course."

"We don't inform the city's army until we're certain," Gisele said. "If the

Empire's Fist catches wind of this, they'll disappear again. No one from House Reinhart who's been briefed on this speaks of it."

"I'll talk to Gregor," Ernald added. "He's the only one who knows. I trust he won't breathe a word."

Sloane inhaled deeply, steadying herself. "Then it's time. Time for the hunters . . . to become the hunted." Her voice was cold steel, sharper than it had been in weeks.

Stefan exchanged a glance with Nemura before addressing Sloane. His expression was firm. "Until it's time to strike, you and I will train together."

Just over a week had passed since they'd uncovered the location of Ressa's hideout. The days that followed had been consumed by meticulous planning and tight-lipped coordination. While the city's army had been given a glimpse of her strategy, Sloane had deliberately kept the finer details—this critical first step—under wraps. She couldn't risk even the possibility of Ressa catching wind of what was coming.

Sloane stood in the narrow shadow of an alley across from the warehouse, flanked by Cristole, Ismeld, and a liaison officer from the army. The night air was still. The building sat quiet and isolated, its proximity to the outer wall making it the perfect infiltration point, and the perfect trap.

Deryk had already taken his position nearby, tasked with signaling when their targets entered the structure. A second surprise awaited once this piece of the plan was executed. Sloane had a crucial role in the next phase, and once she played her part here, she would have to move quickly.

The city officer beside her shifted, his voice barely above a whisper. "General Irileth would like to express his irritation that you waited so long to inform him of this discovery."

Sloane didn't take her eyes off the warehouse. "And if I had told him earlier, would he have shouted it from the ramparts?"

"They clearly have a way of learning these things," Ismeld said softly, her tone sharp. "Whether it's spies or something else, we can't take the risk. But we know they'll be in that building tonight."

Sloane nodded and took a steadying breath. "The building stands alone. I'm going to hit it with almost everything I've got."

She began pulling mana into herself, her core flaring with power. Her fingers tingled as the energy gathered, waiting for the signal.

The liaison's eyes widened in alarm. "Lady Reinhart, I don't think—"

A sharp noise echoed from their flank. Everyone froze.

That was Deryk. "They're here."

Without hesitation, Ismeld reached for her belt and pulled off two grenades. She drew back her arm and threw. They arced silently through the air.

Sloane inhaled sharply and pulled more mana into herself, stacking spell after spell in her mind. She didn't have time to hesitate. The moment the grenades went off, the warehouse would erupt and the window to move would begin closing.

Across the street, a pair of horses waited, her transportation for the second phase of the plan.

Now it was up to her to bring down the hammer.

Ressa moved quietly through the narrow tunnel that connected their concealed entryway to the warehouse. She climbed up into the small side room, her movements practiced and silent. As planned, her team had already begun checking the perimeter from within the building. They moved methodically between the narrow windows, taking care not to expose themselves.

She crossed to the usual spot and focused her mana, conjuring the ladder that would give them access to their hidden crawlspace above. Behind her, Alexi tapped the shoulder of their telv medic, Algor, and motioned toward the opening. One by one, they began the climb.

Ressa stepped aside, heading toward the center of the room to assess. One of her men was peering through a cracked window, eyes scanning the street.

"Anything?" she asked in a low voice, her tone tight.

The man turned just slightly. "No, I don't see—"

The words barely left his mouth before the glass beside another soldier shattered inward. A small object thudded against the wooden floor, coming to a stop near his boot.

"What—?"

They all stared at it for a beat too long. Glowing symbols flickered along the surface. Ressa's eyes widened in horror. *No—*

The device exploded. Purple light and raw force tore through the room, flinging Ressa backward. Agonizing heat and pressure slammed into her chest. She hit the ground hard, a cry ripping from her throat. Another crash of shattering glass sounded.

"Look out!" Alexi shouted.

She rolled, trying to shield her head. A body slammed over her—someone covering her. The second explosion rocked the building. The body on top of her was ripped away, thrown aside like a ragdoll.

Ressa groaned, struggling to push herself upright. Her vision swam. Ears ringing. Breath short. *What just—?*

Darkness swirled in the corners of the ruined room. *Focus. Focus!* She reached for her magic, pulling desperately at the mana around her. *I need to see. I need to see!* Mana flooded her vision, too bright at first, but quickly sharpening. She blinked hard, the warehouse suddenly lit by the pulse of her spell. Dust filled the air, thick and choking. What was left of her team was scrambling through the debris. Then she felt it. *Mana. Rushing. Growing.* Her breath caught.

"We need to get out!" she gasped.

Alexi and Algor were dragging the only other man still on his feet toward the tunnel. Ressa forced herself to her feet, drawing more mana, trying to form a defensive wall.

Too slow. A bolt of purple energy slammed into the outer wall with a deafening crack. Then another. And another.

The force rattled her bones. Arcane power surged—raw, unmistakable. *Her.*

"It's her! Come on!" Alexi shouted. The fourth blast tore through what remained of the weakened wall.

Ressa braced herself, expecting another barrage as she waited for Alexi and the medic to lower their wounded comrade into the tunnel. But nothing came. *They're trying to capture us.*

Two steel orbs clattered through a shattered window, then erupted. Twin flashes of blinding light and sharp, concussive cracks slammed into her senses. Ressa winced and ducked her head, but her mana-infused vision spared her from full blindness. Her ears rang, muffling everything around her. As the light cleared, she turned, scanning the room for her people.

Bodies lay scattered like discarded dolls. The soldier who had shielded her was impaled, his body pinned to the wall by a jagged plank of wood. Ressa snarled and thrust her hand forward, casting her twin spells. A wall of conjured stone rose to protect them with a shimmer of mana just as more explosions shook the building. Smaller, tighter blasts this time—focused. Controlled.

Then silence.

Dust settled around her. No voices. No footsteps. *They're repositioning.* She knew Algor, their medic, was still in the tunnel, tending to the wounded man. She would buy them time. She had to.

A thunderous crash sounded at the far end of the warehouse: a door blasted inward. More magic tore through the air. Ressa heard shouts, then Alexi's voice, calling for her.

"Ressa! Move!"

She didn't hesitate. She turned and jumped down the tunnel, landing hard but balanced. Alexi was already leading them out. They sprinted through the narrow passage, breath ragged, every second precious. At the exit, he turned and swept the area, giving her room to emerge.

Ressa pulled herself into the open and froze. The twin moons were hidden behind thick clouds, casting the city in a blanket of darkness. It should have offered her relief. Safety. But instead, she saw the trap.

One of her men, Nethaniel, stood ready, axe raised, shield angled. Not far off, Algor stood between the injured man and the rest of the world, sword drawn.

A voice echoed into the night, low and mocking. "Our previous fight was not complete before you took flight."

Ressa's breath caught. She didn't need to see the source to know. *Nemura.* She reacted instantly, thrusting her hand forward and cast her twin spells—[**Create Illusion**] and [**Alter Conjuration**]—launching a storm of metal shards toward the sound.

A barrier of shimmering red flared into view, absorbing the attack. Behind it stood the traitor herself: Nemura Kho'lin. Next to her, emerging like a ghost from the gloom, was the orkun knight, Gisele Devereaux. *The Blighter.*

The knight stepped forward, her massive *Zweihänder* gleaming, and raised her left hand. The red mana shielding it pulsed and crackled, illuminating the grim smile on her face. "Amusing," Gisele said. "I was going to say the same thing."

Ressa scanned for others, but no more figures emerged. If this was a trap, it was a small one, or well hidden. She turned her head just enough to speak to Algor. "Get him to safety. Alexi and I will handle this."

The medic hesitated only a second before nodding and moving to lift the wounded man.

Alexi joined her, drawing his mace with practiced ease. His gaze locked onto Nemura. "Nethaniel and I will take the traitor."

Ressa drew her sword, her own eyes fixed on the tall knight. "Then I'll take the Blighter."

The two women before them grinned, their expressions feral. If Ressa were any less, she might have flinched. But she was Empire's Fist. Let them come.

Gisele swept her left hand through the air, and her shield collapsed in a shimmer of red light.

One moment, Nemura was still, and the next, she was slamming her shoulder into Nethaniel's shield with a crash. The man grunted as he skidded backward. Before Nemura could press the advantage, Alexi launched himself into her path, his mace already swinging.

With her target in sight, Ressa acted. She conjured three illusionary arrows and loosed them at the knight. Gisele raised her arm and summoned a red shield—small, buckler-sized, but effective. The arrows struck and vanished harmlessly. The knight's eyes flicked in brief surprise, exactly what Ressa needed.

She surged forward, closing the gap and swinging her sword in a vicious arc. Gisele jumped back, her *Zweihänder* still at the ready, and met Ressa's charge with a counterattack. Their blades clashed, steel singing against steel in a fierce, flurried exchange.

Ressa struck low in a feint, parried a return swing, and thrusted with precision only for another conjured shield to flash into existence between them. Her blade skidded off it with a shriek, and she stumbled as she tried to recover. Another shield burst into being near her foot, and despite her efforts, Ressa couldn't avoid tripping.

Even as she hit the ground, she called up a surge of mana and conjured a flurry of metal arrows. They launched toward Gisele in a staggered wave, forcing the knight to raise another shield and dig in.

Tucking her body, Ressa rolled with the momentum and sprang back to her feet in a smooth motion. She took a deep breath, reset her stance, and locked eyes with her opponent as they began to circle. Gisele moved with a practiced fluidity now. Her coordination with mana was sharper, more refined than before.

She's been training, Ressa noted. *She wasn't this smooth last time.*

A horn sounded in the distance. Ressa's lips curled into a knowing smirk. "Your time is limited. We own everything outside the walls."

Gisele barked a laugh. "I have plenty of time to finish this."

But then the sky lit up in a brilliant wash of purple. An explosion cracked through the night, distant but distinct. Another followed. Ressa's eyes flicked upward just in time to see a blazing sphere of purple energy arcing high above the city. At its peak, it paused, then accelerated downward. She lost sight of it behind the wall, but the resulting blast shook the ground beneath their feet. It came from the direction of the second Vlaredian camp. *No!*

Gisele's voice dripped with satisfaction. "While you were focused on us, Sloane focused on your army."

Another horn blared, closer this time. They all turned. From the field beyond, Vlaredian riders were charging. Reinforcements. Ressa smiled. She seized the moment and conjured a volley of metal darts, sending them hurling at the knight. Another red shield flared to life, catching the attack.

But Gisele's smugness had faded. "Nemura! We need to go!" she shouted.

"I'm a little busy!" came the curt reply.

The large telv woman was locked in a brutal melee with both Alexi and Nethaniel. Despite her strength and precision, Ressa knew it was only a matter of time. They didn't need to defeat her. They just needed to hold her until the cavalry arrived.

With urgency pounding in her chest, Ressa charged toward them. Gisele moved to block her path with another conjured shield, but Ressa slipped past it with practiced ease. She swung her blade at the knight, her strike colliding with steel as Gisele caught it mid-swing. Ressa pressed forward, forcing the knight to take a retreating step before breaking off and pivoting.

Ressa threw out a hand toward the wall and cast her **[Fractured World]**. A surge of mana erupted as conjured bricks sealed off the tunnel behind them, blocking the escape route before she reached the limit of her spell's range.

Gisele's eyes snapped toward the blockade and narrowed in irritation. But instead of retaliating, she spun and bolted toward her allies.

Ressa cursed and unleashed a volley of conjured arrows at the woman's back. A crimson shield flashed into existence just in time, absorbing the barrage. Another, larger shield quickly followed, cutting off Ressa's pursuit entirely.

Then the tide turned. As the first barrier faded, Gisele whipped her hand toward Alexi and Nethaniel, who were still locked in combat with the traitor. Just as Alexi raised his mace for another strike, a red shield intercepted the blow.

He stumbled, caught off guard, only for another shield to form behind his legs, sending him crashing to the ground. A third flared into place to keep him pinned.

The flash of red magic pulled Nethaniel's attention for just a heartbeat. It was all Nemura needed. She surged forward, shield braced, and slammed into him. The young orkun managed to get his own shield up, but the blow rattled him, nearly knocking him off balance.

Ressa growled in fury and summoned another barrage of arrows. She raised them high and fired over Gisele's barriers, targeting the telv traitor. But Gisele moved fast, releasing the shield pinning Alexi and conjuring a fresh one to catch the arrows mid-flight.

The shield in front of Ressa shimmered and vanished. She didn't hesitate, sprinting toward her comrades.

Gisele stepped in, kicking Alexi hard across the face before lunging forward. She raised her hand again, and Ressa dove to the side, narrowly evading yet another crimson shield slamming into the ground where she had been.

"Nethaniel!" Ressa shouted.

The young man turned toward her, but too late. Nemura closed in, slicing a brutal line across his thigh. He bellowed in pain and staggered. Gisele wasted no time, spinning around him and plunging her sword into his back with a precision honed by years of battle. Nethaniel dropped, and did not move again.

But Gisele didn't press toward Ressa or Alexi. Instead, she called out to Nemura, and the two women turned and sprinted for the wall.

Ressa cried out, unleashing another flurry of arrows. One caught Nemura in the side, drawing a gasp. She stumbled and almost dropped. A shield snapped into place behind her, catching the next volley. Without pause, Gisele lifted a hand. Ressa froze.

Steps of glowing red energy materialized midair, a radiant staircase climbing toward the top of the city wall. Ressa could only stare, momentarily stunned by the impossible magic. The two women began to ascend, bounding up the conjured path as if they weighed nothing at all.

Snarling, Ressa shook off the shock and launched spell after spell in rapid succession. Arrows and shards screamed through the air, but Gisele's shields and Nemura's agile form kept them unscathed.

Frustrated beyond words, Ressa dropped her sword and raced to intercept the glowing path.

"Ressa, look out!" Alexi's voice rang out, sharp with urgency.

At the edge of her vision, she caught movement—a ballista swiveling, its barrel slowly aligning with their position. Her heart lurched. Eyes wide, she spun and thrust out a hand, conjuring a wall of stone between them and the siege weapon. The instant it solidified, a bolt launched with a thunderous crack. It punched through her wall like it was paper.

Ressa dove to the side. The bolt struck the ground behind her, then exploded.

She was weightless. Her world flipped and tumbled, the rush of air tearing at her clothes as her vision blurred into darkness. A moment later, the world returned with brutal clarity as she slammed into the ground, pain flaring across her side.

A pair of hands grabbed her. Alexi. He pulled her to her feet with a grunt. "We need to get out of range!"

Horns wailed across the field again, sharp, piercing notes that rattled her already dazed senses. Ressa looked up just in time to see the siege weapon adjusting again, this time locking onto the approaching cavalry. The riders, scattered and maneuvering, were already reacting, trying to outrun the line of fire. Men and mounts screamed as glowing bolts launched one after another, striking the ground in devastating arcs. Fire and smoke blossomed in their wake.

Ressa and Alexi bolted, sprinting toward the riders. Another blast of sound, another bolt arced into the sky. Around them, the battlefield trembled under the weight of magic and fire.

One of the riders leaned low from his saddle, reaching out. Ressa leapt, caught his arm, and used the momentum to swing herself up onto the back of the horse behind him. She landed roughly, gripping the man's armor as the horse thundered forward. Beside her, Alexi had managed the same, though he was hunched, holding his side, injured. But still alive. They were the only ones.

Explosions continued to rock in the distance, echoing from the direction of the second fortified camp. Fire lit up the horizon like a festival gone mad.

"What's happening?" Ressa yelled over the rush of wind.

"The Sovereign reinforcements are here!" the rider shouted back. "The terran—she rode out the gate with a force of riders and attacked the second camp! She's tearing it apart!"

Ressa's stomach dropped. *No . . .*

"We need to get back," she said, voice low, dangerous. "I need to speak with the general—now."

The rider gave a sharp nod and snapped the reins harder. The horse responded, surging ahead with renewed speed. Ressa clung tightly and looked over at Alexi, whose face was tight with pain. Her people. Her squad. Gone.

This entire campaign has been a complete failure.

Sloane kept casting, her hands flowing through spell after spell, the ground around her scorched with mana residue. The Vlaredian army was breaking, pulling back from their demolished forward camp, retreating toward the bulk of their main force. She could see it in their movement: disorder replacing discipline. Panic. The second fortified camp was all but annihilated.

Flanked by a sizable force of city soldiers, along with nearly every member of her house besides Gisele and Nemura, Sloane pressed the offensive. The enemy had not expected a full assault—certainly not from a city under siege. That was their first mistake.

She had pounded the camp with successive artillery spells, arcane shells of condensed mana. Each one had been more refined than the last. After the fifth, something inside her had shifted. She'd felt a surge, a rush of understanding, a clarity of purpose. Her spell's intent had snapped into alignment with her desire. Her magic had evolved—no, it felt like more than that. It felt as if her spell had *upgraded*.

She tightened her grip around her focus, and narrowed her eyes. *I need to study this . . . but later. First, we finish this.* Above her, Tiberius screeched.

"Yes, we're almost there," Sloane called back, voice loud over the distant shouting and clash of steel. "Get up high. Scout the camp. Let me know if there are stragglers. Then we move in."

With a shriek of steel and wind, the mechanical falcon leapt into the sky, wings pumping as he ascended and veered toward the smoking ruins of the enemy encampment.

Sloane exhaled slowly, keeping her mana circulating just beneath her skin. Her eyes remained on the distant silhouettes scrambling to regroup. She'd joined the strike force immediately after launching her barrage at the warehouse in the city—a calculated deception to force Ressa and her squad out of hiding. Nemura and Gisele had waited in ambush, ready to strike. The whole maneuver had been Nemura's idea, and Sloane couldn't help but appreciate the woman's tactical cunning.

Only regret? Not seeing Ressa's face when she realized she'd been played.

But the true victory tonight wasn't in the warehouse. It was here, on the open field. The tide of the war, long stagnant, was finally shifting. The Sovereigns had outmaneuvered the Vlaredians at last. Reinforcements from the city of Barith had moved into position. The enemy's chances of retreat were growing slimmer by the hour.

It had taken weeks of planning, countless messages delivered by Tiberius, and a delicate balancing act of secrecy and misdirection. But it had worked. With General Irileth's guidance, they had coordinated a path for the reinforcements to bypass expected routes and catch the Vlaredian army off guard.

They'd even staged an entire fake encampment to sell the illusion. Scouts had watched the decoy force settle in for the night, completely unaware that the real army had marched through the darkness, bypassing the known roads and scouting points, many of which Tiberius had identified ahead of time.

And now, with their flank exposed and their second camp under siege, the Vlaredians were faltering.

General Irileth believed the enemy's main force would still manage to retreat—barely—but they would bleed for every step they took. That was why Sloane and her team were here: to break them down, to scatter their forces, to delay them. It might not win the war outright, but it would cripple the Empire's campaign here in the west. And it would show the world that Marketbol—and those who defended it—would *not* be broken.

Sloane felt the pull of mana surge again through her fingers, ready for the next cast. Her heart pounded, but not from fear.

She activated her **[Golem Sight]**, choosing to connect directly through her spell rather than using the runic interface built into her watch. Her vision shifted. Tiberius's sensors came online, and her world became his: high above the battlefield, scanning the shattered remains of the second Vlaredian camp.

"Sloane, pay attention," Ismeld said quietly from her side.

"I am. Searching," she murmured, her voice distant as she maintained the spell, not bothering to turn her head.

Tiberius circled once, then held position in the air above her. Through his perspective, she spotted another small formation moving through the rubble—troops trying to escape unnoticed. Sloane reached for her mana, drawing deeply as she prepared her next spell. She was still getting used to the upgraded version of her artillery, the evolved form of her old **[Arcane Explosion]**.

The change had been subtle at first. But after repeated use, combined with the sheer scale of destruction she'd wrought, the spell had shifted. It was no longer simply a burst of force. It had grown into something far more devastating, far more focused. She had dubbed it **[Arcane Mortar]**. It wasn't just more powerful. It *wanted* to destroy.

Not the time to theorize, Sloane . . .

She inhaled sharply and drew the mana into her core. Even from the elevated vantage of Tiberius, she could feel the arcane lines twist and pulse around her, waiting. Her stamina dipped hard as the spell left her, a surge of power that shot skyward in a steep arc.

The orb of condensed arcane force blazed through the night sky, larger and faster than its predecessor. As it reached its apex, it flared with energy, then abruptly adjusted its path, homing in on the fleeing soldiers. The air itself pulsed as the spell accelerated downward.

The impact rocked the earth. A violet flash lit the night, followed by an explosion that consumed the squad in a maelstrom of magic and flame. It was half again as strong as her previous iteration.

Sloane blinked, breath catching in her throat. *I definitely can't cast many of those.*

As Tiberius resumed his patrol, she saw the enemy breaking. The main Vlaredian force was in full retreat, soldiers scattering in every direction. She spotted a group on horseback fleeing from the far side of the city.

She narrowed her eyes. *They're coming from where Gisele and Nemura were.* Sloane released the spell, her vision returning to her own eyes just as the city's soldiers surged forward, charging toward what was left of the enemy camp.

"Ismeld," she said, voice firm, "we need to get to Gisele."

The high elf knight nodded, already turning. Together, they pivoted to rush back toward the city, but what they saw made them pause mid-step. There, above the ruined field, suspended high above the wall, stood two figures atop a shimmering red platform. Gisele and Nemura. Hovering in midair like goddesses of war, framed by the moonlight and mana.

"What in the hell?" Sloane breathed.

Ismeld groaned. "She is such a show-off."

From the walls and streets beyond, the sound of cheering erupted, waves of voices carried on the wind, full of relief, triumph, disbelief. The moment struck Sloane in the chest, heavy and exhilarating all at once. She laughed. The tension that had wrapped itself around her spine for weeks loosened just a little. *We won.*

She turned to look at those around her. Stefan, the knights, her guards, people who had stood beside her through it all. They had come so far, grown so much. There was still a long road ahead, but this? This was a turning point.

She caught Stefan's eye and nodded. Then she looked back up at the two women suspended in the sky, glowing with power and presence. A small, confident smile curved her lips.

Time to continue the search. I can't wait to tell you all about my journey, Gwyn.

Ressa shifted in her saddle, eyes narrowed against the warm summer wind. The last three members of her team rode beside her in silence, their expressions grim. A week had passed since they'd broken away from General Razane's retreating army. What remained of the once formidable force now limped toward Goosebourne.

The defeat at Marketbol marked the Empire's first true setback in the war. A wound not just to their military but also to their ambitions in the region. Without the city, the dream of controlling the central plains was crumbling. Ressa could only hope the campaigns elsewhere were faring better.

Her scowl deepened. *Sloane Reinhart.* The woman had single-handedly turned the tide. It was more than luck or clever tactics, Ressa was sure of that. Reinhart must have coordinated with the southern Sovereigns to open a path through territory that should have been impassable, or at least heavily monitored.

And the magic . . . her magic was terrifying. It had been one thing to hear about the terran's abilities from scattered reports, but another thing entirely to witness what she'd done to the second encampment. The scale, the precision—no one person should have such power at their hands. Unfortunately, Ressa suspected that was where the world was going. Doctrine would need to adapt.

The report she'd filed back to the empress had included her own findings, along with General Razane's notes, outlining Reinhart's instrumental role in fortifying Marketbol's defenses, not to mention the enchantments she had developed. All of it had made one thing clear: *this woman was a threat to the Empire's future.*

The moment the report was sent, they had been ordered to move. No time to regroup, no time to mourn their fallen comrades. Their new destination:

Swanbrook. If her sources were correct, it would be Reinhart's next stop. The coastal city was one of the remaining strategic targets along the inner sea, and if Reinhart embedded herself there, the Vlaredian advance in the west could stall completely.

They couldn't let that happen. But a direct confrontation was off the table after what had happened outside the walls of Marketbol. The traitor Nemura Kho'lin had more than proved herself, and the orkun knight, Devereaux, was a brutal force of nature. Ressa's squad had barely escaped that fight alive. Still, she had learned something important: the knights were planning to part ways with Reinhart. If they did, it would change the dynamics completely.

Ressa turned in her saddle and studied her men. Alexi rode just behind her, the conflict plain on his face. The other two looked just as uneasy. The Empire's Fist did not lose often. And when they did . . . it cut deep. But they weren't broken. Not yet.

"Backs straight," Ressa ordered sharply. "We suffered a setback. That is all. But we will adapt."

All three men sat straighter in their saddles.

"From here to Swanbrook, we train. Every spare moment. We saw what the traitor could do, how she used mana to empower her body. You will learn to do the same. If any of you can touch magic, we'll find out now, not on the battle-field. If we need to face them again, we will be ready."

Her voice was firm, full of conviction. "For the glory of the Ror."

The response came as one, steady and resolute, "And the longing of Vlaredia skies!"

A smile pulled at her lips. They weren't done. Not by a long shot. "We will complete our mission. And we will return with honor." Because the Fist thrived under adversity. And this defeat?

It would forge them into something even stronger.

CHAPTER THIRTY-FIVE

DETOURS IN THE JOURNEY

When the world first stirred with magic, those attuned to black mana walked alone. Their power was quiet, patient, and unkind. The earliest accounts speak not of healing or hope, nor of the awe-inspiring fire or ice, but of shadows walking without breath, of curses spoken in silence, and of minds stripped of sanity. But the most feared and misunderstood was the power that tread on Relena's domain . . . Death.

A History of Mana, 184 SA

Sloane stepped into the auditorium of the Reinhart Center. Everyone was gathered, both those preparing to leave and those staying behind. The moment had finally come: it was time for her to go. The knights, plus Nemura and Stefan, had packed their things.

It felt almost bittersweet. But she had to leave. It was the height of summer now, and they had to reach Swanbrook in time to set sail. She would return, one day, with Gwyn.

Sloane took a long moment to scan the hall. She smiled when she noticed Adaega near the front, her fingers laced with Ernald's. The sun elf and the woman from an Africa of another Earth stood contentedly, joyfully together. They'd soon be moving into Sloane's manor. Adaega's radiant smile as she nodded along to whatever Elodie was saying made Sloane's heart lift. They both deserved every bit of happiness they showed.

At a nearby table, Stefan and Nadia sat locked in quiet conversation. At the bar, Rel was making Kemmy a drink, the tall orkun woman gesturing animatedly while her partner listened with amusement. Laughter drifted between them.

Orthan stood by his father in conversation with—Lady Emerys? She drew her brows together. *Why is she here?* She hadn't expected the noblewoman. They'd spoken only occasionally during the siege, both too busy to follow through on their tentative professional interest. Still, Emerys showing up now was intriguing. A future thread worth pursuing.

Perched on her shoulder, Tiberius turned his head, his metal feathers twitching slightly as he observed the room. The little falcon had grown more intelligent over the past few seasons; his gaze was sharper, more focused, as if he truly *saw*. Sloane reached up and gently patted his head. He chirped in acknowledgment, his glowing eyes glinting with awareness.

I wonder if we can make another. Maybe not with that tea, though. I'm not eager to repeat that particular mistake.

"You're doing it again."

Sloane blinked and turned as Nemura joined her.

"What is the term you use?" the telv woman asked. "Creeping? Yes. You are creeping again."

Sloane sniffed. "I am merely surveying my domain, thank you."

Nemura nudged her shoulder, nearly making her stumble. The woman never seemed to understand just how strong she was. Even being hit by an arrow in the fight against Ressa hadn't affected her much. Sloane turned and looked up at her.

"Nemura," she warned, "we talked about this. You're significantly stronger than everyone around you. It's your stats. Please be careful with your strength."

Nemura grunted. "I'm still not sure about this 'system' you keep talking about."

"You saw it yourself at the church—" She paused, as someone approaching caught her eye. She straightened. "Speaking of . . ."

Nemura's tone shifted instantly. "Praetor Shalas. What an unpleasant surprise. To what do we owe the honor?"

The paladin's expression remained unreadable. She stopped just a few paces away, her attention fixed first on Sloane, then the telv knight beside her. "Nemura Kho'lin. Lady Reinhart. You'll be departing soon, yes?"

Sloane offered a curt nod. "Praetor. We'll be leaving soon, yes." *I really don't like her.*

"Good." Shalas crossed her arms. "You're traveling to the Kingdom of Avira, correct?"

Sloane narrowed her eyes. "I don't recall telling you that."

"It wasn't difficult to figure out," the woman replied flatly. "You're not exactly subtle, and you've told more people than you realize. Regardless, the high priest has a request. He would like you to deliver something to the temple in the Kingdom of Rosale, on your way."

"What is it?" Sloane frowned. "And why can't one of your own people handle it?"

Shalas glanced around the room. "Could we speak in private?"

Sloane started to respond, but Nemura gently touched her shoulder. "We'll hear you out, Praetor," she said.

Sloane sighed but nodded, gesturing toward one of the adjoining rooms. "This way." As she led the two women aside, she caught Gisele's eye across the room. The knight quirked an eyebrow in question. Sloane rolled her eyes and gave a small shake of her head. Gisele sighed theatrically and nodded, making Sloane smile despite herself.

There were a few people conversing in the side room, but as soon as the three women entered, the occupants quietly excused themselves. Sloane offered a warm thanks as they passed. Once the door shut behind them, Nemura took up her post near it, leaning against the wall and crossing her arms. The look she gave the praetor wasn't quite threatening, but only because Sloane knew her.

Shalas stopped mid-step and cast a brief glance back at the big telv before scoffing under her breath. "I've seen the Excerpt of your Journey, Miss Kho'lin. Please don't assume your steps will be enough."

Sloane groaned, loudly and pointedly. "Ugh, I hate that phrasing. Just say what it is: a status screen. 'Excerpt of your Journey' . . . *Honestly.*" She made a mental note, *again*, to figure out how to replicate her watch. *When*, not if, she succeeded, she'd give people a way to see their screens without the church's overblown dramatics.

Nemura just smirked, unbothered by the jab. Sloane shook her head fondly. She remembered the woman's 'Excerpt' from their last visit to the temple.

Nemura Kho'lin
"The Stalwart"
Telv
Path: Stalwart Warrior (Fighter)
Steps: 36
Core Quality: Remarkable
Alignment: Physical
Key Attribute: Constitution

Plenty enough to flatten most threats. Sloane knew that it irked the paladin to be so far behind her and Nemura—at least, from the numbers she knew the woman had during the winter. While she knew that the paladin would still kick *her* ass in a fight since Sloane, as a caster, had a mental alignment, it was not so certain when it came to Nemura. The woman's stats, from what Sloane could tell, were high when it came to physicality. The former Empire's Fist could likely overcome the paladin's skill through sheer stats.

Posturing aside, Sloane decided to steer the conversation back on track so they could return to the others. "So, what did you wish to speak to us privately about?"

The paladin recovered from whatever personal squabble had momentarily distracted her and turned fully to face Sloane. "We would like to formally request that you escort one of our priestesses-in-training to the temple in Calling."

Nemura's eyes widened, and she pushed off the wall, her casual lean vanishing as she stood to full height. "Praetor Shalas, that . . . that is something typically reserved for the Paladins of Alos, is it not?"

Shalas nodded gravely. "It is. But with the war spreading through the region, I was forced to send my paladins out to reinforce nearby temples as the army advanced. There are only four others besides me still in Marketbol. I have no one else to spare."

"Why does she need to leave *now?*" Sloane asked.

"With the unrest within the city, we feel that should certain . . . circumstances come to light, she would be in danger. The high priest would like to get her out of the city as soon as possible to alleviate any future misunderstandings or incidents."

That got Sloane's attention. *What could possibly be wrong with the girl that would have them worried?* She knew that historically on Earth some noble families would send young girls and women who were "problematic" to nunneries to let them live out their lives in seclusion. And thus out of their hair. *Could it be something like that?*

Shalas let out a long breath, tension flickering across her face. "I do not particularly like you, Lady Reinhart. The high priest does—and I acknowledge that you are trustworthy. This request comes from him directly, and while I would prefer otherwise, my personal feelings cannot stand in the way of my duty. Further, you are a mother, which was another reason the high priest believes you are a good choice."

Sloane blinked at the woman's admission. Unexpected, but not unwelcome. "What . . . what does being a mother have to do with anything? What exactly does that have to do with escorting a priestess?"

Shalas met her gaze, her voice quieter now. "Because she is thirteen. Her birthday is in early autumn."

Sloane's breath caught.

"You want us to escort a *child* over half a thousand kilometers to Calling?" Nemura asked, her voice edged with disbelief. "While a war is going on."

"Yes," Shalas said, her tone steady but lacking its earlier conviction. "I would not ask this of you if there were another way. She will be given plain clothes to blend in, and she has been thoroughly instructed to follow your commands without question."

So they'd already told the girl. Sloane glanced at Nemura, catching the flicker of conflict in her expression. She didn't need to ask; Nemura was likely already thinking through the logistics and risks.

Still, Sloane knew she had to ask the question no one else would. "Not to sound callous, but . . . what do we gain from this?"

Praetor Shalas narrowed her eyes slightly, clearly scrutinizing her. Sloane knew she didn't fit neatly into their cultural or religious expectations—being terran had that effect. But this wasn't about disrespect; it was about pragmatism. She wasn't bound by their doctrines, and she needed to safeguard her people.

Finally, Shalas spoke. "We will work with your Center to teach the method for accessing an individual's Excerpt—if you swear to hold the knowledge as a house secret."

Sloane tilted her head thoughtfully, then nodded once. "That is acceptable. However, I want a written manual of the process as well. Something I can preserve. My house must be able to set up this system wherever needed." She hesitated, her gaze flicking to Nemura. *Do I try to involve them? Is it safe?*

Nemura caught it immediately and stepped forward, her voice respectful but firm. "Praetor Shalas, if you'll allow us a moment? I would like to speak privately with my liege."

The paladin inclined her head and silently stepped out of the room.

As the door clicked shut, Sloane let out a quiet breath. "Well. That was unexpected."

"Sloane, what is it?"

"Do you trust the Church?" Sloane asked quietly. "The various churches in my world weren't always trustworthy. If they found Gwyn, would they seek to use that knowledge against me? Would they try to use her to control me? Can *I* trust them?"

Nemura opened her mouth to respond but paused. She crossed her arms and began pacing, deep in thought. After a long moment, she turned and gave Sloane a slow, deliberate nod. "I think you can trust her. For all the tension between you two, she's an honorable woman. The high priest too. The Church, generally speaking, has always tried to present itself as a benevolent and neutral power."

Nemura's tone darkened slightly. "But that neutrality may be slipping. Since the Flash, they've changed. They believe—truly believe—that the gods are intervening. Whether or not that's true, I don't know. But I do know this: they revere children. Always have. That part of their doctrine hasn't changed."

She shifted her stance, now more rigid. "The Paladins of Alos, however, are a different story. They might be politically neutral, but if a nation defies their decrees, they don't hesitate. They will raise arms, call inquisitions, and pursue their aims with zeal. Only a few nations have ever stood firm against them. The Turest Order in the north is one of them. I'd avoid them, by the way—ally to the Empire or not."

Sloane exhaled shakily. It wasn't an easy answer, but it gave her enough. *Seems like I'm going to have to take a leap of faith.* She gave Nemura a small nod. The woman turned and stepped out to retrieve the paladin.

"Have you made a decision?" she asked evenly.

"I have," Sloane said, lifting her chin. "On one condition. In exchange for escorting your priestess, I want you to send word to every temple under your influence—to help me search for my daughter. I'm putting a great deal of trust in you, Shalas . . ."

The paladin's eyes widened slightly. Clearly, she hadn't expected that. She straightened, and for a moment, Sloane saw the same look of compassion the woman had worn back at the temple. "You have my oath that I will treat this matter with the seriousness it deserves. I . . . I apologize for how I've treated you, Lady Reinhart. If you could write down a description of your daughter—what she looked like, what she was wearing when you both arrived—I'll ensure this remains within the Order and only among those we trust."

She hesitated. "If the archpriestess must be told, then so be it. Before you leave, I'll provide you with a sealed letter to deliver to the temple in Maireharbora—they will ensure Empyrea City gets notified. You'll likely arrive in Avira before any messenger of mine, but I give you my word: this message will be sent to every corner of the continent the Church can reach."

"Thank you, Praetor Shalas," Sloane said. "Have the girl here tomorrow at first light. We leave not long after."

"She will be ready." The paladin's expression softened. "Thank you, Lady Reinhart. Truly. I . . . I can assign one of the temple guards to assist, but—"

Nemura raised a hand. "The fewer people, the better. Your guard wouldn't be prepared for this type of mission. Between Stefan, myself, and the army killer here . . ."

Sloane scowled. "Nemura . . ."

The tall woman rolled her eyes. "You saved a lot of people, Sloane. Your magic will help keep the priestess safe. That's all I'm saying."

Shalas nodded. "She's right. I'll take my leave now. I'll return in the morning with the girl." She offered a formal salute, turned on her heel, and exited the room.

As the door closed, Sloane turned to Nemura. "Are we making the right choice?"

"Yes," the telv said without hesitation. "We just gained the support of the Church in your search. That's a reach you couldn't have achieved alone. This turned out better than expected." She paused. "But . . . don't expect much from Stefan or me when it comes to the girl. I—I'm not good with children."

A small laugh escaped Sloane as she looked up at her. "Really, Nemura? I'd have *never* guessed."

The woman wrinkled her nose. "Rude. But fair."

Sloane gave her a warm smile and gestured toward the door. "Come on, let's go say our farewells."

"I'm going to miss you, Sloane. Thank you . . . for everything you've done for me," Adaega said softly, her eyes shining as she glanced at Ernald.

The knight nodded, his expression solemn yet full of quiet joy. "And thank you for what you've given me. I . . . I've finally found what I've been searching for since we left our home. Without you, I'd never have met Adaega. Together, we'll build a home, one worth protecting."

Sloane beamed at the two of them. "I'm so happy for you both. Please, use the manor for as long as you need. It'll be some time before I return—hopefully with Gwyn. I can't wait for you to meet her. And who knows . . . perhaps by then, you two will have someone small for me to meet as well."

Adaega flushed, and Ernald's eyes widened in surprise. The woman from the Unified Kingdom of Yoruba and Delaney stammered, "W-we'll see! Maybe—if . . . if you want that?" She turned shyly toward Ernald.

The sun elf's expression softened, his smile full of affection. He gently squeezed her hand and raised it to his lips. "To build a family with you . . . to spend all our days together? I would be honored, my love."

Sloane chuckled as Adaega stared at him, utterly speechless. She stepped forward and wrapped the smaller woman in a tight hug, leaning down to whisper, "Stay safe, alright? Take care of everything we're building here. I believe in you, Adaega, completely."

Adaega looked up, her eyes shimmering. "Thank you, Sloane." She laughed, wiping at her cheeks. "Funny, isn't it? Seems like just yesterday, the biggest news was a royal heist in my country's capital. Be careful out there. Find Gwyn quickly. We'll hold down the fort until you're back."

Sloane nodded and stepped back. Ernald embraced her briefly, firm and warm, before returning to Adaega's side, their fingers intertwining again.

"I'll miss you both," Sloane said. Her gaze locked with Ernald's. "Keep everyone safe."

"You know me," he said with a grin. "They'll be safer than the city treasury."

Sloane laughed softly.

Gisele and the others approached to say their farewells to their fellow knight, so Sloane stepped away to give them privacy. That goodbye would be its own kind of difficult.

She made her final rounds throughout the center. Rel teared up almost instantly and crushed Sloane in a bone-cracking hug, which made Kemmy laugh as she offered a much gentler pat on the arm. Sloane gasped for breath once she was free, smiling at both.

Koren, ever the quiet professional, bowed and thanked her for the opportunities, wishing her safe travels.

Elodie cried openly, full of emotion, promising with all her heart to uphold the runecard business. Sloane didn't doubt her for a second.

She gave Stefan extra time with his sister but made sure to thank Nadia as well for her continued dedication to House Reinhart.

Eventually, she found herself back in her manor, sipping tea with Nemura in the quiet of the evening.

"Are we ready?" she asked for what felt like the hundredth time.

Nemura raised a brow. "You've asked that five times already, Sloane. Relax. Everything's prepared. We leave in the morning. Try to sleep."

Sloane set her empty cup down with a groan. "Fine. I'll see you in the morning, Nemura. Good night."

"Good night, milady."

An idle thought flitted across her mind about how it was the first time she'd actually slept in the manor. Sleep found her not long after her head touched the pillow.

The morning was cool, the skies a clear stretch of soft blue. Everything was packed and ready—supplies that would carry them to Swanbrook, the port city where they'd sell the wagons in exchange for passage aboard a ship. Sloane kneaded a persistent knot in her lower back, only to wince when it awakened a second one hiding in her shoulder.

Depending on when they arrived, the knights might leave swiftly. Apparently, ships from Blightwych passed through Swanbrook every couple of weeks, and with Gisele's and Ismeld's credentials, they'd be able to board whichever vessel was available.

Stefan yawned beside her, which, of course, triggered Sloane's own yawn—then Maud's, the redhead performing the act with exaggerated flair and a wide-open mouth. When she caught their stares, Maud simply shrugged, utterly unapologetic.

Everyone had gathered near the two wagons, waiting for the paladins to arrive. When they did, it was with far less ceremony than Sloane had imagined. In hindsight, she should've expected that. Discretion was the goal, after all.

Seeing Praetor Shalas out of uniform was something. Sloane had to admit, the paladin cleaned up well. Shalas wore dark gray breeches tucked into black, knee-high leather boots. A cream-colored doublet, its trim adorned with subtle embroidered patterns, hugged her frame with tailored precision. Her sun-kissed hair was tied into a tight bun, and a hint of eyeliner highlighted her hazel eyes with elegant restraint. The woman was striking. Her hand rested casually on the curved sword strapped at her hip.

Two other sun elves, a man and woman, were similarly dressed and carried large, military-style duffel bags that completed their mercenary-like appearance.

Walking between them was a young raithe girl. She wore a knee-length dark-green tunic cinched with a black belt. Silver embroidery decorated the tunic's edges in delicate swirling patterns. Dark brown trousers and black calf-high riding boots completed her traveling attire. A simple leather backpack was slung over her shoulders, looking more like a soft sack with a flap and clasp. Her long, black hair was braided neatly and draped over one shoulder, and her pale-gray skin made her ice-blue eyes all the more luminous. Sloane noticed the tiny fangs peeking beneath her upper lip.

The girl's gaze darted anxiously between those gathered. When she realized Sloane was observing her, she flinched ever so slightly.

Poor kid's terrified. Mom mode, activate. "Good morning, Shalas! How are you today?" Sloane said brightly, stepping forward.

The paladin almost stumbled, and behind her, Sloane could hear both Nemura and Stefan start coughing, clearly trying to suppress laughter.

"I am well, Lady Reinhart," Shalas replied carefully, her posture ever rigid. "Thank you for having us. Please allow me to introduce priestess-in-training Mariel Lunaris, milady." Shalas gestured to the girl and stepped aside.

Sloane offered a warm smile and took a step forward. "It's an absolute pleasure to meet you, Mariel. I'm Sloane. Shalas here tells me you need a ride to Rosale."

The girl tensed, her shoulders lifting, but she managed a soft, "Y-yes, milady. I am in your care."

Still smiling, Sloane shook her head gently. "None of that 'milady' nonsense, please. Call me Sloane." She crouched slightly to meet the girl's eyes. "Tell me, do you enjoy reading? What about art?"

Mariel blinked, uncertain at first. "I enjoy both reading and art . . . Sloane," she added shyly.

"Wonderful!" Sloane beamed. "I picked up a bunch of books for the journey—stories and histories, things I think you'll really like. I also grabbed some supplies to sketch and paint with, if that's your thing. And . . ." She leaned in conspiratorially, cupping a hand over her mouth. "I brought sweets. We can share them. We just have to make sure Nemura doesn't see. She'll steal them."

Mariel giggled behind her hand, eyes sparkling with the first hint of comfort Sloane had seen from her.

"I would like that," the girl said, voice a little steadier.

And just like that, Sloane thought with a small, proud grin, *I'm winning.*

Sloane gently directed Mariel toward Maud, knowing full well the knight-healer had the best temperament for children. The others not so much. She couldn't help but chuckle as Maud's bubbly warmth enveloped the girl almost immediately. The contrast was night and day; Mariel's nervousness softened in the presence of Maud's easy charm.

Sloane turned back toward Praetor Shalas, who stood watching the young priestess walk away with a faint sadness in her eyes. It was a flash of vulnerability Sloane hadn't expected to see.

Shalas looked at her. "Thank you, Lady Reinhart. For putting in the extra effort to make her feel comfortable."

"Of course," Sloane said. "I know how travel can be for kids. They get bored fast, and let's be honest: adults are the *worst.*"

A soft chuckle escaped the woman, her features briefly lit by the memory of something long past. "Yes, that's true. Adults . . ." She trailed off, then turned, summoning the male paladin beside her.

He stepped forward and handed her a small, locked tome and a key. Shalas passed them to Sloane. "This contains everything we have on the Ceremony of Paths, as well as what we've learned about the process. It's all there. As per our agreement, this is to remain a house secret."

Sloane nodded solemnly. "I understand. I'll treat it with the care it deserves." She paused. "Is there anything else I should know about her? Food allergies, temperament . . . any strange latent magical powers that might manifest in her sleep?"

If Sloane hadn't been paying attention, she might have missed Shalas flinching ever so slightly. *Looks like something I'll need to keep an eye out for.*

"She has a journal," the woman said after a pause. "It's locked. It is to be given to the high priest at the temple. I ask that you respect her privacy. Let it remain hers alone." Shalas retrieved a small scroll from a pocket and gave it to her.

Her companion handed over a sealed scroll, which Shalas indicated with a nod. "And that is the letter to present at the temple in Maireharbora." She handed Sloane two more. "The smaller one details which temple she is to go to. It is a small order within the city, one that will be well suited for her. The larger, sealed one, is for the temple in Calling. Give it to the high priest too when you arrive."

Sloane accepted the scrolls, tucking them securely in her satchel. "Understood. We'll get her there safely. You have my word."

Shalas took a long breath and stepped forward, lowering her voice. "I wish I could send someone with her, but there are too many others who need guarding, too many who still look to me. The rioting in the city has been dying down since the siege broke, but the unrest is still bad. Every day we see more and more people flocking to the temple in need of aid and guidance. It is best that she is away from that."

"I understand," Sloane whispered. "She'll be safe. I won't hesitate to use whatever magic I need to keep her unharmed."

The paladin nodded, a flicker of emotion passing across her face. "Good. Please, allow me a moment to say goodbye. I likely won't get the chance again."

Sloane stepped back, giving Shalas space as Nemura collected the duffel bags from the other paladins and loaded them into the wagon.

When it was finally time to leave, Sloane approached Mariel and placed a hand gently on her shoulder. The girl gave Shalas one last, tight hug before stepping back. The paladins turned to go, but Shalas lingered a moment longer.

She stopped beside Sloane, her voice hushed. "If anything . . . unexplainable happens . . ." She hesitated. "Please don't push her away. She's a wonderful child. She's had more than her fair share of cruelty in this world."

She really might wake up with latent magic. Shit. Sloane met the woman's eyes. "Don't worry. I'll treat her like she's my own. We'll be fine."

Shalas gave one final, lingering look to Mariel, then turned without another word and followed her fellow paladins down the road. Mariel watched them until they vanished from view.

Sloane guided the girl gently toward the wagon. As they moved, a small crowd passed by on the street. Someone brushed against her shoulder and offered a quick apology before vanishing into the throng. Sloane frowned, eyes narrowing for a moment, but then refocused. She helped Mariel into the wagon and settled her in beside Maud.

An hour later, they were out of the city and on the road. The Reinhart Center, and all those who had become her friends and found family, remained behind.

Sloane stretched in her seat, her muscles sore from another long day on the road. The wagon rocked gently beneath her as it rolled along the dirt path. From the front, she could hear Stefan and Nemura talking quietly, likely discussing the terrain ahead or trading sharp-witted banter, as they often did.

Across from her, Mariel lay curled on the opposite bench, nose buried in a book. The girl had grown more at ease in the past few weeks, especially around Sloane. She still kept mostly to herself, but she also seemed to enjoy speaking with Maud. The girl apparently remembered the healer from her many visits to the temple during the siege. While she rarely initiated conversation with the others, she was no longer withdrawn or anxious in their company.

She'd clung to Sloane's side in every village and town they passed through, staying quiet during their stops at taverns. Only once had she been questioned, and with commendable poise, she had simply replied that she was a member of Sloane's house.

That had been when Sloane learned something else about the culture of the Sovereign Cities. Subterfuge was often treated as little more than a white lie, an acceptable social tool when discretion called for it. It wasn't seen as deceit so much as practicality. It was a cultural nuance she was slowly learning to appreciate.

For Sloane, most nights on the road were filled with small comforts: quiet conversations with Gisele, sparring with Nemura, or long hours at her workbench tinkering away. Mariel had taken an eager interest in her late-night crafting, watching with wide, curious eyes as Sloane sketched, carved, and etched. Those moments always made her ache for Gwyn. Her daughter would have loved helping, would have been proud.

Her gaze drifted to the notebook open across her lap. The sketches and runic formulas for a new project had nearly filled the page; the design for the answer to Ismeld's lack of magic was coming together.

Sloane had a stash of ink, ingots, and wood reserved for on-the-road crafting, and the time spent traveling had given her an idea. A prototype she was calling a "caster"—a handheld device that would allow Ismeld to cast spells via premade cartridges, not unlike the enchanted grenades Sloane had developed.

It was, for all intents and purposes, a gun. But instead of bullets, the cartridges stored spells. When the hammer struck, the spell would discharge, amplified by internal gems and powered by a mana crystal embedded in the hilt. A polished opal on the exterior would key the device to Ismeld alone, ensuring no one else could wield it.

So far, Sloane had designed cartridges for two spells: |**Mana Bolt**| and |**Arcane Lance**|, a new spell she'd created specifically for the caster. The cartridges had been surprisingly easy to produce, and she already had two small wooden boxes filled with thirty each. But there was a catch: each cartridge could hold only one spell cast before needing to be removed and recharged. And even then, the longevity of the cartridge varied. |**Mana Bolt**| cartridges could be recharged five times, while |**Arcane Lance**| managed only two before the runes began to degrade. Sloane had attempted to design multi-shot cartridges, but the spells weakened too much in the process. That failure had forced her to begin reworking the caster itself.

But progress was progress. And the final device was nearly ready. She flipped the page and jotted a note under her latest diagram: *Test opal resonance. Refine runework for mana signatures of physically aligned users.*

In the end, Sloane opted for a simpler design for the first model of the caster: a breechloader. Clean, functional, and safe. Incremental improvements could come later, after more testing. She had, after all, learned her lesson the hard way: her first attempt, an ambitious revolver-style cylinder, had literally exploded in a rather dramatic fashion. Having the caster detonate in Ismeld's hand was definitely not acceptable.

Building the actual weapon had proved more challenging than expected, especially with her limited tools on the road, but it wasn't beyond her skill. If she stayed on track, it would be completed before they reached Swanbrook.

Creating a custom spell just for Ismeld had been worth it. The knight had practically beamed when Sloane presented the idea. |**Arcane Lance**| was more refined than |**Mana Bolt**| and significantly more focused than the brute-force chaos of |**Arcane Barrage**|. It required more concentration and control—more scalpel than sledgehammer—but that was the point. It was precise, efficient, and elegant. And best of all, it didn't cause the kind of collateral damage that left entire rooms in rubble.

I need more spells like that. Maybe I should start asking the others for ideas before they part ways.

In addition to the caster, Sloane had also worked on enchanting Ismeld's gauntlets, giving each hand its own magical utility. The left now contained |**Protective Shield**|, Gisele's favored spell, allowing the conjuration of a solid mana buckler. A perfect complement for the high elf's fighting style.

Enchanting the right gauntlet had been trickier. Sloane's limited experimentation with white mana had taught her how to cast a rudimentary version of [**Telekinesis**], though the spell had caused her headaches. The main problem was trying to figure out a way to actually target something. She could slow or lift nearby objects, but trying to pull anything to her from a distance had a frustrating range of only a few centimeters.

Still, it had sparked an idea. By combining the runic version of the spell with a |**Connect**| rune—one she'd recently developed—she'd expanded its potential. Now, Ismeld could yank her sword or caster back to her hand from up to five meters away. Apparently, that particular enchantment had made the knight positively giddy.

All in all, their departure from Marketbol had gone smoothly, and the journey thus far had been quiet. Everyone was in good spirits. Sloane was simply relieved to be back on the road, back to her purpose—the search for Gwyn. The anniversary of the Flash was fast approaching at the end of summer, a frustrating reminder of how long it had been.

Wait . . . I completely forgot about my birthday. She groaned, pinching the bridge of her nose. She was now thirty-five and had been for a while now, but with everything that had happened since arriving on Eona, her Earth birthday had come and gone without so much as a second thought. She'd need to sit down and do the math to figure out what her Eonan birthday even was.

But the distraction faded quickly. Her thoughts, as always, returned to her daughter. A full year on Eona, and not a single lead. There'd been no hint that Gwyn was even alive.

But now the Church was helping, too. If anyone could find her, it would be them. Someone in their network had to have seen a girl like Gwyn. They must have. *Please let someone have seen her.*

Sloane set her notebook aside and closed her eyes, letting the rhythm of the wagon lull her into a moment of calm. Swanbrook was just ahead. From there, they'd make their way to the Kingdom of Avira, with a small detour in Rosale first. She didn't mind. It meant more people to question, more places to search. Truthfully, she had begun to doubt her plan of traveling to Avira. But Shalas did have one good idea, that perhaps contacting the Church's leadership there would be of benefit. Hopefully, all of that would be unnecessary and she would find a lead in Rosale. The small coastal kingdom *was* closer to where she'd first arrived on Eona, after all.

I need to focus on positive thoughts. She nodded to herself. *Don't worry, Gwyn. I'm coming. We'll find you.*

CHAPTER THIRTY-SIX

BACK TO SCHOOL

EARLY SPRING

Reme. The capital of Avira, both the duchy and kingdom. The city itself was millennia old, first settled by exiled high elves during the Loreni Diaspora. When the coastal regions were torn apart by war and infighting among their kin, the Avirans had sought refuge inland. They followed the valleys and rivers until they came upon a broad plain, nestled at the convergence of two great rivers. The land formed a natural triangle, bordered by forests, mountains, and a nearby lake.

It was here they built their city. In time, the Valeni were driven back into their forests, and the Avirans solidified their hold on the region, expanding farther inland. When they finally reached the mountains and had nowhere else to go, they turned back. By then, the coastal regions had long been claimed by others. Kingdoms now sat to the south and west of the Aviran domain. So the Avirans did what many growing powers eventually do: they invaded.

At first, it didn't go well. They lost a significant portion of territory to the Kingdom of Edimiss. But the Avirans were patient. They fortified, built up their armies, and waited. When Edimiss grew weary of the war, the Avirans struck a bargain with the king's brother, who, in turn, withdrew his support from the war effort. Once the Edimissan army was stretched thin and exhausted, the Avirans struck. In the aftermath, the Duchy of Edimiss was born. The brother who betrayed his kin was named duke. The king who had trusted him was executed. That pattern of ruthless expansion continued for centuries.

Eventually, the Avirans found themselves facing a formidable rival: the Kingdom of Tiloral, situated to their southwest. War broke out between the two powers. For a people who had been landlocked for generations, the Avirans were finally looking toward the sea. The Tilorals, though not a coastal power themselves, bordered several smaller nations that did have access to the ocean—nations that were deemed ripe for conquest.

But the Tilorals held the advantage of position. The Avirans were boxed in by three Val Forests, still openly hostile to Loreni nations, and two dwarven exclaves.

Though neutral, the dwarves were fiercely protective of their mountainous territories, and any misstep could have brought ruin.

These factors caused numerous setbacks for the kingdom. But after decades of war, the Tilorals made a surprising choice, one that changed the political landscape of the continent. Instead of continuing the fight, they allied with Avira through a political marriage. Their union shocked every nation on the map. With the Tilorals acting as a spearhead, the newly joined kingdoms expanded rapidly.

Together, they conquered the nearby Kingdom of Marsi, nearly doubling the size of the duchy and granting the Avirans their first access to the sea.

From there, the expansion continued. Over time, the duchies of Lis, Nieth, Levosa, and Soraya were added to the kingdom. Though each of these newer territories would change hands no fewer than three times over the coming centuries—

Gwyn looked up from her book at Mister Branigan. "Why do all the duchies keep changing which families rule them? Why are Tiloral and Edimiss different?" she asked, brow furrowed.

The old sun elf scholar regarded her with an almost melancholic expression. "Edimiss's ruling family has actually changed before," he said gently. "But the difference is that the name 'Edimiss' was never about the family, not like Tiloral. Actually, only two duchies utilize the names of the houses that govern them. For Edimiss, like most others, it's the name of the region itself—the land of lakes and rivers surrounding the capital of Roda Alia."

He paused, thoughtful. "Tiloral is different because the duchy cares for its people. Or—no, that's not quite fair. Let's say that the nobles of other duchies often care more about consolidating their own power and influence. In Tiloral, there's a strong cultural identity that fosters a sense of duty. The people are proud to be from there. Proud of their history, their stability, and strength."

"But what about people like Lord Angwin?" Gwyn countered. "He doesn't seem like someone who fits that mold."

"Marquess Angwin *does* care for his people," Branigan replied slowly. "But he's a staunch royalist. I don't doubt that many of his actions are backed—perhaps even directed—by the Crown. That's one of the reasons the Polite War has dragged on so long. It's everywhere now. In every decision, every whisper in court, every alliance made. The Crown wields it like a net, tangling those who try to rise too high or move too freely."

At that, Maya lifted her head from where she had been resting. She yawned and gave her husband a knowing look before speaking. "The royal family learned early that if they wanted to maintain their rule, they needed ways to control both the nobles and the common folk. The Polite War became one of their most effective tools. It allows them to check the power of the duchies—of powerful noble houses—without open conflict. Money and favors shift constantly. Land is traded. Influence is bought. All to keep everything balanced just enough in the Crown's favor."

Her tone darkened slightly. "Even those who claim to oppose the Crown—those working to increase their own power—still use the Polite War to do it. The very nobles who claim to challenge royal authority often do so by playing the same game, just with different stakes."

Gwyn groaned. "And I have to know all of this because people at the Royal Academy are going to try to get me on their side."

Maya nodded. "Yes. You've already chosen a side, whether you realize it or not. By allying yourself with House Tiloral, you've taken a public stance. Historically, they tried to remain neutral. But after Lord Angwin's actions, that neutrality may no longer be an option."

Gwyn frowned, trying to piece it all together. "So . . . what's going to happen?"

Her teachers exchanged a quiet glance before Mister Branigan answered. "Things may get dangerous. The Academy itself will be safe—you'll be safe—but your friend may not be. Roslyn will be far from home and vulnerable. And there are people who might try to exploit that."

Her stomach twisted. *Roslyn could be hurt? No.* "I understand," Gwyn said, her voice firm. "I'll protect her. I'll get stronger. I'll protect everyone."

Maya sat up straighter, alarmed. "Your Highness—Gwyn—you're still just a young girl. This isn't your burden to carry. You should be focused on learning, on growing. Let us protect you."

Gwyn shook her head before Maya even finished speaking. "No. I have magic. And that means I have responsibility. That's what a princess should do." Her eyes burned with conviction. "I have to practice. I have to grow stronger. I'll keep everyone safe—my people, my family. And I'll find my mom."

She didn't miss the glance Mister Branigan and Maya exchanged then, something between worry and resignation. She ignored it.

I have a plan. And I will see it through.

Early the next morning, a soft knock sounded at her carriage door. It creaked open, and Taenya's head peeked in. "Gwyn? Are you awake?" she whispered.

Gwyn looked up. Her ladies-in-waiting were still asleep, their breathing slow and steady in the quiet. A narrow beam of morning light spilled in through a small gap in the curtain she had nudged aside, illuminating the open book in her lap. She had been up for a while, reading. The closer they got to the capital, the more urgent her desire became to learn everything she could about her new home. There was a lot riding on how well she performed at the Royal Academy.

"Yes, Taenya. I'm awake," she said, gently closing her book and setting it aside.

"We're almost at the city," Taenya said softly. "Would you like to come sit on the bench and see it as we approach? Amari and Sabina rode ahead. We'll stop before we reach the Queens' Gate so you can get back inside before anyone sees you."

Gwyn nodded. "Sure." She rose and followed Taenya out into the crisp morning air, blinking against the sunlight. The caravan had set out early to give them the full day to settle into their new home. Guards on horseback offered salutes as she stepped outside. The driver of her carriage, a telv man, quickly dismounted and offered her his hand.

She accepted it, and he helped her climb up to the front bench. "Thank you," she said with a smile, scooting to the far side to make room. Once she was seated and secure, the telv climbed back up and took the reins again.

With the caravan moving at a steady pace, Gwyn had a chance to look around. The landscape was open and wide, with fields of pale green and winter-silver stretching in all directions. Elves and telv worked in large numbers, bundled in cloaks, moving in slow but steady rhythm across the farmland.

Many paused when the caravan passed. A few stared openly. She offered a polite wave to those who lingered too long, and one woman jumped slightly before raising a hesitant hand in return. Gwyn giggled. The driver beside her laughed too.

"They're not used to seeing royalty, Your Highness," he said, amusement warming his tone.

Gwyn squinted. "How do they know I'm royalty?"

The telv tilted his head toward her and grinned. "Your tiara, Princess."

Her hand flew to her head. She gasped. She had completely forgotten she was still wearing it. She'd found herself wearing it more often as they neared the capital; it reminded her of Roslyn. The gesture felt like a tether, something familiar in the face of so much change. She was usually careful to put it away when it wasn't needed, especially when she wasn't using it to help with her magic, but today, she'd simply forgotten.

"Sorry. I forgot I had it on," Gwyn said, lifting her hand to remove the tiara.

But the driver gently stopped her with a shake of his head. "Don't apologize for being who you are, Your Highness," he said with a kind smile. "You should never have to be ashamed or embarrassed to be yourself. Be proud. I know we all are, to be part of your house."

Gwyn blinked, surprised by the warmth in his voice. His words struck deeper than he probably realized. *Be proud. Be who I am* . . . She smiled and dipped her head. "Thank you," she said softly.

"Look, we're here," came Taenya's voice from behind.

Gwyn turned, spotting the knight riding alongside the carriage. Taenya pointed forward, directing her attention ahead.

Beyond the gently rolling fields, dotted with workers and winter-green crops, a massive stone wall dominated the horizon. It was larger than any she'd seen before, even grander than Strathmore's defenses.

Two gatehouses stood side by side in the distance. The larger one was draped in banners and flags, clearly intended for official entries and exits. Flanking the smaller gatehouse were two towering statues of crowned elven women, elegant and regal in their stone stillness. But what truly stole Gwyn's breath was the moment they passed beyond the final line of trees and hedgerows along the road. To the left, following the bend of the river, stretched the largest bridge she had ever seen.

"What is that?" she asked, eyes wide in awe.

The driver chuckled. "That, Your Highness, is the Joshul Bridge. It crosses the entire width of the river."

"Are we going over it?"

He shook his head. "No, Your Highness. The other side of the river is the town of Aldon. We're heading to those gates straight ahead—Westerly Gate and Queens' Gate."

Gwyn looked back at the impressive city entrance, her attention returning to the gate flanked by the statues. "They're beautiful. Who are they?"

"Those are the statues of Queens Sirune and Alavara," he replied with reverence. "The First Queen and the Golden Queen."

The caravan followed the main road as it curved gently through the city outskirts. Soon, they reached a large intersection where three riders waited off to the side. Gwyn spotted Amari first by her crimson armor gleaming in the morning sun, but it was the figure beside her who truly caught her attention. Her face lit up.

"Friedrich!" she called out, waving excitedly as the caravan drew closer.

The blond Austrian knight, with his neatly curled mustache and smartly trimmed goatee, grinned at the sound of her voice. "Princess Gwyn! Welcome to the City of Bridges!"

Sabina, sitting on her mount beside him, gave a soft huff and rolled her eyes. "Welcome to Reme, Your Highness," she said with mock formality.

Gwyn giggled. "Thank you! How are you? How is Roslyn? Is she around?"

Friedrich chuckled warmly. "We will get you settled into your new home first, yes? Then we can visit your friend."

Taenya, now riding up beside the others, nodded. "Agreed. Let's go see the new home Niles and Sir Friedrich acquired for us."

Friedrich straightened proudly in the saddle. "I believe you will be impressed. House Tiloral was quite helpful in securing a residence suitable for a royal of your station, Your Highness."

Gwyn blinked. "What—?"

Amari exchanged a glance with Sabina, who gave a small nod.

"Perhaps we can discuss it once we've arrived," Sabina said smoothly. "This isn't the best place for explanations."

Taenya gave a firm nod. "I agree. Let's see the manor first. Gwyn, would you return to the carriage, please? We're approaching Queens' Gate."

As they rode onward, Gwyn was guided back into the carriage. She watched from the window as they approached one of the most striking entrances she had ever seen. Queens' Gate was a grand entryway reserved exclusively for nobility and royalty. The detailing along the arch was breathtaking, with etched marble and gold filigree. Banners fluttered from the walls.

Her companions finally awakened. Ilyana, Nora, and Lorrena crowded near the small windows, pressing their faces to the glass just as she had done earlier. They chattered excitedly about the city, pointing out the charming cafés, flower-decked courtyards, and tiny shops that lined the boulevard. Gwyn listened quietly, a smile tugging at her lips.

Apparently, this entrance led into one of the wealthiest districts in the capital: Hirwen Row, named after yet another of Avira's long-revered queens. The people here walked with practiced elegance, dressed in styles unlike anything she'd seen in Strathmore.

Everything about Reme felt different. The capital felt ancient, layered, weathered by time and history. There was no unified theme to its design, no consistent structure or pattern. No rhyme or reason to why one street might be narrow cobblestone and the next, a wide brick promenade. But where it lacked uniformity, it overflowed with wealth.

The road they traveled was laid in perfectly cut bricks, each one clean and level. The buildings on either side were freshly painted, some with detailed carvings or gilded trim. Large glass windows proudly displayed bright, luxurious, and expensive wares.

Despite all that, the girls were most excited by the canals. They couldn't stop talking about them, or the bridges that crisscrossed them at seemingly every turn. Gwyn could hardly contain herself. *Back home, Venice was always one of my favorite cities.* If this place came even close to that—if it had shops perched over water, bridges arching over winding channels while boats gently transported people and goods around—she was going to love it here.

The western part of the city was set on the "mainland," built across a series of gently rising hills. It was the newest expansion and home to some of the kingdom's wealthiest families. As the caravan moved beyond it, they neared the city's true heart, where the canals began, threading through neighborhoods like silver ribbons.

Gwyn's eyes danced from storefront to storefront. A bookstore filled with towering shelves, a cosmetics shop with polished mirrors and bottles of perfume, a tailor displaying elegant dresses behind velvet-draped windows. They passed a bakery with trays of bread and pastries stacked high, and a jewelry store glittering with gold and gems. Her head turned so often she nearly made herself dizzy.

Nobles, merchants, messengers, and travelers alike filled the streets. Gwyn lost count of the number of parks and plazas they passed, many adorned with statues, shrines, or small fountains. Guild halls stood proudly near wide-open courtyards, and soldiers marched in tidy formations through main streets. *There's so much to see! I can't wait to explore everything.*

The caravan climbed a winding road that curved up a hill where rows of elegant homes lined either side. Though the buildings were packed closely together—just like in Strathmore—there was a sense of greater density here. Everything felt more compact, more tightly woven into the city's bones. And yet it didn't feel cramped. It felt deliberate. Efficient.

As they neared the top, houses gave way to walled estates, and Gwyn caught glimpses of manicured gardens and grand homes behind iron gates.

Nora leaned forward and explained that they had entered Sterling Heights, a series of rolling hills near the outer canal. It was home to the wealthiest nobles and elite aristocrats, those with money, prestige, and old family names. Gwyn also learned that across the city, nearer to the royal palaces, was another neighborhood: Vermeil Highland. That was where all the ducal palaces were located, nestled on the same island as the famed Old Town.

So this is where I'll live now . . . Gwyn leaned closer to the window, eyes wide. *Not just visit. Live. For several years.*

The Royal Academy was somewhere off in the distance, situated on its own island, a sprawling area filled with schools, shops, restaurants, and dormitories dedicated to one of the most prestigious institutions in the kingdom.

Gwyn smiled as Nora and Lorrena excitedly chattered, eagerly sharing everything they knew about the city. Ilyana, though usually composed, sat wide-eyed beside them, just as awed as Gwyn felt. *I guess I'm not the only one overwhelmed by all this.*

Their voices faded as the caravan began to slow, the creak of wheels and clop of hooves dampened by the crunch of gravel beneath them. The procession came to a stop in front of a large gate and a high stone wall.

Excitement welled up in Gwyn's chest as she spotted the guards standing at attention outside the gate. They wore the colors of *her* house. It brought a welcome familiarity to being somewhere so new.

She held her breath as the guards moved in unison, pulling the gate open. Sir Friedrich, seated tall in his saddle, took the lead. The carriages and wagons followed, trailing behind him as the caravan passed through the entrance.

The gravel path curved gently, drawing them alongside a large, three-story mansion that loomed ahead. When the carriage came to a stop, Gwyn and the girls were carefully helped out by one of the guards. As she stepped onto the path and got her first real look at the building, she gasped.

Sabina and Amari were nearby, directing guards to unload the carriages. Her teachers and several servants had already disembarked and were assisting. Friedrich and Taenya approached from the far side of the yard, the Austrian knight's grin wide.

"Do you like it? It's very *English*, I think," he said proudly.

"Let me get a good look!" Gwyn said, bouncing with excitement. She turned and walked backward along a small stone path that veered away from the mansion, giving herself more space to take in the full view. When she finally reached a spot far enough to see the entire front of the home, she stopped and gasped again. *It's beautiful.*

Her two knights shared a knowing smile, clearly pleased by her reaction.

The manor's light-brown stone was etched with arched designs above each window and entryway. Five steepled roofs lined the top, each crowned with an elegant double window. The structure was perfectly symmetrical, with each end of the house extending outward slightly more than the center, which itself jutted forward just enough to give prominence to the main entrance.

Simple double doors, unassuming yet regal, sat nestled beneath the central steeple, where a tiny bell sat tucked between two chimneys. Actually, now that Gwyn was really looking, there were *a lot* of chimneys. And windows too: tall, elegant windows flanked either end of the building, and above them sat another row of smaller windows. At the very top, the wide, arched double windows seemed to gaze down like watchful eyes.

The two center wings, sandwiched between the entrance and the outer ends, looked like small houses in their own right. They had no doors and were just part of the overall design, giving the entire estate the appearance of depth and structure. But it wasn't just big; it was welcoming. Elegant without being overwhelming. Stately without being cold.

It's like a dream, thought Gwyn. *Our own place in the capital.*

Friedrich stood tall, clearly proud of his role in securing their new home. "It has ten bedrooms spread across the three floors," he began with a flourish. "A formal dining room that seats twenty beside a large fireplace, and an informal dining area for daily use. There's a formal sitting room—grand, of course—and two additional ones for more casual gatherings. Nine washrooms, each with its own privy. And even a sauna." He smiled, hands behind his back. "Your room is especially spacious, Your Highness. I believe you'll be quite pleased with it."

He sounded like a real estate agent giving a grand tour. Gwyn nodded politely as he spoke, though her mind was wandering. She wasn't listening to most of it—she'd made her decision the moment she saw the house.

As soon as he finished, her grin widened. "Let's check it out! Girls! Come on, we can choose your rooms!"

Friedrich chuckled as he stepped aside to let her pass. She dashed for the entrance, slowing only when one of the guards opened the door for her just in time.

"Your Highness, slow down!" Aleanora's voice called from behind, laced with exasperation.

Gwyn glanced back over her shoulder. Lorrena was laughing as she sprinted after her, skirts fluttering in the wind. Ilyana, ever composed, followed with a dignified pace, her posture flawless and regal. Gwyn's smile grew even more.

Home number two. I wonder what Mom will think of this one.

PRESENT

Taenya walked alongside Friedrich and Sabina into the formal sitting room of the manor. The paladin, Amari, followed quietly behind. While the two knights took their seats, both Taenya and Amari chose to remain standing. Taenya kept her posture straight, hands folded behind her back.

"I know we're all busy," she began, her tone calm but focused, "but I wanted to go over some details regarding the near future." She took a slow breath, mentally organizing everything.

Summer had come and gone, and she was glad for it. Somehow, despite being farther north, the capital was even more humid than Strathmore. A miserable kind of damp that clung to armor and refused to let go. They had spent the entire season building the house—recruiting and vetting servants, guards, and support staff. A daunting task that had initially fallen to her and the two house scholars. For a time, Quinn Branigan had assisted, though his lack of patience and strict standards had created more than a few awkward encounters during interviews. The old sun elf had very little tolerance for mediocrity for anyone who would join a royal house, and he made no effort to hide it. Eventually, Maya Rolfe had stepped in to manage the process more directly, reining in her husband's more eccentric tendencies.

By the end of the season, they had formed a capable foundation. The house was in a strong position, and she'd sent a detailed update to Siveril. The process had taken time, but at least their correspondence would remain steady, if infrequent.

Gwyn's birthday the previous week had been a quiet affair. The Tilorals had attended, along with a few notable guests from the capital. It had been a deliberately small and respectful gathering.

Taenya glanced between Sabina and Friedrich. "Gwyn and Lorrena are scheduled to take their entrance exams tomorrow. Ilyana's is set for next week. With all three girls preparing to move into the Academy dormitories, we'll soon find ourselves spread out across the city."

She continued. "Quinn and Maya have rented an apartment in Scholar's Rest, just across the bridge from the Academy. In the meantime, House Tiloral's steward was kind enough to assist us in acquiring a townhouse in Old Town."

She let the statement settle before elaborating. "It's spacious enough for me, Sabina, and any of the girls who wish to stay there over weekends. I imagine they'll want to spend most of their time near their classmates, but we'll maintain a small staff and keep at least one of our security teams stationed with us."

Sabina gave a thoughtful nod. "It's a good location. Close enough to respond quickly if anything arises. There have been murmurs of Crown Prince Kerrell shifting military assets north, toward the border."

Friedrich's thick brows furrowed. "What lies to the north of us?"

"The Turest Order and the Vlaredian Empire," Amari answered smoothly. "Though Turest is directly north, beyond the Duchy of Levosa."

Friedrich nodded slowly, still thinking. "The Vlaredian Empire . . . they're the ones currently at war with the Sovereign Cities, yes?"

"Yes," Taenya confirmed. "Though the conflict is more westward, that war is escalating."

"Thank you. I'm still learning how all the pieces fit," he admitted sincerely.

Taenya gave him a small smile. "We all are, Friedrich. We all are."

Sabina looked at the knight seated beside her. "You've done very well, Sir Friedrich."

The man offered a respectful nod in response, the corners of his mustache twitching with the barest hint of a smile.

Taenya regarded the terran knight carefully. He had come far since arriving in their world, and despite having left behind so much, he'd proved steady and dependable and was fast becoming indispensable.

"Friedrich," she said, "you'll take over stewardship of the manor. I need you to assume all responsibilities necessary to keep House Reinhart supplied and running smoothly here in the capital."

He gave a solemn nod, clearly understanding the weight of the assignment.

"I'll be focusing more on our political ties," she continued. "Meeting with nobles, building our standing. Sabina, keep your ear to the ground—anything that so much as whispers a threat to the princess, I want to know before it breathes." She turned to the paladin.

Amari crossed her arms. "I'll manage temple relations and coordinate with Evocati Khalan. As a paladin, I will have more freedom on Academy grounds. I'll be able to monitor the princess's safety while she's within the institution itself."

Taenya nodded in approval. "Good. I'll ensure we have a rotation of guards with her whenever she's outside the Academy proper."

"I've heard rumors of a group of terrans arriving in the city," Sabina said thoughtfully. "I'd like to meet with them. Friedrich, would you be willing to accompany me?"

"I will," the knight replied without hesitation. "I have hope that one of them might be from the same world as Her Highness, or me."

Taenya let out a quiet sigh. "We can only hope." She looked over the group with calm authority. "Let's get to it. Tomorrow, I'll personally escort the girls to the Academy." *Things are about to get busy again.*

Gwyn sat quietly in the carriage, her thoughts swirling. Everything she'd studied, everything she'd been told, replayed in her mind like a constant loop. They would be arriving at the Academy soon. Then, Taenya would escort them to the examination hall, where they would be tested.

And if they were accepted, it would decide their ranking. *No pressure . . .*

Across from her, Lorrena sat stiffly, hands clenched together in her lap. The girl looked anxious. She'd studied tirelessly for weeks, and everyone around her believed she was ready. Everyone *except* her.

Over the summer, Gwyn had made an effort to get to know her lady-in-waiting better. What she'd learned was that Lorrena struggled with intense anxiety. She loved her family deeply and missed them even more. And most of all, she didn't want to disappoint them.

Gwyn shared a knowing look with Ilyana, who sat next to Lorrena. She reached forward and placed a gentle hand on Lorrena's bouncing knee. "Relax, Lore. You're going to do great."

Lorrena's knee stilled as she looked up. "I know, Your Highness. I just . . . I . . . yes . . ."

"Lore. It's okay."

The girl gave a small nod, but before she could say anything more, the carriage slowed to a stop. Moments later, a knock sounded at the door. Lorrena's breath caught and then quickened.

Gwyn moved to sit beside her just as Taenya opened the carriage door. "Breathe, Lore," Gwyn said gently. "You're going to do fine."

"Lady Lorrena," Taenya added, her voice calm and steady, "deep breaths. In and out. Focus."

Lorrena nodded quickly, still panicked but trying. Gwyn leaned in close, speaking softly, offering reassurance in the same steady rhythm Taenya had taught her. Little by little, Lorrena's shoulders eased. Her breaths came slower. Finally, she inhaled deeply and sat up straighter.

"I'm ready," she said, with determination.

Gwyn gave her a small smile. Together, they stepped out of the carriage and followed Taenya toward the school grounds.

Ilyana, remaining in the carriage, bade them farewell and wished them luck. She would be taking her entrance exam for the Academy's Upper School the following week. For now, she waited for Taenya, who would return shortly to accompany her through the registration process.

They walked along a paved path that cut through a beautifully manicured courtyard. Other students—children around Gwyn's age and older—were also arriving, escorted by parents, guardians, or tutors. The closer they came to the cluster of buildings, the thicker the crowd became.

Gwyn noticed the way Lorrena's posture tightened again with every step. *She's trying so hard,* she thought, staying close beside her. *I'll be right here.*

Unfortunately, focusing on her friend meant she didn't have much of a chance to take in her surroundings, but she didn't mind. *It's okay. We'll be here for a while. I can explore everything later.*

Ahead of them, a large, stately building loomed, its stone facade elegant and old, its windows tall and arched. This was where the prospective students were separated from the adults who had accompanied them. A final line of reassurance. A final moment before things began. Gwyn took a steadying breath.

Taenya slowed their pace and gently guided them aside before they reached the crowd gathering near the main steps.

"I'll be leaving you here," she said, her tone firm but affectionate. "The Academy staff will guide you to where you need to be. I have complete faith that you both will do well."

Gwyn and Lorrena nodded in unison.

Then Taenya leaned closer to Gwyn, her voice dropping to a private whisper. "Remember, you are a princess. No one here stands above you, but that doesn't mean you look down on others. Show respect. Be kind. Some students will judge based on status, on where someone comes from, but you come from a different culture. Don't let yourself fall into their traps. You are the head of your house. We've prepared you for what that means."

Gwyn swallowed and nodded again, listening carefully.

"Amari is working to secure authorization to be present on the Academy grounds," Taenya added. "You'll likely see her later in the week. I'll see you at week's end." Her voice was steady, but her eyes had gone glassy. That, more than anything, set off a familiar tightness in Gwyn's chest.

No. Not yet. Gwyn wrapped her arms tightly around her knight, her protector, her aunt in all but blood. "Thank you, Taenya," she whispered. "I'll make you proud."

Taenya huffed softly, patting the back of Gwyn's head. "You already have."

When Gwyn finally pulled away, Taenya turned her attention to Lorrena, her gaze sharp with a different kind of intensity.

"Lady Lorrena," she said with all the weight of command. "Look out for Her Highness. I leave her in your care. Be her confidante, her support—her friend."

The elven girl straightened and gave a deep nod. "I will, Ser Taenya."

Taenya returned the nod with solemn approval, then gave them both one last look before stepping away.

And just like that, she was gone.

Gwyn turned to look at the gathered students and the lines forming in front of the tall registration building. There were so many people: young nobles saying goodbye to their families, tutors giving last-minute advice, guards waiting respectfully at the edges.

This looks like the right place.

"Let's get in line, Lore," she said quietly.

They made their way through the crowd and found space near the back of one of the lines. Gwyn kept Lorrena distracted, gently steering the conversation toward idle chatter and sneaking in small jokes that managed to coax out a few hesitant laughs. It was enough to keep the girl from spiraling into nerves again.

The line moved slowly, giving Gwyn plenty of time to observe. Most of the students were high elves, though there was a fair number of telv among them. She spotted a few sun elves and even a couple of moon elves and raithe scattered throughout the group. But no dwarves. No orkun either.

Just as she was about to return her attention to Lorrena, something at the edge of her vision caught her eye. Her eyes went wide. She tugged urgently on Lorrena's sleeve.

"Look! Over there." Gwyn pointed subtly at two figures standing off to the side near the back of the line.

Lorrena followed her gaze. The girl's breath caught audibly. "Your Highness, two terrans!"

Gwyn heard gasps from nearby students and felt the weight of stares press down on her, but she ignored them completely. She was just about to whisper to Lorrena that they should go introduce themselves when a voice behind them cut through the murmuring.

"Next," an adult called.

Gwyn turned and found herself looking up at a stern-faced high elf man in a finely tailored Academy uniform.

She blinked. "Me?" she asked, pointing to herself.

The man nodded. "Yes, miss. Please, right this way."

She and Lorrena moved to follow, but the man held up a hand to stop her companion.

"Please wait your turn, miss," he told Lorrena with polite firmness.

Gwyn turned back to her, her voice soft. "I'll see you soon! You've got this. Good luck."

Lorrena's eyes widened slightly, but she managed a small nod.

Gwyn followed the elf into the building, her heart beating a little faster.

They walked down a quiet hallway lined with tall windows that let in slanted beams of morning light, and entered a large room that held a certain quiet gravity. At the front of the room sat five individuals behind a long table, each with neat stacks of paper in front of them.

The man guiding her gestured to a spot in the middle of the room. A symbol was carved into the polished floor—a large sunburst star, radiant and precise. Gwyn stepped into place and stood tall, centering herself over the symbol.

At the center of the table sat a high elf woman who radiated authority. Flanking her were two high elf men, both with unreadable expressions. To the woman's left, seated at the end of the table, was a man with a warm smile. He dipped his head in greeting as their eyes met. It helped. Just enough to take the edge off her nerves.

On the right end sat a telv woman with blonde hair, her expression calm but curious. She seemed to be studying Gwyn with measured, not unkind, interest.

Gwyn returned her attention to the woman in the center. She appeared old—by elven standards—with streaks of silver through her long black hair and eyes like polished emeralds. They were sharp, piercing, assessing. She peered down at Gwyn with cool confidence, and there was no visible reaction to Gwyn's age, race, or title. No condescension. No curiosity. *She's not impressed. But she's not dismissive either. She's just . . . focused.* It was clear to Gwyn that this woman was in charge.

"Name?"

Gwyn took a deep breath, squared her shoulders, and shifted slightly to sit straighter in the chair. Folding her hands neatly in her lap, she answered clearly, "Princess Gwyneth Reinhart."

The reaction was immediate. The group paused, exchanging glances with raised brows and furrowed expressions. One of the men began flipping through a stack of papers. He eventually pulled one free and passed it to the woman in charge.

Silence followed as the woman took her time reading the document, her eyes scanning each line with deliberate focus. Finally, she looked up, her gaze sharp.

"House Reinhart. From the Duchy of Tiloral. A terran."

Gwyn couldn't tell if it was a question or a statement, but she answered with a respectful nod. "Yes, ma'am."

The woman raised a brow and looked back down at the document. "Magic-wielder. Exempt from Kingdom Royal Decree by status as an Honored One, as proclaimed by the archpriestess herself."

That earned audible gasps from two of the examiners. But the leader paid no attention to the reactions around her and remained fixed on the text in front of her. Finally, her gaze returned to Gwyn. "What do you have to say about this?"

Gwyn tilted her head slightly. *Say about what? Magic? My title? The decree?* With a mental shrug, she tossed the question back.

"I don't know what you expect me to say," she replied. "I just want to attend your school."

One of the elf men let out a breathy chuckle. He received a sharp glare, but Gwyn caught a slight twitch of amusement at the corner of his mouth.

The leader, however, remained stone-faced. She studied Gwyn for a long, uncomfortable moment, long enough that Gwyn had to very deliberately stop herself from fidgeting.

Then, at last, the woman reached for a stamp. "Very well. Welcome to the Royal Academy of Avira." With a sharp motion, she pressed it down onto the paper in front of her.

Gwyn froze. Everyone else froze. Gwyn channeled red mana to heat back up. The woman didn't seem to notice. She simply looked up, expression unchanged. "You may go, Miss Reinhart."

Gwyn blinked. "But . . . what about my entrance exam? My rank?"

The woman paused, tapping her quill on the rim of the inkwell before sliding it back inside. She folded her hands neatly on the table.

"You are exempt. Your rank will be assigned accordingly. You are officially on academic probation. The details will be explained later. Please proceed so you may be processed and assigned a guide. We have many other prospective students to assess."

Gwyn took a slow breath, then nodded once and stepped away. The hushed murmurs of the examiners resumed behind her. At the back of the room, a tall telv man offered her a small wave, then gestured toward the door she was to pass through.

A massive amphitheater-style auditorium stretched before her, filled with students already seated in row after row. Laughter, conversation, and youthful energy buzzed in the air. Students of every age and race were scattered across the space, even orkun and dwarves, which surprised her after not seeing any in the registration line.

The man beside her smiled. "Welcome to the Royal Academy. Your progress will be followed with great interest," he said, before turning and disappearing back into the other room.

She looked over the sea of unfamiliar faces, suddenly unsure of where to sit.

Should I wait for Lorrena?

"Gwyn!"

She turned at the sound of her name, heart leaping. A small blonde near the front waved enthusiastically.

Gwyn grinned. *Roslyn!* She drew in a steadying breath, then started down the aisle toward her friend. Confidence bloomed in her chest, her steps growing stronger, lighter.

She didn't know what her rank would be. Or how meeting the other terrans would go. Or what kind of nobles she'd have to navigate within these walls. But she *did* know she'd have her best friend at her side. And Lorrena too.

Finally back in school . . . in another world. Gwyn smiled as mana pulsed through her with quiet strength.

Let's do this.

CHAPTER THIRTY-SEVEN

PROOF OF LIFE

MIDSUMMER

It was another late night within the Banking Guild. With the city finally reopened for trade after the siege, caravans delivering goods and financial reports were arriving almost hourly. This relentless influx required Guild members to work extra shifts, updating and reconciling records from across the region and even the continent at large.

The stop order issued by the Guild just prior to the siege had followed established emergency protocols designed for situations when major branches became inaccessible. Effective though it had been at the time, it now meant that headquarters faced the laborious task of tracking down and rectifying discrepancies caused by the extended communication blackout between regions.

Selven placed his quill carefully into the inkpot and reached for a cup of water. He sipped lightly, soothing his dry throat. Flexing his cramped fingers, he shook out his aching wrist, feeling the strain of repetitive writing creeping up on him.

The oil lamp at his desk flickered, casting wavering shadows across his paperwork. He adjusted the wick to brighten the workspace just as a sharp knock echoed through the quiet office. He glanced around, realizing for the first time that the other five desks in the room sat empty, their occupants having long since departed.

How long have I been working alone? Sighing, he rose stiffly from his chair and crossed the room to open the door. A burly telv man stood outside, breathing heavily and clutching a large chest awkwardly in his arms.

"I was told to bring this up here," the man announced between labored breaths.

Selven sighed again softly. "Right in here, please. Let me help you."

"Thank you."

As Selven grabbed one of the handles, his muscles tightened sharply at the chest's unexpected heft. *What did they make this chest out of?*

With a coordinated grunt, they maneuvered the heavy container onto the floor beside his desk. As they set it down, Selven leaned forward, squinting at the origin panel. Guild Records. Duchy of Lis, Kingdom of Avira. Guild Records. Duchy of Tiloral, Kingdom of Avira. *Of course. Why would they ever think to separate the two? That would only make sense.*

He turned to the telv courier, who lingered awkwardly nearby. "Is there something else?"

The man blinked and straightened abruptly. "No, sorry. I'll be on my way."

Selven watched him leave just as two familiar figures stepped into the office, his fellow clerks finally returning.

"What's that, Selven?" Teya, a high elf woman whose curiosity never seemed to wane, asked with an amused tilt of her head.

"Guild records from the Kingdom of Avira, both the Duchy of Lis and the Duchy of Tiloral. They arrived in one container."

Teya winced sympathetically, clearly recognizing the unnecessary headache. "Of course they did. Why follow procedure?"

The Guild headquarters had issued countless reminders about proper filing protocols. Keeping records distinct by region was more than just bureaucratic preference; it was vital for organization and efficient retrieval. There was no logistical reason the Guild branches from both duchies couldn't have shipped their records simultaneously, yet regulations clearly mandated separate packaging to maintain standards.

Selven rubbed his temples, looking down at the intimidating chest. *Hopefully, they at least sorted them.* He opened the chest and his heart sank. Stacks of documents lay piled inside, utterly devoid of any semblance of order. His hopes for leaving at a reasonable hour vanished instantly.

The telv clerk sighed softly and shook her head in empathetic resignation. "Don't worry, Selven, we'll sort this out. Teya and I can handle the sorting. Could you start processing?"

Selven nodded slowly, gathering his resolve. "I can manage that. Where are the other two? Will they be back soon?"

The high elf shook her head, her expression slightly apologetic. "They were reassigned to help with other duties. It's just us tonight."

Selven glanced to his left, where a mountain of paperwork already awaited him. Behind him sat five more stacks on another desk, neatly sorted but still awaiting filing. He rolled his neck to relieve some tension, as the two women began methodically sorting through the chest. Soon enough, a fresh stack labeled for the Duchy of Tiloral appeared at his elbow.

As he worked through the initial documents, everything seemed standard enough, until he reached his first discrepancy. The assets of a certain house had inexplicably dipped into negative numbers. Such occurrences were rare but not unheard of, typically arising when updates from distant branches lagged behind. Still, this should have been flagged before arriving in Marketbol.

He frowned thoughtfully and stood, retrieving the official ledgers for that particular house from the storage shelves behind him. As he flipped carefully through the pages, the issue quickly became evident. The house had withdrawn funds simultaneously from multiple locations, each transaction seemingly legitimate but collectively suspicious upon closer inspection.

Typical, Selven mused with mild irritation. *Do they really think we won't notice? We always find out.*

Rumors had been circulating within the Guild about an innovative new system developed by a local house in Marketbol, intended specifically to prevent such fraudulent activities. Selven found himself intrigued, quietly hopeful for a more streamlined future.

Stamping the problematic record for review by the fraud department, he placed it aside and moved on. Several more records passed without incident until another unusual occurrence caught his eye: two houses sharing the same name.

Selven examined both records, his lips quirking in amusement. *How curious*—the house originating from the Duchy of Tiloral shared a name with one already established here in Marketbol, the house he'd just been contemplating. Checking further, he noted that the Marketbol-based house originally hailed from the Kingdom of Blightwych. *Funny coincidence,* he thought with a faint smile.

He shrugged lightly, returning his attention to the task at hand. Following established protocol, he carefully adjusted the names within the Guild's records, clearly designating each house by their national origin to avoid confusion.

Grabbing his quill, he diligently recorded the updated names:

House Reinhart – Avira.

House Reinhart – Blightwych.

Satisfied, he meticulously updated the primary Guild records. *Wouldn't want any mix-ups! Could you imagine the chaos of funds going to the wrong house? This is precisely why we have these procedures and protocols.*

A deep yawn escaped him as he reached for the next document. It was indeed shaping up to be another long night.

LATE SUMMER

Elodie entered the Banking Guild and paused briefly to take in the bustling scene before her. It had been weeks since the siege had ended, yet the Guild still seemed overwhelmed with the monumental task of catching up to the rest of the region. Clerks scurried about with documents in hand, while clients waited patiently—or impatiently, as the case might be—for their turn.

She was here on official House Reinhart business, needing to verify the status of several recent financial transactions. The latest transfer from their lucrative contract with the Farum siblings should have arrived, along with the initial payment from their agreement with the Marketbol Smithing Guild.

Securing that particular arrangement had required a fair bit of negotiation, bolstered significantly by Koren's invaluable presence and reputation. But after persistent effort, she'd managed to replicate the favorable terms that Sloane had originally brokered back in Thirdghyll. The long-awaited payments from that earlier deal had already transitioned smoothly to the Guild's new premises in Vilstaf, finally having born fruit a few weeks prior.

As a ruby-tier house, House Reinhart enjoyed preferential treatment within Marketbol. However, Elodie knew well enough that even if they were ranked among the lowest tier (wood), the Banking Guild would still have provided exceptional service. After all, Sloane had quite literally saved the city from ruin. Rumors were even circulating about erecting a statue of Sloane in the Park of Heroes. Elodie wasn't entirely convinced the city council would follow through with such a grand gesture, but it was evident they were eager for Sloane to return once her personal quest had concluded. *Wouldn't surprise me if they offered her a seat on the council to sweeten the deal*, thought Elodie. In an astonishingly short time, Sloane and House Reinhart had become the most significant catalysts for economic growth and innovation the city had ever witnessed.

A familiar high elf clerk, someone she had come to trust through several prior interactions, approached with a professional smile. "Miss Romaris, welcome back! Are you here on House Reinhart business today?"

Elodie nodded gracefully. "Indeed, I am."

The elf gestured politely, inviting her to follow him. They stepped into a small, richly decorated office reserved exclusively for important clientele. Elodie settled comfortably into a plush chair upholstered in luxurious fabric, smiling courteously as the elf clerk took a seat across the polished wooden table. He already held a large portfolio, no doubt containing the comprehensive records of House Reinhart.

"What may the Banking Guild assist House Reinhart with today?" he inquired pleasantly.

Elodie withdrew her planner—a wonderfully practical concept introduced by Sloane—and opened it deftly to the notes section. Setting out her pen and inkwell, she looked up, catching an amused glint in the clerk's eye.

"Oh, sorry," she said with a sheepish smile. "I need to verify the recent status of our account. Specifically, several deposits should have been made within the past two days that I'd like to confirm. One from . . ."

She methodically listed each transaction, and the clerk nodded attentively, opening the portfolio and tracing his finger along the neatly organized records.

"Yes, I see those here," he replied smoothly. He proceeded to detail the amount of each deposit clearly and precisely.

Elodie diligently recorded each figure, her pen moving swiftly and carefully across the page. A subtle, curious sound from the clerk prompted her to glance up. "Sorry, what was that?"

He shook his head lightly, his expression a blend of intrigue and mild puzzlement. "Oh, nothing significant, merely a curiosity."

Elodie tilted her head, narrowing her eyes slightly. She had worked for the Guild—long enough to know that when a clerk called something a 'curiosity,' it usually meant something outside the norm. And House Reinhart didn't need anything outside the norm. Normalcy was vital. Stability was crucial. Their entire growth hinged on it.

"What's so curious?" she asked, her voice calm but edged. "Is it something I should be concerned about?"

The high elf gave a quick shake of his head.

"No, nothing alarming. It's just that the origin of your house name was annotated in the record. That is—"

Elodie froze. Her breath caught in her throat, and her eyes widened. "That means there's another house with the same name."

The elf twitched slightly, the flicker of realization flashing across his face. "Ah. Right. Romaris. I forgot you—"

But her own realization surged ahead of his. She jumped to her feet, the chair scraping loudly against the floor. The high elf's head jerked back in surprise.

Elodie leaned over the table, fire behind her eyes. "Where is the other house?"

He blinked, clearly startled. "Ms. Elodie, you know I can't disclose—"

"Damn it! Tell me where the house is or I swear I'll go straight to the grandmaster!"

The elf inhaled sharply, caught between duty and pressure.

"Avira. The Duchy of Tiloral. But it's probably nothing—"

"I have to go."

She shoved her notes and planner haphazardly into her satchel and burst out of the office at a near sprint, the door slamming behind her. She didn't care about decorum right now.

The high elf remained seated, blinking in stunned silence. He knew he'd have to report the outburst—he just wasn't sure to whom. Or even what exactly he'd be reporting.

Elodie rushed across the polished floors of the Guild's main hall and out into the street, where her carriage waited. She shouted to her guards as she approached, her tone brooking no argument. "We need to get to the campus. Now."

To their credit, the guards didn't ask questions. They reacted instantly, barking orders as the carriage lurched into motion with sudden urgency. It tore through Marketbol's streets at breakneck speed. Pedestrians shouted and leapt out of the way as the guards called ahead, clearing their path. Several mounted city watch joined the pursuit, either to assist or reprimand—Elodie didn't care which.

The carriage came to a skidding halt in front of the Reinhart Center, the horses rearing slightly from the momentum. Elodie was already moving, vaulting out before it had even fully stopped.

The senior guardsman came running, alarmed by the commotion. She pointed sharply at the approaching watchmen. "Handle the city's men. Keep them out."

She didn't wait for a reply. Elodie took a deep breath, steeling herself, and barged into Adaega's office without knocking.

Adaega screamed, leaping backward in shock, while Ernald—who had been standing quite close—whirled around, guilt and embarrassment flashing across his face.

"Shit! Elodie! What are you doing?" Adaega snapped, trying to collect herself.

Elodie barely noticed. Her mind was already racing, her heart pounding. "I found her."

Ernald's eyes narrowed. "Who?" Adaega, clearly about to scold her for the intrusion, froze mid-motion as Elodie cut her off.

"Sloane's daughter."

Both Adaega and Ernald went still. "What?" Ernald asked slowly, his voice thick with disbelief. He and Adaega quickly began pulling their clothing back on, the awkwardness of the moment dulled by the seriousness of Elodie's words.

This is too important. Awkward or not, they need to know.

Elodie took a steadying breath. "There's a second House Reinhart. In Avira. Specifically, the Duchy of Tiloral."

Adaega gasped. "That means—"

Ernald, already nodding, finished for her. "That Sloane will be traveling right through there once she arrives in Avira by sea. They're already too far ahead. There's no way we'll reach Swanbrook before they depart." He paused, thoughtful, stroking his chin. "However . . ."

"What?" Adaega prompted, eyes flicking between them.

"She's escorting that girl from the Church to Calling," Ernald explained. "A courier might make it in time to intercept her en route. It'll be expensive—"

"We can afford it," Elodie cut in without hesitation. "What next?"

Ernald nodded in agreement, while Adaega looked between them with growing urgency. "Then we need to move quickly. We'll have to draft the message carefully—something subtle."

Adaega offered a tight smile. "That's simple. We just tell her that the object of her quest is in Tiloral."

Elodie frowned. "And if the courier misses her? Or can't find her?"

"In that case," Ernald said, folding his arms, "the next best option is to send another courier toward the City of Avira. We at least know her end destination. There's a chance we could intercept her there."

Elodie hesitated for only a breath before a bold idea struck. *It's a bit crazy . . .*

but maybe crazy is what we need. "What if we sent two couriers? One now, to Calling, to try and catch her on the road. And a second to the Duchy of Tiloral . . . but where exactly?"

Silence fell among them as they each tried to puzzle it out. It wasn't simple. If only they'd learned this weeks earlier, before Sloane and her party had set out.

Adaega seemed lost in thought, lips pursed. It didn't surprise Elodie. The terran had adapted incredibly well to life in the city, but there were still gaps in her knowledge. She and Ernald had helped where they could, but this particular situation required familiarity with the region's geography and systems.

Snapping fingers broke the silence. "Huh. Actually, that's simple," Ernald said, a spark of inspiration lighting his features. "The Grand Temple of the Celestials. In Strathmore. Sloane's other arrangement with the Church involved gaining their support. If we send a courier straight to the temple, they might be able to get a message directly to Sloane's daughter."

It was a long shot, but it was the best one they had. All three nodded in agreement. A plan had formed. Elodie exhaled slowly. *Let it work. Please, let it work.*

"Did you see any information about the daughter's house?" Ernald asked, turning back to Elodie.

She shook her head. "No. The Guild would never disclose that kind of detail. I had to threaten the clerk just to find out where she was located."

Ernald chuckled. Elodie and Adaega exchanged glances.

"What's so funny?" Adaega asked, one brow raised.

Ernald smirked. "If I remember correctly, Sloane's daughter is only around twelve, and she's already formed her own house. That's no small feat. And considering everything, the two of them aren't even truly . . ." He trailed off, exhaling through his nose and shaking his head with an admiring grin. "Like mother, like daughter."

Elodie allowed herself a small smile. *Like mother, like daughter, indeed.*

PRESENT

A man sprinted along a mist-laden path until he reached the manor house. The chill of the overcast day pressed in around him, the wind cutting through even his thick cloak. He leaned in, speaking quietly to one of the stationed guards, his words nearly lost to the air.

The guards—stoic in their blue tabards and gleaming silver pauldrons, each embossed with the image of a coiled dragon—stood in tight formation. The polished armor reflected distorted images of the scene around them. The wall of bodies they formed was clear in its intent: none would pass without permission.

This was not the first time they had been posted here like this. Outside the manor, a silent crowd of servants, guards, and family members had been gathered. No one dared to speak. All shivered in quiet discomfort, but none so much as whispered a complaint. The damp earth soaked boots, and the heavy air clung to skin and fabric alike. But none of that mattered.

This was a reckoning. And they were present as witnesses. House Trenlore had been given a chance.

The guard from House Reinhart eased his way through the crowd. As he reached the front, the sight before him brought him to a halt. The baron, Lord Camus Trenlore was in the midst of the dressing down of his life. It was as much ceremony as it was sentence. Two seasons—that's how long he lasted.

Whatever urgent message the guard had come to deliver no longer seemed quite so pressing. He straightened his posture and offered a crisp nod to Ser Theran, who stood nearby and returned the gesture with a silent incline of his head. Now was not the time to interrupt. He would wait.

Siveril Norric, now the count of Galehaven, stood at the base of the steps, composed and commanding, his tone cutting through the cold air like a blade.

"Lord Trenlore. Again you have forgotten your place. You persist in dragging your house toward ruin, and with it, threaten the reputation of House Reinhart—the house to which you pledged your loyalty."

The count's voice, though not raised, carried weight. "I can only assume your mind is failing, for what other excuse could there be? I gave you a warning the last time we stood in this very spot. Do you remember what I said would happen if you failed again?"

Lord Trenlore, a high elf of considerable stature, drew himself to his full height, his gaze narrowed in disdain. He looked down his nose at the count, the smugness in his expression that of a man who believed he still held some measure of control.

He couldn't have been more wrong. Anyone could see that. Two guards of House Reinhart flanked him, while a knight in full plate armor stood imposingly at the top of the manor steps. His own guards, unarmed, stood powerless in the crowd behind him. Not a single one seemed willing to intervene.

"I do not know who you think you are, Ser Norric. But—"

A sharp slap cut the air, echoing across the courtyard. Ser Theran lowered his arm from the strike. "You will address the count with the respect he is due," the knight said, his tone as composed as ever.

Lord Norric sighed, shaking his head in disapproval. His gaze settled once more on the baron, who now knelt, cradling a reddened cheek, the last vestiges of defiance stripped away.

"Very well. By the authority granted to me by our liege, I hereby strip all titles from Lord Camus Trenlore and from any members of his household currently present. House Trenlore shall pass to Lady Ilyana Trenlore upon her age of majority, one week hence. Until her return, Ser Theran will act as steward over house operations."

There it was. The real reason for House Reinhart's presence today. The baron had been granted a final chance, a deadline marked by his daughter's coming of age. He had failed to meet it.

Camus Trenlore scowled, rising to his feet and stepping forward before the guards behind him seized his arms.

Unmoved, Lord Norric turned away. "Remove them from the premises."

The baron's failures had nearly brought shame to House Reinhart through reckless business practices and, more concerning, dealings of questionable legality. But even those offenses weren't what had truly sealed his fate. No, what had pushed Lord Norric beyond forgiveness was what he'd learned about Lady Ilyana's last meal with her family.

Everyone assembled outside the manor ignored the protests and curses hurled by the former baron's family. His wife and children were escorted—some gently, others not so much—from the estate. In more than one case, they had to be physically dragged, still shrieking their outrage and indignation.

As the noise receded, muted by distance and thick stone walls, Lord Norric turned to face the gathered staff. The servants, household retainers, and minor guards stood at stiff attention, chilled by more than just the cold air.

"I regret that you were made to stand outside on this dreary day," Lord Norric began, his tone measured but firm. "I also regret that I was forced to act in such a manner. But understand this: House Reinhart will not tolerate disloyalty or impropriety from those who owe it fealty."

His gaze swept over them all. "You are to maintain this estate and continue your duties in service to your new liege. Ser Theran will oversee all operations and see to it that order is preserved. All knights of House Trenlore will now report directly to him until the day Lady Ilyana returns from her studies and assumes her responsibilities."

A ripple of unease passed through the gathered staff, but none dared speak.

"Now, if you'll excuse me," the count said, his voice cooling. "Urgent matters require my attention."

At those words, the Reinhart guard waiting near the front straightened. Lord Norric was already striding toward him, his steps swift and precise. It shouldn't have surprised the guard that the count had known he was waiting, or that his presence implied urgency.

"You have a message?" the count asked without preamble.

The guard bowed respectfully. "Yes, Your Lordship. Lady Batteux awaits you at the manor. She brings urgent news and has requested your immediate return."

Lord Norric's eyes narrowed. "You rode all the way from Strathmore? Alone?"

"Yes, Your Lordship. Time was of the essence. I departed the moment she informed us."

The count gave a short nod, then turned toward another guard. "See that he and his horse are both rested and well-fed." Then, to a third: "Prepare my carriage. We leave at once."

* * *

The upcoming season marked a new chapter for House Reinhart, which had managed to weather every trial the previous year had thrown at them. Stronger for the challenges, their position within the region was now cemented, and their reputation continued to grow.

Lord Norric knew the work was far from over, but for the first time in a long while, he felt confident that they were on the right path. The princess would soon attend the Royal Academy. The debacle with House Trenlore had been particularly trying, but that too had been resolved.

His own lands in the south, and the town of Galehaven, were thriving after a modest yet effective investment from House Reinhart. The majority of the soldiers promised by the duke were now stationed throughout his county. The rest had been reassigned to protect the princess's assets within the city.

Tensions, however, still simmered two seasons after the incident. He remembered it as if it had happened only yesterday. The message, the disbelief. The news that the princess had been attacked. That an army had been sent against her, and that it had been annihilated. Burned and cut to pieces.

Siveril still wasn't sure how to reconcile that moment. *Those two women let that girl fight an army.* And yet the fact that she had won brought a flicker of warmth to his heart.

When the report reached Tiloral, the duke had summoned the marquess Angwin immediately and demanded an explanation. What followed had been a direct and unmistakable blow aimed at the crown prince. The marquess was censured in public record and confined to house arrest within his march. None of his retainers, family members, or employees were permitted to leave his lands without express permission from the duke.

The Crown had not taken that lightly. In retaliation, they had levied increased taxes on sea-based imports and raised entrance fees for all foreign visitors entering through the duchy's ports. Taxes and fees that only applied to the Duchy of Tiloral.

Lord Norric stepped from his carriage and ascended the steps of Reinhart Manor. The grand doors opened without delay, and he made his way through the familiar halls until he reached the parlor.

Inside, Guildmistress Maeva Batteux of the Banking Guild sat in an armchair near the fire, sipping tea with the composed elegance that defined her. As he entered, she turned, the firelight painting her features in warm gold and crimson.

"Guildmistress Batteux, to what do we owe the pleasure? I was told your message was urgent," he said.

Lady Batteux offered him a warm smile and gestured to the chair beside her. "Please, sit, Siveril. And call me Maeva. I believe this is a conversation best had sitting down."

Siveril exhaled slowly, pushing aside his instinct to leap to conclusions.

Instead, he nodded and took the seat across from her. "Maeva. Why are you here?"

Setting her cup gently on the table, the high elf met his gaze. "We've received an update from Marketbol. As part of our routine record exchange, we were informed of a recent change to your account. The Banking Guild now lists your house under the designation Reinhart — Avira."

Siveril squinted. "And that means?"

Maeva drew a slow breath. "It means there is another House Reinhart."

He froze.

She didn't wait for him to speak. "Judging from your expression, you already understand the implication. We've located the girl's mother. And given how carefully she's hidden herself, I can only conclude that you were unaware of her whereabouts."

Siveril tilted his head, uncertain. "What exactly are you saying, Maeva?"

"The head of House Reinhart — Blightwych is the baroness Lady Sloane Reinhart," she explained. "It took me some time to piece everything together, but once I did, the connections fell into place. It appears Queen Reinhart understood that claiming the title of queen upon arrival would place her at a disadvantage—no land, no army, no power base to justify the claim. Your princess, by contrast, has been lucky. She now leads a modest house, one that can destroy armies, apparently. But I digress."

Maeva leaned back slightly. "Instead of drawing attention, the princess's mother chose a status that wouldn't raise suspicion, that of baroness. It's a common rank in Western Ikios, especially in Blightwych. It gave her cover. Legitimacy without fanfare."

Siveril nodded slowly. It made sense. *Blightwych . . .* He frowned and looked up, a question forming on his lips.

Maeva's smile widened slightly, her eyes gleaming with satisfaction. "It appears you've come to the same conclusion I have. I looked into why the update originated from Marketbol rather than Blightwych. It seems the duchy's recent port troubles have severely hindered communication through Maireharbora. In fact, the last report we received from Blightwych predates this update entirely."

She folded her hands together. "It's apparent that my counterpart in the Blightwych Guild has chosen to cut us out of the loop until our interregional issues are resolved. I've already submitted a formal complaint to Marketbol regarding the breach in protocol, but I suspect it'll be some time before we see any kind of meaningful resolution."

Siveril couldn't bring himself to care about the inner politics of the Guild. Not right now. The only thing that mattered was the revelation Maeva had brought to him. "Do you know where to find this other House Reinhart in Blightwych?"

Maeva shook her head with a trace of disappointment. "No, unfortunately. The Guild's records only maintain national origin, not specific locations, unless it is a major subdivision such as a duchy. However, Blightwych isn't particularly large. If I were you, I'd start your search in the capital—Arginwych."

Siveril rose from his seat, his mind already racing ahead. "Maeva, thank you for bringing this to my attention. I also request—"

But she stood with him, lifting a hand gently to cut him off. "Don't worry, Siveril. I'll keep this information between us." Her smile turned knowing. "Besides, I haven't even told you the best part."

He narrowed his eyes. "Go on."

"House Reinhart — Blightwych is registered as a ruby-tier house. And baronesses do not receive that status." She paused to let the weight of that settle. "It's clear the Guild recognizes the importance of the princess's mother. Damaging that relationship—especially when your house has already fostered a strong one—would be unwise."

She was right. The ruby-tier was a designation typically reserved for ducal houses or individuals of equal stature. Only royalty warranted a higher classification—such as his house and liege. *And if Gwyn's mother is trying to remain discreet, claiming such a lofty status openly would only draw unwanted attention.*

"Thank you again for your insight and discretion, Maeva. It seems I suddenly have quite a bit more work ahead of me. If you'll excuse me . . ." He allowed a faint smile to cross his face. "Perhaps we might speak again soon? Over tea?"

Maeva returned the smile, her voice warm. "That would be lovely, Lord Norric."

"Then I look forward to it, Lady Batteux."

"So, we need to send a team to search for this House Reinhart within Blightwych," Theran clarified, his tone already shifting into action mode.

Siveril nodded firmly. "Yes. As soon as possible. We'll also dispatch at least two couriers to the capital. Her Highness must be informed."

Theran offered a crisp nod. "I'll gather two teams and have them on the road by nightfall."

"Good."

Theran paused. Then, with a faint smile tugging at his lips, he said, "I imagine Her Highness will be thrilled by this news."

Siveril chuckled. "*I'm* excited for her. But yes, keeping her in the Academy after this will be a challenge. Fortunately, that's Taenya's problem."

They wouldn't need to say much at first. Just enough to tell the princess they had narrowed down her mother's location. Once they confirmed it, they could send word again. *If I were her mother, I'd be racing to the capital the moment I heard.* Siveril leaned back in his chair and let the flicker of a smile touch his face. *Things are finally looking up. Especially for that girl. She's endured far more than any child should.*

He glanced over at Theran. "Let's get to work."

The knight gave a short, respectful bow. "Understood. I'll assemble the teams immediately."

"Good. And once that's done, begin drafting a preliminary framework for a house merger. It doesn't hurt to be prepared." *Certainly not. If Gwyn has gathered this much support already, what has her mother built in the meantime?*

Siveril watched as Theran exited the chamber, his footsteps echoing down the hall. The count leaned back once more, thoughtful, the embers of the fire casting a warm glow over his expression.

So many doors had just opened. So many new paths. For the first time in what felt like an age, he allowed himself a flicker of genuine hope. He chuckled under his breath.

"Like mother, like daughter."

A CASE FOR AGENCY

The headmaster rubbed her temples, a dull ache forming behind her eyes. She had chosen to personally sit in on the entrance panel for the terran princess, and as it turned out, that had been a wise decision. Even within these supposedly neutral halls, the crown prince's influence loomed large. Three of the five members of the panel would have denied the girl's admission, citing one petty interest or another, had she not asked this year's chair to step aside.

Fortunately, the princess wasn't the only terran seeking admission. It was, after all, the first year that terrans had even been considered for enrollment, and a surprising number had applied. Given the unique situation, it had made sense for her to invoke her prerogative and chair the terran applicant panel herself. And now, to add to her day, one of the Church's paladins had arrived with a formal request to enter the grounds and carry out their duties.

A knock sounded at the door. Her secretary stepped in, composed as always. "Headmaster, they're here to speak with you."

She raised an eyebrow. "They?"

The telv woman nodded. "Yes, Headmaster. Two Paladins of Alos."

Her eyes narrowed slightly. This was escalating. *Now there are two of them?*

The doors opened wider and two figures entered, clad in the unmistakable crimson plate of the Paladins of Alos. They moved with the kind of unwavering confidence that often bordered on arrogance, something the headmaster had come to expect from members of the Holy Order. She had never been overly fond of the paladins, but even nations bent to their will when they made demands.

The man and woman, both sun elves, halted in front of her desk. Sun elves made up the majority of the order's ranks, thanks to its proximity to their ancestral lands, so it wasn't their presence that drew her attention but, rather, their rank.

The subtle detailing on their armor identified them as Evocatis—paladins of respectable standing, neither initiates nor commanders. They were the kind of field operatives sent alone on missions that required tact, skill, and judgment.

It's rare to see two Evocatis assigned together. Her curiosity bloomed, tempering her annoyance. She offered a practiced smile. "What can I do for the Holy Order, Evocatis?"

If either of them was surprised she recognized their rank, they didn't show it. Instead, the man spoke, his tone clipped and sure.

"I am Evocati Khalan, and this is Evocati Amari. We have each been assigned an Honored One to protect. Both are scheduled to attend the Royal Academy this year. We will be brief: inform your Guard that we will be onsite to perform our duties."

His certainty was absolute. As if approval were already granted. *Not that he's wrong.* Still, something didn't add up. *Two Honored Ones?*

The headmaster frowned, eyes narrowing slightly. "Who is the second Honored One? I am aware of only the terran girl."

The female paladin narrowed her eyes. "I suppose her status is no longer a secret."

The headmaster arched a brow. *No longer a secret?* Everyone even remotely connected to the capital had heard of the fire-wielding princess, the Displaced girl who had scorched her way into the center of national attention. As headmaster, it was her responsibility to be informed of any notable applicant to the Academy. Never mind that the Church itself had escorted the girl to the capital. And that the girl had certainly not kept a low profile. She'd spent ample time in Avira—enough for the city's whispers to evolve into policy debates.

"Everyone knows who the princess is, Evocati," she said, tone dry. "Subtlety was never part of her strategy. She blasted her way into the public eye and practically reignited the Polite War. Her methods may be controversial, but they're effective. That's not even counting the fact she *literally* scorched her opposition. I hear even the Crown has taken notice." *That's an understatement. The Crown is actively working to sabotage her. All because of her connection to—*

Her eyes widened slightly as realization struck, and she turned her attention sharply to the male paladin. "Your charge is Lady Roslyn Tiloral," she said slowly. "She's the other Honored One. Interesting."

The man nodded once. "She is, indeed. Both girls require protection. The archpriestess was very clear."

"The archpriestess does not—"

"Tut-tut, Headmistress," the woman interrupted sharply. "I advise you not to finish that sentence. I will bring the entire Aviran contingent of the Holy Order down upon this Academy if I must. Those girls *will* be protected."

The headmaster inhaled deeply and exhaled through her nose. She had already gone to great lengths to ensure the terran girl could attend the Academy. Two paladins were better than a larger entourage, but still, this came with complications.

"You will not interfere with academic proceedings," she said firmly. "Their

Church status is the sole reason you are being granted access. Do not hinder the Academy Guard in the execution of their duties. There's a reason we've been able to maintain neutrality through all the brutality of this nation's politics. They are that reason, so coordinate with the Guard. Ensure your presence is complementary, not disruptive. I will prepare documentation authorizing your presence, no more. Keep it with you. Despite your stance, it will prevent future misunderstandings."

She reached for a pre-filled authorization letter, which she had wisely prepared earlier. Adding the names of both paladins, she signed it with a practiced flourish. The security office would copy the documents and file the original. She extended the parchment across the desk, and the woman took it without hesitation.

The male paladin gave a respectful nod. "Thank you, Headmistress."

She rolled her eyes. "It is *Headmaster.*"

Evocati Amari smirked. "As you say, Headmistress. Thank you."

When they finally left, the headmaster pressed her fingers to her temples again.

A short while later, another knock sounded, and the head of the Academy Guard stepped in. The middle-aged high elf looked as if he hadn't slept properly in days—which, given his responsibilities, wouldn't have been surprising. He was tasked with the security of not just her school, but the entirety of the Academy, both Lower and Upper campuses.

"Headmaster," he greeted. "These paladins . . . should the Guard be preparing for trouble?"

She let out a rueful chuckle. "Yes," she replied simply. "There's no doubt in my mind they'll bring trouble. I imagine most of it will be through no fault of their own." She closed her eyes for a moment, then reopened them with a deep breath. "Watch the princess. Keep the fire brigade on standby."

He blinked. "We will be prepared."

I sure hope so. I hope we all are.

Swanbrook. A city where coin reigned supreme. One of the few urban centers overseen by the Merchant Guild, it was a place where—for the right price—anything could be bought. It also boasted a significant presence of the Blades Guild. Laws existed more in theory than in practice, eroded by years of systemic corruption.

A city that would thrive under imperial rule, thought Ressa. She stepped out of the local guard house, the transaction complete, and slipped her coin pouch into an inner pocket of her coat. She ensured it went into the correct one, the one designed to let a decoy pouch be lifted first. Swanbrook was also home to the Thieves Guild, and one of their favorite pastimes was robbing the riskiest-looking foreigners. It was almost a sport.

Her team waited for her at a nearby plaza, blending into the crowd of the market square. The streets were lively despite Swanbrook being on the newly established front line of the war. Unlike in Marketbol, which had suffered a full siege, Swanbrook's army remained active and engaged. Battles raged just west of the city, across the river, where three bridges served as critical supply and defense points. Forty kilometers away, the Sovereigns' troops were holding out against a slightly larger imperial force. *They will soon be sorely disappointed.*

The presence of ongoing combat suggested one undeniable truth: Weltonsden, a city perched at the northern mouth of the bay, had fallen to imperial control. It was only a matter of time before her people established a blockade around the bay inlet. The only remaining obstacle for the imperial navy would be the Cartaelk fleet to the south.

Together, Weltonsden, Swanbrook, and Cartaelk formed what was known as the Gearldine Triangle. The triad of port cities had deliberately structured their economies to avoid competition with one another, and as a result, the bay had become one of the most prosperous trade regions in the Sovereign Cities. It was impressive, until you realized that Parholm—the City of Merchants—alone surpassed the entire region.

In the plaza's center, she found her team lounging beside a glittering fountain. Alexi was nibbling on a skewer of grilled meat, while the team's medic sipped water. A crumpled wax wrapper on the ground indicated he'd also indulged.

When Alexi saw her, he stood abruptly, shoving the remainder of his snack into his mouth and chewing furiously.

"Is that good?" she asked, voice neutral.

He gave an enthusiastic nod. "Delicious," he mumbled through a mouthful. "What was it?"

He shrugged, a grin forming. "Knowing Swanbrook? Probably rat."

A rare chuckle escaped her. "The report we needed on the City Guard is handled. When our friends arrive, they'll face more resistance than expected."

Alexi's expression grew serious. "Good. Different strategy this time?"

Ressa exhaled and shook her head. "Yes. We'll be more . . . *restrained.* Our objective isn't to confront the woman directly but to disrupt her ability to assist the city. If that means hiring the Blades, we will."

"Good," Alexi said. "The last city didn't go well. That wasn't our best performance."

She couldn't argue. Marketbol had been a string of missteps, failure after failure. But Swanbrook would be different. This time, they were better prepared. No action would be taken until the Knights of Haven's Hope had departed. Ressa could only hope they *did* leave the terran behind. Her team was severely outnumbered otherwise. As much as she wanted to kill that terran, she had to remain professional. Going in unhinged would only get more people killed. This time, they'd take it slow. No rash decisions. No forced confrontations.

Ressa would use the time to learn more about her own magic, mana, and how to fight the growing power of her enemies. There was work to do. And she intended to see it through.

Amanda Levings let out a low groan as she rolled over on the narrow cot that served as her bed. Today was supposed to be her recovery day. Every muscle in her body ached.

For the past few weeks—though it had felt like months—Ser Weylind had pushed her through increasingly brutal training sessions. She had been taught everything from hand-to-hand combat to the many ways one could kill with a dagger. On top of that, the elven knight had drilled academic topics into her mind with unrelenting precision: etiquette, politics, medicine, alchemy, poison. The list felt endless. She hated every second of it. But every time she considered quitting, a strange, uncontrollable drive would seize her—an overwhelming desire to master the art of killing. So, she kept saying yes. Kept pushing herself beyond her limits.

She had thought the training before Avira had been grueling. Since arriving, it had become much worse. Lady Racine had promised she would be helping her grandson. She hadn't said what else would be required.

Every time Amanda felt that familiar pressure in her skull, she knew what would follow: pain, exhaustion, obedience. How long had she been trapped in this cycle? Weeks? Months? She wasn't sure anymore. All she knew was what she was told, what she was made to do. Every day followed the same script—except, theoretically, on recovery days.

Wake up. Eat. Classroom instruction. The endless parade of subjects they deemed essential. Afterward, a brief break to eat again. Then came the worst of it: combat training. And no matter how much she wanted to stop, *needed* to stop, she couldn't. It was like her body wasn't hers anymore. Like her very identity was slipping away with each passing day. Her sense of self was unraveling. *I just want to go home.*

After training came a mandatory bath, and then her time with Lord Racine. The boy treated her like garbage. But to be fair, he treated *everyone* like garbage. She was required to obey his every whim, regardless of how menial, or disturbing, the request.

When did I stop being a guest? When did I become just a servant?

Many of his requests had become increasingly twisted. There was something deeply wrong with the boy. But he would soon be attending the Royal Academy. And Amanda would return to training.

A sudden bang at the door made her shoot upright. Her body screamed in protest as she stood.

An elf with piercing green eyes entered. Ser Weylind. He was a strict taskmaster. But the pain he inflicted was always in training, never beyond it. Any serious injury was promptly treated by physicians.

A gilded cage is still a cage. Pressure welled up behind her eyes, nearly buckling her knees. She fought to stay upright. Showing weakness would only prolong her punishment.

The knight stared at her in silence, then turned and exited the room. She followed without a word. He led her through the manor's cold halls until they reached the young lord's suite.

When they entered, Amanda's breath caught—but the old Amanda, the one who would have gasped or screamed, was long gone. She didn't flinch. She didn't cry. That girl was dead. She was being reforged into something new. A weapon.

Two guards were lifting the corpse of the boy's former tutor. The man's lifeless eyes stared blankly at the ceiling. Blood had run down his cheeks, dark and glistening like tears.

Lord Racine stood off to the side, eyes narrowed in contempt. "Amanda? Ser Weylind, you got *her*? What is *she* supposed to teach me? Terrans don't know anything."

We know more than this shit world—

Pain surged through her head. Ser Weylind turned to her and spoke coolly. "She will be adequate, my lord. I have ensured her training is sufficient."

The boy groaned exaggeratedly. "Fine."

The knight gave her a subtle nod. Amanda approached the desk, where several books lay scattered. She picked up the one already opened—hopefully the one they'd been using—and sat without acknowledging the guards as they carried the body away.

Basic material. First-year Academy coursework. Simple enough. She glanced between the knight and the boy. The young lord sat beside her, still grumbling. She wished she could return to training. At least that pain made sense.

Another wave of pressure struck her. She winced, but the boy didn't notice.

Amanda silently resumed her new role within House Racine. House Racine had invested a great deal in her. She was safe. For now.

Even if the tasks she was required to perform made her stomach turn.

But such was life.

The burden of leadership was not something all men could bear. It was not something that could be learned overnight or simply assumed; it had to be bred, honed from birth, forged through tradition and discipline. The other paths—bureaucracy, populism—were inefficient distractions. Avira had bureaucracy, of course. One could not rule the largest kingdom on the continent without it. But the moment governance was left solely in the hands of bureaucrats, the nation began to stagnate.

Never mind the foolish experiments in collective or representative rule. Give power to the masses, and a nation would spiral into chaos. Stability demanded control. The people needed order. There was a reason every nation of consequence was either a kingdom or an empire. It was also why the nobility, with their end-less attempts to steal power from the throne, had to be brought to heel.

For Kerrell, crown prince of Avira, this was more than duty: it was destiny. As his father aged, the process of transferring day-to-day authority had begun. While Kerrell had not yet ascended the throne, the king had increasingly entrusted governance to his son.

His court had moved swiftly to expand his influence. Alliances were forged, deals made, and in two short years, many had already borne fruit. Some had not, but where the vine withered, it had to be pruned, to preserve the rest.

Then came the Displaced—the terrans—and the emergence of magic. Kerrell needed only glance at the western front, where the dwarves had suffered immense losses, to understand the potential devastation magic could bring. He knew that magic itself wasn't the problem; when properly harnessed, it could be a powerful asset. The danger was in its accessibility—that it could be learned by *anyone.* You did not arm peasants like you armed knights. That path led only to rebellion.

No, magic had to be controlled. Regulated. The magi would be trained and bound to the throne. If that meant creating an entirely new social class to contain them, so be it. Avira had done so before. The Crown would do it again.

Then came the girl. A terran. A *princess,* barely of age, and already permitted into the Royal Academy. She was dangerous not because of her power—though that was significant—but because of her alliances. House Tiloral had seized upon her presence, using her to embolden their quiet rebellion. The old rivalries between their houses had flared anew.

Lord Angwin, a minor but loyal supporter in Tiloral, had acted too soon. He'd attempted to take vengeance on this House Reinhart, blaming them for his son's death. But what came next was humiliating. His forces were utterly destroyed by the girl and her paladin protectors, who brought down a force reminiscent of an inquisition. And to make matters worse, the Church had *sanctioned* it. They had taken a side. Such overt political interference from the Church was unheard of . . . and intolerable. It would take time and consider-able resources to devise a proper response. And even more troubling was that the Church had aligned itself not only with the terran girl but also with the heir to House Tiloral.

Everywhere Kerrell turned, incompetence and failure flanked him. No matter. His own children, the twins, would soon begin their education at the Academy. He would ensure they understood their role. After all, the matter of succession remained undecided. The title of heir was still up for contention.

Kerrell entered the council chamber, and the assembled men stood as he approached. Only once he had taken his place at the head of the table did they sit. He surveyed them. *More sycophants. A purge may be in order.*

"Your Highness," said the general of the northern armies. "There's news from our agents in the north." The high elf general glanced at the spymaster, who nodded.

"Yes, Your Highness," said the graying man. "We've gained ground in Turest. Something is happening along their northern border with the Norsval Forest. Our spies haven't identified the exact cause, but their attention has shifted. Their focus on us has waned. We believe now is the time to act."

Likely the work of his subordinate, Kerrell thought. The old spymaster's apprentice had been carrying the weight of the intelligence network for years. He nodded. "Good. Proceed. And what of our position regarding the war between the Sovereigns and the Vlaredians?"

The noble representing the Duchy of Lis cleared his throat. "Lis stands ready, Your Highness. As discussed, we will move to 'liberate' Rallan. The city has been under siege by the Vlaredians for some time and is cut off from the Sovereigns."

"Has Armanval reacted to our use of the pass?" Kerrell asked. The Armanval Forest was temperamental. The Valeni who lived within were generally content to remain in their cloistered enclaves, but Avira had learned—through blood and shadow—what lay beneath their ancient groves.

Knowledge paid for in lives. And kept secret ever since.

The telv noble shook his head. "No, Your Highness. The forest remains quiet."

"Good. Proceed. Lis will gain a valuable holding. Send the Crown's regards to the duchess."

The noble bowed. "Her Grace looks forward to deepening her ties with the Crown, and enjoying the benefits that come with it."

Kerrell resisted the urge to roll his eyes. He ended the council and departed the chamber, his mind already shifting to his next priority: a private meeting with the king. They would discuss the terrans, how to classify them, whether to treat them as a single group. Kerrell believed they should not. Why give them a banner to rally behind? To do so was to invite solidarity. Resistance. Rebellion.

One noble had already made that mistake. A large group of terrans had seized a castle, using their shared knowledge to hold it against a local count's army. Kerrell had gone himself to witness it under parlay. Their leader had told him that *might makes right*. That terrans would build their own nation. That had stayed with him. *Such a quaint phrase.*

His status gave him the power to decide not just his future but also the futures of others. It was a burden he wore proudly. The great game of politics was his battlefield, and he was born to master it.

After ordering the castle razed and its defenders slain, Kerrell had reflected on the encounter. *That terran had spirit. But he misunderstood one crucial truth: the Loreni have lived by that phrase for millennia.*

It had birthed dynasties and ended them.

It had made legends of kings—and monsters of men.

And it would crush any who dared stand in the path of inevitability.

ACKNOWLEDGMENTS

Book three is where I finally started to find my rhythm. Turning the rough early draft into what you're holding took time, stubborn effort, and a lot of help.

First, to my beta readers, old and new: you've walked with me for literal years now. You've been sounding boards, first-line editors, and kind critics when those first drafts needed it most. Your notes shaped scenes, fixed missteps, and kept me honest. This book is sharper because of you.

To the crew at Podium, past and present, thank you for everything you do behind the scenes to make Manabound real. Cass, you were an invaluable guide for almost two years and helped me grow book by book. Tierney, thanks for stepping in as the current production editor for Manabound and for your patience as I tweak and retweak. Christina, my author relations manager, thank you for keeping so many moving parts aligned. Leah, for coordinating the art and wrangling the nitpicky details I throw your way. And Jodie, your narration keeps giving these characters breath and heartbeat. You make them live.

Bri, thank you for the advice, the support, the late-night "talk me through this" chats, and for keeping me on track when I drift. Still the MVP. To my daughter, thanks for the maps, the names, and the worldbuilding sessions that turned into adventures of their own. You made this one more fun.

To everyone who reads, reviews, recommends, or simply waits for the next chapter: you keep me going. Thank you.

ABOUT THE AUTHOR

Travis Albrecht spent twenty years traveling the globe, and afterward found he immensely enjoyed reading and imagining tales set in other worlds. He lives in California with his family.

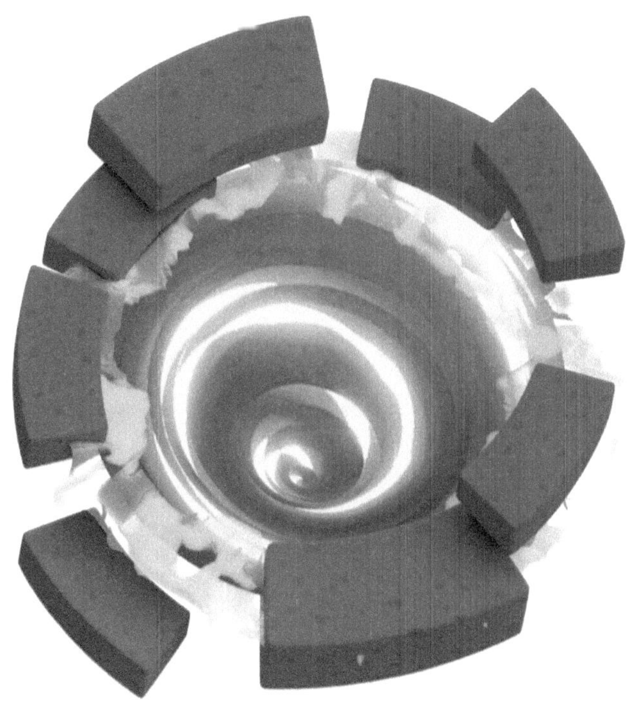

RESPAWN YOUR CURIOSITY

follow us on our socials

 podiumentertainment.com

 @podiumentertainment

 /podiumentertainment

 @podium_ent

 @podiumentertainment

www.ingramcontent.com/pod-product-compliance
Lightning Source LLC
Chambersburg PA
CBHW020639120726
47906CB00001B/44